"THE TEXT PULSES WITH MENACE, MYSTERY, AND VIOLENCE, AND WITH SENSUALITY VERGING ON EROTICA."
—*Publishers Weekly*

A feat of mesmeric storytelling, a chilling entertainment, *The Queen of the Damned* unleashes Akasha, the Queen herself, who has risen from a six-thousand-year sleep to let loose the powers of the night. Akasha has a marvelously devious plan to "save" mankind and destroy Lestat—in this extraordinarily sensual novel of the complex, erotic, electrifying world of the undead.

"A welcome chance to catch up with old fiends . . . Fascinating . . . When we emerge from its folds, there's good news on the last page: 'The chronicle of the vampires will continue.' Yum."
—*Philadelphia Inquirer*

The QUEEN
OF THE
DAMNED

THE QUEEN OF THE DAMNED

THE THIRD BOOK
IN THE
VAMPIRE CHRONICLES

by

ANNE RICE

Ballantine Books
New York

Copyright © 1988 by Anne O'Brien Rice
Untitled poem copyright © 1988 by Stan Rice

All rights reserved under International and Pan-American Copyright Conventions. Published in the United States by Ballantine Books, a division of Random House, Inc., New York, and simultaneously in Canada by Random House of Canada Limited, Toronto.

Poems by Stan Rice quoted in this book were originally published in:

Some Lamb by Stan Rice. Copyright © 1975 by Stan Rice. Published by The Figures. Reprinted by permission of Stan Rice.

Whiteboy by Stan Rice. Copyright © 1976 by Stan Rice. Published by Mudra. Reprinted by permission of Stan Rice.

Body of Work by Stan Rice. Copyright © 1983 by Stan Rice. Reprinted by permission of Lost Roads Publishers.

http://www.randomhouse.com

Library of Congress Catalog Card Number: 97-93891

ISBN: 0-345-41962-6

This edition published by arrangement with Alfred A. Knopf, Inc.

Manufactured in the United States of America

First International Ballantine Books Edition: August 1989
First Ballantine Books Mass Market Edition: October 1989
First Ballantine Books Trade Paperback Edition: October 1997

10 9 8 7 6 5 4 3 2 1

This book is dedicated
with love
to
Stan Rice, Christopher Rice,
and John Preston

And to the memory
of
my beloved editors:
John Dodds
and
William Whitehead

TRAGIC RABBIT

Tragic rabbit, a painting.
The caked ears green like rolled corn.
The black forehead pointing at the stars.
A painting on my wall, alone

as rabbits are
and aren't. Fat red cheek,
all Art, trembling nose,
a habit hard to break as not.

You too can be a tragic rabbit; green and red
your back, blue your manly little chest.
But if you're ever goaded into being one
beware the True Flesh, it

will knock you off your tragic horse
and break your tragic colors like a ghost
breaks marble; your wounds will heal
so quickly water

will be jealous.
Rabbits on white paper painted
outgrow all charms against their breeding wild;
and their rolled corn ears become horns.

So watch out if the tragic life feels fine—
caught in that rabbit trap
all colors look like sunlight's swords,
and scissors like The Living Lord.

STAN RICE
Some Lamb (1975)

THE QUEEN
OF THE
DAMNED

'M THE Vampire Lestat. Remember me? The vampire who became a super rock star, the one who wrote the autobiography? The one with the blond hair and the gray eyes, and the insatiable desire for visibility and fame? You remember. I wanted to be a symbol of evil in a shining century that didn't have any place for the literal evil that I am. I even figured I'd do some good in that fashion—playing the devil on the painted stage.

And I was off to a good start when we talked last. I'd just made my debut in San Francisco—first "live concert" for me and my mortal band. Our album was a huge success. My autobiography was doing respectably with both the dead and the undead.

Then something utterly unforeseen took place. Well, at least *I* hadn't seen it coming. And when I left you, I was hanging from the proverbial cliff, you might say.

Well, it's all over now—what followed. I've survived, obviously. I wouldn't be talking to you if I hadn't. And the cosmic dust has finally settled; and the small rift in the world's fabric of rational beliefs has been mended, or at least closed.

I'm a little sadder for all of it, and a little meaner and a little more conscientious as well. I'm also infinitely more powerful, though the human in me is closer to the surface than ever—an anguished and hungry being who both loves and detests this invincible immortal shell in which I'm locked.

The blood thirst? Insatiable, though physically I have never needed the blood less. Possibly I could exist now without it altogether. But the lust I feel for everything that walks tells me that this will never be put to the test.

You know, it was never merely the need for the blood anyway, though the blood is all things sensual that a creature could desire; it's the intimacy of that moment—drinking, killing—the great heart-to-heart dance that takes place as the victim weakens and I feel myself expanding, swallowing the death which, for a split second, blazes as large as the life.

That's deceptive, however. No death can be as large as a life. And that's why I keep taking life, isn't it? And I'm as far from salvation now as I could ever get. The fact that I know it only makes it worse.

Of course I can still pass for human; all of us can, in one way or another, no matter how old we are. Collar up, hat down, dark glasses, hands in pockets—it usually does the trick. I like slim leather jackets and tight jeans for this disguise now, and a pair of plain black boots that are good for walking on any terrain. But now and then I wear the fancier silks which people like in these southern climes where I now reside.

If someone does look too closely, then there is a little telepathic razzle-dazzle: *Perfectly normal, what you see.* And a flash of the old smile, fang teeth easily concealed, and the mortal goes his way.

Occasionally I throw up all the disguises; I just go out the way I am. Hair long, a velvet blazer that makes me think of the olden times, and an emerald ring or two on my right hand. I walk fast right through the downtown crowds in this lovely corrupt southern city; or stroll slowly along the beaches, breathing the warm southern breeze, on sands that are as white as the moon.

Nobody stares for more than a second or two. There are too many other inexplicable things around us—horrors, threats, mysteries that draw you in and then inevitably disenchant you. Back to the predictable and humdrum. The prince is never going to come, everybody knows that; and maybe Sleeping Beauty's dead.

It's the same for the others who have survived with me, and who share this hot and verdant little corner of the universe—the southeastern tip of the North American continent, the glistering metropolis of Miami, a happy hunting ground for bloodthirsting immortals if ever there was such a place.

It's good to have them with me, the others; it's crucial, really—and what I always thought I wanted: a grand coven of the wise, the enduring, the ancient, and the careless young.

But ah, the agony of being anonymous among mortals has never been worse for me, greedy monster that I am. The soft murmur of preternatural voices can't distract me from it. That taste of mortal recognition was too seductive—the record albums in the windows, the fans leaping and clapping in front of the stage. Never mind that they didn't really believe I was a vampire; for that moment we were together. They were calling my name!

Now the record albums are gone, and I will never listen to those songs again. My book remains—along with *Interview with the Vampire*—safely disguised as fiction, which is, perhaps, as it should be. I caused enough trouble, as you will see.

Disaster, that's what I wrought with my little games. The vampire who would have been a hero and a martyr finally for one moment of pure relevance . . .

You'd think I'd learn something from it, wouldn't you? Well, I did, actually. I really did.

But it's just so painful to shrink back into the shadows—Lestat, the sleek and nameless gangster ghoulie again creeping up on helpless mortals who know nothing of things like me. So hurtful to be again the outsider, forever on the fringes, struggling with good and evil in the age-old private hell of body and soul.

In my isolation now I dream of finding some sweet young thing in a moonlighted chamber—one of those tender teenagers, as they call them now, who read my book and listened to my songs; one of the idealistic lovelies who wrote me fan letters on scented paper, during that brief period of ill-fated glory, talking of poetry and the power of illusion, saying she wished I was real; I dream of stealing into her darkened room, where maybe my book lies on a bedside table, with a pretty velvet marker in it, and I dream of touching her shoulder and smiling as our eyes meet. "Lestat! I always believed in you. I always knew you would come!"

I clasp her face in both hands as I bend to kiss her. "Yes, darling," I answer, "and you don't know how I need you, how I love you, how I always have."

Maybe she would find me more charming on account of what's befallen me—the unexpected horror I've seen, the inevitable pain I've endured. It's an awful truth that suffering can deepen us, give a greater luster to our colors, a richer resonance to our words. That is, if it doesn't destroy us, if it doesn't burn away the optimism and the spirit, the capacity for visions, and the respect for simple yet indispensable things.

Please forgive me if I sound bitter.

I don't have any right to be. I started the whole thing; and I got out in one piece, as they say. And so many of our kind did not. Then there were the mortals who suffered. That part was inexcusable. And surely I shall always pay for that.

But you see, I still don't really fully understand what happened. I don't know whether or not it was a tragedy, or merely a meaningless venture. Or whether or not something absolutely magnificent might have been born of my blundering, something that could have lifted me right out of irrelevance and nightmare and into the burning light of redemption after all.

I may never know, either. The point is, it's over. And our world—our little private realm—is smaller and darker and safer than ever. It will never again be what it was.

It's a wonder that I didn't foresee the cataclysm, but then I never really envision the finish of anything that I start. It's the risk that fascinates, the moment of infinite possibility. It lures me through eternity when all other charms fail.

After all, I was like that when I was alive two hundred years ago—the restless one, the impatient one, the one who was always spoiling for love and a good brawl. When I set out for Paris in the 1780s to be an actor, all I dreamed of were beginnings—the moment each night when the curtain went up.

Maybe the old ones are right. I refer now to the true immortals—the blood drinkers who've survived the millennia—who say that none of us really changes over time; we only become more fully what we are.

To put it another way, you do get wiser when you live for hundreds of years; but you also have more time to turn out as badly as your enemies always said you might.

And I'm the same devil I always was, the young man who would have center stage, where you can best see me, and maybe love me. One's no good without the other. And I want so much to amuse you, to enthrall you, to make you forgive me everything. . . . Random moments of secret contact and recognition will never be enough, I'm afraid.

But I'm jumping ahead now, aren't I?

If you've read my autobiography then you want to know what I'm talking about. What was this disaster of which I speak?

Well, let's review, shall we? As I've said, I wrote the book and made the album because I wanted to be visible, to be seen for what I am, even if only in symbolic terms.

As to the risk that mortals might really catch on, that they might realize I was exactly what I said I was—I was rather excited by that possibility as well. Let them hunt us down, let them destroy us, that was in a way my fondest wish. We don't deserve to exist; they ought to kill us. And think of the battles! Ah, fighting those who really know what I am.

But I never really expected such a confrontation; and the rock musician persona, it was too marvelous a cover for a fiend like me.

It was my own kind who took me literally, who decided to punish me for what I had done. And of course I'd counted on that too.

After all, I'd told our history in my autobiography; I'd told our deepest secrets, things I'd been sworn never to reveal. And I was strutting before the hot lights and the camera lenses. And what if some scientist had gotten hold of me, or more likely a zealous police officer on a minor traffic violation five minutes before sunup, and somehow I'd been incarcerated, inspected, identified, and classified—all during the daylight hours while I lay helpless—to the satisfaction of the worst mortal skeptics worldwide?

Granted, that wasn't very likely. Still isn't. (Though it could be such fun, it really could!)

Yet it was inevitable that my own kind should be infuriated by the risks I was taking, that they would try to burn me alive, or chop me up in little immortal pieces. Most of the young ones, they were too stupid to realize how safe we were.

And as the night of the concert approached, I'd found myself dreaming of those battles, too. Such a pleasure it was going to be to destroy those who were as evil as I was; to cut a swathe through the guilty; to cut down my own image again and again.

Yet, you know, the sheer joy of being out there, making music, making theater, making magic!—that's what it was all about in the end. I wanted to be alive, finally. I wanted to be simply human. The mortal actor who'd gone to Paris two hundred years ago and met death on the boulevard, would have his moment at last.

But to continue with the review—the concert was a success. I had my moment of triumph before fifteen thousand screaming mortal fans; and two of my greatest immortal loves were there with me—Gabrielle and Louis— my fledglings, my paramours, from whom I'd been separated for too many dark years.

Before the night was over, we licked the pesty vampires who tried to punish me for what I was doing. But we'd had an invisible ally in these little skirmishes; our enemies burst into flames before they could do us harm.

As morning approached, I was too elated by the whole night to take the question of danger seriously. I ignored Gabrielle's impassioned warnings—too sweet to hold her once again; and I dismissed Louis's dark suspicions as I always had.

And then the jam, the cliffhanger . . .

Just as the sun was rising over Carmel Valley and I was closing my eyes as vampires must do at that moment, I realized I wasn't alone in my underground lair. It wasn't only the young vampires I'd reached with my music; my songs had roused from their slumber the very oldest of our kind in the world.

And I found myself in one of those breathtaking instants of risk and possibility. What was to follow? Was I to die finally, or perhaps to be reborn?

Now, to tell you the full story of what happened after that, I must move back a little in time.

I have to begin some ten nights before the fatal concert and I have to let you slip into the minds and hearts of other beings who were responding to my music and my book in ways of which I knew little or nothing at the time.

In other words, a lot was going on which I had to reconstruct later. And it is the reconstruction that I offer you now.

So we will move out of the narrow, lyrical confines of the first person singular; we will jump as a thousand mortal writers have done into the brains and souls of "many characters." We will gallop into the world of "third person" and "multiple point of view."

And by the way, when these other characters think or say of me that I am beautiful or irresistible, etc., don't think I put these words in their heads. I didn't! It's what was told to me after, or what I drew out of their minds with infallible telepathic power; I wouldn't lie about that or anything else. I can't help being a gorgeous fiend. It's just the card I drew. The bastard monster who made me what I am picked me on account of my good looks. That's the long and short of it. And accidents like that occur all the time.

We live in a world of accidents finally, in which only aesthetic principles have a consistency of which we can be sure. Right and wrong we will struggle with forever, striving to create and maintain an ethical balance; but the shimmer of summer rain under the street lamps or the great flashing glare of artillery against a night sky—such brutal beauty is beyond dispute.

Now, be assured: though I am leaving you, I will return with full flair at the appropriate moment. The truth is, I hate not being the first person narrator all the way through! To paraphrase David Copperfield, I don't know whether I'm the hero or the victim of this tale. But either way, shouldn't I dominate it? I'm the one really telling it, after all.

Alas, my being the James Bond of vampires isn't the whole issue. Vanity must wait. I want you to know what really took place with us, even if you never believe it. In fiction if nowhere else, I must have a little meaning, a little coherence, or I will go mad.

So until we meet again, I am thinking of you always; I love you; I wish you were here . . . in my arms.

CONTENTS

PROEM

Declaration in the Form of Graffiti

*—written in black felt-tip pen on a red wall in
the back room of a bar called Dracula's Daughter
in San Francisco—*

Children of Darkness
Be Advised of the Following:

Book One: *Interview with the Vampire,* published in 1976, was a true story. Any one of us could have written it—an account of becoming what we are, of the misery and the searching. Yet Louis, the two-hundred-year-old immortal who reveals all, insists on mortal sympathy. Lestat, the villain who gave Louis the Dark Gift, gave him precious little else in the way of explanations or consolation. Sound familiar? Louis hasn't given up the search for salvation yet, though even Armand, the oldest immortal he was ever to find, could tell him nothing of why we are here or who made us. Not very surprising, is it, vampire boys and girls? After all, there has never been a Baltimore Catechism for vampires.

That is, there wasn't until the publication of:

Book Two: *The Vampire Lestat,* this very week. Subtitle: His "early education and adventures." You don't believe it? Check with the nearest mortal bookseller. Then go into the nearest record store and ask to see the album which has only just arrived—also entitled *The Vampire Lestat,* with predictable modesty. Or if all else fails, switch on your cable TV, if you don't disdain such things, and wait for one of Lestat's numerous rock video films which began to air with nauseating frequency only yesterday. You will know Lestat for what he is immediately. And it may not surprise you to be told that he plans to compound these unprecedented outrages by appearing "live" on stage in a debut concert in this very city. Yes, on Halloween, you guessed it.

But let us forget for the moment the blatant insanity of his preternatural eyes flashing from every record store window, or his powerful voice singing out the secret names and stories of the most ancient among us. Why is he doing all this? What do his songs tell us? It is spelled out in his book. He has given us not only a catechism but a Bible.

And deep into biblical times we are led to confront our first parents: Enkil and Akasha, rulers of the valley of the Nile before it was ever called Egypt. Kindly disregard the gobbledygook of how they became the first bloodsuckers on the face of the earth; it makes only a little more sense than the story of how life formed on this planet in the first place, or how human fetuses develop from microscopic cells within the wombs of their mortal mothers. The truth is we are descended from this venerable pair, and like it or no, there is considerable reason to believe that the primal generator of all our delicious and indispensable powers resides in one or the other of their ancient bodies. What does this mean? To put it bluntly, if Akasha and Enkil should ever walk hand in hand into a furnace, we should all burn with them. Crush them to glittering dust, and we are annihilated.

Ah, but there's hope. The pair haven't moved in over fifty centuries! Yes, that's correct. Except of course that Lestat claims to have wakened them both by playing a violin at the foot of their shrine. But if we dismiss his extravagant tale that Akasha took him in her arms and shared with him her primal blood, we are left with the more likely state of affairs, corroborated by stories of old, that the two have not batted an eyelash since before the fall of the Roman Empire. They've been kept all this time in a nice private crypt by Marius, an ancient Roman vampire, who certainly knows what's best for all of us. And it was he who told the Vampire Lestat never to reveal the secret.

Not a very trustworthy confidant, the Vampire Lestat. And what are his motives for the book, the album, the films, the concert? Quite impossible to know what goes on in the mind of this fiend, except that what he wants to do he does, with reliable consistency. After all, did he not make a vampire child? And a vampire of his own mother, Gabrielle, who for years was his loving companion? He may set his sights upon the papacy, this devil, out of sheer thirst for excitement!

So that's the gist: Louis, a wandering philosopher whom none of us can find, has confided our deepest moral secrets to countless strangers. And Lestat has dared to reveal our history to the world, as he parades his supernatural endowments before the mortal public.

Now the Question: Why are these two still in existence? Why have we not destroyed them already? Oh, the danger to us from the great mortal herd is by no means a certainty. The villagers are not yet at the door, torches in hand, threatening to burn the castle. But the monster is courting a change in mortal perspective. And though we are too clever to corroborate for the human record his foolish fabrications, the outrage exceeds all precedent. It cannot go unpunished.

Further observations: If the story the Vampire Lestat has told is true—and there are many who swear it is, though on what account they cannot tell you—may not the two-thousand-year-old Marius come forward to punish Lestat's disobedience? Or perhaps the King and Queen, if they have ears to hear, will waken at the sound of their names carried on radio waves around the planet. What might happen to us all if this should occur? Shall we prosper under their new reign? Or will they set the time for universal destruction? Whatever the case, might not the swift destruction of the Vampire Lestat avert it?

The Plan: Destroy the Vampire Lestat and all his cohorts as soon as they dare to show themselves. Destroy all those who show him allegiance.

A Warning: Inevitably, there are other very old blood drinkers out there. We have all from time to time glimpsed them, or felt their presence. Lestat's revelations do not shock so much as they rouse some unconscious awareness within us. And surely with their great powers, these old ones can hear Lestat's music. What ancient and terrible beings, incited by history, purpose, or mere recognition, might be moving slowly and inexorably to answer his summons?

Copies of this Declaration have to been sent to every meeting place on the Vampire Connection, and to coven houses the world over. But you must take heed and spread the word: The Vampire Lestat is to be destroyed and with him his mother, Gabrielle, his cohorts, Louis and Armand, and any and all immortals who show him loyalty.

Happy Halloween, vampire boys and girls. We shall see you at the concert. We shall see that the Vampire Lestat never leaves it.

THE blond-haired figure in the red velvet coat read the declaration over again from his comfortable vantage point in the far corner. His eyes were almost invisible behind his dark tinted glasses and the brim of his gray hat. He wore gray suede gloves, and his arms were folded over his chest as he leaned back against the high black wainscoting, one boot heel hooked on the rung of his chair.

"Lestat, you are the damnedest creature!" he whispered under his breath. "You are a brat prince." He gave a little private laugh. Then he scanned the large shadowy room.

Not unpleasing to him, the intricate black ink mural drawn with such skill, like spiderwebs on the white plaster wall. He rather enjoyed the ruined castle, the graveyard, the withered tree clawing at the full moon. It was the cliché reinvented as if it were not a cliché, an artistic gesture he invariably appreciated. Very fine too was the molded ceiling with its frieze of prancing devils and hags upon broomsticks. And the incense, sweet—an old Indian mixture which he himself had once burnt in the shrine of Those Who Must Be Kept centuries ago.

Yes, one of the more beautiful of the clandestine meeting places.

Less pleasing were the inhabitants, the scattering of slim white figures who hovered around candles set on small ebony tables. Far too many of them for this civilized modern city. And they knew it. To hunt tonight, they would have to roam far and wide, and young ones always have to hunt. Young ones have to kill. They are too hungry to do it any other way.

But they thought only of him just now—who was he, where had he come from? Was he very old and very strong, and what would he do before he left here? Always the same questions, though he tried to slip into their "vampire bars" like any vagrant blood drinker, eyes averted, mind closed.

Time to leave their questions unanswered. He had what he wanted, a fix on their intentions. And Lestat's small audio cassette in his jacket pocket. He would have a tape of the video rock films before he went home.

He rose to go. And one of the young ones rose also. A stiff silence fell, a silence in thoughts as well as words as he and the young one both approached the door. Only the candle flames moved, throwing their shimmer on the black tile floor as if it were water.

"Where do you come from, stranger?" asked the young one politely. He couldn't have been more than twenty when he died, and that could not have been ten years ago. He painted his eyes, waxed his lips, streaked his hair with barbaric color, as if the preternatural gifts were not enough. How extravagant he looked, how unlike what he was, a spare and powerful revenant who could with luck survive the millennia.

What had they promised him with their modern jargon? That he should know the Bardo, the Astral Plane, etheric realms, the music of the spheres, the sound of one hand clapping?

Again he spoke: "Where do you stand on the Vampire Lestat, on the Declaration?"

"You must forgive me. I'm going now."

"But surely you know what Lestat's done," the young one pressed, slipping between him and the door. Now, this was not good manners.

He studied this brash young male more closely. Should he do something to stir them up? To have them talking about it for centuries? He couldn't repress a smile. But no. There'd be enough excitement soon, thanks to his beloved Lestat.

"Let me give you a little piece of advice in response," he said quietly to the young inquisitor. "You cannot destroy the Vampire Lestat; no one can. But why that is so, I honestly can't tell you."

The young one was caught off guard, and a little insulted.

"But let me ask you a question now," the other continued. "Why this obsession with the Vampire Lestat? What about the content of his revelations? Have you fledglings no desire to seek Marius, the guardian of Those Who Must Be Kept? To see for yourselves the Mother and the Father?"

The young one was confused, then gradually scornful. He could not form a clever answer. But the true reply was plain enough in his soul—in the souls of all those listening and watching. Those Who Must Be Kept might or might not exist; and Marius perhaps did not exist either. But the Vampire Lestat was real, as real as anything this callow immortal knew, and the Vampire Lestat was a greedy fiend who risked the secret prosperity of all his kind just to be loved and seen by mortals.

He almost laughed in the young one's face. Such an insignificant battle. Lestat understood these faithless times so beautifully, one had to admit it. Yes, he'd told the secrets he'd been warned to keep, but in so doing, he had betrayed nothing and no one.

"Watch out for the Vampire Lestat," he said to the young one finally with a smile. "There are very few true immortals walking this earth. He may be one of them."

Then he lifted the young one off his feet and set him down out of the way. And he went out the door into the tavern proper.

The front room, spacious and opulent with its black velvet hangings and fixtures of lacquered brass, was packed with noisy mortals. Cinema vampires glared from their gilt frames on satin-lined walls. An organ poured out the passionate Toccata and Fugue of Bach, beneath a babble of conversation and violent riffs of drunken laughter. He loved the sight of so much exuberant life. He loved even the age-old smell of the malt and the wine, and the perfume of the cigarettes. And as he made his way to the front, he loved the crush of the soft fragrant humans against him. He loved the fact that the living took not the slightest notice of him.

At last the moist air, the busy early evening pavements of Castro Street. The sky still had a polished silver gleam. Men and women rushed to and fro to escape the faint slanting rain, only to be clotted at the corners, waiting for great bulbous colored lights to wink and signal.

The speakers of the record store across the street blared Lestat's voice over the roar of the passing bus, the hiss of wheels on the wet asphalt:

> In my dreams, I hold her still,
> Angel, lover, Mother.
> And in my dreams, I kiss her lips,
> Mistress, Muse, Daughter.
>
> She gave me life
> I gave her death
> My beautiful Marquise.
>
> And on the Devil's Road we walked
> Two orphans then together.
>
> And does she hear my hymns tonight
> of Kings and Queens and Ancient truths?
> Of broken vows and sorrow?
>
> Or does she climb some distant path
> where rhyme and song can't find her?
>
> Come back to me, my Gabrielle
> My Beautiful Marquise.
> The castle's ruined on the hill
> The village lost beneath the snow
> But you are mine forever.

Was she here already, his mother?

The voice died away in a soft drift of electric notes to be swallowed finally by the random noise around him. He wandered out into the wet breeze and made his way to the corner. Pretty, the busy little street. The flower vendor still sold his blooms beneath the awning. The butcher was thronged with after-work shoppers. Behind the café windows, mortals took their evening meals or lingered with their newspapers. Dozens waited for a downhill bus, and a line had formed across the way before an old motion picture theater.

She was here, Gabrielle. He had a vague yet infallible sense of it.

When he reached the curb, he stood with his back against the iron street lamp, breathing the fresh wind that came off the mountain. It was a good view of downtown, along the broad straight length of Market Street. Rather like a boulevard in Paris. And all around the gentle urban slopes covered with cheerful lighted windows.

Yes, but where was she, precisely? Gabrielle, he whispered. He closed his eyes. He listened. At first there came the great boundless roar of thousands of voices, image crowding upon image. The whole wide world threatened to open up, and to swallow him with its ceaseless lamentations. *Gabrielle.* The thunderous clamor slowly died away. He caught a glimmer of pain from a mortal passing near. And in a high building on the hill, a dying woman dreamed of childhood strife as she sat listless at her window. Then in a dim steady silence, he saw what he wanted to see: Gabrielle, stopped in her tracks. She'd heard his voice. She knew that she was watched. A tall blond female, hair in a single braid down her back, standing in one of the clean deserted streets of downtown, not far from him. She wore a khaki jacket and pants, a worn brown sweater. And a hat not unlike his own that covered her eyes, only a bit of her face visible above her upturned collar. Now she closed her mind, effectively surrounding herself with an invisible shield. The image vanished.

Yes, here, waiting for her son, Lestat. Why had he ever feared for her—the cold one who fears nothing for herself, only for Lestat. All right. He was pleased. And Lestat would be also.

But what about the other? Louis, the gentle one, with the black hair and green eyes, whose steps made a careless sound when he walked, who even whistled to himself in dark streets so that mortals heard him coming. *Louis, where are you?*

Almost instantly, he saw Louis enter an empty drawing room. He had only just come up the stairs from the cellar where he had slept by day in a vault behind the wall. He had no awareness at all of anyone watching. He moved with silky strides across the dusty room, and stood looking down through the soiled glass at the thick flow of passing cars. Same old house on Divisadero Street. In fact, nothing changed much at all with this elegant and sensuous creature who had caused such a little tumult with his story in *Interview with the Vampire.* Except that now he was waiting for Lestat. He had had troubling dreams; he was fearful for Lestat, and full of old and unfamiliar longings.

Reluctantly, he let the image go. He had a great affection for that one, Louis. And the affection was not wise because Louis had a tender, educated soul and none of the dazzling power of Gabrielle or her devilish son. Yet Louis might survive as long as they, he was sure of that. Curious the kinds of courage which made for endurance. Maybe it had to do with acceptance. But then how account for Lestat, beaten, scarred, yet risen again? Lestat who never accepted anything?

They had not found each other yet, Gabrielle and Louis. But it was all right. What was he to do? Bring them together? The very idea. . . . Besides, Lestat would do that soon enough.

But now he was smiling again. "Lestat, you are the damnedest creature! Yes, a brat prince." Slowly, he reinvoked every detail of Lestat's face and form. The ice-blue eyes, darkening with laughter; the generous smile; the way the eyebrows came together in a boyish scowl; the sudden flares of high spirits and blasphemous humor. Even the catlike poise of the body he could envisage. So uncommon in a man of muscular build. Such strength, always such strength and such irrepressible optimism.

The fact was, he did not know his own mind about the entire enterprise, only that he was amused and fascinated. Of course there was no thought of vengeance against Lestat for telling his secrets. And surely Lestat had counted upon that, but then one never knew. Maybe Lestat truly did not care. He knew no more than the fools back there in the bar, on that score.

What mattered to him was that for the first time in so many years, he found himself thinking in terms of past and future; he found himself most keenly aware of the nature of this era. Those Who Must Be Kept were fiction even to their own children! Long gone were the days when fierce rogue blood drinkers searched for their shrine and their powerful blood. Nobody believed or even cared any longer!

And there lay the essence of the age; for its mortals were of an even more practical ilk, rejecting at every turn the miraculous. With unprecedented courage, they had founded their greatest ethical advances squarely upon the truths embedded in the physical.

Two hundred years since he and Lestat had discussed these very things on an island in the Mediterranean—the dream of a godless and truly moral world where love of one's fellow man would be the only dogma. *A world in which we do not belong.* And now such a world was almost realized. And the Vampire Lestat had passed into popular art where all the old devils ought to go, and would take with him the whole accused tribe, including Those Who Must Be Kept, though they might never know it.

It made him smile, the symmetry of it. He found himself not merely in awe but strongly seduced by the whole idea of what Lestat had done. He could well understand the lure of fame.

Why, it had thrilled him shamelessly to see his own name scrawled on the wall of the bar. He had laughed; but he had enjoyed the laughter thoroughly.

Leave it to Lestat to construct such an inspiring drama, and that's what it was, all right. Lestat, the boisterous boulevard actor of the ancien régime, now risen to stardom in this beauteous and innocent era.

But had he been right in his little summation to the fledgling in the bar, that no one could destroy the brat prince? That was sheer romance. Good advertising. *The fact is, any of us can be destroyed . . . one way or another. Even Those Who Must Be Kept, surely.*

They were weak, of course, those fledgling "Children of Darkness," as they styled themselves. The numbers did not increase their strength significantly. But what of the older ones? If only Lestat had not used the names of Mael and Pandora. But were there not blood drinkers older even than that, ones of whom he himself knew nothing? He thought of that warning on the wall: "ancient and terrible beings . . . moving slowly and inexorably to answer his summons."

A frisson startled him; coldness, yet for an instant he thought he saw a jungle—a green, fetid place, full of unwholesome and smothering warmth. Gone, without explanation, like so many sudden signals and messages he received. He'd learned long ago to shut out the endless flow of voices and images that his mental powers enabled him to hear; yet now and then something violent and unexpected, like a sharp cry, came through.

Whatever, he had been in this city long enough. He did not know that he meant to intervene, no matter what happened! He was angry with his own sudden warmth of feeling. He wanted to be home now. He had been away from Those Who Must Be Kept for too long.

But how he loved to watch the energetic human crowd, the clumsy parade of shining traffic. Even the poison smells of the city he did not mind. They were no worse than the stench of ancient Rome, or Antioch, or Athens—when piles of human waste fed the flies wherever you looked, and the air reeked of inevitable disease and hunger. No, he liked the clean pastel-colored cities of California well enough. He could have lingered forever among their clear-eyed and purposeful inhabitants.

But he must go home. The concert was not for many nights, and he would see Lestat then, if he chose. . . . How delicious not to know precisely what he might do, any more than others knew, others who didn't even believe in him!

He crossed Castro Street and went swiftly up the wide pavement of

Market. The wind had slackened; the air was almost warm. He took up a brisk pace, even whistling to himself the way that Louis often did. He felt good. Human. Then he stopped before the store that sold television sets and radios. Lestat was singing on each and every screen, both large and small.

He laughed under his breath at the great concert of gesture and movement. The sound was off, buried in tiny glowing seeds within the equipment. He'd have to search to receive it. But wasn't there a charm in merely watching the antics of the yellow-haired brat prince in merciless silence?

The camera drew back to render the full figure of Lestat who played a violin as if in a void. A starry darkness now and then enclosed him. Then quite suddenly a pair of doors were opened—it was the old shrine of Those Who Must Be Kept, quite exactly! And there—Akasha and Enkil, or rather actors made up to play the part, white-skinned Egyptians with long black silken hair and glittering jewelry.

Of course. Why hadn't he guessed that Lestat would carry it to this vulgar and tantalizing extreme? He leant forward, listening for the transmission of the sound. He heard the voice of Lestat above the violin:

> Akasha! Enkil!
> Keep your secrets
> Keep your silence
> It is a better gift than truth.

And now as the violin player closed his eyes and bore down on his music, Akasha slowly rose from the throne. The violin fell from Lestat's hands as he saw her; like a dancer, she wrapped her arms around him, drew him to her, bent to take the blood from him, while pressing his teeth to her own throat.

It was rather better than he had ever imagined—such clever craft. Now the figure of Enkil awakened, rising and walking like a mechanical doll. Forward he came to take back his Queen. Lestat was thrown down on the floor of the shrine. And there the film ended. The rescue by Marius was not part of it.

"Ah, so I do not become a television celebrity," he whispered with a faint smile. He went to the entrance of the darkened store.

The young woman was waiting to let him in. She had the black plastic video cassette in her hand.

"All twelve of them," she said. Fine dark skin and large drowsy brown eyes. The band of silver around her wrist caught the light. He found it enticing. She took the money gratefully, without counting it. "They've been playing them on a dozen channels. I caught them all over, actually. Finished it yesterday afternoon."

"You've served me well," he answered. "I thank you." He produced another thick fold of bills.

"No big thing," she said. She didn't want to take the extra money. *You will.*

She took it with a shrug and put it in her pocket.

No big thing. He loved these eloquent modern expressions. He loved the sudden shift of her luscious breasts as she'd shrugged, and the lithe twist of her hips beneath the coarse denim clothes that made her seem all the more smooth and fragile. An incandescent flower. As she opened the door for him, he touched the soft nest of her brown hair. Quite unthinkable to feed upon one who has served you; one so innocent. He would not do this! Yet he turned her around, his gloved fingers slipping up through her hair to cradle her head:

"The smallest kiss, my precious one."

Her eyes closed; his teeth pierced the artery instantly and his tongue lapped at the blood. Only a taste. A tiny flash of heat that burnt itself out in his heart within a second. Then he drew back, his lips resting against her frail throat. He could feel her pulse. The craving for the full draught was almost more than he could bear. Sin and atonement. He let her go. He smoothed her soft, springy curls, as he looked into her misted eyes.

Do not remember.

"Good-bye now," she said, smiling.

He stood motionless on the deserted sidewalk. And the thirst, ignored and sullen, gradually died back. He looked at the cardboard sheath of the video cassette.

"A dozen channels," she had said. "I caught them all over, actually." Now if that was so, his charges had already seen Lestat, inevitably, on the large screen positioned before them in the shrine. Long ago, he'd set the satellite dish on the slope above the roof to bring them broadcasts from all the world. A tiny computer device changed the channel each hour. For years, they'd stared expressionless as the images and colors shifted before their lifeless eyes. Had there been the slightest flicker when they heard Lestat's voice, or saw their very own image? Or heard their own names sung as if in a hymn?

Well, he would soon find out. He would play the video cassette for them. He would study their frozen, gleaming faces for something—anything—besides the mere reflection of the light.

"Ah, Marius, you never despair, do you? You are no better than Lestat, with your foolish dreams."

. . .

IT WAS midnight before he reached home.

He shut the steel door against the driving snow, and, standing still for a moment, let the heated air surround him. The blizzard through which he'd passed had lacerated his face and his ears, even his gloved fingers. The warmth felt so good.

In the quiet, he listened for the familiar sound of the giant generators, and the faint electronic pulse of the television set within the shrine many hundreds of feet beneath him. Could that be Lestat singing? Yes. Undoubtedly, the last mournful words of some other song.

Slowly he peeled off his gloves. He removed his hat and ran his hand through his hair. He studied the large entrance hall and the adjacent drawing room for the slightest evidence that anyone else had been here.

Of course that was almost an impossibility. He was miles from the nearest outpost of the modern world, in a great frozen snow-covered waste. But out of force of habit, he always observed everything closely. There were some who could breach this fortress, if only they knew where it was.

All was well. He stood before the giant aquarium, the great room-sized tank which abutted the south wall. So carefully he had constructed this thing, of the heaviest glass and the finest equipment. He watched the schools of multicolored fishes dance past him, then alter their direction instantly and totally in the artificial gloom. The giant sea kelp swayed from one side to another, a forest caught in a hypnotic rhythm as the gentle pressure of the aerator drove it this way and that. It never failed to captivate him, to lock him suddenly to its spectacular monotony. The round black eyes of the fish sent a tremor through him; the high slender trees of kelp with their tapering yellow leaves thrilled him vaguely; but it was the movement, the constant movement that was the crux.

Finally he turned away from it, glancing back once into that pure, unconscious, and incidentally beautiful world.

Yes, all was well here.

Good to be in these warm rooms. Nothing amiss with the soft leather furnishings scattered about the thick wine-colored carpet. Fireplace piled with wood. Books lining the walls. And there the great bank of electronic equipment waiting for him to insert Lestat's tape. That's what he wanted to do, settle by the fire and watch each rock film in sequence. The craft intrigued him as well as the songs themselves, the chemistry of old and new—how Lestat had used the distortions of media to disguise himself so perfectly as another mortal rock singer trying to appear a god.

He took off his long gray cloak and threw it on the chair. Why did the whole thing give him such an unexpected pleasure! Do we all long to blaspheme, to shake our fists in the faces of the gods? Perhaps so. Centuries ago, in what is now called "ancient Rome," he, the well-mannered boy, had always laughed at the antics of bad children.

He should go to the shrine before he did anything else, he knew that. Just for a few moments, to make certain things were as they should be. To check the television, the heat, and all the complex electrical systems. To place fresh coals and incense in the brazier. It was so easy to maintain a paradise for them now, with the livid lights that gave the nutrients of the sun to trees and flowers that had never seen the natural lights of heaven. But the incense, that must be done by hand, as always. And never did he sprinkle it over the coals that he did not think of the first time he'd ever done it.

Time to take a soft cloth, too, and carefully, respectfully, wipe the dust from the parents—from their hard unyielding bodies, even from their lips and their eyes, their cold unblinking eyes. And to think, it had been a full month. It seemed shameful.

Have you missed me, my beloved Akasha and Enkil? Ah, the old game.

His reason told him, as it always had, that they did not know or care whether he came or went. But his pride always teased with another possibility. Does not the crazed lunatic locked in the madhouse cell feel something for the slave who brings it water? Perhaps it wasn't an apt comparison. Certainly not one that was kind.

Yes, they had moved for Lestat, the brat prince, that was true—Akasha to offer the powerful blood and Enkil to take vengeance. And Lestat could make his video films about it forever. But had it not merely proved once and for all that there was no mind left in either of them? Surely no more than an atavistic spark had flared for an instant; it had been too simple to drive them back to silence and stillness on their barren throne.

Nevertheless, it had embittered him. After all, it had never been his goal to transcend the emotions of a thinking man, but rather to refine them, reinvent them, enjoy them with an infinitely perfectible understanding. And he had been tempted at the very moment to turn on Lestat with an all-too-human fury.

Young one, why don't you take Those Who Must Be Kept since they have shown you such remarkable favor? I should like to be rid of them now. I have only had this burden since the dawn of the Christian era.

But in truth that wasn't his finer feeling. Not then, not now. Only a temporary indulgence. Lestat he loved as he always had. Every realm needs a brat prince. And the silence of the King and Queen was as much a blessing as a curse, perhaps. Lestat's song had been quite right on that point. But who would ever settle the question?

Oh, he would go down later with the video cassette and watch for himself, of course. And if there were just the faintest flicker, the faintest shift in their eternal gaze.

But there you go again. . . . Lestat makes you young and stupid. Likely to feed on innocence and dream of cataclysm.

How many times over the ages had such hopes risen, only to leave him wounded, even heartbroken. Years ago, he had brought them color films of the rising sun, the blue sky, the pyramids of Egypt. Ah, such a miracle! Before their very eyes the sun-drenched waters of the Nile flowed. He himself had wept at the perfection of illusion. He had even feared the cinematic sun might hurt him, though of course he knew that it could not. But such had been the caliber of the invention. That he could stand there, watching the sunrise, as he had not seen it since he was a mortal man.

But Those Who Must Be Kept had gazed on in unbroken indifference, or was it wonder—great undifferentiated wonder that held the particles of dust in the air to be a source of endless fascination?

Who will ever know? They had lived four thousand years before he was ever born. Perhaps the voices of the world roared in their brains, so keen was their telepathic hearing; perhaps a billion shifting images blinded them to all else. Surely such things had almost driven him out of his mind until he'd learned to control them.

It had even occurred to him that he would bring modern medical tools to bear on the matter, that he would hook electrodes to their very heads to test the patterns of their brains! But it had been too distasteful, the idea of such callous and ugly instruments. After all, they were his King and his Queen, the Father and Mother of us all. Under his roof, they had reigned without challenge for two millennia.

One fault he must admit. He had an acid tongue of late in speaking to them. He was no longer the High Priest when he entered the chamber. No. There was something flippant and sarcastic in his tone, and that should be beneath him. Maybe it was what they called "the modern temper." How could one live in a world of rockets to the moon without an intolerable self-consciousness threatening every trivial syllable? And he had never been oblivious to the century at hand.

Whatever the case, he had to go to the shrine now. And he would purify his thoughts properly. He would not come with resentment or despair. Later, after he had seen the videos, he would play the tape for them. He would remain there, watching. But he did not have the stamina for it now.

He entered the steel elevator and pressed the button. The great electronic whine and the sudden loss of gravity gave him a faint sensuous pleasure. The world of this day and age was full of so many sounds that had never been heard before. It was quite refreshing. And then there was the lovely ease of plummeting hundreds of feet in a shaft through solid ice to reach the electrically lighted chambers below.

He opened the door and stepped into the carpeted corridor. It was Lestat again singing within the shrine, a rapid, more joyful song, his voice battling a thunder of drums and the twisted undulating electronic moans.

But something was not quite right here. Merely looking at the long corridor he sensed it. The sound was too loud, too clear. The antechambers leading to the shrine were open!

He went to the entrance immediately. The electric doors had been unlocked and thrown back. How could this be? Only he knew the code for the tiny series of computer buttons. The second pair of doors had been opened wide as well and so had the third. In fact he could see into the shrine itself, his view blocked by the white marble wall of the small alcove. The red and blue flicker of the television screen beyond was like the light of an old gas fireplace.

And Lestat's voice echoed powerfully over the marble walls, the vaulted ceilings.

> *Kill us, my brothers and sisters*
> *The war is on.*
>
> *Understand what you see,*
> *When you see me.*

He took a slow easy breath. No sound other than the music, which was fading now to be replaced by characterless mortal chatter. And no outsider here. No, he would have known. No one in his lair. His instincts told him that for certain.

There was a stab of pain in his chest. He even felt a warmth in his face. How remarkable.

He walked through the marble antechambers and stopped at the door of the alcove. Was he praying? Was he dreaming? He knew what he would soon see—Those Who Must be Kept—just as they had always been. And some dismal explanation for the doors, a shorted circuit or a broken fuse, would soon present itself.

Yet he felt not fear suddenly but the raw anticipation of a young mystic on the verge of a vision, that at last he would see the living Lord, or in his own hands the bloody stigmata.

Calmly, he stepped into the shrine.

For a moment it did not register. He saw what he expected to see, the long room filled with trees and flowers, and the stone bench that was the throne, and beyond it the large television screen pulsing with eyes and mouths and unimportant laughter. Then he acknowledged the fact: there was only one figure seated on the throne; and this figure was almost completely transparent! The violent colors of the distant television screen were passing right through it!

No, but this is quite out of the question! *Marius, look carefully. Even your senses are not infallible.* Like a flustered mortal he put his hands to his head as if to block out all distraction.

He was gazing at the back of Enkil, who, save for his black hair, had become some sort of milky glass statue through which the colors and the lights moved with faint distortion. Suddenly an uneven burst of light caused the figure to radiate, to become a source of faint glancing beams.

He shook his head. Not possible. Then he gave himself a little shake all over. "All right, Marius," he whispered. "Proceed slowly."

But a dozen unformed suspicions were sizzling in his mind. Someone had come, someone older and more powerful than he, someone who had discovered Those Who Must Be Kept, and done something unspeakable! And all this was Lestat's doing! Lestat, who had told the world his secret.

His knees were weak. Imagine! He had not felt such mortal debilities in so long that he had utterly forgotten them. Slowly he removed a linen handkerchief from his pocket. He wiped at the thin layer of blood sweat that covered his forehead. Then he moved towards the throne, and went round it, until he stood staring directly at the figure of the King.

Enkil as he had been for two thousand years, the black hair in long tiny plaits, hanging to his shoulders. The broad gold collar lying against his smooth, hairless chest, the linen of his kilt immaculate with its pressed pleats, the rings still on his motionless fingers.

But the body itself was glass! And it was utterly hollow! Even the huge shining orbs of the eyes were transparent, only shadowy circles defining the irises. No, wait. Observe everything. And there, you can see the bones, turned to the very same substance as the flesh, they are there, and also the fine crazing of veins and arteries, and something like lungs inside, but it is all transparent now, it is all of the same texture. But what had been done to him!

And the thing was changing still. Before his very eyes, it was losing its milky cast. It was drying up, becoming ever more transparent.

Tentatively, he touched it. Not glass at all. A husk.

But his careless gesture had upset the thing. The body teetered, then fell over onto the marble tile, its eyes locked open, its limbs rigid in their former position. It made a sound like the scraping of an insect as it settled.

Only the hair moved. The soft black hair. But it too was changed. It was breaking into fragments. It was breaking into tiny shimmering splinters. A cool ventilating current was scattering it like straw. And as the hair fell away from the throat, he saw two dark puncture wounds in it. Wounds that had not healed as they might have done because all the healing blood had been drawn out of the thing.

"Who has done this?" He whispered aloud, tightening the fingers of his right fist as if this would keep him from crying out. Who could have taken every last drop of life from him?

And the thing was dead. There wasn't the slightest doubt of it. And what was revealed by this awful spectacle?

Our King is destroyed, our Father. And I still live; I breathe. And this can only mean that *she* contains the primal power. She was the first, and it has always resided in her. *And someone has taken her!*

Search the cellar. Search the house. But these were frantic, foolish thoughts. No one had entered here, and he knew it. Only one creature could have done this deed! Only one creature would have known that such a thing was finally possible.

He didn't move. He stared at the figure lying on the floor, watching it lose the very last trace of opacity. And would that he could weep for the thing, for surely someone should. Gone now with all that it had ever known, all that it had ever witnessed. This too coming to an end. It seemed beyond his ability to accept it.

But he wasn't alone. Someone or something had just come out of the alcove, and he could feel it watching him.

For one moment—one clearly irrational moment—he kept his eyes on the fallen King. He tried to comprehend as calmly as he could everything that was occurring around him. The thing was moving towards him now, without a sound; it was becoming a graceful shadow in the corner of his eye, as it came around the throne and stood beside him.

He knew who it was, who it had to be, and that it had approached with the natural poise of a living being. Yet, as he looked up, nothing could prepare him for the moment.

Akasha, standing only three inches away from him. Her skin was white and hard and opaque as it had always been. Her cheek shone like pearl as she smiled, her dark eyes moist and enlivened as the flesh puckered ever so slightly around them. They positively glistered with vitality.

Speechless, he stared. He watched as she lifted her jeweled fingers to touch his shoulder. He closed his eyes, then opened them. Over thousands of years he had spoken to her in so many tongues—prayers, pleas, complaints, confessions—and now he said not a word. He merely looked at her mobile lips, at the flash of white fang teeth, and the cold glint of recognition in her eyes, and the soft yielding cleft of the bosom moving beneath the gold necklace.

"You've served me well," she said. "I thank you." Her voice was low, husky, beautiful. But the intonation, the words; it was what he'd said hours ago to the girl in the darkened store in the city!

The fingers tightened on his shoulder.

"Ah, Marius," she said, imitating his tone perfectly again, "you never despair, do you? You are no better than Lestat, with your foolish dreams."

His own words again, spoken to himself on a San Francisco street. She mocked him!

Was this terror? Or was it hatred that he felt—hatred that had lain waiting in him for centuries, mixed with resentment and weariness, and grief for his human heart, hatred that now boiled to a heat he could never have imagined. He didn't dare move, dare speak. The hate was fresh and astonishing and it had taken full possession of him and he could do nothing to control it or understand it. All judgment had left him.

But she knew. Of course. She knew everything, every thought, word, deed, that's what she was telling him. She had always known, everything and anything that she chose to know! And she'd known that the mindless thing beside her was past defending itself. And this, which should have been a triumphant moment, was somehow a moment of horror!

She laughed softly as she looked at him. He could not bear the sound of it. He wanted to hurt her. He wanted to destroy her, all her monstrous children be damned! Let us all perish with her! If he could have done it, he would have destroyed her!

It seemed she nodded, that she was telling him she understood. The monstrous insult of it. Well, he did not understand. And in another moment, he would be weeping like a child. Some ghastly error had been made, some terrible miscarriage of purpose.

"My dear servant," she said, her lips lengthening in a faint bitter smile. "You have never had the power to stop me."

"What do you want! What do you mean to do!"

"You must forgive me," she said, oh, so politely, just as he had said the very words to the young one in the back room of the bar. "I'm going now."

He heard the sound before the floor moved, the shriek of tearing metal. He was falling, and the television screen had blown apart, the glass piercing his flesh like so many tiny daggers. He cried out, like a mortal man, and this time it was fear. The ice was cracking, roaring, as it came down upon him.

"Akasha!"

He was dropping into a giant crevasse, he was plunging into scalding coldness.

"Akasha!" he cried again.

But she was gone, and he was still falling. Then the broken tumbling ice caught him, surrounded him, and buried him, as it crushed the bones of his arms, his legs, his face. He felt his blood pouring out against the searing surface, then freezing. He couldn't move. He couldn't breathe. And the pain was so intense that he couldn't bear it. He saw the jungle again, inexplicably for an instant, as he had seen it earlier. The hot fetid jungle, and something moving through it. Then it was gone. And when he cried out this time, it was to Lestat: *Danger. Lestat, beware. We are all in danger.*

Then there was only the cold and the pain, and he was losing consciousness. A dream coming, a lovely dream of warm sun shining on a grassy clearing. Yes, the blessed sun. The dream had him now. And the women, how lovely their red hair. But what was it, the thing that was lying there, beneath the wilted leaves, on the altar?

PART I

THE ROAD TO THE VAMPIRE LESTAT

Tempting to place in coherent collage
    the bee, the mountain range, the shadow
    of my hoof—
tempting to join them, enlaced by logical
    vast & shining molecular thought-thread
    thru all Substance—
. . . .

              Tempting
to say I see in all I see
the place where the needle
began in the tapestry—but ah,
it all looks whole and *part—*
long live the eyeball and the lucid heart.

STAN RICE
from "Four Days in Another City"
Some Lamb (1975)

1

THE LEGEND
OF THE TWINS

Tell it
in rhythmic
continuity.
Detail by detail
the living creatures.
Tell it
as must, the rhythm
solid in the shape.
Woman. Arms lifted. Shadow eater.

STAN RICE
from "Elegy"
Whiteboy (1976)

ALL her for me," he said. "Tell her I have had the strangest dreams, that they were about the twins. You must call her!"

His daughter didn't want to do it. She watched him fumble with the book. His hands were his enemies now, he often said. At ninety-one, he could scarcely hold a pencil or turn a page.

"Daddy," she said, "that woman's probably dead."

Everybody he had known was dead. He'd outlived his colleagues; he'd outlived his brothers and sisters, and even two of his children. In a tragic way, he had outlived the twins, because no one read his book now. No one cared about "the legend of the twins."

"No, you call her," he said. "You must call her. You tell her that I dreamed of the twins. I *saw* them in the dream."

"Why would she want to know that, Daddy?"

His daughter took the little address book and paged through it slowly. Dead all these people, long dead. The men who had worked with her father on so many expeditions, the editors and photographers who had worked with him on his book. Even his enemies who had said his life was wasted, that his research had come to nothing; even the most scurrilous, who had accused him of doctoring pictures and lying about the caves, which her father had never done.

Why should she be still alive, the woman who had financed his long-ago expeditions, the rich woman who had sent so much money for so many years?

"You must ask her to come! Tell her it's very important. I must describe to her what I've seen."

To come? All the way to Rio de Janeiro because an old man had had strange dreams? His daughter found the page, and yes, there was the name and the number. And the date beside it, only two years old.

"She lives in Bangkok, Daddy." What time was it in Bangkok? She had no idea.

"She'll come to me. I know she will."

He closed his eyes and settled back onto the pillow. He was small now, shrunken. But when he opened his eyes, there was her father looking at her, in spite of the shriveling yellowed skin, the dark spots on the backs of his wrinkled hands, the bald head.

He appeared to be listening to the music now, the soft singing of the Vampire Lestat, coming from her room. She would turn it down if it kept him awake. She wasn't much for American rock singers, but this one she'd rather liked.

"Tell her I must speak to her!" he said suddenly, as though coming back to himself.

"All right, Daddy, if you want me to." She turned off the lamp by the bed. "You go back to sleep."

"Don't give up till you find her. Tell her . . . the twins! I've seen the twins."

But as she was leaving, he called her back again with one of those sudden moans that always frightened her. In the light from the hall, she could see he was pointing to the books on the far wall.

"Get it for me," he said. He was struggling to sit up again.

"The book, Daddy?"

"The twins, the pictures . . ."

She took down the old volume and brought it to him and put it in his lap. She propped the pillows up higher for him and turned on the lamp again.

It hurt her to feel how light he was as she lifted him; it hurt her to see him struggle to put on his silver-rimmed glasses. He took the pencil in hand, to read with it, ready to write, as he had always done, but then he let it fall and she caught it and put it back on the table.

"You go call her!" he said.

She nodded. But she stayed there, just in case he needed her. The music from her study was louder now, one of the more metallic and raucous songs. But he didn't seem to notice. Very gently she opened the book for him, and turned to the first pair of color pictures, one filling the left page, the other the right.

How well she knew these pictures, how well she remembered as a little girl making the long climb with him to the cave on Mount Carmel, where he had led her into the dry dusty darkness, his flashlight lifted to reveal the painted carvings on the wall.

"There, the two figures, you see them, the red-haired women?"

It had been difficult at first to make out the crude stick figures in the dim beam of the flashlight. So much easier later to study what the close-up camera so beautifully revealed.

But she would never forget that first day, when he had shown her each small drawing in sequence: the twins dancing in rain that fell in tiny dashes from a scribble of cloud; the twins kneeling on either side of the altar upon which a body lay as if in sleep or death; the twins taken prisoner and standing before a tribunal of scowling figures; the twins running away. And then the damaged pictures of which nothing could be recovered; and finally the one twin alone weeping, her tears falling in tiny dashes, like the rain, from eyes that were tiny black dashes too.

They'd been carved in the rock, with pigments added—orange for the hair, white chalk for the garments, green for the plants that grew around them, and even blue for the sky over their heads. Six thousand years had passed since they had been created in the deep darkness of the cave.

And no less old were the near identical carvings, in a shallow rock chamber high on the slope of Huayna Picchu, on the other side of the world.

She had made that journey also with her father, a year later, across the Urubamba River and up through the jungles of Peru. She'd seen for herself the same two women in a style remarkably similar though not the same.

There again on the smooth wall were the same scenes of the rain falling, of the red-haired twins in their joyful dance. And then the somber altar scene in loving detail. It was the body of a woman lying on the altar, and in their hands the twins held two tiny, carefully drawn plates. Soldiers bore down upon the ceremony with swords uplifted. The twins were taken into bondage, weeping. And then came the hostile tribunal and the familiar escape. In another picture, faint but still discernible, the twins held an infant between them, a small bundle with dots for eyes and the barest bit of red hair; then to others they entrusted their treasure as once more the menacing soldiers appeared.

And lastly, the one twin, amid the full leafy trees of the jungle, her arms out as if reaching for her sister, the red pigment of her hair stuck to the stone wall with dried blood.

How well she could recall her excitement. She had shared her father's ecstasy, that he had found the twins a world apart from each other, in these ancient pictures, buried in the mountain caves of Palestine and Peru.

It seemed the greatest event in history; nothing could have been so important. Then a year later a vase had been discovered in a Berlin museum that bore the very same figures, kneeling, plates in hand before the stone bier. A crude thing it was, without documentation. But what did that matter? It had been dated 4000 B.C. by the most reliable methods, and there unmistakably, in the newly translated language of ancient Sumer, were the words that meant so much to all of them:

"The Legend of the Twins"

Yes, so terribly significant, it had all seemed. The foundation of a life's work, until he presented his research.

They'd laughed at him. Or ignored him. Not believable, such a link between the Old World and the New. Six thousand years old, indeed! They'd relegated him to the "crazy camp" along with those who talked of ancient astronauts, Atlantis, and the lost kingdom of Mu.

How he'd argued, lectured, begged them to believe, to journey with him to the caves, to see for themselves! How he'd laid out the specimens of pigment, the lab reports, the detailed studies of the plants in the carvings and even the white robes of the twins.

Another man might have given it up. Every university and foundation had turned him away. He had no money even to care for his children. He took a teaching position for bread and butter, and, in the evenings, wrote letters to museums all over the world. And a clay tablet, covered with drawings, was found in Manchester, and another in London, both clearly depicting the twins! On borrowed money he journeyed to photograph these artifacts. He wrote papers on them for obscure publications. He continued his search.

Then she had come, the quiet-spoken and eccentric woman who had listened to him, looked at his materials, and then given him an ancient papyrus, found early in this century in a cave in Upper Egypt, which contained some of the very same pictures, and the words "The Legend of the Twins."

"A gift for you," she'd said. And then she'd bought the vase for him from the museum in Berlin. She obtained the tablets from England as well.

But it was the Peruvian discovery that fascinated her most of all. She gave him unlimited sums of money to go back to South America and continue his work.

For years he'd searched cave after cave for more evidence, spoken to villagers about their oldest myths and stories, examined ruined cities, temples, even old Christian churches for stones taken from pagan shrines.

But decades passed and he found nothing.

It had been the ruin of him finally. Even she, his patron, had told him to give it up. She did not want to see his life spent on this. He should leave it now to younger men. But he would not listen. This was his discovery! The Legend of the Twins! And so she wrote the checks for him, and he went on until he was too old to climb the mountains and hack his way through the jungle anymore.

In the last years, he lectured only now and then. He could not interest the new students in this mystery, even when he showed the papyrus, the vase, the tablets. After all, these items did not fit anywhere really, they were of no definable period. And the caves, could anyone have found them now?

But she had been loyal, his patron. She'd bought him this house in Rio, created a trust for him which would come to his daughter when he died. Her money had paid for his daughter's education, for so many other things. Strange that they lived in such comfort. It was as if he had been successful after all.

"Call her," he said again. He was becoming agitated, empty hands scraping at the photographs. After all, his daughter had not moved. She stood at his shoulder looking down at the pictures, at the figures of the twins.

"All right, Father." She left him with his book.

It was late afternoon the next day when his daughter came in to kiss him. The nurse said that he'd been crying like a child. He opened his eyes as his daughter squeezed his hand.

"I know now what they did to them," he said. "I've seen it! It was sacrilege what they did."

His daughter tried to quiet him. She told him that she had called the woman. The woman was on her way.

"She wasn't in Bangkok, Daddy. She's moved to Burma, to Rangoon. But I reached her there, and she was so glad to hear from you. She said she'd leave within a few hours. She wants to know about the dreams."

He was so happy. She was coming. He closed his eyes and turned his head into the pillow. "The dreams will start again, after dark," he whispered. "The whole tragedy will start again."

"Daddy, rest," she said. "Until she comes."

SOMETIME during the night he died. When his daughter came in, he was already cold. The nurse was waiting for her instructions. He had the dull, half-lidded stare of dead people. His pencil was lying on the coverlet, and there was a piece of paper—the flyleaf of his precious book—crumpled under his right hand.

She didn't cry. For a moment she didn't do anything. She remembered the cave in Palestine, the lantern. "Do you see? The two women?"

Gently, she closed his eyes, and kissed his forehead. He'd written something on the piece of paper. She lifted his cold, stiff fingers and removed the paper and read the few words he'd scrawled in his uneven spidery hand:

"IN THE JUNGLES—WALKING."

What could it mean?

And it was too late to reach the woman now. She would probably arrive sometime that evening. All that long way. . . .

Well, she would give her the paper, if it mattered, and tell her the things he'd said about the twins.

2

THE SHORT HAPPY LIFE OF BABY JENKS AND THE FANG GANG

The Murder Burger
is served right here.
You need not wait
at the gate of Heaven
for unleavened death.
You can be a goner
on this very corner.
Mayonnaise, onions, dominance of flesh.
If you wish to eat it
you must feed it.
"Yall come back."
"You bet."

STAN RICE
from "Texas Suite"
Some Lamb (1975)

BABY Jenks pushed her Harley to seventy miles an hour, the wind freezing her naked white hands. She'd been fourteen last summer when they'd done it to her, made her one of the Dead, and "dead weight" she was eighty-five pounds max. She hadn't combed out her hair since it happened—didn't have to—and her two little blond braids were swept back by the wind, off the shoulders of her black leather jacket. Bent forward, scowling with her little pouting mouth turned down, she looked mean, and deceptively cute. Her big blue eyes were vacant.

The rock music of *The Vampire Lestat* was blaring through her earphones, so she felt nothing but the vibration of the giant motorcycle under her, and the mad lonesomeness she had known all the way from Gun Barrel City five nights ago. And there was a dream that was bothering her, a dream she kept having every night right before she opened her eyes.

She'd see these redheaded twins in the dream, these two pretty ladies, and then all these terrible things would go down. No, she didn't like it one damn bit and she was so lonely she was going out of her head.

The Fang Gang hadn't met her south of Dallas as they had promised. She had waited two nights by the graveyard, then she had known that something was really, really wrong. They would never have headed out to California without her. They were going to see the Vampire Lestat on stage in San Francisco, but they'd had plenty of time. No, something was wrong. She knew it.

Even when she had been alive, Baby Jenks could feel things like that. And now that she was Dead it was ten times what it had been then. She knew the Fang Gang was in deep trouble. Killer and Davis would never have dumped her. Killer said he loved her. Why the hell else would he have ever made her, if he didn't love her? She would have died in Detroit if it hadn't been for Killer.

She'd been bleeding to death, the doctor had done it to her all right, the baby was gone and all, but she was going to die too, he'd cut something in there, and she was so high on heroin she didn't give a damn. And then that funny thing happened. Floating up to the ceiling and looking down at her body! And it wasn't the drugs either. Seemed to her like a whole lot of other things were about to happen.

But down there, Killer had come into the room and from up where she was floating she could see that he was a Dead guy. Course she didn't know what he called himself then. She just knew he wasn't alive. Otherwise he just looked kind of ordinary. Black jeans, black hair, real deep black eyes. He had "Fang Gang" written on the back of his leather jacket. He'd sat down on the bed by her body and bent over it.

"Ain't you cute, little girl!" he'd said. Same damn thing the pimp had said to her when he made her braid her hair and put plastic barrettes in it before she went out on the street.

Then whoom! She was back in her body all right, and she was just full of something warmer and better than horse and she heard him say: "You're not going to die, Baby Jenks, not ever!" She had her teeth in his goddamn neck, and boy, was that heaven!

But the never dying part? She wasn't so sure now.

Before she'd lit out of Dallas, giving up on the Fang Gang for good, she'd seen the coven house on Swiss Avenue burnt to timbers. All the glass blown out of the windows. It had been the same in Oklahoma City. What the hell had happened to all those Dead guys in those houses? And they were the big city bloodsuckers, too, the smart ones that called themselves vampires.

How she'd laughed when Killer and Davis had told her that, that those Dead guys went around in three-piece suits and listened to classical music and called themselves vampires. Baby Jenks could have laughed herself to death. Davis thought it was pretty funny too, but Killer just kept warning her about them. Stay away from them.

Killer and Davis, and Tim and Russ, had taken her by the Swiss Avenue coven house just before she left them to go to Gun Barrel City.

"You got to always know where it is," Davis had said. "Then stay away from it."

They'd showed her the coven houses in every big city they hit. But it was when they showed her the first one in St. Louis that they'd told her the whole story.

She'd been real happy with the Fang Gang since they left Detroit, feeding off the men they lured out of the roadside beer joints. Tim and Russ were OK guys, but Killer and Davis were her special friends and they were the leaders of the Fang Gang.

Now and then they'd gone into town and found some little shack of a place, all deserted, with maybe two bums in there or something, men who looked kinda like her dad, wearing bill caps and with real calloused hands from the work they did. And they'd have a feast in there on those guys. You could always live off that kind, Killer told her, because nobody gives a damn what happens to them. They'd strike fast, kachoom!—drinking the blood quick, draining them right down to the last heartbeat. It wasn't fun to torture people like that, Killer said. You had to feel sorry for them. You did what you did, then you burnt down the shack, or you took them outside and dug a hole real deep and stuck them down there. And if you couldn't do anything like that to cover it up, you did this little trick: cut your finger, let your Dead blood run over the bite where you'd sucked them dry, and look at that, the little puncture wounds just like to vanished. Flash! No-body'd ever figure it out; it looked like stroke or heart attack.

Baby Jenks had been having a ball. She could handle a full-sized Harley, carry a dead body with one arm, leap over the hood of a car, it was fantastic. And she hadn't had the damn dream then, the dream that had started up in Gun Barrel City—with those redheaded twins and that woman's body lying on an altar. *What were they doing?*

What would she do now if she couldn't find the Fang Gang? Out in California the Vampire Lestat was going on stage two nights from now. And every Dead guy in creation would be there, leastways that's how she figured it, and that's how the Fang Gang had figured it and they were all supposed to be together. So what the hell was she doing lost from the Fang Gang and headed for a jerkwater city like St. Louis?

All she wanted was for everything to be like it had been before, goddamn it. Oh, the blood was good, yum, it was so good, even now that she was alone and had to work up her nerve, the way it had been this evening, to pull into a gas station and lure the old guy out back. Oh, yeah, snap, when she'd gotten her hands on his neck, and the blood came, it had been just fine, it was hamburgers and french fries and strawberry shakes, it was beer and chocolate sundaes. It was mainline, and coke and hash. It was better than screwing! It was all of it.

But everything had been better when the Fang Gang was with her. And they had understood when she got tired of the chewed-up old guys and said she wanted to taste something young and tender. No problem. Hey, it was a nice little runaway kid she needed, Killer said. Just close your eyes and wish. And sure enough, like that, they found him hitchhiking on the main road, just five miles out of some town in northern Missouri, name of Parker. Real pretty boy with long shaggy black hair, just twelve years old, but real tall for his age, with some beard on his chin, and trying to pass for sixteen. He'd climbed on her bike and they'd taken him into the woods. Then Baby Jenks laid down with him, real gentle like, and slurp, that was it for Parker.

It was delicious all right, juicy was the word. But she didn't know really whether it was any better than the mean old guys when you got down to it. And with them it was more sport. Good ole boy blood, Davis called it.

Davis was a black Dead guy and one damned good-looking black Dead guy, as Baby Jenks saw it. His skin had a gold glow to it, the Dead glow which in the case of white Dead guys made them look like they were standing in a fluorescent light all the time. Davis had beautiful eyelashes too, just damn near unbelievably long and thick, and he decked himself out in all the gold he could find. He stole the gold rings and watches and chains and things off the victims.

Davis loved to dance. They all loved to dance. But Davis could out-dance any of them. They'd go to the graveyards to dance, maybe round three a.m., after they'd all fed and buried the dead and all that jazz. They'd set the ghetto blaster radio on a tombstone and turn it way up, with the Vampire Lestat roaring. "The Grand Sabbat" song, that was the one that was good for dancing. And oh, man, how good it felt, twisting and turning and leaping in the air, or just watching Davis move and Killer move and Russ spinning in circles till he fell down. Now that was real Dead guy dancing.

Now if those big city bloodsuckers weren't hip to that, they were crazy.

God, she wished now that she could tell Davis about this dream she'd been having since Gun Barrel City. How it had come to her in her mom's trailer, zap, the first time when she'd been sitting waiting. It was so clear for a dream, those two women with the red hair, and the body lying there with its skin all black and crackled like. And what the hell was that on the plates in the dream? Yeah, it had been a heart on one plate and a brain on the other. Christ. All those people kneeling around that body and those plates. It was creepy. And she'd had it over and over again since then. Why, she was having it every goddamn time she shut her eyes and again right before she dug her way out of wherever she'd been hiding by daylight.

Killer and Davis would understand. They'd know if it meant something. They wanted to teach her everything.

When they first hit St. Louis on their way south, the Fang Gang had headed off the boulevard into one of those big dark streets with iron gates that they call "a private place" in St. Louis. It was the Central West End down here, they said. Baby Jenks had liked those big trees. There just aren't enough big trees in south Texas. There wasn't much of nothing in south Texas. And here the trees were so big their branches made a roof over your head. And the streets were full of noisy rustling leaves and the houses were big, with peaked roofs and the lights buried deep inside them. The coven house was made of brick and had what Killer called Moorish arches.

"Don't go any closer," Davis had said. Killer just laughed. Killer wasn't scared of the big city Dead. Killer had been made sixty years ago, he was old. He knew everything.

"But they will try to hurt you, Baby Jenks," he said, walking his Harley just a little farther up the street. He had a lean long face, wore a gold earring in his ear, and his eyes were small, kind of thoughtful. "See, this one's an old coven, been in St. Louis since the turn of the century."

"But why would they want to hurt us?" Baby Jenks had asked. She was real curious about that house. What did the Dead do who lived in houses? What kind of furniture did they have? Who paid the bills, for God's sakes?

Seems like she could see a chandelier in one of those front rooms, through the curtains. A big fancy chandelier. Man! Now that's living.

"Oh, they got all that down," said Davis, reading her mind. "You don't think the neighbors think they're real people? Look at that car in the drive, you know what that is? That's a Bugatti, baby. And the other one beside it, a Mercedes-Benz."

What the hell was wrong with a pink Cadillac? That's what she'd like to have, a big gas-guzzling convertible that she could push to a hundred and twenty on the open stretch. And that's what had got her into trouble, got her to Detroit, an asshole with a Cadillac convertible. But just 'cause you were Dead didn't mean you had to drive a Harley and sleep in the dirt every day, did it?

"We're free, darlin'," Davis said, reading her thoughts. "Don't you see? There's a lotta baggage goes with this big city life. Tell her, Killer. And you ain't getting me in no house like that, sleeping in a box under the floorboards."

He broke up. Killer broke up. She broke up too. But what the hell was it like in there? Did they turn on the late show and watch the vampire movies? Davis was really rolling on the ground.

"The fact is, Baby Jenks," Killer said, "we're rogues to them, they wanna run everything. Like they don't think we have a right to be Dead. Like when they make a new vampire as they call it, it's a big ceremony."

"Like what happens, like a wedding or something you mean?"

More laughter from those two.

"Not exactly," Killer said, "more like a funeral!"

They were making too much noise. Surely those Dead guys in the house were going to hear them. But Baby Jenks wasn't afraid if Killer wasn't afraid. Where were Russ and Tim, gone off hunting?

"But the point is, Baby Jenks," said Killer, "they have all these rules, and I'll tell you what, they're spreading it all over that they're going to get the Vampire Lestat the night of his concert, but you know what, they're reading his book like it was the Bible. They're using all that language he used, Dark Gift, Dark Trick, I tell you it's the stupidest thing I've ever seen, they're going to burn the guy at the stake and then use his book like it was Emily Post or Miss Manners—"

"They'll never get Lestat," Davis had sneered. "No way, man. You can't kill the Vampire Lestat, that is flat out impossible. It has been tried, you see, and it has failed. Now that is one cat who is utterly and completely immortal."

"Hell, they're going out there same as we are," Killer said, "to join up with the cat if he wants us."

Baby Jenks didn't understand the whole thing. She didn't know who Emily Post was or Miss Manners either. And weren't we all supposed to be immortal? And why would the Vampire Lestat want to be running around with the Fang Gang? I mean he was a rock star, for Chrissakes. Probably had his own limousine. And was he ever one adorable-looking guy, Dead or alive! Blond hair to die for and a smile that just made you wanna roll over and let him bite your goddamn neck!

She'd tried to read the Vampire Lestat's book—the whole history of

Dead guys back to ancient times and all—but there were just too many big words and konk, she was asleep.

Killer and Davis said she'd find out she could read real fast now if she just stuck with it. They carried copies of Lestat's book around with them, and the first one, the one with the title she could never get straight, something like "conversations with the vampire," or "talking with the vampire," or "getting to meet the vampire," or something like that. Davis would read out loud from that one sometimes, but Baby Jenks couldn't take it in, snore! The Dead Guy, Louis, or whoever he was, had been made Dead down in New Orleans and the book was full of stuff about banana leaves and iron railings and Spanish moss.

"Baby Jenks, they know everything, the old European ones," Davis had said. "They know how it started, they know we can go on and on if we hang in there, live to be a thousand years old and turn into white marble."

"Gee, that's just great, Davis," Baby Jenks said. "It's bad enough now not being able to walk into a Seven Eleven under those lights without people looking at you. Who wants to look like white marble?"

"Baby Jenks, you don't need anything anymore from the Seven Eleven," Davis said real calmly. But he got the point.

Forget the books. Baby Jenks did love the Vampire Lestat's music, and those songs just kept giving her a lot, especially that one about Those Who Must Be Kept—the Egyptian King and Queen—though to tell the truth she didn't know what the hell it meant till Killer explained.

"They're the parents of all vampires, Baby Jenks, the Mother and the Father. See, we're all an unbroken line of blood coming down from the King and the Queen in ancient Egypt who are called Those Who Must Be Kept. And the reason you gotta keep them is if you destroy them, you destroy all of us, too."

Sounded like a bunch of bull to her.

"Lestat's seen the Mother and the Father," Davis said. "Found them hidden on a Greek island, so he knows that it's the truth. That's what he's been telling everybody with these songs—and it's the truth."

"And the Mother and the Father don't move or speak or drink blood, Baby Jenks," Killer said. He looked real thoughtful, sad, almost. "They just sit there and stare like they've done for thousands of years. Nobody knows what those two know."

"Probably nothing," Baby Jenks had said disgustedly. "And I tell you, this is some kind of being immortal! What do you mean the big city Dead guys can kill us? Just how can they manage that?"

"Fire and sun can always do it," Killer answered just a touch impatient. "I told you that. Now mind me, please. You can always fight the big city Dead guys. You're tough. Fact is, the big city Dead are as scared of you as you will ever be of them. You just beat it when you see a Dead guy you don't know. That's a rule that's followed by everybody who's Dead."

After they'd left the coven house, she'd got another big surprise from Killer: he'd told her about the vampire bars. Big fancy places in New York and San Francisco and New Orleans, where the Dead guys met in the back rooms while the damn fool human beings drank and danced up front. In there, no other Dead guy could kill you, city slicker, European, or rogue like her.

"You run for one of those places," he told her, "if the big city Dead guys ever get on your case."

"I'm not old enough to go in a bar," Baby Jenks said.

That really did it. He and Davis laughed themselves sick. They were falling off their motorcycles.

"You find a vampire bar, Baby Jenks," Killer said, "you just give them the Evil Eye and say 'Let me in.' "

Yeah, she'd done that Evil Eye on people and made them do stuff, it worked OK. And truth was, they'd never seen the vampire bars. Just heard about them. Didn't know where they were. She'd had lots of questions when they finally left St. Louis.

But as she made her way north towards the same city now, the only thing in the world she cared about was getting to that same damned coven house. Big city Dead guys, here I come. She'd go clean out of her head if she had to go on alone.

The music in the earphones stopped. The tape had run out. She couldn't stand the silence in the roar of the wind. The dream came back; she saw those twins again, the soldiers coming. Jesus. If she didn't block it out, the whole damn dream would replay itself like the tape.

Steadying the bike with one hand, she reached in her jacket to open the little cassette player. She flipped the tape over. "Sing on, man!" she said, her voice sounding shrill and tiny to her over the roar of the wind, if she heard it at all.

> *Of Those Who Must Be Kept*
> *What can we know?*
> *Can any explanation save us?*

Yes sir, that was the one she loved. That's the one she'd been listening to when she fell asleep waiting for her mother to come home from work in Gun Barrel City. It wasn't the words that got to her, it was the way he sang it, groaning like Bruce Springsteen into the mike and making it just break your heart.

It was kind of like a hymn in a way. It had that kind of sound, yet Lestat was right there in the middle of it, singing to her, and there was a steady drumbeat that went to her bones.

"OK, man, OK, you're the only goddamn Dead guy I've got now, Lestat, keep singing!"

Five minutes to St. Louis, and there she was thinking about her mother again, how strange it had all been, how bad.

Baby Jenks hadn't even told Killer or Davis why she was going home, though they knew, they understood.

Baby Jenks had to do it, she had to get her parents before the Fang Gang went out west. And even now she didn't regret it. Except for that strange moment when her mother was dying there on the floor.

Now Baby Jenks had always hated her mother. She thought her mother was just a real fool, making crosses every day of her life with little pink seashells and bits of glass and then taking them to the Gun Barrel City Flea Market and selling them for ten dollars. And they were ugly, too, just real ready-made junk, those things with a little twisted-up Jesus in the middle made up of tiny red and blue beads and things.

But it wasn't just that, it was everything her mother had ever done that got to Baby Jenks and made her disgusted. Going to church, that was bad enough, but talking the way she did to people so sweet and just putting up with her husband's drinking and always saying nice things about everybody.

Baby Jenks never bought a word of it. She used to lie there on her bunk in the trailer thinking to herself, What really makes that lady tick? When is she going to blow up like a stick of dynamite? Or is she just too stupid? Her mother had stopped looking Baby Jenks in the eye years ago. When Baby Jenks was twelve she'd come in and said, "You know I done it, don't you? I hope to God you don't think I'm no virgin." And her mother just faded out, like, just looked away with her eyes wide and empty and stupid, and went back to her work, humming like always as she made those seashell crosses.

One time some big city person told her mother that she made real folk art. "They're making a fool of you," Baby Jenks had said. "Don't you know that? They didn't buy one of those ugly things, did they? You know what those things look like to me? I'll tell you what they look like. They look like great big dime-store earrings!"

No arguing. Just turning the other cheek. "You want some supper, honey?"

It was like an open and shut case, Baby Jenks figured. So she had headed out of Dallas early, making Cedar Creek Lake in less than an hour, and there was the familiar sign that meant her sweet little old home town: WELCOME TO GUN BARREL CITY. WE SHOOT STRAIGHT WITH YOU.

She hid her Harley behind the trailer when she got there, nobody home, and lay down for a nap, Lestat singing in the earphones, and the steam iron ready by her side. When her mother came in, slam bam, thank you, ma'am, she'd take her out with it.

Then the dream happened. Why, she wasn't even asleep when it started. It was like Lestat faded out, and the dream pulled her down and snap:

She was in a place full of sunlight. A clearing on the side of a mountain. And these two twins were there, beautiful women with soft wavy red hair, and they knelt like angels in church with their hands folded. Lots of people around, people in long robes, like people in the Bible. And there was music, too, a creepy thumping and the sound of a horn playing, real mournful. But the worst part was the dead body, the burned body of the woman on a stone slab. Why, she looked like she'd been cooked, lying there! And on the plates, there was a fat shiny heart and a brain. Yep, sure thing, that was a heart and a brain.

Baby Jenks had woken up, scared. To hell with that. Her mother was standing in the door. Baby Jenks jumped up and banged her with the steam iron till she stopped moving. Really bashed in her head. And she should have been dead, but she wasn't yet, and then that crazy moment came.

Her mother was lying there on the floor, half dead, staring, just like her daddy would be later. And Baby Jenks was sitting in the chair, one blue jean leg thrown over the arm, leaning on her elbow, or twirling one of her braids, just waiting, thinking about the twins in the dream sort of, and the body and the things on the plates, what was it all for? But mostly just waiting. Die, you stupid bitch, go on, die, I'm not slamming you again!

Even now Baby Jenks wasn't sure what had happened. It was like her mother's thoughts had changed, grown wider, bigger. Maybe she was floating up on the ceiling somewhere the way Baby Jenks had been when she nearly died before Killer saved her. But whatever was the cause, the thoughts were just amazing. Just flat out amazing. Like her mother knew everything! All about good and bad and how important it was to love, really love, and how it was so much more than just all the rules about don't drink, don't smoke, pray to Jesus. It wasn't preacher stuff. It was just gigantic.

Her mother, lying there, had thought about how the lack of love in her daughter, Baby Jenks, had been as awful as a bad gene that made Baby Jenks blind and crippled. Yet it didn't matter. It was going to be all right.

Baby Jenks would rise out of what was going on now, just as she had almost done before Killer had got to her, and there would be a finer understanding of everything. What the hell did that mean? Something about everything around us being part of one big thing, the fibers in the carpet, the leaves outside the window, the water dripping in the sink, the clouds moving over Cedar Creek Lake, and the bare trees, and they weren't really so ugly as Baby Jenks had thought. No, the whole thing was almost too beautiful to describe suddenly. And Baby Jenks' mother had always known about this! Seen it that way. Baby Jenks' mother forgave Baby Jenks everything. Poor Baby Jenks. She didn't know. She didn't know about the green grass. Or the seashells shining in the light of the lamp.

Then Baby Jenks' mother had died. Thank God! Enough! But Baby Jenks had been crying. Then she'd carried the body out of the trailer and buried it in back, real deep, feeling how good it was to be one of the Dead and so strong and able to just heft those shovels full of dirt.

Then her father came home. This one's really for fun! She buried him while he was still alive. She'd never forget the look on his face when he came in the door and saw her with the fire ax. "Well, if it ain't Lizzie Borden."

Who the hell was Lizzie Borden?

Then the way his chin stuck out, and his fist came flying towards her, he was so sure of himself! "You little slut!" She split his goddamn forehead in half. Yeah, that part was great, feeling the skull cave—"Go down, you bastard!"—and so was shoveling dirt on his face while he was still looking at her. Paralyzed, couldn't move, thinking he was a kid again on a farm or something in New Mexico. Just baby talk. *You son of a bitch, I always knew you had shit for brains. Now I can smell it!*

But why the hell had she ever gone down there? Why had she left the Fang Gang?

If she'd never left them, she'd be with them now in San Francisco, with Killer and Davis, waiting to see Lestat on the stage. They might have even made the vampire bar out there or something. Leastways, if they had ever gotten there. If something wasn't really really wrong.

And what the hell was she doing now backtracking? Maybe she should have gone along out west. Two nights, that was all that was left.

Hell, maybe she'd rent a motel room when the concert happened, so she could watch it on TV. But before that, she had to find some Dead guys in St. Louis. She couldn't go on alone.

How to find the Central West End. Where was it?

This boulevard looked familiar. She was cruising along, praying no meddling cop would start after her. She'd outrun him of course, she always did, though she dreamed of getting just one of those damn sons-a-bitches on a lonely road. But the fact was she didn't want to be chased out of St. Louis.

Now this looked like something she knew. Yeah, this was the Central West End or whatever they called it and she turned off now to the right and went down an old street with those big cool leafy trees all around her. Made her think of her mother again, the green grass, the clouds. Little sob in her throat.

If she just wasn't so damn lonesome! But then she saw the gates, yeah, this was the street. Killer had told her that Dead guys never really forget anything. Her brain would be like a little computer. Maybe it was true. These were the gates all right, great big iron gates, opened wide and covered with dark green ivy. Guess they never really close up "a private place."

She slowed to a rumbling crawl, then cut the motor altogether. Too noisy in this dark valley of mansions. Some bitch might call the cops. She had to get off to walk her bike. Her legs weren't long enough to do it any other way. But that was OK. She liked walking in these deep dead leaves. She liked this whole quiet street.

Boy, if I was a big city vampire I'd live here too, she thought, and then far off down the street, she saw the coven house, saw the brick walls and the white Moorish arches. Her heart was really going!

Burnt up!

At first she didn't believe it! Then she saw it was true all right, big streaks of black on the bricks, and the windows all blown out, not a pane of glass left anywhere. Jesus Christ! She was going crazy. She walked her bike up closer, biting her lip so hard she could taste her own blood. Just look at it. Who the hell was doing it! Teeny bits of glass all over the lawn and even in the trees so the whole place was kind of sparkling in a way that human beings probably couldn't make out. Looked to her like nightmare Christmas decorations. And the stink of burning wood. It was just hanging there.

She was going to cry! She was going to start screaming! But then she heard something. Not a real sound, but the things that Killer had taught her to listen for. There was a Dead guy in there!

She couldn't believe her luck, and she didn't give a damn what happened, she was going in there. Yeah, somebody in there. It was real faint. She went a few more feet, crunching real loud in the dead leaves. No light but something moving in there, and it knew she was coming. And as she stood there, heart hammering, afraid, and frantic to go in, somebody came out on the front porch, a Dead guy looking right at her.

Praise the Lord, she whispered. And he wasn't no jerkoff in a three-piece suit, either. No, he was a young kid, maybe no more than two years older than her when they did it to him, and he looked real special. Like he had silver hair for one thing, just real pretty short curly gray hair, and that always looked great on a young person. And he was tall too, about six feet, and skinny, a real elegant guy, the way she saw it. He had an icy look to his skin it was so white, and he wore a dark brown turtleneck shirt, real smooth across his chest, and a fancy cut brown leather jacket and pants, nothing at all like biker leather. Really boss, this guy, and cuter than any Dead guy in the Fang Gang.

"Come inside!" he said in a hiss. "Hurry."

She like to flew up the steps. The air was still full of tiny ashes, and it hurt her eyes and made her cough. Half the porch had fallen in. Carefully she made her way into the hallway. Some of the stairs was left, but the roof way above was wide open. And the chandelier had fallen down, all crushed and full of soot. Real spooky, like a haunted house this place.

The Dead guy was in the living room or what was left of it, kicking and picking through burnt-up stuff, furniture and things, sort of in a rage, it looked like.

"Baby Jenks, is it?" he said, flashing her a weird fake smile, full of pearly teeth including his little fangs, and his gray eyes glittering kind of. "And you're lost, aren't you?"

OK, another goddamn mind reader like Davis. And one with a foreign accent.

"Yeah, so what?" she said. And real surprising, she caught his name like as if it was a ball and he'd tossed it to her: Laurent. Now that was a classy name, French sounding.

"Stay right there, Baby Jenks," he said. The accent was French too, probably. "There were three in this coven and two were incinerated. The police can't detect the remains but you will know them if you step on them and you will not like it."

Christ! And he was telling her the truth, 'cause there was one of them right there, no jive, at the back of the hall, and it looked like a half-burnt suit of clothes lying there, kind of vaguely in the outline of a man, and sure thing, she could tell by the smell, there'd been a Dead guy in the clothes, and just the sleeves and the pant legs and shoes were left. In the middle of it all there was a kind of grayish messy stuff, looked more like grease and powder than ashes. Funny the way the shirt sleeve was still neatly sticking out of the coat sleeve. Now that had been a three-piece suit maybe.

She was getting sick. Could you get sick when you were Dead? She wanted to get out of here. What if whatever had done this was coming back? Immortal, tie a can to it!

"Don't move," the Dead guy said to her, "and we'll be leaving together just as soon as we can."

"Like now, OK!" she said. She was shaking, goddamn it. This is what they meant when they said cold sweat!

He'd found a tin box and he was taking all the unburnt money out of it.

"Hey, man, I'm splitting," she said. She could feel something around here, and it had nothing to do with that grease spot on the floor. She was thinking of the burnt-up coven houses in Dallas and Oklahoma City, the way the Fang Gang had vanished on her. He got all that, she could tell. His face got soft, real cute again. He threw down the box and came towards her so fast it scared her worse.

"Yes, *ma chère*," he said in a real nice voice, "all those coven houses, exactly. The East Coast has been burnt out like a circuit of lights. There is no answer at the coven house in Paris or the coven house in Berlin."

He took her arm as they headed for the front door.

"Who the hell's doing this!" she said.

"Who the hell knows, *chérie?* It destroys the houses, the vampire bars, whatever rogues it finds. We have got to get out of here. Now make the bike go."

But she had come to a halt. *Something out here.* She was standing at the edge of the porch. Something. She was as scared to go on as she was to go back in the house.

"What's wrong?" he asked her in a whisper.

How dark this place was with these great big trees and the houses, they all looked haunted, and she could hear something, something real low like . . . like something's breathing. Something like that.

"Baby Jenks? Move it now!"

"But where are we going?" she asked. This thing, whatever it was, it was almost a sound.

"The only place we can go. To him, darling, to the Vampire Lestat. He is out there in San Francisco waiting, unharmed!"

"Yeah?" she said, staring at the dark street in front of her. "Yeah, right, to the Vampire Lestat." Just ten steps to the bike. Take it, Baby Jenks. He was about to leave without her. "No, don't you do that, you son of a bitch, don't you touch my bike!"

But it was a sound now, wasn't it? Baby Jenks had never heard anything quite like it. But you hear a lot of things when you're Dead. You hear trains miles away, and people talking on planes over your head.

The Dead guy heard it. No, he heard her hearing it! "What is it?" he whispered. Jesus, he was scared. And now he heard it all by himself too.

He pulled her down the steps. She stumbled and almost fell, but he lifted her off her feet and put her on the bike.

The noise was getting really loud. It was coming in beats like music. And it was so loud now she couldn't even hear what this Dead guy was saying to her. She twisted the key, turned the handles to give the Harley gas, and the Dead guy was on the bike behind her, but Jesus, the noise, she couldn't think. She couldn't even hear the engine of the bike!

She looked down, trying to see what the hell was going on, was it running, she couldn't even feel it. Then she looked up and she knew she was looking towards the thing that was sending the noise. It was in the darkness, behind the trees.

The Dead guy had leaped off the bike, and he was jabbering away at it, as if he could see it. But no, he was looking around like a crazy man talking to himself. But she couldn't hear a word. She just knew it was there, it was looking at them, and the crazy guy was wasting his breath!

She was off the Harley. It had fallen over. The noise stopped. Then there was a loud ringing in her ears.

"—anything you want!" the Dead guy next to her was saying, "just anything, name it, we will do it. We are your servants—!" Then he ran past Baby Jenks, nearly knocking her over and grabbing up her bike.

"Hey!" she shouted, but just as she started for him, he burst into flames! He screamed.

And then Baby Jenks screamed too. She screamed and screamed. The burning Dead guy was turning over and over on the ground, just pinwheeling. And behind her, the coven house exploded. She felt the heat on her back. She saw stuff flying through the air. The sky looked like high noon.

Oh, sweet Jesus, let me live, let me live!

For one split second she thought her heart had burst. She meant to look down to see if her chest had broken open and her heart was spewing out blood like molten lava from a volcano, but then the heat built up inside her head and swoosh! she was gone.

She was rising up and up through a dark tunnel, and then high above she floated, looking down on the whole scene.

Oh yeah, just like before. And there it was, the thing that had killed them, a white figure standing in a thicket of trees. And there was the Dead guy's clothes smoking on the pavement. And her own body just burning away.

Through the flames she could see the pure black outline of her own skull and her bones. But it didn't frighten her. It didn't really seem that interesting at all.

It was the white figure that amazed her. It looked just like a statue, like the Blessed Virgin Mary in the Catholic church. She stared at the sparkling silver threads that seemed to move out from the figure in all directions, threads made out of some kind of dancing light. And as she moved higher, she saw that the silver threads stretched out, tangling with other threads, to make a giant net all over the whole world. All through the net were Dead guys, caught, like helpless flies in a web. Tiny pinpoints of light, pulsing, and connected to the white figure, and almost beautiful, the sight of it, except it was so sad. Oh, poor souls of all the Dead guys locked in indestructible matter unable to grow old or die.

But she was free. The net was way far away from her now. She was seeing so many things.

Like there were thousands and thousands of other dead people floating up here, too, in a great hazy gray layer. Some were lost, others were fighting with each other, and some were looking back down to where they'd died, so pitiful, like they didn't know or wouldn't believe they were dead. There was even a couple of them trying to be seen and heard by the living, but that they could not do.

She knew she was dead. This had happened before. She was just passing through this murky lair of sad lingering people. She was on her way! And the pitifulness of her life on earth caused her sorrow. But it was not the important thing now.

The light was shining again, the magnificent light she'd glimpsed when she'd almost died that first time around. She moved towards it, into it. And this was truly beautiful. Never had she seen such colors, such radiance, never had she heard the pure music that she was hearing now. There were no words to describe this; it was beyond any language she'd ever known. And this time nobody would bring her back!

Because the one coming towards her, to take her and to help her—it was her mother! And her mother wouldn't let her go.

Never had she felt such love as she felt for her mother; but then love surrounded her; the light, the color, the love—these things were utterly indistinguishable.

Ah, that poor Baby Jenks, she thought as she looked down to earth just one last time. But she wasn't Baby Jenks now. No, not at all.

3

THE GODDESS PANDORA

Once we had the words.
Ox and Falcon. Plow.
There was clarity.
Savage as horns
curved.
We lived in stone rooms.
We hung our hair out the windows and up it climbed the men.
A garden behind the ears, the curls.
On each hill a king
of that hill. At night the threads were pulled out
of the tapestries. The unravelled men screamed.
All moons revealed. We had the words.
. . . .

STAN RICE
from "The Words Once"
Whiteboy (1976)

SHE was a tall creature, clad in black, with only her eyes uncovered, her strides long as she moved with inhuman speed up the treacherous snow-covered path.

Almost clear this night of tiny stars in the high thin air of the Himalayas, and far ahead—beyond her powers of reckoning distance—loomed the massive pleated flank of Everest, splendidly visible above a thick wreath of turbulent white cloud. It took her breath away each time she glanced at it, not only because it was so beautiful, but because it was so seemingly full of meaning, though no true meaning was there.

Worship this mountain? Yes, one could do that with impunity, because the mountain would never answer. The whistling wind that chilled her skin was the voice of nothing and no one. And this incidental and utterly indifferent grandeur made her want to cry.

So did the sight of the pilgrims far below her, a thin stream of ants it seemed, winding their way up an impossibly narrow road. Too unspeakably sad their delusion. Yet she moved towards the same hidden mountain temple. She moved towards the same despicable and deceiving god.

She was suffering from the cold. Frost covered her face, her eyelids. It clung in tiny crystals to her eyelashes. And each step in the driving wind was hard even for her. Pain or death it couldn't cause her, really; she was too old for that. It was something mental, her suffering. It came from the tremendous resistance of the elements, from seeing nothing for hours but the sheer white and dazzling snows.

No matter. A deep shiver of alarm had passed through her nights ago, in the crowded stinking streets of Old Delhi, and every hour or so since had repeated itself, as if the earth had begun to tremble at its core.

At certain moments, she was sure that the Mother and the Father must be waking. Somewhere far away in a crypt where her beloved Marius had placed them, Those Who Must Be Kept had stirred at last. Nothing less than such a resurrection could transmit this powerful yet vague signal— Akasha and Enkil rising, after six thousand years of horrifying stillness, from the throne they shared.

But that was fancy, wasn't it? Might as well ask the mountain to speak. For these were no mere legend to her, the ancient parents of all blood drinkers. Unlike so many of their spawn, she had seen them with her own eyes. At the door of their shrine she had been made immortal; she had crept forward on her knees and touched the Mother; she had pierced the smooth shining surface that had once been the Mother's human skin and caught in her open mouth the gushing stream of the Mother's blood. What a miracle it had been even then, the living blood pouring forth from the lifeless body before the wounds miraculously closed.

But in those early centuries of magnificent belief she had shared Marius's conviction that the Mother and Father merely slumbered, that the time would come when they would wake and speak to their children once again.

In the candlelight, she and Marius had sung hymns to them together; she herself had burnt the incense, placed before them the flowers; she had sworn never to reveal the location of the sanctuary lest other blood drinkers come to destroy Marius, to steal his charges and feast gluttonously on the original and most powerful blood.

But that was long ago when the world was divided among tribes and empires, when heroes and emperors were made gods in a day. In that time elegant philosophical ideas had caught her fancy.

She knew now what it meant to live forever. Tell it to the mountain.

Danger. She felt it again coursing through her, a scorching current. Then gone. And then a glimpse of a green and humid place, a place of soft earth and stifling growth. But it vanished almost immediately.

She paused, the moonlit snow blinding her for a moment, and she raised her eyes to the stars, twinkling through a thin fleece of passing cloud. She listened for other immortal voices. But she heard no clear and vital transmission—only a dim throb from the temple to which she was going, and from far behind her, rising out of the dark warrens of a dirty over-crowded city, the dead, electronic recordings of that mad blood drinker, "the rock star," the Vampire Lestat.

Doomed that impetuous modern fledgling who had dared to fashion garbled songs of bits and pieces of old truths. She had seen countless young ones rise and fall.

Yet his audacity intrigued her, even as it shocked her. Could it be that the alarm she heard was somehow connected to his plaintive yet raucous songs?

Akasha, Enkil
Hearken to your children

How dare he speak the ancient names to the mortal world? It seemed impossible, an offense to reason, that such a creature not be dismissed out of hand. Yet the monster, reveling in improbable celebrity, revealed secrets he could have learned only from Marius himself. And where was Marius, who for two thousand years had taken Those Who Must Be Kept from one secret sanctuary to another? Her heart would break if she let herself think of Marius, of the quarrels that had long ago divided them.

But the recorded voice of Lestat was gone now, swallowed by other faint electric voices, vibrations rising from cities and villages, and the ever audible cry of mortal souls. As so often happened, her powerful ears could separate no one signal. The rising tide had overwhelmed her—shapeless, horrific—so that she closed herself off. Only the wind again.

Ah, what must the collective voices of the earth be to the Mother and the Father whose powers had grown, inevitably, from the dawn of recorded time? Had they the power, as she had still, to shut off the flow, or to select from time to time the voices they might hear? Perhaps they were as passive in this regard as in any other, and it was the unstoppable din that kept them fixed, unable to reason, as they heard the endless cries, mortal and immortal, of the entire world.

She looked at the great jagged peak before her. She must continue. She tightened the covering over her face. She walked on.

And as the trail led her to a small promontory, she saw her destination at last. Across an immense glacier, the temple rose from a high cliff, a stone structure of near invisible whiteness, its bell tower disappearing into the swirling snow that had just begun to fall.

How long would it take her to reach it, even fast as she could walk? She knew what she must do, yet she dreaded it. She must lift her arms, defy the laws of nature and her own reason, and rise over the gulf that separated her from the temple, gently descending only when she had reached the other side of the frozen gorge. No other power she possessed could make her feel so insignificant, so inhuman, so far from the common earthly being she had once been.

But she wanted to reach the temple. She had to. And so she did raise her arms slowly, with conscious grace. Her eyes closed for the moment as she willed herself upwards, and she felt her body rising immediately as if it were weightless, a force seemingly unfettered by substance, riding by sheer intention the wind itself.

For a long moment she let the winds buffet her; she let her body twist, drift. She rose higher and higher, allowing herself to turn away from the earth altogether, the clouds flying past her, as she faced the stars. How heavy her garments felt; was she not ready to become invisible? Would that not be the next step? A speck of dust in the eye of God, she thought. Her heart was aching. The horror of this, to be utterly unconnected. . . . The tears welled in her eyes.

And as always happened in such moments, the vague shining human past she clung to seemed more than ever a myth to be cherished as all practical belief died away. *That I lived, that I loved, that my flesh was warm.* She saw Marius, her maker, not as he was now, but then, a young immortal burning with a supernatural secret: "Pandora, my dearest . . ." "Give it to me, I beg you." "Pandora, come with me to ask the blessing of the Mother and the Father. Come into the shrine."

Unanchored, in despair, she might have forgotten her destination. She could have let herself drift towards the rising sun. But the alarm came again, the silent, pulsating signal of *Danger,* to remind her of her purpose. She spread out her arms, willed herself to face the earth again, and saw the temple courtyard with its smoking fires directly below. *Yes, there.*

The speed of her descent astonished her; momentarily, it shattered her reason. She found herself standing in the courtyard, her body aching for one flashing instant, and then cold and still.

The scream of the wind was distant. The music of the temple came through the walls, a dizzying throb, the tambourines and drums driving with it, voices melding into one gruesome and repetitive sound. And before her were the pyres, spitting, crackling, the dead bodies darkening as they lay heaped on the burning wood. The stench sickened her. Yet for a long time, she watched the flames working slowly at the sizzling flesh, the blackening stumps, the hair that gave off sudden wisps of white smoke. The smell suffocated her; the cleansing mountain air could not reach her here.

She stared at the distant wooden door to the inner sanctum. She would test the power again, bitterly. *There.* And she found herself moving over the threshold, the door opened, the light of the inner chamber dazzling her, along with the warm air and the deafening chant.

"Azim! Azim! Azim!" the celebrants sang over and over, their backs turned to her as they pressed to the center of the candle-lighted hall, their hands raised, twisting at the wrists in rhythm with their rocking heads. "Azim! Azim! Azim-Azim-Azim! Ahhhh Zeeeem!" Smoke rose from the censers; an endless swarm of figures turned, circling in place on their bare feet, but they did not see her. Their eyes were closed, their dark faces smooth, only their mouths moving as they repeated the revered name.

She pushed into the thick of them, men and women in rags, others in gorgeous colored silks and clattering gold jewelry, all repeating the invocation in horrifying monotony. She caught the smell of fever, starvation, dead bodies fallen in the press, unheeded in the common delirium. She clung to a marble column, as if to anchor herself in the turbulent stream of movement and noise.

And then she saw Azim in the middle of the crush. His dark bronze skin was moist and gleaming in the light of the candles, his head bound in a black silk turban, his long embroidered robes stained with a mingling of mortal and immortal blood. His black eyes, ringed in kohl, were enormous. To the hard underlying beat of the drums, he danced, undulating, thrusting his fists forward and drawing them back as though pounding upon an invisible wall. His slippered feet tapped the marble in frenzied rhythm. Blood oozed from the corners of his mouth. His expression was one of utter mindless absorption.

Yet he knew that she had come. And from the center of his dance, he looked directly at her, and she saw his blood-smeared lips curl in a smile.

Pandora, my beautiful immortal Pandora. . . .

Glutted with the feast he was, plump and heated with it as she had seldom ever seen an immortal become. He threw back his head, spun round, and gave a shrill cry. His acolytes came forward, slashing at his outstretched wrists with their ceremonial knives.

And the faithful surged against him, mouths uplifted to catch the sacred blood as it gushed out. The chant grew louder, more insistent over the strangled cries of those nearest him. And suddenly, she saw him being lifted, his body stretched out full length on the shoulders of his followers, golden slippers pointed to the high tessellated ceiling, the knives slashing at his ankles and again at his wrists where the wounds had already closed.

The maddened crowd seemed to expand as its movements grew more frantic, reeking bodies slamming against her, oblivious to the coldness and hardness of the ancient limbs beneath her soft shapeless wool clothes. She did not move. She let herself be surrounded, drawn in. She saw Azim lowered to the ground once more; bled, moaning, wounds already healed. He beckoned to her to join him. Silently she refused.

She watched as he reached out and snatched a victim, blindly, at random, a young woman with painted eyes and dangling golden earrings, gashing open her slender throat.

The crowd had lost the perfect shape of the syllables it chanted; it was now a simple wordless cry that came from every mouth.

Eyes wide as if in horror at his own power, Azim sucked the woman dry of blood in one great draught, then dashed the body on the stones before him where it lay mangled as the faithful surrounded it, hands out in supplication to their staggering god.

She turned her back; she went out in the cold air of the courtyard, moving away from the heat of the fires. Stink of urine, offal. She stood against the wall, gazing upwards, thinking of the mountain, paying no heed when the acolytes dragged past her the bodies of the newly dead and threw them into the flames.

She thought of the pilgrims she had seen on the road below the temple, the long chain that moved sluggishly day and night through the uninhabited mountains to this unnamed place. How many died without ever reaching this precipice? How many died outside the gates, waiting to be let in?

She loathed it. And yet it did not matter. It was an ancient horror. She waited. Then Azim called her.

She turned and moved back through the door and then through another into a small exquisitely painted antechamber where, standing on a red carpet bordered with rubies, he waited silently for her, surrounded by random treasures, offerings of gold and silver, the music in the hall lower, full of languor and fear.

"Dearest," he said. He took her face in his hands and kissed her. A heated stream of blood flowed out of his mouth into her, and for one rapturous moment her senses were filled with the song and dance of the faithful, the heady cries. Flooding warmth of mortal adoration, surrender. Love.

Yes, love. She saw Marius for one instant. She opened her eyes, and stepped back. For a moment she saw the walls with their painted peacocks, lilies; she saw the heaps of shimmering gold. Then she saw only Azim.

He was changeless as were his people, changeless as were the villages from which they had come, wandering through snow and waste to find this horrid, meaningless end. One thousand years ago, Azim had begun his rule in this temple from which no worshiper ever departed alive. His supple golden skin nourished by an endless river of blood sacrifice had paled only slightly over the centuries, whereas her own flesh had lost its human blush in half the time. Only her eyes, and her dark brown hair perhaps, gave an immediate appearance of life. She had beauty, yes, she knew that, but he had a great surpassing vigor. *Evil.* Irresistible to his followers, shrouded in legend, he ruled, without past or future, as incomprehensible to her now as he had ever been.

She didn't want to linger. The place repelled her more than she wanted him to know. She told him silently of her purpose, the alarm that she had heard. Something wrong somewhere, something changing, something that has never happened before! And she told him too of the young blood drinker who recorded songs in America, songs full of truths about the Mother and the Father, whose names he knew. It was a simple opening of her mind, without drama.

She watched Azim, sensing his immense power, the ability with which he'd glean from her any random thought or idea, and shield from her the secrets of his own mind.

"Blessed Pandora," he said scornfully. "What do I care about the Mother and the Father? What are they to me? What do I care about your precious Marius? That he calls for help over and over! This is nothing to me!"

She was stunned. Marius calling for help. Azim laughed.

"Explain what you're saying," she said.

Again laughter. He turned his back to her. There was nothing she could do but wait. Marius had made her. All the world could hear Marius's voice, but she could not hear it. Was it an echo that had reached her, dim in its deflection, of a powerful cry that the others had heard? *Tell me, Azim. Why make an enemy of me?*

When he turned to her again, he was thoughtful, his round face plump, human-looking as he yielded to her, the backs of his hands fleshy and dimpled as he pressed them together just beneath his moist lower lip. He wanted something of her. There was no scorn or malice now.

"It's a warning," he said. "It comes over and over, echoing through a chain of listeners who carry it from its origins in some far-off place. We are all in danger. Then it is followed by a call for help, which is weaker.

Help him that he may try to avert the danger. But in this there is little conviction. It is the warning above all that he would have us heed."

"The words, what are they?"

He shrugged. "I do not listen. I do not care."

"Ah!" She turned her back now on him. She heard him come towards her, felt his hands on her shoulders.

"You must answer *my* question now," he said. He turned her to face him. "It is the dream of the twins that concerns me. What does this mean?"

Dream of the twins. She didn't have an answer. The question didn't make sense to her. She had had no such dream.

He regarded her silently, as if he believed she was lying. Then he spoke very slowly, evaluating her response carefully.

"Two women, red hair. Terrible things befall them. They come to me in troubling and unwelcome visions just before I would open my eyes. I see these women raped before a court of onlookers. Yet I do not know who they are or where this outrage takes place. And I am not alone in my questioning. Out there, scattered through the world, there are other dark gods who have these dreams and would know why they come to us now."

Dark gods! We are not gods, she thought contemptuously.

He smiled at her. Were they not standing in his very temple? Could she not hear the moaning of the faithful? Could she not smell their blood?

"I know nothing of these two women," she said. Twins, red hair. No. She touched his fingers gently, almost seductively. "Azim, don't torment me. I want you to tell me about Marius. From where does his call come?"

How she hated him at this moment, that he might keep this secret from her.

"From where?" he asked her defiantly. "Ah, that is the crux, isn't it? Do you think he would dare to lead us to the shrine of the Mother and the Father? If I thought that, I would answer him, oh, yes, oh, truly. I would leave my temple to find him, of course. But he cannot fool us. He would rather see himself destroyed than reveal the shrine."

"From where is he calling?" she asked patiently.

"These dreams," he said, his face darkening with anger. "The dreams of the twins, this I would have explained!"

"And I would tell you who they are and what they mean, if only I knew." She thought of the songs of Lestat, the words she'd heard. Songs of Those Who Must Be Kept and crypts beneath European cities, songs of questing, sorrow. Nothing there of red-haired women, nothing. . . .

Furious, he gestured for her to stop. "The Vampire Lestat," he said, sneering. "Do not speak of this abomination to me. Why hasn't he been destroyed already? Are the dark gods asleep like the Mother and the Father?"

He watched her, calculating. She waited.

"Very well. I believe you," he said finally. "You've told me what you know."

"Yes."

"I close my ears to Marius. I told you. Stealer of the Mother and the Father, let him cry for help until the end of time. But you, Pandora, for you I feel love as always, and so I will soil myself with these affairs. Cross the sea to the New World. Look in the frozen north beyond the last of the woodlands near the western sea. And there you may find Marius, trapped in a citadel of ice. He cries that he is unable to move. As for his warning, it is as vague as it is persistent. We are in danger. We must help him so that he may stop the danger. So that he may go to the Vampire Lestat."

"Ah. So it is the young one who has done this!"

The shiver passed through her, violent, painful. She saw in her mind's eye the blank, senseless faces of the Mother and the Father, indestructible monsters in human form. She looked at Azim in confusion. He had paused, but he wasn't finished. And she waited for him to go on.

"No," he said, his voice dropping, having lost its sharp edge of anger. "There is a danger, Pandora, yes. Great danger, and it does not require Marius to announce it. It has to do with the red-haired twins." How uncommonly earnest he was, how unguarded. "This I know," he said, "because I was old before Marius was made. The twins, Pandora. Forget Marius. And hearken to your dreams."

She was speechless, watching him. He looked at her for a long moment, and then his eyes appeared to grow smaller, to become solid. She could feel him drawing back, away from her and all the things of which they'd spoken. Finally, he no longer saw her.

He heard the insistent wails of his worshipers; he felt thirst again; he wanted hymns and blood. He turned and started out of the chamber, then he glanced back.

"Come with me, Pandora! Join me but for an hour!" His voice was drunken, unclear.

The invitation caught her off guard. She considered. It had been years since she had sought the exquisite pleasure. She thought not merely of the blood itself, but of the momentary union with another soul. And there it was, suddenly, waiting for her, among those who had climbed the highest mountain range on earth to seek this death. She thought also of the quest that lay before her—to find Marius—and of the sacrifices it would entail.

"Come, dearest."

She took his hand. She let herself be led out of the room and into the center of the crowded hall. The brightness of the light startled her; yes, the blood again. The smell of humans pressed in on her, tormenting her.

The cry of the faithful was deafening. The stamp of human feet seemed to shake the painted walls, the glimmering gold ceiling. The incense burned her eyes. Faint memory of the shrine, eons ago, of Marius embracing her. Azim stood before her as he removed her outer cloak, revealing her face, her naked arms, the plain gown of black wool she wore, and her long brown hair. She saw herself reflected in a thousand pairs of mortal eyes.

"The goddess Pandora!" he cried out, throwing back his head.

Screams rose over the rapid thudding of drums. Countless human hands stroked her. "Pandora, Pandora, Pandora!" The chant mingled with the cries of "Azim!"

A young brown-skinned man danced before her, white silk shirt plastered to the sweat of his dark chest. His black eyes, gleaming under low dark brows, were fired with the challenge. *I am your victim! Goddess!* She could see nothing suddenly in the flickering light and drowning noise but his eyes, his face. She embraced him, crushing his ribs in her haste, her teeth sinking deep into his neck. *Alive.* The blood poured into her, reached her heart and flooded its chambers, then sent its heat through all her cold limbs. It was beyond remembrance, this glorious sensation—and the exquisite lust, the wanting again! The death shocked her, knocked the breath out of her. She felt it pass into her brain. She was blinded, moaning. Then instantly, the clarity of her vision was paralyzing. The marble columns lived and breathed. She dropped the body, and took hold of another young male, half starved, naked to the waist, his strength on the verge of death maddening her.

She broke his tender neck as she drank, hearing her own heart swell, feeling even the surface of her skin flooded with blood. She could see the color in her own hands just before she closed her eyes, yes, human hands, the death slower, resistant, and then yielding in a rush of dimming light and roaring sound. *Alive.*

"Pandora! Pandora! Pandora!"

God, is there no justice, is there no end?

She stood rocking back and forth, human faces, each discrete, lurid, dancing in front of her. The blood inside her was boiling as it sought out every tissue, every cell. She saw her third victim hurling himself against her, sleek young limbs enfolding her, so soft this hair, this fleece on the back of his arms, the fragile bones, so light, as if she were the real being and these were but creatures of the imagination.

She ripped the head half off the neck, staring at the white bones of the broken spinal cord, then swallowing the death instantly with the violent spray of blood from the torn artery. But the heart, the beating heart, she would see it, taste it. She threw the body back over her right arm, bones cracking, while with her left hand she split the breast bone and tore open the ribs, and reached through the hot bleeding cavity to pull the heart free.

Not dead yet this, not really. And slippery, glistening like wet grapes. The faithful crushed against her as she held it up over her head, squeezing it gently so that the living juice ran down her fingers and into her open mouth. Yes, this, forever and ever.

"Goddess! Goddess!"

Azim was watching her, smiling at her. But she did not look at him. She stared at the shriveled heart as the last droplets of blood left it. A pulp. She let it fall. Her hands glowed like living hands, smeared with blood. She could feel it in her face, the tingling warmth. A tide of memory threatened, a tide of visions without understanding. She drove it back. This time it wouldn't enslave her.

She reached for her black cloak. She felt it enclosing her, as warm, solicitous human hands brought the soft wool covering up over her hair, over the lower part of her face. And ignoring the heated cries of her name all around her, she turned and went out, her limbs accidentally bruising the frenzied worshipers who stumbled into her path.

So deliciously cold the courtyard. She bent her head back slightly, breathing a vagrant wind as it gusted down into the enclosure, where it fanned the pyres before carrying their bitter smoke away. The moonlight was clear and beautiful falling on the snow-covered peaks beyond the walls.

She stood listening to the blood inside her, and marveling in a crazed, despairing way that it could still refresh her and strengthen her, even now. Sad, grief-stricken, she looked at the lovely stark wilderness encircling the temple, she looked up at the loose and billowing clouds. How the blood gave her courage, how it gave her a momentary belief in the sheer rightness of the universe—fruits of a ghastly, unforgivable act.

If the mind can find no meaning, then the senses give it. Live for this, wretched being that you are.

She moved towards the nearest pyre and, careful not to singe her clothes, reached out to let the fire cleanse her hands, burn away the blood, the bits of heart. The licking flames were nothing to the heat of the blood inside her. When finally the faintest beginning of pain was there, the faintest signal of change, she drew back and looked down at her immaculate white skin.

But she must leave here now. Her thoughts were too full of anger, new resentment. Marius needed her. *Danger.* The alarm came again, stronger than ever before, because the blood made her a more powerful receptor. And it did not seem to come from one. Rather it was a communal voice, the dim clarion of a communal knowledge. She was afraid.

She allowed her mind to empty itself, as tears blurred her vision. She lifted her hands, just her hands, delicately. And the ascent was begun. Soundlessly, swiftly, as invisible to mortal eyes, perhaps, as the wind itself.

High over the temple, her body pierced a soft thin agitated mist. The degree of light astonished her. Everywhere the shining whiteness. And below the crenellated landscape of stone peak and blinding glacier descending to a soft darkness of lower forests and vale. Nestled here and there were clusters of sparkling lights, the random pattern of villages or towns. She could have gazed on this forever. Yet within seconds an undulating fleece of cloud had obscured all of it. And she was with the stars alone.

The stars—hard, glittering, embracing her as though she were one of their own. But the stars claimed nothing, really, and no one. She felt terror. Then a deepening sorrow, not unlike joy, finally. No more struggle. No more grief.

Scanning the splendid drift of the constellations, she slowed her ascent and reached out with both hands to the west.

The sunrise lay nine hours behind her. And so she commenced her journey away from it, in time with the night on its way to the other side of the world.

4

THE STORY OF DANIEL, THE DEVIL'S MINION, OR THE BOY FROM INTERVIEW WITH THE VAMPIRE

Who are these shades we wait for and believe
will come some evening in limousines
from Heaven?
The rose
though it knows
is throatless
and cannot say.
My mortal half laughs.
The code and the message are not the same.
And what is an angel
but a ghost in drag?

STAN RICE
from "Of Heaven"
Body of Work (1983)

 E WAS a tall, slender young man, with ashen hair and violet eyes. He wore a dirty gray sweat shirt and jeans, and in the icy wind whipping along Michigan Avenue at five o'clock, he was cold.

Daniel Molloy was his name. He was thirty-two, though he looked younger, a perennial student, not a man, that kind of youthful face. He murmured aloud to himself as he walked. "Armand, I need you. Armand, that concert is tomorrow night. And something terrible is going to happen, something terrible. . . ."

He was hungry. Thirty-six hours had passed since he'd eaten. There was nothing in the refrigerator of his small dirty hotel room, and besides, he had been locked out of it this morning because he had not paid the rent. Hard to remember everything at once.

Then he remembered the dream that he kept having, the dream that came every time he closed his eyes, and he didn't want to eat at all.

He saw the twins in the dream. He saw the roasted body of the woman before them, her hair singed away, her skin crisped. Her heart lay glistening like a swollen fruit on the plate beside her. The brain on the other plate looked exactly like a cooked brain.

Armand knew about it, he had to know. It was no ordinary dream, this. Something to do with Lestat, definitely. And Armand would come soon.

God, he was weak, delirious. Needed something, a drink at least. In his pocket there was no money, only an old crumpled royalty check for the book *Interview with the Vampire,* which he had "written" under a pseudonym over twelve years ago.

Another world, that, when he had been a young reporter, roaming the bars of the world with his tape recorder, trying to get the flotsam and jetsam of the night to tell him some truth. Well, one night in San Francisco he had found a magnificent subject for his investigations. And the light of ordinary life had suddenly gone out.

Now he was a ruined thing, walking too fast under the lowering night sky of Chicago in October. Last Sunday he had been in Paris, and the Friday before that in Edinburgh. Before Edinburgh, he had been in Stockholm and before that he couldn't recall. The royalty check had caught up with him in Vienna, but he did not know how long ago that was.

In all these places he frightened those he passed. The Vampire Lestat had a good phrase for it in his autobiography: "One of those tiresome mortals who has seen spirits . . ." *That's me!*

Where was that book, *The Vampire Lestat?* Ah, somebody had stolen it off the park bench this afternoon while Daniel slept. Well, let them have it. Daniel had stolen it himself, and he'd read it three times already.

But if only he had it now, he could sell it, maybe get enough for a glass of brandy to make him warm. And what was his net worth at this moment, this cold and hungry vagabond that shuffled along Michigan Avenue, hating the wind that chilled him through his worn and dirty clothes? Ten million? A hundred million? He didn't know. Armand would know.

You want money, Daniel? I'll get it for you. It's simpler than you think.

A thousand miles south Armand waited on their private island, the island that belonged in fact to Daniel alone. And if only he had a quarter now, just a quarter, he could drop it into a pay phone and tell Armand that he wanted to come home. Out of the sky, they'd come to get him. They always did. Either the big plane with the velvet bedroom on it or the smaller one with the low ceiling and the leather chairs. Would anybody on this street lend him a quarter in exchange for a plane ride to Miami? Probably not.

Armand, now! I want to be safe with you when Lestat goes on that stage tomorrow night.

Who would cash this royalty check? No one. It was seven o'clock and the fancy shops along Michigan Avenue were for the most part closed, and he had no identification because his wallet had somehow disappeared day before yesterday. So dismal this glaring gray winter twilight, the sky boiling silently with low metallic clouds. Even the stores had taken on an uncommon grimness, with their hard facades of marble or granite, the wealth within gleaming like archaeological relics under museum glass. He plunged his hands in his pockets to warm them, and he bowed his head as the wind came with greater fierceness and the first sting of rain.

He didn't give a damn about the check, really. He couldn't imagine pressing the buttons of a phone. Nothing here seemed particularly real to him, not even the chill. Only the dream seemed real, and the sense of impending disaster, that the Vampire Lestat had somehow set into motion something that even he could never control.

Eat from a garbage can if you have to, sleep somewhere even if it's a park. None of that matters. But he'd freeze if he lay down again in the open air, and besides the dream would come back.

It was coming now every time he closed his eyes. And each time, it was longer, more full of detail. The red-haired twins were so tenderly beautiful. He did not want to hear them scream.

The first night in his hotel room he'd ignored the whole thing. Meaningless. He'd gone back to reading Lestat's autobiography, and glancing up now and then as Lestat's rock video films played themselves out on the little black and white TV that came with that kind of dump.

He'd been fascinated by Lestat's audacity; yet the masquerade as rock star was so simple. Searing eyes, powerful yet slender limbs, and a mischievous smile, yes. But you really couldn't tell. Or could you? He had never laid eyes on Lestat.

But he was an expert on Armand, wasn't he, he had studied every detail of Armand's youthful body and face. Ah, what a delirious pleasure it had been to read about Armand in Lestat's pages, wondering all the while if Lestat's stinging insults and worshipful analyses had put Armand himself into a rage.

In mute fascination, Daniel had watched that little clip on MTV portraying Armand as the coven master of the old vampires beneath the Paris cemetery, presiding over demonic rituals until the Vampire Lestat, the eighteenth-century iconoclast, had destroyed the Old Ways.

Armand must have loathed it, his private history laid bare in flashing images, so much more crass than Lestat's more thoughtful written history. Armand, whose eyes scanned perpetually the living beings around him, refusing even to speak of the undead. But it was impossible that he did not know.

And all this for the multitudes—like the paperback report of an anthropologist, back from the inner circle, who sells the tribe's secrets for a slot on the best-seller list.

So let the demonic gods war with each other. This mortal has been to the top of the mountain where they cross swords. And he has come back. He has been turned away.

The next night, the dream had returned with the clarity of a hallucination. He knew that it could not have been invented by him. He had never seen people quite like that, seen such simple jewelry made of bone and wood.

The dream had come again three nights later. He'd been watching a Lestat rock video for the fifteenth time, perhaps—this one about the ancient and immovable Egyptian Father and Mother of the vampires, Those Who Must Be Kept:

> *Akasha and Enkil,*
> *We are your children,*
> *but what do you give us?*
> *Is your silence*
> *A better gift than truth?*

And then Daniel was dreaming. And the twins were about to begin the feast. They would share the organs on the earthen plates. One would take the brain, the other the heart.

He'd awakened with a sense of urgency, dread. Something terrible going to happen, something going to happen to all of us . . . And that was the first time he'd connected it with Lestat. He had wanted to pick up the phone then. It was four o'clock in the morning in Miami. Why the hell hadn't he done it? Armand would have been sitting on the terrace of the villa, watching the tireless fleet of white boats wend its way back and forth from the Night Island. "Yes, Daniel?" That sensuous, mesmerizing voice. "Calm down and tell me where you are, Daniel."

But Daniel hadn't called. Six months had passed since he had left the

Night Island, and this time it was supposed to be for good. He had once and for all forsworn the world of carpets and limousines and private planes, of liquor closets stocked with rare vintages and dressing rooms full of exquisitely cut clothing, of the quiet overwhelming presence of his immortal lover who gave him every earthly possession he could want.

But now it was cold and he had no room and no money, and he was afraid.

You know where I am, you demon. You know what Lestat's done. And you know I want to come home.

What would Armand say to that?

But I don't know, Daniel. I listen. I try to know. I am not God, Daniel.

Never mind. Just come, Armand. Come. It's dark and cold in Chicago. And tomorrow night the Vampire Lestat will sing his songs on a San Francisco stage. And something bad is going to happen. This mortal knows.

Without slowing his pace, Daniel reached down under the collar of his sagging sweat shirt and felt the heavy gold locket he always wore—the amulet, as Armand called it with his unacknowledged yet irrepressible flair for the dramatic—which held the tiny vial of Armand's blood.

And if he had never tasted that cup would he be having this dream, this vision, this portent of doom?

People turned to look at him; he was talking to himself again, wasn't he? And the wind made him sigh loudly. He had the urge for the first time in all these years to break open the locket and the vial, to feel that blood burn his tongue. *Armand, come!*

The dream had visited him in its most alarming form this noon.

He'd been sitting on a bench in the little park near the Water Tower Place. A newspaper had been left there, and when he opened it he saw the advertisement: "Tomorrow Night: The Vampire Lestat Live on Stage in San Francisco." The cable would broadcast the concert at ten o'clock Chicago time. How nice for those who still lived indoors, could pay their rent, and had electricity. He had wanted to laugh at the whole thing, delight in it, revel in it, Lestat surprising them all. But the chill had passed through him, becoming a deep jarring shock.

And what if Armand does not know? But the record stores on the Night Island must have *The Vampire Lestat* in their windows. In the elegant lounges, they must be playing those haunting and hypnotic songs.

It had even occurred to Daniel at that moment to go on to California on his own. Surely he could work some miracle, get his passport from the hotel, go into any bank with it for identification. Rich, yes so very rich, this poor mortal boy. . . .

But how could he think of something so deliberate? The sun had been warm on his face and shoulders as he'd lain down on the bench. He'd folded the newspaper to make of it a pillow.

And there was the dream that had been waiting all the time. . . .

Midday in the world of the twins: the sun pouring down onto the clearing. Silence, except for the singing of the birds.

And the twins kneeling quite still together, in the dust. Such pale women, their eyes green, their hair long and wavy and coppery red. Fine clothes they wore, white linen dresses that had come all the way from the markets of Nineveh, bought by the villagers to honor these powerful witches, whom the spirits obey.

The funeral feast was ready. The mud bricks of the oven had been torn down and carried away, and the body lay steaming hot on the stone slab, the yellow juices running out of it where the crisp skin had broken, a black and naked thing with only a covering of cooked leaves. It horrified Daniel.

But it horrified no one present, this spectacle, not the twins or the villagers who knelt to watch the feast begin.

This feast was the right and the duty of the twins. *This was their mother, the blackened body on the stone slab.* And what was human must remain with the human. A day and night it may take to consume the feast, but all will keep watch until it is done.

Now a current of excitement passes through the crowd around the clearing. One of the twins lifts the plate on which the brain rests together with the eyes, and the other nods and takes the plate that holds the heart.

And so the division has been made. The beat of a drum rises, though Daniel cannot see the drummer. Slow, rhythmic, brutal.

"Let the banquet begin."

But the ghastly cry comes, just as Daniel knew it would. *Stop the soldiers.* But he can't. All this has happened somewhere, of that he is now certain. It is no dream, it is a vision. And he is not there. The soldiers storm the clearing, the villagers scatter, the twins set down the plates and fling themselves over the smoking feast. But this is madness.

The soldiers tear them loose so effortlessly, and as the slab is lifted, the body falls, breaking into pieces, and the heart and the brain are thrown down into the dust. The twins scream and scream.

But the villagers are screaming too, the soldiers are cutting them down as they run. The dead and the dying litter the mountain paths. The eyes of the mother have fallen from the plate into the dirt, and they, along with the heart and brain, are trampled underfoot.

One of the twins, her arms pulled behind her back, cries to the spirits for vengeance. And they come, they do. It is a whirlwind. But not enough.

If only it were over. But Daniel can't wake up.

Stillness. The air is full of smoke. Nothing stands where these people have lived for centuries. The mud bricks are scattered, clay pots are broken, all that will burn has burned. Infants with their throats slit lie naked on the ground as the flies come. No one will roast these bodies, no one will consume this flesh. It will pass out of the human race, with all its power and its mystery. The jackals are already approaching. And the soldiers have gone. Where are the twins! He hears the twins crying, but he cannot find them. A great storm is rumbling over the narrow road that twists down through the valley towards the desert. The spirits make the thunder. The spirits make the rain.

His eyes opened. Chicago, Michigan Avenue at midday. The dream had gone out like a light turned off. He sat there shivering, sweating.

A radio had been playing near him, Lestat singing in that haunting mournful voice of Those Who Must Be Kept.

> *Mother and Father.*
> *Keep your silence,*
> *Keep your secrets,*
> *But those of you with tongues,*
> *sing my song.*
>
> *Sons and daughters*
> *Children of darkness*
> *Raise your voices*
> *Make a chorus*
> *Let heaven hear us*
>
> *Come together,*
> *Brother and sisters,*
> *Come to me.*

He had gotten up, started walking. Go into the Water Tower Place, so like the Night Island with its engulfing shops, endless music and lights, shining glass.

And now it was almost eight o'clock and he had been walking continuously, running from sleep and from the dream. He was far from any music and light. How long would it go on next time? Would he find out whether they were alive or dead? My beauties, my poor beauties. . . .

He stopped, turning his back to the wind for a moment, listening to the chimes somewhere, then spotting a dirty clock above a dime store lunch counter; yes, Lestat had risen on the West Coast. Who is with him? Is Louis there? And the concert, a little over twenty-four hours. Catastrophe! *Armand, please.*

The wind gusted, pushed him back a few steps on the pavement, left him shivering violently. His hands were frozen. Had he ever been this cold in his life? Doggedly, he crossed Michigan Avenue with the crowd at the stoplight and stood at the plate glass windows of the bookstore, where he could see the book, *The Vampire Lestat,* on display.

Surely Armand had read it, devouring every word in that eerie, horrible way he had of reading, of turning page after page without pause, eyes flashing over the words, until the book was finished, and then tossing it aside. How could a creature shimmer with such beauty yet incite such . . . what was it, revulsion? No, he had never been revolted by Armand, he had to admit it. What he always felt was ravening and hopeless desire.

A young girl inside the warmth of the store picked up a copy of Lestat's book, then stared at him through the window. His breath made steam on the glass in front of him. *Don't worry, my darling, I am a rich man. I could buy this whole store full of books and make it a present to you. I am lord and master of my own island, I am the Devil's minion and he grants my every wish. Want to come take my arm?*

It had been dark for hours on the Florida coast. The Night Island was already thronged.

The shops, restaurants, bars had opened their broad, seamless plate glass doors at sunset, on five levels of richly carpeted hallway. The silver escalators had begun their low, churning hum. Daniel closed his eyes and envisioned the walls of glass rising above the harbor terraces. He could almost hear the great roar of the dancing fountains, see the long narrow beds of daffodils and tulips blooming eternally out of season, hear the hypnotic music that beat like a heart beneath it all.

And Armand, he was probably roaming the dimly lighted rooms of the villa, steps away from the tourists and the shoppers, yet utterly cut off by steel doors and white walls—a sprawling palace of floor-length windows and broad balconies, perched over white sand. Solitary, yet near to the endless commotion, its vast living room facing the twinkling lights of the Miami shore.

Or maybe he had gone through one of the many unmarked doors into the public galleria itself. "To live and breathe among mortals" as he called it in this safe and self-contained universe which he and Daniel had made. How Armand loved the warm breezes of the Gulf, the endless springtime of the Night Island.

No lights would go out until dawn.

"Send someone for me, Armand, I need you! You know you want me to come home."

Of course it had happened this way over and over again. It did not need strange dreams, or Lestat to reappear, roaring like Lucifer from tape and film.

Everything would go all right for months as Daniel felt compelled to move from city to city, walking the pavements of New York or Chicago or New Orleans. Then the sudden disintegration. He'd realize he had not moved from his chair in five hours. Or he'd wake suddenly in a stale and unchanged bed, frightened, unable to remember the name of the city where he was, or where he'd been for days before. Then the car would come for him, then the plane would take him home.

Didn't Armand cause it? Didn't he somehow drive Daniel to these periods of madness? Didn't he by some evil magic dry up every source of pleasure, every fount of sustenance until Daniel welcomed the sight of the familiar chauffeur come to drive him to the airport, the man who was never shocked by Daniel's demeanor, his unshaven face, his soiled clothes?

When Daniel finally reached the Night Island, Armand would deny it.

"You came back to me because you wanted to, Daniel," Armand always said calmly, face still and radiant, eyes full of love. "There is nothing for you now, Daniel, except me. You know that. Madness waits out there."

"Same old dance," Daniel invariably answered. And all that luxury, so intoxicating, soft beds, music, the wine glass placed in his hand. The rooms were always full of flowers, the foods he craved came on silver trays.

Armand lay sprawled in a huge black velvet wing chair gazing at the television, Ganymede in white pants and white silk shirt, watching the news, the movies, the tapes he'd made of himself reading poetry, the idiot sitcoms, the dramas, the musicals, the silent films.

"Come in, Daniel, sit down. I never expected you back so soon."

"You son of a bitch," Daniel would say. "You wanted me here, you summoned me. I couldn't eat, sleep, nothing, just wander and think of you. You did it."

Armand would smile, sometimes even laugh. Armand had a rich, beautiful laugh, always eloquent of gratitude as well as humor. He looked and sounded mortal when he laughed. "Calm yourself, Daniel. Your heart's racing. It frightens me." Small crease to the smooth forehead, the voice for a moment deepened by compassion. "Tell me what you want, Daniel, and I'll get it for you. Why do you keep running away?"

"Lies, you bastard. Say that you wanted me. You'll torment me forever, won't you, and then you'll watch me die, and you'll find that interesting, won't you? It was true what Louis said. You watch them die, your mortal slaves, they mean nothing to you. You'll watch the colors change in my face as I die."

"That's Louis's language," Armand said patiently. "Please don't quote that book to me. I'd rather die than see you die, Daniel."

"Then give it to me! Damn you! Immortality that close, as close as your arms."

"No, Daniel, because I'd rather die than do that, too."

But even if Armand did not cause this madness that brought Daniel home, surely he always knew where Daniel was. He could hear Daniel's call. The blood connected them, it had to—the precious tiny drinks of burning preternatural blood. Never enough to do more than awaken dreams in Daniel, and the thirst for eternity, to make the flowers in the wallpaper sing and dance. Whatever, Armand could always find him, of that he had no doubt.

IN THE early years, even before the blood exchange, Armand had pursued Daniel with the cunning of a harpy. There had been no place on earth that Daniel could hide.

Horrifying yet tantalizing, their beginning in New Orleans, twelve years ago when Daniel had entered a crumbling old house in the Garden District and known at once that it was the vampire Lestat's lair.

Ten days before he'd left San Francisco after his night-long interview with the vampire Louis, suffering from the final confirmation of the frightening tale he had been told. In a sudden embrace, Louis had demonstrated his supernatural power to drain Daniel almost to the point of death. The puncture wounds had disappeared, but the memory had left Daniel near to madness. Feverish, sometimes delirious, he had traveled no more than a few hundred miles a day. In cheap roadside motels, where he forced himself to take nourishment, he had duplicated the tapes of the interview one by one, sending the copies off to a New York publisher, so that a book was in the making before he ever stood before Lestat's gate.

But that had been secondary, the publication, an event connected with the values of a dimming and distant world.

He had to find the vampire Lestat. He had to unearth the immortal who had made Louis, the one who still survived somewhere in this damp, decadent, and beautiful old city, waiting perhaps for Daniel to awaken him, to bring him out into the century that had terrified him and driven him underground.

It was what Louis wanted, surely. Why else had he given this mortal emissary so many clues as to where Lestat could be found? Yet some of the details were misleading. Was this ambivalence on Louis's part? It did not matter, finally. In the public records, Daniel had found the title to the property, and the street number, under the unmistakable name: Lestat de Lioncourt.

The iron gate had not even been locked, and once he'd hacked his way through the overgrown garden, he had managed easily to break the rusted lock on the front door.

Only a small pocket flash helped him as he entered. But the moon had been high, shining its full white light here and there through the oak branches. He had seen clearly the rows and rows of books stacked to the ceiling, making up the very walls of every room. No human could or would have done such a mad and methodical thing. And then in the upstairs bedroom, he had knelt down in the thick dust that covered the rotting carpet and found the gold pocket watch on which was written the name Lestat.

Ah, that chilling moment, that moment when the pendulum swung away from ever increasing dementia to a new passion—he would track to the ends of the earth these pale and deadly beings whose existence he had only glimpsed.

What had he wanted in those early weeks? Did he hope to possess the splendid secrets of life itself? Surely he would gain from this knowledge no purpose for an existence already fraught with disappointment. No, he wanted to be swept away from everything he had once loved. He longed for Louis's violent and sensuous world.

Evil. He was no longer afraid.

Maybe he was like the lost explorer who, pushing through the jungle, suddenly sees the wall of the fabled temple before him, its carvings overhung with spiderwebs and vines; no matter that he may not live to tell his story; he has beheld the truth with his own eyes.

But if only he could open the door a little further, see the full magnificence. If they would only let him in! Maybe he just wanted to live forever. Could anyone fault him for that?

He had felt good and safe standing alone in the ruin of Lestat's old house, with the wild roses crawling at the broken window and the four-poster bed a skeleton, its hangings rotting away.

Near them, near to their precious darkness, their lovely devouring gloom. How he had loved the hopelessness of it all, the moldering chairs with their bits of carving, shreds of velvet, and the slithering things eating the last of the carpet away.

But the relic; ah, the relic was everything, the gleaming gold watch that bore an immortal's name!

After a while, he had opened the armoire; the black frock coats fell to pieces when he touched them. Withered and curling boots lay on the cedar boards.

But Lestat, you are here. He had taken the tape recorder out, set it down, put in the first tape, and let the voice of Louis rise softly in the shadowy room. Hour by hour, the tapes played.

Then just before dawn he had seen a figure in the hallway, and known that he was meant to see it. And he had seen the moon strike the boyish face, the auburn hair. The earth tilted, the darkness came down. The last word he uttered had been the name Armand.

He should have died then. Had a whim kept him alive?

He'd awakened in a dark, damp cellar. Water oozed from the walls. Groping in the blackness, he'd discovered a bricked-up window, a locked door plated with steel.

And what was his comfort, that he had found yet another god of the secret pantheon—Armand, the oldest of the immortals whom Louis had described, Armand, the coven master of the nineteenth-century Theater of the Vampires in Paris, who had confided his terrible secret to Louis: of our origins nothing is known.

For three days and nights, perhaps, Daniel had lain in this prison. Impossible to tell. He had been near to dying certainly, the stench of his own urine sickening him, the insects driving him mad. Yet his was a religious fervor. He had come ever nearer to the dark pulsing truths that Louis had revealed. Slipping in and out of consciousness, he dreamed of Louis, Louis talking to him in that dirty little room in San Francisco, *there have always been things such as we are, always,* Louis embracing him, his green eyes darkening suddenly as he let Daniel see the fang teeth.

The fourth night, Daniel had awakened and known at once that someone or something was in the room. The door lay open to a passage. Water was flowing somewhere fast as if in a deep underground sewer. Slowly his eyes grew accustomed to the dirty greenish light from the doorway and then he saw the pale white-skinned figure standing against the wall.

So immaculate the black suit, the starched white shirt—like the imitation of a twentieth-century man. And the auburn hair clipped short and the fingernails gleaming dully even in this semidarkness. Like a corpse for the coffin—that sterile, that well prepared.

The voice had been gentle with a trace of an accent. Not European; something sharper yet softer at the same time. Arabic or Greek perhaps, that kind of music. The words were slow and without anger.

"Get out. Take your tapes with you. They are there beside you. I know of your book. No one will believe it. Now you will go and take these things."

Then you won't kill me. And you won't make me one of you either. Desperate, stupid thoughts, but he couldn't stop them. He had seen the power! No lies, no cunning here. And he'd felt himself crying, so weakened by fear and hunger, reduced to a child.

"Make you one of us?" The accent thickened, giving a fine lilt to the words. "Why would I do that?" Eyes narrowing. "I would not do that to those whom I find to be despicable, whom I would see burning in hell as a matter of course. So why should I do it to an innocent fool—like you?"

I want it. I want to live forever. Daniel had sat up, climbed to his feet slowly, struggling to see Armand more clearly. A dim bulb burned somewhere far down the hall. *I want to be with Louis and with you.*

Laughter, low, gentle. But contemptuous. "I see why he chose you for his confidant. You are naive and beautiful. But the beauty could be the only reason, you know."

Silence.

"Your eyes are an unusual color, almost violet. And you are strangely defiant and beseeching in the same breath."

Make me immortal. Give it to me!

Laughter again. Almost sad. Then silence, the water rushing fast in that distant someplace. The room had become visible, a filthy basement hole. And the figure more nearly mortal. There was even a faint pink tinge to the smooth skin.

"It was all true, what he told you. But no one will ever believe it. And you will go mad in time from this knowledge. That's what always happens. But you're not mad yet."

No. This is real, it's all happening. You're Armand and we're talking together. And I'm not mad..

"Yes. And I find it rather interesting . . . interesting that you know my name and that you're alive. I have never told my name to anyone who is alive." Armand hesitated. "I don't want to kill you. Not just now."

Daniel had felt the first touch of fear. If you looked closely enough at these beings you could see what they were. It had been the same with Louis. No, they weren't living. They were ghastly imitations of the living. And this one, the gleaming manikin of a young boy!

"I am going to let you leave here," Armand had said. So politely, softly. "I want to follow you, watch you, see where you go. As long as I find you interesting, I won't kill you. And of course, I may lose interest altogether and not bother to kill you. That's always possible. You have hope in that. And maybe with luck I'll lose track of you. I have my limitations, of course. You have the world to roam, and you can move by day. Go now. Start running. I want to see what you do, I want to know what you are."

Go now, start running!

He'd been on the morning plane to Lisbon, clutching Lestat's gold watch in his hand. Yet two nights later in Madrid, he'd turned to find Armand seated on a city bus beside him no more than inches away. A week later in Vienna he'd looked out the window of a café to see Armand watching him from the street. In Berlin, Armand slipped into a taxi beside him, and sat there staring at him, until finally Daniel had leapt out in the thick of the traffic and run away.

Within months, however, these shattering silent confrontations had given way to more vigorous assaults.

He woke in a hotel room in Prague to find Armand standing over him, crazed, violent. "Talk to me now! I demand it. Wake up. I want you to walk with me, show me things in this city. Why did you come to this particular place?"

Riding on a train through Switzerland, he looked up suddenly to see Armand directly opposite watching him over the upturned cover of his fur-lined coat. Armand snatched the book out of his hand and insisted that he explain what it was, why he read it, what did the picture on the cover mean?

In Paris Armand pursued him nightly through the boulevards and the back streets, only now and then questioning him on the places he went, the things he did. In Venice, he'd looked out of his room at the Danieli, to see Armand staring from a window across the way.

Then weeks passed without a visitation. Daniel vacillated between terror and strange expectation, doubting his very sanity again. But there was Armand waiting for him in the New York airport. And the following night in Boston, Armand was in the dining room of the Copley when Daniel came in. Daniel's dinner was already ordered. Please sit down. Did Daniel know that *Interview with the Vampire* was in the bookstores?

"I must confess I enjoy this small measure of notoriety," Armand had said with exquisite politeness and a vicious smile. "What puzzles me is that you do not want notoriety! You did not list yourself as the 'author,' which means that you are either very modest or a coward. Either explanation would be very dull."

"I'm not hungry, let's get out of here," Daniel had answered weakly. Yet suddenly dish after dish was being placed on the table; everyone was staring.

"I didn't know what you wanted," Armand confided, the smile becoming absolutely ecstatic. "So I ordered everything that they had."

"You think you can drive me crazy, don't you?" Daniel had snarled. "Well, you can't. Let me tell you. Every time I lay eyes on you, I realize that I didn't invent you, and that I'm sane!" And he had started eating, lustily, furiously—a little fish, a little beef, a little veal, a little sweetbreads, a little cheese, a little everything, put it all together, what did he care, and Armand had been so delighted, laughing and laughing like a schoolboy as he sat watching, with folded arms. It was the first time Daniel had ever heard that soft, silky laughter. So seductive. He got drunk as fast as he could.

The meetings grew longer and longer. Conversations, sparring matches, and downright fights became the rule. Once Armand had dragged Daniel out of bed in New Orleans and shouted at him: "That telephone, I want you to dial Paris, I want to see if it can really talk to Paris."

"Goddamn it, do it yourself," Daniel had roared. "You're five hundred years old and you can't use a telephone? Read the directions. What are you, an immortal idiot? I will do no such thing!"

How surprised Armand had looked.

"All right, I'll call Paris for you. But you pay the bill."

"But of course," Armand had said innocently. He had drawn dozens of hundred-dollar bills out of his coat, sprinkling them on Daniel's bed.

More and more they argued philosophy at these meetings. Pulling Daniel out of a theater in Rome, Armand had asked what did Daniel really think that death was? People who were still living knew things like that! Did Daniel know what Armand truly feared?

As it was past midnight and Daniel was drunk and exhausted and had been sound asleep in the theater before Armand found him, he did not care.

"I'll tell you what I fear," Armand had said, intense as any young student. "That it's chaos after you die, that it's a dream from which you can't wake. Imagine drifting half in and out of consciousness, trying vainly to remember who you are or what you were. Imagine straining forever for the lost clarity of the living. . . ."

It had frightened Daniel. Something about it rang true. Weren't there tales of mediums conversing with incoherent yet powerful presences? He didn't know. How in hell could he know? Maybe when you died there was flat out nothing. That terrified Armand, no effort expended to conceal the misery.

"You don't think it terrifies me?" Daniel had asked, staring at the white-faced figure beside him. "How many years do I have? Can you tell just by looking at me? Tell me."

When Armand woke him up in Port-au-Prince, it was war he wanted to talk about. What did men in this century actually think of war? Did Daniel know that Armand had been a boy when this had begun for him? Seventeen years old, and in those times that was young, very young.

Seventeen-year-old boys in the twentieth century were virtual monsters; they had beards, hair on their chests, and yet they were children. Not then. Yet children worked as if they were men.

But let us not get sidetracked. The point was, Armand didn't know what men felt. He never had. Oh, of course he'd known the pleasures of the flesh, that was par for the course. Nobody then thought children were innocent of sensuous pleasures. But of true aggression he knew little. He killed because it was his nature as a vampire; and the blood was irresistible. But why did men find war irresistible? What was the desire to clash violently against the will of another with weapons? What was the physical need to destroy?

At such times, Daniel did his best to answer: for some men it was the need to affirm one's own existence through the annihilation of another. Surely Armand knew these things.

"Know? Know? What does that matter if you don't understand," Armand had asked, his accent unusually sharp in his agitation, "if you cannot proceed from one perception to another? Don't you see, this is what I cannot do."

When he found Daniel in Frankfurt, it was the nature of history, the impossibility of writing any coherent explanation of events that was not in itself a lie. The impossibility of truth being served by generalities, and the impossibility of learning proceeding without them.

Now and then these meetings had not been entirely selfish. In a country inn in England Daniel woke to the sound of Armand's voice warning him to leave the building at once. A fire destroyed the inn in less than an hour.

Another time he had been in jail in New York, picked up for drunkenness and vagrancy when Armand appeared to bail him out, looking all too human as he always did after he had fed, a young lawyer in a tweed coat and flannel pants, escorting Daniel to a room in the Carlyle, where he left him to sleep it off with a suitcase full of new clothes waiting, and a wallet full of money hidden in a pocket.

Finally, after a year and a half of this madness, Daniel began to question Armand. What had it really been like in those days in Venice? Look at this film, set in the eighteenth century, tell me what is wrong.

But Armand was remarkably unresponsive. "I cannot tell you those things because I have no experience of them. You see, I have so little ability to synthesize knowledge; I deal in the immediate with a cool intensity. What was it like in Paris? Ask me if it rained on the night of Saturday, June 5, 1793. Perhaps I could tell you that."

Yet at other moments, he spoke in rapid bursts of the things around him, of the eerie garish cleanliness of this era, of the horrid acceleration of change.

"Behold, earthshaking inventions which are useless or obsolete within the same century—the steamboat, the railroads; yet do you know what these meant after six thousand years of galley slaves and men on horseback? And now the dance hall girl buys a chemical to kill the seed of her lovers, and lives to be seventy-five in a room full of gadgets which cool the air and veritably eat the dust. And yet for all the costume movies and the paperback history thrown at you in every drugstore, the public has no accurate memory of anything; every social problem is observed in relation to 'norms' which in fact never existed, people fancy themselves 'deprived' of luxuries and peace and quiet which in fact were never common to any people anywhere at all."

"But the Venice of your time, tell me. . . ."

"What? That it was dirty? That it was beautiful? That people went about in rags with rotting teeth and stinking breath and laughed at public executions? You want to know the key difference? There is a horrifying loneliness at work in this time. No, listen to me. We lived six and seven to a room in those days, when I was still among the living. The city streets were seas of humanity; and now in these high buildings dim-witted souls hover in luxurious privacy, gazing through the television window at a faraway world of kissing and touching. It is bound to produce some great fund of common knowledge, some new level of human awareness, a curious skepticism, to be so alone."

Daniel found himself fascinated, sometimes trying to write down the things Armand told him. Yet Armand continued to frighten him. Daniel was ever on the move.

He wasn't quite sure how long it had gone on before he stopped running, though the night itself was quite impossible to forget.

Maybe four years had passed since the game had begun. Daniel had spent a long quiet summer in southern Italy during which he had not seen his demon familiar even once.

In a cheap hotel only a half block from the ruins of ancient Pompeii, he had spent his hours reading, writing, trying to define what his glimpse of the supernatural had done to him, and how he must learn again to want, to envision, to dream. Immortality on this earth was indeed possible. This he knew without question, but what did it matter if immortality was not Daniel's to have?

By day he walked the broken streets of the excavated Roman city. And when the moon was full he wandered there, alone, by night as well. It seemed sanity had come back to him. And life might soon come back too. Green leaves smelled fresh when he crushed them in his fingers. He looked up at the stars and did not feel resentful so much as sad.

Yet at other times, he burned for Armand as if for an elixir without which he could not go on. The dark energy that had fired him for four years was now missing. He dreamed Armand was near him; he awoke weeping stupidly. Then the morning would come and he would be sad but calm.

Then Armand had returned.

It was late, perhaps ten o'clock in the evening, and the sky, as it is so often in southern Italy, was a brilliant dark blue overhead. Daniel had been walking alone down the long road that leads from Pompeii proper to the Villa of the Mysteries, hoping no guards would come to drive him away.

As soon as he'd reached the ancient house, a stillness had descended. No guards here. No one living. Only the sudden silent appearance of Armand before the entrance. Armand again.

He'd come silently out of the shadows into the moonlight, a young boy in dirty jeans and worn denim jacket, and he had slipped his arm around Daniel and gently kissed Daniel's face. Such warm skin, full of the fresh blood of the kill. Daniel fancied he could smell it, the perfume of the living clinging to Armand still.

"You want to come into this house?" Armand had whispered. No locks ever kept Armand from anything. Daniel had been trembling, on the edge of tears. And why was that? So glad to see him, touch him, ah, damn him!

They had entered the dark, low-ceilinged rooms, the press of Armand's arm against Daniel's back oddly comforting. Ah, yes, this intimacy, because that's what it is, isn't it? You, my secret . . .

Secret lover.

Yes.

Then the realization had come to Daniel as they stood together in the ruined dining room with its famous murals of ritual flagellation barely visible in the dark: He isn't going to kill me after all. He isn't going to do it. Of course he won't make me what he is, but he isn't going to kill me. The dance will not end like that.

"But how could you not know such a thing," Armand had said, reading his thoughts. "I love you. If I hadn't grown to love you, I would have killed you before now, of course."

The moonlight poured through the wooden lattices. The lush figures of the murals came to life against their red backdrop, the color of dried blood.

Daniel stared hard at the creature before him, this thing that looked human and sounded human but was not. There was a horrid shift in his consciousness; he saw this being like a great insect, a monstrous evil predator who had devoured a million human lives. And yet he loved this thing. He loved its smooth white skin, its great dark brown eyes. He loved it not because it looked like a gentle, thoughtful young man, but because it was ghastly and awful and loathsome, and beautiful all at the same time. He loved it the way people love evil, because it thrills them to the core of their souls. Imagine, killing like that, just taking life any time you want it, just doing it, sinking your teeth into another and taking all that that person can possibly give.

Look at the garments he wore. Blue cotton shirt, brass-buttoned denim jacket. Where had he gotten them? Off a victim, yes, like taking out his knife and skinning the kill while it was still warm? No wonder they reeked of salt and blood, though none was visible. And the hair trimmed just as if it weren't going to grow out within twenty-four hours to its regular shoulder length. This is evil. This is illusion. *This is what I want to be, which is why I cannot stand to look at him.*

Armand's lips had moved in a soft, slightly concealed smile. And then his eyes had misted and closed. He had bent close to Daniel, pressed his lips to Daniel's neck.

And once again, as he had in a little room on Divisadero Street in San Francisco with the vampire Louis, Daniel felt the sharp teeth pierce the surface of his skin. Sudden pain and throbbing warmth. "Are you killing me finally?" He grew drowsy, on fire, filled with love. "Do it, yes."

But Armand had taken only a few droplets. He'd released Daniel and pressed gently on his shoulders, forcing Daniel down to his knees. Daniel had looked up to see the blood flowing from Armand's wrist. Great electric shocks had passed through Daniel at the taste of that blood. It had seemed in a flash that the city of Pompeii was full of a whispering, a crying, some vague and pulsing imprint of long-ago suffering and death. Thousands perishing in smoke and ash. Thousands dying together. *Together.* Daniel had clung to Armand. But the blood was gone. Only a taste—no more.

"You are mine, beautiful boy," Armand had said.

The following morning when he awoke in bed at the Excelsior in Rome, Daniel knew that he would not run away from Armand ever again. Less than an hour after sunset, Armand came to him. They would go to London now, the car was waiting to take them to the plane. But there was time enough, wasn't there, for another embrace, another small exchange of blood. "Here from my throat," Armand had whispered, cradling Daniel's head in his hand. A fine soundless throbbing. The light of the lamps expanded, brightened, obliterated the room.

Lovers. Yes, it had become an ecstatic and engulfing affair.

"You are my teacher," Armand told him. "You will tell me everything about this century. I am learning secrets already that have eluded me since the beginning. You'll sleep when the sun rises, if you wish, but the nights are mine."

INTO the very midst of life they plunged. At pretense Armand was a genius, and killing early on any given evening, he passed for human everywhere that they went. His skin was burning hot in those early hours, his face full of passionate curiosity, his embraces feverish and quick.

It would have taken another immortal to keep up with him. Daniel nodded off at symphonies and operas or during the hundreds upon hundreds of films that Armand dragged him to see. Then there were the endless parties, the cluttered noisy gatherings from Chelsea to Mayfair where Armand argued politics and philosophy with students, or women of fashion, or anyone who would give him the slightest chance. His eyes grew moist with excitement, his voice lost its soft preternatural resonance and took on the hard human accent of the other young men in the room.

Clothes of all kinds fascinated him, not for their beauty but for what he thought they meant. He wore jeans and sweat shirts like Daniel; he wore cable-knit sweaters and workmen's brogans, leather windbreakers, and mirrored sunglasses pushed up on his head. He wore tailored suits, and dinner jackets, and white tie and tails when the fancy suited him; his hair was cut short one night so he looked like any young man down from Cambridge, and left curly and long, an angel's mane, the next.

It seemed that he and Daniel were always walking up four unlighted flights of stairs to visit some painter, sculptor, or photographer, or to see some special never-released yet revolutionary film. They spent hours in the cold-water flats of dark-eyed young women who played rock music and made herbal tea which Armand never drank.

Men and women fell in love with Armand, of course, "so innocent, so passionate, so brilliant!" You don't say. In fact, Armand's power to seduce was almost beyond his control. And it was Daniel who must bed these unfortunates, if Armand could possibly arrange it, while he watched from a chair nearby, a dark-eyed Cupid with a tender approving smile. Hot, nerve-searing, this witnessed passion, Daniel working the other body with ever greater abandon, aroused by the dual purpose of every intimate gesture. Yet he lay empty afterwards, staring at Armand, resentful, cold.

. . .

IN NEW YORK they went tearing to museum openings, cafés, bars, adopted a young dancer, paying all his bills through school. They sat on the stoops in SoHo and Greenwich Village whiling the hours away with anybody who would stop to join them. They went to night classes in literature, philosophy, art history, and politics. They studied biology, bought microscopes, collected specimens. They studied books on astronomy and mounted giant telescopes on the roofs of the buildings in which they lived for a few days or a month at most. They went to boxing matches, rock concerts, Broadway shows.

Technological inventions began to obsess Armand, one after the other. First it was kitchen blenders, in which he made frightful concoctions mostly based on the colors of the ingredients; then microwave ovens, in which he cooked roaches and rats. Garbage disposers enchanted him; he fed them paper towels and whole packages of cigarettes. Then it was telephones. He called long distance all over the planet, speaking for hours with "mortals" in Australia or India. Finally television caught him up utterly, so that the flat was full of blaring speakers and flickering screens.

Anything with blue skies enthralled him. Then he must watch news programs, prime time series, documentaries, and finally every film, regardless of merit, ever taped.

At last particular movies struck his fancy. Over and over he watched Ridley Scott's *Blade Runner*, fascinated by Rutger Hauer, the powerfully built actor who, as the leader of the rebel androids, confronts his human maker, kisses him, and then crushes his skull. It would bring a slow and almost impish laugh from Armand, the bones cracking, the look in Hauer's ice-cold blue eye.

"That's your friend, Lestat, there," Armand whispered once to Daniel. "Lestat would have the . . . how do you say? . . . guts? . . . to do that!"

After *Blade Runner* it was the idiotic and hilarious *Time Bandits*, a British comedy in which five dwarfs steal a "Map of Creation" so they can travel through the holes in Time. Into one century after another they tumble, thieving and brawling, along with a little boy companion, until they all wind up in the devil's lair.

Then one scene in particular became Armand's favorite: the dwarfs on a broken-down stage in Castelleone singing "Me and My Shadow" for Napoleon really sent Armand out of his mind. He lost all supernatural composure and became utterly human, laughing till the tears rose in his eyes.

Daniel had to admit there was a horrible charm to it, the "Me and My

Shadow" number, with the dwarfs stumbling, fighting with each other, finally lousing up the whole proceedings, and the dazed eighteenth-century musicians in the pit not knowing what to make of the twentieth-century song. Napoleon was stupefied, then delighted! A stroke of comic genius, the entire scene. But how many times could a mortal watch it? For Armand there seemed no end.

Yet within six months he had dropped the movies for video cameras and must make his own films. All over New York he dragged Daniel, as he interviewed people on the nighttime streets. Armand had reels of himself reciting poetry in Italian or Latin, or merely staring with his arms folded, a gleaming white presence slipping in and out of focus in eternally dim bronze light.

Then somewhere, somehow, in a place unbeknownst to Daniel, Armand made a long tape of himself lying in the coffin during his daytime deathlike sleep. Daniel found this impossible to look at. Armand sat before the slow-moving film for hours, watching his own hair, cut at sunrise, slowly growing against the satin as he lay motionless with closed eyes.

Next it was computers. He was filling disk after disk with his secret writings. He rented additional apartments in Manhattan to house his word processors and video game machines.

Finally he turned to planes.

Daniel had always been a compulsive traveler, he had fled Armand to cities worldwide, and certainly he and Armand had taken planes together. Nothing new in that. But now it was a concentrated exploration; they must spend the entire night in the air. Flying to Boston, then Washington, then to Chicago, then back to New York City, was not unusual. Armand observed everything, passengers, stewardesses; he spoke with the pilots; he lay back in the deep first-class seats listening to the engines roar. Double-decker jets particularly enchanted him. He must try longer, more daring adventures: all the way to Port-au-Prince or San Francisco, or Rome, or Madrid or Lisbon, it didn't matter, as long as Armand was safely landed by dawn.

Armand virtually disappeared at dawn. Daniel was never to know where Armand actually slept. But then Daniel was dead on his feet by daybreak anyway. Daniel didn't see high noon for five years.

Often Armand had been in the room some time before Daniel awakened. The coffee would be perking, the music going—Vivaldi or honky-tonk piano, as Armand loved both equally—and Armand would be pacing, ready for Daniel to get up.

"Come, lover, we're going to the ballet tonight. I want to see Baryshnikov. And after that, down to the Village. You remember that jazz band

I loved last summer, well, they've come back. Come on, I'm hungry, my beloved. We must go."

And if Daniel was sluggish, Armand would push him into the shower, soap him all over, rinse him off, drag him out, dry him thoroughly, then shave his face as lovingly as an old-fashioned barber, and finally dress him after carefully selecting from Daniel's wardrobe of dirty and neglected clothes.

Daniel loved the feel of the hard gleaming white hands moving over his naked flesh, rather like satin gloves. And the brown eyes that seemed to draw Daniel out of himself; ah, the delicious disorientation, the certainty that he was being carried downwards, out of all things physical, and finally the hands closing on his throat gently, and the teeth breaking through the skin.

He closed his eyes, his body heating slowly, only to burn truly when Armand's blood touched his lips. He heard the distant sighs again, the crying, was it of lost souls? It seemed a great luminous continuity was there, as if all his dreams were suddenly connected and vitally important, yet it was all slipping away. . . .

Once he'd reached out, held Armand with all his strength, and tried to gash the skin of his throat. Armand had been so patient, making the tear for him, and letting him close his mouth on it for the longest time—yes, this—then guiding him gently away.

Daniel was past all decision. Daniel lived only in two alternating states: misery and ecstasy, united by love. He never knew when he'd be given the blood. He never knew if things looked different because of it—the carnations staring at him from their vases, skyscrapers hideously visible like plants sprung up from steel seeds overnight—or because he was just going out of his mind.

Then had come the night when Armand said he was ready to enter this century in earnest, he understood enough about it now. He wanted "incalculable" wealth. He wanted a vast dwelling full of all those things he'd come to value. And yachts, planes, cars—millions of dollars. He wanted to buy Daniel everything that Daniel might ever desire.

"What do you mean, millions!" Daniel had scoffed. "You throw your clothes away after you wear them, you rent apartments and forget where they are. Do you know what a zip code is, or a tax bracket? I'm the one who buys all the goddamned airline tickets. Millions. How are we going to get millions! Steal another Maserati and be done with it, for God's sakes!"

"Daniel, you are a gift to me from Louis," Armand had said tenderly. "What would I do without you? You misunderstand everything." His eyes were large, childlike. "I want to be in the vital center of things the way I was years ago in Paris in the Theater of the Vampires. Surely you remember. I want to be a canker in the very eye of the world."

DANIEL had been dazzled by the speed with which things happened.

It had begun with a treasure find in the waters off Jamaica, Armand chartering a boat to show Daniel where salvage operations must begin. Within days a sunken Spanish galleon loaded with bullion and jewels had been discovered. Next it was an archaeological find of priceless Olmec figurines. Two more sunken ships were pinpointed in rapid succession. A cheap piece of South American property yielded a long forgotten emerald mine.

They purchased a mansion in Florida, yachts, speedboats, a small but exquisitely appointed jet plane.

And now they must be outfitted like princes for all occasions. Armand himself supervised the measurements for Daniel's custom-made shirts, suits, shoes. He chose the fabrics for an endless parade of sports coats, pants, robes, silk foulards. Of course Daniel must have for colder climes mink-lined raincoats, and dinner jackets for Monte Carlo, and jeweled cuff links, and even a long black suede cloak, which Daniel with his "twentieth-century height" could carry off quite well.

At sunset when Daniel awoke, his clothes had already been laid out for him. Heaven help him if he were to change a single item, from the linen handkerchief to the black silk socks. Supper awaited in the immense dining room with its windows open to the pool. Armand was already at his desk in the adjoining study. There was work to do: maps to consult, more wealth to be acquired.

"But how do you do it!" Daniel had demanded, as he watched Armand making notes, writing directions for new acquisitions.

"If you can read the minds of men, you can have anything that you want," Armand had said patiently. Ah, that soft reasonable voice, that open and almost trusting boyish face, the auburn hair always slipping into the eye a bit carelessly, the body so suggestive of human serenity, of physical ease.

"Give *me* what I want," Daniel had demanded.

"I'm giving you everything you could ever ask for."

"Yes, but not what I *have* asked for, not what I want!"

"Be alive, Daniel." A low whisper, like a kiss. "Let me tell you from my heart that life is better than death."

"I don't want to be alive, Armand, I want to live forever, and then *I* will tell *you* whether life is better than death."

The fact was, the riches were maddening him, making him feel his mortality more keenly than ever before. Sailing the warm Gulf Stream with Armand under a clear night sky, sprinkled with countless stars, he was desperate to possess all of this forever. With hatred and love he watched Armand effortlessly steering the vessel. Would Armand really let him die?

The game of acquisition continued.

Picassos, Degas, Van Goghs, these were but a few of the stolen paintings Armand recovered without explanation and handed over to Daniel for resales or rewards. Of course the recent owners would not dare to come forward, if in fact they had survived Armand's silent nocturnal visit to the sanctums where these stolen treasures had been displayed. Sometimes no clear title to the work in question existed. At auction, they brought millions. But even this was not enough.

Pearls, rubies, emeralds, diamond tiaras, these he brought to Daniel. "Never mind, they were stolen, no one will claim them." And from the savage narcotics traders off the Miami coast, Armand stole anything and everything, guns, suitcases full of money, even their boats.

Daniel stared at the piles and piles of green bills, as the secretaries counted them and wrapped them for coded accounts in European banks.

Often Daniel watched Armand go out alone to hunt the warm southern waters, a youth in soft black silk shirt and black pants, manning a sleek unlighted speedboat, the wind whipping his uncut long hair. Such a deadly foe. Somewhere far out there, beyond sight of land, he finds his smugglers and he strikes—the lone pirate, death. Are the victims dropped into the deep, hair billowing perhaps for one moment while the moon can still illuminate them as they look up for a last glimpse at what has been their ruin? This boy! They thought they were the evil ones. . . .

"Would you let me go with you? Would you let me see it when you do it?"

"No."

Finally enough capital had been amassed; Armand was ready for real action.

He ordered Daniel to make purchases without counsel or hesitation: a fleet of cruise ships, a chain of restaurants and hotels. Four private planes were now at their disposal. Armand had eight phones.

And then came the final dream: the Night Island, Armand's own personal creation with its five dazzling glass stories of theaters, restaurants, and shops. He drew the pictures for the architects he'd chosen. He gave them endless lists of the materials he wanted, the fabrics, the sculptures for the fountains, even the flowers, the potted trees.

Behold, the Night Island. From sunset till dawn, the tourists mobbed it, as boat after boat brought them out from the Miami docks. The music played eternally in the lounges, on the dance floors. The glass elevators never stopped their climb to heaven; ponds, streams, waterfalls glittered amid banks of moist, fragile blooms.

You could buy anything on the Night Island—diamonds, a Coca-Cola, books, pianos, parrots, designer fashions, porcelain dolls. All the fine cuisines of the world awaited you. Five films played nightly in the cinemas. Here was English tweed and Spanish leather, Indian silk, Chinese carpets, sterling silver, ice-cream cones or cotton candy, bone china, and Italian shoes.

Or you could live adjacent to it, in secret luxury, slipping in and out of the whirl at will.

"All this is yours, Daniel," Armand said, moving slowly through the spacious airy rooms of their very own Villa of the Mysteries, which covered three stories—and cellars verboten to Daniel—windows open to the distant burning nightscape of Miami, to the dim high clouds rolling above.

Gorgeous the skilled mixture of old and new. Elevator doors rolling back on broad rectangular rooms full of medieval tapestries and antique chandeliers; giant television sets in every room. Renaissance paintings filled Daniel's suite, where Persian rugs covered the parquet. The finest of the Venetian school surrounded Armand in his white carpeted study full of shining computers, intercoms, and monitors. The books, magazines, newspapers came from all over the world.

"This is your home, Daniel."

And so it had been and Daniel had loved it, he had to admit that, and what he had loved even more was the freedom, the power, and the luxury that attended him everywhere that he went.

He and Armand had gone into the depths of the Central American jungles by night to see the Mayan ruins; they had gone up the flank of Annapurna to glimpse the distant summit under the light of the moon. Through the crowded streets of Tokyo they had wandered together, through Bangkok and Cairo and Damascus, through Lima and Rio and Kathmandu. By day Daniel wallowed in comfort at the best of the local hostelries; by night he wandered fearless with Armand at his side.

Now and then, however, the illusion of civilized life would break down. Sometimes in some far-flung place, Armand sensed the presence of other immortals. He explained that he had thrown his shield around Daniel, yet it worried him. Daniel must stay at his side.

"Make me what you are and worry no more."

"You don't know what you're saying," Armand had answered. "Now you're one of a billion faceless humans. If you were one of us, you'd be a candle burning in the dark."

Daniel wouldn't accept it.

"They would spot you without fail," Armand continued. He had become angry, though not at Daniel. The fact was he disliked any talk at all of the undead. "Don't you know the old ones destroy the young ones out of hand?" he'd asked. "Didn't your beloved Louis explain that to you? It's what I do everywhere that we settle—I clean them out, the young ones, the vermin. But I am not invincible." He'd paused as though debating whether or not he should continue. Then: "I'm like any beast on the prowl. I have enemies who are older and stronger who would try to destroy me if it interested them to do so, I am sure."

"Older than you are? But I thought you were the oldest," Daniel had said. It had been years since they'd spoken of *Interview with the Vampire.* They had, in fact, never discussed its contents in detail.

"No, of course I'm not the oldest," Armand had answered. He seemed slightly uneasy. "Merely the oldest your friend Louis was ever to find. There are others. I don't know their names, I've seldom seen their faces. But at times, I feel them. You might say that we feel each other. We send our silent yet powerful signals. 'Keep away from me.' "

The following night, he'd given Daniel the locket, the amulet as he called it, to wear. He'd kissed it first and rubbed it in his hands as if to warm it. Strange to witness this ritual. Stranger still to see the thing itself with the letter A carved on it, and inside the tiny vial of Armand's blood.

"Here, snap the clasp if they come near you. Break the vial instantly. And they will feel the power that protects you. They will not dare—"

"Ah, you'll let them kill me. You know you will," Daniel had said coldly. Shut out. "Give me the power to fight for myself."

But he had worn the locket ever since. Under the lamp, he'd examined the A and the intricate carvings all over the thing to find they were tiny twisted human figures, some mutilated, others writhing as if in agony, some dead. Horrid thing actually. He had dropped the chain down into his shirt, and it was cold against his naked chest, but out of sight.

Yet Daniel was never to see or sense the presence of another supernatural being. He remembered Louis as if he'd been a hallucination, something known in a fever. Armand was Daniel's single oracle, his merciless and all-loving demonic god.

More and more his bitterness increased. Life with Armand inflamed him, maddened him. It had been years since Daniel had even thought of his family, of the friends he used to know. Checks went out to kin, of that he'd made certain, but they were just names now on a list.

"You'll never die, and yet you look at me and you watch me die, night after night, you watch it."

Ugly fights, terrible fights, finally, Armand broken down, glassy-eyed with silent rage, then crying softly but uncontrollably as if some lost emotion had been rediscovered which threatened to tear him apart. "I will not do it, I cannot do it. Ask me to kill you, it would be easier than that. You don't know what you ask for, don't you see? It is always a damnable error! Don't you realize that any one of us would give it up for one human lifetime?"

"Give up immortality, just to live one life? I don't believe you. This is the first time you have told me an out-and-out lie."

"How dare you!"

"Don't hit me. You might kill me. You're very strong."

"I'd give it up. If I weren't a coward when it gets right down to it, if I weren't after five hundred greedy years in this whirlwind still terrified to the marrow of my bones of death."

"No, you wouldn't. Fear has nothing to do with it. Imagine one lifetime back then when you were born. And all this lost? The future in which you know power and luxury of which Genghis Khan never dreamed? But forget the technical miracles. Would you settle for ignorance of the world's destiny? Ah, don't tell me you would."

No resolution in words was ever reached. It would end with the embrace, the kiss, the blood stinging him, the shroud of dreams closing over him like a great net, hunger! I love you! Give me more! Yes, more. But never enough.

It was useless.

What had these transfusions done to his body and soul? Made him see the descent of the falling leaf in greater detail? Armand was not going to give it to him!

Armand would see Daniel leave time and again, and drift off into the terrors of the everyday world, risk that, rather than do it. There was nothing Daniel could do, nothing he could give.

And the wandering started, the escaping, and Armand did not follow him. Armand would wait each time until Daniel begged to come back. Or until Daniel was beyond calling, until Daniel was on the verge of death itself. And then and only then, Armand would bring him back.

THE rain hit the wide pavements of Michigan Avenue. The bookstore was empty, the lights had gone out. Somewhere a clock had struck the hour of nine. He stood against the glass watching the traffic stream past in front of him. Nowhere to go. Drink the tiny drop of blood inside the locket. Why not?

And Lestat in California, on the prowl already, perhaps stalking a victim even now. And they were preparing the hall for the concert, weren't they? Mortal men rigging up lights, microphones, concession stands, oblivious to the secret codes being given, the sinister audience that would conceal itself in the great indifferent and inevitably hysterical human throng. Ah, maybe Daniel had made a horrible miscalculation. Maybe Armand was there!

At first it seemed an impossibility, then a certainty. Why hadn't Daniel realized this before?

Surely Armand had gone! If there was any truth at all in what Lestat had written, Armand would go for a reckoning, to witness, to search perhaps for those he'd lost over the centuries now drawn to Lestat by the same call.

And what would a mortal lover matter then, a human who'd been no more than a toy for a decade? No. Armand had gone on without him. And this time there would be no rescue.

He felt cold, small, as he stood there. He felt miserably alone. It didn't matter, his premonitions, how the dream of the twins descended upon him and then left him with foreboding. These were things that were passing him by like great black wings. You could feel the indifferent wind as they swept over. Armand had proceeded without him towards a destiny that Daniel would never fully understand.

It filled him with horror, with sadness. Gates locked. The anxiety aroused by the dream mingled with a dull sickening fear. He had come to the end of the line. What would he do? Wearily, he envisioned the Night Island locked against him. He saw the villa behind its white walls, high above the beach, impossible to reach. He imagined his past gone, along with his future. Death was the understanding of the immediate present: that there is finally nothing else.

He walked on a few steps; his hands were numb. The rain had drenched his sweat shirt. He wanted to lie down on the very pavement and let the twins come again. And Lestat's phrases ran through his head. The Dark Trick he called the moment of rebirth. The Savage Garden he called the world that could embrace such exquisite monsters, ah, yes.

But let me be a lover in the Savage Garden with you, and the light that went out of life would come back in a great burst of glory. Out of mortal flesh I would pass into eternity. I would be one of you.

Dizzy. Did he almost fall? Someone talking to him, someone asking if he was all right. No, of course not. Why should I be?

But there was a hand on his shoulder.

Daniel.

He looked up.

Armand stood at the curb.

At first he could not believe it, he wanted it so badly, but there was no denying what he saw. Armand stood there. He was peering silently from the unearthly stillness he seemed to carry with him, his face flushed beneath the faintest touch of unnatural pallor. How normal he looked, if beauty is ever normal. And yet how strangely set apart from the material things touching him, the rumpled white coat and pants he wore. Behind him the big gray hulk of a Rolls waited, like an ancillary vision, droplets teeming on its silver roof.

Come on, Daniel. You made it hard for me this time, didn't you, so hard.

Why the urgency of the command when the hand that pulled him forward was so strong? Such a rare thing to see Armand truly angry. Ah, how Daniel loved this anger! His knees went out from under him. He felt himself lifted. And then the soft velvet of the back seat of the car spread out under him. He fell over on his hands. He closed his eyes.

But Armand gently pulled him upright, held him. The car rocked gently, deliciously as it moved forward. So nice to sleep at last in Armand's arms. But there was so much he must tell Armand, so much about the dream, the book.

"Don't you think I know?" Armand whispered. A strange light in the eye, what was it? Something raw and tender in the way Armand looked, all the composure stripped away. He lifted a tumbler half full of brandy and put it in Daniel's hand.

"And you running from me," he said, "from Stockholm and Edinburgh and Paris. What do you think I am that I can follow you at such speed down so many pathways? And such danger—"

Lips against Daniel's face, suddenly, ah, that's better, I like kissing. And snuggling with dead things, yes, hold me. He buried his face in Armand's neck. *Your blood.*

"Not yet, my beloved." Armand pushed him forward, pressing his fingers to Daniel's lips. Such uncommon feeling in the low, controlled voice. "Listen to what I'm saying to you. All over the world, our kind are being destroyed."

Destroyed. It sent a current of panic through him, so that his body tensed in spite of his exhaustion. He tried to focus on Armand, but he saw the red-haired twins again, the soldiers, the blackened body of the mother being overturned in the ashes. But the meaning, the continuity . . . Why?

"I cannot tell you," Armand said. And he meant the dream when he spoke, because he'd had the dream too. He lifted the brandy to Daniel's lips.

Oh, so warm, yes. He would slip into unconsciousness if he didn't hold tight. They were racing silently along the freeway now, out of Chicago, the rain flooding the windows, locked together in this warm, velvet-lined little place. Ah, such lovely silver rain. And Armand had turned away, distracted, as if listening to some faraway music, his lips parted, frozen on the verge of speech.

I'm with you, safe with you.

"No, Daniel, not safe," he answered. "Maybe not even for a night or so much as an hour."

Daniel tried to think, to form a question, but he was too weak, too drowsy. The car was so comfortable, the motion of it so soothing. And the twins. The beautiful red-haired twins wanted in now! His eyes closed for a split second and he sank against Armand's shoulder, feeling Armand's hand on his back.

Far away he heard Armand's voice: "What do I do with you, my beloved? Especially now, when I myself am so afraid."

Darkness again. He held fast to the taste of the brandy in his mouth, to the touch of Armand's hand, but he was already dreaming.

The twins were walking in the desert; the sun was high above. It burned their white arms, their faces. Their lips were swollen and cracked from thirst. Their dresses were stained with blood.

"Make the rain fall," Daniel whispered aloud, "you can do it, make the rain fall." One of the twins fell down on her knees, and her sister knelt and put her arms around her. Red hair and red hair.

Somewhere far off he heard Armand's voice again. Armand said that they were too deep in the desert. Not even their spirits could make rain in such a place.

But why? Couldn't spirits do anything?

He felt Armand kiss him gently again.

The twins have now entered a low mountain pass. But there is no shade because the sun is directly above them, and the rocky slopes are too treacherous for them to climb. On they walk. Can't someone help them? They stumble and fall every few steps now. The rocks look too hot to touch. Finally one of them falls face down in the sand, and the other lies over her, sheltering her with her hair.

Oh, if only evening would come, with its cold winds.

Suddenly the twin who is protecting her sister looks up. Movement on the cliffs. Then stillness again. A rock falls, echoes with a soft clear shuffling sound. And then Daniel sees the men moving over the precipices, desert people as they have looked for thousands of years with their dark skin and heavy white robes.

The twins rise on their knees together as these men approach. The men offer them water. They pour the cool water over the twins. Suddenly the twins are laughing and talking hysterically, so great is their relief, but the men don't understand. Then it is gestures, so purely eloquent, as one twin points to the belly of her sister, and then folding her arms makes the universal sign for rocking a child. Ah, yes. The men lift the pregnant woman. And all move together towards the oasis, round which their tents stand.

At last by the light of a fire outside the tent, the twins sleep, safe, among the desert people, the Bedouins. Could it be that the Bedouins are so very ancient, that their history goes back thousands and thousands of years? At dawn, one of the twins rises, the one who does not carry a child. As her sister watches, she walks out towards the olive trees of the oasis. She lifts her arms, and at first it seems she is only welcoming the sun. Others have awakened; they gather to see. Then a wind rises, gently, moving the branches of the olive trees. And the rain, the light sweet rain begins to fall.

He opened his eyes. He was on the plane.

HE RECOGNIZED the small bedroom immediately by the white plastic walls and the soothing quality of the dim yellow light. Everything synthetic, hard and gleaming like the great rib bones of prehistoric creatures. Have things come full circle? Technology has recreated Jonah's chamber deep within the belly of the whale.

He was lying on the bed that had no head or foot or legs or frame to it. Someone had washed his hands and his face. He was clean-shaven. Ah, that felt so good. And the roar of the engines was a huge silence, the whale breathing, slicing through the sea. That made it possible for him to see things around him very distinctly. A decanter. Bourbon. He wanted it. But he was too exhausted to move. And something not right, something. . . . He reached up, felt his neck. The amulet was gone! But it didn't matter. He was with Armand.

Armand sat at the little table near the whale's eye window, the white plastic lid pulled all the way down. He had cut his hair. And he wore black wool now, neat and fine, like the corpse again dressed for the funeral even to the shining black shoes. Grim all this. Someone will now read the Twenty-third Psalm. Bring back the white clothes.

"You're dying," Armand said softly.

" 'And though I walk through the valley of the shadow of death,' et cetera," Daniel whispered. His throat was so dry. And his head ached. Didn't matter saying what was really on his mind. All been said long ago.

Armand spoke again silently, a laser beam touching Daniel's brain:

Shall we bother with the particulars? You weigh no more than a hundred and thirty pounds now. And the alcohol is eating at your insides. You are half mad. There is almost nothing left in the world that you enjoy.

"Except talking to you now and then. It's so easy to hear everything you say."

If you were never to see me again, that would only make things worse. If you go on as you are, you won't live another five days.

Unbearable thought, actually. But if that's so, then why have I been running away?

No response.

How clear everything seemed. It wasn't only the roar of the engines, it was the curious movement of the plane, that never-ending irregular undulation as if it rode the air in bumps and dips and over curbs and now and then uphill. The whale speeding along on the whale path, as Beowulf called it.

Armand's hair was brushed to one side, neatly. Gold watch on his wrist, one of those high-tech numbers he so adored. Think of that thing flashing its digits inside a coffin during the day. And the black jacket, old-fashioned rather with narrow lapels. The vest was black silk, it looked like that anyway. But his face, ah, he had fed all right. Fed plenty.

Do you remember anything I said to you earlier?

"Yes," Daniel said. But the truth is he had trouble remembering. Then it came back suddenly, oppressively. "Something about destruction everywhere. But I'm dying. They're dying, I'm dying. They got to be immortal before it happened; I am merely alive. See? I remember. I would like to have the bourbon now."

There is nothing I can do to make you want to live, isn't that so?

"Not that again. I will jump out of the plane if you go on."

Will you listen to me, then? Really listen?

"How can I help it? I can't get away from your voice when you want me to listen; it's like a tiny microphone inside my head. What is this, tears? You're going to weep over me?"

For one second, he looked so young. What a travesty.

"Damn you, Daniel," he said, so that Daniel heard the words aloud.

A chill passed over Daniel. Horrid to see him suffering. Daniel said nothing.

"What we are," Armand said, "it wasn't meant to be, you know that. You didn't have to read Lestat's book to find it out. Any one of us could have told you it was an abomination, a demonic fusion—"

"Then what Lestat wrote was true." A demon going into the ancient

Egyptian Mother and the Father. Well, a spirit anyway. They had called it a demon back then.

"Doesn't matter whether or not it's true. The beginning is no longer important. What matters is that the end may be at hand."

Deep tightening of panic, the atmosphere of the dream returning, the shrill sound of the twins' screams.

"Listen to me," Armand said patiently, calling him back away from the two women. "Lestat has awakened something or someone—"

"Akasha . . . Enkil."

"Perhaps. It may be more than one or two. No one knows for certain. There is a vague repeated cry of danger, but no one seems to know whence it comes. They only know that we are being sought out and annihilated, that coven houses, meeting places, go up in flames."

"I've heard the cry of danger," Daniel whispered. "Sometimes very strong in the middle of the night, and then at other moments like an echo." Again he saw the twins. It had to be connected to the twins. "But how do you know these things, about the coven houses, about—"

"Daniel, don't try me. There isn't much time left. I know. The others know. It's like a current, running through the wires of a great web."

"Yes." Whenever Daniel had tasted the vampiric blood, he had glimpsed for one instant that great glittering mesh of knowledge, connections, half-understood visions. And it was true then. The web had begun with the Mother and the Father—

"Years ago," Armand interrupted, "it wouldn't have mattered to me, all this."

"What do you mean?"

"But I don't want it to end now. I don't want to continue unless you—" His face changed slightly. Faint look of surprise. "I don't want you to die."

Daniel said nothing.

Eerie the stillness of this moment. Even with the plane riding the air currents gently. Armand sitting there, so self-contained, so patient, with the words belying the smooth calm of the voice.

"I'm not afraid, because you're here," Daniel said suddenly.

"You're a fool then. But I will tell you another mysterious part of it."

"Yes?"

"Lestat is still in existence. He goes on with his schemes. And those who've gathered near him are unharmed."

"But how do you know for certain?"

Short little velvet laugh. "There you go again. So irrepressibly human. You overestimate me or underestimate me. Seldom do you ever hit the mark."

"I work with limited equipment. The cells in my body are subject to deterioration, to a process called aging and—"

"They're gathered in San Francisco. They crowd the back rooms of a tavern called Dracula's Daughter. Perhaps I know because others know it and one powerful mind picks up images from another and unwittingly or deliberately passes those images along. Perhaps one witness telegraphs the image to many. I can't tell. Thoughts, feelings, voices, they're just there. Traveling the web, the threads. Some are clear, others clouded. Now and then the warning overrides everything. *Danger.* It is as if our world falls silent for one instant. Then other voices rise again."

"And Lestat. Where is Lestat?"

"He's been seen but only in glimpses. They can't track him to his lair. He's too clever to let that happen. But he teases them. He races his black Porsche through the streets of San Francisco. He may not know all that's happened."

"Explain."

"The power to communicate varies. To listen to the thoughts of others is often to be heard oneself. Lestat is concealing his presence. His mind may be completely cut off."

"And the twins? The two women in the dream, who are they?"

"I don't know. Not all have had these dreams. But many know of them, and all seem to fear them, to share the conviction that somehow Lestat is to blame. For all that's happened, Lestat is to blame."

"A real devil among devils." Daniel laughed softly.

With a subtle nod, Armand acknowledged the little jest wearily. He even smiled.

Stillness. Roar of the engines.

"Do you understand what I'm telling you? There have been attacks upon our kind everywhere but there."

"Where Lestat is."

"Precisely. But the destroyer moves erratically. It seems it must be near to the thing it would destroy. It may be waiting for the concert in order to finish what it has begun."

"It can't hurt you. It would have already—"

The short, derisive laugh again, barely audible. A telepathic laugh?

"Your faith touches me as always, but don't be my acolyte just now. The thing is not omnipotent. It can't move with infinite speed. You have to understand the choice I've made. We're going to him because there isn't any other safe place to go. It has found rogues in far-flung places and burnt them to ashes—"

"And because you want to be with Lestat."

No answer.

"You know you do. You want to see him. You want to be there if he needs you. If there's going to be a battle . . ."

No answer.

"And if Lestat caused it, maybe he can stop it."

Still Armand didn't answer. He appeared confused.

"It is simpler than that," he said finally. "I *have* to go."

The plane seemed a thing suspended on a spume of sound. Daniel looked drowsily at the ceiling, at the light moving.

To see Lestat at last. He thought of Lestat's old house in New Orleans. Of the gold watch he'd recovered from the dusty floor. And now it was back to San Francisco, back to the beginning, back to Lestat. God, he wanted the bourbon. Why wouldn't Armand give it to him? He was so weak. They'd go to the concert, he'd see Lestat—

But then the sense of dread came again, deepening, the dread which the dreams inspired. "Don't let me dream any more of them," he whispered suddenly.

He thought he heard Armand say yes.

Suddenly Armand stood beside the bed. His shadow fell over Daniel. The whale's belly seemed smaller, no more than the light surrounding Armand.

"Look at me, beloved," he said.

Darkness. And then the high iron gates opening, and the moon flooding down on the garden. *What is this place?*

Oh, Italy, it had to be, with this gentle embracing warm air and a full moon shining down on the great sweep of trees and flowers, and beyond, the Villa of the Mysteries at the very edge of ancient Pompeii.

"But how did we get here!" He turned to Armand, who stood beside him dressed in strange, old-fashioned velvet clothes. For one moment he could do nothing but stare at Armand, at the black velvet tunic he wore and the leggings, and his long curling auburn hair.

"We aren't really here," Armand said. "You know we aren't." He turned and walked into the garden towards the villa, his heels making the faintest sound on the worn gray stones.

But it was real! Look at the crumbling old brick walls, and the flowers in their long deep beds, and the path itself with Armand's damp footprints! And the stars overhead, the stars! He turned around and reached up into the lemon tree and broke off a single fragrant leaf.

Armand turned, reached back to take his arm. The smell of freshly turned earth rose from the flower beds. *Ah, I could die here.*

"Yes," said Armand, "you could. And you will. And you know, I've never done it before. I told you but you never believed me. Now Lestat's told you in his book. I've never done it. Do you believe him?"

"Of course I believed you. The vow you made, you explained everything. But Armand, this is my question, to whom did you make this vow?"

Laughter.

Their voices carried over the garden. Such roses and chrysanthemums,
how enormous they were. And light poured from the doorways of the Villa
of the Mysteries. Was there music playing? Why, the whole ruined place
was brilliantly illuminated under the incandescent blue of the night sky.

"So you would have me break my vow. You would have what you
think you want. But look well at this garden, because once I do it, you'll
never read my thoughts or see my visions again. A veil of silence will come
down."

"But we'll be brothers, don't you see?" Daniel asked.

Armand stood so close to him they were almost kissing. The flowers
were crushed against them, huge drowsing yellow dahlias and white gladi-
oli, such lovely drenching perfume. They had stopped beneath a dying tree
in which the wisteria grew wild. Its delicate blossoms shivered in clusters,
its great twining arms white as bone. And beyond voices poured out of the
Villa. Were there people singing?

"But where are we really?" Daniel asked. "Tell me!"

"I told you. It's just a dream. But if you want a name, let me call it
the gateway of life and death. I'll bring you with me through this gateway.
And why? Because I am a coward. And I love you too much to let you go."

Such joy Daniel felt, such cold and lovely triumph. And so the moment was his, and he was lost no more in the awesome free fall of time. No
more one of the teeming millions who would sleep in this dank odoriferous
earth, beneath the broken withered flowers, without name or knowledge,
all vision lost.

"I promise you nothing. How can I? I've told you what lies ahead."

"I don't care. I'll go towards it with you."

Armand's eyes were reddened, weary, old. Such delicate clothes these
were, hand sewn, dusty, like the clothes of a ghost. Were they what the
mind conjured effortlessly when it wanted to be purely itself?

"Don't cry! It's not fair," Daniel said. "This is my rebirth. How can
you cry? Don't you know what this means? Is it possible you never knew?"
He looked up suddenly, to catch the whole sweep of this enchanted landscape, the distant Villa, the rolling land above and below. And then he
turned his face upwards, and the heavens astonished him. Never had he
seen so many stars.

Why, it seemed as if the sky itself went up and up forever with stars
so plentiful and bright that the constellations were utterly lost. No pattern.
No meaning. Only the gorgeous victory of sheer energy and matter. But
then he saw the Pleiades—the constellation beloved of the doomed red-

haired twins in the dream—and he smiled. He saw the twins together on a mountaintop, and they were happy. It made him so glad.

"Say the word, my love," Armand said. "I'll do it. We'll be in hell together after all."

"But don't you see," Daniel said, "all human decisions are made like this. Do you think the mother knows what will happen to the child in her womb? Dear God, we are lost, I tell you. What does it matter if you give it to me and it's wrong! There is no wrong! There is only desperation, and I would *have it!* I want to live forever with you."

He opened his eyes. The ceiling of the cabin of the plane, the soft yellow lights reflected in the warm wood-paneled walls, and then around him the garden, the perfume, the sight of the flowers almost breaking loose from their stems.

They stood beneath the dead tree twined full of airy purple wisteria blossoms. And the blossoms stroked his face, the clusters of waxy petals. Something came back to him, something he had known long ago—that in the language of an ancient people the word for flowers was the same as the word for blood. He felt the sudden sharp stab of the teeth in his neck.

His heart was caught suddenly, wrenched in a powerful grip! The pressure was more than he could bear. Yet he could see over Armand's shoulder and the night was sliding down around him, the stars growing as large as these moist and fragrant blooms. Why, they were rising into the sky!

For a split second he saw the Vampire Lestat, driving, plunging through the night in his long sleek black car. How like a lion Lestat looked with his mane of hair blown back by the wind, his eyes filled with mad humor and high spirits. And then he turned and looked at Daniel, and from his throat came a deep soft laugh.

Louis was there too. Louis was standing in a room on Divisadero Street looking out of the window, waiting, and then he said, "Yes, come, Daniel, if that is what must happen."

But they didn't know about the burnt-out coven houses! They didn't know about the twins! About the cry of danger!

They were all in a crowded room, actually, inside the Villa, and Louis was leaning against the mantel in a frock coat. Everyone was there! Even the twins were there! "Thank God, you've come," Daniel said. He kissed Louis on one cheek and then the other decorously. "Why, my skin is as pale as yours!"

He cried out suddenly as his heart was let go, and the air filled his lungs. The garden again. The grass was all around him. The garden grew up over his head. *Don't leave me here, not here against the earth.*

"Drink, Daniel." The priest said the Latin words as he poured the Holy Communion wine into his mouth. The red-haired twins took the sacred plates—the heart, the brain. "This the brain and the heart of my mother I devour with all respect for the spirit of my mother—"

"God, give it to me!" He'd knocked the chalice to the marble floor of the church, so clumsy, but God! The blood!

He sat up, crushing Armand to him, drawing it out of him, draught after draught. They had fallen over together in the soft bank of flowers. Armand lay beside him, and his mouth was open on Armand's throat, and the blood was an unstoppable fount.

"Come into the Villa of the Mysteries," said Louis to him. Louis was touching his shoulder. "We're waiting." The twins were embracing each other, stroking each other's long curling red hair.

The kids were screaming outside the auditorium because there were no more tickets. They would camp in the parking lot until tomorrow night.

"Do we have tickets?" he asked. "Armand, the tickets!"

Danger. Ice. It's coming from the one trapped beneath the ice! Something hit him, hard. He was floating.

"Sleep, beloved."

"I want to go back to the garden, the Villa." He tried to open his eyes. His belly was hurting. Strangest pain, it seemed so far away.

"You know he's buried under the ice?"

"Sleep," Armand said, covering him with the blanket. "And when you wake, you'll be just like me. Dead."

SAN FRANCISCO. He knew he was there before he even opened his eyes. And such a ghastly dream, he was glad to leave it—suffocating, blackness, and riding the rough and terrifying current of the sea! But the dream was fading. A dream without sight, and only the sound of the water, the feel of the water! A dream of unspeakable fear. He'd been a woman in it, helpless, without a tongue to scream.

Let it go away.

Something about the wintry air on his face, a white freshness that he could almost taste. San Francisco, of course. The cold moved over him like a tight garment, yet inside he was deliciously warm.

Immortal. Forever.

He opened his eyes. Armand had put him here. Through the viscid darkness of the dream, he'd heard Armand telling him to remain. Armand had told him that here he would be safe.

Here.

The French doors stood open all along the far wall. And the room itself, opulent, cluttered, one of those splendid places that Armand so often found, so dearly loved.

Look at the sheer lace panel blown back from the French doors. Look at the white feathers curling and glowing in the Aubusson carpet. He climbed to his feet and went out through the open doors.

A great mesh of branches rose between him and the wet shining sky. Stiff foliage of the Monterey cypress. And down there, through the branches, against a velvet blackness, he saw the great burning arc of the Golden Gate Bridge. The fog poured like thick white smoke past the immense towers. In fits and gusts it tried to swallow the pylons, the cables, then vanished as if the bridge itself with its glittering stream of traffic burnt it away.

Too magnificent, this spectacle—and the deep dark outline of the distant hills beneath their mantle of warm lights. Ah, but to take one tiny detail—the damp rooftops spilling downhill away from him, or the gnarled branches rising in front of him. Like elephant hide, this bark, this living skin.

Immortal . . . forever.

He ran his hands back through his hair and a gentle tingling passed through him. He could feel the soft imprint of his fingers on his scalp after he had taken his hands away. The wind stung him exquisitely. He remembered something. He reached up to find his fang teeth. Yes, they were beautifully long and sharp.

Someone touched him. He turned so quickly he almost lost his balance. Why, this was all so inconceivably different! He steadied himself, but the sight of Armand made him want to cry. Even in deep shadow, Armand's dark brown eyes were filled with a vibrant light. And the expression on his face, so loving. He reached out very carefully and touched Armand's eyelashes. He wanted to touch the tiny fine lines in Armand's lips. Armand kissed him. He began to tremble. The way it felt, the cool silky mouth, like a kiss of the brain, the electric purity of a thought!

"Come inside, my pupil," Armand said. "We have less than an hour left."

"But the others—"

Armand had gone to discover something very important. What was it? Terrible things happening, coven houses burned. Yet nothing at the moment seemed more important than the warmth inside him, and the tingling as he moved his limbs.

"They're thriving, plotting," Armand said. Was he speaking out loud? He must have been. But the voice was so clear! "They're frightened of the wholesale destruction, but San Francisco isn't touched. Some say Lestat has done it to drive everyone to him. Others that it's the work of Marius, or even the twins. Or Those Who Must Be Kept, who strike with infinite power from their shrine."

The twins! He felt the darkness of the dream again around him, a woman's body, tongueless, terror, closing him in. Ah, nothing could hurt him now. Not dreams or plots. He was Armand's child.

"But these things must wait," Armand said gently. "You must come and do as I tell you. We must finish what was begun."

"Finish?" It was finished. He was reborn.

Armand brought him in out of the wind. Glint of the brass bed in the darkness, of a porcelain vase alive with gilded dragons. Of the square grand piano with its keys like grinning teeth. Yes, touch it, feel the ivory, the velvet tassels hanging from the lampshade. . . .

The music, where did the music come from? A low, mournful jazz trumpet, playing all alone. It stopped him, this hollow melancholy song, the notes flowing slowly into one another. He did not want to move just now. He wanted to say he understood what was happening, but he was absorbing each broken sound.

He started to say thank you for the music, but again, his voice sounded so unaccountably strange—sharper, yet more resonant. Even the feel of his tongue, and out there, the fog, look at it, he pointed, the fog blowing right past the terrace, the fog eating the night!

Armand was patient. Armand understood. Armand brought him slowly through the darkened room.

"I love you," Daniel said.

"Are you certain?" Armand answered.

It made him laugh.

They had come into a long high hallway. A stairs descending in deep shadow. A polished balustrade. Armand urged him forward. He wanted to look at the rug beneath him, a long chain of medallions woven with lilies, but Armand had brought him into a brightly lighted room.

He caught his breath at the sheer flood of illumination, light moving over the low-slung leather couches, chairs. Ah, but the painting on the wall!

So vivid the figures in the painting, formless creatures who were actually great thick smears of glaring yellow and red paint. Everything that looked alive was alive, that was a distinct possibility. You painted armless beings, swimming in blinding color, and they had to exist like that forever. Could they see you with all those tiny, scattered eyes? Or did they see only the heaven and hell of their own shining realm, anchored to the studs in the wall by a piece of twisted wire?

He could have wept to think of it, wept at the deep-throated moan of the trumpet—and yet he wasn't weeping. He had caught a strong seductive aroma. *God, what is it?* His whole body seemed to harden inexplicably. Then suddenly he was staring at a young girl.

She sat in a small gilded straight-back chair watching him, ankles crossed, her thick brown hair a gleaming mop around her white face. Her scant clothes were dirty. A little runaway with her torn jeans and soiled shirt. What a perfect picture, even to the sprinkling of freckles across her nose, and the greasy backpack that lay at her feet. But the shape of her little arms, the way her legs were made! And her eyes, her brown eyes! He was laughing softly, but it was humorless, crazed. It had a sinister sound to it; how strange! He realized he had taken her face in his hands and she was staring up at him, smiling, and a faint scarlet blush came in her warm little cheeks.

Blood, that was the aroma! His fingers were burning. Why, he could even see the blood vessels beneath her skin! And the sound of her heart, he could hear it. It was getting louder, it was such a . . . a moist sound. He backed away from her.

"God, get her out of here!" he cried.

"Take her," Armand whispered. "And do it now."

5

KHAYMAN, MY KHAYMAN

No one is listening.
Now you may sing the selfsong,
as the bird does, not for territory
or dominance,
but for self-enlargement.
Let something
come from nothing.
. . .

STAN RICE
from "Texas Suite"
Body of Work (1983)

UNTIL this night, this awful night, he'd had a little joke about himself: He didn't know who he was, or where he'd come from, but he knew what he liked.

And what he liked was all around him—the flower stands on the corners, the big steel and glass buildings full of milky evening light, the trees, of course, the grass beneath his feet. And the bought things of shining plastic and metal—toys, computers, telephones—it didn't matter. He liked to figure them out, master them, then crush them into tiny hard multicolored balls which he could then juggle or toss through plate glass windows when nobody was about.

He liked piano music, the motion pictures, and the poems he found in books.

He also liked the automobiles that burnt oil from the earth like lamps. And the great jet planes that flew on the same scientific principles, above the clouds.

He always stopped and listened to the people laughing and talking up there when one of the planes flew overhead.

Driving was an extraordinary pleasure. In a silver Mercedes-Benz, he had sped on smooth empty roads from Rome to Florence to Venice in one night. He also liked television—the entire electric process of it, with its tiny bits of light. How soothing it was to have the company of television, the intimacy with so many artfully painted faces speaking to you in friendship from the glowing screen.

The rock and roll, he liked that too. He liked all music. He liked the Vampire Lestat singing "Requiem for the Marquise." He didn't pay attention to the words much. It was the melancholy, and the dark undertone of drums and cymbals. Made him want to dance.

He liked giant yellow machines that dug into the earth late at night in the big cities with men in uniforms crawling all over them; he liked the double-decker buses of London, and the people—the clever mortals everywhere—he liked them, too, of course.

He liked walking in Damascus during the evening, and seeing in sudden flashes of disconnected memory the city of the ancients. Romans, Greeks, Persians, Egyptians in these streets.

He liked the libraries where he could find photographs of ancient monuments in big smooth good-smelling books. He took his own photographs of the new cities around him and sometimes he could put images on these pictures which came from his thoughts. For example, in his photograph of Rome there were Roman people in tunics and sandals superimposed upon the modern versions in their thick ungraceful clothes.

Oh, yes, much to like all around him always—the violin music of Bartók, little girls in snow white dresses coming out of the church at midnight having sung at the Christmas mass.

He liked the blood of his victims too, of course. That went without saying. It was no part of his little joke. Death was not funny to him. He stalked his prey in silence; he didn't want to know his victims. All a mortal had to do was speak to him and he was turned away. Not proper, as he saw it, to talk to these sweet, soft-eyed beings and then gobble their blood, break their bones and lick the marrow, squeeze their limbs to a dripping pulp. And that was the way he feasted now, so violently. He felt no great need for blood anymore; but he wanted it. And the desire overpowered him in all its ravening purity, quite apart from thirst. He could have feasted upon three or four mortals a night.

Yet he was sure, absolutely sure, that he had been a human being once. Walking in the sun in the heat of the day, yes, he had once done that, even though he certainly couldn't do it now. He envisioned himself sitting at a plain wood table and cutting open a ripe peach with a small copper knife. Beautiful the fruit before him. He knew the taste of it. He knew the taste of bread and beer. He saw the sun shining on the dull yellow sand that stretched for miles and miles outside. "Lie down and rest in the heat of the day," someone had once said to him. Was this the last day that he had been alive? Rest, yes, because tonight the King and the Queen will call all the court together and something terrible, something. . . .

But he couldn't really remember.

No, he just knew it, that is, until this night. This night . . .

Not even when he'd heard the Vampire Lestat did he remember. The character merely fascinated him a little—a rock singer calling himself a blood drinker. And he did look unearthly, but then that was television, wasn't it? Many humans in the dizzying world of rock music appeared unearthly. And there was such human emotion in the Vampire Lestat's voice.

It wasn't merely emotion; it was human ambition of a particular sort. The Vampire Lestat wanted to be heroic. When he sang, he said: "Allow me my significance! I am the symbol of evil; and if I am a true symbol, then I do good."

Fascinating. Only a human being could think of a paradox like that. And he himself knew this, because he'd been human, of course.

Now he did have a supernatural understanding of things. That was true. Humans couldn't look at machines and perceive their principles as he could. And the manner in which everything was "familiar" to him—that had to do with his superhuman powers as well. Why, there was nothing that surprised him really. Not quantum physics or theories of evolution or the paintings of Picasso or the process by which children were inoculated with germs to protect them from disease. No, it was as if he'd been aware of things long before he remembered being here. Long before he could say: "I think; therefore I am."

But disregarding all that, he still had a human perspective. That no one would deny. He could feel human pain with an eerie and frightening perfection. He knew what it meant to love, and to be lonely, ah, yes, he knew that above all things, and he felt it most keenly when he listened to the Vampire Lestat's songs. That's why he didn't pay attention to the words.

And another thing. The more blood he drank the more human-looking he became.

When he'd first appeared in this time—to himself and others—he hadn't looked human at all. He'd been a filthy skeleton, walking along the highway in Greece towards Athens, his bones enmeshed in tight rubbery veins, the whole sealed beneath a layer of toughened white skin. He'd terrified people. How they had fled from him, gunning the engines of their little cars. But he'd read their minds—seen himself as they saw him—and he understood, and he was so sorry, of course.

In Athens, he'd gotten gloves, a loose wool garment with plastic buttons, and these funny modern shoes that covered up your whole foot. He'd wrapped rags around his face with only holes for his eyes and mouth. He'd covered his filthy black hair with a gray felt hat.

They still stared but they didn't run screaming. At dusk, he roamed through the thick crowds in Omonia Square and no one paid him any mind. How nice the modern bustle of this old city, which in long ago ages had been just as vital, when students came there from all over the world to study philosophy and art. He could look up at the Acropolis and see the Parthenon as it had been then, perfect, the house of the goddess. Not the ruin it was today.

The Greeks as always were a splendid people, gentle and trusting, though they were darker of hair and skin now on account of their Turkish blood. They didn't mind his strange clothes. When he talked in his soft, soothing voice, imitating their language perfectly—except for a few apparently hilarious mistakes—they loved him. And in private, he had noticed that his flesh was slowly filling out. It was hard as a rock to the touch. Yet it was changing. Finally, one night when he unwrapped the ragged covering, he had seen the contours of a human face. So this is what he looked like, was it?

Big black eyes with fine soft wrinkles at the corners and rather smooth lids. His mouth was a nice, smiling mouth. The nose was neat and finely made; he didn't disdain it. And the eyebrows: he liked these best of all because they were very black and straight, not broken or bushy, and they were drawn high enough above his eyes so that he had an open expression, a look of veiled wonder that others might trust. Yes, it was a very pretty young male face.

After that he'd gone about uncovered, wearing modern shirts and pants. But he had to keep to the shadows. He was just too smooth and too white.

He said his name was Khayman when they asked him. But he didn't know where he'd gotten it. And he had been called Benjamin once, later, he knew that, too. There were other names. . . . But when? Khayman. That was the first and secret name, the one he never forgot. He could draw two tiny pictures that meant Khayman, but where these symbols had come from he had no idea.

His strength puzzled him as much as anything else. He could walk through plaster walls, lift an automobile and hurl it into a nearby field. Yet he was curiously brittle and light. He drove a long thin knife right through his own hand. Such a strange sensation! And blood everywhere. Then the wounds closed and he had to open them again to pull the knife out.

As for the lightness, well, there was nothing that he could not climb. It was as though gravity had no control over him once he decided to defy it. And one night after climbing a tall building in the middle of the city, he flew off the top of it, descending gently to the street below.

Lovely, this. He knew he could traverse great distances if only he dared. Why, surely he had once done it, moving into the very clouds. But then . . . maybe not.

He had other powers as well. Each evening as he awakened, he found himself listening to voices from all over the world. He lay in the darkness bathed in sound. He heard people speaking in Greek, English, Romanian, Hindustani. He heard laughter, cries of pain. And if he lay very still, he could hear thoughts from people—a jumbled undercurrent full of wild exaggeration that frightened him. He did not know where these voices came from. Or why one voice drowned out another. Why, it was as if he were God and he were listening to prayers.

And now and then, quite distinct from the human voices, there came to him immortal voices too. Others like him out there, thinking, feeling, sending a warning? Far away their powerful silvery cries, yet he could easily separate them from the human warp and woof.

But this receptiveness hurt him. It brought back some awful memory of being shut up in a dark place with only these voices to keep him company for years and years and years. Panic. He would not remember that. Some things one doesn't want to remember. Like being burned, imprisoned. Like remembering everything and crying, terrible anguished crying.

Yes, bad things had happened to him. He had been here on this earth under other names and at other times. But always with this same gentle and optimistic disposition, loving things. Was his a migrant soul? No, he had always had this body. That's why it was so light and so strong.

Inevitably he shut off the voices. In fact, he remembered an old admonition: If you do not learn to shut out the voices, they will drive you mad. But with him now, it was simple. He quieted them simply by rising, opening his eyes. Actually, it would have required an effort to listen. They just went on and on and became one irritating noise.

The splendor of the moment awaited him. And it was easy to drown out the thoughts of mortals close at hand. He could sing, for instance, or fix his attention hard upon anything around him. Blessed quiet. In Rome there were distractions everywhere. How he loved the old Roman houses painted ocher and burnt sienna and dark green. How he loved the narrow stone streets. He could drive a car very fast through the broad boulevard full of wreckless mortals, or wander the Via Veneto until he found a woman with whom to fall in love for a little while.

And he did so love the clever people of this time. They were still people, but they knew so much. A ruler was murdered in India, and within the hour all the world could mourn. All manner of disasters, inventions, and medical miracles weighed down upon the mind of the ordinary man. People played with fact and fancy. Waitresses wrote novels at night that would make them famous. Laborers fell in love with naked movie queens in rented cassette films. The rich wore paper jewelry, and the poor bought tiny diamonds. And princesses sallied forth onto the Champs Elysées in carefully faded rags.

Ah, he wished he was human. After all, what was he? What were the others like?—the ones whose voices he shut out. Not the First Brood, he was sure of it. The First Brood could never contact each other purely through the mind. But what the hell was the First Brood? He couldn't remember! A little panic seized him. Don't think of those things. He wrote poems in a notebook—modern and simple, yet he knew that they were in the earliest style he'd ever known.

He moved ceaselessly about Europe and Asia Minor, sometimes walking, sometimes rising into the air and willing himself to a particular place. He charmed those who would have interfered with him and slumbered carelessly in dark hiding places by day. After all, the sun didn't burn him anymore. But he could not function in the sunlight. His eyes began to close as soon as he saw light in the morning sky. Voices, all those voices, other blood drinkers crying in anguish—then nothing. And he awoke at sunset, eager to read the age-old pattern of the stars.

Finally he grew brave with his flying. On the outskirts of Istanbul he went upwards, shooting like a balloon far over the roofs. He tossed and tumbled, laughing freely, and then willed himself to Vienna, which he reached before dawn. Nobody saw him. He moved too fast for them to see him. And besides he did not try these little experiments before prying eyes.

He had another interesting power too. He could travel without his body. Well, not really travel. He could send out his vision, as it were, to look at things far away. Lying still, he would think, for example, of a distant place that he would like to see, and suddenly he was there before it. Now, there were some mortals who could do that too, either in their dreams or when they were awake, with great and deliberate concentration. Occasionally he passed their sleeping bodies and perceived that their souls were traveling elsewhere. But the souls themselves he could never see. He could not see ghosts or any kind of spirit for that matter. . . .

But he knew they were there. They *had* to be.

And some old awareness came to him, that once as a mortal man, in the temple, he had drunk a strong potion given to him by the priests, and had traveled in the very same way, up out of his body, and into the firmament. The priests had called him back. He had not wanted to come. He was with those among the dead whom he loved. But he had known he must return. That was what was expected of him.

He'd been a human being then, all right. Yes, definitely. He could remember the way the sweat had felt on his naked chest when he lay in the dusty room and they brought the potion to him. Afraid. But then they all had to go through it.

Maybe it was better to be what he was now, and be able to fly about with body and soul together.

But not knowing, not really remembering, not understanding how he could do such things or why he lived off the blood of humans—all this caused him intense pain.

In Paris, he went to "vampire" movies, puzzling over what seemed true and what was false. Familiar all this, though much of it was silly. The Vampire Lestat had taken his garments from these old black and white films. Most of the "creatures of the night" wore the same costume—the black cloak, the stiff white shirt, the fine black jacket with tails, the black pants.

Nonsense of course, yet it comforted him. After all, these were blood drinkers, beings who spoke gently, liked poetry, and yet killed mortals all the time.

He bought the vampire comics and cut out certain pictures of beautiful gentlemen blood drinkers like the Vampire Lestat. Maybe he himself should try this lovely costume; again, it would be a comfort. It would make him feel that he was part of something, even if the something didn't really exist.

In London, past midnight in a darkened store, he found his vampire clothes. Coat and pants, and shining patent leather shoes; a shirt as stiff as new papyrus with a white silk tie. And oh, the black velvet cloak, magnificent, with its lining of white satin; it hung down to the very floor.

He did graceful turns before the mirrors. How the Vampire Lestat would have envied him, and to think, he, Khayman, was no human pretending; he was real. He brushed out his thick black hair for the first time. He found perfumes and unguents in glass cases and anointed himself properly for a grand evening. He found rings and cuff links of gold.

Now he was beautiful, as he had once been in other garments long ago. And immediately in the streets of London people adored him! This had been the right thing to do. They followed him as he walked along smiling and bowing, now and then, and winking his eye. Even when he killed it was better. The victim would stare at him as if seeing a vision, as if *understanding*. He would bend—as the Vampire Lestat did in the television songs—and drink first, gently, from the throat, before ripping the victim apart.

Of course this was all a joke. There was something frightfully trivial about it. It had nothing to do with being a blood drinker, that was the dark secret, nothing to do with the faint things he only half remembered, now and then, and pushed from his mind. Nevertheless it was fun for the moment to be "somebody" and "something."

Yes, the moment, the moment was splendid. And the moment was all he ever had. After all, he would forget this time too, wouldn't he? These nights with their exquisite details would vanish from him; and in some even more complex and demanding future he would be loosed again, remembering only his name.

Home to Athens he went finally.

Through the museum by night he roamed with a stub of candle, inspecting the old tombstones with their carved figures which made him cry. The dead woman seated—always the dead are seated—reaches out for the living baby she has left behind, who is held in her husband's arm. Names came back to him, as if bats were whispering in his ear. *Go to Egypt; you'll remember.* But he would not. Too soon to beg for madness and forgetfulness. Safe in Athens, roaming the old cemetery beneath the Acropolis, from which they'd taken all the stele; never mind the traffic roaring by; the earth here is beautiful. And it still belongs to the dead.

He acquired a wardrobe of vampire garments. He even bought a coffin, but he did not like to get inside. For one thing, it was not shaped like a person, this coffin, and it had no face on it, and no writings to guide the soul of the dead. Not proper. Rather like a box for jewelry, as he saw it. But still, being a vampire, well, he thought he should have it and it was fun. Mortals who came to the flat loved it. He served them bloodred wine in crystal glasses. He recited "The Rime of the Ancient Mariner" for them or sang songs in strange tongues which they loved. Sometimes he read his poems. What good-hearted mortals. And the coffin gave them something to sit on in a flat that contained nothing else.

But gradually the songs of the American rock singer, the Vampire Lestat, had begun to disturb him. They weren't fun anymore. Neither were the silly old films. But the Vampire Lestat really bothered him. What blood drinker would dream of acts of purity and courage? Such a tragic tone to the songs.

Blood drinker. . . . Sometimes when he awoke, alone on the floor of the hot airless flat with the last light of day fading through the curtained windows, he felt a heavy dream lift from him in which creatures sighed and groaned in pain. Had he been following through a ghastly nightscape the path of two beautiful red-haired women who suffered unspeakable injustice, twin beauties to whom he reached out again and again? After they cut out her tongue, the red-haired woman in the dream snatched the tongue back from the soldiers and ate it. Her courage had astonished them—

Ah, do not look at such things!

His face hurt, as if he had been crying also or miserably anxious. He let himself relax slowly. Behold the lamp. The yellow flowers. Nothing. Just Athens with its miles and miles of undistinguished stucco buildings, and the great broken temple of Athena on the hill, looming over all despite the smoke-filled air. Evening time. The divine rush as thousands in their drab workaday clothes poured down the escalators to the underground trains. Syntagma Square scattered with the lazy drinkers of retsina or ouzo, suffering beneath the early evening heat. And the little kiosks selling magazines and papers from all lands.

He didn't listen to any more of the Vampire Lestat's music. He left the American dance halls where they played it. He moved away from the students who carried small tape players clipped to their belts.

Then one night in the heart of the Plaka, with its glaring lights and noisy taverns, he saw other blood drinkers hurrying through the crowds. His heart stopped. Loneliness and fear overcame him. He could not move or speak. Then he tracked them through the steep streets, in and out of one dancing place after another where the electronic music blared. He studied them carefully as they rushed on through the crush of tourists, not aware that he was there.

Two males and a female in scant black silk garments, the woman's feet strapped painfully into high-heeled shoes. Silver sunglasses covered their eyes; they whispered together and gave out sudden piercing bursts of laughter; decked with jewels and scent, they flaunted their shining preternatural skin and hair.

But never mind these superficial matters, they were very different from him. They were nothing as hard and white, to begin with. In fact they were made up of so much soft human tissue that they were animated corpses still. Beguilingly pink and weak. And how they needed the blood of their victims. Why, they were suffering agonies of thirst right now. And surely this was their fate nightly. Because the blood had to work endlessly on all the soft human tissue. It worked not merely to animate the tissue, but to convert it slowly into something else.

As for him, he was all made up of that something else. He had no soft human tissue left. Though he lusted for blood, it was not needed for this conversion. Rather he realized suddenly that the blood merely refreshed him, increased his telepathic powers, his ability to fly, or to travel out of his body, or his prodigious strength. Ah, he understood it! For the nameless power that worked in all of them, he was now a nearly perfected host.

Yes, that was it exactly. And they were younger, that's all. They had merely begun their journey towards true vampiric immortality. Didn't he remember—? Well, not actually, but he *knew* it, that they were fledglings, no more than one or two hundred years along the way! That was the dangerous time, when you first went mad from it, or the others got you, shut you up, burned you, that sort of thing. Many did not survive those years. And how long ago it had been for him, of the First Brood. Why, the amount of time was almost inconceivable! He stopped beside the painted wall of a garden, reaching up to rest his hand on a gnarled branch, letting the cool fleecy green leaves touch his face. He felt himself washed in sadness suddenly, sadness more terrible than fear. He heard someone crying, not here but in his head. Who was it? Stop!

Well, he would not hurt them, these tender children! No, he wanted only to know them, to embrace them. After all, we are of the same family, blood drinkers, you and I!

But as he drew nearer, as he sent out his silent yet exuberant greeting, they turned and looked at him with undisguised terror. They fled. Through a dark tangle of hillside lanes they descended, away from the lights of the Plaka, and nothing he could say or do would make them stop.

He stood rigid and silent, feeling a sharp pain he had not known before. Then a curious and terrible thing happened. He went after them till he had them in sight again. He became angry, really angry. *Damn you. Punish you that you hurt me!* And lo and behold he felt a sudden sensation in his forehead, a cold spasm just behind the bone. Out of him, a power seemed to leap as if it were an invisible tongue. Instantly it penetrated the hindmost of the fleeing trio, the female, and her body burst into flame.

Stupefied he watched this. Yet he realized what had happened. He had penetrated her with some sharply directed force. It had kindled the powerful combustible blood that he and she had in common, and at once the fire had shot through the circuit of her veins. Invading the marrow of her bones, it had caused her body to explode. In seconds, she was no more.

Ye gods! He had done this! In grief and terror, he stood staring down at her empty clothes, unburnt, yet blackened and stained with grease. Only a little of her hair was left on the stones, and this burnt away to wisps of smoke as he watched.

Maybe there was some mistake. But no, he knew he'd done it. He'd felt himself doing it. And she had been so afraid!

In shocked silence, he made his way home. He knew he'd never used this power before, or even been aware of it. Had it come to him only now, after centuries of the blood working, drying out his cells, making them thin and white and strong like the chambers of a wasps' nest?

Alone in his flat, with the candles and incense burning to comfort him, he pierced himself again with his knife and watched the blood gush. Thick and hot it was, pooling on the table before him, glittering in the light of the lamp as if it was alive. And it was!

In the mirror, he studied the darkening radiance which had returned to him after so many weeks of dedicated hunting and drinking. A faint yellow tinge to his cheeks, a trace of pink to his lips. But never mind, he was as the abandoned skin of the snake lying on the rock—dead and light and crisp save for the constant pumping of this blood. This vile blood. And his brain, ah, his brain, what did it look like now? Translucent as a thing made of crystal with the blood surging through its tiny compartments? And therein the power lived, did it not, with its invisible tongue?

Going out again, he tried this newfound force upon animals, upon the cats, for which he had an unreasonable loathing—evil things, those creatures—and upon rats, which all men disdain. Not the same. He killed these creatures with the invisible tongue flick of energy, but they didn't catch fire. Rather the brains and hearts suffered some sort of fatal rupture, but the natural blood in them, it was not combustible. And so they did not burn.

This fascinated him in a cold, harrowing fashion. "What a subject I am for study," he whispered, eyes shining suddenly with unwelcome tears. Capes, white ties, vampire movies, what was this to him! *Who in hell was he?* The fool of the gods, roaming the road from moment to moment through eternity? When he saw a great lurid poster of the Vampire Lestat mocking him in a video store window, he turned and with the tongue flick of energy shattered the glass.

Ah, lovely, lovely. Give me the forests, the stars. He went to Delphi that night, ascending soundlessly above the darkened land. Down into the moist grass he went to walk where the oracle had once sat, in this the ruin of the god's house.

But he would not leave Athens. He must find the two blood drinkers, and tell them he was sorry, that he would never, never use this power against them. They must talk to him! They must be with him—! Yes.

The next night upon awakening, he listened for them. And an hour later, he heard them as they rose from their graves. A house in the Plaka was their lair, with one of those noisy, smoky taverns open to the street. In its cellars they slept by day, he realized, and came up by dark to watch the mortals of the tavern sing and dance. Lamia, the old Greek word for vampire, was the name of this establishment in which the electric guitars played the primitive Greek music, and the young mortal men danced with one another, hips churning with all the seductiveness of women, as the retsina flowed. On the walls hung pictures from the vampire movies—Bela Lugosi as Dracula, the pale Gloria Holden as his daughter—and posters of the blond and blue-eyed Vampire Lestat.

So they too had a sense of humor, he thought gently. But the vampire pair, stunned with grief and fear, sat together, staring at the open door as he peered in. How helpless they looked!

They did not move when they saw him standing on the threshold with his back to the white glare of the street. What did they think when they saw his long cloak? A monster come alive from their own posters to bring them destruction when so little else on earth could?

I come in peace. I only wish to speak with you. Nothing shall anger me. I come in . . . love.

The pair appeared transfixed. Then suddenly one of them rose from the table, and both gave a spontaneous and horrid cry. Fire blinded him as it blinded the mortals who pushed past him in their sudden stampede to the street. The blood drinkers were in flames, dying, caught in a hideous dance with twisted arms and legs. The house itself was burning, rafters smoking, glass bottles exploding, orange sparks shooting up to the lowering sky.

Had he done this! Was he death to the others, whether he willed such a thing or not?

Blood tears flowed down his white face onto his stiff shirt front. He lifted his arm to shield his face with his cloak. It was a gesture of respect for the horror happening before him—the blood drinkers dying within.

No, couldn't have done it, couldn't. He let the mortals push him and shove him out of the way. Sirens hurt his ears. He blinked as he tried to see, despite the flashing lights.

And then in a moment of violent understanding he knew that he had not done it. Because he saw the being who had! There covered in a cloak of gray wool, and half hidden in a dark alleyway, stood the one, silently watching him.

And as their eyes met, she softly whispered his name:

"Khayman, my Khayman!"

His mind went blank. Wiped clean. It was as though a white light descended on him, burning out all detail. He felt nothing for one serene moment. He heard no noise of the raging fire, nothing of those who still jostled him as they went past.

He merely stared at this thing, this beautiful and delicate being, exquisite as ever she had been. An unsupportable horror overcame him. He remembered everything—everything he had ever seen or been or known.

The centuries opened before him. The millennia stretched out, going back and back to the very beginning. *First Brood.* He knew it all. He was shuddering, crying. He heard himself say with all the rancor of an accusation:

"You!"

Suddenly, in a great withering flash he felt the full force of her undisguised power. The heat struck him in the chest, and he felt himself staggering backwards.

Ye gods, you will kill me, too! But she could not hear his thoughts! He was knocked against the whitewashed wall. A fierce pain collected in his head.

Yet he continued to see, to feel, to think! And his heart beat steadily as before. He was not burning!

And then with sudden calculation, he gathered his strength and fought this unseen energy with a violent thrust of his own.

"Ah, it is malice again, my sovereign," he cried out in the ancient language. How human the sound of his voice!

But it was finished. The alleyway was empty. She was gone.

Or more truly she had taken flight, rising straight upwards, just as he himself had often done, and so fast that the eye could not see. Yes, he felt her receding presence. He looked up and, without effort, found her—a tiny pen stroke moving towards the west above the bits and pieces of pale cloud.

Raw sounds shocked him—sirens, voices, the crackle of the burning house as its last timbers collapsed. The little narrow street was jam-crowded; the bawling music of the other taverns had not stopped. He drew back, away from the place, weeping, with one backward glance for the domain of the dead blood drinkers. Ah, how many thousands of years he could not count, and yet it was still the same war.

For hours he wandered the dark back streets.

Athens grew quiet. People slept behind wooden walls. The pavements shone in the mist that came as thick as rain. Like a giant snail shell was his history, curling and immense above him, pressing him down to the earth with its impossible weight.

Up a hill he moved finally, and into the cool luxurious tavern of a great modern steel and glass hotel. Black and white this place, just as he was, with its checkered dance floor, black tables, black leather banquettes.

Unnoticed he sank down on a bench in the flickering dimness, and he let his tears flow. Like a fool he cried, with his forehead pressed to his arm.

Madness did not come to him; neither did forgetfulness. He was wandering the centuries, revisiting the places he had known with tender thoughtless intimacy. He cried for all those he had known and loved.

But what hurt him above all things was the great suffocating sense of the beginning, the true beginning, even before that long ago day when he had lain down in his house by the Nile in the noon stillness, knowing he must go to the palace that night.

The true beginning had been a year before when the King had said to him, "But for my beloved Queen, I would take my pleasure of these two women. I would show that they are not witches to be feared. You will do this in my stead."

It was as real as this moment; the uneasy court gathered there watching; black-eyed men and women in their fine linen skirts and elaborate black wigs, some hovering behind the carved pillars, others proudly close to the throne. And the red-haired twins standing before him, his beautiful prisoners whom he had come to love in their captivity. *I cannot do this.* But he had done it. As the court waited, as the King and the Queen waited, he had put on the King's necklace with its gold medallion, to act for the King. And he had gone down the steps from the dais, as the twins stared at him, and he had defiled them one after the other.

Surely this pain couldn't last.

Into the womb of the earth he would have crawled, if he had had the strength for it. Blessed ignorance, how he wanted it. Go to Delphi, wander in the high sweet-smelling green grass. Pick the tiny wild flowers. Ah, would they open for him, as for the light of the sun, if he held them beneath the lamp?

But then he did not want to forget at all. Something had changed; something had made this moment like no other. *She* had risen from her long slumber! He had seen her in an Athens street with his own eyes! Past and present had become one.

As his tears dried, he sat back, listening, thinking.

Dancers writhed on the lighted checkerboard before him. Women smiled at him. Was he a beautiful porcelain Pierrot to them, with his white face and red-stained cheeks? He raised his eyes to the video screen pulsing and glittering above the room. His thoughts grew strong like his physical powers.

This was now, the month of October, in the late twentieth century after the birth of Christ. And only a handful of nights ago, he had seen the twins in his dreams! No. There was no retreat. For him the true agony was just beginning, but that did not matter. He was more *alive* than he had ever been.

He wiped his face slowly with a small linen handkerchief. He washed his fingers in the glass of wine before him, as if to consecrate them. And he looked up again to the high video screen where the Vampire Lestat sang his tragic song.

Blue-eyed demon, yellow hair flung wild about him, with the powerful arms and chest of a young man. Jagged yet graceful his movements, lips seductive, voice full of carefully modulated pain.

And all this time you have been telling me, haven't you? Calling me! Calling her name!

The video image seemed to stare at him, respond to him, sing to him, when of course it could not see him at all. *Those Who Must Be Kept! My King and my Queen.* Yet he listened with his full attention to each syllable carefully articulated above the din of horns and throbbing drums.

And only when the sound and the image faded did he rise and leave the tavern to walk blindly through the cool marble corridors of the hotel and into the darkness outside.

Voices called out to him, voices of blood drinkers the world over, signaling. Voices that had always been there. They spoke of calamity, of converging to prevent some horrid disaster. *The Mother Walks.* They spoke of the dreams of the twins which they did not understand. And he had been deaf and blind to all this!

"How much you do not understand, Lestat," he whispered.

He climbed to a dim promontory finally and gazed at the High City of temples far beyond—broken white marble gleaming beneath the feeble stars.

"Damn you, my sovereign!" he whispered. "Damn you into hell for what you did, to all of us!" And to think that in this world of steel and gasoline, of roaring electronic symphonies and silent gleaming computer circuitry, we wander still.

But another curse came back to him, far stronger than his own. It had come a year after the awful moment when he had raped the two women—a curse screamed within the courtyard of the palace, under a night sky as distant and uncaring as this.

"Let the spirits witness: for theirs is the knowledge of the future—both what it would be, *and what I will:* You are the Queen of the Damned, that's what you are! Evil is your only destiny. But at your greatest hour, it is I who will defeat you. Look well on my face. It is I who will bring you down."

How many times during the early centuries had he remembered those words? In how many places across desert and mountains and through fertile river valleys had he searched for the two red-haired sisters? Among the Bedouins who had once sheltered them, among the hunters who wore skins still and the people of Jericho, the oldest city in the world. They were already legend.

And then blessed madness had descended; he had lost all knowledge, rancor, and pain. He was Khayman, filled with love for all he saw around him, a being who understood the word *joy.*

Could it be that the hour had come? That the twins had somehow endured just as he had? And for this great purpose his memory had been restored?

Ah, what a lustrous and overwhelming thought, that the First Brood would come together, that the First Brood would finally know victory.

But with a bitter smile, he thought of the Vampire Lestat's human hunger for heroism. *Yes, my brother, forgive me for my scorn. I want it too, the goodness, the glory. But there is likely no destiny, and no redemption. Only what I see before me as I stand above this soiled and ancient landscape—just birth and death, and horrors await us all.*

He took one last look at the sleeping city, the ugly and careworn modern place where he had been so content, wandering over countless old graves.

And then he went upwards, rising within seconds above the clouds. Now would come the greatest test of this magnificent gift, and how he loved the sudden sense of purpose, illusory though it might be. He moved west, towards the Vampire Lestat, and towards the voices that begged for understanding of the dreams of the twins. He moved west as she had moved before him.

His cloak flared like sleek wings, and the delicious cold air bruised him and made him laugh suddenly as if for one moment he were the happy simpleton again.

6

THE *STORY* OF JESSE,
THE GREAT FAMILY,
AND THE TALAMASCA

i.

The dead don't share.
Though they reach towards us
from the grave (I swear
they do) they do
not hand their hearts to you.
They hand their heads,
the part that stares.

STAN RICE
from "Their Share"
Body of Work (1983)

ii.

Cover her face; mine eyes dazzle; she died young.

JOHN WEBSTER

iii.

THE TALAMASCA

Investigators of the Paranormal
We watch
And we are always here.

London   Amsterdam   Rome

ESSE was moaning in her sleep. She was a delicate woman of thirty-five with long curly red hair. She lay deep in a shapeless feather mattress, cradled in a wooden bed which hung from the ceiling on four rusted chains.

Somewhere in the big rambling house a clock chimed. She must wake up. Two hours until the Vampire Lestat's concert. But she could not leave the twins now.

This was new to her, this part unfolding so rapidly, and the dream was maddeningly dim as all the dreams of the twins had been. Yet she knew the twins were in the desert kingdom again. The mob surrounding the twins was dangerous. And the twins, how different they looked, how pale. Maybe it was an illusion, this phosphorescent luster, but they appeared to glow in the semidarkness, and their movements were languid, almost as if they were caught in the rhythm of a dance. Torches were thrust at them as they embraced one another; but look, something was wrong, very wrong. One of them was now blind.

Her eyelids were shut tight, the tender flesh wrinkled and sunken. Yes, they have plucked out her eyes. And the other one, why does she make those terrible sounds? "Be still, don't fight anymore," said the blind one, in the ancient language which was always understandable in the dreams. And out of the other twin came a horrid, guttural moaning. She couldn't speak. They'd cut out her tongue!

I don't want to see any more, I want to wake up. But the soldiers were pushing their way through the crowd, something dreadful was to happen, and the twins became suddenly very still. The soldiers took hold of them, dragged them apart.

Don't separate them! Don't you know what this means to them? Get the torches away. Don't set them on fire! Don't burn their red hair.

The blind twin reached out for her sister, screaming her name: "Mekare!" And Mekare, the mute one, who could not answer, roared like a wounded beast.

The crowd was parting, making way for two immense stone coffins, each carried on a great heavy bier. Crude these sarcophagi, yet the lids had the roughened shape of human faces, limbs. What have the twins done to be put in these coffins? I can't stand it, the biers being set down, the twins dragged towards the coffins, the crude stone lids being lifted. Don't do it! The blind one is fighting as if she can see it, yet they are overpowering her, lifting her and putting her inside the stone box. In mute terror, Mekare is watching, though she herself is being dragged to the other bier. Don't lower the lid, or I will scream for Mekare! For both of them—

Jesse sat up, her eyes open. She had screamed.

Alone in this house, with no one to hear her, she'd screamed, and she could feel the echo still. Then nothing but the quiet settling around her, and the faint creaking of the bed as it moved on its chains. The song of the birds outside in the forest, the deep forest; and her own curious awareness that the clock had struck six.

The dream was fading rapidly. Desperately she tried to hold on to it, to see the details that always slipped away—the clothing of these strange people, the weapons the soldiers carried, the faces of the twins! But it was already gone. Only the spell remained and an acute awareness of what had happened—and the certainty that the Vampire Lestat was linked to these dreams.

Sleepily, she checked her watch. No time left. She wanted to be in the auditorium when the Vampire Lestat entered; she wanted to be at the very foot of the stage.

Yet she hesitated, staring at the white roses on the bedside table. Beyond, through the open window, she saw the southern sky full of a faint orange light. She picked up the note that lay beside the flowers and she read it through once more.

My darling,

I have only just received your letter, as I am far from home and it took some time for this to reach me. I understand the fascination which this creature, Lestat, holds for you. They are playing his music even in Rio. I have already read the books which you have enclosed. And I know of your investigation of this creature for the Talamasca. As for your dreams of the twins, this we must talk about together. It is of the utmost importance. For there are others who have had such dreams. But I beg you—no, I order you not to go to this concert. You must remain at the Sonoma compound until I get there. I am leaving Brazil as soon as I can.

Wait for me. I love you.

Your aunt Maharet

"Maharet, I'm sorry," she whispered. But it was unthinkable that she not go. And if anyone in the world would understand, it was Maharet.

The Talamasca, for whom she'd worked for twelve long years, would never forgive her for disobeying their orders. But Maharet knew the reason; *Maharet was the reason.* Maharet would forgive.

Dizzy. The nightmare still wouldn't let go. The random objects of the room were disappearing in the shadows, yet the twilight burned so clear suddenly that even the forested hills were giving back the light. And the roses were phosphorescent, like the white flesh of the twins in the dream.

White roses, she tried to remember something she'd heard about white roses. You send white roses for a funeral. But no, Maharet could not have meant that.

Jesse reached out, took one of the blossoms in both hands, and the petals came loose instantly. Such sweetness. She pressed them to her lips, and a faint yet shining image came back to her from that long ago summer of Maharet in this house in a candle-lighted room, lying on a bed of rose petals, so many white and yellow and pink rose petals, which she had gathered up and pressed to her face and her throat.

Had Jesse really seen such a thing? So many rose petals caught in Maharet's long red hair. Hair like Jesse's hair. Hair like the hair of the twins in the dream—thick and wavy and streaked with gold.

It was one of a hundred fragments of memory which she could never afterwards fit into a whole. But it no longer mattered, what she could or could not remember of that dreamy lost summer. The Vampire Lestat waited: there would be a finish if not an answer, not unlike the promise of death itself.

She got up. She put on the worn hacking jacket that was her second skin these days, along with the boy's shirt, open at the neck, and the jeans she wore. She slipped on her worn leather boots. Ran the brush through her hair.

Now to take leave of the empty house she'd invaded this morning. It hurt her to leave it. But it had hurt her more to come at all.

AT THE first light, she'd arrived at the edge of the clearing, quietly stunned to discover it unchanged after fifteen years, a rambling structure built into the foot of the mountain, its roofs and pillared porches veiled in blue morning glory vines. High above, half hidden in the grassy slopes, a few tiny secret windows caught the first flash of morning light.

Like a spy she'd felt as she came up the front steps with the old key in her hand. No one had been here in months, it seemed. Dust and leaves wherever she looked.

Yet there were the roses waiting in their crystal vase, and the letter for her pinned to the door, with the new key in the envelope.

For hours, she'd wandered, revisited, explored. Never mind that she was tired, that she'd driven all night. She had to walk the long shaded galleries, to move through the spacious and overwhelming rooms. Never had the place seemed so much like a crude palace with its enormous timbers shouldering the rough-sawn plank ceilings, the rusted smokestack chimneys rising from the round stone hearths.

Even the furnishings were massive—the millstone tables, chairs and couches of unfinished lumber piled with soft down pillows, bookshelves and niches carved into the unpainted adobe walls.

It had the crude medieval grandeur, this place. The bits and pieces of Mayan art, the Etruscan cups and Hittite statues, seemed to belong here, amid the deep casements and stone floors. It was like a fortress. It felt safe.

Only Maharet's creations were full of brilliant color as if they'd drawn it from the trees and sky outside. Memory hadn't exaggerated their beauty in the least. Soft and thick the deep hooked wool rugs carrying the free pattern of woodland flower and grass everywhere as if the rug were the earth itself. And the countless quilted pillows with their curious stick figures and odd symbols, and finally the giant hanging quilts—modern tapestries that covered the walls with childlike pictures of fields, streams, mountains and forests, skies full of sun and moon together, of glorious clouds and even falling rain. They had the vibrant power of primitive painting with their myriad tiny bits of fabric sewn so carefully to create the detail of cascading water or falling leaf.

It had killed Jesse to see all this again.

By noon, hungry and light-headed from the long sleepless night, she'd gotten the courage to lift the latch from the rear door that led into the secret windowless rooms within the mountain itself. Breathless, she had followed the stone passage. Her heart pounded as she found the library unlocked and switched on the lamps.

Ah, fifteen years ago, simply the happiest summer of her life. All her wonderful adventures afterwards, ghost hunting for the Talamasca, had been nothing to that magical and unforgettable time.

She and Maharet in this library together, with the fire blazing. And the countless volumes of the family history, amazing her and delighting her. The lineage of "the Great Family," as Maharet always called it—"the thread we cling to in the labyrinth which is life." How lovingly she had taken down the books for Jesse, unlocked for her the caskets that contained the old parchment scrolls.

Jesse had not fully accepted it that summer, the implications of all she'd seen. There had been a slow confusion, a delicious suspension of ordinary reality, as if the papyruses covered with a writing she could not classify belonged more truly to dream. After all, Jesse had already become a trained archaeologist by that time. She'd done her time on digs in Egypt and at Jericho. Yet she could not decipher those strange glyphs. *In the name of God, how old were these things?*

For years after, she'd tried to remember other documents she'd seen. Surely she had come into the library one morning and discovered a back room with an open door.

Into a long corridor, she'd gone past other unlighted rooms. She'd found a light switch finally, and seen a great storage place full of clay tablets—clay tablets covered with tiny pictures! Without doubt, she'd held these things in her hands.

Something else had happened; something she had never really wanted to recall. Was there another hallway? She knew for certain that there had been a curving iron stairway which took her down into lower rooms with plain earthen walls. Tiny bulbs were fixed in old porcelain light sockets. She had pulled chains to turn them on.

Surely she had done that. Surely she had opened a heavy redwood door . . .

For years after, it had come back to her in little flashes—a vast, low-ceilinged room with oak chairs, a table and benches that looked as if they were made from stone. And what else? Something that at first seemed utterly familiar. And then—

Later that night, she'd remembered nothing but the stairway. Suddenly it was ten o'clock, and she'd just awakened and Maharet was standing at the foot of her bed. Maharet had come to her and kissed her. Such a lovely warm kiss; it had sent a low throbbing sensation through her. Maharet said they'd found her down by the creek, asleep in the clearing, and at sunset, they'd brought her in.

Down by the creek? For months after, she'd actually "remembered" falling asleep there. In fact, it was a rather rich "recollection" of the peace and stillness of the forest, of the water singing over the rocks. But it had never happened, of that she was now sure.

But on this day, some fifteen years later, she had found no evidence one way or the other of these half-remembered things. Rooms were bolted against her. Even the neat volumes of the family history were in locked glass cases which she dared not disturb.

Yet never had she believed so firmly in what she could recall. Yes, clay tablets covered with nothing but tiny stick figures for persons, trees, animals. She'd seen them, taken them off the shelves and held them under the feeble overhead light. And the stairway, and the room that frightened her, no, terrified her, yes . . . all there.

Nevertheless, it had been paradise here, in those warm summer days and nights, when she had sat by the hour talking to Maharet, when she had danced with Mael and Maharet by the light of the moon. Forget for now the pain afterwards, trying to understand why Maharet had sent her back home to New York never to come here again.

My darling,
The fact is I love you too much. My life will engulf yours if we are not separated. You must have freedom, Jesse, to devise your own plans, ambitions, dreams . . .

It was not to relive the old pain that she had returned, it was to know again, for a little while, the joy that had gone before.

FIGHTING weariness this afternoon, she'd wandered out of the house finally, and down the long lane through the oaks. So easy to find the old paths through the dense redwoods. And the clearing, ringed in fern and clover on the steep rocky banks of the shallow rushing creek.

Here Maharet had once guided her through total darkness, down into the water and along a path of stones. Mael had joined them. Maharet had poured the wine for Jesse, and they had sung together a song Jesse could never recall afterwards, though now and then she would find herself humming this eerie melody with inexplicable accuracy, then stop, aware of it, unable to find the proper note again.

She might have fallen asleep near the creek in the deep mingled sounds of the forest, so like the false "recollection" of years ago.

So dazzling the bright green of the maples, catching the rare shafts of light. And the redwoods, how monstrous they seemed in the unbroken quiet. Mammoth, indifferent, soaring hundreds of feet before their somber lacy foliage closed on the frayed margin of sky.

And she'd known what the concert tonight, with Lestat's screaming fans, would demand of her. But she'd been afraid that the dream of the twins would start again.

FINALLY, she'd gone back to the house, and taken the roses and the letter with her. Her old room. Three o'clock. Who wound the clocks of this place that they knew the hour? The dream of the twins was stalking her. And she was simply too tired to fight anymore. The place felt so good to her. No ghosts here of the kind she'd encountered so many times in her work. Only the peace. She'd lain down on the old hanging bed, on the quilt that

she herself had made so carefully with Maharet that summer. And sleep—
and the twins—had come together.

Now she had two hours to get to San Francisco, and she must leave this
house, maybe in tears, again. She checked her pockets. Passport, papers,
money, keys.

She picked up her leather bag, slung it over her shoulder, and hurried
through the long passage to the stairs. Dusk was coming fast, and when
darkness did cover the forest, nothing would be visible at all.

There was still a bit of sunlight in the main hall when she reached it.
Through the western windows, a few long dusty rays illuminated the giant
tapestry quilt on the wall.

Jesse caught her breath as she looked at it. Always her favorite, for its
intricacy, its size. At first it seemed a great mass of random tiny prints and
patches—then gradually the wooded landscape emerged from the myriad
pieces of cloth. One minute you saw it; the next it was gone. That's how
it had happened over and over again that summer when, drunk with wine,
she had walked back and forth before it, losing the picture, then recovering
it: the mountain, the forest, a tiny village nestled in the green valley below.

"I'm sorry, Maharet," she whispered again softly. She had to go. Her
journey was nearly ended.

But as she looked away, something in the quilted picture caught her
eye. She turned back, studied it again. Were there figures there, which she
had never seen? Once more it was a swarm of stitched-together fragments.
Then slowly the flank of the mountain emerged, then the olive trees, and
finally the rooftops of the village, no more than yellow huts scattered on
the smooth valley floor. The figures? She could not find them. That is, until
she again turned her head away. In the corner of her eye, they were visible
for a split second. Two tiny figures holding each other, women with red
hair!

Slowly, almost cautiously she turned back to the picture. Her heart
was skipping. Yes, there. But was it an illusion?

She crossed the room until she stood directly before the quilt. She
reached up and touched it. Yes! Each little rag-doll being had a tiny pair
of green buttons for its eyes, a carefully sewn nose and red mouth! And
the hair, the hair was red yarn, crimped into jagged waves and delicately
sewn over the white shoulders.

She stared at it, half disbelieving. Yet there they were—the twins! And
as she stood there, petrified, the room began to darken. The last light had
slipped below the horizon. The quilt was fading before her eyes into an
unreadable pattern.

In a daze, she heard the clock strike the quarter hour. Call the Talamasca. Call David in London. Tell him part of it, anything— But that was out of the question and she knew it. And it broke her heart to realize that no matter what did happen to her tonight, the Talamasca would never know the whole story.

She forced herself to leave, to lock the door behind her and walk across the deep porch and down the long path.

She didn't fully understand her feelings, why she was so shaken and on the verge of tears. It confirmed her suspicions, all she thought she knew. And yet she was frightened. She was actually crying.

Wait for Maharet.

But that she could not do. Maharet would charm her, confuse her, drive her away from the mystery in the name of love. That's what had happened in that long ago summer. The Vampire Lestat withheld nothing. The Vampire Lestat was the crucial piece in the puzzle. To see him and touch him was to validate everything.

The red Mercedes roadster started instantly. And with a spray of gravel she backed up, turned, and made for the narrow unpaved road. The convertible top was down; she'd be frozen by the time she reached San Francisco, but it didn't matter. She loved the cold air on her face, she loved to drive fast.

The road plunged at once into the darkness of the woods. Not even the rising moon could penetrate here. She pushed to forty, swinging easily into the sudden turns. Her sadness grew heavier suddenly, but there were no more tears. The Vampire Lestat . . . almost there.

When at last she hit the county road, she was speeding, singing to herself in syllables she could hardly hear above the wind. Full darkness came just as she roared through the pretty little city of Santa Rosa and connected with the broad swift current of Highway 101 south.

The coastal fog was drifting in. It made ghosts of the dark hills to the east and west. Yet the bright flow of tail lamps illuminated the road ahead of her. Her excitement was mounting. One hour to the Golden Gate. The sadness was leaving her. All her life she'd been confident, lucky; and sometimes impatient with the more cautious people she'd known. And despite her sense of fatality on this night, her keen awareness of the dangers she was approaching, she felt her usual luck might be with her. She wasn't really afraid.

SHE'D been born lucky, as she saw it, found by the side of the road minutes after the car crash that had killed her seven-months-pregnant teenaged mother—a baby spontaneously aborted from the dying womb, and screaming loudly to clear her own tiny lungs when the ambulance arrived.

She had no name for two weeks as she languished in the county hospital, condemned for hours to the sterility and coldness of machines; but the nurses had adored her, nicknaming her "the sparrow," and cuddling her and singing to her whenever allowed.

Years later they were to write to her, sending along the snapshots they'd taken, telling her little stories, which had greatly amplified her early sense of having been loved.

It was Maharet who at last came for her, identifying her as the sole survivor of the Reeves family of South Carolina and taking her to New York to live with cousins of a different name and background. There she was to grow up in a lavish old two-story apartment on Lexington Avenue with Maria and Matthew Godwin, who gave her not only love but everything she could want. An English nanny had slept in her room till Jesse was twelve years old.

She could not remember when she'd learned that her aunt Maharet had provided for her, that she could go on to any college and any career she might choose. Matthew Godwin was a doctor, Maria was a sometime dancer and teacher; they were frank about their attachment to Jesse, their dependence upon her. She was the daughter they had always wanted, and these had been rich and happy years.

The letters from Maharet started before she was old enough to read. They were wonderful, often full of colorful postcards and odd pieces of currency from the countries where Maharet lived. Jesse had a drawerful of rupees and lire by the time she was seventeen. But more important, she had a friend in Maharet, who answered every line she ever wrote with feeling and care.

It was Maharet who inspired her in her reading, encouraged her music lessons and painting classes, arranged her summer tours of Europe and finally her admission to Columbia, where Jesse studied ancient languages and art.

It was Maharet who arranged her Christmas visits with European cousins—the Scartinos of Italy, a powerful banking family who lived in a villa outside Siena, and the humbler Borchardts of Paris, who welcomed her to their overcrowded but cheerful home.

The summer that Jesse turned seventeen she went to Vienna to meet the Russian émigré branch of the family, young fervent intellectuals and musicians whom she greatly loved. Then it was off to England to meet the Reeves family, directly connected to the Reeveses of South Carolina, who had left England centuries ago.

When she was eighteen, she'd gone to visit the Petralona cousins in their villa on Santorini, rich and exotic-looking Greeks. They had lived in near feudal splendor, surrounded by peasant servants, and had taken Jesse with them on a spur-of-the-moment voyage aboard their yacht to Istanbul, Alexandria, and Crete.

Jesse had almost fallen in love with young Constantin Petralona. Maharet had let her know the marriage would have everyone's blessing, but she must make her own decision. Jesse had kissed her lover good-bye and flown back to America, the university, and preparation for her first archaeological dig in Iraq.

But even through the college years, she remained as close to the family as ever. Everyone was so good to her. But then everyone was good to everyone else. Everyone believed in the family. Visits among the various branches were common; frequent intermarriage had made endless entanglements; every family house contained rooms in constant readiness for relatives who might drop in. Family trees seemed to go back forever; people passed on funny stories about famous relatives who had been dead for three or four hundred years. Jesse had felt a great communion with these people, no matter how different they seemed.

In Rome she was charmed by the cousins who drove their sleek Ferraris at breakneck speed, stereos blaring, and went home at night to a charming old palazzo where the plumbing didn't work and the roof leaked. The Jewish cousins in southern California were a dazzling bunch of musicians, designers, and producers who had one way or the other been connected with the motion pictures and the big studios for fifty years. Their old house off Hollywood Boulevard was home to a score of unemployed actors. Jesse could live in the attic if she wanted to; dinner was served at six to anybody and everybody who walked in.

But who was this woman Maharet, who had always been Jesse's distant but ever attentive mentor, who guided her studies with frequent and thoughtful letters, who gave her the personal direction to which she so productively responded and which she secretly craved?

To all the cousins whom Jesse was ever to visit, Maharet was a palpable presence though her visits were so infrequent as to be remarkable. She was the keeper of the records of the Great Family, that is, all the branches under many names throughout the world. It was she who frequently brought members together, even arranging marriages to unite different branches, and the one who could invariably provide help in times of trouble, help that could sometimes mean the difference between life and death.

Before Maharet, there had been her mother, now called Old Maharet, and before that Great-aunt Maharet and so forth and so on as long as anybody could remember. "There will always be a Maharet" was an old family saying, rattled off in Italian as easily as in German or Russian or Yiddish or Greek. That is, a single female descendant in each generation would take the name and the record-keeping obligations, or so it seemed, anyhow, for no one save Maharet herself really knew those details.

"When will I meet you?" Jesse had written many times over the years. She had collected the stamps off the envelopes from Delhi and Rio and Mexico City, from Bangkok, and Tokyo and Lima and Saigon and Moscow.

All the family were devoted to this woman and fascinated by her, but with Jesse there was another secret and powerful connection.

From her earliest years, Jesse had had "unusual" experiences, unlike those of the people around her.

For example, Jesse could read people's thoughts in a vague, wordless way. She "knew" when people disliked her or were lying to her. She had a gift for languages because she frequently understood the "gist" even when she did not know the vocabulary.

And she saw ghosts—people and buildings that could not possibly be there.

When she was very little she often saw the dim gray outline of an elegant town house across from her window in Manhattan. She'd known it wasn't real, and it made her laugh at first, the way it came and went, sometimes transparent, other times as solid as the street itself, with lights behind its lace-curtained windows. Years passed before she learned that the phantom house had once been the property of architect Stanford White. It had been torn down decades ago.

The human images she saw were not at first so well formed. On the contrary, they were brief flickering apparitions that often compounded the inexplicable discomfort she felt in particular places.

But as she got older these ghosts became more visible, more enduring. Once on a dark rainy afternoon, the translucent figure of an old woman had ambled towards her and finally passed right through her. Hysterical, Jesse had run into a nearby shop, where clerks had called Matthew and Maria. Over and over Jesse tried to describe the woman's troubled face, her bleary-eyed stare which seemed utterly blind to the real world about her.

Friends often didn't believe Jesse when she described these things. Yet they were fascinated and begged her to repeat the stories. It left Jesse with an ugly vulnerable feeling. So she tried not to tell people about the ghosts, though by the time she was in her early teens she was seeing these lost souls more and more often.

Even walking in the dense crowds of Fifth Avenue at midday she glimpsed these pale searching creatures. Then one morning in Central Park, when Jesse was sixteen, she saw the obvious apparition of a young man sitting on a bench not far from her. The park was crowded, noisy; yet the figure seemed detached, a part of nothing around it. The sounds around Jesse began to go dim as if the thing were absorbing them. She prayed for it to go away. Instead it turned and fixed its eyes on her. It tried to speak to her.

Jesse ran all the way home. She was in a panic. These things knew her now, she told Matthew and Maria. She was afraid to leave the apartment. Finally Matthew gave her a sedative and told her she would be able to sleep. He left the door of her room open so she wouldn't be frightened.

As Jesse lay there halfway between dream and waking, a young girl came in. Jesse realized she knew this young girl; of course, she was one of the family, she'd always been here, right by Jesse, they'd talked lots of times, hadn't they, and no surprise at all that she was so sweet, so loving, and so familiar. She was just a teenager, no older than Jesse.

She sat on Jesse's bed and told Jesse not to worry, that these spirits could never hurt her. No ghost had ever hurt anybody. They didn't have the power. They were poor pitiful weak things. "You write to Aunt Maharet," the girl said, and then she kissed Jesse and brushed the hair back out of Jesse's face. The sedative was really working then. Jesse couldn't even keep her eyes open. There was a question she wanted to ask about the car wreck when she was born, but she couldn't think of it. "Good-bye, sweetheart," said the girl and Jesse was asleep before the girl had left the room.

When she woke up it was two o'clock in the morning. The flat was dark. She began her letter to Maharet immediately, recounting every strange incident that she could remember.

It wasn't until dinnertime that she thought of the young girl with a start. Impossible that such a person had been living here and was familiar and had always been around. How could she have accepted such a thing? Even in her letter she had said, "Of course Miriam was here and Miriam said . . ." And who was Miriam? A name on Jesse's birth certificate. Her mother.

Jesse told no one what had happened. Yet a comforting warmth enveloped her. She could feel Miriam here, she was sure of it.

Maharet's letter came five days later. Maharet believed her. These spirit apparitions were nothing surprising at all. Such things most certainly did exist, and Jesse was not the only person who saw them:

Our family over the generations has contained many a seer of spirits. And as you know these were the sorcerers and witches of ages past.

Frequently this power appears in those who are blessed with your physical attributes: your green eyes, pale skin, and red hair. It would seem the genes travel together. Maybe science one day will explain this to us. But for now be assured that your powers are entirely natural.

This does not mean, however, that they are constructive. Though spirits are real, they make almost no difference in the scheme of things! They can be childish, vindictive, and deceitful. By and large you cannot help the entities who try to communicate with you, and sometimes you are merely gazing at a lifeless ghost—that is, a visual echo of a personality no longer present.

Don't fear them, but do not let them waste your time. For that they love to do, once they know that you can see them. As for Miriam, you must tell me if you see her again. But as you have done as she asked in writing to me I do not think she will find it necessary to return. In all probability she is quite above the sad antics of those whom you see most often. Write to me about these things whenever they frighten you. But try not to tell others. Those who do not see will never believe you.

This letter proved invaluable to Jesse. For years she carried it with her, in her purse or pocket wherever she went. Not only had Maharet believed her, but Maharet had given her a way to understand and survive this troublesome power. Everything that Maharet said had made sense.

After that Jesse was occasionally frightened again by spirits; and she did share these secrets with her closest friends. But by and large she did as Maharet had instructed her, and the powers ceased to bother her. They seemed to go dormant. She forgot them for long periods.

Maharet's letters came with ever greater frequency. Maharet was her confidante, her best friend. As Jesse entered college, she had to admit that Maharet was more real to her through the letters than anyone else she had ever known. But she had long come to accept that they might never see each other.

Then one evening during Jesse's third year at Columbia she had opened the door of her apartment to discover the lights burning, and a fire going under the mantel, and a tall, thin red-haired woman standing at the andirons with the poker.

Such beauty! That had been Jesse's first overwhelming impression. Skillfully powdered and painted, the face had an Oriental artifice, save for the remarkable intensity of the green eyes and the thick curly red hair pouring down over the shoulders.

"My darling," the woman said. "It's Maharet."

Jesse had rushed into her arms. But Maharet had caught her, gently holding her apart as if to look at her. Then she'd covered Jesse with kisses, as if she dared not touch her in any other way, her gloved hands barely holding Jesse's arms. It had been a lovely and delicate moment. Jesse had stroked Maharet's soft thick red hair. So like her own.

"You are my child," Maharet had whispered. "You are everything I had hoped you would be. Do you know how happy I am?"

Like ice and fire, Maharet had seemed that night. Immensely strong, yet irrepressibly warm. A thin, yet statuesque creature with a tiny waist and flowing skirts, she had the high-toned mystery of fashion manikins, the eerie glamour of women who have made of themselves sculpture, her long brown wool cape moving with sweeping grace as they left the flat together. Yet how easy with one another they had been.

It had been a long night on the town; they'd gone to galleries, the theater, and then to a late night supper though Maharet had wanted nothing. She was too excited, she said. She did not even remove her gloves. She wanted only to listen to all that Jesse had to tell her. And Jesse had talked unendingly about everything—Columbia, her work in archaeology, her dreams of fieldwork in Mesopotamia.

So different from the intimacy of letters. They had even walked through Central Park in the pitch darkness together, Maharet telling Jesse there was not the slightest reason to be afraid. And it had seemed entirely normal then, hadn't it? And so beautiful, as if they were following the paths of an enchanted forest, fearing nothing, talking in excited yet hushed voices. How divine to feel so safe! Near dawn, Maharet left Jesse at the apartment with promises to bring her to visit in California very soon. Maharet had a house there, in the Sonoma mountains.

But two years were to pass before the invitation ever came. Jesse had just finished her bachelor's degree. She was scheduled to work on a dig in Lebanon in July.

"You must come for two weeks," Maharet had written. The plane ticket was enclosed. Mael, "a dear friend," would fetch her from the airport.

Though Jesse hadn't admitted it at the time, there had been strange things happening from the start.

Mael, for instance, a tall overpowering man with long wavy blond hair and deep-set blue eyes. There had been something almost eerie about the way he moved, the timbre of his voice, the precise way he handled the car as they drove north to Sonoma County. He'd worn the rawhide clothes of a rancher it seemed, even to the alligator boots, except for a pair of exquisite black kid gloves and a large pair of gold-rimmed blue-tinted glasses.

And yet he'd been so cheerful, so glad to see her, and she'd liked him immediately. She'd told him the story of her life before they reached Santa Rosa. He had the most lovely laugh. But Jesse had gotten positively dizzy looking at him once or twice. Why?

The compound itself was unbelievable. Who could have built such a place? It was at the end of an impossible unpaved road, to begin with; and its back rooms had been dug out of the mountain, as if by enormous machines. Then there were the roof timbers. Were they primeval redwood? They must have been twelve feet in girth. And the adobe walls, positively ancient. Had there been Europeans in California so long ago that they could have . . . but what did it matter? The place was magnificent, finally. She loved the round iron hearths and animal-skin rugs, and the huge library and the crude observatory with its ancient brass telescope.

She had loved the good-hearted servants who came each morning from Santa Rosa to clean, do laundry, prepare the sumptuous meals. It did not even bother her that she was alone so much. She loved walking in the forest. She went into Santa Rosa for novels and newspapers. She studied the tapestried quilts. There were ancient artifacts here she could not classify; she loved examining these things.

And the compound had every convenience. Aerials high on the mountain brought television broadcasts from far and wide. There was a cellar movie theater complete with projector, screen, and an immense collection of films. On warm afternoons she swam in the pond to the south of the house. As dusk fell bringing the inevitable northern California chill, huge fires blazed in every hearth.

Of course the grandest discovery for her had been the family history, that there were countless leather volumes tracing the lineage of all the branches of the Great Family for centuries back. She was thrilled to discover photograph albums by the hundreds, and trunks full of painted portraits, some no more than tiny oval miniatures, others large canvases now layered with dust.

At once she devoured the history of the Reeveses of South Carolina, her own people—rich before the Civil War, and ruined after. Their photographs were almost more than she could bear. Here at last were the forebears she truly resembled; she could see her features in their faces. They had her pale skin, even her expression! And two of them had her long curly red hair. To Jesse, an adopted child, this had a very special significance.

It was only towards the end of her stay that Jesse began to realize the implications of the family records, as she opened scrolls covered with ancient Latin, Greek, and finally Egyptian hieroglyphs. Never afterwards was she able to pinpoint the discovery of the clay tablets deep within the cellar room. But the memory of her conversations with Maharet were never clouded. They'd talked for hours about the family chronicles.

Jesse had begged to work with the family history. She would have given up school for this library. She wanted to translate and adapt the old records and feed them into computers. Why not publish the story of the Great Family? For surely such a long lineage was highly unusual, if not absolutely unique. Even the crowned heads of Europe could not trace themselves back before the Dark Ages.

Maharet had been patient with Jesse's enthusiasm, reminding her that it was time-consuming and unrewarding work. After all, it was only the story of one family's progress through the centuries; sometimes there were only lists of names in the record, or short descriptions of uneventful lives, tallies of births and deaths, and records of migration.

Good memories, those conversations. And the soft mellow light of the library, the delicious smells of the old leather and parchment, of the candles and the blazing fire. And Maharet by the hearth, the lovely manikin, her pale green eyes covered with large faintly tinted glasses, cautioning Jesse that the work might engulf her, keep her from better things. It was the Great Family that mattered, not the record of it, it was the vitality in each generation, and the knowledge and love of one's kin. The record merely made this possible.

Jesse's longing for this work was greater than anything she'd ever known. Surely Maharet would let her stay here! She'd have years in this library, discovering finally the very origins of the family!

Only afterwards did she see it as an astounding mystery, and one among many during that summer. Only afterwards, had so many little things preyed on her mind.

For example, Maharet and Mael simply never appeared until after dark, and the explanation—they slept all day—was no explanation at all. And where did they sleep?—that was another question. Their rooms lay empty all day with the doors open, the closets overflowing with exotic and spectacular clothes. At sunset they would appear almost as if they'd materialized. Jesse would look up. Maharet would be standing by the hearth, her makeup elaborate and flawless, her clothes dramatic, her jeweled earrings and neck-lace sparkling in the broken light. Mael, dressed as usual in soft brown buckskin jacket and pants, stood silently against the wall.

But when Jesse asked about their strange hours, Maharet's answers were utterly convincing! They were pale beings, they detested sunlight, and they did stay up so late! True. Why, at four in the morning, they were still arguing with each other about politics or history, and from such a bizarre and grand perspective, calling cities by their ancient names, and sometimes speaking in a rapid, strange tongue that Jesse could not classify, let alone understand. With her psychic gift, she sometimes knew what they were saying; but the strange sounds baffled her.

And something about Mael rankled Maharet, it was obvious. Was he her lover? It did not really seem so.

Then it was the way that Mael and Maharet kept speaking to each other, as if they were reading each other's minds. All of a sudden, Mael would say, "But I told you not to worry," when in fact Maharet had not said a word out loud. And sometimes they did it with Jesse too. One time, Jesse was certain, Maharet had called her, asked her to come down to the main dining hall, though Jesse could have sworn she heard the voice only in her head.

Of course Jesse was psychic. But were Mael and Maharet both powerful psychics as well?

Dinner: that was another thing—the way that Jesse's favorite dishes appeared. She didn't have to tell the servants what she liked and didn't like. They knew! Escargots, baked oysters, fettucini alla carbonara, beef Wellington, any and all her favorites were the nightly fare. And the wine, she had never tasted such delicious vintages. Yet Maharet and Mael ate like birds, or so it seemed. Sometimes they sat out the entire meal with their gloves on.

And the strange visitors, what about them? Santino, for instance, a black-haired Italian, who arrived one evening on foot, with a youthful companion named Eric. Santino had stared at Jesse as if she were an exotic animal, then he'd kissed her hand and given her a gorgeous emerald ring, which had disappeared without explanation several nights later. For two hours Santino had argued with Maharet in that same unusual language, then left in a rage, with the flustered Eric.

Then there were the strange nighttime parties. Hadn't Jesse awakened twice at three or four in the morning to find the house full of people? There had been people laughing and talking in every room. And all of these people had something in common. They were very pale with remarkable eyes, much like Mael and Maharet. But Jesse had been so sleepy. She couldn't even remember going back to bed. Only that at one point she had been surrounded by several very beautiful young men who filled a glass of wine for her, and the next thing she knew it was morning. She was in bed. The sun was pouring through the window. The house was empty.

Also, Jesse had heard things at odd hours. The roar of helicopters, small planes. Yet no one said a word about such things.

But Jesse was so happy! These things seemed of no consequence! Maharet's answers would banish Jesse's doubts in an instant. Yet how unusual that Jesse would change her mind like that. Jesse was such a confident person. Her own feelings were often known to her at once. She was actually rather stubborn. And yet she always had two attitudes towards various things Maharet told her. On the one hand, "Why, that's ridiculous," and on the other, "Of course!"

But Jesse was having too much fun to care. She spent the first few evenings of her visit talking with Maharet and Mael about archaeology. And Maharet was a fund of information though she had some very strange ideas.

For example, she maintained that the discovery of agriculture had actually come about because tribes who lived very well by hunting wanted to have hallucinogenic plants ever available to them for religious trances. And also they wanted beer. Never mind that there wasn't a shred of archaeological evidence. Just keep digging. Jesse would find out.

Mael read poetry out loud beautifully; Maharet sometimes played the piano, very slowly, meditatively. Eric reappeared for a couple of nights, joining them enthusiastically in their singing.

He'd brought films with him from Japan and Italy, and they'd had a splendid time watching these. *Kwaidan*, in particular, had been quite impressive, though frightening. And the Italian *Juliet of the Spirits* had made Jesse break into tears.

All of these people seemed to find Jesse interesting. In fact, Mael asked her incredibly odd questions. Had she ever in her life smoked a cigarette? What did chocolate taste like? How could she dare to go with young men alone in automobiles or to their apartments? Didn't she realize they might kill her? She had almost laughed. No, but seriously, that could happen, he insisted. He worked himself into a state over it. Look at the papers. Women of the modern cities were hunted by men like deer in the wood.

Best to get him off that subject, and onto his travels. His descriptions of all the places he'd been were marvelous. He'd lived for years in the jungles of the Amazon. Yet he would not fly in "an aeroplane." That was too dangerous. What if it exploded? And he didn't like "cloth garments" because they were too fragile.

Jesse had a very peculiar moment with Mael. They'd been talking together at the dining table. She'd been explaining about the ghosts she sometimes saw, and he had referred to these crossly as the addlebrained dead, or the insane dead, which had made her laugh in spite of herself. But it was true; ghosts did behave as if they were a little addlebrained, that was the horror of it. Do we cease to exist when we die? Or do we linger in a stupid state, appearing to people at odd moments and making nonsensical remarks to mediums? When had a ghost ever said anything interesting?

"But they are merely the earthbound, of course," Mael had said. "Who knows where we go when we at last let loose of the flesh and all its seductive pleasures?"

Jesse had been quite drunk by this time, and she felt a a terrible dread coming over her—thoughts of the old ghost mansion of Stanford White, and the spirits roaming the New York crowds. She'd focused sharply upon Mael, who for once was not wearing his gloves or his tinted glasses. Handsome Mael, whose eyes were very blue except for a bit of blackness at the centers.

"Besides," Mael had said, "there are other spirits who have always been here. They were never flesh and blood; and it makes them so angry."

What a curious idea. "How do you know this?" Jesse had asked, still staring at Mael. Mael was beautiful. The beauty was the sum of the faults— the hawk nose, the too prominent jaw, the leanness of the face with the wild wavy straw-colored hair around it. Even the eyes were too deep-set, yet all the more visible for it. Yes, beautiful—to embrace, to kiss, to invite to bed . . . In fact, the attraction she'd always felt to him was suddenly overwhelming.

Then, an odd realization had seized her. *This isn't a human being.* This is something pretending to be a human being. It was so clear. But it was also ridiculous! If it wasn't a human being, what the hell was it? It certainly was no ghost or spirit. That was obvious.

"I guess we don't know what's real or unreal," she had said without meaning to. "You stare at anything long enough and suddenly it looks monstrous." She had in fact turned away from him to stare at the bowl of flowers in the middle of the table. Old tea roses, falling to pieces amid the baby's breath and fern and purple zinnias. And they did look absolutely alien, these things, the way that insects always do, and sort of horrible! What were these things, really? Then the bowl broke into pieces and the water went everywhere. And Mael had said quite sincerely, "Oh, forgive me. I didn't mean to do that."

Now that had happened, without question. Yet it had made not the slightest impact. Mael had slipped away for a walk in the woods, kissing her forehead before he went, his hand trembling suddenly as he reached to touch her hair and then apparently thought the better of it.

Of course, Jesse had been drinking. In fact, Jesse drank too much the entire time she was there. And no one seemed to notice.

Now and then they went out and danced in the clearing under the moon. It was not an organized dancing. They would move singly, in circles, gazing up at the sky. Mael would hum or Maharet would sing songs in the unknown language.

What had been her state of mind to do such things for hours? And why had she never questioned, even in her mind, Mael's strange manner of wearing gloves about the house, or walking in the dark with his sunglasses on?

Then one morning well before dawn, Jesse had gone to bed drunk and had a terrible dream. Mael and Maharet were fighting with each other. Mael kept saying over and over:

"But what if she dies? What if somebody kills her, or a car hits her? What if, what if, what if . . ." It had become a deafening roar.

Then several nights later the awful and final catastrophe had begun. Mael had been gone for a while, but then he'd returned. She'd been drinking burgundy all evening long, and she was standing on the terrace with him and he had kissed her and she had lost consciousness and yet she knew what was going on. He was holding her, kissing her breasts, yet she was slipping down through a fathomless darkness. Then the girl had come again, the teenaged girl who'd come to her that time in New York when she was so afraid. Only Mael couldn't see the girl, and of course Jesse knew exactly who she was, Jesse's mother, Miriam, and that Miriam was afraid. Mael had suddenly released Jesse.

"Where is she!" he'd cried out angrily.

Jesse had opened her eyes. Maharet was there. She struck Mael so hard he flew backwards over the railing of the terrace. And Jesse screamed, pushing aside the teenaged girl accidentally as she ran to look over the edge.

Far down there in the clearing Mael stood, unhurt. Impossible, yet obviously the case. He was on his feet already, and he made Maharet a deep ceremonial bow. He stood in the light falling from the windows of the lower rooms, and he blew a kiss to Maharet. Maharet looked sad, but she smiled. She'd said something under her breath and made a little dismissive gesture to Mael, as if to say she wasn't angry.

Jesse was in a panic that Maharet would be angry with her, but when she looked into Maharet's eyes she knew that there was no cause for worry. Then Jesse looked down and saw that the front of her dress was torn. She felt a sharp pain where Mael had been kissing her, and when she turned to Maharet, she became disoriented, unable to hear her own words.

She was sitting on her bed somehow, propped against the pillows, and she wore a long flannel gown. She was telling Maharet that her mother had come again, she'd seen her on the terrace. But that was only part of what she'd been saying because she and Maharet had been talking for hours about the whole thing. But what whole thing? Maharet told her she would forget.

Oh, God, how she tried to recall after. Bits and pieces had tormented her for years. Maharet's hair was down, and it was very long and full. They had moved through the dark house together, like ghosts, she and Maharet, Maharet holding her, and now and then stopping to kiss her, and she had hugged Maharet. Maharet's body felt like stone that could breathe.

They were high up in the mountain in a secret room. Massive computers were there, with their reels and red lights, giving off a low electronic hum. And there, on an immense rectangular screen that stretched dozens of feet up the wall, was an enormous family tree drawn electronically by means of light. This was the Great Family, stretching back through all the millennia. Ah, yes, to one root! The plan was matrilineal, which had always been the way with the ancient peoples—as it had been with the Egyptians, yes, descent through the princesses of the royal house. And as it was, after a fashion, with the Hebrew tribes to this day.

All the details had been plain to Jesse at this moment—ancient names, places, the beginning!—God, had she known even the beginning?—the staggering reality of hundreds of generations charted before her eyes! She had seen the progress of the family through the ancient countries of Asia Minor and Macedonia and Italy and finally up through Europe and then to the New World! And this could have been the chart of any human family!

Never after was she able to reinvoke the details of that electronic map. No, Maharet had told her she would forget it. The miracle was that she remembered anything at all.

But what else had happened? What had been the real thrust of their long talk?

Maharet crying, that she remembered. Maharet weeping with the soft feminine sound of a young girl. Maharet had never appeared so alluring; her face had been softened, yet luminous, the lines so few and so delicate. But it had been shadowy then, and Jesse could scarcely see anything clearly. She remembered the face burning like a white ember in the darkness, the pale green eyes clouded yet vibrant, and the blond eyelashes glistening as if the tiny hairs had been stroked with gold.

Candles burning in her room. The forest rising high outside the window. Jesse had been begging, protesting. But what in God's name was the argument about?

You will forget this. You will remember nothing.

She'd known when she opened her eyes in the sunlight that it was over; they had gone. Nothing had come back to her in those first few moments, except that something irrevocable had been said.

Then she had found the note on the bedside table:

My darling,

It is no longer good for you to be around us. I fear we have all become too enamored of you and would sweep you off your feet and take you away from those things which you have set out to do.

You will forgive us for leaving so suddenly. I am confident that this is best for you. I have arranged for the car to take you to the airport. Your plane leaves at four o'clock. Your cousins Maria and Matthew will meet you in New York.

Be assured I love you more than words can say. My letter will be waiting for you when you reach home. Some night many years from now we will discuss the family history again. You may become my helper with these records if you still wish it. But for now this must not engulf you. It must not lead you away from life itself.

Yours always,
with unquestioning love,
Maharet

JESSE had never seen Maharet again.

Her letters came with the same old regularity, full of affection, concern, advice. But never again was there to be a visit. Never was Jesse invited back to the house in the Sonoma forest.

In the following months, Jesse had been showered with presents—a beautiful old town house on Washington Square in Greenwich Village, a new car, a heady increase in income, and the usual plane tickets to visit members of the family all over the world. Eventually, Maharet underwrote a substantial part of Jesse's archaeological work at Jericho. In fact, as the years passed she gave Jesse anything and everything Jesse could possibly desire.

Nevertheless, Jesse had been damaged by that summer. Once in Damascus she had dreamed of Mael and awakened crying.

SHE was in London, working at the British Museum, when the memories began to come back with full force. She never knew what triggered them. Maybe the effect of Maharet's admonition—*You will forget*—had simply worn off. But there might have been another reason. One evening in

Trafalgar Square, she'd seen Mael or a man who looked exactly like him. The man, who stood many feet away, had been staring at her when their eyes met. Yet when she'd waved, he'd turned his back and walked off without the slightest recognition. She'd run after him trying to catch up with him; but he was gone as if he'd never been there.

It had left her hurt and disappointed. Yet three days later she'd received an anonymous gift, a bracelet of hammered silver. It was an ancient Celtic relic, she soon found out, and probably priceless. Could Mael have sent her this precious and lovely thing? She wanted so to believe it.

Holding the bracelet tightly in her hand she felt his presence. She remembered the long ago night when they'd spoken of addlebrained ghosts. She smiled. It was as if he were there, holding her, kissing her. She told Maharet about the gift when she wrote. She wore the bracelet ever after that.

Jesse kept a diary of the memories that came back to her. She wrote down dreams, fragments she saw in flashes. But she did not mention any of this in her letters to Maharet.

She had a love affair while she was in London. It ended badly, and she felt rather alone. It was at that time that the Talamasca contacted her and the course of her life was changed forever.

JESSE had been living in an old house in Chelsea, not far from where Oscar Wilde had once lived. James McNeill Whistler had once shared the neighborhood and so had Bram Stoker, the author of *Dracula*. It was a place that Jesse loved. But unbeknownst to her, the house in which she'd leased her rooms had been haunted for many years. Jesse saw several strange things within the first few months. They were faint, flickering, apparitions of the kind one frequently sees in such places; echoes, as Maharet had called them, of people who'd been there years before. Jesse ignored them.

However when a reporter stopped her one afternoon, explaining that he was doing a story on the haunted house, she told him rather matter-of-factly about the things she'd seen. Common enough ghosts for London—an old woman carrying a pitcher from the pantry, a man in a frock coat and top hat who would appear for a second or more on the stair.

It made for a rather melodramatic article. Jesse had talked too much, obviously. She was called a "psychic" or "natural medium" who saw these things all the time. One of the Reeves family in Yorkshire called to tease her a little about it. Jesse thought it was funny too. But other than that, she didn't much care. She was deep into her studies at the British Museum. It just didn't matter at all.

Then the Talamasca, having read the paper, came to call.

Aaron Lightner, an old-fashioned gentleman with white hair and exquisite manners, asked to take Jesse to lunch. In an old but meticulously maintained Rolls Royce, he and Jesse were driven through London to a small and elegant private club.

Surely it was one of the strangest meetings Jesse had ever had. In fact, it reminded her of the long ago summer, not because it was like it, but because both experiences were so unlike anything else that had ever happened to Jesse.

Lightner was a bit on the glamorous side, as Jesse saw it. His white hair was quite full and neatly groomed, and he wore an impeccably tailored suit of Donegal tweed. He was the only man she'd ever seen with a silver walking stick.

Rapidly and pleasantly he explained to Jesse that he was a "psychic detective"; he worked for a "secret order called the Talamasca," whose sole purpose was to collect data on "paranormal" experiences and maintain those records for the study of such phenomena. The Talamasca held out its hand to people with paranormal powers. And to those of extremely strong ability, it now and then offered membership, a career in "psychic investigation," which was in fact more truly a vocation, as the Talamasca demanded full devotion, loyalty, and obedience to its rules.

Jesse almost laughed. But Lightner was apparently prepared for her skepticism. He had a few "tricks" he always used at such introductory meetings. And to Jesse's utter amazement, he managed to move several objects on the table without touching them. A simple power, he said, which functioned as a "calling card."

As Jesse watched the salt shaker dance back and forth of its own volition, she was too amazed to speak. But the real surprise came when Lightner confessed he knew all about her. He knew where she'd come from, where she'd studied. He knew that she'd seen spirits when she was a little girl. It had come to the attention of the order years ago through "routine channels," and a file had been created for Jesse. She must not be offended.

Please understand the Talamasca proceeded in its investigations with the utmost respect for the individual. The file contained only hearsay reports of things that Jesse had told neighbors, teachers, and school friends. Jesse could see the file any time she wanted. That was always the way it was with the Talamasca. Contact was always eventually attempted with subjects under observation. Information was freely given to the subject, though it was otherwise confidential.

Jesse questioned Lightner rather relentlessly. It soon became clear that he did know a great deal about her, but he knew nothing whatsoever about Maharet or the Great Family.

And it was this combination of knowledge and ignorance that lured Jesse. One mention of Maharet and she would have turned her back on the Talamasca forever, for to the Great Family Jesse was unfailingly loyal. But the Talamasca cared only about Jesse's abilities. And Jesse, in spite of Maharet's advice, had always cared about them, too.

Then the history of the Talamasca itself proved powerfully attractive. Was this man telling the truth? A secret order, which traced its existence back to the year 758, an order with records of witches, sorcerers, mediums, and seers of spirits going back to that remote period? It dazzled her as the records of the Great Family had once dazzled her.

And Lightner graciously withstood another round of relentless questioning. He knew his history and his geography, that was clear enough. He spoke easily and accurately of the persecution of the Cathars, the suppression of the Knights Templar, the execution of Grandier, and a dozen other historical "events." In fact, Jesse couldn't stump him. On the contrary, he referred to ancient "magicians" and "sorcerers" of whom she had never heard.

That evening, when they arrived at the Motherhouse outside London, Jesse's fate was pretty much sealed. She didn't leave the Motherhouse for a week, and then only to close up her flat in Chelsea and return to the Talamasca.

The Motherhouse was a mammoth stone structure built in the 1500s and acquired by the Talamasca "only" two hundred years ago. Though the sumptuous paneled libraries and parlors had been created in the eighteenth century, along with appropriate plasterwork and friezes, the dining room and many of the bedchambers dated back to the Elizabethan period.

Jesse loved the atmosphere immediately, the dignified furnishings, the stone fireplaces, the gleaming oak floors. Even the quiet civil members of the order appealed to her, as they greeted her cheerfully, then returned to their discussions or the reading of the evening papers, as they sat about the vast, warmly lighted public rooms. The sheer wealth of the place was startling. It lent substance to Lightner's claims. And the place felt good. Psychically good. People here were what they said they were.

But it was the libraries themselves that finally overwhelmed her, and brought her back to that tragic summer when another library and its ancient treasures had been shut against her. Here were countless volumes chronicling witch trials and hauntings and poltergeist investigations, cases of possession, of psychokinesis, reincarnation, and the like. Then there were museums beneath the building, rooms crammed with mysterious objects connected with paranormal occurrences. There were vaults to which no one was admitted except the senior members of the order. Delicious, the prospect of secrets revealed only over a period of time.

"So much work to be done, always," Aaron had said casually. "Why, all these old records, you see, are in Latin, and we can no longer demand that the new members read and write Latin. It's simply out of the question in this day and age. And these storage rooms, you see, the documentation on most of these objects hasn't been reevaluated in four centuries—".

Of course Aaron knew that Jesse could read and write not only Latin, but Greek, ancient Egyptian, and ancient Sumerian as well. What he didn't know was that here Jesse had found a replacement for the treasures of that lost summer. She had found another "Great Family."

That night a car was sent to get Jesse's clothing and whatever she might want from the Chelsea flat. Her new room was in the southwest corner of the Motherhouse, a cozy little affair with a coffered ceiling and a Tudor fireplace.

Jesse never wanted to leave this house, and Aaron knew it. On Friday of that week, only three days after her arrival, she was received into the order as a novice. She was given an impressive allowance, a private parlor adjacent to her bedroom, a full-time driver, and a comfortable old car. She left her job at the British Museum as soon as possible.

The rules and regulations were simple. She would spend two years in full-time training, traveling with other members when and where necessary throughout the world. She could talk about the order to members of her family or friends, of course. But all subjects, files, and related details remained confidential. And she must never seek to publish anything about the Talamasca. In fact, she must never contribute to any "public mention" of the Talamasca. References to specific assignments must always omit names and places, and remain vague.

Her special work would be within the archives, translating and "adapting" old chronicles and records. And in the museums she would work on organizing various artifacts and relics at least one day of each week. But fieldwork—investigations of hauntings and the like—would take precedence over research at any time.

It was a month before she wrote to Maharet of her decision. And in her letter she poured out her soul. She loved these people and their work. Of course the library reminded her of the family archive in Sonoma, and the time when she'd been so happy. Did Maharet understand?

Maharet's answer astonished her. Maharet knew what the Talamasca was. In fact, Maharet seemed quite thoroughly familiar with the history of the Talamasca. She said without preamble that she admired enormously the efforts of the order during the witchcraft persecutions of the fifteenth and sixteenth centuries to save the innocent from the stake.

Surely they have told you of their "underground railroad" by means of which many accused persons were taken from the villages and hamlets where they might have been burnt and given refuge in Amsterdam, an enlightened city, where the lies and foolishness of the witchcraft era were not long believed.

Jesse hadn't known anything about this, but she was soon to confirm every detail. However, Maharet had her reservations about the Talamasca:

Much as I admire their compassion for the persecuted of all eras, you must understand that I do not think their investigations amount to much. To clarify: spirits, ghosts, vampires, werewolves, witches, entities that defy description—all these may exist and the Talamasca may spend another millennium studying them, but what difference will this make to the destiny of the human race?

Undoubtedly there have been, in the distant past, individuals who saw visions and spoke to spirits. And perhaps as witches or shamans, these people had some value for their tribes or nations. But complex and fanciful religions have been founded upon such simple and deceptive experiences, giving mythical names to vague entities, and creating an enormous vehicle for compounded superstitious belief. Have not these religions been more evil than good?

Allow me to suggest that, however one interprets history, we are now well past the point where contact with spirits can be of any use. A crude but inexorable justice may be at work in the skepticism of ordinary individuals regarding ghosts, mediums, and like company. The supernatural, in whatever form it exists, *should not* interfere in human history.

In sum, I am arguing that, except for comforting a few confused souls here and there, the Talamasca compiles records of things that are not important and should not be important. The Talamasca is an interesting organization. But it cannot accomplish great things.

I love you. I respect your decision. But I hope for your sake that you tire of the Talamasca—and return to the real world—very soon.

Jesse thought carefully before answering. It tortured her that Maharet didn't approve of what she had done. Yet Jesse knew there was a recrimination in her decision. Maharet had turned her away from the secrets of the family; the Talamasca had taken her in.

When she wrote, she assured Maharet that the members of the order had no illusions about the significance of their work. They had told Jesse it was largely secret; there was no glory, sometimes no real satisfaction. They would agree in full with Maharet's opinions about the insignificance of mediums, spirits, ghosts.

But did not millions of people think that the dusty finds of archaeologists were of little significance as well? Jesse begged Maharet to understand what this meant to her. And lastly she wrote, much to her own surprise, the following lines:

I will never tell the Talamasca anything about the Great Family. I will never tell them about the house in Sonoma and the mysterious things that happened to me while I was there. They would be too hungry for this sort of mystery. And my loyalty is to you. But some day, I beg you, let me come back to the California house. Let me talk to you about the things that I saw. I've remembered things lately. I have had puzzling dreams. But I trust your judgment in these matters. You've been so generous to me. I don't doubt that you love me. Please understand how much I love you.

Maharet's response was brief.

Jesse, I am an eccentric and willful being; very little has ever been denied me. Now and then I deceive myself as to the effect I have upon others. I should never have brought you to the Sonoma house; it was a selfish thing to do, for which I cannot forgive myself. But you must soothe my conscience for me. Forget the visit ever took place. Do not deny the truth of what you recall; but do not dwell on it either. Live your life as if it had never been so recklessly interrupted. Some day I will answer all your questions, but never again will I try to subvert your destiny. I congratulate you on your new vocation. You have my unconditional love forever.

Elegant presents soon followed. Leather luggage for Jesse's travels and a lovely mink-lined coat to keep her warm in "the abominable British weather." It is a country "only a Druid could love," Maharet wrote.

Jesse loved the coat because the mink was inside and didn't attract attention. The luggage served her well. And Maharet continued to write twice and three times a week. She remained as solicitous as ever.

But as the years passed, it was Jesse who grew distant—her letters brief and irregular—because her work with the Talamasca was confidential. She simply could not describe what she did.

Jesse still visited members of the Great Family, at Christmas and Easter. Whenever cousins came to London, she met them for sight-seeing or lunch. But all such contact was brief and superficial. The Talamasca soon became Jesse's life.

A WORLD was revealed to Jesse in the Talamasca archives as she began her translations from the Latin: records of psychic families and individuals, cases of "obvious" sorcery, "real" *maleficia*, and finally the repetitive yet horribly fascinating transcripts of actual witchcraft trials which invariably involved the innocent and the powerless. Night and day she worked, translating directly into the computer, retrieving invaluable historical material from crumbling parchment pages.

But another world, even more seductive, was opening up to her in the field. Within a year of joining the Talamasca, Jesse had seen poltergeist hauntings frightening enough to send grown men running out of the house and into the street. She had seen a telekinetic child lift an oak table and send it crashing through a window. She had communicated in utter silence with mind readers who received any message she sent to them. She had seen ghosts more palpable than anything she had ever believed could exist. Feats of psychometry, automatic writing, levitation, trance mediumship—all these she witnessed, jotting down her notes afterwards, and forever marveling at her own surprise.

Would she never get used to it? Take it for granted? Even the older members of the Talamasca confessed that they were continually shocked by the things they witnessed.

And without doubt Jesse's power to "see" was exceptionally strong. With constant use it developed enormously. Two years after entering the Talamasca, Jesse was being sent to haunted houses all over Europe and the United States. For every day or two spent in the peace and quiet of the library, there was a week in some drafty hallway watching the intermittent appearances of a silent specter who had frightened others.

Jesse seldom came to any conclusions about these apparitions. Indeed, she learned what all members of the Talamasca knew: there was no single theory of the occult to embrace all the strange things one saw or heard. The work was tantalizing, but ultimately frustrating. Jesse was unsure of herself when she addressed these "restless entities," or addlebrained spirits as Mael had once rather accurately described them. Yet Jesse advised them to move on to "higher levels," to seek peace for themselves and thereby leave mortals at peace also.

It seemed the only possible course to take, though it frightened her that she might be forcing these ghosts out of the only life that remained to them.

What if death were the end, and hauntings came about only when tenacious souls would not accept it? Too awful to think of that—of the spirit world as a dim and chaotic afterglow before the ultimate darkness.

Whatever the case, Jesse dispelled any number of hauntings. And she was constantly comforted by the relief of the living. There developed in her a profound sense of the specialness of her life. It was exciting. She wouldn't have swapped it for anything in the world.

Well, not for almost anything. After all, she might have left in a minute if Maharet had appeared on her doorstep and asked her to return to the Sonoma compound and take up the records of the Great Family in earnest. And then again perhaps not.

Jesse did have one experience with the Talamasca records, however, which caused her considerable personal confusion regarding the Great Family.

In transcribing the witch documents Jesse eventually discovered that the Talamasca had monitored for centuries certain "witch families" whose fortunes appeared to be influenced by supernatural intervention of a verifiable and predictable sort. The Talamasca was watching a number of such families right now! There was usually a "witch" in each generation of such a family, and this witch could, according to the record, attract and manipulate supernatural forces to ensure the family's steady accumulation of wealth and other success in human affairs. The power appeared to be hereditary—i.e., based in the physical—but no one knew for sure. Some of these families were now entirely ignorant as to their own history; they did not understand the "witches" who had manifested in the twentieth century. And though the Talamasca attempted regularly to make "contact" with such people, they were often rebuffed, or found the work too "dangerous" to pursue. After all, these witches could work actual *maleficia*.

Shocked and incredulous, Jesse did nothing after this discovery for several weeks. But she could not get the pattern out of her mind. It was too like the pattern of Maharet and the Great Family.

Then she did the only thing she could do without violating her loyalty to anybody. She carefully reviewed the records of every witch family in the Talamasca files. She checked and double-checked. She went back to the oldest records in existence and went over them minutely.

No mention of anyone named Maharet. No mention of anyone connected to any branch or surname of the Great Family that Jesse had ever heard of. No mention of anything even vaguely suspicious.

Her relief was enormous, but in the end, she was not surprised. Her instincts had told her she was on the wrong track. Maharet was no witch. Not in this sense of the word. *There was more to it than that.*

Yet in truth, Jesse never tried to figure it all out. She resisted theories about what had happened as she resisted theories about everything. And it occurred to her, more than once, that she had sought out the Talamasca in order to lose this personal mystery in a wilderness of mysteries. Surrounded by ghosts and poltergeists and possessed children, she thought less and less about Maharet and the Great Family.

BY THE time Jesse became a full member, she was an expert on the rules of the Talamasca, the procedures, the way to record investigations, when and how to help the police in crime cases, how to avoid all contact with the press. She also came to respect that the Talamasca was not a dogmatic organization. It did not require its members to believe *anything*, merely to be honest and careful about all the phenomena that they observed.

Patterns, similarities, repetitions—these fascinated the Talamasca. Terms abounded, but there was no rigid vocabulary. The files were merely cross-referenced in dozens of different ways.

Nevertheless members of the Talamasca studied the theoreticians. Jesse read the works of all the great psychic detectives, mediums, and mentalists. She studied anything and everything related to the occult.

And many a time she thought of Maharet's advice. What Maharet had said was true. Ghosts, apparitions, psychics who could read minds and move objects telekinetically—it was all fascinating to those who witnessed it firsthand. But to the human race at large it meant very little. There was not now, nor would there ever be, any great occult discovery that would alter human history.

But Jesse never tired of her work. She became addicted to the excitement, even the secrecy. She was within the womb of the Talamasca, and though she grew accustomed to the elegance of her surroundings—to antique lace and poster beds and sterling silver, to chauffeured cars and servants—she herself became ever more simple and reserved.

At thirty she was a fragile-looking light-skinned woman with her curly red hair parted in the middle and kept long so that it would fall behind her shoulders and leave her alone. She wore no cosmetics, perfume, or jewelry, except for the Celtic bracelet. A cashmere blazer was her favorite garment, along with wool pants, or jeans if she was in America. Yet she was an attractive person, drawing a little more attention from men than she thought was best. Love affairs she had, but they were always short. And seldom very important.

What mattered more were her friendships with the other members of the order; she had so many brothers and sisters. And they cared about her as she cared about them. She loved the feeling of the community surrounding her. At any hour of the night, one could go downstairs to a lighted parlor where people were awake—reading, talking, arguing perhaps in a subdued way. One could wander into the kitchen where the night cook was ever ready to prepare an early breakfast or a late dinner, whatever one might desire.

Jesse might have gone on forever with the Talamasca. Like a Catholic religious order, the Talamasca took care of its old and infirm. To die within the order was to know every luxury as well as every medical attention, to spend your last moments the way you wanted, alone in your bed, or with other members near you, comforting you, holding your hand. You could go home to your relatives if that was your choice. But most, over the years, chose to die in the Motherhouse. The funerals were dignified and elaborate. In the Talamasca, death was a part of life. A great gathering of black-dressed men and women witnessed each burial.

Yes, these had become Jesse's people. And in the natural course of events she would have remained forever.

But when she reached the end of her eighth year, something happened that was to change everything, something that led eventually to her break with the order.

Jesse's accomplishments up to that point had been impressive. But in the summer of 1981, she was still working under the direction of Aaron Lightner and she had seldom even spoken to the governing council of the Talamasca or the handful of men and women who were really in charge.

So when David Talbot, the head of the entire order, called her up to his office in London, she was surprised. David was an energetic man of sixty-five, heavy of build, with iron-gray hair and a consistently cheerful manner. He offered Jesse a glass of sherry and talked pleasantly about nothing for fifteen minutes before getting to the point.

Jesse was being offered a very different sort of assignment. He gave her a novel called *Interview with the Vampire*. He said, "I want you to read this book."

Jesse was puzzled. "The fact is, I have read it," she said. "It was a couple of years ago. But what does a novel like this have to do with us?"

Jesse had picked up a paperback copy at the airport and devoured it on a long transcontinental flight. The story, supposedly told by a vampire to a young reporter in present-day San Francisco, had affected Jesse rather like a bad dream. She wasn't sure she liked it. Matter of fact, she'd thrown it away later, rather than leave it on a bench at the next airport for fear some unsuspecting person might find it.

The main characters of the work—rather glamorous immortals when you got right down to it—had formed an evil little family in antebellum New Orleans where they preyed on the populace for over fifty years. Lestat was the villain of the piece, and the leader. Louis, his anguished subordinate, was the hero, and the one telling the tale. Claudia, their exquisite vampire "daughter," was a truly tragic figure, her mind maturing year after year while her body remained eternally that of a little girl. Louis's fruitless quest for redemption had been the theme of the book, obviously, but Claudia's hatred for the two male vampires who had made her what she was, and her own eventual destruction, had had a much stronger effect upon Jesse.

"The book isn't fiction," David explained simply. "Yet the purpose of creating it is unclear. And the act of publishing it, even as a novel, has us rather alarmed."

"Not fiction?" Jesse asked. "I don't understand."

"The author's name is a pseudonym," David continued, "and the royalty checks go to a nomadic young man who resists all our attempts at contact. He was a reporter, however, much like the boy interviewer in the novel. But that's neither here nor there at the moment. Your job is to go to New Orleans and document the events in the story which took place there before the Civil War."

"Wait a minute. You're telling me there are vampires? That these characters—Louis and Lestat and the little girl Claudia—are real!"

"Yes, exactly," David answered. "And don't forget about Armand, the mentor of the Théâtre des Vampires in Paris. You do remember Armand."

Jesse had no trouble remembering Armand or the theater. Armand, the oldest immortal in the novel, had had the face and form of an adolescent boy. As for the theater, it had been a gruesome establishment where human beings were killed on stage before an unsuspecting Parisian audience as part of the regular fare.

The entire nightmarish quality of the book was coming back to Jesse. Especially the parts that dealt with Claudia. Claudia had died in the Theater of the Vampires. The coven, under Armand's command, had destroyed her.

"David, am I understanding you correctly? You're saying these creatures exist?"

"Absolutely," David answered. "We've been observing this type of being since we came into existence. In a very real way, the Talamasca was formed to observe these creatures, but that's another story. In all probability, there are no fictional characters in this little novel whatsoever, but that would be your assignment, you see—to document the existence of the New Orleans coven, as described here—Claudia, Louis, Lestat."

Jesse laughed. She couldn't help it. She really laughed. David's patient expression only made her laugh more. But she wasn't surprising David, any more than her laughter had surprised Aaron Lightner eight years ago when they first met.

"Excellent attitude," David said, with a little mischievous smile. "We wouldn't want you to be too imaginative or trusting. But this field requires great care, Jesse, and strict obedience to the rules. Believe me when I say that this is an area which can be extremely dangerous. You are certainly free to turn down the assignment right now."

"I'm going to start laughing again," Jesse said. She had seldom if ever heard the word "dangerous" in the Talamasca. She had seen it in writing only in the witch family files. Now, she could believe in a witch family without much difficulty. Witches were human beings, and spirits could be manipulated, most probably. But vampires?

"Well, let's approach it this way," David said. "Before you make up your mind, we'll examine certain artifacts pertaining to these creatures which we have in the vaults."

The idea was irresistible. There were scores of rooms beneath the Motherhouse to which Jesse had never been admitted. She wasn't going to pass up this opportunity.

As she and David went down the stairs together, the atmosphere of the Sonoma compound came back to her unexpectedly and rather vividly. Even the long corridor with its occasional dim electric bulbs reminded her of Maharet's cellar. She found herself all the more excited.

She followed David silently through one locked storage room after another. She saw books, a skull on a shelf, what seemed old clothing heaped on the floor, furniture, oil paintings, trunks and strongboxes, dust.

"All this paraphernalia," David said, with a dismissive gesture, "is in one way or another connected to our blood-drinking immortal friends. They tend to be a rather materialistic lot, actually. And they leave behind them all sorts of refuse. It is not unknown for them to leave an entire household, complete with furnishings, clothing, and even coffins—very ornate and interesting coffins—when they tire of a particular location or identity. But there are some specific things which I must show you. It will all be rather conclusive, I should think."

Conclusive? There was something conclusive in this work? This was certainly an afternoon for surprises.

David led her into a final chamber, a very large room, paneled in tin and immediately illuminated by a bank of overhead lights.

She saw an enormous painting against the far wall. She placed it at once as Renaissance, and probably Venetian. It was done in egg tempera on wood. And it had the marvelous sheen of such paintings, a gloss that no synthetic material can create. She read the Latin title along with the name of the artist, in small Roman-style letters painted in the lower right corner.

"The Temptation of Amadeo"
by Marius

She stood back to study it.

A splendid choir of black-winged angels hovered around a single kneeling figure, that of a young auburn-haired boy. The cobalt sky behind them, seen through a series of arches, was splendidly done with masses of gilded clouds. And the marble floor before the figures had a photographic perfection to it. One could feel its coldness, see the veins in the stone.

But the figures were the true glory of the picture. The faces of the angels were exquisitely modeled, their pastel robes and black feathered wings extravagantly detailed. And the boy, the boy was very simply alive! His dark brown eyes veritably glistened as he stared forward out of the painting. His skin appeared moist. He was about to move or speak.

In fact, it was all too realistic to be Renaissance. The figures were particular rather than ideal. The angels wore expressions of faint amusement, almost bitterness. And the fabric of the boy's tunic and leggings, it was too exactly rendered. She could even see the mends in it, a tiny tear, the dust on his sleeve. There were other such details—dried leaves here and there on the floor, and two paintbrushes lying to one side for no apparent reason.

"Who is this Marius?" she whispered. The name meant nothing. And never had she seen an Italian painting with so many disturbing elements. Black-winged angels . . .

David didn't answer. He pointed to the boy. "It's the boy I want you to observe," he said. "He's not the real subject of your investigation, merely a very important link."

Subject? Link. . . . She was too engrossed in the picture. "And look, bones in the corner, human bones covered with dust, as if someone had merely swept them out of the way. But what on earth does it all mean?"

"Yes," David murmured. "When you see the word 'temptation,' usually there are devils surrounding a saint."

"Exactly," she answered. "And the craft is exceptional." The more she stared at the picture, the more disturbed she became. "Where did you get this?"

"The order acquired it centuries ago," David answered. "Our emissary in Venice retrieved it from a burnt-out villa on the Grand Canal. These vampires are endlessly associated with fires, by the way. It is the one weapon they can use effectively against one another. There are always fires. In *Interview with the Vampire,* there were several fires, if you recall. Louis set fire to a town house in New Orleans when he was trying to destroy his maker and mentor, Lestat. And later, Louis burned the Theater of the Vampires in Paris after Claudia's death."

Claudia's death. It sent a shiver through Jesse, startling her slightly.

"But look at this boy carefully," David said. "It's the boy we're discussing now."

Amadeo. It meant "one who loves God." He was a handsome creature, all right. Sixteen, maybe seventeen, with a square, strongly proportioned face and a curiously imploring expression.

David had put something in her hand. Reluctantly she took her eyes off the painting. She found herself staring at a tintype, a late-nineteenth-century photograph. After a moment, she whispered: "This is the same boy!"

"Yes. And something of an experiment," David said. "It was most likely taken just after sunset in impossible lighting conditions which might not have worked with another subject. Notice not much is really visible but his face."

True, yet she could see the style of the hair was of the period.

"You might look at this as well," David said. And this time he gave her an old magazine, a nineteenth-century journal, the kind with narrow columns of tiny print and ink illustrations. There was the same boy again alighting from a barouche—a hasty sketch, though the boy was smiling.

"The article's about him, and about his Theater of the Vampires. Here's an English journal from 1789. That's a full eighty years earlier, I believe. But you will find another very thorough description of the establishment and the same young man."

"The Theater of the Vampires . . ." She stared up at the auburn-haired boy kneeling in the painting. "Why, this is Armand, the character in the novel!"

"Precisely. He seems to like that name. It may have been Amadeo when he was in Italy, but it became Armand by the eighteenth century and he's used Armand ever since."

"Slow down, please," Jesse said. "You're telling me that the Theater of the Vampires has been documented? By our people?"

"Thoroughly. The file's enormous. Countless memoirs describe the theater. We have the deeds to the property as well. And here we come to another link with our files and this little novel, *Interview with the Vampire.* The name of the owner of the theater was Lestat de Lioncourt, who purchased it in 1789. And the property in modern Paris is in the hands of a man by the same name even now."

"This is verified?" Jesse said.

"It's all in the file," David said, "photostats of the old records and the recent ones. You can study the signature of Lestat if you like. Lestat does everything in a big way—covers half the page with his magnificent lettering. We have photostats of several examples. We want you to take those photostats to New Orleans with you. There's a newspaper account of the fire which destroyed the theater exactly as Louis described it. The date is consistent with the facts of the story. You must go over everything, of course. And the novel, do read it again carefully."

By the end of the week, Jesse was on a plane for New Orleans. She was to annotate and document the novel, in every way possible, searching property titles, transfers, old newspapers, journals—anything she could find to support the theory that the characters and events were real.

But Jesse still didn't believe it. Undoubtedly there was "something here," but there had to be a catch. And the catch was in all probability a clever historical novelist who had stumbled upon some interesting research and woven it into a fictional story. After all, theater tickets, deeds, programs, and the like do not prove the existence of bloodsucking immortals.

As for the rules Jesse had to follow, she thought they were a scream. She was not allowed to remain in New Orleans except between the hours of sunrise and four p.m. At four p.m. she had to drive north to the city of Baton Rouge and spend the nights safe within a sixteenth-story room in a modern hotel. If she should have the slightest feeling that someone was watching her or following her, she was to make for the safety of a large crowd at once. From a well-lighted and populated place, she was to call the Talamasca long distance in London immediately.

Never, under any circumstances, must she attempt a "sighting" of one of these vampire individuals. The parameters of vampiric power were not known to the Talamasca. But one thing was certain: the beings could read minds. Also, they could create mental confusion in human beings. And there was considerable evidence that they were exceptionally strong. Most certainly they could kill.

Also some of them, without doubt, knew of the existence of the Talamasca. Over the centuries, several members of the order had disappeared during this type of investigation.

Jesse was to read the daily papers scrupulously. The Talamasca had reason to believe that there were no vampires in New Orleans at present.

Or Jesse would not be going there. But at any time, Lestat, Armand, or Louis might appear. If Jesse came across an article about a suspicious death she was to get out of the city and not return.

Jesse thought all this was hilarious. Even a handful of old items about mysterious deaths did not impress her or frighten her. After all, these people could have been the victims of a satanic cult. And they were all too human.

But Jesse had wanted this assignment.

On the way to the airport, David had asked her why. "If you really can't accept what I'm telling you, then why do you want to investigate the book?"

She'd taken her time in answering. "There is something obscene about this novel. It makes the lives of these beings seem attractive. You don't realize it at first; it's a nightmare and you can't get out of it. Then all of a sudden you're comfortable there. You want to remain. Even the tragedy of Claudia isn't really a deterrent."

"And?"

"I want to prove it's fiction," Jesse said.

That was good enough for the Talamasca, especially coming from a trained investigator.

But on the long flight to New York, Jesse had realized there was something she couldn't tell David. She had only just faced it herself. *Interview with the Vampire* "reminded" her of that long ago summer with Maharet, though Jesse didn't know why. Again and again she stopped her reading to think about that summer. And little things were coming back to her. She was even dreaming about it again. Quite beside the point, she told herself. Yet there was some connection, something to do with the atmosphere of the book, the mood, even the attitudes of the characters, and the whole manner in which things seemed one way and were really not that way at all. But Jesse could not figure it out. Her reason, like her memory, was curiously blocked.

Jesse's first few days in New Orleans were the strangest in her entire psychic career.

The city had a moist Caribbean beauty, and a tenacious colonial flavor that charmed her at once. Yet everywhere Jesse went she "felt" things. The entire place seemed haunted. The awesome antebellum mansions were seductively silent and gloomy. Even the French Quarter streets, crowded with tourists, had a sensuous and sinister atmosphere that kept her forever walking out of her way or stopping for long periods to dream as she sat slumped on a bench in Jackson Square.

She hated to leave the city at four o'clock. The high-rise hotel in Baton Rouge provided a divine degree of American luxury. Jesse liked that well enough. But the soft lazy ambience of New Orleans clung to her. She awoke each morning dimly aware that she'd dreamed of the vampire characters. And of Maharet.

Then, four days into her investigation, she made a series of discoveries that sent her directly to the phone. There most certainly had been a Lestat de Lioncourt on the tax rolls in Louisiana. In fact, in 1862 he had taken possession of a Royal Street town house from his business partner, Louis de Pointe du Lac. Louis de Pointe du Lac had owned seven different pieces of Louisiana property, and one of them had been the plantation described in *Interview with the Vampire*. Jesse was flabbergasted. She was also delighted.

But there were even more discoveries. Somebody named Lestat de Lioncourt owned houses all over the city right now. And this person's signature, appearing in records dated 1895 and 1910, was identical to the eighteenth-century signatures.

Oh, this was too marvelous. Jesse was having a wonderful time.

At once she set out to photograph Lestat's properties. Two were Garden District mansions, clearly uninhabitable and falling to ruin behind rusted gates. But the rest, including the Royal Street town house—the very same deeded to Lestat in 1862—were rented by a local agency which made payment to an attorney in Paris.

This was more than Jesse could bear. She cabled David for money. She must buy out the tenants in Royal Street, for this was surely the house once inhabited by Lestat, Louis, and the child Claudia. They may or may not have been vampires, but they lived there!

David wired the money immediately, along with strict instructions that she mustn't go near the ruined mansions she'd described. Jesse answered at once that she'd already examined these places. Nobody had been in them for years.

It was the town house that mattered. By week's end she'd bought out the lease. The tenants left cheerfully with fists full of cash. And early on a Monday morning, Jesse walked into the empty second-floor flat.

Deliciously dilapidated. The old mantels, moldings, doors all there!

Jesse went to work with a screwdriver and chisel in the front rooms. Louis had described a fire in these parlors in which Lestat had been badly burnt. Well, Jesse would find out.

Within an hour she had uncovered the burnt timbers! And the plasterers—bless them—when they had come to cover up the damage, they had stuffed the holes with old newspapers dated 1862. This fitted with Louis's account perfectly. He'd signed the town house over to Lestat, made plans to leave for Paris, then came the fire during which Louis and Claudia had fled.

Of course Jesse told herself she was still skeptical, but the characters of the book were becoming curiously real. The old black telephone in the hall had been disconnected. She had to go out to call David, which annoyed her. She wanted to tell him everything right now.

But she didn't go out. On the contrary, she merely sat in the parlor for hours, feeling the warm sun on the rough floorboards around her, listening to the creaking of the building. A house of this age is never quiet, not in a humid climate. It feels like a living thing. No ghosts here, not that she could see anyway. Yet she didn't feel alone. On the contrary, there was an embracing warmth. Someone shook her to wake her up suddenly. No, of course not. No one here but her. A clock chiming four . . .

The next day she rented a wallpaper steamer and went to work in the other rooms. She must get down to the original coverings. Patterns could be dated, and besides she was looking for something in particular. But there was a canary singing nearby, possibly in another flat or shop, and the song distracted her. So lovely. Don't forget the canary. The canary will die if you forget it. Again, she fell asleep.

It was well after dark when she awakened. She could hear the nearby music of a harpsichord. For a long time, she'd listened before opening her eyes. Mozart, very fast. Too fast, but what skill. A great rippling riff of notes, a stunning virtuosity. Finally she forced herself to get up and turn on the overhead lights and plug in the steamer again.

The steamer was heavy; the hot water dripped down her arm. In each room she stripped a section of wall to the original plaster, then she moved on. But the droning noise of the thing bothered her. She seemed to hear voices in it—people laughing, talking to one another, someone speaking French in a low urgent whisper, and a child crying—or was it a woman?

She'd turn the damn thing off. Nothing. Just a trick of the noise itself in the empty echoing flat.

She went back to work with no consciousness of time, or that she had not eaten, or that she was getting drowsy. On and on she moved the heavy thing until quite suddenly in the middle bedroom she found what she'd been seeking—a hand-painted mural on a bare plaster wall.

For a moment, she was too excited to move. Then she went to work in a frenzy. Yes, it was the mural of the "magical forest" that Lestat had commissioned for Claudia. And in rapid sweeps of the dripping steamer she uncovered more and more.

"Unicorns and golden birds and laden fruit trees over sparkling streams." It was exactly as Louis had described it. Finally she had laid bare a great portion of the mural running around all four walls. Claudia's room, this, without question. Her head was spinning. She was weak from not eating. She glanced at her watch. One o'clock.

One o'clock! She'd been here half the night. She should go now, immediately! This was the first time in all these years that she'd broken a rule!

Yet she could not bring herself to move. She was so tired, in spite of her excitement. She was sitting against the marble mantel, and the light from the ceiling bulb was so dreary, and her head hurt, too. Yet she kept staring at the gilded birds, the small, wonderfully wrought flowers and trees. The sky was a deep vermilion, yet there was a full moon in it and no sun, and a great drifting spread of tiny stars. Bits of hammered silver still clinging to the stars.

Gradually she noticed a stone wall painted in the background in one corner. There was a castle behind it. How lovely to walk through the forest towards it, to go through the carefully painted wooden gate. Pass into another realm. She heard a song in her head, something she'd all but forgotten, something Maharet used to sing.

Then quite abruptly she saw that the gate was painted over an actual opening in the wall!

She sat forward. She could see the seams in the plaster. Yes, a square opening, which she had not seen, laboring behind the heavy steamer. She knelt down in front of it and touched it. A wooden door. Immediately she took the screwdriver and tried to pry it open. No luck. She worked on one edge and then the other. But she was only scarring the picture to no avail.

She sat back on her heels and studied it. A painted gate covering a wooden door. And there was a worn spot right where the painted handle was. Yes! She reached out and gave the worn spot a little jab. The door sprang open. It was as simple as that.

She lifted her flashlight. A compartment lined in cedar. And there were things there. A small white leather-bound book! A rosary, it looked like, and a doll, a very old porcelain doll.

For a moment she couldn't bring herself to touch these objects. It was like desecrating a tomb. And there was a faint scent there as of perfume. She wasn't dreaming, was she? No, her head hurt too much for this to be a dream. She reached into the compartment, and removed the doll first.

The body was crude by modern standards, yet the wooden limbs were well jointed and formed. The white dress and lavender sash were decaying, falling into bits and pieces. But the porcelain head was lovely, the large blue paperweight eyes perfect, the wig of flowing blond hair still intact.

"Claudia," she whispered.

Her voice made her conscious of the silence. No traffic now at this hour. Only the old boards creaking. And the soft soothing flicker of an oil lamp on a nearby table. And then that harpsichord from somewhere, someone playing Chopin now, the Minute Waltz, with the same dazzling skill she'd heard before. She sat still, looking down at the doll in her lap. She wanted to brush its hair, fix its sash.

The climactic events of *Interview with the Vampire* came back to her—Claudia destroyed in Paris. Claudia caught by the deadly light of the rising sun in a brick-lined airshaft from which she couldn't escape. Jesse felt a dull shock, and the rapid silent beat of her heart against her throat. Claudia gone, while the others continued. Lestat, Louis, Armand. . . .

Then with a start, she realized she was looking at the other things inside the compartment. She reached for the book.

A diary! The pages were fragile, spotted. But the old-fashioned sepia script was still readable, especially now that the oil lamps were all lighted, and the room had a cozy brightness to it. She could translate the French effortlessly. The first entry was September 21, 1836:

This is my birthday present from Louis. Use as I like, he tells me. But perhaps I should like to copy into it those occasional poems which strike my fancy, and read these to him now and then?

I do not understand entirely what is meant by birthday. Was I born into this world on the 21st of September or was it on that day that I departed all things human to become this?

My gentlemen parents are forever reluctant to illuminate such simple matters. One would think it bad taste to dwell on such subjects. Louis looks puzzled, then miserable, before he returns to the evening paper. And Lestat, he smiles and plays a little Mozart for me, then answers with a shrug: "It was the day you were born *to us.*"

Of course, he gave me a doll as usual, the replica of me, which as always wears a duplicate of my newest dress. To France he sends for these dolls, he wants me to know. And what should I do with it? Play with it as if I were really a child?

"Is there a message here, my beloved father?" I asked him this evening. "That I shall be a doll forever myself?" He has given me thirty such dolls over the years if recollection serves me. And recollection never does anything else. Each doll has been exactly like the rest. They would crowd me out of my bedroom if I kept them. But I do not keep them. I burn them, sooner or later. I smash their china faces with the poker. I watch the fire eat their hair. I can't say that I like doing this. After all, the dolls are beautiful. And they do resemble me. Yet, it becomes the appropriate gesture. The doll expects it. So do I.

And now he has brought me another, and he stands in my doorway staring at me afterwards, as if my question cut him. And the expression on his face is so dark suddenly, I think, this cannot be my Lestat.

I wish that I could hate him. I wish that I could hate them both. But they defeat me not with their strength but with their weakness. They are so loving! And so pleasing to look at. Mon Dieu, how the women go after them!

As he stood there watching me, watching me examine this doll he had given me, I asked him sharply:

"Do you like what you see?"

"You don't want them anymore, do you?" he whispered.

"Would you want them," I asked, "if you were me?"

The expression on his face grew even darker. Never have I seen him the way he looked. A scorching heat came into his face, and it seemed he blinked to clear his vision. His perfect vision. He left me and went into the parlor. I went after him. In truth, I couldn't bear to see him the way he was, yet I pursued him. "Would you like them," I asked, "if you were me?"

He stared at me as if I frightened him, and he a man of six feet and I a child no more than half that, at best.

"Am I beautiful to you?" I demanded.

He went past me down the hall, out the back door. But I caught up with him. I held tight to his sleeve as he stood at the top of the stairs. "Answer me!" I said to him. "Look at me. What do you see?"

He was in a dreadful state. I thought he'd pull away, laugh, flash his usual brimming colors. But instead he dropped to his knees before me and took hold of both my arms. He kissed me roughly on the mouth. "I love you," he whispered. "I love you!" As if it were a curse he laid on me, and then he spoke this poetry to me:

> *Cover her face;*
> *mine eyes dazzle;*
> *she died young.*

Webster it is, I am almost certain. One of those plays Lestat so loves. I wonder . . . will Louis be pleased by this little poem? I cannot imagine why not. It is small but very pretty.

Jesse closed the book gently. Her hand was trembling. She lifted the doll and held it against her breast, her body rocking slightly as she sat back against the painted wall.

"Claudia," she whispered.

Her head throbbed, but it didn't matter. The light of the oil lamps was so soothing, so different from the harsh electric bulb. She sat still, caressing the doll with her fingers almost in the manner of a blind woman, feeling its soft silken hair, its stiff starched little dress. The clock chimed again, loudly, each somber note echoing through the room. She must not faint here. She must get up somehow. She must take the little book and the doll and the rosary and leave.

The empty windows were like mirrors with the night behind them. Rules broken. Call David, yes, call David now. But the phone was ringing. At this hour, imagine. The phone ringing. And David didn't have any number for this flat because the phone. . . . She tried to ignore it, but it went on and on ringing. All right, answer it!

She kissed the doll's forehead. "Be right back, my darling," she whispered.

Where was the damn phone in this flat anyway? In the niche in the hallway, of course. She had almost reached it when she saw the wire with the frayed end, curled around it. It wasn't connected. She could see it wasn't connected. Yet it was ringing, she could hear it, and it was no auditory hallucination, the thing was giving one shrill pulse after another! And the oil lamps! My God, there were no oil lamps in this flat!

All right, you've seen things like this before. Don't panic, for the love of God. Think! What should you do? But she was about to scream. The phone would not stop ringing! If you panic, you will lose control utterly. You must turn off these lamps, stop this phone! But the lamps can't be real. And the living room at the end of the hall—the furniture's not real! The flicker of the fire, not real! And the person moving in there, who is it, a man? Don't look up at him! She reached out and shoved the phone out of the niche so that it fell to the floor. The receiver rolled on its back. Tiny and thin, a woman's voice came out of it.

"Jesse?"

In blind terror, she ran back to the bedroom, stumbling over the leg of a chair, falling against the starched drapery of a four-poster bed. Not real. Not there. Get the doll, the book, the rosary! Stuffing them in her canvas bag, she climbed to her feet and ran out of the flat to the back stairway. She almost fell as her feet hit the slippery iron. The garden, the fountain— But you know there's nothing there but weeds. There was a wrought-iron gate blocking her path. Illusion. Go through it! Run!

It was the proverbial nightmare and she was caught in it, the sounds of horses and carriages thudding in her ears as she ran down the cobblestone pavement. Each clumsy gesture stretched over eternity, her hands struggling to get the car keys, to get the door open, and then the car refusing to start.

By the time she reached the edge of the French Quarter, she was sobbing and her body was drenched with sweat. On she drove through the shabby garish downtown streets towards the freeway. Blocked at the on-ramp, she turned her head. Back seat empty. OK, they didn't follow. And the canvas bag was in her lap; she could feel the hard porcelain head of the doll against her breast. She floored it to Baton Rouge.

She was sick by the time she reached the hotel. She could barely walk to the desk. An aspirin, a thermometer. Please help me to the elevator.

When she woke up eight hours later, it was noon. The canvas bag was still in her arms. Her temperature was 104. She called David, but the connection was dreadful. He called her back; it was still no good. Nevertheless she tried to make herself understood. The diary, it was Claudia's, absolutely, it confirmed everything! And the phone, it wasn't connected, yet she heard the woman's voice! The oil lamps, they'd been burning when she ran out of the flat. The flat had been filled with furniture; there'd been fires in the grates. Could they burn down the flat, these lamps and fires? David must do something! And he was answering her, but she could barely hear him. She had the bag, she told him, he must not worry.

It was dark when she opened her eyes. The pain in her head had woken her up. The digital clock on the dresser said ten thirty. Thirst, terrible thirst, and the glass by the bed was empty. *Someone else was in the room.*

She turned over on her back. Light through the thin white curtains. Yes, there. A child, a little girl. She was sitting in the chair against the wall.

Jesse could just see the outline clearly—the long yellow hair, the puff-sleeved dress, the dangling legs that didn't touch the floor. She tried to focus. Child . . . not possible. Apparition. No. Something occupying space. Something malevolent. Menace— And the child was looking at her.

Claudia.

She scrambled out of the bed, half falling, the bag in her arms still as she backed up against the wall. The little girl got up. There was the clear sound of her feet on the carpet. The sense of menace seemed to grow stronger. The child moved into the light from the window as she came towards Jesse, and the light struck her blue eyes, her rounded cheeks, her soft naked little arms.

Jesse screamed. Clutching the bag against her, she rushed blindly in the direction of the door. She clawed at the lock and chain, afraid to look over her shoulder. The screams were coming out of her uncontrollably. Someone was calling from the other side, and finally she had the door open and she was stumbling out into the hallway.

People surrounded her; but they couldn't stop her from getting away from the room. But then someone was helping her up because apparently she'd fallen again. Someone else had gotten a chair. She cried, trying to be quiet, yet unable to stop it, and she held the bag with the doll and the diary in both hands.

When the ambulance arrived, she refused to let them take the bag away from her. In the hospital they gave her antibiotics, sedatives, enough dope to drive anyone to insanity. She lay curled up like a child in the bed with the bag beside her under the covers. If the nurse so much as touched it, Jesse woke at once.

When Aaron Lightner arrived two days later, she gave it to him. She was still sick when she got on the plane for London. The bag was in his lap, and he was so good to her, calming her, caring for her, as she slept on and off on the long flight home. It was only just before they landed that she realized her bracelet was gone, her beautiful silver bracelet. She'd cried softly with her eyes closed. Mael's bracelet gone.

THEY pulled her off the assignment.

She knew even before they told her. She was too young for this work, they said, too inexperienced. It had been their mistake, sending her. It was simply too dangerous for her to continue. Of course what she had done was of "immense value." And the haunting, it had been one of unusual power. The spirit of a dead vampire? Entirely possible. And the ringing phone, well, there were many reports of such things—entities used various means to "communicate" or frighten. Best to rest now, put it out of her mind. Others would continue the investigation.

As for the diary, it included only a few more entries, nothing more significant than what she herself had read. The psychometrics who had examined the rosary and the doll learned nothing. These things would be stored with utmost care. But Jesse really must remove her mind from all this immediately.

Jesse argued. She begged to go back. She threw a scene of sorts, finally. But it was like talking to the Vatican. Some day, ten years from now, maybe twenty, she could enter this particular field again. No one was ruling out such a possibility, but for the present the answer was no. Jesse was to rest, get better, forget what had taken place.

Forget what had taken place. . . .

She was sick for weeks. She wore white flannel gowns all day long and drank endless cups of hot tea. She sat in the window seat of her room. She looked out on the soft deep greenery of the park, at the heavy old oak trees.

She watched the cars come and go, tiny bits of soundless color moving on the distant gravel road. Lovely here, such stillness. They brought her delicious things to eat, to drink. David came and talked softly to her of anything but the vampires. Aaron filled her room with flowers. Others came.

She talked little, or not at all. She could not explain to them how deeply this hurt her, how it reminded her of the long ago summer when she'd been pushed away from other secrets, other mysteries, other documents in vaults. It was the same old story. She'd glimpsed something of inestimable importance, only to have it locked away.

And now she would never understand what she'd seen or experienced. She must remain here in silence with her regrets. Why hadn't she picked up that phone, spoken into it, listened to the voice on the other end?

And the child, what had the spirit of the child wanted! Was it the diary or the doll! No, Jesse had been meant to find them and remove them! And yet she had turned away from the spirit of the child! She who had addressed so many nameless entities, who had stood bravely in darkened rooms talking to weak flickering things when others fled in panic. She who comforted others with the old assurance: these beings, whatever they are, cannot do us harm!

One more chance, she pleaded. She went over everything that had happened. She must return to that New Orleans flat. David and Aaron were silent. Then David came to her and put his arm around her.

"Jesse, my darling," he said. "We love you. But in this area above all others, one simply does not break the rules."

At night she dreamed of Claudia. Once she woke at four o'clock and went to the window and looked out over the park straining to see past the dim lights from the lower windows. There was a child out there, a tiny figure beneath the trees, in a red cloak and hood, a child looking up at her. She had run down the stairs, only to find herself stranded finally on the empty wet grass with the cold gray morning coming.

IN THE spring they sent her to New Delhi.

She was to document evidence of reincarnation, reports from little children in India that they remembered former lives. There had been much promising work done in this field by a Dr. Ian Stevenson. And Jesse was to undertake an independent study on behalf of the Talamasca which might produce equally fruitful results.

Two elder members of the order met her in Delhi. They made her right at home in the old British mansion where they lived. She grew to love the work; and after the initial shocks and minor discomforts, she grew to love India as well. By the end of the year she was happy—and useful—again.

And something else happened, a rather small thing, yet it seemed a good omen. In a pocket of her old suitcase—the one Maharet had sent her years ago—she'd found Mael's silver bracelet.

Yes, happy she had been.

But she did not forget what had happened. There were nights when she would remember so vividly the image of Claudia that she would get up and turn on every light in the room. At other times she thought she saw around her in the city streets strange white-faced beings very like the characters in *Interview with the Vampire*. She felt she was being watched.

Because she could not tell Maharet about this strange adventure, her letters became even more hurried and superficial. Yet Maharet was as faithful as ever. When members of the family came to Delhi, they visited Jesse. They tried to keep her in the fold. They sent her news of weddings, births, funerals. They begged her to visit during the holidays. Matthew and Maria wrote from America, begging Jesse to come home soon. They missed her.

JESSE spent four happy years in India. She documented over three hundred individual cases which included startling evidence of reincarnation. She worked with some of the finest psychic investigators she had ever known. And she found her work continuously rewarding, almost comforting. Very unlike the chasing of haunts which she had done in her early years.

In the fall of her fifth year, she finally yielded to Matthew and Maria. She would come home to the States for a four-week visit. They were overjoyed.

The reunion meant more to Jesse than she had ever thought it would. She loved being back in the old New York apartment. She loved the late night dinners with her adopted parents. They didn't question her about her work. Left alone during the day, she called old college friends for lunch or took long solitary walks through the bustling urban landscape of all her childhood hopes and dreams and griefs.

Two weeks after her return, Jesse saw *The Vampire Lestat* in the window of a bookstore. For a moment, she thought she'd made a mistake. Not possible. But there it was. The bookstore clerk told her of the record album by the same name, and the upcoming San Francisco concert. Jesse bought a ticket on the way home at the record store where she purchased the album.

All day Jesse lay alone in her room reading the book. It was as if the nightmare of *Interview with the Vampire* had returned and, once again, she could not get out of it. Yet she was strangely compelled by every word. *Yes, real, all of you.* And how the tale twisted and turned as it moved back in time to the Roman coven of Santino, to the island refuge of Marius, and to the Druid grove of Mael. And finally to Those Who Must Be Kept, alive yet hard and white as marble.

Ah, yes, she had touched that stone! She had looked into Mael's eyes; she had felt the clasp of Santino's hand. She had seen the painting done by Marius in the vault of the Talamasca!

When she closed her eyes to sleep, she saw Maharet on the balcony of the Sonoma compound. The moon was high above the tips of the redwoods. And the warm night seemed unaccountably full of promise and danger. Eric and Mael were there. So were others whom she'd never seen except in Lestat's pages. All of the same tribe; eyes incandescent, shimmering hair, skin a poreless shining substance. On her silver bracelet she had traced a thousand times the old Celtic symbols of gods and goddesses to whom the Druids spoke in woodland groves like that to which Marius had once been taken prisoner. How many links did she require between these esoteric fictions and the unforgettable summer?

One more, without question. The Vampire Lestat himself—in San Francisco, where she would see him and touch him—that would be the final link. She would know then, in that physical moment, the answer to everything.

The clock ticked. Her loyalty to the Talamasca was dying in the warm quiet. She could tell them not a word of it. And such a tragedy it was, when they would have cared so much and so selflessly; they would have doubted none of it.

The lost afternoon. She was there again. Going down into Maharet's cellar by the spiral stairway. Could she not push back the door? Look. See what you saw then. Something not so horrible at first glance—merely those she knew and loved, asleep in the dark, asleep. But Mael lies on the cold floor as if dead and Maharet sits against the wall, upright like a statue. Her eyes are open!

She awoke with a start, her face flushed, the room cold and dim around her. "Miriam," she said aloud. Gradually the panic subsided. She had drawn closer, so afraid. She had touched Maharet. Cold, petrified. And Mael dead! The rest was darkness.

New York. She lay on the bed with the book in her hand. And Miriam didn't come to her. Slowly, she climbed to her feet and walked across the bedroom to the window.

There, opposite in the dirty afternoon gloom, stood the high narrow phantom town house of Stanford White. She stared until the bulky image gradually faded.

From the album cover propped on the dresser the Vampire Lestat smiled at her.

She closed her eyes. She envisioned the tragic pair of Those Who Must Be Kept. Indestructible King and Queen on their Egyptian throne, to whom the Vampire Lestat sang his hymns out of the radios and the juke-boxes and from the little tapes people carried with them. She saw Maharet's white face glowing in the shadows. Alabaster. The stone that is always full of light.

Dusk falling, suddenly as it does in the late fall, the dull afternoon fading into the sharp brightness of evening. Traffic roared through the crowded street, echoing up the sides of the buildings. Did ever traffic sound so loud as in the streets of New York? She leaned her forehead against the glass. Stanford White's house was visible in the corner of her eye. There were figures moving inside it.

JESSE left New York the next afternoon, in Matt's old roadster. She paid him for the car in spite of his arguments. She knew she'd never bring it back. Then she embraced her parents and, as casually as she could, she told them all the simple heartfelt things she'd always wanted them to know.

That morning, she had sent an express letter to Maharet, along with the two "vampire" novels. She explained that she had left the Talamasca, she was going to the Vampire Lestat's concert out west, and she wanted to stop at the Sonoma compound. She had to see Lestat, it was of crucial importance. Would her old key fit the lock of the Sonoma house? Would Maharet allow her to stop there?

It was the first night in Pittsburgh that she dreamed of the twins. She saw the two women kneeling before the altar. She saw the cooked body ready to be devoured. She saw one twin lift the plate with the heart; the other the plate with the brain. Then the soldiers, the sacrilege.

By the time she reached Salt Lake City she had dreamed of the twins three times. She had seen them raped in a hazy and terrifying scene. She had seen a baby born to one of the sisters. She had seen the baby hidden when the twins were again hunted down and taken prisoner. Had they been killed? She could not tell. The red hair. If only she could see their faces, their eyes! The red hair tormented her.

Only when she called David from a roadside pay phone did she learn that others had had these dreams—psychics and mediums the world over. Again and again the connection had been made to the Vampire Lestat. David told Jesse to come home immediately.

Jesse tried to explain gently. She was going to the concert to see Lestat for herself. She had to. There was more to tell, but it was too late now. David must try to forgive her.

"You will not do this, Jessica," David said. "What is happening is no simple matter for records and archives. You must come back, Jessica. The truth is, you are needed here. You are needed desperately. It's unthinkable that you should attempt this 'sighting' on your own. Jesse, listen to what I'm telling you."

"I can't come back, David. I've always loved you. Loved you all. But tell me. It's the last question I'll ever ask you. How can you not come yourself?"

"Jesse, you're not listening to me."

"David, the truth. Tell me the truth. Have you ever really believed in them? Or has it always been a question of artifacts and files and paintings in vaults, things you can see and touch! You know what I'm saying, David. Think of the Catholic priest, when he speaks the words of consecration at Mass. Does he really believe Christ is on the altar? Or is it just a matter of chalices and sacramental wine and the choir singing?"

Oh, what a liar she had been to keep so much from him yet press him so hard. But his answer had not disappointed her.

"Jesse, you've got it wrong. I know what these creatures are. I've always known. There's never been the slightest doubt with me. And on account of that, no power on earth could induce me to attend this concert. It is you who can't accept the truth. You'll have to see it to believe it! Jesse, the danger's real. Lestat is exactly what he professes to be, and there will be others there, even more dangerous, others who may spot you for what you are and try to hurt you. Realize this and do as I tell you. Come home now."

What a raw and painful moment. He was striving to reach her, and she was only telling him farewell. He had said other things, that he would tell her "the whole story," that he would open the files to her, that she was needed on this very matter by them all.

But her mind had been drifting. She couldn't tell him her "whole story," that was the sorrow. She'd been drowsy again, the dream threatening as she hung up the phone. She'd seen the plates, the body on the altar. Their mother. Yes, their mother. Time to sleep. The dream wants in. And then go on.

. . .

HIGHWAY 101. Seven thirty-five p.m. Twenty-five minutes until the concert.

She had just come through the mountain pass on the Waldo Grade and there was the old miracle—the great crowded skyline of San Francisco tumbling over the hills, far beyond the black glaze of the water. The towers of the Golden Gate loomed ahead of her, the ice cold wind off the Bay freezing her naked hands as she gripped the steering wheel.

Would the Vampire Lestat be on time? It made her laugh to think of an immortal creature having to be *on time*. Well, she would be on time; the journey was almost ended.

All grief was gone now, for David and Aaron and those she'd loved. There was no grief either for the Great Family. Only the gratitude for all of it. Yet maybe David was right. Perhaps she had not accepted the cold frightening truth of the matter, but had merely slipped into the realm of memories and ghosts, of pale creatures who were the proper stuff of dreams and madness.

She was walking towards the phantom town house of Stanford White, and it didn't matter now who lived there. She would be welcome. They had been trying to tell her that ever since she could remember.

PART II

ALL HALLOW'S EVE

Very little is
more worth our time
than understanding
the talent of Substance.
. . .
A bee, a living bee,
at the windowglass, trying to get out, doomed,
it can't understand.

STAN RICE
Untitled Poem
from
Pig's Progress (1976)

Daniel

LONG curving lobby; the crowd was like liquid sloshing against the colorless walls. Teenagers in Halloween costume poured through the front doors; lines were forming to purchase yellow wigs, black satin capes—"Fang teeth, fifty cents!"—glossy programs. Whiteface everywhere he looked. Painted eyes and mouths. And here and there bands of men and women carefully done up in authentic nineteenth-century clothes, their makeup and coiffed hair exquisite.

A velvet-clad woman tossed a great shower of dead rosebuds into the air above her head. Painted blood flowed down her ashen cheeks. Laughter.

He could smell the greasepaint, and the beer, so alien now to his senses: rotten. The hearts beating all around him made a low, delicious thunder against the tender tympana of his ears.

He must have laughed out loud, because he felt the sharp pinch of Armand's fingers on his arm. "Daniel!"

"Sorry, boss," he whispered. Nobody was paying a damn bit of attention anyway; every mortal within sight was disguised; and who were Armand and Daniel but two pale nondescript young men in the press, black sweaters, jeans, hair partially hidden under sailor's caps of blue wool, eyes behind dark glasses. "So what's the big deal? I can't laugh out loud, especially now that everything is so funny?"

Armand was distracted; listening again. Daniel couldn't get it through his head to be afraid. He had what he wanted now. None of you my brothers and sisters!

Armand had said to him earlier, "You take a lot of teaching." That was during the hunt, the seduction, the kill, the flood of blood through his greedy heart. But he had become a natural at being unnatural, hadn't he, after the clumsy anguish of the first murder, the one that had taken him from shuddering guilt to ecstasy within seconds. Life by the mouthful. He'd woken up thirsting.

And thirty minutes ago, they'd taken two exquisite little vagabonds in the ruins of a derelict school by the park where the kids lived in boarded-up rooms with sleeping bags and rags and little cans of Sterno to cook the food they stole from the Haight-Ashbury dumpsters. No protests this time around. No, just the thirsting and the ever increasing sense of the perfection and the inevitability of it, the preternatural memory of the taste faultless. Hurry. Yet there had been such an art to it with Armand, none of the rush of the night before when time had been the crucial element.

Armand had stood quietly outside the building, scanning it, waiting for "those who wanted to die"; that was the way he liked to do it; you called to them silently and they came out. And the death had a serenity to it. He'd tried to show that trick to Louis long ago, he'd said, but Louis had found it distasteful.

And sure enough the denim-clad cherubs had come wandering through the side door, as if hypnotized by the music of the Pied Piper. "Yes, you came, we knew you'd come. . . ." Dull flat voices welcoming them as they were led up the stairs and into a parlor made out of army blankets on ropes. To die in this garbage in the sweep of the passing headlights through the cracks in the plywood.

Hot dirty little arms around Daniel's neck; reek of hashish in her hair; he could scarcely stand it, the dance, her hips against him, then driving his fangs into the flesh. "You love me, you know you do," she'd said. And he'd answered yes with a clear conscience. Was it going to be this good forever? He'd clasped her chin with his hand, underneath, pushing her head back, and then, the death like a doubled fist going down his throat, to his gut, the heat spreading, flooding his loins and his brain.

He'd let her drop. Too much and not enough. He'd clawed at the wall for a moment thinking it must be flesh and blood, too, and were it flesh and blood it could be his. Then such a shock to know he wasn't hungry anymore. He was filled and complete and the night waited, like something made out of pure light, and the other one was dead, folded up like a baby in sleep on the grimy floor, and Armand, glowing in the dark, just watching.

It was getting rid of the bodies after that had been hard. Last night that had been done out of his sight, as he wept. Beginner's luck. This time Armand said "no trace means no trace." So they'd gone down together to bury them deep beneath the basement floor in the old furnace room, carefully putting the paving stones back in place. Lots of work even with such strength. So loathsome to touch the corpse like that. Only for a second did it flicker in his mind: *who were they?* Two fallen beings in a pit. No more *now,* no destiny. And the waif last night? Was somebody looking for her somewhere? He'd been crying suddenly. He'd heard it, then reached up and touched the tears coming out of his eyes.

"What do you think this is?" Armand had demanded, making him help with the paving stones. "A penny dreadful novel? You don't feed if you can't cover it up."

The building had been crawling with gentle humans who noticed not a thing as they'd stolen the clothes they now wore, uniforms of the young, and left by a broken door into an alley. Not my brothers and sisters anymore. The woods have always been filled with these soft doe-eyed things, with hearts beating for the arrow, the bullet, the lance. And now at last I reveal my secret identity: I have always been the huntsman.

"Is it all right, the way I am now?" he'd asked Armand. "Are you happy?" Haight Street, seven thirty-five. Bumper-to-bumper traffic, junkies screaming on the corner. Why didn't they just go on to the concert? Doors open already. He couldn't bear the anticipation.

But the coven house was near, Armand had explained, big tumble-down mansion one block from the park, and some of them were still hanging back in there plotting Lestat's ruin. Armand wanted to pass close, just for a moment, know what was going on.

"Looking for someone?" Daniel had asked. "Answer me, are you pleased with me or not?"

What had he seen in Armand's face? A sudden flare of humor, lust? Armand had hurried him along the dirty stained pavements, past the bars, the cafés, the stores crowded with stinking old clothes, the fancy clubs with their gilded letters on the greasy plate glass and overhead fans stirring the fumes with gilded wooden blades, while the potted ferns died a slow death in the heat and the semidarkness. Past the first little children—"Trick or treat!"—in their taffeta and glitter costumes.

Armand had stopped, at once surrounded by tiny upturned faces covered in store-bought masks, plastic spooks, ghouls, witches; a lovely warm light had filled his brown eyes; with both hands he'd dropped shiny silver dollars in their little candy sacks, then taken Daniel by the arm and led him on.

"I love it well enough the way you turned out," he had whispered with a sudden irrepressible smile, the warmth still there. "You're my firstborn," he'd said. Was there a catch in his throat, a sudden glancing from right to left as if he'd found himself cornered? Back to the business at hand. "Be patient. I am being afraid for us both, remember?"

Oh, we shall go to the stars together! Nothing can stop us. All the ghosts running through these streets are mortal!

Then the coven house had blown up.

He'd heard the blast before he saw it—and a sudden rolling plume of flame and smoke, accompanied by a shrill sound he would never before have detected: preternatural screams like silver paper curling in the heat. Sudden scatter of shaggy-haired humans running to see the blaze.

Armand had shoved Daniel off the street, into the stagnant air of a narrow liquor store. Bilious glare; sweat and reek of tobacco; mortals, oblivious to the nearby conflagration, reading the big glossy girlie magazines. Armand had pushed him to the very rear of the tiny corridor. Old lady buying tiny carton of milk and two cans of cat food out of the icebox. No way out of here.

But how could one hide from the thing that was passing over, from the deafening sound that mortals could not even hear? He'd lifted his hands to his ears, but that was foolish, useless. Death out there in alleyways. Things like him running through the debris of backyards, caught, burnt in their tracks. He saw it in sputtering flashes. Then nothing. Ringing silence. The clanging bells and squealing tires of the mortal world.

Yet he'd been too enthralled still to be afraid. Every second was eternal, the frost on the icebox door beautiful. The old lady with the milk in her hand, eyes like two small cobalt stones.

Armand's face had gone blank beneath the mask of his dark glasses, hands slipped into his tight pants pockets. The tiny bell on the door jangled as a young man entered, bought a single bottle of German beer, and went out.

"It's over, isn't it?"

"For now," Armand had answered.

Not until they'd gotten in the cab did he say more.

"It knew we were there; it heard us."

"Then why didn't it—?"

"I don't know. I only know it knew we were there. It knew before we found shelter."

AND now, push and shove inside the hall, and he loved it, the crowd carrying them closer and closer to the inner doors. He could not even raise his arms, so tight was the press; yet young men and women elbowed past him, buffeted him with delicious shocks; he laughed again as he saw the life-sized posters of Lestat plastered to the walls.

He felt Armand's fingers against his back; he felt a subtle change in Armand's whole body. A red-haired woman up ahead had turned around and was facing them as she was moved along towards the open door.

A soft warm shock passed through Daniel. "Armand, the red hair." So like the twins in the dream! It seemed her green eyes locked on him as he said, "Armand, the twins!"

Then her face vanished as she turned away again and disappeared inside the hall.

"No," Armand whispered. Small shake of his head. He was in a silent fury, Daniel could feel it. He had the rigid glassy look he always got when profoundly offended. "Talamasca," he whispered, with a faint uncharacteristic sneer.

"Talamasca." The word struck Daniel suddenly as beautiful. Talamasca. He broke it down from the Latin, understood its parts. Somewhere out of his memory bank it came: animal mask. Old word for witch or shaman.

"But what does it really mean?" he asked.

"It means Lestat is a fool," Armand said. Flicker of deep pain in his eyes. "But it makes no difference now."

Khayman

KHAYMAN watched from the archway as the Vampire Lestat's car entered the gates of the parking lot. Almost invisible Khayman was, even in the stylish denim coat and pants he'd stolen earlier from a shop manikin. He didn't need the silver glasses that covered his eyes. His glowing skin didn't matter. Not when everywhere he looked he saw masks and paint, glitter and gauze and sequined costumes.

He moved closer to Lestat, as if swimming through the wriggling bodies of the youngsters who mobbed the car. At last he glimpsed the creature's blond hair, and then his violet blue eyes as he smiled and blew kisses to his adorers. Such charm the devil had. He drove the car himself, gunning the motor and forcing the bumper against these tender little humans even as he flirted, winked, seduced, as if he and his foot on the gas pedal weren't connected to each other.

Exhilaration. Triumph. That's what Lestat felt and knew at this moment. And even his reticent companion, Louis, the dark-haired one in the car beside him, staring timidly at the screaming children as if they were birds of paradise, didn't understand what was truly happening.

Neither knew that the Queen had waked. Neither knew the dreams of the twins. Their ignorance was astonishing. And their young minds were so easy to scan. Apparently the Vampire Lestat, who had hidden himself quite well until this night, was now prepared to do battle with everyone. He wore his thoughts and intentions like a badge of honor.

"Hunt us down!" That's what he said aloud to his fans, though they didn't hear. "Kill us. We're evil. We're bad. It's perfectly fine to cheer and sing with us now. But when you catch on, well, then the serious business will begin. And you'll remember that I never lied to you."

For one instant his eyes and Khayman's eyes met. *I want to be good! I would die for that!* But there was no recognition of who or what received this message.

Louis, the watcher, the patient one, was there on account of love pure and simple. The two had found each other only last night, and theirs had been an extraordinary reunion. Louis would go where Lestat led him. Louis would perish if Lestat perished. But their fears and hopes for this night were heartbreakingly human.

They did not even guess that the Queen's wrath was close at hand, that she'd burnt the San Francisco coven house within the hour. Or that the infamous vampire tavern on Castro Street was burning now, as the Queen hunted down those fleeing from it.

But then the many blood drinkers scattered throughout this crowd did not know these simple facts either. They were too young to hear the warnings of the old, to hear the screams of the doomed as they perished. The dreams of the twins had only confused them. From various points, they glared at Lestat, overcome with hatred or religious fervor. They would destroy him or make of him a god. They did not guess at the danger that awaited them.

But what of the twins themselves? What was the meaning of the dreams?

Khayman watched the car move on, forcing its way towards the back of the auditorium. He looked up at the stars overhead, the tiny pinpricks of light behind the mist that hung over the city. He thought he could feel the closeness of his old sovereign.

He turned back towards the auditorium and made his way carefully through the press. To forget his strength in such a crowd as this would have been disaster. He would bruise flesh and break bones without even feeling it.

He took one last look at the sky, and then he went inside, easily befuddling the ticket taker as he went through the little turnstile and towards the nearest stairway.

The auditorium was almost filled. He looked about himself thoughtfully, savoring the moment somewhat as he savored everything. The hall itself was nothing, a shell of a place to hold light and sound—utterly modern and unredeemably ugly.

But the mortals, how pretty they were, glistering with health, their pockets full of gold, sound bodies everywhere, in which no organ had been eaten by the worms of disease, no bone ever broken.

In fact the sanitized well-being of this entire city rather amazed Khayman. True, he'd seen wealth in Europe such as he could never have imagined, but nothing equaled the flawless surface of this small and over-populated place, even to the San Francisco peasantry, whose tiny stucco cottages were choked with luxuries of every description. Driveways here were jammed with handsome automobiles. Paupers drew their money from bank machines with magic plastic cards. No slums anywhere. Great towers the city had, and fabulous hostelries; mansions in profusion; yet girded as it was by sea and mountains and the glittering waters of the Bay, it seemed not so much a capital as a resort, an escape from the world's greater pain and ugliness.

No wonder Lestat had chosen this place to throw down the gauntlet. In the main, these pampered children were good. Deprivation had never wounded or weakened them. They might prove perfect combatants for real evil. That is, when they came to realize that the symbol and the thing were one and the same. Wake up and smell the blood, young ones.

But would there be time for that now?

Lestat's great scheme, whatever it truly was, might be stillborn; for surely the Queen had a scheme of her own, and Lestat knew nothing of it.

Khayman made his way now to the top of the hall. To the very last row of wooden seats where he had been earlier. He settled comfortably in the same spot, pushing aside the two "vampire books," which still lay on the floor, unnoticed.

Earlier, he had devoured the texts—Louis's testament: "Behold, the void." And Lestat's history: "And this and this and this, and it means nothing." They had clarified for him many things. And what Khayman had divined of Lestat's intentions had been confirmed completely. But of the mystery of the twins, of course, the book told nothing.

And as for the Queen's true intent, that continued to baffle him.

She had slain hundreds of blood drinkers the world over, yet left others unharmed.

Even now, Marius lived. In destroying her shrine, she had punished him but not killed him, which would have been simple. He called to the older ones from his prison of ice, warning, begging for assistance. And effortlessly, Khayman sensed two immortals moving to answer Marius's call, though one, Marius's own child, could not even hear it. Pandora was that one's name; she was a lone one, a strong one. The other, called Santino, did not have her power, but he could hear Marius's voice, as he struggled to keep pace with her.

Without doubt the Queen could have struck them down had she chosen to do it. Yet on and on they moved, clearly visible, clearly audible, yet unmolested.

How did the Queen make such choices? Surely there were those in this very hall whom she had spared for some purpose. . . .

Daniel

THEY had reached the doors, and now had to push the last few feet down a narrow ramp into the giant open oval of the main floor.

The crowd loosened, like marbles rolling in all directions.

Daniel moved towards the center, his fingers hooked around Armand's belt so as not to lose him, his eyes roaming over the horseshoe-shaped theater, the high banks of seats rising to the ceiling. Mortals everywhere swarmed the cement stairs, or hung over iron railings, or flowed into the milling crowd around him.

A blur it was suddenly, the noise of it like the low grind of a giant machine. But then in the moment of deliberately distorted vision, he saw *the others.* He saw the simple, inescapable difference between the living and the dead. Beings like himself in every direction, concealed in the mortal forest, yet shining like the eyes of an owl in the light of the moon. No paint or dark glasses or shapeless hats or hooded capes could ever conceivably hide them from each other. And it wasn't merely the unearthly sheen to their faces or hands. It was the slow, lissome grace of their movements, as if they were more spirit than flesh.

Ah, my brothers and sisters, at last!

But it was hatred he felt around him. A rather dishonest hatred! They loved Lestat and condemned him simultaneously. They loved the very act of hating, punishing. Suddenly, he caught the eye of a powerful hulking creature with greasy black hair who bared his fangs in an ugly flash and then revealed the plan in stunning completeness. Beyond the prying eyes of mortals, they would hack Lestat's limbs from his body; they would sever his head; then the remains would be burnt on a pyre by the sea. The end of the monster and his legend. *Are you with us or against us?*

Daniel laughed out loud. "You'll never kill him," Daniel said. Yet he gaped as he glimpsed the sharpened scythe the creature held against his chest inside his coat. Then the beast turned and vanished. Daniel gazed upwards through the smoky light. *One of them now. Know all their secrets!* He felt giddy, on the verge of madness.

Armand's hand closed on his shoulder. They had come to the very center of the main floor. The crowd was getting denser by the second. Pretty girls in black silk gowns shoved and pushed against the crude bikers in their worn black leather. Soft feathers brushed his cheek; he saw a red devil with giant horns; a bony skeleton face topped with golden curls and pearl combs. Random cries rose in the bluish gloom. The bikers howled like wolves; someone shouted "Lestat" in a deafening voice, and others took up the call instantly.

Armand again had the lost expression, the expression that belonged to deep concentration, as if what he saw before him meant nothing at all.

"Thirty perhaps," he whispered in Daniel's ear, "no more than that, and one or two so old they could destroy the rest of us in an instant."

"Where, tell me where?"

"Listen," Armand said. "And see for yourself. There is no hiding from them."

Khayman

AHARET'S *child. Jessica.* The thought caught Khayman off guard. *Protect Maharet's child. Somehow escape from here.*

He roused himself, senses sharpened. He'd been listening to Marius again, Marius trying to reach the young untuned ears of the Vampire Lestat, who preened backstage, before a broken mirror. What could this mean, Maharet's child, Jessica, and when the thoughts pertained, without doubt, to a mortal woman?

It came again, the unexpected communication of some strong yet unveiled mind: *Take care of Jesse. Somehow stop the Mother . . . .* But there were no words really—it was no more than a shining glimpse into another's soul, a sparkling overflow.

Khayman's eyes moved slowly over the balconies opposite, over the swarming main floor. Far away in some remote corner of the city, an old one wandered, full of fear of the Queen yet longing to look upon her face. He had come here to die, but to know her face in the final instant.

Khayman closed his eyes to shut this out.

Then he heard it again suddenly. *Jessica, my Jessica.* And behind the soulful call, the knowledge of Maharet! The sudden vision of Maharet, enshrined in love, and ancient and white as he himself was. It was a moment of stunning pain. He slumped back in the wooden seat and bowed his head just a little. Then he looked out again over the steel rafters, the ugly tangles of black wire and rusted cylindrical lights. *Where are you?*

There, far away against the opposite wall, he saw the figure from whom the thoughts were coming. Ah, the oldest he had seen so far. A giant Nordic blood drinker, seasoned and cunning, dressed in coarse brown rawhide garments, with flowing straw-colored hair, his heavy brows and small deep-set eyes giving him a brooding expression.

The being was tracking a small mortal woman who fought her way through the crowds of the main floor. Jesse, Maharet's mortal daughter.

Maddened, disbelieving, Khayman focused tightly on the small woman. He felt his eyes mist with tears as he saw the astonishing resemblance. Here was Maharet's long coppery red hair, curling, thick, and the same tall birdlike frame, the same clever and curious green eyes, sweeping the scene as the female let herself be turned around and around by those who pushed against her.

Maharet's profile. Maharet's skin, which had been so pale and almost luminous in life, so like the inner lining of a seashell.

In a sudden vivid memory, he saw Maharet's skin through the mesh of his own dark fingers. As he had pushed her face to the side during the rape, his fingertips had touched the delicate folds of flesh over her eyes. Not till a year later had they plucked out her eyes and he had been there remembering the moment, the feel of the flesh. That is before he had picked up the eyes themselves and . . . .

He shuddered. He felt a sharp pain in his lungs. His memory wasn't going to fail him. He would not slip away from this moment, the happy clown remembering nothing.

Maharet's child, all right. But how? Through how many generations had these characteristics survived to flower again in this small female who appeared to be fighting her way towards the stage at the end of the hall?

It was not impossible, of course. He quickly realized it. Perhaps three hundred ancestors stood between this twentieth-century woman and the long ago afternoon when he had put on the King's medallion and stepped down from the dais to commit the King's rape. Maybe even less than that. A mere fraction of this crowd, to put it more neatly in perspective.

But more astonishing than this, that Maharet knew her own descendants. And know this woman Maharet did. The tall blood drinker's mind yielded that fact immediately.

He scanned the tall Nordic one. Maharet, alive. Maharet, the guardian of her mortal family. Maharet, the embodiment of illimitable strength and will. Maharet who had given him, this blond servant, no explanation of the dreams of the twins, but had sent him here instead to do her bidding: save Jessica.

Ah, but she lives, Khayman thought. She lives, and if she lives then in a real way, they both live, the red-haired sisters!

Khayman studied the creature even more intently, probing even deeper. But all he caught now was the fierce protectiveness. Rescue Jesse, not merely from the danger of the Mother but from this place altogether, where Jesse's eyes would see what no one could ever explain away.

And how he loathed the Mother, this tall, fair being with the posture of a warrior and a priest in one. He loathed that the Mother had disrupted the serenity of his timeless and melancholy existence; loathed that his sad, sweet love for this woman, Jessica, exacerbated the alarm he felt for himself. He knew the extent of the destruction too, that every blood drinker from one end of this continent to the other had been destroyed, save for a precious few, most of whom were under this roof, never dreaming of the fate that threatened them.

He knew as well of the dreams of the twins, but he did not understand them. After all, two redheaded sisters he had never known; only one red-haired beauty ruled his life. And once again Khayman saw Maharet's face, a vagrant image of softened weary human eyes peering from a porcelain mask: *Mael, do not ask me anything more. But do as I tell you.*

Silence. The blood drinker was aware of the surveillance suddenly. With a little jerk of his head he looked around the hall, trying to spot the intruder.

The name had done it, as names so often do. The creature had felt himself known, recognized. And Khayman had recognized the name at once, connecting it with the Mael of Lestat's pages. Undoubtedly they were one and the same—this was the Druid priest who had lured Marius into the sacred grove where the blood god had made him one of its own, and sent him off to Egypt to find the Mother and the Father.

Yes, this was the same Mael. And the creature felt himself recognized and hated it.

After the initial spasm of rage, all thought and emotion vanished. A rather dizzying display of strength, Khayman conceded. He relaxed in the chair. But the creature couldn't find him. Two dozen other white faces he picked out of the crowd, but not Khayman.

Intrepid Jessica had meantime reached her destination. Ducking low, she'd slipped through the heavy-muscled motorcycle riders who claimed the space before the stage as their own, and had risen to take hold of the lip of the wooden platform.

Flash of her silver bracelet in the light. And that might as well have been a tiny dagger to the mental shield of Mael, because his love and his thoughts were wholly visible again for one fluid instant.

This one is going to die, too, if he doesn't become wise, Khayman thought. He'd been schooled by Maharet, no doubt, and perhaps nourished by her powerful blood; yet his heart was undisciplined, and his temper beyond his control, it was obvious.

Then some feet behind Jesse, in the swirling color and noise, Khayman spied another intriguing figure, much younger, yet almost as powerful in his own fashion as the Gaul, Mael.

Khayman sought for the name, but the creature's mind was a perfect blank; not so much as a glimmer of personality escaped from it. A boy he'd been when he died, with straight dark auburn hair, and eyes a little too big for his face. But it was easy, suddenly, to filch the being's name from Daniel, his newborn fledgling who stood beside him. Armand. And the fledgling, Daniel, was scarcely dead. All the tiny molecules of his body were dancing with the demon's invisible chemistry.

Armand immediately attracted Khayman. Surely he was the same Armand of whom Louis and Lestat had both written—the immortal with the form of a youth. And this meant that he was no more than five hundred years old, yet he veiled himself completely. Shrewd, cold he seemed, yet without flair—a stance that required no room in which to display itself. And now, sensing infallibly that he was watched, he turned his large soft brown eyes upward and fixed instantly upon the remote figure of Khayman.

"No harm meant to you or your young one," Khayman whispered, so that his lips might shape and control the thoughts. "No friend to the Mother."

Armand heard but gave no answer. Whatever terror he felt at the sight of one so old, he masked completely. One would have thought he was looking at the wall behind Khayman's head, at the steady stream of laughing and shouting children who poured down the steps from the topmost doorways.

And, quite inevitably, this oddly beguiling little five-hundred-year-old being fixed his eyes upon Mael as the gaunt one felt another irresistible surge of concern for his fragile Jesse.

Khayman understood this being, Armand. He felt he understood him and liked him completely. As their eyes met again, all that had been written of this creature in the two little histories was informed and balanced by the creature's innate simplicity. The loneliness which Khayman had felt in Athens was now very strong.

"Not unlike my own simple soul," Khayman whispered. "You're lost in all this because you know the terrain too well. And that no matter how far you walk, you come again to the same mountains, the same valley."

No response. Of course. Khayman shrugged and smiled. To this one he'd give anything that he could; and guilelessly, he let Armand know it.

Now the question was, how to help them, these two that might have some hope of sleeping the immortal sleep until another sunset. And most important of all, how to reach Maharet, to whom the fierce and distrusting Mael was unstintingly devoted.

To Armand, Khayman said with the slightest movement of his lips: "No friend of the Mother. I told you. And keep with the mortal crowd. She'll pick you out when you step apart. It's that simple."

Armand's face registered no change. Beside him, the fledgling Daniel was happy, glorying in the pageant that surrounded him. He knew no fear, no plans or dreams. And why not? He had this extremely powerful creature to take care of him. He was a damn sight luckier than the rest.

Khayman rose to his feet. It was the loneliness as much as anything else. He would be near to one of these two, Armand or Mael. That's what he had wanted in Athens when all this glorious remembering and knowing had begun. To be near another like himself. To speak, to touch . . . something.

He moved along the top aisle of the hall, which circled the entire room, save for a margin at the far end behind the stage which belonged to the giant video screen.

He moved with slow human grace, careful not to crush the mortals who pushed against him. And also he wanted this slow progress because he must give Mael the opportunity to see him.

He knew instinctively that if he snuck up on this proud and quarrelsome thing, the insult would never be borne. And so he proceeded, only picking up his pace when he realized Mael was now aware of his approach.

Mael couldn't hide his fear as Armand could. Mael had never seen a blood drinker of Khayman's age save for Maharet; he was gazing at a potential enemy. Khayman sent the same warm greeting he had sent to Armand—Armand who watched—but nothing in the old warrior's stance changed.

The auditorium was now full and locked; outside children screamed and beat upon the doors. Khayman heard the whine and belch of the police radios.

The Vampire Lestat and his cohorts stood spying upon the hall through the holes in a great serge curtain.

Lestat embraced his companion Louis, and they kissed on the mouth, as the mortal musicians put their arms around both of them.

Khayman paused to feel the passion of the crowd, the very air charged with it.

Jessica had rested her arms on the edge of the platform. She had rested her chin upon the back of her hands. The men behind her, hulking creatures clothed in shiny black leather, shoved her brutally, out of carelessness and drunken exuberance, but they couldn't dislodge her.

Neither could Mael, should he make the attempt.

And something else came clear to Khayman suddenly, as he looked down at her. It was the single word Talamasca. This woman belonged to them; she was part of the order.

Not possible, he thought again, then laughed silently at his own foolish innocence. This was a night of shocks, was it not? Yet it seemed quite incredible that the Talamasca should have survived from the time he had known it centuries before, when he had played with its members and tormented them, and then turned his back on them out of pity for their fatal combination of innocence and ignorance.

Ah, memory was too ghastly a thing. Let his past lives slip into oblivion! He could see the faces of those vagabonds, those secular monks of the Talamasca who had so clumsily pursued him across Europe, recording glimpses of him in great leather-bound books, their quill pens scratching late into the night. Benjamin had been his name in that brief respite of consciousness, and Benjamin the Devil they had labeled him in their fancy Latin script, sending off crackling parchment epistles with big sloppy wax seals to their superiors in Amsterdam.

It had been a game to him, to steal their letters and add his notes to them; to frighten them; to crawl out from under their beds in the night and grab them by the throats and shake them; it had been fun; and what was not? When the fun stopped, he'd always lost his memory again.

But he had loved them; not exorcists they, or witch-hunting priests, or sorcerers who hoped to chain and control his power. It had even occurred to him once that when it came time to sleep, he would choose the vaults beneath their moldy Motherhouse. For all their meddlesome curiosity, they would never have betrayed him.

And now to think that the order had survived, with the tenacity of the Church of Rome, and this pretty mortal woman with the shining bracelet on her arm, beloved of Maharet and Mael, was one of their special breed. No wonder she had fought her way to the front ranks, as if to the bottom step of the altar.

Khayman drew closer to Mael, but he stopped short of him by several feet, the crowd passing ceaselessly in front of them. This he did out of respect for Mael's apprehension, and the shame the creature felt for being afraid. It was Mael who approached and stood at Khayman's side.

The restless crowd passed them as if they were the wall itself. Mael leant close to Khayman, which in its own way was a greeting, an offering of trust. He looked out over the hall, where no empty seat was visible, and the main floor was a mosaic of flashing colors and glistening hair and tiny upthrust fists. Then he reached out and touched Khayman as if he couldn't prevent himself from doing it. With his fingertips he touched the back of Khayman's left hand. And Khayman remained still to allow this little exploration.

How many times had Khayman seen such a gesture between immortals, the young one verifying for himself the texture and hardness of the elder's flesh. Hadn't some Christian saint slipped his hand in Christ's wounds because the sight of them had not been sufficient? More mundane comparisons made Khayman smile. It was like two fierce dogs tentatively examining each other.

Far below, Armand remained impassive as he kept his eyes upon the two figures. Surely he saw Mael's sudden disdainful glance, but he did not acknowledge it.

Khayman turned and embraced Mael, and smiled at him. But this merely frightened Mael, and Khayman felt the disappointment heavily. Politely, he stepped away. For a moment he was painfully confused. He stared down at Armand. Beautiful Armand who met his gaze with utter passivity. But it was time to say now what he'd come to say.

"You must make your shield stronger, my friend," he explained to Mael gently. "Don't let your love for that girl expose you. The girl will be perfectly safe from our Queen if you curb your thoughts of the girl's origins and her protector. That name is anathema to the Queen. It always has been."

"And where is the Queen?" Mael asked, his fear surging again, along with the rage that he needed to fight it.

"She's close."

"Yes, but where?"

"I cannot say. She's burnt their tavern house. She hunts the few rogues who haven't come to the hall. She takes her time with it. And this I've learned through the minds of her victims."

Khayman could see the creature shudder. He could see subtle changes in him that marked his ever increasing anger. Well and good. The fear withered in the heat of the anger. But what a basically quarrelsome creature this one was. His mind did not make sophisticated distinctions.

"And why do you give me this warning," demanded Mael, "when she can hear every word we speak to each other?"

"But I don't think that she can," Khayman replied calmly. "I am of the First Brood, friend. To hear other blood drinkers as we hear mortal men, that curse belongs only to distant cousins. I could not read her mind if she stood on this spot; and mine is closed to her as well, you can be sure of it. And so it was with all our kind through the early generations."

That clearly fascinated the blond giant. So Maharet could not hear the Mother! Maharet had not admitted this to him.

"No," Khayman said, "and the Mother can only know of her through your thoughts, so kindly guard them. Speak to me now in a human voice, for this city is a wilderness of such voices."

Mael considered, brows puckered in a frown. He glared at Khayman as if he meant to hit him.

"And this will defeat her?"

"Remember," Khayman said, "that excess can be the very opposite of essence." He looked back at Armand as he spoke. "She who hears a multitude of voices may not hear any one voice. And she who would listen closely to one, must shut out the others. You are old enough to know the trick."

Mael didn't answer out loud. But it was clear that he understood. The telepathic gift had always been a curse to him, too, whether he was besieged by the voices of blood drinkers or humans.

Khayman gave a little nod. The telepathic gift. Such nice words for the madness that had come on him eons ago, after years of listening, years of lying motionless, covered with dust in the deep recesses of a forgotten Egyptian tomb, listening to the weeping of the world, without knowledge of himself or his condition.

"Precisely my point, my friend," he said. "And for two thousand years you have fought the voices while our Queen may well have been drowned by them. It seems the Vampire Lestat has outshouted the din; he has, as it were, snapped his fingers in the corner of her eye and brought her to attention. But do not overestimate the creature who sat motionless for so long. It isn't useful to do so."

These ideas startled Mael somewhat. But he saw the logic of them. Below, Armand remained attentive.

"She can't do all things," Khayman said, "whether she herself knows it or not. She was always one to reach for the stars, and then draw back as if in horror."

"How so?" Mael said. Excited, he leaned closer. "What is she really like!" he whispered.

"She was full of dreams and high ideals. She was like Lestat." Khayman shrugged. "The blond one down there who would be good and do good and gather to himself the needy worshipers."

Mael smiled, coldly, cynically.

"But what in the name of hell does she mean to do?" he asked. "So he has waked her with his abominable songs. Why does she destroy us?"

"There's a purpose, you can be sure of it. With our Queen there has always been a purpose. She could not do the smallest thing without a grand purpose. And you must know we do not really change over time; we are as flowers unfolding; we merely become more nearly ourselves." He glanced again at Armand. "As for what her purpose may be, I can give you only speculations . . ."

"Yes, tell me."

"This concert will take place because Lestat wants it. And when it is finished, she will slaughter more of our kind. But she will leave some, some to serve this purpose, some perhaps to witness."

Khayman gazed at Armand. Marvelous how his expressionless face conveyed wisdom, while the harried, weary face of Mael did not. And who can say which one understood the most? Mael gave a little bitter laugh.

"To witness?" Mael asked. "I think not. I think she is cruder than that. She spares those whom Lestat loves, it's that simple."

This hadn't occurred to Khayman.

"Ah, yes, think on it," Mael said, in the same sharply pronounced English. "Louis, Lestat's companion. Is he not alive? And Gabrielle, the mother of the fiend, she is near at hand, waiting to rendezvous with her son as soon as it is wise to do so. And Armand, down there, whom you so like to look at, it seems Lestat would see him again, so he is alive, and that outcast with him, the one who published the accursed book, the one the others would tear limb from limb if only they guessed . . ."

"No, there's more to it than that. There has to be," Khayman said. "Some of us she can't kill. And those who go to Marius now, Lestat knows nothing of them but their names."

Mael's face changed slightly; it underwent a deep, human flush, as his eyes narrowed. It was clear to Khayman that Mael would have gone to Marius if he could. He would have gone this very night, if only Maharet had come to protect Jessica. He tried now to banish Maharet's name from his thoughts. He was afraid of Maharet, deeply afraid.

"Ah, yes, you try to hide what you know," Khayman said. "And this is just what you must reveal to me."

"But I can't," Mael said. The wall had gone up. Impenetrable. "I am not given answers, only orders, my friend. And my mission is to survive this night, and to take my charge safely out of here."

Khayman meant to press, to demand. But he did neither. He had felt a soft, subtle change in the atmosphere around him, a change so insignificant yet pure that he couldn't call it movement or sound.

She was coming. She was moving close to the hall. He felt himself slip away from his body into pure listening; yes, it was she. All the sounds of the night rose to confuse him, yet he caught it; a low irreducible sound which she could not veil, the sound of her breathing, of the beat of her heart, of a force moving through space at tremendous and unnatural speed, causing the inevitable tumult amid the visible and the invisible.

Mael sensed it; so did Armand. Even the young one beside Armand heard it, though so many other young ones did not. Even some of the more finely tuned mortals seemed to feel it and to be distracted by it.

"I must go, friend," Khayman said. "Remember my advice." Impossible to say more now.

She was very close. Undoubtedly she scanned; she listened.

He felt the first irresistible urge to see her, to scan for the minds of those hapless souls out there in the night whose eyes might have passed over her.

"Good-bye, friend," he said. "It's no good for me to be near you."

Mael looked at him in confusion. Below, Armand gathered Daniel to him and made for the edge of the crowd.

The hall went dark suddenly; and for one split second Khayman thought it was her magic, that some grotesque and vengeful judgment would now be made.

But the mortal children all around him knew the ritual. The concert was about to begin! The hall went mad with shrieks, and cheers, and stomping. Finally it became a great collective roar. He felt the floor tremble.

Tiny flames appeared as mortals struck their matches, ignited their chemical lighters. And a drowsy beautiful illumination once again revealed the thousands upon thousands of moving forms. The screams were a chorus from all sides.

"I am no coward," Mael whispered suddenly, as if he could not remain silent. He took hold of Khayman's arm, then let it go as if the hardness of it repelled him.

"I know," Khayman said.

"Help me. Help Jessica."

"Don't speak her name again. Stay away from her as I've told you. You are conquered again, Druid. Remember? Time to fight with cunning, not rage. Stay with the mortal herd. I will help you when and if I can."

There was so much more he wanted to say! Tell me where Maharet is! But it was too late now for that. He turned away and moved along the aisle swiftly until he came to an open place above a long narrow flight of cement stairs.

Below on the darkened stage, the mortal musicians appeared, darting over wires and speakers to gather their instruments from the floor.

The Vampire Lestat came striding through the curtain, his black cloak flaring around him, as he moved to the very front of the platform. Not three feet from Jesse he stood with microphone in hand.

The crowd had gone into ecstasies. Clapping, hooting, howling, it was a noise such as Khayman had never actually heard. He laughed in spite of himself at the stupid frenzy, at the tiny smiling figure down there who loved it utterly, who was laughing even as Khayman laughed.

Then in a great white flash, light flooded the small stage. Khayman stared, not at the small figures strutting in their finery, but at the giant video screen that rose behind them to the very roof. The living image of the Vampire Lestat, thirty feet in height, blazed before Khayman. The creature smiled; he lifted his arms, and shook his mane of yellow hair; he threw back his head and howled.

The crowd was on its feet in delirium; the very structure rumbled; but it was the howl that filled all ears. The Vampire Lestat's powerful voice swallowed every other sound in the auditorium.

Khayman closed his eyes. In the heart of the monstrous cry of the Vampire Lestat, he listened again for the sound of the Mother, but he could no longer find it.

"My Queen," he whispered, searching, scanning, hopeless though it was. Did she stand up there on some grassy slope listening to the music of her troubadour? He felt the soft damp wind and saw the gray starless sky as random mortals felt and saw these things. The lights of San Francisco, its spangled hills and glowing towers, these were the beacons of the urban night, as terrible suddenly as the moon or the drift of the galaxies.

He closed his eyes. He envisioned her again as she'd been in the Athens street watching the tavern burn with her children in it; her tattered cape had hung loose over her shoulders, the hood thrown back from her plaited hair. Ah, the Queen of Heaven she'd seemed, as she had once so loved to be known, presiding over centuries of litany. Her eyes had been shining and empty in the electric light; her mouth soft, guileless. The sheer sweetness of her face had been infinitely beautiful.

The vision carried him back now over the centuries to a dim and awful moment, when he'd come, a mortal man, heart pounding to hear her will. His Queen, now cursed and consecrated to the moon, the demon in her demanding blood, his Queen who would not allow even the bright lamps to be near to her. How agitated she had been, pacing the mud floor, the colored walls around her full of silent painted sentinels.

"These twins," she'd said, "these evil sisters, they have spoken such abominations."

"Have mercy," he had pleaded. "They meant no harm, I swear they tell the truth. Let them go again, Your Highness. They cannot change it now."

Oh, such compassion he had felt for all of them! The twins, and his afflicted sovereign.

"Ah, but you see, we must put it to the test, their revolting lies," she had said. "You must come closer, my devoted steward, you who have always served me with such devotion—"

"My Queen, my beloved Queen, what do you want of me?"

And with the same lovely expression on her face, she had lifted her icy hands to touch his throat, to hold him fast suddenly with a strength that terrified him. In shock, he'd watched her eyes go blank, her mouth open. The two tiny fang teeth he'd seen, as she rose on tiptoe with the eerie grace of nightmare. *Not me. You would not do this to me! My Queen, I am Khayman!*

He should have perished long before now, as so many blood drinkers had afterwards. Gone without a trace, like the nameless multitudes dissolved within the earth of all lands and nations. But he had not perished. And the twins—at least one—had lived on also.

Did she know it? Did she know those terrible dreams? Had they come to her from the minds of all the others who had received them? Or had she traveled the night around the world, dreamless, and without cease, and bent upon one task, since her resurrection?

They live, my Queen, they live on in the one if not in the two together. Remember the old prophecy! If only she could hear his voice!

He opened his eyes. He was back again in the moment, with this ossified thing that was his body. And the rising music saturated him with its remorseless rhythm. It pounded against his ears. The flashing lights blinded him.

He turned his back and put his hand against the wall. Never had he been so engulfed by sound. He felt himself losing consciousness, but Lestat's voice called him back.

With his fingers splayed across his eyes, Khayman looked down at the fiery white square of the stage. Behold the devil dance and sing with such obvious joy. It touched Khayman's heart in spite of himself.

Lestat's powerful tenor needed no electric amplification. And even the immortals lost among their prey were singing with him, it was so contagious, this passion. Everywhere he looked Khayman saw them caught up, mortal and immortal alike. Bodies twisted in time with the bodies on the stage. Voices rose; the hall swayed with one wave of movement after another.

The giant face of Lestat expanded on the video screen as the camera moved in upon it. The blue eye fixed upon Khayman and winked.

"WHY DON'T YOU KILL ME! YOU KNOW WHAT I AM!"
Lestat's laughter rose above the twanging scream of the guitars.
"DON'T YOU KNOW EVIL WHEN YOU SEE IT?"

Ah, such a belief in goodness, in heroism. Khayman could see it even in the creature's eyes, a dark gray shadow there of tragic need. Lestat threw back his head and roared again; he stamped his feet and howled; he looked to the rafters as if they were the firmament.

Khayman forced himself to move; he had to escape. He made his way clumsily to the door, as if suffocating in the deafening sound. Even his sense of balance had been affected. The blasting music came after him into the stairwell, but at least he was sheltered from the flashing lights. Leaning against the wall, he tried to clear his vision.

Smell of blood. Hunger of so many blood drinkers in the hall. And the throb of the music through the wood and the plaster.

He moved down the steps, unable to hear his own feet on the concrete, and sank down finally on a deserted landing. He wrapped his arms around his knees and bowed his head.

The music was like the music of old, when all songs had been the songs of the body, and the songs of the mind had not yet been invented.

He saw himself dancing; he saw the King—the mortal king he had so loved—turn and leap into the air; he heard the beat of the drums; the rise of the pipes; the King put the beer in Khayman's hand. The table sagged beneath its wealth of roasted game and glistening fruit, its steaming loaves of bread. The Queen sat in her golden chair, immaculate and serene, a mortal woman with a tiny cone of scented wax atop her elaborate hair, melting slowly in the heat to perfume her plaited tresses.

Then someone had put the coffin in his hand; the tiny coffin that was passed now among those who feasted; the little reminder: Eat. Drink. For Death awaits all of us.

He held it tight; should he pass it now to the King?

He felt the King's lips against his face suddenly. "Dance, Khayman. Drink. Tomorrow we march north to slay the last of the flesh eaters." The King didn't even look at the tiny coffin as he took it; he slipped it into the Queen's hands and she, without looking down, gave it to another.

The last of the flesh eaters. How simple it had all seemed; how good. Until he had seen the twins kneeling before that altar.

The great rattle of drums drowned out Lestat's voice. Mortals passed Khayman, hardly noticing him huddled there; a blood drinker ran quickly by without the slightest heed of him.

The voice of Lestat rose again, singing of the Children of Darkness, hidden beneath the cemetery called Les Innocents in superstition and fear.

Into the light
We've come
My Brothers and Sisters!

KILL US!
My Brothers and Sisters!

Sluggishly, Khayman rose. He was staggering, but he moved on, downward until he had come out in the lobby where the noise was just a little muted, and he rested there, across from the inner doors, in a cooling draft of fresh air.

Calm was returning to him, but only slowly, when he realized that two mortal men had paused nearby and were staring at him as he stood against the wall with his hands in his pockets, his head bowed.

He saw himself suddenly as they saw him. He sensed their apprehension, mingled with a sudden irrepressible sense of victory. Men who had known about his kind, men who had lived for a moment such as this, yet dreaded it, and never truly hoped for it.

Slowly, he looked up. They stood some twenty feet away from him, near to the cluttered concession stand, as if it could hide them—proper British gentlemen. They were old, in fact, learned, with heavily creased faces and prim formal attire. Utterly out of place here their fine gray overcoats, the bit of starched collar showing, the gleaming knot of silk tie. They seemed explorers from another world among the flamboyant youth that moved restlessly to and fro, thriving on the barbaric noise and broken chatter.

And with such natural reticence they stared; as if they were too polite to be afraid. Elders of the Talamasca looking for Jessica.

Know us? Yes, you do of course. No harm. Don't care.

His silent words drove the one called David Talbot back a pace. The man's breathing became hurried, and there was a sudden dampness on his forehead and upper lip. Yet such elegant composure. David Talbot narrowed his eyes as if he would not be dazzled by what he saw; as if he would see the tiny dancing molecules in the brightness.

How small it seemed suddenly the span of a human life; look at this fragile man, for whom education and refinement have only increased all risks. So simple to alter the fabric of his thought, his expectations. Should Khayman tell them where Jesse was? Should he meddle? It would make no difference ultimately.

He sensed now that they were afraid to go or to remain, that he had them fixed almost as if he'd hypnotized them. In a way, it was respect that kept them there, staring at him. It seemed he had to offer something, if only to end this awful scrutiny.

Don't go to her. You'd be fools if you did. She has others like me now to look after her. Best leave here. I would if I were you.

Now, how would all this read in the archives of the Talamasca? Some night he might find out. To what modern places had they removed their old documents and treasures?

Benjamin, the Devil. That's who I am. Don't you know me? He smiled at himself. He let his head droop, staring at the floor. He had not known he possessed this vanity. And suddenly he did not care what this moment meant to them.

He thought listlessly of those olden times in France when he had played with their kind. "Allow us but to speak to you!" they'd pleaded. Dusty scholars with pale eternally red-rimmed eyes and worn velvet clothing, so unlike these two fine gentlemen, for whom the occult was a matter of science, not philosophy. The hopelessness of that time suddenly frightened him; the hopelessness of this time was equally frightening.

Go away.

Without looking up, he saw that David Talbot had nodded. Politely, he and his companion withdrew. Glancing back over their shoulders, they hurried down the curve of the lobby, and into the concert.

Khayman was alone again, with the rhythm of the music coming from the doorway, alone and wondering why he had come here, what it was he wanted; wishing that he could forget again; that he was in some lovely place full of warm breezes and mortals who didn't know what he was, and twinkling electric lights beneath the faded clouds, and flat endless city pavements to walk until morning.

Jesse

ET me alone, you son of a bitch!" Jesse kicked the man beside her, the one who had hooked his arm around her waist and lifted her away from the stage. "You bastard!" Doubled over with the pain in his foot, he was no match for her sudden shove. He toppled and went down.

Five times she'd been swept back from the stage. She ducked and pushed through the little cluster that had taken her place, sliding against their black leather flanks as if she were a fish and rising up again to grab the apron of unpainted wood, one hand taking hold of the strong synthetic cloth that decorated it, and twisting it into a rope.

In the flashing lights she saw the Vampire Lestat leap high into the air and come down without a palpable sound on the boards, his voice rising again without benefit of the mike to fill the auditorium, his guitar players prancing around him like imps.

The blood ran in tiny rivulets down his white face, as if from Christ's Crown of Thorns, his long blond hair flying out as he turned full circle, his hand ripping at his shirt, tearing it open down his chest, the black tie loose and falling. His pale crystalline blue eyes were glazed and shot with blood as he screamed the unimportant lyrics.

Jesse felt her heart knocking again as she stared up at him, at the rocking of his hips, the tight cloth of the black pants revealing the powerful muscles of his thighs. He leapt again, rising effortlessly, as if he would ascend to the very ceiling of the hall.

Yes, you see it, and there is no mistake! No other explanation!

She wiped at her nose. She was crying again. But touch him, damn it, you have to! In a daze she watched him finish the song, stomping his foot to the last three resounding notes, as the musicians danced back and forth, taunting, tossing their hair over their heads, their voices lost in his as they struggled to meet his pace.

God, how he loved it! There was not the slightest pretense. He was bathed in the adoration he was receiving. He was soaking it up as if it were blood.

And now as he went into the frenzied opening of another song, he ripped off the black velvet cloak, gave it a great twirl, and sent it flying into the audience. The crowd wailed, shifted. Jesse felt a knee in her back, a boot scraping her heel, but this was her chance, as the guards jumped down off the boards to stop the melee.

With both hands pressed down hard on the wood, she sprang up and over on her belly and onto her feet. She ran right towards the dancing figure whose eyes suddenly looked into hers.

"Yes, you! You!" she cried out. In the corner of her eye was the approaching guard. She threw her full weight at the Vampire Lestat. Shutting her eyes, she locked her arms around his waist. She felt the cold shock of his silky chest against her face, she tasted the blood suddenly on her lip!

"Oh, God, real!" she whispered. Her heart was going to burst, but she hung on. Yes, Mael's skin, like this, and Maharet's skin, like this, and all of them. Yes, this! Real, not human. Always. And it was all here in her arms and she knew and it was too late for them to stop her now!

Her left hand went up, and caught a thick tangle of his hair, and as she opened her eyes, she saw him smiling down at her, saw the poreless gleaming white skin, and the tiny fang teeth.

"You devil!" she whispered. She was laughing like a mad woman, crying and laughing.

"Love you, Jessica," he whispered back at her, smiling at her as if he were teasing her, the wet blond hair tumbling down into his eyes.

Astonished, she felt his arm around her, and then he lifted her on his hip, swinging her in a circle. The screaming musicians were a blur; the lights were violent streaks of white, red. She was moaning; but she kept looking up at him, at his eyes, yes, real. Desperately she hung on, for it seemed he meant to throw her high into the air over the heads of the crowd. And then as he set her down and bowed his head, his hair falling against her cheek, she felt his mouth close on hers.

The throbbing music went dim as if she'd been plunged into the sea. She felt him breathe into her, sigh against her, his smooth fingers sliding up her neck. Her breasts were pressed against the beat of his heart; and a voice was speaking to her, purely, the way a voice had long ago, a voice that knew her, a voice that understood her questions and knew how they must be answered.

Evil, Jesse. As you have always known.

Hands pulled her back. Human hands. She was being separated from him. She screamed.

Bewildered, he stared at her. He was reaching deep, deep into his dreams for something he only faintly remembered. The funeral feast; the red-haired twins kneeling on either side of the altar. But it was no more than a split second; then gone; he was baffled; his smile flashed again, impersonal, like one of the lights that were constantly blinding her. "Beautiful Jesse!" he said, his hand lifted as if in farewell. They were carrying her backwards away from him, off the stage.

She was laughing when they set her down.

Her white shirt was smeared with blood. Her hands were covered with it—pale streaks of salty blood. She felt she knew the taste of it. She threw back her head and laughed; and it was so curious not to be able to hear it, only to feel it, to feel the shudder running through her, to know she was crying and laughing at the same time. The guard said something rough to her, something crude, threatening. But that didn't matter.

The crowd had her again. It just swallowed her, tumbling against her, driving her out of the center. A heavy shoe crushed her right foot. She stumbled, and turned, and let herself be pushed along ever more violently, towards the doors.

Didn't matter now. *She knew.* She knew it all. Her head spun. She could not have stood upright if it were not for the shoulders knocking against her. And never had she felt such wondrous abandon. Never had she felt such release.

The crazy cacophonous music went on; faces flickered and disappeared in a wash of colored light. She smelled the marijuana, the beer. Thirst. Yes, something cold to drink. Something cold. So thirsty. She lifted her hand again and licked at the salt and the blood. Her body trembled, vibrated, the way it so often did on the verge of sleep. A soft delicious tremor that meant that dreams were coming. She licked at the blood again and closed her eyes.

Quite suddenly she felt herself pass into an open place. No one shoving her. She looked up and saw that she had come to the doorway, to the slick ramp that led some ten feet into the lobby below. The crowd was behind her, above her. And she could rest here. She was all right.

She ran her hand along the greasy wall, stepping over the crush of paper cups, a fallen wig with cheap yellow curls. She lay her head back suddenly and merely rested, the ugly light from the lobby shining in her eyes. The taste of the blood was on the tip of her tongue. It seemed she was going to cry again, and it was a perfectly fine thing to do. For the moment, there was no past or present, no necessity, and all the world was changed, from the simplest things to the grandest. She was floating, as if in the center of the most seductive state of peace and acceptance that she had ever known. Oh, if only she could tell David these things; if only somehow she could share this great and overwhelming secret.

Something touched her. Something hostile to her. Reluctantly she turned and saw a hulking figure at her side. *What?* She struggled to see it clearly.

Bony limbs, black hair slicked back, red paint on the twisted ugly mouth, but the skin, the same skin. And the fang teeth. Not human. One of them!

Talamasca?

It came at her like a hiss. It struck her in the chest. Instinctively her arms rose, crossing over her breasts, fingers locking on her shoulders.

Talamasca?

It was soundless yet deafening in its rage.

She moved to back away, but his hand caught her, fingers biting into her neck. She tried to scream as she was lifted off her feet.

Then she was flying across the lobby and she was screaming until her head slammed into the wall.

Blackness. She saw the pain. It flashed yellow and then white as it traveled down her backbone and then spread out as if into a million branches in her limbs. Her body went numb. She hit the floor with another shocking pain in her face and in the open palms of her hands and then she rolled over on her back.

She couldn't see. Maybe her eyes were closed, but the funny thing was, if they were, she couldn't open them. She heard voices, people shouting. A whistle blew, or was it the clang of a bell? There was a thunderous noise, but that was the crowd inside applauding. People near her argued.

Someone close to her ear said:

"Don't touch her. Her neck's broken!"

Broken? Can you live when your neck is broken?

Someone laid a hand on her forehead. But she couldn't really feel it so much as a tingling sensation, as if she were very cold, walking in snow, and all real feeling had left her. *Can't see.*

"Listen, honey." A young man's voice. One of those voices you could hear in Boston or New Orleans or New York City. Firefighter, cop, saver of the injured. "We're taking care of you, honey. The ambulance is on its way. Now lie still, honey, don't you worry."

Someone touching her breast. No, taking the cards out of her pocket. Jessica Miriam Reeves. Yes.

She stood beside Maharet and they were looking up at the giant map with all the tiny lights. And she understood. Jesse born of Miriam, who was born of Alice, who was born of Carlotta, who was born of Jane Marie, who was born of Anne, who was born of Janet Belle, who was born of Elizabeth, who was born of Louise, who was born of Frances, who was born of Frieda, who was born of—

"If you will allow me, please, we are her friends—"

David.

They were lifting her; she heard herself scream, but she had not meant to scream. She saw the screen again and the great tree of names. "Frieda born of Dagmar, born of . . ."

"Steady now, steady! Goddamn it!"

The air changed; it went cool and moist; she felt the breeze moving over her face; then all feeling left her hands and feet completely. She could feel her eyelids but not move them.

Maharet was talking to her. ". . . came out of Palestine, down into Mesopotamia and then up slowly through Asia Minor and into Russia and then into Eastern Europe. Do you see?"

This was either a hearse or an ambulance and it seemed too quiet to be the latter, and the siren, though steady, was too far away. What had happened to David? He wouldn't have let her go, unless she was dead. But then how could David have been there? David had told her nothing could induce him to come. David wasn't here. She must have imagined it. And the odd thing was, Miriam wasn't here either. "Holy Mary, Mother of God . . . now and at the hour of our death . . . ."

She listened: they were speeding through the city; she felt them turn the corner; but where was her body? She couldn't feel it. Broken neck. That meant surely that one had to be dead.

What was that, the light she could see through the jungle? A river? It seemed too wide to be a river. How to cross it. But it wasn't Jesse who was walking through the jungle, and now along the bank of the river. It was somebody else. Yet she could see the hands out in front of her, moving aside the vines and the wet sloppy leaves, as if they were her hands. She could see red hair when she looked down, red hair in long curling tangles, full of bits of leaf and earth. . . .

"Can you hear me, honey? We've got you. We're taking care of you. Your friends are in the car behind us. Now don't you worry."

He was saying more. But she had lost the thread. She couldn't hear him, only the tone of it, the tone of loving care. Why did he feel so sorry for her? He didn't even know her. Did he understand that it wasn't her blood all over her shirt? Her hands? *Guilty.* Lestat had tried to tell her it was evil, but that had been so unimportant to her, so impossible to relate to the whole. It wasn't that she didn't care about what was good and what was right; it was that this was bigger for the moment. *Knowing.* And he'd been talking as if she meant to do something and she hadn't meant to do anything at all.

That's why dying was probably just fine. If only Maharet would understand. And to think, David was with her, in the car behind them. David knew some of the story, anyway, and they would have a file on her: Reeves, Jessica. And it would be more evidence. "One of our devoted members, definitely the result of . . . most dangerous . . . must not under any circumstances attempt a sighting . . . ."

They were moving her again. Cool air again, and smells rising of gasoline and ether. She knew that just on the other side of this numbness, this darkness, there was terrible pain and it was best to lie very still and not try to go there. Let them carry you along; let them move the gurney down the hallway.

Someone crying. A little girl.

"Can you hear me, Jessica? I want you to know that you're in the hospital and that we are doing everything we can for you. Your friends are outside. David Talbot and Aaron Lightner. We've told them that you must lie very still. . . ."

Of course. When your neck is broken you are either dead or you die if you move. That was it. Years ago in a hospital she had seen a young girl with a broken neck. She remembered now. And the girl's body had been tied to a huge aluminum frame. Every now and then a nurse would move the frame to change the girl's position. Will you do that to me?

He was talking again but this time he was farther away. She walked a little faster through the jungle, to get closer, to hear over the sound of the river. He was saying . . . .

". . . of course we can do all that, we can run those tests, of course, but you must understand what I'm saying, this situation is terminal. The back of the skull is completely crushed. You can see the brain. And the obvious injury to the brain is enormous. Now, in a few hours the brain will begin to swell, if we even have a few hours. . . ."

Bastard, you killed me. You threw me against the wall. If I could move anything—my eyelids, my lips. But I'm trapped inside here. I have no body anymore yet I'm trapped in here! When I was little, I used to think it would be like this, death. You'd be trapped in your head in the grave, with no eyes to see and no mouth to scream. And years and years would pass.

Or you roamed the twilight realm with the pale ghosts; thinking you were alive when you were really dead. Dear God, I have to know when I'm dead. I have to know when it's begun!

Her lips. There was the faintest sensation. Something moist, warm. Something parting her lips. But there's no one here, is there? They were out in the hallway, and the room was empty. She would have known if someone was here. Yet now she could taste it, the warm fluid flowing into her mouth.

What is it? What are you giving me? I don't want to go under.

Sleep, my beloved.

I don't want to. I want to feel it when I die. I want to know!

But the fluid was filling her mouth, and she was swallowing. The muscles of her throat were alive. Delicious the taste of it, the saltiness of it. She knew this taste! She knew this lovely, tingling sensation. She sucked harder. She could feel the skin of her face come alive, and the air stirring around her. She could feel the breeze moving through the room. A lovely warmth was moving down her spine. It was moving through her legs and her arms, taking exactly the path the pain had taken, and all her limbs were coming back.

Sleep, beloved.

The back of her head tingled; and the tingling moved through the roots of her hair.

Her knees were bruised but her legs weren't hurt and she'd be able to walk again, and she could feel the sheet under her hand. She wanted to reach up, but it was too soon for that, too soon to move.

Besides she was being lifted, carried.

And it was best to sleep now. Because if this was death . . . well, it was just fine. The voices she could barely hear, the men arguing, threatening, they didn't matter now. It seemed David was calling out to her. But what did David want her to do? To die? The doctor was threatening to call the police. The police couldn't do anything now. That was almost funny.

Down and down the stairs they went. Lovely cold air.

The sound of the traffic grew louder; a bus roaring past. She had never liked these sounds before but now they were like the wind itself, that pure. She was being rocked again, gently, as if in a cradle. She felt the car move forward with a sudden lurch, and then the smooth easy momentum. Miriam was there and Miriam wanted Jesse to look at her, but Jesse was too tired now.

"I don't want to go, Mother."

"But Jesse. Please. It's not too late. You can still come!" Like David calling. "Jessica."

Daniel

ABOUT halfway through, Daniel understood. The white-faced brothers and sisters would circle each other, eye each other, even threaten each other all during the concert, but nobody would do anything. The rule was too hard and fast: leave no evidence of what we are—not victims, not a single cell of our vampiric tissue.

Lestat was to be the only kill and that was to be done most carefully. Mortals were not to see the scythes unless it was unavoidable. Snatch the bastard when he tried to take his leave, that was the scheme; dismember him before the cognoscenti only. That is, unless he resisted, in which case he must die before his fans, and the body would have to be destroyed completely.

Daniel laughed and laughed. Imagine Lestat allowing such a thing to happen.

Daniel laughed in their spiteful faces. Pallid as orchids, these vicious souls who filled the hall with their simmering outrage, their envy, their greed. You would have thought they hated Lestat if for no other reason than his flamboyant beauty.

Daniel had broken away from Armand finally. Why not?

Nobody could hurt him, not even the glowing stone figure he'd seen in the shadows, the one so hard and so old he looked like the Golem of legend. What an eerie thing that was, that stone one staring down at the wounded mortal woman who lay with her neck broken, the one with the red hair who looked like the twins in the dream. And probably some stupid human being had done that to her, broken her neck like that. And the blond vampire in the buckskin, pushing past them to reach the scene, he had been an awe-inspiring sight as well, with the hardened veins bulging on his neck and on the backs of his hands when he reached the poor broken victim. Armand had watched the men take the red-haired woman away with the most unusual expression on his face, as if he should somehow intervene; or maybe it was only that the Golem thing, standing idly by, made him wary. Finally, he'd shoved Daniel back into the singing crowd. But there was no need to fear. It was sanctuary for *them* in this place, this cathedral of sound and light.

And Lestat was Christ on the cathedral cross. How describe his overwhelming and irrational authority? His face would have been cruel if it hadn't been for the childlike rapture and exuberance. Pumping his fist into the air, he bawled, pleaded, roared at the powers that be as he sang of his downfall—Lelio, the boulevard actor turned into a creature of night against his will!

His soaring tenor seemed to leave his body utterly as he recounted his defeats, his resurrections, the thirst inside him which no measure of blood could ever quench. "Am I not the devil in you all!" he cried, not to the moonflower monsters in the crowd but to the mortals who adored him.

And even Daniel was screaming, bellowing, leaping off his feet as he cried in agreement, though the words meant nothing finally; it was merely the raw force of Lestat's defiance. Lestat cursed heaven on behalf of all who had ever been outcasts, all who had ever known violation, and then turned, in guilt and malice, on their own kind.

It seemed to Daniel at the highest moments as though it were an omen that he should find immortality on the eve of this great Mass. The Vampire Lestat was God; or the nearest thing he had ever known to it. The giant on the video screen gave his benediction to all that Daniel had ever desired.

How could the others resist? Surely the fierceness of their intended victim made him all the more inviting. The final message behind all Lestat's lyrics was simple: Lestat had the gift that had been promised to each of them; Lestat was unkillable. He devoured the suffering forced upon him and emerged all the stronger. To join with him was to live forever:

This is my Body. This is my Blood.

Yet the hate boiled among the vampire brothers and sisters. As the concert came to a close, Daniel felt it keenly—an odor rising from the crowd—an expanding hiss beneath the strum of the music.

Kill the god. Tear him limb from limb. Let the mortal worshipers do as they have always done—mourn for him who was meant to die. "Go, the Mass is ended."

The houselights went on. The fans stormed the wooden stage, tearing down the black serge curtain to follow the fleeing musicians.

Armand grabbed Daniel's arm. "Out the side door," he said. "Our only chance is to get to him quickly."

Khayman

T WAS just as he had expected. She struck out at the first of those who struck at him. Lestat had come through the back door, Louis at his side, and made a dash for his black Porsche when the assassins set upon him. It seemed a rude circle sought to close, but at once the first, with scythe raised, went up in flames. The crowd panicked, terrified children stampeding in all directions. Another immortal assailant was suddenly on fire. And then another.

Khayman slipped back against the wall as the clumsy humans hurtled past him. He saw a tall elegant female blood drinker slice unnoticed through the mob, and slide behind the wheel of Lestat's car, calling to Louis and Lestat to join her. It was Gabrielle, the fiend's mother. And logically enough the lethal fire did not harm her. There wasn't a particle of fear in her cold blue eyes as she readied the vehicle with swift, decisive gestures.

Lestat meantime turned around and around in a rage. Maddened, robbed of the battle, he finally climbed into the car only because the others forced him to do so.

And as the Porsche plowed viciously through the rushing youngsters, blood drinkers burst into flame everywhere. In a horrid silent chorus, their cries rose, their frantic curses, their final questions.

Khayman covered his face. The Porsche was halfway to the gates before the crowd forced it to stop. Sirens screamed; voices roared commands; children had fallen with broken limbs. Mortals cried in misery and confusion.

Get to Armand, Khayman thought. But what was the use? He saw them burning everywhere he looked in great writhing plumes of orange and blue flame that changed suddenly to white in their heat as they released the charred clothes which fell to the pavements. How could he come between the fire and Armand? How could he save the young one, Daniel?

He looked up at the distant hills, at a tiny figure glowing against the dark sky, unnoticed by all who screamed and fled and cried for help around him.

Suddenly he felt the heat; he felt it touch him as it had in Athens. He felt it dance about his face, he felt his eyes watering. Steadily he regarded the distant tiny source. And then for reasons that he might never himself understand, he chose not to drive back the fire, but rather to see what it might do to him. Every fiber of his being said, Give it back. Yet he remained motionless, washed of thought, and feeling the sweat drip from him. The fire circled him, embraced him. And then it moved away, leaving him alone, cold, and wounded beyond his wildest imagining. Quietly he whispered a prayer: *May the twins destroy you.*

Daniel

IRE!" Daniel caught the rank greasy stench just as he saw the flames themselves breaking out here and there all through the multitude. What protection was the crowd now? Like tiny explosions the fires were, as groups of frantic teenagers stumbled to get away from them, and ran in senseless circles, colliding helplessly with one another.

The sound. Daniel heard it again. It was moving above them. Armand pulled him back against the building. It was useless. They could not get to Lestat. And they had no cover. Dragging Daniel after him, Armand retreated into the hall again. A pair of terrified vampires ran past the entrance, then exploded into tiny conflagrations.

In horror, Daniel watched the skeletons glowing as they melted within the pale yellow blaze. Behind them in the deserted auditorium a fleeing figure was suddenly caught in the same ghastly flames. Twisting, turning, he collapsed on the cement floor, smoke rising from his empty clothing. A pool of grease formed on the cement, then dried up even as Daniel stared at it.

Out into the fleeing mortals, they ran again, this time towards the distant front gates over yards and yards of asphalt.

And suddenly they were traveling so fast that Daniel's feet had left the ground. The world was nothing but a smear of color. Even the piteous cries of the frightened fans were stretched, softened. Abruptly they stopped at the gates, just as Lestat's black Porsche raced out of the parking lot, past them, and onto the avenue. Within seconds it was gone, like a bullet traveling south towards the freeway.

Armand made no attempt to follow it; he seemed not even to see it. He stood near the gatepost looking back over the heads of the crowd, beyond the curved roof of the hall to the distant horizon. The eerie telepathic noise was deafening now. It swallowed every other sound in the world; it swallowed every sensation.

Daniel couldn't keep his hands from going to his ears, couldn't keep his knees from buckling. He felt Armand draw close. But he could no longer see. He knew that if it was meant to happen it would be now, yet still he couldn't feel the fear; still he couldn't believe in his own death; he was paralyzed with wonder and confusion.

Gradually the sound faded. Numb, he felt his vision clear; he saw the great red shape of a lumbering ladder truck approach, the firemen shouting for him to move out of the gateway. The siren came as if from another world, an invisible needle through his temples.

Armand was gently pulling him out of the path. Frightened people thundered past as if driven by a wind. He felt himself fall. But Armand caught him. Into the warm crush of mortals, outside the fence they passed, slipping among those who peered through the chain mesh at the melee.

Hundreds still fled. Sirens, sour and discordant, drowned out their cries. One fire engine after another roared up to the gates, to nudge its way through dispersing mortals. But these sounds were thin and distant, dulled still by the receding supernatural noise. Armand clung to the fence, his eyes closed, his forehead pressed against the metal. The fence shuddered, as if it alone could hear the thing as they heard it.

It was gone.

An icy quiet descended. The quiet of shock, emptiness. Though the pandemonium continued, it did not touch them.

They were alone, the mortals loosening, milling, moving away. And the air carried those lingering preternatural cries like burning tinsel again; more dying, but where?

Across the avenue he moved at Armand's side. Unhurried. And down a dark side street they made their way, past faded stucco houses and shabby corner stores, past sagging neon signs and over cracked pavements.

On and on, they walked. The night grew cold and still around them. The sound of the sirens was remote, almost mournful.

As they came to a broad garish boulevard, a great lumbering trolleybus appeared, flooded with a greenish light. Like a ghost it seemed, proceeding towards them, through the emptiness and the silence. Only a few forlorn mortal passengers peered from its smeared and dirty windows. The driver drove as if in his sleep.

Armand raised his eyes, wearily, as if only to watch it pass. And to Daniel's amazement the bus came to a halt for them.

They climbed aboard together, ignoring the little coin box, and sank down side by side on the long leather bench seat. The driver never turned his head from the dark windshield before him. Armand sat back against the window. Dully, he stared at the black rubber floor. His hair was tousled, his cheek smudged with soot. His lower lip protruded ever so slightly. Lost in thought, he seemed utterly unconscious of himself.

Daniel looked at the lackluster mortals: the prune-faced woman with a slit for a mouth who looked at him angrily; the drunken man, with no neck, who snored on his chest; and the small-headed teenage woman with the stringy hair and the sores at the corners of her mouth who held a giant toddler on her lap with skin like bubblegum. Why, something was horribly wrong with each of them. And there, the dead man on the back seat, with his eyes half mast and the dried spit on his chin. Did nobody know he was dead? The urine stank as it dried beneath him.

Daniel's own hands look dead, lurid. Like a corpse with one live arm, the driver seemed, as he turned the wheel. Was this a hallucination? The bus to hell?

No. Only a trolleybus like a million he had taken in his lifetime, on which the weary and the down-and-out rode the city's streets through the late hours. He smiled suddenly, foolishly. He was going to start laughing, thinking of the dead man back there, and these people just riding along, and the way the light made everyone look, but then a sense of dread returned.

The silence unnerved him. The slow rocking of the bus unnerved him; the parade of dingy houses beyond the windows unnerved him; the sight of Armand's listless face and empty stare was unbearable.

"Will she come back for us?" he asked. He could not endure it any longer.

"She knew we were there," Armand said, eyes dull, voice low. "She passed us over."

Khayman

E HAD retreated to the high grassy slope, with the cold Pacific beyond it.

It was like a panorama now; death at a distance, lost in the lights, the vapor-thin wails of preternatural souls interwoven with the darker, richer voices of the human city.

The fiends had pursued Lestat, forcing the Porsche over the edge of the freeway. Unhurt, Lestat had emerged from the wreck, spoiling for battle; but the fire had struck again to scatter or destroy those who surrounded him.

Finally left alone with Louis and Gabrielle, he had agreed to retreat, uncertain of who or what had protected him.

And unbeknownst to the trio, the Queen pursued their enemies for them.

Over the roofs, her power moved, destroying those who had fled, those who had tried to hide, those who had lingered near fallen companions in confusion and anguish.

The night stank of their burning, these wailing phantoms that left nothing on the empty pavement but their ruined clothes. Below, under the arc lamps of the abandoned parking lots, the lawmen searched in vain for bodies; the firefighters looked in vain for those to assist. The mortal youngsters cried piteously.

Small wounds were treated; the crazed were narcotized and taken away gently. So efficient the agencies of this plentiful time. Giant hoses cleaned the lots. They washed away the scorched rags of the burnt ones.

Tiny beings down there argued and swore that they had witnessed these immolations. But no evidence remained. She had destroyed completely her victims.

And now she moved on far away from the hall, to search the deepest recesses of the city. Her power turned corners and entered windows and doorways. There would be a tiny burst of flame out there like the striking of a sulphur match; then nothing.

The night grew quieter. Taverns and shops shut their doors, winking out in the thickening darkness. Traffic thinned on the highways.

The ancient one she caught in the North Beach streets, the one who had wanted but to see her face; she had burned him slowly as he crawled along the sidewalk. His bones turned to ash, the brain a mass of glowing embers in its last moments. Another she struck down upon a high flat roof, so that he fell like a shooting star out over the glimmering city. His empty clothes took flight like dark paper when it was finished.

And south Lestat went, to his refuge in Carmel Valley. Jubilant, drunk on the love he felt for Louis and Gabrielle, he spoke of old times and new dreams, utterly oblivious to the final slaughter.

"Maharet, where are you?" Khayman whispered. The night gave no answer. If Mael was near, if Mael heard the call, he gave no sign of it. Poor, desperate Mael, who had run out into the open after the attack upon Jessica. Mael, who might have been slain now, too. Mael staring helplessly as the ambulance carried Jesse away from him.

Khayman could not find him.

He combed the light-studded hills, the deep valleys in which the beat of souls was like a thunderous whisper. "Why have I witnessed these things?" he asked. "Why have the dreams brought me here?"

He stood listening to the mortal world.

The radios chattered of devil worship, riots, random fires, mass hallucinations. They whined of vandalism and crazed youth. But it was a big city for all its geographic smallness. The rational mind had already encapsulated the experience and disregarded it. Thousands took no notice. Others slowly and painstakingly revised in memory the impossible things they had seen. The Vampire Lestat was a human rock star and nothing more, his concert the scene of predictable though uncontrollable hysteria.

Perhaps it was part of the Queen's design to so smoothly abort Lestat's dreams. To burn his enemies off the earth before the frail blanket of human assumptions could be irreparably damaged. If this was so, would she punish the creature himself finally?

No answer came to Khayman.

His eyes moved over the sleepy terrain. An ocean fog had swept in, settling in deep rosy layers beneath the tops of the hills. The whole had a fairy-tale sweetness to it now in the first hour past midnight.

Collecting his strongest power, he sought to leave the confines of his body, to send his vision out of himself like the wandering *ka* of the Egyptian dead, to see those whom the Mother might have spared, to draw close to them.

"Armand," he said aloud. And then the lights of the city went dim. He felt the warmth and illumination of another place, and Armand was there before him.

He and his fledgling, Daniel, had come safely again to the mansion where they would sleep beneath the cellar floor unmolested. Groggily the young one danced through the large and sumptuous rooms, his mind full of Lestat's songs and rhythms. Armand stared out into the night, his youthful face as impassive as before. He saw Khayman! He saw him standing motionless on the faraway hill, yet felt him near enough to touch. Silently, invisibly, they studied one another.

It seemed Khayman's loneliness was more than he could bear; but the eyes of Armand held no emotion, no trust, no welcome.

Khayman moved on, drawing on ever greater strength, rising higher and higher in his search, so far from his body now that he could not for the moment even locate it. To the north he went, calling the names Santino, Pandora.

In a blasted field of snow and ice he saw them, two black figures in the endless whiteness—Pandora's garments shredded by the wind, her eyes full of blood tears as she searched for the dim outline of Marius's compound. She was glad of Santino at her side, this unlikely explorer in his fine clothes of black velvet. The long sleepless night through which Pandora had circled the world had left her aching in every limb and near to collapsing. All creatures must sleep; must dream. If she did not lie down soon in some dark place, her mind would be unable to fight the voices, the images, the madness. She did not want to take to the air again, and this Santino could not do such things, and so she walked beside him.

Santino cleaved to her, feeling only her strength, his heart shrunken and bruised from the distant yet inescapable cries of those whom the Queen had slaughtered. Feeling the soft brush of Khayman's gaze, he pulled his black cloak tight around his face. Pandora took no notice whatsoever.

Khayman veered away. Softly, it hurt him to see them touch; it hurt him to see the two of them together.

In the mansion on the hill, Daniel slit the throat of a wriggling rat and let its blood flow into a crystal glass. "Lestat's trick," he said studying it in the light. Armand sat still by the fire, watching the red jewel of blood in the glass as Daniel lifted it to his lips lovingly.

Back into the night Khayman moved, wandering higher again, far from the city lights as if in a great orbit.

Mael, answer me. Let me know where you are. Had the Mother's cold fiery beam struck him, too? Or did he mourn now so deeply for Jesse that he hearkened to nothing and no one? Poor Jesse, dazzled by miracles, struck down by a fledgling in the blink of an eye before anyone could prevent it. *Maharet's child, my child!*

Khayman was afraid of what he might see, afraid of what he dared not seek to alter. But maybe the Druid was simply too strong for him now; the Druid concealed himself and his charge from all eyes and all minds. Either that or the Queen had had her way and it was finished.

Jesse

SO QUIET here. She lay on a bed that was hard and soft, and her body felt floppy like that of a rag doll. She could lift her hand but then it would drop, and still she could not see, except in a vague ghostly way things that might have been an illusion.

For example lamps around her; ancient clay lamps shaped like fish and filled with oil. They gave a thick odoriferous perfume to the room. Was this a funeral parlor?

It came again, the fear that she was dead, locked in the flesh yet disconnected. She heard a curious sound; what was it? A scissors cutting. It was trimming the edges of her hair; the feel of it traveled to her scalp. She felt it even in her intestines.

A tiny vagrant hair was plucked suddenly from her face; one of those annoying hairs, quite out of place, which women so hate. She was being groomed for the coffin, wasn't she? Who else would take such care, lifting her hand now, and inspecting her fingernails so carefully.

But the pain came again, an electric flash moving down her back and she screamed. She screamed aloud in this room where she'd been only hours before in this very bed with the chains creaking.

She heard a gasp from someone near her. She tried to see, but she only saw the lamps again. And some dim figure standing in the window. Miriam watching.

"Where?" he asked. He was startled, trying to see the vision. Hadn't this happened before?

"Why can't I open my eyes?" she asked. He could look forever and he would never see Miriam.

"Your eyes are open," he said. How raw and tender his voice sounded. "I can't give you any more unless I give it all. We are not healers. We are slayers. It's time for you to tell me what you want. There is no one to help me."

I don't know what I want. All I know is I don't want to die! I don't want to stop living. What cowards we are, she thought, what liars. A great fatalistic sadness had accompanied her all the way to this night, yet there had been the secret hope of this always! Not merely to see, to know, but to be part of . . . .

She wanted to explain, to hone it carefully with audible words, but the pain came again. A fiery brand touched to her spine, the pain shooting into her legs. And then the blessed numbness. It seemed the room she couldn't see grew dark and the flames of the ancient lamps sputtered. Outside the forest whispered. The forest writhed in the dark. And Mael's grip on her wrist was weak suddenly, not because he had let her go but because she couldn't any longer feel it.

"Jesse!"

He shook her with both his hands, and the pain was like lightning shattering the dark. She screamed through her clenched teeth. Miriam, stony-eyed and silent, glared from the window.

"Mael, do it!" she cried.

With all her strength, she sat up on the bed. The pain was without shape or limit; the scream strangled inside her. But then she opened her eyes, truly opened them. In the hazy light, she saw Miriam's cold unmerciful expression. She saw the tall bent figure of Mael towering over the bed. And then she turned to the open door. Maharet was coming.

Mael didn't know, didn't realize, till she did. With soft silky steps, Maharet came up the stairs, her long skirts moving with a dark rustling sound; she came down the corridor.

Oh, after all these years, these long years! Through her tears, Jesse watched Maharet move into the light of the lamps; she saw her shimmering face, and the burning radiance of her hair. Maharet gestured for Mael to leave them.

Then Maharet approached the bed. She lifted her hands, palms open, as if in invitation; she raised her hands as if to receive a baby.

"Yes, do it."

"Say farewell then, my darling, to Miriam."

IN OLDEN times there was a terrible worship in the city of Carthage. To the great bronze god Baal, the populace offered in sacrifice their little children. The small bodies were laid on the statue's outstretched arms, and then by means of a spring, the arms would rise and the children would fall into the roaring furnace of the god's belly.

After Carthage was destroyed, only the Romans carried the old tale, and as the centuries passed wise men came not to believe it. Too terrible, it seemed, the immolation of these children. But as the archaeologists brought their shovels and began to dig, they found the bones of the small victims in profusion. Whole necropolises they unearthed of nothing but little skeletons.

And the world knew the old legend was true; that the men and women of Carthage had brought their offspring to the god and stood in obeisance as their children tumbled screaming into the fire. It was religion.

Now as Maharet lifted Jesse, as Maharet's lips touched her throat, Jesse thought of the old legend. Maharet's arms were like the hard metal arms of the god Baal, and in one fiery instant Jesse knew unspeakable torment.

But it was not her own death that Jesse saw; it was the deaths of others—the souls of the immolated undead, rising upwards away from terror and the physical pain of the flames that consumed their preternatural bodies. She heard their cries; she heard their warnings; she saw their faces as they left the earth, dazzling as they carried with them still the stamp of human form without its substance; she felt them passing from misery into the unknown; she heard their song just beginning.

And then the vision paled, and died away, like music half heard and half remembered. She was near to death; her body gone, all pain gone, all sense of permanence or anguish.

She stood in the clearing in the sunshine looking down at the mother on the altar. "In the flesh," Maharet said. "In the flesh all wisdom begins. Beware the thing that has no flesh. Beware the gods, beware the *idea*, beware the devil."

Then the blood came; it poured through every fiber of her body; she was legs and arms again as it electrified her limbs, her skin stinging with the heat; and the hunger making her body writhe as the blood sought to anchor her soul to substance forever.

They lay in each other's arms, she and Maharet, and Maharet's hard skin warmed and softened so that they became one wet and tangled thing, hair enmeshed, Jesse's face buried in Maharet's neck as she gnawed at the fount, as one shock of ecstasy passed through her after another.

Suddenly Maharet drew away and turned Jesse's face against the pillow. Maharet's hand covered Jesse's eyes, and Jesse felt the tiny razor-sharp teeth pierce her skin; she felt it all being taken back, drawn out. Like the whistling wind, the sensation of being emptied, of being devoured; of being nothing!

"Drink again, my darling." Slowly she opened her eyes; she saw the white throat and the white breasts; she reached out and caught the throat in her hands, and this time it was she who broke the flesh, she tore it. And when the first spill of blood hit her tongue, she pulled Maharet down under her. Utterly compliant Maharet was; hers; Maharet's breasts against her breasts; Maharet's lips against her face, as she sucked the blood, sucked it harder and harder. *You are mine, you are utterly and completely mine.* All images, voices, visions, gone now.

They slept, or almost slept, folded against one another. It seemed the pleasure left its shimmer; it seemed that to breathe was to feel it again; to shift against the silken sheets or against Maharet's silken skin was to begin again.

The fragrant wind moved through the room. A great collective sigh rose from the forest. No more Miriam, no more the spirits of the twilight realm, caught between life and death. She had found her place; her eternal place.

As she closed her eyes, she saw the thing in the jungle stop and look at her. The red-haired thing saw her and saw Maharet in her arms; it saw the red hair; two women with red hair; and the thing veered and moved towards them.

Khayman

DEAD quiet the peace of Carmel Valley. So happy were the little coven in the house, Lestat, Louis, Gabrielle, so happy to be together. Lestat had rid himself of his soiled clothes and was resplendent again in shining "vampire attire," even to the black velvet cloak thrown casually over one shoulder. And the others, how animated they were, the woman Gabrielle unbraiding her yellow hair rather absently as she talked in an easy, passionate manner. And Louis, the human one, silent, yet profoundly excited by the presence of the other two, entranced, as it were, by their simplest gestures.

At any other time, how moved Khayman would have been by such happiness. He would have wanted to touch their hands, look into their eyes, tell them who he was and what he had seen, he would have wanted just to be with them.

But she was near. And the night was not finished.

The sky paled and the faintest warmth of the morning crept across the fields. Things stirred in the growing light. The trees shifted, their leaves uncurling ever so slowly.

Khayman stood beneath the apple tree, watching the color of the shadows change; listening to the morning. She was here, without question.

She concealed herself, willfully, and powerfully. But Khayman she could not deceive. He watched; he waited, listening to the laughter and talk of the small coven.

At the doorway of the house, Lestat embraced his mother, as she took leave of him. Out into the gray morning she came, with a sprightly step, in her dusty neglected khaki clothes, her thick blond hair brushed back, the picture of a carefree wanderer. And the black-haired one, the pretty one, Louis, was beside her.

Khayman watched them cross the grass, the female moving on into the open field before the woods where she meant to sleep within the earth itself, while the male entered the cool darkness of a small outbuilding. Something so refined about that one, even as he slipped beneath the floorboards, something about the way that he lay down as if in the grave; the way he composed his limbs, falling at once into utter darkness.

And the woman; with stunning violence, she made her deep and secret hiding place, the leaves settling as if she had never been there. The earth held her outstretched arms, her bent head. Into the dreams of the twins she plunged, into images of jungle and river she would never remember.

So far so good. Khayman did not want them to die, to burn up.

Exhausted, he stood with his back to the apple tree, the pungent green fragrance of the apples enveloping him.

Why was she here? And where was she hiding? When he opened himself to it, he felt the low radiant sound of her presence, rather like an engine of the modern world, giving off some irrepressible whisper of itself and its lethal power.

Finally Lestat emerged from the house and hurried towards the lair he had made for himself beneath the acacia trees against the hillside. Through a trapdoor he descended, down earthen steps, and into a dank chamber.

So it was peace for them all, peace until tonight when he would be the bringer of bad tidings.

The sun rose closer to the horizon; the first deflected rays appeared, which always dulled Khayman's vision. He focused upon the soft deepening colors of the orchard as all the rest of the world lost its distinct lines and shapes. He closed his eyes for a moment, realizing that he must go into the house, that he must seek some cool and shadowy place where mortals were unlikely to disturb him.

And when the sun set, he'd be waiting for them when they woke. He would tell them what he knew; he would tell them about the others. With a sudden stab of pain he thought of Mael, and of Jesse, whom he could not find, as if the earth had devoured them.

He thought of Maharet and he wanted to weep. But he made his way towards the house now. The sun was warm on his back; his limbs were heavy. Tomorrow night, whatever else came to pass, he wouldn't be alone. He would be with Lestat and his cohorts; and if they turned him away, he would seek out Armand. He would go north to Marius.

He heard the sound first—a loud, crackling roar. He turned, shielding his eyes from the rising sun. A great spray of earth shot up from the floor of the forest. The acacias swayed as if in a storm, limbs cracking, roots heaved up from the soil, trunks falling helter-skelter.

In a dark streak of windblown garments the Queen rose with ferocious speed, the limp body of Lestat dangling from her arms as she made for the western sky away from the sunrise.

Khayman gave a loud cry before he could stop himself. And his cry rang out over the stillness of the valley. So she had taken her lover.

Oh, poor lover, oh, poor beautiful blond-haired prince . . . .

But there was no time to think or to act or to know his own heart; he turned to the shelter of the house; the sun had struck the clouds and the horizon had become an inferno.

DANIEL stirred in the dark. The sleep seemed to lift like a blanket that had been about to crush him. He saw the gleam of Armand's eye. He heard Armand's whisper: "She's taken him."

JESSE moaned aloud. Weightless, she drifted in the pearly gloom. She saw the two rising figures as if in a dance—the Mother and the Son. Like saints ascending on the painted ceiling of a church. Her lips formed the words "the Mother."

IN THEIR deep-dug grave beneath the ice, Pandora and Santino slept in each other's arms. Pandora heard the sound. She heard Khayman's cry. She saw Lestat with his eyes closed and his head thrown back, rising in Akasha's embrace. She saw Akasha's black eyes fixed upon his sleeping face. Pandora's heart stopped in terror.

MARIUS closed his eyes. He could keep them open no longer. Above the wolves howled; the wind tore at the steel roof of the compound. Through the blizzard the feeble rays of the sun came as if igniting the swirling snow, and he could feel the dulling heat move down through layer upon layer of ice to numb him.

He saw the sleeping figure of Lestat in her arms; he saw her rising into the sky. "Beware of her, Lestat," he whispered with his last conscious breath. "Danger."

ON THE cool carpeted floor, Khayman stretched out and buried his face in his arm. And a dream came at once, a soft silky dream of a summer night in a lovely place, where the sky was big over the city lights, and they were all together, these immortals whose names he knew and held to his heart now.

PART III

AS IT WAS IN
THE BEGINNING,
IS NOW, AND EVER
SHALL BE...

*Hide me
from me.
Fill these
holes with eyes
for mine are not
mine. Hide
me head & need
for I am no good
so dead in life
so much time.
Be wing, and
shade my me
from my desire
to be
hooked fish.
That worm
wine
looks sweet and
makes my me
blind. And, too,
my heart hide
for I shall at
this rate it also
eat in time.*

STAN RICE
"Cannibal"
Some Lamb (1975)

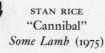

1

LESTAT:
IN THE ARMS OF
THE GODDESS

I CAN'T say when I awoke, when I first came to my senses.
I remember knowing that she and I had been together for a long time, that I'd been feasting on her blood with an animal abandon, that Enkil was destroyed and she alone held the primeval power; and that she was causing me to see things and understand things that made me cry like a child.

Two hundred years ago, when I'd drunk from her in the shrine, the blood had been silent, eerily and magnificently silent. Now it was an utter transport of images—ravishing the brain just as the blood itself ravished the body; I was learning everything that had happened; I was there as the others died one by one in that horrible way.

And then there were the voices: the voices that rose and fell, seemingly without purpose, like a whispering choir in a cave.

It seemed there was a lucid moment in which I connected everything—the rock concert, the house in Carmel Valley, her radiant face before me. And the knowledge that I was here now with her, in this dark snowy place. I'd waked her. Or rather I had given her the reason to rise as she had said it. The reason to turn and stare back at the throne on which she'd sat and take those first faltering steps away from it.

Do you know what it meant to lift my hand and see it move in the light? Do you know what it meant to hear the sudden sound of my own voice echoing in that marble chamber?

Surely we had danced together in the dark snow-covered wood, or was it only that we had embraced over and over again?

Terrible things had happened. Over the whole world, terrible things. The execution of those who should never have been born. *Evil spawn.* The massacre at the concert had been only the finish.

Yet I was in her arms in this chilling darkness, in the familiar scent of winter, and her blood was mine again, and it was enslaving me. When she drew away, I felt agony. I had to clear my thoughts, had to know whether or not Marius was alive, whether or not Louis and Gabrielle, and Armand, had been spared. I had to find myself again, somehow.

But the voices, the rising tide of voices! Mortals near and far. Distance made no difference. Intensity was the measure. It was a million times my old hearing, when I could pause on a city street and hear the tenants of some dark building, each in his own chamber, talking, thinking, praying, for as long and as closely as I liked.

Sudden silence when she spoke:

"Gabrielle and Louis are safe. I've told you this. Do you think I would hurt those you love? Look into my eyes now and listen only to what I say. I have spared many more than are required. And this I did for you as well as for myself, that I may see myself reflected in immortal eyes, and hear the voices of my children speaking to me. But I chose the ones you love, the ones you would see again. I could not take that comfort from you. But now you are with me, and you must see and know what is being revealed to you. You must have courage to match mine."

I couldn't endure it, the visions she was giving me—that horrid little Baby Jenks in those last moments; had it been a desperate dream the moment of her death, a string of images flickering within her dying brain? I couldn't bear it. And Laurent, my old companion Laurent, drying up in the flames on the pavement; and on the other side of the world, Felix, whom I had known also at the Theater of the Vampires, driven, burning, through the alleyways of Naples, and finally into the sea. And the others, so many others, the world over; I wept for them; I wept for all of it. Suffering without meaning.

"A life like that," I said of Baby Jenks, crying.

"That's why I showed you all of it," she answered. "That's why it is finished. The Children of Darkness are no more. And we shall have only angels now."

"But the others," I asked. "What has happened to Armand?" And the voices were starting again, the low humming that could mount to a deafening roar.

"Come now, my prince," she whispered. Silence again. She reached up and held my face in her hands. Her black eyes grew larger, the white face suddenly supple and almost soft. "If you must see it, I'll show you those who still live, those whose names will become legend along with yours and mine."

Legend?

She turned her head ever so slightly; it seemed a miracle when she closed her eyes; because then the visible life went out of her altogether. A dead and perfect thing, fine black eyelashes curling exquisitely. I looked down at her throat; at the pale blue of the artery beneath the flesh, suddenly visible as if she meant for me to see it. The lust I felt was unsupportable. The goddess, mine! I took her roughly with a strength that would have hurt a mortal woman. The icy skin seemed absolutely impenetrable and then my teeth broke through it and the hot fount was roaring into me again.

The voices came, yet they died back at my command. And there was nothing then but the low rush of the blood and her heart beating slowly next to my own.

Darkness. A brick cellar. A coffin made of oak and polished to a fine luster. Locks of gold. The magic moment; the locks opened as if sprung by an invisible key. The lid rose, revealing the satin lining. There was a faint scent of Eastern perfume. I saw Armand lying on the white satin pillow, a seraph with long full auburn hair; head to one side, eyes blank, as if to wake was unfailingly startling. I watched him rise from the coffin, with slow, elegant gestures; our gestures, for we are the only beings who routinely rise from coffins. I saw him close the lid. Across the damp brick floor, he walked to yet another coffin. And this one he opened reverently, as if it were a casket containing a rare prize. Inside, a young man lay sleeping; lifeless, yet dreaming. Dreaming of a jungle where a red-haired woman walked, a woman I could not clearly see. And then the most bizarre scene, something I'd glimpsed before, but where? Two women kneeling beside an altar. That is, I thought it was an altar. . . .

A tensing in her; a tightening. She shifted against me like a statue of the Virgin ready to crush me. I swooned; I thought I heard her speak a name. But the blood came in another gush and my body was throbbing again with the pleasure; no earth; no gravity.

The brick cellar once more. A shadow had fallen over the young man's body. Another had come into the cellar and placed a hand on Armand's shoulder. Armand knew him. Mael was his name. *Come.*

But where is he taking them?

Purple evening in the redwood forest. Gabrielle was walking in that careless, straight-backed, unstoppable way of hers, her eyes like two chips of glass, giving back nothing to what she saw around her, and there was Louis beside her, struggling gracefully to keep up. Louis looked so touchingly civilized in the wilderness; so hopelessly out of place. The vampire guise of last night had been discarded; yet he seemed even more the gentleman in his worn old clothing, merely a little down on his luck. Out of his league with her, and does she know it? Will she take care of him? *But they're both afraid, afraid for me!*

The tiny sky above was turning to polished porcelain; the trees seemed to bring the light down their massive trunks almost to the roots. I could hear a creek rushing in the shadows. Then I saw it. Gabrielle walked right into the water in her brown boots. *But where are they going?* And who was the third one with them, who came into view only as Gabrielle turned back to look at him?—my God, such a face, and so placid. Ancient, powerful, yet letting the two young ones walk before him. Through the trees I could see a clearing, a house. On a high stone veranda stood a red-haired woman; the woman whom I'd seen in the jungle? Ancient expressionless mask of a face like the face of the male in the forest who was looking up at her; face like the face of my Queen.

Let them come together. I sighed as the blood poured into me. *It will make it all the simpler.* But who were they, these ancient ones, these creatures with countenances washed as clean as her own?

The vision shifted. This time the voices were a soft wreath around us, whispering, crying. And for one moment I wanted to listen, to try to detach from the monstrous chorus one fleeting mortal song. Imagine it, voices from all over, from the mountains of India, from the streets of Alexandria, from the tiny hamlets near and far.

But another vision was coming.

Marius. Marius was climbing up out of a bloodstained pit of broken ice with Pandora and Santino to aid him. They had just managed to reach the jagged shelf of a basement floor. The dried blood was a crust covering half of Marius's face; he looked angry, bitter, eyes dull, his long yellow hair matted with blood. With a limp he went up a spiraling iron stairs, Pandora and Santino in his wake. It was like a pipe through which they ascended. When Pandora tried to help him he brushed her aside roughly.

Wind. Bitter cold. Marius's house lay open to the elements as if an earthquake had broken it apart. Sheets of glass were shattered into dangerous fragments; rare and beautiful tropical fish were frozen on the sand floor of a great ruined tank. Snow blanketed the furnishings and lay heaped against the bookshelves, against the statues, against the racks of records and tapes. The birds were dead in their cages. The green plants were dripping with icicles. Marius stared at the dead fish in the murky margin of ice in the bottom of the tank. He stared at the great dead stalks of seaweed that lay among the shards of gleaming glass.

Even as I watched, I saw him healing; the bruises seemed to melt from his face; I saw the face itself regain its natural shape. His leg was mending. He could stand almost straight. In rage he stared at the tiny blue and silver fish. He looked up at the sky, at the white wind that obliterated the stars completely. He brushed the flakes of dried blood from his face and hair.

Thousands of pages had been scattered about by the wind—pages of parchment, old crumbling paper. The swirling snow came down now lightly into the ruined parlor. There Marius took up the brass poker for a walking stick, and stared out through the ruptured wall at the starving wolves howling in their pen. No food for them since he, their master, had been buried. Ah, the sound of the wolves howling. I heard Santino speak to Marius, try to tell him that they must go, they were expected, that a woman waited for them in the redwood forest, a woman as old as the Mother, and the meeting could not begin until they had come. A chord of alarm went through me. What was this meeting? Marius understood but he didn't answer. He was listening to the wolves. To the wolves. . . .

The snow and the wolves. I dreamed of wolves. I felt myself drift away, back into my own mind, into my own dreams and memories. I saw a pack of fleet wolves racing over the newly fallen snow.

I saw myself as a young man fighting them—a pack of wolves that had come in deep winter to prey upon my father's village two hundred years ago. I saw myself, the mortal man, so close to death that I could smell it. But I had cut down the wolves one by one. Ah, such coarse youthful vigor, the pure luxury of thoughtless irresistible life! Or so it seemed. At the time it had been misery, hadn't it? The frozen valley, my horse and dogs slain. But now all I could do was remember, and ah, to see the snow covering the mountains, my mountains, my father's land.

I opened my eyes. She had let me go and forced me back a pace. For the first time I understood where we really were. Not in some abstract night, but in a real place and a place that had once, for all purposes, been mine.

"Yes," she whispered. "Look around you."

I knew it by the air, by the smell of winter, and as my vision cleared again, I saw the broken battlements high above, and the tower.

"This is my father's house!" I whispered. "This is the castle in which I was born."

Stillness. The snow shining white over the old floor. This had been the great hall, where we now stood. God, to see it in ruins; to know that it had been desolate for so long. Soft as earth the old stones seemed; and here had been the table, the great long table fashioned in the time of the Crusades; and there had been the gaping hearth, and there the front door.

The snow was not falling now. I looked up and I saw the stars. The tower had its round shape still, soaring hundreds of feet above the broken roof, though all the rest was as a fractured shell. My father's house . . . .

Lightly she stepped away from me, across the shimmering whiteness of the floor, turning slowly in a circle, her head back, as if she were dancing.

To move, to touch solid things, to pass from the realm of dreams into the real world, of all these joys she'd spoken earlier. It took my breath away, watching her. Her garments were timeless, a black silk cloak, a gown of silken folds that swirled gently about her narrow form. Since the dawn of history women have worn such garments, and they wear them now into the ballrooms of the world. I wanted to hold her again, but she forbade it with a soft sudden gesture. What had she said? *Can you imagine it? When I realized that he could no longer keep me there? That I was standing before the throne, and he had not stirred! That not the faintest response came from him?*

She turned; she smiled; the pale light of the sky struck the lovely angles of her face, the high cheekbones, the gentle slope of her chin. Alive she looked, utterly alive.

Then she vanished!

"Akasha!"

"Come to me," she said.

But where was she? Then I saw her far, far away from me at the very end of the hall. A tiny figure at the entrance to the tower. I could scarce make out the features of her face now, yet I could see behind her the black rectangle of the open door.

I started to walk towards her.

"No," she said. "Time to use the strength I've given you. Merely come!"

I didn't move. My mind was clear. My vision was clear. And I knew what she meant. But I was afraid. I'd always been the sprinter, the leaper, the player of tricks. Preternatural speed that baffled mortals, that was not new to me. But she asked for a different accomplishment. I was to leave the spot where I stood and locate myself suddenly beside her, with a speed which I myself could not track. It required a surrender, to try such a thing.

"Yes, surrender," she said gently. "Come."

For a tense moment I merely looked at her, her white hand gleaming on the edge of the broken door. Then I made the decision to be standing at her side. It was as if a hurricane touched me, full of noise and random force. Then I was there! I felt myself shudder all over. The flesh of my face hurt a little, but what did that matter! I looked down into her eyes and I smiled.

Beautiful she was, so beautiful. The goddess with her long black plaited hair. Impulsively I took her in my arms and kissed her; kissed her cold lips and felt them yield to me just a little.

Then the blasphemy of it struck me. It was like the time I'd kissed her in the shrine. I wanted to say something in apology, but I was staring at her throat again, hungry for the blood. It tantalized me that I could drink it and yet she was who she was; she could have destroyed me in a second with no more than the wish to see me die. That's what she had done to the others. The danger thrilled me, darkly. I closed my fingers round her arms, felt the flesh give ever so slightly. I kissed her again, and again. I could taste blood in it.

She drew back and placed her finger on my lips. Then she took my hand and led me through the tower door. Starlight fell through the broken roof hundreds of feet above us, through a gaping hole in the floor of the highest room.

"Do you see?" she said. "The room at the very top is still there? The stairs are gone. The room is unreachable. Except for you and me, my prince."

Slowly she started to rise. Never taking her eyes off me she traveled upwards, the sheer silk of her gown billowing only slightly. I watched in astonishment as she rose higher and higher, her cloak ruffled as if by a faint breeze. She passed through the opening and then stood on the very edge.

Hundreds of feet! Not possible for me to do this . . . .

"Come to me, my prince," she said, her soft voice carrying in the emptiness. "Do as you have already done. Do it quickly, and as mortals so often say, don't look down." Whispered laughter.

Suppose I got a fifth of the way up—a good leap, the height, say, of a four-story building, which was rather easy for me but also the limit of—Dizziness. Not possible. Disorientation. How had we come to be here? It was all spinning again. I saw her but it was dreamlike, and the voices were intruding. I didn't want to lose this moment. I wanted to remain connected with time in a series of linked moments, to understand this on my terms.

"Lestat!" she whispered. "Now." Such a tender thing, her small gesture to me to be quick.

I did what I had done before; I looked at her and decided that I should instantly be at her side.

The hurricane again, the air bruising me; I threw up my arms and fought the resistance. I think I saw the hole in the broken boards as I passed through it. Then I was standing there, shaken, terrified I would fall.

It sounded as if I were laughing; but I think I was just going mad a little. Crying actually. "But how?" I said. "I have to know how I did it."

"You know the answer," she said. "The intangible thing which animates you has much more strength now than it did before. It moved you as it has always moved you. Whether you take a step or take flight, it is simply a matter of degree."

"I want to try it again," I said.

She laughed very softly, but spontaneously. "Look about this room," she said. "Do you remember it?"

I nodded. "When I was a young man, I came here all the time," I said. I moved away from her. I saw piles of ruined furniture—the heavy benches and stools that had once filled our castle, medieval work so crude and strong it was damn near indestructible, like the trees that fall in the forest and remain for centuries, the bridges over streams, their trunks covered with moss. So these things had not rotted away. Even old caskets remained, and armor. Oh, yes, the old armor, ghosts of past glory. And in the dust I saw a faint bit of color. Tapestries, but they were utterly destroyed.

In the revolution, these things must have been brought here for safe-keeping and then the stairs had fallen away.

I went to one of the tiny narrow windows and I looked out on the land. Far below, nestled in the mountainside, were the electric lights of a little city, sparse, yet there. A car made its way down the narrow road. Ah, the modern world so close yet far away. The castle was the ghost of itself.

"Why did you bring me here?" I asked her. "It's so painful to see this, as painful as everything else."

"Look there, at the suits of armor," she said. "At what lies at their feet. You remember the weapons you took with you the day you went out to kill the wolves?"

"Yes. I remember them."

"Look at them again. I will give you new weapons, infinitely more powerful weapons with which you will kill for me now."

"Kill?"

I glanced down at the cache of arms. Rusted, ruined it seemed; save for the old broadsword, the fine one, which had been my father's and given to him by his father, who had got it from his father, and so forth and so on, back to the time of St. Louis. The lord's broadsword, which I, the seventh son, had used on that long ago morning when I'd gone out like a medieval prince to kill the wolves.

"But whom will I kill?" I asked.

She drew closer. How utterly sweet her face was, how brimming with innocence. Her brows came together; there was that tiny vertical fold of flesh in her forehead, just for an instant. Then all went smooth again.

"I would have you obey me without question," she said gently. "And then understanding would follow. But this is not your way."

"No," I confessed. "I've never been able to obey anyone, not for very long."

"So fearless," she said, smiling.

She opened her right hand gracefully; and quite suddenly she was holding the sword. It seemed I'd felt the thing moving towards her, a tiny change of atmosphere, no more. I stared at it, at the jeweled scabbard and the great bronze hilt that was of course a cross. The belt still hung from it, the belt I'd bought for it, during some long ago summer, of toughened leather and plaited steel.

It was a monster of a weapon, as much for battering as for slashing or piercing. I remembered the weight of it, the way it had made my arm ache when I had slashed again and again at the attacking wolves. Knights in battle had often held such weapons with two hands.

But then what did I know of such battles? I'd been no knight. I'd skewered an animal with this weapon. My only moment of mortal glory, and what had it got me? The admiration of an accursed bloodsucker who chose to make me his heir.

She placed the sword in my hands.

"It's not heavy now, my prince," she said. "You are immortal. Truly immortal. My blood is in you. And you will use your new weapons for me as you once used this sword."

A violent shudder went through me as I touched the sword; it was as if the thing held some latent memory of what it had witnessed; I saw the wolves again; I saw myself standing in the blackened frozen forest ready to kill.

And I saw myself a year later in Paris, dead, immortal; a monster, and on account of those wolves. "Wolfkiller," the vampire had called me. He had picked me from the common herd because I had slain those cursed wolves! And worn their fur so proudly through the winter streets of Paris.

How could I feel such bitterness even now? Did I want to be dead and buried down below in the village graveyard? I looked out of the window again at the snow-covered hillside. Wasn't the same thing happening now? Loved for what I'd been in those early thoughtless mortal years. Again I asked, "But whom or what will I kill?"

No answer.

I thought of Baby Jenks again, that pitiful little thing, and all the blood drinkers who were now dead. And I had wanted a war with them, a little war. And they were all dead. All who had responded to the battle call—dead. I saw the coven house in Istanbul burning; I saw an old one she had caught and burned so slowly; one who had fought her and cursed her. I was crying again.

"Yes, I took your audience from you," she said. "I burnt away the arena in which you sought to shine. I stole the battle! But don't you see?

I offer you finer things than you have ever reached for. I offer you the world, my prince."

"How so?"

"Stop the tears you shed for Baby Jenks, and for yourself. Think on the mortals you should weep for. Envision those who have suffered through the long dreary centuries—the victims of famine and deprivation and ceaseless violence. Victims of endless injustice and endless battling. How then can you weep for a race of monsters, who without guidance or purpose played the devil's gambit on every mortal they chanced to meet!"

"I know. I understand—"

"Do you? Or do you merely retreat from such things to play your symbolic games? Symbol of evil in your rock music. That is nothing, my prince, nothing at all."

"Why didn't you kill me along with the rest of them?" I asked, belligerently, miserably. I grasped the hilt of the sword in my right hand. I fancied I could see the dried blood of the wolf still on it. I pulled the blade free of the leather scabbard. Yes, the blood of the wolf. "I'm no better than they are, am I?" I said. "Why spare any of us?"

Fear stopped me suddenly. Terrible fear for Gabrielle and Louis and Armand. For Marius. Even for Pandora and Mael. Fear for myself. There isn't a thing made that doesn't fight for life, even when there is no real justification. I wanted to live; I always had.

"I would have you love me," she whispered tenderly. Such a voice. In a way, it was like Armand's voice; a voice that could caress you when it spoke to you. Draw you into itself. "And so I take time with you," she continued. She put her hands on my arms, and looked up into my eyes. "I want you to understand. You are my instrument! And so the others shall be if they are wise. Don't you see? There has been a design to all of it—your coming, my waking. For now the hopes of the millennia can be realized at last. Look on the little town below, and on this ruined castle. This could be Bethlehem, my prince, my savior. And together we shall realize all the world's most enduring dreams."

"But how could that possibly be?" I asked. Did she know how afraid I was? That her words moved me from simple fear into terror? Surely she did.

"Ah, you are so strong, princeling," she said. "But you were destined for me, surely. Nothing defeats you. You fear and you don't fear. For a century I watched you suffer, watched you grow weak and finally go down in the earth to sleep, and I then saw you rise, the very image of my own resurrection."

She bowed her head now as if she were listening to sounds from far away. The voices rising. I heard them too, perhaps because she did. I heard the ringing din. And then, annoyed, I pushed them away.

"So strong," she said. "They cannot drag you down into them, the voices, but do not ignore this power; it's as important as any other you possess. They are praying to you just as they have always prayed to me."

I understood her meaning. But I didn't want to hear their prayers; what could I do for them? What had prayers to do with the thing that I was?

"For centuries they were my only comfort," she continued. "By the hour, by the week, by the year I listened; it seemed in early times that the voices I heard had woven a shroud to make of me a dead and buried thing. Then I learned to listen more carefully. I learned to select one voice from the many as if picking a thread from the whole. To that voice alone I would listen and through it I knew the triumph and ruin of a single soul."

I watched her in silence.

"Then as the years passed, I acquired a greater power—to leave my body invisibly and to go to the single mortal whose voice I listened to, to see then through that mortal's eyes. I would walk in the body of this one, or that one. I would walk in sunshine and in darkness; I would suffer; I would hunger; I would know pain. Sometimes I walked in the bodies of immortals as I walked in the body of Baby Jenks. Often, I walked with Marius. Selfish, vain Marius, Marius who confuses greed with respect, who is ever dazzled by the decadent creations of a way of life as selfish as he is. Oh, don't suffer so. I loved him. I love him now; he cared for me. My keeper." Her voice was bitter but only for that instant. "But more often I walked with one among the poor and the sorrowful. It was the rawness of true life I craved."

She stopped; her eyes clouded; her brows came together and the tears rose in her eyes. I knew the power of which she spoke, but only slightly. I wanted so to comfort her but when I reached out to embrace her she motioned for me to be still.

"I would forget who I was, where I was," she continued. "I would be that creature, the one whose voice I had chosen. Sometimes for years. Then the horror would return, the realization that I was a motionless, purposeless thing condemned to sit forever in a golden shrine! Can you imagine the horror of waking suddenly to that realization? That all you have seen and heard and been is nothing but illusion, the observation of another's life? I would return to myself. I would become again what you see before you. This idol with a heart and brain."

I nodded. Centuries ago when I had first laid eyes upon her, I had imagined unspeakable suffering locked within her. I had imagined agonies without expression. And I had been right.

"I knew he kept you there," I said. I spoke of Enkil. Enkil who was now gone, destroyed. A fallen idol. I was remembering the moment in the shrine when I'd drunk from her and he'd come to claim her and almost finished me then and there. Had he known what he meant to do? Was all reason gone even then?

She only smiled in answer. Her eyes were dancing as she looked out into the dark. The snow had begun again, swirling almost magically, catching the light of the stars and the moon and diffusing it through all the world, it seemed.

"It was meant, what happened," she answered finally. "That I should pass those years growing ever more strong. Growing so strong finally that no one . . . no one can be my equal." She stopped. Just for a moment her conviction seemed to waver. But then she grew confident again. "He was but an instrument in the end, my poor beloved King, my companion in agony. His mind was gone, yes. And I did not destroy him, not really. I took into myself what was left of him. And at times I had been as empty, as silent, as devoid of the will even to dream as he was. Only for him there was no returning. He had seen his last visions. He was of no use anymore. He has died a god's death because it only made me stronger. And it was all meant, my prince. All meant from start to finish."

"But how? By whom?"

"Whom?" She smiled again. "Don't you understand? You need look no further for the cause of anything. I am the fulfillment and I shall from this moment on be the cause. There is nothing and no one now who can stop me." Her face hardened for a second. That wavering again. "Old curses mean nothing. In silence I have attained such power that no force in nature could harm me. Even my first brood cannot harm me though they plot against me. It was meant that those years should pass before you came."

"How did I change it?"

She came a step closer. She put her arm around me and it felt soft for the moment, not like the hard thing it truly was. We were just two beings standing near to each other, and she looked indescribably lovely to me, so pure and otherworldly. I felt the awful desire for the blood again. To bend down, to kiss her throat, to have her as I had had a thousand mortal women, yet she the goddess, she with the immeasurable power. I felt the desire rising, cresting.

Again, she put her finger on my lips, as if to say be still.

"Do you remember when you were a boy here?" she asked. "Think back now on the time when you begged them to send you to the monastery school. Do you remember the things the brothers taught you? The prayers, the hymns, the hours you worked in the library, the hours in the chapel when you prayed alone?"

"I remember, of course." I felt the tears coming again. I could see it so vividly, the monastery library, and the monks who had taught me and believed I could be a priest. I saw the cold little cell with its bed of boards; I saw the cloister and the garden veiled in rosy shadow; God, I didn't want to think now of those times. But some things can never be forgotten.

"Do you remember the morning that you went into the chapel," she continued, "and you knelt on the bare marble floor, with your arms out in the form of the cross, and you told God you would do anything if only he would make you good?"

"Yes, good . . . ." Now it was my voice that was tinged with bitterness.

"You said you would suffer martyrdom; torments unspeakable; it did not matter; if only you were to be someone who was good."

"Yes, I remember." I saw the old saints; I heard the hymns that had broken my heart. I remembered the morning my brothers had come to take me home, and I had begged them on my knees to let me stay there.

"And later, when your innocence was gone, and you took the high road to Paris, it was the same thing you wanted; when you danced and sang for the boulevard crowds, you wanted to be good."

"I was," I said haltingly. "It was a good thing to make them happy and for a little while I did."

"Yes, happy," she whispered.

"I could never explain to Nicolas, my friend, you know, that it was so important to . . . believe in a concept of goodness, even if we make it up ourselves. We don't really make it up. It's there, isn't it?"

"Oh, yes, it's there," she said. "It's there because we put it there."

Such sadness. I couldn't speak. I watched the falling snow. I clasped her hand and felt her lips against my cheek.

"You were born for me, my prince," she said. "You were tried and perfected. And in those first years, when you went into your mother's bedchamber and brought her into the world of the undead with you, it was but a prefigurement of your waking me. I am your true Mother, the Mother who will never abandon you, and I have died and been reborn, too. All the religions of the world, my prince, sing of you and of me."

"How so?" I asked. "How can that be?"

"Ah, but you know. *You know!*" She took the sword from me and examined the old belt slowly, running it across the open palm of her right hand. Then she dropped it down into the rusted heap—the last remnants on earth of my mortal life. And it was as if a wind touched these things, blowing them slowly across the snow-covered floor, until they were gone.

"Discard your old illusions," she said. "Your inhibitions. They are no more of use than these old weapons. Together, we will make the myths of the world real."

A chill cut through me, a dark chill of disbelief and then confusion; but her beauty overcame it.

"You wanted to be a saint when you knelt in that chapel," she said. "Now you shall be a god with me."

There were words of protest on the tip of my tongue; I was frightened; some dark sense overcame me. Her words, what could they possibly mean?

But suddenly I felt her arm around me, and we were rising out of the tower up through the shattered roof. The wind was so fierce it cut my eyelids. I turned towards her. My right arm went round her waist and I buried my head against her shoulder.

I heard her soft voice in my ear telling me to sleep. It would be hours before the sun set on the land to which we were going, to the place of the first lesson.

Lesson. Suddenly I was weeping again, clinging to her, weeping because I was lost, and she was all there was to cling to. And I was in terror now of what she would ask of me.

MARIUS: COMING TOGETHER

T HEY met again at the edge of the redwood forest, their clothes tattered, their eyes tearing from the wind. Pandora stood to the right of Marius, Santino to the left. And from the house across the clearing, Mael came towards them, a lanky figure almost loping over the mown grass.

Silently, he embraced Marius.

"Old friend," Marius said. But his voice had no vitality. Exhausted, he looked past Mael towards the lighted windows of the house. He sensed a great hidden dwelling within the mountain behind the visible structure with its peaked and gabled roof.

And what lay there waiting for him? For all of them? If only he had the slightest spirit for it; if only he could recapture the smallest part of his own soul.

"I'm weary," he said to Mael. "I'm sick from the journey. Let me rest here a moment longer. Then I'll come."

Marius did not despise the power to fly, as he knew Pandora did, nevertheless it invariably chastened him. He had been defenseless against it on this night of all nights; and he had now to feel the earth under him, to smell the forest, and to scan the distant house in a moment of uninterrupted quiet. His hair was tangled from the wind and still matted with dried blood. The simple gray wool jacket and pants he had taken from the ruins of his house barely gave him warmth. He brought the heavy black cloak close around him, not because the night here required it, but because he was still chilled and sore from the wind.

Mael appeared not to like his hesitation, but to accept it. Suspiciously he gazed at Pandora, whom he had never trusted, and then with open hostility he stared at Santino, who was busy brushing off his black garments and combing his fine, neatly trimmed black hair. For one second, their eyes met, Santino bristling with viciousness, then Mael turned away.

Marius stood still listening, thinking. He could feel the last bit of healing in his body; it rather amazed him that he was once again whole. Even as mortals learn year by year that they are older and weaker, so immortals must learn that they are stronger than ever they imagined they would be. It maddened him at the moment.

Scarcely an hour had passed since he was helped from the icy pit by Santino and Pandora, and now it was as if he had never been there, crushed and helpless, for ten days and nights, visited again and again by the nightmares of the twins. Yet nothing could ever be as it had been.

The twins. The red-haired woman was inside the house waiting. Santino had told him this. Mael knew it too. But who was she? And why did he not want to know the answers? Why was this the blackest hour he had ever known? His body was fully healed, no doubt about it; but what was going to heal his soul?

Armand in this strange wooden house at the base of the mountain? Armand again after all this time? Santino had told him about Armand also, and that the others—Louis and Gabrielle—had also been spared.

Mael was studying him. "He's waiting for you," he said. "Your Amadeo." It was respectful, not cynical or impatient.

And out of the great bank of memories that Marius carried forever with him, there came a long neglected moment, startling in its purity— Mael coming to the palazzo in Venice in the contented years of the fifteenth century, when Marius and Armand had known such happiness, and Mael seeing the mortal boy at work with the other apprentices on a mural which Marius had only lately left to their less competent hands. Strange how vivid, the smell of the egg tempera, the smell of the candles, and that familiar smell—not unpleasant now in remembering—which permeated all Venice, the smell of the rottenness of things, of the dark and putrid waters of the canals. "And so you would make that one?" Mael had asked with simple directness. "When it's time," Marius had said dismissively, "when it's time." Less than a year later, he had made his little blunder. "Come into my arms, young one, I can live without you no more."

Marius stared at the distant house. *My world trembles and I think of him, my Amadeo, my Armand.* The emotions he felt were suddenly as bittersweet as music, the blended orchestral melodies of recent centuries, the tragic strains of Brahms or Shostakovich which he had come to love.

But this was no time for cherishing this reunion. No time to feel the keen warmth of it, to be glad of it, and to say all the things to Armand that he so wanted to say.

Bitterness was something shallow compared to his present state of mind. *Should have destroyed them, the Mother and the Father. Should have destroyed us all.*

"Thank the gods," Mael said, "that you did not."

"And why?" Marius demanded. "Tell me why?"

Pandora shuddered. He felt her arm come around his waist. And why did that make him so angry? He turned sharply to her; he wanted to strike her, push her away. But what he saw stopped him. She wasn't even looking at him; and her expression was so distant, so soul weary that he felt his own exhaustion all the more heavily. He wanted to weep. The well-being of Pandora had always been crucial to his own survival. He did not need to be near her—better that he was not near her—but he had to know that she was somewhere, and continuing, and that they might meet again. What he saw now in her—had seen earlier—filled him with foreboding. If he felt bitterness, then Pandora felt despair.

"Come," Santino said, "they're waiting." It was said with courtly politeness.

"I know," Marius answered.

"Ah, what a trio we are!" Pandora whispered suddenly. She was spent, fragile, hungering for sleep and dreams, yet protectively she tightened her grip on Marius's waist.

"I can walk unaided, thank you," he said with uncharacteristic meanness, and to this one, the one he most loved.

"Walk, then," she answered. And just for a second, he saw her old warmth, even a spark of her old humor. She gave him a little shove, and then started out alone towards the house.

Acid. His thoughts were acid as he followed. He could not be of use to these immortals. Yet he walked on with Mael and Santino into the light streaming from the windows beyond. The redwood forest receded into shadow; not a leaf moved. But the air was good here, warm here, full of fresh scents and without the sting of the north.

Armand. It made him want to weep.

Then he saw the woman appear in the doorway. A sylph with her long curly red hair catching the hallway light.

He did not stop, but surely he felt a little intelligent fear. Old as Akasha she was, certainly. Her pale eyebrows were all but faded into the radiance of her countenance. Her mouth had no color anymore. And her eyes . . . . Her eyes were not really her eyes. No, they had been taken from a mortal victim and they were already failing her. She could not see very well as she looked at him. Ah, the blinded twin from the dreams, she was. And she felt pain now in the delicate nerves connected to the stolen eyes.

Pandora stopped at the edge of the steps.

Marius went past her and up onto the porch. He stood before the red-haired woman, marveling at her height—she was as tall as he was—and at the fine symmetry of her masklike face. She wore a flowing gown of black wool with a high neck and full dagged sleeves. In long loose gores the cloth fell from a slender girdle of braided black cord just beneath her small breasts. A lovely garment really. It made her face seem all the more radiant and detached from everything around it, a mask with the light behind it, glowing in a frame of red hair.

But there was a great deal more to marvel at than these simple attributes which she might have possessed in one form or another six thousand years ago. The woman's vigor astonished him. It gave her an air of infinite flexibility and overwhelming menace. Was she the true immortal?—the one who had never slept, never gone silent, never been released by madness? One who had walked with a rational mind and measured steps through all the millennia since she had been born?

She let him know, for what it was worth, that this was exactly what she was.

He could see her immeasurable strength as if it were incandescent light; yet he could sense an immediate informality, the immediate receptivity of a clever mind.

How to read her expression, however. How to know what she really felt.

A deep, soft femininity emanated from her, no less mysterious than anything else about her, a tender vulnerability that he associated exclusively with women though now and then he found it in a very young man. In the dreams, her face had evinced this tenderness; now it was something invisible but no less real. At another time it would have charmed him; now he only took note of it, as he noted her gilded fingernails, so beautifully tapered, and the jeweled rings she wore.

"All those years you knew of me," he said politely, speaking in the old Latin. "You knew I kept the Mother and the Father. Why didn't you come to me? Why didn't you tell me who you were?"

She considered for a long moment before answering, her eyes moving back and forth suddenly over the others who drew close to him now.

Santino was terrified of this woman, though he knew her very well. And Mael was afraid of her too, though perhaps a little less. In fact, it seemed that Mael loved her and was bound to her in some subservient way. As for Pandora, she was merely apprehensive. She drew even closer to Marius as if to stand with him, regardless of what he meant to do.

"Yes, I knew of you," the woman said suddenly. She spoke English in the modern fashion. But it was the unmistakable voice of the twin in the dream, the blind twin who had cried out the name of her mute sister, Mekare, as both had been shut up in stone coffins by the angry mob.

Our voices never really change, Marius thought. The voice was young, pretty. It had a reticent softness as she spoke again.

"I might have destroyed your shrine if I had come," she said. "I might have buried the King and the Queen beneath the sea. I might even have destroyed them, and so doing, destroyed all of us. And this I didn't want to do. And so I did nothing. What would you have had me do? I couldn't take your burden from you. I couldn't help you. So I did not come."

It was a better answer than he had expected. It was not impossible to like this creature. On the other hand, this was merely the beginning. And her answer—it wasn't the whole truth.

"No?" she asked him. Her face revealed a tracery of subtle lines for an instant, the glimpse of something that had once been human. "What is the whole truth?" she asked. "That I owed you nothing, least of all the knowledge of my existence and that you are impertinent to suggest that I should have made myself known to you? I have seen a thousand like you. I know when you come into being. I know when you perish. What are you to me? We come together now because we have to. We are in danger. All living things are in danger! And maybe when this is finished we will love each other and respect each other. And maybe not. Maybe we'll all be dead."

"Perhaps so," he said quietly. He couldn't help smiling. She was right. And he liked her manner, the bone-hard way in which she spoke.

It had been his experience that all immortals were irrevocably stamped by the age in which they were born. And so it was true, also, of even this ancient one, whose words had a savage simplicity, though the timbre of the voice had been soft.

"I'm not myself," he added hesitantly. "I haven't survived all this as well as I should have survived it. My body's healed—the old miracle." He sneered. "But I don't understand my present view of things. The bitterness, the utter—" He stopped.

"The utter darkness," she said.

"Yes. Never has life itself seemed so senseless," he added. "I don't mean for us. I mean—to use your phrase—for all living things. It's a joke, isn't it? Consciousness, it's a kind of joke."

"No," she said. "That's not so."

"I disagree with you. Will you patronize me? Tell me now how many thousands of years you've lived before I was born? How much you know that I don't know?" He thought again of his imprisonment, the ice hurting him, the pain shooting through his limbs. He thought of the immortal voices that had answered him; the rescuers who had moved towards him, only to be caught one by one by Akasha's fire. He had heard them die, if he had not seen them! And what had sleep meant for him? The dreams of the twins.

She reached out suddenly and caught his right hand gently in both of hers. It was rather like being held in the maw of a machine; and though Marius had inflicted that very impression upon many young ones himself over the years, he had yet to feel such overpowering strength himself.

"Marius, we need you now," she said warmly, her eyes glittering for an instant in the yellow light that poured out of the door behind her, and out of the windows to the right and to the left.

"For the love of heaven, why?"

"Don't jest," she answered. "Come into the house. We must talk while we have time."

"About what?" he insisted. "About why the Mother has allowed us to live? I know the answer to that question. It makes me laugh. You she cannot kill, obviously, and we . . . we are spared because Lestat wants it. You realize this, don't you? Two thousand years I cared for her, protected her, worshiped her, and she has spared me now on account of her love for a two-hundred-year-old fledgling named Lestat."

"Don't be so sure of it!" Santino said suddenly.

"No," the woman said. "It's not her only reason. But there are many things we must consider—"

"I know you're right." he said. "But I haven't the spirit for it. My illusions are gone, you see, and I didn't even know they were illusions. I thought I had attained such wisdom! It was my principal source of pride. I was with the eternal things. Then, when I saw her standing there in the shrine, I knew that all my deepest hopes and dreams had come true! She was alive inside that body. Alive, while I played the acolyte, the slave, the eternal guardian of the tomb!"

But why try to explain it? Her vicious smile, her mocking words to him, the ice falling. The cold darkness afterwards and the twins. Ah, yes, the twins. That was at the heart of it as much as anything else, and it occurred to him suddenly that the dreams had cast a spell on him. He should have questioned this before now. He looked at her, and the dreams seemed to surround her suddenly, to take her out of the moment back to those stark times. He saw sunlight; he saw the dead body of the mother; he saw the twins poised above the body. So many questions . . .

"But what have these dreams to do with this catastrophe!" he demanded suddenly. He had been so defenseless against those endless dreams.

The woman looked at him for a long moment before answering. "This I will tell you, insofar as I know. But you must calm yourself. It's as if you've got your youth back, and what a curse it must be."

He laughed. "I was never young. But what do you mean by this?"

"You rant and rave. And I can't console you."

"And you would if you could?"

"Yes."

He laughed softly.

But very gracefully she opened her arms to him. The gesture shocked him, not because it was extraordinary but because he had seen her so often go to embrace her sister in this manner in the dreams. "My name is Maharet," she said. "Call me by my name and put away your distrust. Come into my house."

She leant forward, her hands touching the sides of his face as she kissed him on the cheek. Her red hair touched his skin and the sensation confused him. The perfume rising from her clothes confused him—the faint Oriental scent that made him think of incense, which always made him think of the shrine.

"Maharet," he said angrily. "If I am needed, why didn't you come for me when I lay in that pit of ice? Could she have stopped *you?*"

"Marius, I have come," she said. "And you are here now with us." She released him, and let her hands fall, gracefully clasped before her skirts. "Do you think I had nothing to do during these nights when all our kind were being destroyed? To the left and right of me, the world over, she slew those I had loved or known. I could not be here and there to protect these victims. Cries reached my ears from every corner of the earth. And I had my own quest, my own sorrow—" Abruptly she stopped.

A faint carnal blush came over her; in a warm flash the normal expressive lines of her face returned. She was in pain, both physical and mental, and her eyes were clouding with thin blood tears. Such a strange thing, the fragility of the eyes in the indestructible body. And the suffering emanating from her—he could not bear it—it was like the dreams themselves. He saw a great riff of images, vivid yet wholly different. And quite suddenly he realized—

"You aren't the one who sent the dreams to us!" he whispered. "You are not the source."

She didn't answer.

"Ye gods, where is your sister! What does all this mean?"

There was a subtle recoiling, as if he'd struck her heart. She tried to veil her mind from him; but he felt the unquenchable pain. In silence, she stared at him, taking in all of his face and figure slowly and obviously, as if to let him know that he had unforgivably transgressed.

He could feel the fear coming from Mael and Santino, who dared to say nothing. Pandora drew even closer to him and gave him a little warning signal as she clasped his hand.

Why had he spoken so brutally, so impatiently? *My quest, my own sorrow* . . . . But damn it all!

He watched her close her eyes, and press her fingers tenderly to her eyelids as if she would make the ache in her eyes go away, but she could not.

"Maharet," he said with a soft, honest sigh. "We're in a war and we stand about on the battlefield speaking harsh words to each other. I am the worst offender. I only want to understand."

She looked up at him, her head still bowed, her hand hovering before her face. And the look was fierce, almost malicious. Yet he found himself staring senselessly at the delicate curve of her fingers, at the gilded nails and the ruby and emerald rings which flashed suddenly as if sparked with electric light.

The most errant and awful thought came to him, that if he didn't stop being so damned stupid he might never see Armand. She might drive him out of here or worse. . . . And he wanted so—before it was over—to see Armand.

"You come in now, Marius," she said suddenly, her voice polite, forgiving. "You come with me, and be reunited with your old child, and then we'll gather with the others who have the same questions. We will begin."

"Yes, my old child . . . ." he murmured. He felt the longing for Armand again like music, like Bartók's violin phrases played in a remote and safe place where there was all the time in the world to hear. Yet he hated her; he hated all of them. He hated himself. The other twin, where was the other twin? Flashes of heated jungle. Flashes of the vines torn and the saplings breaking underfoot. He tried to reason, but he couldn't. Hatred poisoned him.

Many a time he had witnessed this black denial of life in mortals. He had heard the wisest of them say, "Life is not worth it," and he had never fathomed it; well, he understood it now.

Vaguely he knew she had turned to those around him. She was welcoming Santino and Pandora into the house.

As if in a trance, he saw her turn to lead the way. Her hair was so long it fell to her waist in back, a great mass of soft red curls. And he felt the urge to touch it, see if it was as soft as it looked. How positively remarkable that he could be distracted by something lovely at this moment, something impersonal, and that it could make him feel all right; as if nothing had happened; as if the world were good. He beheld the shrine intact again; the shrine at the center of his world. Ah, the idiot human brain, he thought, how it seizes whatever it can. And to think Armand was waiting, so near . . . .

She led them through a series of large, sparely furnished rooms. The place for all its openness had the air of a citadel; the ceiling beams were enormous; the fireplaces, each with a roaring blaze, were no more than open stone hearths.

So like the old meeting halls of Europe in the dark times, when the Roman roads had fallen to ruin and the Latin tongue had been forgotten, and the old warrior tribes had risen again. The Celts had been triumphant in the end really. They were the ones who conquered Europe; its feudal castles were no more than Celtic encampments; even in the modern states, the Celtic superstitions, more than Roman reason, lived on.

But the appointments of this place hearkened back to even earlier times. Men and women had lived in cities built like this before the invention of writing; in rooms of plaster and wood; among things woven, or hammered by hand.

He rather liked it; ah, the idiot brain again, he thought, that he could like something at such a time. But the places built by immortals always intrigued him. And this one was a place to study slowly, to come to know over a great span of time.

Now they passed through a steel door and into the mountain itself. The smell of the raw earth enclosed him. Yet they walked in new metal corridors, with walls of tin. He could hear the generators, the computers, all the sweet humming electrical sounds that had made him feel so safe in his own house.

Up an iron stairs they went. It doubled back upon itself again and again as Maharet led them higher and higher. Now roughened walls revealed the innards of the mountain, its deep veins of colored clay and rock. Tiny ferns grew here; but where did the light come from? A skylight high above. Little portal to heaven. He glanced up thankfully at the bare glimmer of blue light.

Finally they emerged on a broad landing and entered a small darkened room. A door lay open to a much larger chamber where the others waited; but all Marius could see for the moment was the bright shock of distant firelight, and it made him turn his eyes away.

Someone was waiting here in this little room for him, someone whose presence he had been unable, except by the most ordinary means, to detect. A figure who stood behind him now. And as Maharet went on into the large room, taking Pandora and Santino and Mael with her, he understood what was about to happen. To brace himself he took a slow breath and closed his eyes.

How trivial all his bitterness seemed; he thought of this one whose existence had been for centuries unbroken suffering; whose youth with all its needs had been rendered truly eternal; this one whom he had failed to save, or to perfect. How many times over the years had he dreamed of such a reunion, and he had never had the courage for it; and now on this battlefield, in this time of ruin and upheaval, they were at last to meet.

"My love," he whispered. He felt himself chastened suddenly as he had been earlier when he had flown up and up over the snowy wastes past the realm of the indifferent clouds. Never had he spoken words more heartfelt. "My beautiful Amadeo," he said.

And reaching out he felt the touch of Armand's hand.

Supple still this unnatural flesh, supple as if it were human, and cool and so soft. He couldn't help himself now. He was weeping. He opened his eyes to see the boyish figure standing before him. Oh, such an expression. So accepting, so yielding. Then he opened his arms.

Centuries ago in a palazzo in Venice, he had tried to capture in imperishable pigment the quality of this love. What had been its lesson? That in all the world no two souls contain the same secret, the same gift of devotion or abandon; that in a common child, a wounded child, he had found a blending of sadness and simple grace that would forever break his heart? This one had understood him! This one had loved him as no other ever had.

Through his tears he saw no recrimination for the grand experiment that had gone wrong. He saw the face that he had painted, now darkened slightly with the thing we naively call wisdom; and he saw the same love he had counted upon so totally in those lost nights.

If only there were time, time to seek the quiet of the forest—some warm, secluded place among the soaring redwoods—and there talk together by the hour through long unhurried nights. But the others waited; and so these moments were all the more precious, and all the more sad.

He tightened his arms around Armand. He kissed Armand's lips, and his long loose vagabond hair. He ran his hand covetously over Armand's shoulders. He looked at the slim white hand he held in his own. Every detail he had sought to preserve forever on canvas; every detail he had certainly preserved in death.

"They're waiting, aren't they?" he asked. "They won't give us more than a few moments now."

Without judgment, Armand nodded. In a low, barely audible voice, he said, "It's enough. I always knew that we would meet again." Oh, the memories that the timbre of the voice brought back. The palazzo with its coffered ceilings, beds draped in red velvet. The figure of this boy rushing up the marble staircase, his face flushed from the winter wind off the Adriatic, his brown eyes on fire. "Even in moments of the greatest jeopardy," the voice continued, "I knew we would meet before I would be free to die."

"Free to die?" Marius responded. "We are always free to die, aren't we? What we must have now is the courage to do it, if indeed it is the right thing to do."

Armand appeared to think on this for a moment. And the soft distance that crept into his face brought back the sadness again to Marius. "Yes, that's true," he said.

"I love you," Marius whispered suddenly, passionately as a mortal man might. "I have always loved you. I wish that I could believe in anything other than love at this moment; but I can't."

Some small sound interrupted them. Maharet had come to the door.

Marius slipped his arm around Armand's shoulder. There was one final moment of silence and understanding between them. And then they followed Maharet into an immense mountaintop room.

ALL of glass it was, except for the wall behind him, and the distant iron chimney that hung from the ceiling above the blazing fire. No other light here save the blaze, and above and beyond, the sharp tips of the monstrous redwoods, and the bland Pacific sky with its vaporous clouds and tiny cowardly stars.

But it was beautiful still, wasn't it? Even if it was not the sky over the Bay of Naples, or seen from the flank of Annapurna or from a vessel cast adrift in the middle of the blackened sea. The mere sweep of it was beautiful, and to think that only moments ago he had been high up there, drifting in the darkness, seen only by his fellow travelers and by the stars themselves. The joy came back to him again as it had when he looked at Maharet's red hair. No sorrow as when he thought of Armand beside him; just joy, impersonal and transcendent. A reason to remain alive.

It occurred to him suddenly that he wasn't very good at bitterness or regret, that he didn't have the stamina for them, and if he was to recapture his dignity, he had better shape up fast.

A little laugh greeted him, friendly, unobtrusive; a little drunken maybe, the laugh of a fledgling who lacked common sense. He smiled in acknowledgment, darting a glance at the amused one, Daniel. Daniel the anonymous "boy" of *Interview with the Vampire*. It hit him quickly that this was Armand's child, the only child Armand had ever made. A good start on the Devil's Road this creature had, this exuberant and intoxicated being, strengthened with all that Armand had to give.

Quickly he surveyed the others who were gathered around the oval table.

To his right and some distance away, there was Gabrielle, with her blond hair in a braid down her back and her eyes full of undisguised anguish; and beside her, Louis, unguarded and passive as always, staring at Marius mutely as if in scientific inquiry or worship or both; then came his beloved Pandora, her rippling brown hair free over her shoulders and still speckled with the tiny sparkling droplets of melted frost. Santino sat to her right, finally, looking composed once more, all the dirt gone from his finely cut black velvet clothes.

On his left sat Khayman, another ancient one, who gave his name silently and freely, a horrifying being, actually, with a face even smoother than that of Maharet. Marius found he couldn't take his eyes off this one. Never had the faces of the Mother and the Father so startled him, though they too had had these black eyes and jet black hair. It was the smile, wasn't it? The open, affable expression fixed there in spite of all the efforts of time to wash it away. The creature looked like a mystic or a saint, yet he was a savage killer. Recent feasts of human blood had softened his skin just a little, and given a faint blush to his cheeks.

Mael, shaggy and unkempt as always, had taken the chair to Khayman's left. And after him came another old one, Eric, past three thousand years by Marius's reckoning, gaunt and deceptively fragile in appearance, perhaps thirty when he died. His soft brown eyes regarded Marius thoughtfully. His handmade clothes were like exquisite replicas of the store-bought goods men of business wore today.

But what was this other being? The one who sat to the right of Maharet, who stood directly opposite Marius at the far end? Now, this one truly gave him a shock. The other twin was his first rash conjecture as he stared at her green eyes and her coppery red hair.

But this being had been alive yesterday, surely. And he could find no explanation for her strength, her frigid whiteness; the piercing manner in which she stared at him; and the overwhelming telepathic power that emanated from her, a cascade of dark and finely delineated images which she seemed unable to control. She was seeing with uncanny accuracy the painting he had done centuries ago of his Amadeo, surrounded by black-winged angels as he knelt in prayer. A chill passed over Marius.

"In the crypt of the Talamasca," he whispered. "My painting?" He laughed, rudely, venomously. "And so it's there!"

The creature was frightened; she hadn't meant to reveal her thoughts. Protective of the Talamasca, and hopelessly confused, she shrank back into herself. Her body seemed to grow smaller and yet to redouble its power. A monster. A monster with green eyes and delicate bones. Born yesterday, yes, exactly as he had figured it; there was living tissue in her; and suddenly he understood all about her. This one, named Jesse, had been made by

Maharet. This one was an actual human descendant of the woman; and now she had become the fledgling of her ancient mother. The scope of it astonished him and frightened him slightly. The blood racing through the young one's veins had a potency that was unimaginable to Marius. She was absolutely without thirst; yet she wasn't even really dead.

But he must stop this, this merciless and rummaging appraisal. They were, after all, waiting for him. Yet he could not help but wonder where in God's name were his own mortal descendants, spawn of the nephews and nieces he had so loved when he was alive? For a few hundred years, true, he had followed their progress; but finally, he could no longer recognize them; he could no longer recognize Rome itself. And he had let it all go into darkness, as Rome had passed into darkness. Yet surely there were those walking the earth today who had that old family blood in their veins.

He continued to stare at the red-haired young one. How she resembled her great mother; tall, yet frail of bone, beautiful yet severe. *Some great secret here, something to do with the lineage, the family. . . .* She wore soft dark clothes rather similar to those of the ancient one; her hands were immaculate; she wore no scent or paint.

They were all of them magnificent in their own way. The tall heavily built Santino was elegant in his priestly black, with his lustrous black eyes and a sensuous mouth. Even the unkempt Mael had a savage and overpowering presence as he glowered at the ancient woman with an obvious mixture of love and hate. Armand's angelic face was beyond description; and the boy Daniel, a vision with his ashen hair and gleaming violet eyes.

Was nobody ugly ever given immortality? Or did the dark magic simply make beauty out of whatever sacrifice was thrown into the blaze? But Gabrielle had been a lovely thing in life surely, with all her son's courage and none of his impetuosity, and Louis, ah, well, Louis of course had been picked for the exquisite bones of his face, for the depth of his green eyes. He had been picked for the inveterate attitude of somber appreciation that he revealed now. He looked like a human being lost among them, his face softened with color and feeling; his body curiously defenseless; his eyes wondering and sad. Even Khayman had an undeniable perfection of face and form, horrifying as the total effect had come to be.

As for Pandora, he saw her alive and mortal when he looked at her, he saw the eager innocent woman who had come to him so many eons ago in the ink-black nighttime streets of Antioch, begging to be made immortal, not the remote and melancholy being who sat so still now in her simple biblical robes, staring through the glass wall opposite her at the fading galaxy beyond the thickening clouds.

Even Eric, bleached by the centuries and faintly radiant, retained, as Maharet did, an air of great human feeling, made all the more appealing by a beguiling androgynous grace.

The fact was, Marius had never laid eyes on such an assemblage—a gathering of immortals of all ages from the newborn to the most ancient; and each endowed with immeasurable powers and weaknesses, even to the delirious young man whom Armand had skillfully created with all the unspent virtue of his virgin blood. Marius doubted that such a "coven" had ever come together before.

And how did he fit into the picture, he who had been the eldest of his own carefully controlled universe in which the ancients had been silent gods? The winds had cleansed him of the dried blood that had clung to his face and shoulder-length hair. His long black cloak was damp from the snows from which he'd come. And as he approached the table, as he waited belligerently for Maharet to tell him he might be seated, he fancied he looked as much the monster as the others did, his blue eyes surely cold with the animosity that was burning him from within.

"Please," she said to him graciously. She gestured to the empty wooden chair before him, a place of honor obviously, at the foot of the table; that is, if one conceded that she stood at the head.

Comfortable it was, not like so much modern furniture. Its curved back felt good to him as he seated himself, and he could rest his hand on the arm, that was good, too. Armand took the empty chair to his right.

Maharet seated herself without a sound. She rested her hands with fingers folded on the polished wood before her. She bowed her head as if collecting her thoughts to begin.

"Are we all that is left?" Marius asked. "Other than the Queen and the brat prince and—" He paused.

A ripple of silent confusion passed through the others. The mute twin, where was she? What was the mystery?

"Yes," Maharet answered soberly. "Other than the Queen, and the brat prince, and my sister. Yes, we are the only ones left. Or the only ones left who count."

She paused as if to let her words have their full effect. Her eyes gently took in the complete assembly.

"Far off," she said, "there may be others—old ones who choose to remain apart. Or those she hunts still, who are doomed. But we are what remains in terms of destiny or decision. Or intent."

"And my son," Gabrielle said. Her voice was sharp, full of emotion, and subtle disregard for those present. "Will none of you tell me what she's done with him and where he is?" She looked from the woman to Marius, fearlessly and desperately. "Surely you have the power to know where he is."

Her resemblance to Lestat touched Marius. It was from this one that Lestat had drawn his strength, without doubt. But there was a coldness in her that Lestat would never understand.

"He's with her, as I've already told you," Khayman said, his voice deep and unhurried. "But beyond that she doesn't let us know."

Gabrielle did not believe it, obviously. There was a pulling away in her, a desire to leave here, to go off alone. Nothing could have forced the others away from the table. But this one had made no such commitment to the meeting, it was clear.

"Allow me to explain this," Maharet said, "because it's of the utmost importance. The Mother is skillful at cloaking herself, of course. But we of the early centuries have never been able to communicate silently with the Mother and the Father or with each other. We are all simply too close to the source of the power that makes us what we are. We are deaf and blind to each other's minds just as master and fledgling are among you. Only as time passed and more and more blood drinkers were created did they acquire the power to communicate silently with each other as we have done with mortals all along."

"Then Akasha couldn't find you," Marius said, "you or Khayman—if you weren't with us."

"That's so. She must see us through your minds or not at all. And so we must see her through the minds of others. Except of course for a certain sound we hear now and then on the approach of the powerful, a sound that has to do with a great exertion of energy, and with breath and blood."

"Yes, that sound," Daniel murmured softly. "That awful relentless sound."

"But is there nowhere *we* can hide from her?" Eric asked. "Those of us she can hear and see?" It was a young man's voice, of course, and with a heavy undefinable accent, each word rather beautifully intoned.

"You know there isn't," Maharet answered with explicit patience. "But we waste time talking of hiding. You are here either because she cannot kill you or she chooses not to. And so be it. We must go on."

"Or she hasn't finished," Eric said disgustedly. "She hasn't made up her infernal mind on the matter of who shall die and who shall live!"

"I think you are safe here," Khayman said. "She had her chance with everyone present, did she not?"

But that was just it, Marius realized. It was not at all clear that the Mother had had her chance with Eric, Eric who traveled, apparently, in the company of Maharet. Eric's eyes locked on Maharet. There was some quick silent exchange but it wasn't telepathic. What came clear to Marius was that Maharet had made Eric, and neither knew for certain whether Eric was too strong now for the Mother. Maharet was pleading for calm.

"But Lestat, you can read *his* mind, can't you?" Gabrielle said. "Can't you discover them both through him?"

"Not even I can always cover a pure and enormous distance," Maharet answered. "If there were other blood drinkers left who could pick up Lestat's thoughts and relay them to me, well, then of course I could find him in an instant. But in the main, those blood drinkers are no more. And Lestat has always been good at cloaking his presence; it's natural to him. It's always that way with the strong ones, the ones who are self-sufficient and aggressive. Wherever he is now, he instinctively shuts us out."

"She's taken him," Khayman said. He reached across the table and laid his hand on Gabrielle's hand. "She'll reveal everything to us when she is ready. And if she chooses to harm Lestat in the meantime there is absolutely nothing that any of us can do."

Marius almost laughed. It seemed these ancient ones thought statements of absolute truth were a comfort; what a curious combination of vitality and passivity they were. Had it been so at the dawn of recorded history? When people sensed the inevitable, they stood stock-still and accepted it? It was difficult for him to grasp.

"The Mother won't harm Lestat," he said to Gabrielle, to all of them. "She loves him. And at its core it's a common kind of love. She won't harm him because she doesn't want to harm herself. And she knows all his tricks, I'll wager, just as we know them. He won't be able to provoke her, though he's probably foolish enough to try."

Gabrielle gave a little nod at that with a trace of a sad smile. It was her considered opinion that Lestat could provoke anyone, finally, given enough time and opportunity; but she let it pass.

She was neither consoled nor resigned. She sat back in the wooden chair and stared past them as if they no longer existed. She felt no allegiance to this group; she felt no allegiance to anyone but Lestat.

"All right then," she said coldly. "Answer the crucial question. If I destroy this monster who's taken my son, do we all die?"

"How the hell are you going to destroy her?" Daniel asked in amazement.

Eric sneered.

She glanced at Daniel dismissively. Eric she ignored. She looked at Maharet. "Well, is the old myth true? If I waste this bitch, to use the vernacular, do I waste the rest of us too?"

There was faint laughter in the gathering. Marius shook his head. But Maharet gave a little smile of acknowledgment as she nodded:

"Yes. It was tried in the earlier times. It was tried by many a fool who didn't believe it. The spirit who inhabits her animates us all. Destroy the host, you destroy the power. The young die first; the old wither slowly; the eldest perhaps would go last. But she is the Queen of the Damned, and the Damned can't live without her. Enkil was only her consort, and that is why it does not matter now that she has slain him and drunk his blood to the last drop."

"The Queen of the Damned." Marius whispered it aloud softly. There had been a strange inflection when Maharet had said it, as if memories had stirred in her, painful and awful, and undimmed by time. Undimmed as the dreams were undimmed. Again he had a sense of the starkness and severity of these ancient beings, for whom language perhaps, and all the thoughts governed by it, had not been needlessly complex.

"Gabrielle," Khayman said, pronouncing the name exquisitely, "we cannot help Lestat. We must use this time to make a plan." He turned to Maharet. "The dreams, Maharet. Why have the dreams come to us now? This is what we all want to know."

There was a protracted silence. All present had known, in some form, these dreams. Only lightly had they touched Gabrielle and Louis, so lightly in fact that Gabrielle had, before this night, given no thought to them, and Louis, frightened by Lestat, had pushed them out of his mind. Even Pandora, who confessed no personal knowledge of them, had told Marius of Azim's warning. Santino had called them horrid trances from which he couldn't escape.

Marius knew now that they had been a noxious spell for the young ones, Jesse and Daniel, almost as cruel as they had been for him.

Yet Maharet did not respond. The pain in her eyes had intensified; Marius felt it like a soundless vibration. He felt the spasms in the tiny nerves.

He bent forward slightly, folding his hands before him on the table. "Maharet," he said. "Your sister is sending the dreams. Isn't this so?" No answer.

"Where is Mekare?" he pushed.

Silence again.

He felt the pain in her. And he was sorry, very sorry once more for the bluntness of his speech. But if he was to be of use here, he must push things to a conclusion. He thought of Akasha in the shrine again, though why he didn't know. He thought of the smile on her face. He thought of Lestat—protectively, desperately. But Lestat was just a symbol now. A symbol of himself. Of them all.

Maharet was looking at him in the strangest way, as if he were a mystery to her. She looked at the others. Finally she spoke:

"You witnessed our separation," she said quietly. "All of you. You saw it in the dreams. You saw the mob surround me and my sister; you saw them force us apart; in stone coffins they placed us, Mekare unable to cry out to me because they had cut out her tongue, and I unable to see her for the last time because they had taken my eyes.

"But I saw through the minds of those who hurt us. I knew it was to the seashores that we were being taken. Mekare to the west; and I to the east.

"Ten nights I drifted on the raft of pitch and logs, entombed alive in the stone coffin. And finally when the raft sank and the water lifted the stone lid, I was free. Blind, ravenous, I swam ashore and stole from the first poor mortal I encountered the eyes to see and the blood to live.

"But Mekare? Into the great western ocean she had been cast—the waters that ran to the end of the world.

"Yet from that first night on I searched for her; I searched through Europe, through Asia, through the southern jungles and the frozen lands of the north. Century after century I searched, finally crossing the western ocean when mortals did to take my quest to the New World as well.

"I never found my sister. I never found a mortal or immortal who had set eyes upon her or heard her name. Then in this century, in the years after the second great war, in the high mountain jungles of Peru, the indisputable evidence of my sister's presence was discovered by a lone archaeologist on the walls of a shallow cave—pictures my sister had created—of stick figures and crude pigment which told the tale of our lives together, the sufferings you all know.

"But six thousand years ago these drawings had been carved into the stone. And six thousand years ago my sister had been taken from me. No other evidence of her existence was ever found.

"Yet I have never abandoned the hope of finding my sister. I have always known, as only a twin might, that she walks this earth still, that I am not here alone.

"And now, within these last ten nights, I have, for the first time, proof that my sister is still with me. It has come to me through the dreams.

"These are Mekare's thoughts; Mekare's images; Mekare's rancor and pain."

Silence. All eyes were fixed on her. Marius was quietly stunned. He feared to be the one to speak again, but this was worse than he had imagined and the implications were now entirely clear.

The origin of these dreams was almost certainly not a conscious survivor of the millennia; rather the visions had—very possibly—come from one who had no more mind now than an animal in whom memory is a spur to action which the animal does not question or understand. It would explain their clarity; it would explain their repetition.

And the flashes he had seen of something moving through the jungles, this was Mekare herself.

"Yes," Maharet said immediately. " 'In the jungles. Walking,' " she whispered. "The words of the dying archaeologist, scribbled on a piece of paper and left for me to find when I came. 'In the jungles. Walking.' But where?"

It was Louis who broke the silence.

"Then the dreams may not be a deliberate message," he said, his words marked by a slight French accent. "They may simply be the outpouring of a tortured soul."

"No. They are a message," Khayman said. "They are a warning. They are meant for all of us, and for the Mother as well."

"But how can you say this?" Gabrielle asked him. "We don't know what her mind is now, or that she even knows that we are here."

"You don't know the whole story," Khayman said. "I know it. Maharet will tell it." He looked to Maharet.

"I saw her," Jesse said unobtrusively, her voice tentative as she looked at Maharet. "She's crossed a great river; she's coming. I saw her! No, that's not right. I saw as if I were she."

"Yes," Marius answered. "Through her eyes!"

"I saw her red hair when I looked down," Jesse said. "I saw the jungle giving way with each step."

"The dreams must be a communication," Mael said with sudden impatience. "For why else would the message be so strong? Our private thoughts don't carry such power. She raises her voice; she wants someone or something to know what she is thinking. . . ."

"Or she is obsessed and acting upon that obsession," Marius answered. "And moving towards a certain goal." He paused. "To be united with you, her sister! What else could she possibly want?"

"No," Khayman said. "That is not her goal." Again he looked at Maharet. "She has a promise to keep to the Mother, and that is what the dreams mean."

Maharet studied him for a moment in silence; it seemed this was almost beyond her endurance, this discussion of her sister, yet she fortified herself silently for the ordeal that lay ahead.

"We were there in the beginning," Khayman said. "We were the first children of the Mother; and in these dreams lies the story of how it began."

"Then you must tell us . . . all of it," Marius said as gently as he could.

"Yes." Maharet sighed. "And I will." She looked at each of them in turn and then back to Jesse. "I must tell you the whole story," she said, "so that you can understand what we may be powerless to avert. You see, this is not merely the story of the beginning. It may be the story of the end as well." She sighed suddenly as if the prospect were too much for her. "Our world has never seen such upheaval," she said, looking at Marius. "Lestat's music, the rising of the Mother, so much death."

She looked down for a moment, as if collecting herself again for the effort. And then she glanced at Khayman and at Jesse, who were the ones she most loved.

"I have never told it before," she said as if pleading for indulgence. "It has for me now the hard purity of mythology—those times when I was alive. When I could still see the sun. But in this mythology is rooted all the truths that I know. And if we go back, we may find the future, and the means to change it. The very least that we can do is seek to understand."

A hush fell. All waited with respectful patience for her to begin.

"In the beginning," she said, "we were witches, my sister and I. We talked to the spirits and the spirits loved us. Until she sent her soldiers into our land."

3

LESTAT:
THE QUEEN OF HEAVEN

S HE let me go. Instantly I began to plummet; the wind was a roar in my ears. But the worst part was that I couldn't see! I heard her say *Rise.*

There was a moment of exquisite helplessness. I was plunging towards the earth and nothing was going to stop it; then I looked up, my eyes stinging, the clouds closing over me, and I remembered the tower, and the feeling of rising. I made the decision. *Go up!* And my descent stopped at once.

It was as if a current of air had caught me. I went up hundreds of feet in one instant, and then the clouds were below me—a white light that I could scarcely see. I decided to drift. Why did I have to go anywhere for the moment? Maybe I could open my eyes fully, and see through the wind, if I wasn't afraid of the pain.

She was laughing somewhere—in my head or over it, I didn't know which. *Come on, prince, come higher.*

I spun around and shot upwards again, until I saw her coming towards me, her garments swirling about her, her heavy plaits lifted more gently by the wind.

She caught me and kissed me. I tried to steady myself, holding onto her, to look down and really see something through the breaks in the clouds. Mountains, snow-covered and dazzling in the moonlight, with great bluish flanks that disappeared into deep valleys of fathomless snow.

"Lift me now," she whispered in my ear. "Carry me to the northwest."

"I don't know the direction."

"Yes, you do. The body knows it. Your mind knows it. Don't ask them which way it is. Tell them that is the way you wish to go. You know the principles. When you lifted your rifle, you looked at the wolf running; you didn't calculate the distance or the speed of the bullet; you fired; the wolf went down."

I rose again with that same incredible buoyancy; and then I realized she had become a great weight in my arm. Her eyes were fixed on me; she was making me carry her. I smiled. I think I laughed aloud. I lifted her and kissed her again, and continued the ascent without interruption. *To the northwest.* That is to the right and to the right again and higher. My mind did know it; it knew the terrain over which we'd come. I made a little artful turn and then another; I was spinning, clutching her close to me, rather loving the weight of her body, the press of her breasts against me, and her lips again closing delicately on mine.

She drew close to my ear. "Do you hear it?" she asked.

I listened; the wind seemed annihilating; yet there came a dull chorus from the earth, human voices chanting; some in time with each other, others at random; voices praying aloud in an Asian tongue. Far far away I could hear them, and then near at hand. Important to distinguish the two sounds. First, there was a long procession of worshipers ascending through the mountain passes and over the cliffs, chanting to keep themselves alive as they trudged on in spite of weariness and cold. And within a building, a loud, ecstatic chorus, chanting fiercely over the clang of cymbals and drums.

I gathered her head close to mine and looked down, but the clouds had become a solid bed of whiteness. Yet I could see through the minds of the worshipers the brilliant vision of a courtyard and a temple of marble arches and vast painted rooms. The procession wound towards the temple.

"I want to see it!" I said. She didn't answer, but she didn't stop me as I drifted downward, stretching out on the air as if I were a bird flying, yet descending until we were in the very middle of the clouds. She had become light again, as if she were nothing.

And as we left the sea of whiteness, I saw the temple gleaming below, a tiny clay model of itself, it seemed, the terrain buckling here and there beneath its meandering walls. The stench of burning bodies rose from its blazing pyres. And towards this cluster of roofs and towers, men and women wound their way along perilous paths from as far as I could see.

"Tell me who is inside, my prince," she said. "Tell me who is the god of this temple."

See it! Draw close to it. The old trick, but all at once I began to fall. I let out a terrible cry. She caught me.

"More care, my prince," she said, steadying me.

I thought my heart was going to burst.

"You cannot move out of your body to look into the temple and fly at the same time. Look through the eyes of the mortals the way you did it before."

I was still shaking, clutching hold of her.

"I'll drop you again if you don't calm yourself," she said gently. "Tell your heart to do as you would have it do."

I gave a great sigh. My body ached suddenly from the constant force of the wind. And my eyes, they were stinging so badly again, I couldn't see anything. But I tried to subdue these little pains; or rather to ignore them as if they didn't exist. I took hold of her firmly and started down, telling myself to go slowly; and then again I tried to find the minds of the mortals and see what they saw:

Gilded walls, cusped arches, every surface glittering with decoration; incense rising, mingling with the scent of fresh blood. In blurred snatches I saw him, "the god of the temple."

"A vampire," I whispered. "A bloodsucking devil. He draws them to himself, and slaughters them at his leisure. The place reeks of death."

"And so there shall be more death," she whispered, kissing my face again tenderly. "Now, very fast, so fast mortal eyes can't see you. Bring us down to the courtyard beside the funeral pyre."

I could have sworn it was done before I'd decided it; I'd done no more than consider the idea! And there I was fallen against a rough plaster wall, with hard stones under my feet, trembling, my head reeling, my innards grinding in pain. My body wanted to keep going down, right through solid rock.

Sinking back against the wall, I heard the chanting before I could see anything. I smelt the fire, the bodies burning; then I saw the flames.

"That was very clumsy, my prince," she said softly. "We almost struck the wall."

"I don't exactly know how it happened."

"Ah, but that's the key," she said, "the word 'exact.' The spirit in you obeys swiftly and completely. Consider a little more. You don't cease to hear and see as you descend; it merely happens faster than you realize. Do you know the pure mechanics of snapping your fingers? No, you do not. Yet you can do it. A mortal child can do it."

I nodded. The principle was clear all right, as it had been with the target and the gun.

"Merely a matter of degrees," I said.

"And of surrender, fearless surrender."

I nodded. The truth was I wanted to fall on a soft bed and sleep. I blinked my eyes at the roaring fire, the sight of the bodies going black in the flames. One of them wasn't dead; an arm was raised, fingers curled. Now he was dead. Poor devil. All right.

Her cold hand touched my cheek. It touched my lips, and then she smoothed back the tangled hair of my head.

"You've never had a teacher, have you?" she asked. "Magnus orphaned you the night he made you. Your father and brothers were fools. As for your mother, she hated her children."

"I've always been my own teacher," I said soberly. "And I must confess I've always been my favorite pupil as well."

Laughter.

"Maybe it was a little conspiracy," I said. "Of pupil and teacher. But as you said, there was never anyone else."

She was smiling at me. The fire was playing in her eyes. Her face was luminous, frighteningly beautiful.

"Surrender," she said, "and I'll teach you things you never dreamed of. You've never known battle. Real battle. You've never felt the purity of a righteous cause."

I didn't answer. I felt dizzy, not merely from the long journey through the air, but from the gentle caress of her words, and the fathomless blackness of her eyes. It seemed a great part of her beauty was the sweetness of her expression, the serenity of it, the way that her eyes held steady even when the glistening white flesh of her face moved suddenly with a smile or a subtle frown. I knew if I let myself, I'd be terrified of what was happening. She must have known it too. She took me in her arms again. "Drink, prince," she whispered. "Take the strength you need to do as I would have you do."

I don't know how many moments passed. When she pulled away, I was drugged for an instant, then the clarity was as always overwhelming. The monotonous music of the temple was thundering through the walls.

"Azim! Azim! Azim!"

As she drew me along after her, it seemed my body didn't exist anymore except as a vision I kept in place. I felt of my own face, the bones beneath my skin, to touch something solid that was myself; but this skin, this sensation. It was utterly new. What was left of me?

The wooden doors opened as if by magic before us. We passed silently into a long corridor of slender white marble pillars and scalloped arches, but this was but the outer border of an immense central room. And the room was filled with frenzied, screaming worshipers who did not even see us or sense our presence as they continued to dance, to chant, to leap into the air in the hopes of glimpsing their one and only god.

"Keep at my side, Lestat," she said, the voice cutting through the din as if I'd been touched by a velvet glove.

The crowd parted, violently, bodies thrust to right and left. Screaming replaced the chant immediately; the room was in chaos, as a path lay open for us to the center of the room. The cymbals and drums were silenced; moans and soft piteous cries surrounded us.

Then a great sigh of wonder rose as Akasha stepped forward and threw back her veil.

Many feet away, in the center of the ornate floor stood the blood god, Azim, clothed in a black silk turban and jeweled robes. His face was disfigured with fury as he stared at Akasha, as he stared at me.

Prayers rose from the crowd around us; a shrill voice cried out an anthem to "the eternal mother."

"Silence!" Azim commanded. I didn't know the language; but I understood the word.

I could hear the sound of human blood in his voice; I could see it rushing through his veins. Never in fact had I seen any vampire or blood drinker so choked with human blood as was this one; he was as old as Marius, surely, yet his skin had a dark golden gleam. A thin veil of blood sweat covered it completely, even to the backs of his large, soft-looking hands.

"You dare to come into my temple!" he said, and again the language itself eluded me but the meaning was telepathically clear.

"You will die now!" Akasha said, the voice even softer than it had been a moment ago. "You who have misled these hopeless innocents; you who have fed upon their lives and their blood like a bloated leech."

Screams rose from the worshipers, cries for mercy. Again, Azim told them to be quiet.

"What right have you to condemn my worship," he cried, pointing his finger at us, "you who have sat silent on your throne since the beginning of time!"

"Time did not begin with you, my cursed beauty," Akasha answered. "I was old when you were born. And I am risen now to rule as I was meant to rule. And you shall die as a lesson to your people. You are my first great martyr. You shall die now!"

He tried to run at her; and I tried to step between them; but it was all too fast to be seen. She caught him by some invisible means and shoved him backwards so that his feet slid across the marble tile and he teetered, almost falling and then dancing as he sought to right himself, his eyes rolling up into his head.

A deep gurgling cry came out of him. He was burning. His garments were burning; and then the smoke rose from him gray and thin and writhing in the gloom as the terrified crowd gave way to screams and wails. He was twisting as the heat consumed him; then suddenly, bent double, he rose, staring at her, and flew at her with his arms out.

It seemed he would reach her before she thought what to do. And again, I tried to step before her, and with a quick shove of her right hand she threw me back into the human swarm. There were half-naked bodies all around, struggling to get away from me as I caught my balance.

I spun around and saw him poised not three feet from her, snarling at her, and trying to reach her over some invisible and unsurmountable force.

"Die, damnable one!" she cried out. (I clamped my hands over my ears.) "Go into the pit of perdition. I create it for you now."

Azim's head exploded. Smoke and flame poured out of his ruptured skull. His eyes turned black. With a flash, his entire frame ignited; yet he went down in a human posture, his fist raised against her, his legs curling as if he meant to try to stand again. Then his form disappeared utterly in a great orange blaze.

Panic descended upon the crowd, just as it had upon the rock fans outside the concert hall when the fires had broken out and Gabrielle and Louis and I had made our escape.

Yet it seemed the hysteria here reached a more dangerous pitch. Bodies crashed against the slender marble pillars. Men and women were crushed instantly as others rushed over them to the doors.

Akasha turned full circle, her garments caught in a brief dance of black and white silk around her; and everywhere human beings were caught as if by invisible hands and flung to the floor. Their bodies went into convulsions. The women, looking down at the stricken victims, wailed and tore their hair.

It took me a moment to realize what was happening, that she was killing the men. It wasn't fire. It was some invisible attack upon the vital organs. Blood poured from their ears and their eyes as they expired. Enraged, several of the women ran at her, only to meet the same fate. The men who attacked her were vanquished instantly.

Then I heard her voice inside my head:

Kill them, Lestat. Slaughter the males to the last one.

I was paralyzed. I stood beside her, lest one of them get close to her. But they didn't have a chance. This was beyond nightmare, beyond the stupid horrors to which I'd been a party all of my accursed life.

Suddenly she was standing in front of me, grasping my arms. Her soft icy voice had become an engulfing sound in my brain.

My prince, my love. You will do this for me. Slaughter the males so that the legend of their punishment will surpass the legend of the temple. They are the henchmen of the blood god. The women are helpless. Punish the males in my name.

"Oh, God help me, please don't ask this of me," I whispered. "They are pitiful humans!"

The crowd seemed to have lost its spirit. Those who had run into the rear yard were trapped. The dead and the mourning lay everywhere around us, while from the ignorant multitude at the front gates there rose the most piteous pleas.

"Let them go, Akasha, please," I said to her. Had I ever in my life begged for anything as I did now? What had these poor beings to do with us?

She drew closer to me. I couldn't see anything now but her black eyes.

"My love, this is divine war. Not the loathsome feeding upon human life which you have done night after night without scheme or reason save to survive. You kill now in my name and for my cause and I give you the greatest freedom ever given man: I tell you that to slay your mortal brother is right. Now use the new power I've given you. Choose your victims one by one, use your invisible strength or the strength of your hands."

My head was spinning. Had I this power to make men drop in their tracks? I looked around me in the smoky chamber where the incense still poured from the censers and bodies tumbled over one another, men and women embracing each other in terror, others crawling into corners as if there they would be safe.

"There is no life for them now, save in the lesson," she said. "Do as I command."

It seemed I saw a vision; for surely this wasn't from my heart or mind; I saw a thin emaciated form rise before me; I gritted my teeth as I glared at it, concentrating my malice as if it were a laser, and then I saw the victim rise off his feet and tumble backwards as the blood came out of his mouth. Lifeless, withered, he fell to the floor. It had been like a spasm; and then as effortless as shouting, as throwing one's voice out unseen yet powerful, over a great space.

Yes, kill them. Strike for the tender organs; rupture them; make the blood flow. You know that you have always wanted to do it. To kill as if it were nothing, to destroy without scruple or regret!

It was true, so true; but it was also forbidden, forbidden as nothing else on earth is forbidden. . . .

My love, it is as common as hunger; as common as time. And now you have my power and command. You and I shall put an end to it through what we will do now.

A young man rushed at me, crazed, hands out to catch my throat. *Kill him.* He cursed me as I drove him backwards with the invisible power, feeling the spasm deep in my throat and my belly; and then a sudden tightening in the temples; I *felt* it touching him, I felt it pouring out of me; I felt it as surely as if I had penetrated his skull with my fingers and was squeezing his brain. Seeing it would have been crude; there was no need to see it. All I needed to see was the blood spurting from his mouth and his ears, and down his naked chest.

Oh, was she ever right, how I had wanted to do it! How I had dreamed of it in my earliest mortal years! The sheer bliss of killing them, killing them under all their names which were the same name—*enemy*—those who deserved killing, those who were born for killing, killing with full force, my body turning to solid muscle, my teeth clenched, my hatred and my invisible strength made one.

In all directions they ran, but that only further inflamed me. I drove them back, the power slamming them into the walls. I aimed for the heart with this invisible tongue and heard the heart when it burst. I turned round and round, directing it carefully yet instantly at this one, and that one, and then another as he ran through the doorway, and yet another as he rushed down the corridor, and yet another as he tore the lamp from its chains and hurled it foolishly at me.

Into the back rooms of the temple I pursued them, with exhilarating ease through the heaps of gold and silver, tossing them over on their backs as if with long invisible fingers, then clamping those invisible fingers on their arteries until the blood gushed through the bursting flesh.

The women crowded together weeping; others fled. I heard bones break as I walked over the bodies. And then I realized that she too was killing them; that we were doing it together, and the room was now littered with the mutilated and the dead. A dark, rank smell of blood permeated everything; the fresh cold wind could not dispel it; the air was filled with soft, despairing cries.

A giant of a man raced at me, eyes bulging as he tried to stop me with a great curved sword. In rage I snatched the sword from him and sliced through his neck. Right through the bone the blade went, breaking as it did so, and head and broken blade fell at my feet.

I kicked aside the body. I went in the courtyard and stared at those who shrank from me in terror. I had no more reason, no more conscience. It was a mindless game to chase them, corner them, thrust aside the women behind whom they hid, or who struggled so pitifully to hide them, and aim the power at the right place, to pump the power at that vulnerable spot until they lay still.

The front gates! She was calling me. The men in the courtyard were dead; the women were tearing their hair, sobbing. I walked through the ruined temple, through the mourners and the dead they mourned. The crowd at the gates was on its knees in the snow, ignorant of what had gone on inside, voices raised in desperate entreaty.

Admit me to the chamber; admit me to the vision and the hunger of the lord.

At the sight of Akasha, their cries rose in volume. They reached out to touch her garments as the locks broke and the gates swung open. The wind howled down the mountain pass; the bell in the tower above gave a faint hollow sound.

Again I shoved them down, rupturing brains and hearts and arteries. I saw their thin arms flung out in the snow. The wind itself stank of blood. Akasha's voice cut through the horrid screams, telling the women to draw back and away and they would be safe.

Finally I was killing so fast I couldn't even see it anymore: The males. The males must die. I was rushing towards completion, that every single male thing that moved or stirred or moaned should be dead.

Like an angel I moved on down the winding path, with an invisible sword. And finally all the way down the cliff they dropped to their knees and waited for death. In a ghastly passivity they accepted it!

Suddenly I felt her holding me though she was nowhere near me. I heard her voice in my head:

Well done, my prince.

I couldn't stop. This invisible thing was one of my limbs now. I couldn't withdraw it and bring it back into myself. It was as if I was poised to take a breath, and if I did not take that breath I should die. But she held me motionless, and a great calm was coming over me, as if a drug had been fed into my veins. Finally I grew still and the power concentrated itself within me and became part of me and nothing more.

Slowly I turned around. I looked at the clear snowy peaks, the perfectly black sky, and at the long line of dark bodies that lay on the path from the temple gates. The women were clinging to one another, sobbing in disbelief, or giving off low and terrible moans. I smelled death as I have never smelled it; I looked down at the bits of flesh and gore that had splashed my garments. But my hands! My hands were so white and clean. *Dear God, I didn't do it! Not me. I didn't. And my hands, they are clean!*

Oh, but I had! And what am I that I could do it? That I loved it, loved it beyond all reason, loved it as men have always loved it in the absolute moral freedom of war—

It seemed a silence had fallen.

If the women still cried I didn't hear them. I didn't hear the wind either. I was moving, though why I didn't know. I had dropped down to my knees and I reached out for the last man I had slain, who was flung like broken sticks in the snow, and I put my hand into the blood on his mouth and then I smeared this blood all over both my hands and pressed them to my face.

Never had I killed in two hundred years that I hadn't tasted the blood, and taken it, along with the life, into myself. And that was a monstrous thing. But more had died here in these few ghastly moments than all those I'd ever sent to their untimely graves. And it had been done with the ease of thought and breath. Oh, this can never be atoned for! This can never never be justified!

I stood staring at the snow, through my bloody fingers; weeping and yet hating that as well. Then gradually I realized that some change had taken place with the women. Something was happening around me, and I could feel it as if the cold air had been warmed and the wind had risen and left the steep slope undisturbed.

Then the change seemed to enter into me, subduing my anguish and even slowing the beat of my heart.

The crying *had* ceased. Indeed the women were moving by twos and threes down the path as if in a trance, stepping over the dead. It seemed that sweet music was playing, and that the earth had suddenly yielded spring flowers of every color and description, and that the air was full of perfume.

Yet these things weren't happening, were they? In a haze of muted colors, the women passed me, in rags and silks, and dark cloaks. I shook myself all over. I had to think clearly! This was no time for disorientation. This power and these dead bodies were no dream and I could not, absolutely could not, yield to this overwhelming sense of well-being and peace.

"Akasha!" I whispered.

Then lifting my eyes, not because I wanted to, but because I had to, I saw her standing on a far promontory, and the women, young and old, were moving towards her, some so weak from the cold and from hunger that others had to carry them over the frozen ground.

A hush had fallen over all things.

Without words she began to speak to those assembled before her. It seemed she addressed them in their own language, or in something quite beyond specific language. I couldn't tell.

In a daze, I saw her stretch out her arms to them. Her black hair spilled down on her white shoulders, and the folds of her long simple gown barely moved in the soundless wind. It struck me that never in all my life had I beheld anything quite as beautiful as she was, and it was not merely the sum of her physical attributes, it was the pure serenity, the essence that I perceived with my innermost soul. A lovely euphoria came over me as she spoke.

Do not be afraid, she told them. The bloody reign of your god is over, and now you may return to the truth.

Soft anthems rose from the worshipers. Some dipped their foreheads to the ground before her. And it appeared that this pleased her or at least that she would allow it.

You must return now to your villages, she said. You must tell those who knew of the blood god that he is dead. The Queen of Heaven has destroyed him. The Queen will destroy all those males who still believe in him. The Queen of Heaven will bring a new reign of peace on earth. There will be death for the males who have oppressed you, but you must wait for my sign.

As she paused the anthems rose again. The Queen of Heaven, the Goddess, the Good Mother—the old litany sung in a thousand tongues the world over was finding a new form.

I shuddered. I made myself shudder. I had to penetrate that spell! It was a trick of the power, just as the killing had been a trick of the power—something definable and measurable, yet I remained drugged by the sight of her, and by the anthems. By the soft embrace of this feeling: all is well; all is as it should be. We are all safe.

Somewhere, from the sunlit recesses of my mortal memory a day came back, a day like many before it, when in the month of May in our village we had crowned a statue of the Virgin amid banks of sweet-smelling flowers, when we had sung exquisite hymns. Ah, the loveliness of that moment, when the crown of white lilies had been lifted to the Virgin's veiled head. I'd gone home that night singing those hymns. In an old prayer book, I'd found a picture of the Virgin, and it had filled me with enchantment and wondrous religious fervor such as I felt now.

And from somewhere deeper in me even, where the sun had never penetrated, came the realization that if I believed in her and what she was saying, then this unspeakable thing, this slaughter that I had committed against fragile and helpless mortals would somehow be redeemed.

You kill now in my name and for my cause and I give you the greatest freedom ever given man: I tell you that to slay your brother is right.

"Go on," she said aloud. "Leave this temple forever. Leave the dead to the snow and the winds. Tell the people. A new era is coming when those males who glorify death and killing shall reap their reward; and the era of peace shall be yours. I will come again to you. I will show you the way. Await my coming. And I will tell you then what you must do. For now, believe in me and what you have seen here. And tell others that they too may believe. Let the men come and see what awaits them. Wait for signs from me."

In a body they moved to obey her command; they ran down the mountain path towards those distant worshipers who had fled the massacre; their cries rose thin and ecstatic in the snowy void.

The wind gusted through the valley; high on the hill, the temple bell gave another dull peal. The wind tore at the scant garments of the dead. The snow had begun to fall, softly and then thickly, covering brown legs and arms and faces, faces with open eyes.

The sense of well-being had dissipated, and all the raw aspects of the moment were clear and inescapable again. These women, this visitation. . . . Bodies in the snow! Undeniable displays of power, disruptive and overwhelming.

Then a soft little sound broke the silence; things shattering in the temple above; things falling, breaking apart.

I turned and looked at her. She stood still on the little promontory, the cloak very loose over her shoulders, her flesh as white as the falling snow. Her eyes were fixed on the temple. And as the sounds continued, I knew what was happening within.

Jars of oil breaking; braziers falling. The soft whisper of cloth exploding into flame. Finally the smoke rose, thick and black, billowing from the bell tower, and from over the rear wall.

The bell tower trembled; a great roaring noise echoed against the far cliffs; and then the stones broke loose; the tower collapsed. It fell down into the valley, and the bell, with one final peal, disappeared into the soft white abyss.

The temple was consumed in fire.

I stared at it, my eyes watering from the smoke that blew down over the path, carrying with it tiny ashes and bits of soot.

Vaguely, I was aware that my body wasn't cold despite the snow. That it wasn't tired from the exertion of killing. Indeed my flesh was whiter than it had been. And my lungs took in the air so efficiently that I couldn't hear my own breathing; even my heart was softer, steadier. Only my soul was bruised and sore.

For the first time ever in my life, either mortal or immortal, I was afraid that I might die. I was afraid that she might destroy me and with reason, because I simply could not do again what I'd just done. I could not be part of this design. And I prayed I couldn't be made to do it, that I would have the strength to refuse.

I felt her hands on my shoulders.

"Turn and look at me, Lestat," she said.

I did as she asked. And there it was again, the most seductive beauty I'd ever beheld.

And I am yours, my love. You are my only true companion, my finest instrument. You know this, do you not?

Again, a deliberate shudder. Where in God's name are you, Lestat! Are you going to shrink from speaking your heart?

"Akasha, help me," I whispered. "Tell me. Why did you want me to do this, this killing? What did you mean when you told them that the males would be punished? That there would be a reign of peace on earth?" How stupid my words sounded. Looking into her eyes, I could believe she was the goddess. It was as if she drew my conviction out of me, as if it were merely blood.

I was quaking suddenly with fear. Quaking. I knew what the word meant for the first time. I tried to say more but I merely stammered. Finally I blurted it out:

"In the name of what morality will all this be done?"

"In the name of *my* morality!" she answered, the faint little smile as beautiful as before. "I am the reason, the justification, the right by which it is done!" Her voice was cold with anger, but her blank, sweet expression had not changed. "Now, listen to me, beautiful one," she said. "I love you. You've awakened me from my long sleep and to my great purpose; it gives me joy merely to look at you, to see the light in your blue eyes, and to hear the sound of your voice. It would wound me beyond your understanding of pain to see you die. But as the stars are my witness, you will aid me in my mission. Or you will be no more than the instrument for the commencement, as Judas was to Christ. And I shall destroy you as Christ destroyed Judas once your usefulness is past."

Rage overcame me. I couldn't help myself. The shift from fear to anger was so fast, I was boiling inside.

"But how do you dare to do these things!" I asked. "To send these ignorant souls abroad with mad lies!"

She stared at me in silence; it seemed she would strike out at me; her face became that of a statue again; and I thought, Well, the moment is now. I will die the way I saw Azim die. I can't save Gabrielle or Louis. I can't save Armand. I won't fight because it's useless. I won't move when it happens. I'll go deep into myself, perhaps, if I must run from the pain. I'll find some last illusion like Baby Jenks did and cling to it until I am no longer Lestat.

She didn't move. The fires on the hill were burning down. The snow was coming more thickly and she had become like a ghost standing there in the silent snowfall, white as the snow was white.

"You really aren't afraid of anything, are you?" she said.

"I'm afraid of you," I said.

"Oh, no, I do not think so."

I nodded. "I am. And I'll tell you what else I am. Vermin on the face of the earth. Nothing more than that. A loathsome killer of human beings. But I *know* that's what I am! I do not pretend to be what I am not! You have told these ignorant people that you are the Queen of Heaven! How do you mean to redeem those words and what they will accomplish among stupid and innocent minds?"

"Such arrogance," she said softly. "Such incredible arrogance, and yet I love you. I love your courage, even your rashness, which has always been your saving grace. I even love your stupidity. Don't you understand? There is no promise now that I cannot keep! I shall make the myths over! I *am* the Queen of Heaven. And Heaven shall reign on earth finally. I am anything that I say I am!"

"Oh, lord, God," I whispered.

"Do not speak those hollow words. Those words that have never meant anything to anyone! You stand in the presence of the only goddess you will ever know. You are the only god these people will ever know! Well, you must think like a god now, my beauty. You must reach for something beyond your selfish little ambitions. Don't you realize what's taken place?"

I shook my head. "I don't know anything. I'm going mad."

She laughed. She threw back her head and laughed. "We are what they dream of, Lestat. We cannot disappoint them. If we did, the truth implicit in the earth beneath our feet would be betrayed."

She turned away from me. She went back up again to the small outcropping of snow-covered rock where she had stood before. She was looking down into the valley, at the path that cut along the sheer cliff beneath her, at the pilgrims turning back now as the fleeing women gave them the word.

I heard cries echo off the stone face of the mountain. I heard the men dying down there, as she, unseen, struck them with that power, that great seductive and easy power. And the women stammering madly of miracles and visions. And then the wind rose, swallowing everything, it seemed; the great indifferent wind. I saw her shimmering face for an instant; she came towards me; I thought this is death again, this is death coming, the woods and the wolves coming, and no place to hide; and then my eyes closed.

WHEN I awoke I was in a small house. I didn't know how we'd gotten here, or how long ago the slaughter in the mountains had been. I'd been drowning in the voices, and now and then a dream had come to me, a terrible yet familiar dream. I had seen two redheaded women in this dream. They knelt beside an altar where a body lay waiting for them to perform some ritual, some crucial ritual. And I'd been struggling desperately to understand the dream's content, for it seemed that everything depended upon it; I must not forget it again.

But now all that faded. The voices, the unwelcome images; the moment pressed in.

The place where I lay was dark and dirty, and full of foul smells. In little dwellings all around us, mortals lived in misery, babies crying in hunger, amid the smell of cooking fires and rancid grease.

There was war in this place, true war. Not the debacle of the mountainside, but old-fashioned twentieth-century war. From the minds of the afflicted I caught it in viscid glimpses—an endless existence of butchery and menace—buses burned, people trapped inside beating upon the locked windows; trucks exploding, women and children running from machine gun fire.

I lay on the floor as if someone had flung me there. And Akasha stood in the doorway, her cloak wrapped tightly around her, even to her eyes, as she peered out into the dark.

When I had climbed to my feet and come up beside her, I saw a mud alley full of puddles and other small dwellings, some with roofs of tin and others with roofs of sagging newspaper. Against the filthy walls men slept, wrapped from head to toe as if in shrouds. But they were not dead; and the rats they sought to avoid knew it. And the rats nibbled at the wrappings, and the men twitched and jerked in their sleep.

It was hot here, and the warmth cooked the stenches of the place— urine, feces, the vomit of dying children. I could even smell the hunger of the children, as they cried in spasms. I could smell the deep dank sea smell of the gutters and the cesspools.

This was no village; it was a place of hovels and shacks, of hopelessness. Dead bodies lay between the dwellings. Disease was rampant; and the old and the sick sat silent in the dark, dreaming of nothing, or of death perhaps, which was nothing, as the babies cried.

Down the alley there came now a tottering child with a swollen belly, screaming as it rubbed with a small fist its swollen eye.

It seemed not to see us in the darkness. From door to door it went crying, its smooth brown skin glistening in the dim flicker of the cooking fires as it moved away.

"Where are we?" I asked her.

Astonished, I saw her turn and lift her hand tenderly to stroke my hair and my face. Relief washed through me. But the raw suffering of this place was too great for that relief to matter. So she had not destroyed me; she had brought me to hell. What was the purpose? All around me I felt the misery, the despair. What could alter the suffering of these abject people?

"My poor warrior," she said. Her eyes were full of blood tears. "Don't you know where we are?"

I didn't answer.

She spoke slowly, close to my ear. "Shall I recite the poetry of names?" she asked. "Calcutta, if you wish, or Ethiopia; or the streets of Bombay; these poor souls could be the peasants of Sri Lanka; of Pakistan; of Nicaragua, of El Salvador. It does not matter what it is; it matters how much there is of it; that all around the oases of your shining Western cities it exists; it is three-fourths of the world! Open your ears, my darling; listen to their prayers; listen to the silence of those who've learned to pray for nothing. For nothing has always been their portion, whatever the name of their nation, their city, their tribe."

We walked out together into the mud street; past piles of dung and filthy puddles and the starving dogs that came forth, and the rats that darted across our path. Then we came to the ruins of an ancient palace. Reptiles slithered among the stones. The blackness swarmed with gnats. Derelicts slept in a long row beside a running gutter. Beyond in the swamp, bodies rotted, bloated and forgotten.

Far away on the highway, the trucks passed, sending their rumble through the stifling heat like thunder. The misery of the place was like a gas, poisoning me as I stood there. This was the ragged edge of the savage garden of the world in which hope could not flower. This was a sewer.

"But what can we do?" I whispered. "Why have we come here?" Again, I was distracted by her beauty, the look of compassion that suddenly infected her and made me want to weep.

"We can reclaim the world," she said, "as I've told you. We can make the myths real; and the time will come when this will be a myth, that humans ever knew such degradation. We shall see to that, my love."

"But this is for them to solve, surely. It isn't only their obligation, it's their right. How can we aid in such a thing? How can our interference not lead to catastrophe?"

"We shall see that it does not," she said calmly. "Ah, but you don't begin to comprehend. You don't realize the strength we now possess. Nothing can stop us. But you must watch now. You are not ready and I would not push you again. When you kill again for me you must have perfect faith and perfect conviction. Be assured that I love you and I know that a heart can't be educated in the space of a night. But *learn* from what you see and hear."

She went back out in the street. For one moment she was merely a frail figure, moving through the shadows. Then suddenly I could hear beings roused in the tiny hovels all around us, and I saw the women and children emerge. Around me the sleeping forms began to stir. I shrank back into the dark.

I was trembling. I wanted desperately to do something, to beg her to have patience!

But again that sense of peace descended, that spell of perfect happiness, and I was traveling back through the years to the little French church of my childhood as the hymns began. Through my tears I saw the shining altar. I saw the icon of the Virgin, a gleaming square of gold above the flowers; I heard the Aves whispered as if they were a charm. Under the arches of Notre Dame de Paris I heard the priests singing "Salve Regina."

Her voice came, clear, inescapable as it had been before, as if it were inside my brain. Surely the mortals heard it with the same irresistible power. The command itself was without words; and the essence was beyond dispute—that a new order was to begin, a new world in which the abused and injured would know peace and justice finally. The women and the children were exhorted to rise, and to slay all males within this village. All males save one in a hundred should be killed, and all male babies save one in a hundred should also be slaughtered immediately. Peace on earth would follow once this had been done far and wide; there would be no more war; there would be food and plenty.

I was unable to move, or to voice my terror. In panic I heard the frenzied cries of the women. Around me, the sleeping derelicts rose from their wrappings, only to be driven back against the walls, dying as I had seen the men die in Azim's temple.

The street rang with cries. In clouded flashes, I saw people running; I saw the men rushing out of the houses, only to drop in the mud. On the distant road the trucks went up in flames, wheels screeching as the drivers lost control. Metal was hurled against metal. Gas tanks exploded; the night was full of magnificent light. Rushing from house to house, the women surrounded the men and beat them with any weapon they could find. Had the village of shanties and hovels ever known such vitality as it did now in the name of death?

And she, the Queen of Heaven, had risen and was hovering above the tin rooftops, a stark delicate figure burning against the clouds as if made of white flame.

I closed my eyes and turned towards the wall, fingers clutching at the crumbling rock. To think that we were solid as this, she and I. Yet not of it. No, never of it. And we did not belong here! We had no right.

But even as I wept, I felt the soft embrace of the spell again; the sweet drowsy sensation of being surrounded by flowers, of slow music with its inevitable and enthralling rhythm. I felt the warm air as it passed into my lungs; I felt the old stone tiles beneath my feet.

Soft green hills stretched out before me in hallucinatory perfection—a world without war or deprivation in which women roamed free and unafraid, women who even under provocation would shrink from the common violence that lurks in the heart of every man.

Against my will I lingered in this new world, ignoring the thud of bodies hitting the wet earth, and the final curses and cries of those who were being killed.

In great dreamy flashes, I saw whole cities transformed; I saw streets without fear of the predatory and the senselessly destructive; streets in which beings moved without urgency or desperation. Houses were no longer fortresses; gardens no longer needed their walls.

"Oh, Marius, help me," I whispered, even as the sun poured down on the tree-lined pathways and endless green fields. "Please, please help me."

And then another vision shocked me, crowding out the spell. I saw fields again, but there was no sunlight; this was a real place somewhere—and I was looking through the eyes of someone or something walking in a straight line with strong strides at incredible speed. But who was this someone? What was this being's destination? Now, this vision was being sent; it was powerful, refusing to be ignored. But why?

It was gone as quickly as it had come.

I was back in the crumbling palace arcade, among the scattered dead; staring through the open archway at the rushing figures; hearing the high-pitched cries of victory and jubilation.

Come out, my warrior, where they can see you. Come to me.

She stood before me with her arms extended. God, what did they think they were seeing? For a moment I didn't move, then I went towards her, stunned and compliant, feeling the eyes of the women, their worshipful gaze. They fell down on their knees as she and I came together. I felt her hand close too tightly; I felt my heart thudding. *Akasha, this is a lie, a terrible lie. And the evil sown here will flourish for a century.*

Suddenly the world tilted. We weren't standing on the ground anymore. She had me in her embrace and we were rising over the tin roofs, and the women below were bowing and waving their arms, and touching their foreheads to the mud.

"Behold the miracle, behold the Mother, behold the Mother and her Angel . . ."

Then in an instant, the village was a tiny scattering of silver roofs far below us, all that misery alchemized into images, and we were traveling once again on the wind.

I glanced back, trying in vain to recognize the specific location—the dark swamps, the lights of the nearby city, the thin strip of road where the overturned trucks still burned. But she was right, it really didn't matter.

Whatever was going to happen had now begun, and I did not know what could possibly stop it.

4

THE STORY OF THE TWINS
PART I

ALL eyes were fixed on Maharet as she paused. Then she began again, her words seemingly spontaneous, though they came slowly and were carefully pronounced. She seemed not sad, but eager to reexamine what she meant to describe.

"Now, when I say that my sister and I were witches, I mean this: we inherited from our mother—as she had from her mother—the power to communicate with the spirits, to get them to do our bidding in small and significant ways. We could feel the presence of the spirits—which are in the main invisible to human eyes—and the spirits were drawn to us.

"And those with such powers as we had were greatly revered amongst our people, and sought after for advice and miracles and glimpses into the future, and occasionally for putting the spirits of the dead to rest.

"What I am saying is that we were perceived as good; and we had our place in the scheme of things.

"There have always been witches, as far as I know. And there are witches now, though most no longer understand what their powers are or how to use them. Then there are those known as clairvoyants or mediums, or channelers. Or even psychic detectives. It is all the same thing. These are people who for reasons we may never understand attract spirits. Spirits find them downright irresistible; and to get the notice of these people, the spirits will do all kinds of tricks.

"As for the spirits themselves, I know that you're curious about their nature and properties, that you did not—all of you—believe the story in Lestat's book about how the Mother and the Father were made. I'm not sure that Marius himself believed it, when he was told the old story, or when he passed it on to Lestat."

Marius nodded. Already he had numerous questions. But Maharet gestured for patience. "Bear with me," she said. "I will tell you all we knew of the spirits then, which is the same as what I know of them now. Understand of course that others may use a different name for these entities. Others may define them more in the poetry of science than I will do.

"The spirits spoke to us only telepathically; as I have said, they were invisible; but their presence could be felt; they had distinct personalities, and our family of witches had over many generations given them various names.

"We divided them as sorcerers have always done into the good and the evil; but there is no evidence that they themselves have a sense of right and wrong. The evil spirits were those who were openly hostile to human beings and who liked to play malicious tricks such as the throwing of stones, the making of wind, and other such pesty things. Those who possess humans are often 'evil' spirits; those who haunt houses and are called poltergeists fall into this category, too.

"The good spirits could love, and wanted by and large to be loved as well. Seldom did they think up mischief on their own. They would answer questions about the future; they would tell us what was happening in other, remote places; and for very powerful witches such as my sister and me, for those whom the good spirits really loved, they would do their greatest and most taxing trick: they would make the rain.

"But you can see from what I'm saying that labels such as good and evil were self-serving. The good spirits were useful; the bad spirits were dangerous and nerve-wracking. To pay attention to the bad spirits—to invite them to hang about—was to court disaster, because ultimately they could not be controlled.

"There was also abundant evidence that what we called bad spirits envied us that we were fleshly and also spiritual—that we had the pleasures and powers of the physical while possessing spiritual minds. Very likely, this mixture of flesh and spirit in human beings makes all spirits curious; it is the source of our attraction for them; but it rankles the bad spirits; the bad spirits would know sensuous pleasure, it seems; yet they cannot. The good spirits did not evince such dissatisfaction.

"Now, as to where these spirits came from—they used to tell us that they had always been here. They would brag that they had watched human beings change from animals into what they were. We didn't know what they meant by such remarks. We thought they were being playful or just lying. But now, the study of human evolution makes it obvious that the spirits had witnessed this development. As for questions about their nature—how they were made or by whom—well, these they never answered. I don't think they understood what we were asking. They seemed insulted by the questions or even slightly afraid, or even thought the questions were humorous.

"I suspect that someday the scientific nature of spirits will be known. I suspect that they are matter and energy in sophisticated balance as is everything else in our universe, and that they are no more magical than electricity or radio waves, or quarks or atoms, or voices over the telephone—the things that seemed supernatural only two hundred years ago. In fact the poetry of modern science has helped me to understand them in retrospect better than any other philosophical tool. Yet I cling to my old language rather instinctively.

"It was Mekare's contention that she could now and then see them, and that they had tiny cores of physical matter and great bodies of whirling energy which she compared to storms of lightning and wind. She said there were creatures in the sea which were equally exotic in their organization; and insects who resembled the spirits, too. It was always at night that she saw their physical bodies, and they were never visible for more than a second, and usually only when the spirits were in a rage.

"Their size was enormous, she said, but then they said this too. They told us we could not imagine how big they were; but then they love to brag; one must constantly sort from their statements the part which makes sense.

"That they exert great force upon the physical world is beyond doubt. Otherwise how could they move objects as they do in poltergeist hauntings? And how could they have brought together the clouds to make the rain? Yet very little is really accomplished by them for all the energy they expend. And that was a key, always, to controlling them. There is only so much they can do, and no more, and a good witch was someone who understood that perfectly.

"Whatever their material makeup is, they have no apparent biological needs, these entities. They do not age; they do not change. And the key to understanding their childish and whimsical behavior lies in this. They have no *need* to do anything; they drift about unaware of time, for there is no physical reason to care about it, and they do whatever strikes the fancy. Obviously they see our world; they are part of it; but how it looks to them I can't guess.

"Why witches attract them or interest them I don't know either. But that's the crux of it; they see the witch, they go to her, make themselves known to her, and are powerfully flattered when they are noticed; and they do her bidding in order to get more attention; and in some cases, in order to be loved.

"And as this relationship progresses, they are made for the love of the witch to concentrate on various tasks. It exhausts them but it also delights them to see human beings so impressed.

"But imagine now, how much fun it is for them to listen to prayers and try to answer them, to hang about altars and make thunder after sacrifices are offered up. When a clairvoyant calls upon the spirit of a dead ancestor to speak to his descendants, they are quite thrilled to start chattering away in pretense of being the dead ancestor, though of course they are not that person; and they will telepathically extract information from the brains of the descendants in order to delude them all the more.

"Surely all of you know the pattern of their behavior. It's no different now than it was in our time. But what is different is the attitude of human beings to what spirits do; and that difference is crucial.

"When a spirit in these times haunts a house and makes predictions through the vocal cords of a five-year-old child, no one much believes it except those who see and hear it. It does not become the foundation of a great religion.

"It is as if the human species has grown immune to such things; it has evolved perhaps to a higher stage where the antics of spirits no longer befuddle it. And though religions linger—old religions which became entrenched in darker times—they are losing their influence among the educated very rapidly.

"But I'll say more on this later on. Let me continue now to define the properties of a witch, as such things relate to me and my sister, and to what happened to us.

"It was an inherited thing in our family. It may be physical for it seemed to run in our family line through the women and to be coupled invariably with the physical attributes of green eyes and red hair. As all of you know—as you've come to learn in one way or another since you entered this house—my child, Jesse, was a witch. And in the Talamasca she used her powers often to comfort those who were plagued by spirits and ghosts.

"Ghosts, of course, are spirits too. But they are without question spirits of those who have been human on earth; whereas the spirits I have been speaking of are not. However, one can never be too sure on this point. A very old earthbound ghost could forget that he had ever been alive; and possibly the very malevolent spirits are ghosts; and that is why they hunger so for the pleasures of the flesh; and when they possess some poor human being they belch obscenities. For them, the flesh is filth and they would have men and women believe that erotic pleasures and malice are equally dangerous and evil.

"But the fact is, given the way spirits lie—if they don't want to tell you—there's no way to know why they do what they do. Perhaps their obsession with the erotic is merely something abstracted from the minds of men and women who have always felt guilty about such things.

"To return to the point, it was mostly the women in our family who were witches. In other families it passes through both men and women. Or it can appear full-blown in a human being for reasons we can't grasp.

"Be that as it may, ours was an old, old family of witches. We could count witches back fifty generations, to what was called The Time Before the Moon. That is, we claimed to have lived in the very early period of earth history before the moon had come into the night sky.

"The legends of our people told of the coming of the moon, and the floods, storms, and earthquakes that attended it. Whether such a thing really happened I don't know. We also believed that our sacred stars were the Pleiades, or the Seven Sisters, that all blessings came from that constellation, but why, I never knew or cannot remember.

"I talk of old myths now, beliefs that were old before I was born. And those who commune with spirits become for obvious reasons rather skeptical of things. '

"Yet science even now cannot deny or verify the tales of The Time Before the Moon. The coming of the moon—its subsequent gravitational pull—has been used theoretically to explain the shifting of the polar caps and the late ice ages. Maybe there was truth in the old stories, truths that will someday be clarified for us all.

"Whatever the case, ours was an old line. Our mother had been a powerful witch to whom the spirits told numerous secrets, reading men's minds as they do. And she had a great effect upon the restless spirits of the dead.

"In Mekare and me, it seemed her power had been doubled, as is often true with twins. That is, each of us was twice as powerful as our mother. As for the power we had together, it was incalculable. We talked to the spirits when we were in the cradle. We were surrounded by them when we played. As twins, we developed our own secret language, which not even our mother understood. But the spirits knew it. The spirits would understand anything we said to them; they could even speak our secret language back to us.

"Understand, I don't tell you all this out of pride. That would be absurd. I tell you so that you will grasp what we were to each other and to our own people before the soldiers of Akasha and Enkil came into our land. I want you to understand why this evil—this making of the blood drinkers—eventually happened!

"We were a great family. We had lived in the caves of Mount Carmel for as long as anybody knew. And our people had always built their encampments on the valley floor at the foot of the mountain. They lived by herding goats and sheep. And now and then they hunted; and they grew a few crops, for the making of the hallucinogenic drugs we took to make trances—this was part of our religion—and also for the making of beer. They cut down the wild wheat which grew then in profusion.

"Small round mud-brick houses with thatched roofs made up our village, but there were others which had grown into small cities, and some in which all the houses were entered from the roofs.

"Our people made a highly distinctive pottery which they took to the markets of Jericho for trade. From there they brought back lapis lazuli, ivory, incense, and mirrors of obsidian and other such fine things. Of course we knew of many other cities, vast and beautiful as Jericho, cities which are now buried completely under the earth and which may never be found.

"But by and large we were simple people. We knew what writing was—that is, the concept of it. But it did not occur to us to use such a thing, as words had a great power and we would not have dared to write our names, or curses or truths that we knew. If a person had your name, he could call on the spirits to curse you; he could go out of his body in a trance and travel to where you were. Who could know what power you would put into his hands if he could write your name on stone or papyrus? Even for those who weren't afraid, it was distasteful at the very least.

"And in the large cities, writing was largely used for financial records which we of course could keep in our heads.

"In fact, all knowledge among our people was committed to memory; the priests who sacrificed to the bull god of our people—in whom we did not believe, by the way—committed his traditions and beliefs to memory and taught them to the young priests by rote and by verse. Family histories were told from memory, of course.

"We did however paint pictures; they covered the walls of the bull shrines in the village.

"And my family, living in the caves on Mount Carmel as we had always, covered our secret grottoes with paintings which no one saw but us. Therein we kept a kind of record. But this was done with caution. I never painted or drew the image of myself, for example, until after catastrophe had struck and I and my sister were the things which we all are.

"But to return to our people, we were peaceful; shepherds, sometime craftsmen, sometime traders, no more, no less. When the armies of Jericho went to war, sometimes our young men joined them; but that was what they wanted to do. They wanted to be young men of adventure, and to be soldiers and know glory of that sort. Others went to the cities, to see the great markets, the majesty of the courts, or the splendor of the temples. And some went to ports of the Mediterranean to see the great merchant ships. But for the most part life went on in our villages as it had for many centuries without change. And Jericho protected us, almost indifferently, because it was the magnet which drew an enemy's force unto itself.

"Never, never, did we hunt men to eat their flesh! This was not our custom! And I cannot tell you what an abomination such cannibalism would have been to us, the eating of enemy flesh. Because we were cannibals, and the eating of the flesh had a special significance—we ate the flesh of our dead."

Maharet paused for a moment as if she wanted the significance of these words to be plain to all.

Marius saw the image again of the two red-haired women kneeling before the funeral feast. He felt the warm midday stillness, and the solemnity of the moment. He tried to clear his mind and see only Maharet's face.

"Understand," Maharet said. "We believed that the spirit left the body at death; but we also believed that the residue of all living things contains some tiny amount of power after life itself is gone. For example, a man's personal belongings retain some bit of his vitality; and the body and bones, surely. And of course when we consumed the flesh of our dead this residue, so to speak, would be consumed as well.

"But the real reason we ate the dead was out of respect. It was in our view the proper way to treat the remains of those we loved. We took into ourselves the bodies of those who'd given us life, the bodies from which our bodies had come. And so a cycle was completed. And the sacred remains of those we loved were saved from the awful horror of putrefaction within the earth, or from being devoured by wild beasts, or burnt as if they were fuel or refuse.

"There is a great logic to it if you think on it. But the important thing to realize is that it was part and parcel of us as a people. The sacred duty of every child was to consume the remains of his parents; the sacred duty of the tribe was to consume the dead.

"Not a single man, woman, or child died in our village whose body was not consumed by kith or kin. Not a single man, woman, or child of our village had not consumed the flesh of the dead."

Again, Maharet paused, her eyes sweeping the group slowly before she went on.

"Now, it was not a time of great wars," she said. "Jericho had been at peace for as long as anyone could remember. And Nineveh had been at peace as well.

"But far away, to the southwest in the Nile Valley, the savage people of that land made war as they had always done upon the jungle peoples south of them so that they might bring back captives for their spits and pots. For not only did they devour their own dead with all proper respect as we did, they ate the bodies of their enemies; they gloried in it. They believed the strength of the enemy went into their bodies when they consumed his flesh. Also they liked the taste of the flesh.

"We scorned what they did, for the reasons I've explained. How could anyone want the flesh of an enemy? But perhaps the crucial difference between us and the warlike dwellers of the Nile Valley was not that they ate their enemies, but that they were warlike and we were peaceful. We did not have any enemies.

"Now, about the time that my sister and I reached our sixteenth year, a great change occurred in the Nile Valley. Or so we were told.

"The aging Queen of that realm died without a daughter to carry on the royal blood. And amongst many ancient peoples the royal blood went only through the female line. Since no male can ever be certain of the paternity of his wife's child, it was the Queen or the Princess who brought with her the divine right to the throne. This is why Egyptian pharaohs of a later age often married their sisters. It was to secure their royal right.

"And so it would have been with this young King Enkil if he had had a sister, but he did not. He did not even have a royal cousin or aunt to marry. But he was young and strong and determined to rule his land. Finally, he settled upon a new bride, not from his own people, but from those of the city of Uruk in the Tigris and Euphrates Valley.

"And this was Akasha, a beauty of the royal family, and a worshiper of the great goddess Inanna, and one who could bring into Enkil's kingdom the wisdom of her land. Or so the gossip went in the marketplaces of Jericho and Nineveh and with the caravans that came to trade for our wares.

"Now the people of the Nile were farmers already, but they tended to neglect this to hunt to make war for human flesh. And this horrified the beautiful Akasha, who set about at once to turn them away from this barbaric habit as possibly anyone of higher civilization might do.

"She probably also brought with her writing, as the people of Uruk had it—they were great keepers of records—but as writing was something largely scorned by us, I do not know this for sure. Perhaps the Egyptians had already begun to write on their own.

"You cannot imagine the slowness with which such things affect a culture. Records of taxation might be kept for generations before anyone commits to a clay tablet the words of a poem. Peppers and herbs might be cultivated by a tribe for two hundred years before anyone thinks to grow wheat or corn. As you know, the Indians of South America had toys with wheels when the Europeans swept down upon them; and jewelry they had, made of metal. But they had no wheels in use in any other form whatsoever; and they did not use metal for their weapons. And so they were defeated by the Europeans almost at once.

"Whatever the case, I don't know the full story of the knowledge Akasha brought with her from Uruk. I do know that our people heard great gossip about the ban upon all cannibalism in the Nile Valley, and how those who disobeyed were cruelly put to death. The tribes who had hunted for flesh for generations were infuriated that they could no longer enjoy this sport; but even greater was the fury of all the people that they could not eat their own dead. Not to hunt, that was one thing, but to commit one's ancestors to the earth was a horror to them as it would have been to us.

"So in order that Akasha's edict would be obeyed, the King decreed that all the bodies of the dead must be treated with unguents and wrapped up. Not only could one not eat the sacred flesh of mother or father, but it must be secured in linen wrappings at great expense, and these intact bodies must be displayed for all to see, and then placed in tombs with proper offerings and incantation of the priest.

"The sooner the wrapping was done the better; because no one could then get to the flesh.

"And to further assist the people in this new observance, Akasha and Enkil convinced them that the spirits of the dead would fare better in the realm to which they had gone if their bodies were preserved in these wrappings on earth. In other words, the people were told, 'Your beloved ancestors are not neglected; rather they are well kept.'

"We thought it was very amusing when we heard it—wrapping the dead and putting them away in furnished rooms above or below the desert sand. We thought it amusing that the spirits of the dead should be helped by the perfect maintenance of their bodies on earth. For as anyone knows who has ever communicated with the dead, it is better that they forget their bodies; it is only when they relinquish their earthly image that they can rise to the higher plane.

"And now in Egypt in the tombs of the very rich and very religious, there lay these things—these mummies in which the flesh rotted away.

"If anyone had told us that this custom of mummification would become entrenched in that culture, that for four thousand years the Egyptians would practice it, that it would become a great and enduring mystery to the entire world—that little children in the twentieth century would go into museums to gaze at mummies—we would not have believed such a thing.

"However, it did not matter to us, really. We were very far from the Nile Valley. We could not even imagine what these people were like. We knew their religion had come out of Africa, that they worshiped the god Osiris, and the sun god, Ra, and animal gods as well. But we really didn't understand these people. We didn't understand their land of inundation and desert. When we held in our hands fine objects which they had made, we knew some faint shimmer of their personalities, but it was alien. We felt sorry for them that they could not eat their dead.

"When we asked the spirits about them, the spirits seemed mightily amused by the Egyptians. They said the Egyptians had 'nice voices' and 'nice words' and that it was pleasurable to visit their temples and altars; they liked the Egyptian tongue. Then they seemed to lose interest in the question, and to drift off as was often the case.

"What they said fascinated us but it didn't surprise us. We knew how the spirits liked our words and our chants and our songs. So the spirits were playing gods there for the Egyptians. The spirits did that sort of thing all the time.

"As the years passed, we heard that Enkil, to unite his kingdom and stop the rebellion and resistance of the die-hard cannibals, had made a great army and embarked on conquests to north and south. He had launched ships in the great sea. It was an old trick: get them all to fight an enemy and they'll stop quarreling at home.

"But again, what had this to do with us? Ours was a land of serenity and beauty, of laden fruit trees and fields of wild wheat free for anyone to cut with the scythe. Ours was a land of green grass and cool breezes. But there wasn't anything that anyone would want to take from us. Or so we believed.

"My sister and I continued to live in perfect peace on the gentle slopes of Mount Carmel, often speaking to our mother and to each other silently, or with a few private words, which we understood perfectly; and learning from our mother all she knew of the spirits and men's hearts.

"We drank the dream potions made by our mother from the plants we grew on the mountain, and in our trances and dream states, we traveled back into the past and spoke with our ancestors—very great witches whose names we knew. In sum, we lured the spirits of these ancient ones back to earth long enough to give us some knowledge. We also traveled out of our bodies and high over the land.

"I could spend these hours telling what we saw in these trances; how once Mekare and I walked hand in hand through the streets of Nineveh, gazing on wonders which we had not imagined; but these things are not important now.

"Let me say only what the company of the spirits meant to us—the soft harmony in which we lived with all living things around us and with the spirits; and how at moments, the love of the spirits was palpable to us, as Christian mystics have described the love of God or his saints.

"We lived in bliss together, my sister and I and our mother. The caves of our ancestors were warm and dry; and we had all things that we needed—fine robes and jewelry and lovely combs of ivory and sandals of leather—brought to us by the people as offerings, for no one ever paid us for what we did.

"And every day the people of our village came to consult with us, and we would put their questions to the spirits. We would try to see the future, which of course the spirits can do after a fashion, insofar as certain things tend to follow an inevitable course.

"We looked into minds with our telepathic power and we gave the best wisdom that we could. Now and then those possessed were brought to us. And we drove out the demon, or the bad spirit, for that is all it was. And when a house was bedeviled, we went there and ordered the bad spirit away.

"We gave the dream potion to those who requested it. And they would fall into the trance, or sleep and dream heavily in vivid images, which we sought then to interpret or explain.

"For this we didn't really need the spirits though sometimes we sought their particular advice. We used our own powers of understanding and deep vision, and often the information handed down to us, as to what various images mean.

"But our greatest miracle—which took all our power to accomplish, and which we could never guarantee—was the bringing down of the rain.

"Now, in two basic ways we worked this miracle—'little rain,' which was largely symbolic and a demonstration of power and a great healing thing for our people's souls. Or 'big rain,' which was needed for the crops, and which was very hard, indeed, to do if we could do it at all.

"Both required a great wooing of the spirits, a great calling of their names, and demanding that they come together and concentrate and use their force at our command. 'Little rain' was often done by our most familiar spirits, those who loved Mekare and me particularly, and had loved our mother and her mother, and all our ancestors before us, and could always be counted upon to do hard tasks out of love.

"But many spirits were required for 'big rain' and since some of these spirits seemed to loathe each other and to loathe cooperation, a great deal of flattery had to be thrown into the bargain. We had to do chants, and a great dance. For hours, we worked at it as the spirits gradually took interest, came together, became enamored of the idea, and then finally set to work.

"Mekare and I were able to accomplish 'big rain' only three times. But what a lovely thing it was to see the clouds gather over the valley, to see the great blinding sheets of rain descend. All our people ran out into the downpour; the land itself seemed to swell, to open, to give thanks.

" 'Little rain' we did often; we did it for others, we did it for joy.

"But it was the making of 'big rain' that really spread our fame far and wide. We had always been known as the witches of the mountain; but now people came to us from the cities of the far north, from lands whose names we didn't know.

"Men waited their turn in the village to come to the mountain and drink the potion and have us examine their dreams. They waited their turn to seek our counsel or sometimes merely to see us. And of course our village served them meat and drink and took an offering for this, and all profited, or so it seemed. And in this regard what we did was not so different from what doctors of psychology do in this century; we studied images; we interpreted them; we sought for some truth from the subconscious mind; and the miracles of 'little rain' and 'big rain' merely bolstered the faith of others in our abilities.

"One day, half a year I think before our mother was to die, a letter came into our hands. A messenger had brought it from the King and Queen of Kemet, which was the land of Egypt as the Egyptians called it themselves. It was a letter written on a clay tablet as they wrote in Jericho and Nineveh, and there were little pictures in the clay, and the beginnings of what men would later call cuneiform.

"Of course we could not read it; in fact, we found it frightening, and thought that it might be a curse. We did not want to touch it, but touch it we had to do if we were to understand anything about it that we should know.

"The messenger said that his sovereigns Akasha and Enkil had heard of our great power and would be honored if we would visit at their court; they had sent a great escort to accompany us to Kemet, and they would send us home with great gifts.

"We found ourselves, all three, distrustful of this messenger. He was speaking the truth as far as he knew it, but there was more to the whole thing.

"So our mother took the clay tablet into her hands. Immediately, she felt something from it, something which passed through her fingers and gave her great distress. At first she wouldn't tell us what she had seen; then taking us aside, she said that the King and Queen of Kemet were evil, great shedders of blood, and very disregarding of others' beliefs. And that a terrible evil would come to us from this man and woman, no matter what the writing said.

"Then Mekare and I touched the letter and we too caught the presentiment of evil. But there was a mystery here, a dark tangle, and caught up with the evil was an element of courage and what seemed good. In sum this was no simple plot to steal us and our power; there was some genuine curiosity and respect.

"Finally we asked the spirits—those two spirits which Mekare and I most loved. They came near to us and they read the letter which was a very easy thing for them to do. They said that the messenger had told the truth. But some terrible danger would come to us if we were to go to the King and Queen of Kemet.

" 'Why?' we asked the spirits.

" 'Because the King and Queen will ask you questions,' the spirits answered, 'and if you answer truthfully, which you will, the King and Queen will be angry with you, and you will be destroyed.'

"Of course we would never have gone to Egypt anyway. We didn't leave our mountain. But now we knew for sure that we must not. We told the messenger with all respect that we could not leave the place where we had been born, that no witch of our family had ever left here, and we begged him to tell this to the King and Queen.

"And so the messenger left and life returned to its normal routine.

"Except that several nights later, an evil spirit came to us, one which we called Amel. Enormous, powerful, and full of rancor, this thing danced about the clearing before our cave trying to get Mekare and me to take notice of him, and telling us that we might soon need his help.

"We were long used to the blandishments of evil spirits; it made them furious that we would not talk to them as other witches and wizards might. But we knew these entities to be untrustworthy and uncontrollable and we had never been tempted to use them and thought that we never would.

"This Amel, in particular, was maddened by our 'neglect' of him, as he called it. And he declared over and over again that he was 'Amel, the powerful,' and 'Amel, the invincible,' and we should show him some respect. For we might have great need of him in the future. We might need him more than we could imagine, for trouble was coming our way.

"At this point, our mother came out of the cave and demanded of this spirit what was this trouble that he saw.

"This shocked us because we had always been forbidden by her to speak to evil spirits; and when she had spoken to them it was always to curse them or drive them away; or to confuse them with riddles and trick questions so that they got angry, felt stupid, and gave up.

"Amel, the terrible, the evil, the overwhelming—whatever he called himself, and his boasting was endless—declared only that great trouble was coming and we should pay him the proper respect if we were wise. He then bragged of all the evil he had worked for the wizards of Nineveh. That he could torment people, bedevil them, and even prick them as if he were a swarm of gnats! He could draw blood from humans, he declared; and he liked the taste of it; and he would draw blood for us.

"My mother laughed at him. 'How could you do such a thing?' she demanded. 'You are a spirit; you have no body; you can taste nothing!' she said. And this is the sort of language which always made spirits furious, for they envy us the flesh, as I've said.

"Well, this spirit, to demonstrate his power, came down upon our mother like a gale; and immediately her good spirits fought him and there was a terrible commotion over the clearing, but when it had died away and Amel had been driven back by our guardian spirits, we saw that there were tiny pricks upon our mother's hand. Amel, the evil one, had drawn blood from her, exactly as he had said he would—as if a swarm of gnats had tormented her with little bites.

"My mother looked at these tiny pinprick wounds; the good spirits went mad to see her treated with such disrespect, but she told them to be still. Silently she pondered this thing, how it could be possible, and how this spirit might taste the blood that he had drawn.

"And it was then that Mekare explained her vision that these spirits had infinitesimal material cores at the very center of their great invisible bodies, and it was possibly through this core that the spirit tasted the blood. Imagine, Mekare said, the wick of a lamp, but a tiny thing within a flame. The wick might absorb blood. And so it was with the spirit who appeared to be all flame but had that tiny wick in it.

"Our mother was scornful but she did not like this thing. She said ironically that the world was full of wonders enough without evil spirits with a taste for blood. 'Be gone, Amel,' she said, and laid curses on him, that he was trivial, unimportant, did not matter, was not to be recognized, and might as well blow away. In other words the things she always said to get rid of pesty spirits—the things which priests say even now in slightly different form when they seek to exorcise children who are possessed.

"But what worried our mother more than Amel's antics was his warning, that evil was coming our way. It deepened the distress she had felt when she took hold of the Egyptian tablet. Yet she did not ask the good spirits for comfort or advice. Maybe she knew better than to ask them. But this I can never know. Whatever was the case, our mother knew something was going to happen, and clearly she felt powerless to prevent it. Perhaps she understood that sometimes, when we seek to prevent disaster, we play into its hands.

"Whatever was the truth of it, she grew sick in the days that followed, then weak, and then unable to speak.

"For months she lingered, paralyzed, half asleep. We sat by her night and day and sang to her. We brought flowers to her and we tried to read her thoughts. The spirits were in a terrible state of agitation as they loved her. And they made the wind blow on the mountain; they tore the leaves from the trees.

"All the village was in sorrow. Then one morning the thoughts of our mother took shape again; but they were fragments. We saw sunny fields and flowers and images of things she'd known in childhood; and then only brilliant colors and little more.

"We knew our mother was dying, and the spirits knew it. We did our best to calm them, but some of them had gone into a rage. When she died, her ghost would rise and pass through the realm of the spirits and they would lose her forever and go mad for a while in their grief.

"But finally it happened, as it was perfectly natural and inevitable, and we came out of the cave to tell the villagers our mother had gone to higher realms. All the trees of the mountain were caught in the wind made by the spirits; the air was full of green leaves. My sister and I wept; and for the first time in my life I thought I heard the spirits; I thought I heard their cries and lamentations over the wind.

"At once the villagers came to do what must be done.

"First our mother was laid out on a stone slab as was the custom so that all could come and pay their respects. She was dressed in the white gown she so loved in life, of Egyptian linen, and all her fine jewelry from Nineveh and the rings and necklaces of bone which contained tiny bits of our ancestors, and which would soon come to us.

"And after ten hours had passed, and hundreds had come to visit, both from our village and all the surrounding villages, we then prepared the body for the funeral feast. For any other dead person of our village, the priests would have done this honor. But we were witches and our mother was a witch; and we alone could touch her. And in privacy, and by the light of oil lamps, my sister and I removed the gown from our mother and covered her body completely with fresh flowers and leaves. We sawed open her skull and lifted the top carefully so that it remained intact at the forehead, and we removed her brain and placed it on a plate with her eyes. Then with an equally careful incision we removed the heart and placed it on another plate. Then these plates were covered with heavy domes of clay to protect them.

"And the villagers came forward and built a brick oven around the body of our mother on the stone slab, with the plates beside her, and they put the fire in the oven, beneath the slab, between the rocks upon which it rested, and the roasting began.

"All night it took place. The spirits had quieted because the spirit of our mother was gone. I don't think the body mattered to them; what we did now did not matter, but it certainly mattered to us.

"Because we were witches and our mother was a witch, we alone would partake of her flesh. It was all ours by custom and right. The villagers would not assist in the feast as they might have done at any other where only two offspring were left with the obligation. No matter how long it took we would consume our mother's flesh. And the villagers would keep watch with us.

"But as the night wore on, as the remains of our mother were prepared in the oven, my sister and I deliberated over the heart and the brain. We would divide these organs of course; and which should take which organ, that was what concerned us; for we had strong beliefs about these organs and what resided in each.

"Now to many peoples of that time, it was the heart that mattered. To the Egyptians, for example, the heart was the seat of conscience. This was even so to the people of our village; but we as witches believed that the brain was the residence of the human spirit: that is, the spiritual part of each man or woman that was like unto the spirits of the air. And our belief that the brain was important came from the fact that the eyes were connected to the brain; and the eyes were the organs of sight. And *seeing* is what we did as witches; we *saw* into hearts, we saw into the future; we saw into the past. Seer, that was the word for what we were in our language; that is what 'witch' meant.

"But again, this was largely ceremony of which we spoke; we believed our mother's spirit had gone. Out of respect for her, we consumed these organs so that they should not rot. So it was easy for us to reach agreement; Mekare would take the brain and the eyes; and I would take the heart.

"Mekare was the more powerful witch; the one born first; and the one who always took the lead in things; the one who spoke out immediately; the one who acted as the older sister, as one twin invariably does. It seemed right that she should take the brain and the eyes; and I, who had always been quieter of disposition, and slower, should take the organ which was associated with deep feeling, and love—the heart.

"We were pleased with the division and as the morning sky grew light we slept for a few hours, our bodies weak from hunger and the fasting that prepared us for the feast.

"Sometime before dawn the spirits waked us. They were making the wind come again. I went out of the cave; the fire glowed in the oven. The villagers who kept watch were asleep. Angrily I told the spirits to keep quiet. But one of them, that one which I most loved, said that strangers were gathered on the mountain, many many strangers who were most impressed with our power and dangerously curious about the feast.

" 'These men want something of you and Mekare,' the spirit told me. 'These men are not for the good.'

"I told him that strangers always came here; that this was nothing, and that he must be quiet now, and let us do what we had to do. But then I went to one of the men of our village and asked that the village be ready in case some trouble was to happen, that the men bring their arms with them when they gathered for the feast to begin.

"It wasn't such a strange request. Most men carried their weapons with them wherever they went. Those few who had been professional soldiers or could afford swords frequently wore them; those with knives kept them tucked in their belt.

"But in the main I was not concerned about such things; after all, strangers from far and wide came to our village; it was only natural that they would for this special event—the death of a witch.

"But you know what was to happen. You saw it in your dreams. You saw the villagers gather around the clearing as the sun rose towards the high point of noon. Maybe you saw the bricks taken down slowly from the cooling oven; or only the body of our mother, darkened, shriveled, yet peaceful as in sleep, revealed on the warm slab of stone. You saw the wilted flowers covering her, and you saw the heart and the brain and the eyes upon their plates.

"You saw us kneel on either side of our mother's body. And you heard the musicians begin to play.

"What you could not see, but you know now, is that for thousands of years our people had gathered at such feasts. For thousands of years we had lived in that valley and on the slopes of the mountain where the high grass grew and the fruit fell from the trees. This was our land, our custom, our moment.

"Our sacred moment.

"And as Mekare and I knelt opposite each other, dressed in the finest robes we possessed and wearing now the jewelry of our mother as well as our own adornments, we saw before us, not the warnings of the spirits, or the distress of our mother when she had touched the tablet of the King and Queen of Kemet. We saw our own lives—with hope, long and happy—to be lived here among our own.

"I don't know how long we knelt there; how long we prepared our souls. I remember that finally, in unison, we lifted the plates which contained the organs of our mother; and the musicians began to play. The music of the flute and the drum filled the air around us; we could hear the soft breath of the villagers; we could hear the song of the birds.

"And then the evil came down upon us; came so suddenly with the tramp of feet and loud shrill war cries of the Egyptian soldiers, that we scarce knew what was happening. Over our mother's body, we threw ourselves, seeking to protect the sacred feast; but at once they had pulled us up and away, and we saw the plates falling into the dirt, and the slab overturned!

"I heard Mekare screaming as I had never heard a human scream. But I too was screaming, screaming as I saw my mother's body thrown down into the ashes.

"Yet curses filled my ears; men denouncing us as flesh eaters, cannibals, men denouncing us as savages and those who must be put to the sword.

"Only no one harmed us. Screaming, struggling, we were bound and kept helpless, though all of our kith and kin were slaughtered before our eyes. Soldiers tramped on the body of our mother; they tramped on her heart and her brain and her eyes. They tramped back and forth in the ashes, while their cohorts skewered the men and women and children of our village.

"And then, through the chorus of screams, through the hideous outcry of all those hundreds dying on the side of the mountain, I heard Mekare call on our spirits for vengeance, call on them to punish the soldiers for what they had done.

"But what was wind or rain to such men as these? The trees shook; it seemed the earth itself trembled; leaves filled the air as they had the night before. Rocks rolled down the mountain; dust rose in clouds. But there was no more than a moment's hesitation, before the King, Enkil, himself stepped forth and told his men that these were but tricks that all men had witnessed, and we and our demons could do no more.

"It was all too true, this admonition; and the massacre went on unabated. My sister and I were ready to die. But they did not kill us. It was not their intention to kill us, and as they dragged us away, we saw our village burning, we saw the fields of wild wheat burning, we saw all the men and women of our tribe lying dead, and we knew their bodies would be left there for the beasts and the earth to consume, in utter disregard and abandon."

Maharet stopped. She had made a small steeple of her hands and now she touched the tips of her fingers to her forehead, and rested it seemed before she went on. When she continued, her voice was roughened slightly and lower, but steady as it had been before.

"What is one small nation of villages? What is one people—or even one life?

"Beneath the earth a thousand such peoples are buried. And so our people are buried to this day.

"All we knew, all we had been, was laid waste within the space of an hour. A trained army had slaughtered our simple shepherds, our women, and our helpless young. Our villages lay in ruins, huts pulled down; everything that could burn was burned.

"Over the mountain, over the village that lay at the foot of it, I felt the presence of the spirits of the dead; a great haze of spirits, some so agitated and confused by the violence done them that they clung to the earth in terror and pain; and others rising above the flesh to suffer no more.

"And what could the spirits do?

"All the way to Egypt, they followed our procession; they bedeviled the men who kept us bound and carried us by means of a litter on their shoulders, two weeping women, snuggling close to each other in terror and grief.

"Each night when the company made camp, the spirits sent wind to tear up their tents and scatter them. Yet the King counseled his soldiers not to be afraid. The King said the gods of Egypt were more powerful than the demons of the witches. And as the spirits were in fact doing all that they were capable of, as things got no worse, the soldiers obeyed.

"Each night the King had us brought before him. He spoke our language, which was a common one in the world then, spoken all through the Tigris and Euphrates Valley and along the flanks of Mount Carmel. 'You are great witches,' he would say, his voice gentle and maddeningly sincere. 'I have spared your life on this account though you were flesh eaters as were your people, and you were caught in the very act by me and my men. I have spared you because I would have the benefit of your wisdom. I would learn from you, and my Queen would learn as well. Tell me what I can give you to ease your suffering and I will do it. You are under my protection now; I am your King.'

"Weeping, refusing to meet his eyes, saying nothing, we stood before him until he tired of all this, and sent us back to sleep in the small crowded litter—a tiny rectangle of wood with only small windows—as we had been before.

"Alone once more, my sister and I spoke to each other silently, or by means of our language, the twin language of gestures and abbreviated words that only we understood. We recalled what the spirits had said to our mother; we remembered that she had taken ill after the letter from the King of Kemet and she had never recovered. Yet we weren't afraid.

"We were too stricken with grief to be afraid. It was as if we were already dead. We'd seen our people massacred, we'd seen our mother's body desecrated. We did not know what could be worse. We were together; maybe separation would be worse.

"But during this long journey to Egypt, we had one small consolation which we were not later to forget. Khayman, the King's steward, looked upon us with compassion, and did everything that he could, in secret, to ease our pain."

Maharet stopped again and looked at Khayman, who sat with his hands folded before him on the table and his eyes down. It seemed he was deep in his recollection of the things which Maharet described. He accepted this tribute but it didn't seem to console him. Then finally he looked to Maharet in acknowledgment. He seemed dazed and full of questions. But he didn't ask them. His eyes passed over the others, acknowledging their glances as well, acknowledging the steady stare of Armand, and of Gabrielle, but again, he said nothing.

Then Maharet continued:

"Khayman loosened our bonds whenever possible; he allowed us to walk about in the evening; he brought us meat and drink. And there was a great kindness in that he didn't speak to us when he did these things; he did not ask for our gratitude. He did these things with a pure heart. It was simply not to his taste to see people suffer.

"It seemed we traveled ten days to reach the land of Kemet. Maybe it was more; maybe it was less. Some time during that journey the spirits tired of their tricks; and we, dejected and without courage, did not call upon them. We sank into silence finally, only now and then looking into each other's eyes.

"At last we came into a kingdom the like of which we had never seen. Over scorching desert we were brought to the rich black land that bordered the Nile River, the black earth from which the word Kemet derives; and then over the mighty river itself by raft we were taken as was all the army, and into a sprawling city of brick buildings with grass roofs, of great temples and palaces built of the same coarse materials, but all very fine.

"This was long before the time of the stone architecture for which the Egyptians would become known—the temples of the pharaohs which have stood to this day.

"But already there was a great love of show and decoration, a movement towards the monumental. Unbaked bricks, river reeds, matting—all of these simple materials had been used to make high walls which were then whitewashed and painted with lovely designs.

"Before the palace into which we were taken as royal prisoners were great columns made from enormous jungle grasses, which had been dried and bound together and plastered with river mud; and within a closed court a lake had been made, full of lotus blossoms and surrounded by flowering trees.

"Never had we seen people so rich as these Egyptians, people decked out with so much jewelry, people with beautifully plaited hair and painted eyes. And their painted eyes tended to unnerve us. For the paint hardened their stare; it gave an illusion of depth where perhaps there was no depth; instinctively, we shrank from this artifice.

"But all we saw merely inspired further misery in us. How we hated everything around us. And we could sense from these people—though we didn't understand their strange tongue—that they hated and feared us too. It seemed our red hair caused great confusion among them; and that we were twins, this too produced fear.

"For it had been the custom among them now and then to kill twin children; and the red-haired were invariably sacrificed to the gods. It was thought to be lucky.

"All this came clear to us in wanton flashes of understanding; imprisoned, we waited grimly to see what would be our fate.

"As before, Khayman was our only consolation in those first hours. Khayman, the King's chief steward, saw that we had comforts in our imprisonment. He brought us fresh linen, and fruit to eat and beer to drink. He brought us even combs for our hair and clean dresses; and for the first time he spoke to us; he told us that the Queen was gentle and good, and we must not be afraid.

"We knew that he was speaking the truth, there was no doubt of it; but something was wrong, as it had been months before with the words of the King's messenger. Our trials had only begun.

"We also feared the spirits had deserted us; that maybe they did not want to come into this land on our behalf. But we didn't call upon the spirits; because to call and not to be answered—well, that would have been more than we could bear.

"Then evening came and the Queen sent for us; and we were brought before the court.

"The spectacle overwhelmed us, even as we despised it: Akasha and Enkil upon their thrones. The Queen was then as she is now—a woman of straight shoulders and firm limbs with a face almost too exquisite to evince intelligence, a being of enticing prettiness with a soft treble voice. As for the King, we saw him now not as a soldier but as a sovereign. His hair was plaited, and he wore his formal kilt and jewels. His black eyes were full of earnestness as they had always been; but it was clear, within a moment, that it was Akasha who ruled this kingdom and always had. Akasha had the language—the verbal skill.

"At once, she told us that our people had been properly punished for their abominations; that they had been dealt with mercifully, as all flesh eaters are savages, and they should have, by right, suffered a slow death. And she said that we had been shown mercy because we were great witches, and the Egyptians would learn from us; they would know what wisdom of the realms of the invisible we had to impart.

"Immediately, as if these words were nothing, she went into her questions. Who were our demons? Why were some good, if they were demons? Were they not gods? How could we make the rain fall?

"We were too horrified by her callousness to respond. We were bruised by the spiritual coarseness of her manner, and had begun to weep again. We turned away from her and into each other's arms.

"But something else was also coming clear to us—something very plain from the manner in which this person spoke. The speed of her words, their flippancy, the emphasis she put upon this or that syllable—all this made known to us that she was lying and did not herself know that she lied.

"And looking deep into the lie, as we closed our eyes, we saw the truth which she herself would surely deny:

"She had slaughtered our people in order to bring us here! She had sent her King and her soldiers upon this 'holy war' simply because we had refused her earlier invitation, and she wanted us at her mercy. *She was curious about us.*

"This was what our mother had seen when she held the tablet of the King and Queen in her hands. Perhaps the spirits in their own way had foreseen it. We only understood the full monstrousness of it now.

"Our people had died because we had attracted the interest of the Queen just as we attracted the interest of the spirits; we had brought this evil upon all.

"Why, we wondered, hadn't the soldiers merely taken us from our helpless villagers? Why had they brought to ruin all that our people were?

"But that was the horror! A moral cloak had been thrown over the Queen's purpose, a cloak through which she could not see any more than anyone else.

"She had convinced herself that our people should die, yes, that their savagery merited it, even though they were not Egyptians and our land was far from her home. And oh, wasn't it rather convenient, that then we should be shown mercy and brought here to satisfy her curiosity at last. And we should, of course, be grateful by then and willing to answer her questions.

"And even deeper beyond her deception, we beheld the mind that made such contradictions possible.

"This Queen had no true morality, no true system of ethics to govern the things which she did. This Queen was one of those many humans who sense that perhaps there is nothing and no reason to anything that can ever be known. Yet she cannot bear the thought of it. And so she created day in and day out her ethical systems, trying desperately to believe in them, and they were all cloaks for things she did for merely pragmatic reasons. Her war on the cannibals, for instance, had stemmed more from her *dislike* of such customs than anything else. Her people of Uruk hadn't eaten human flesh; and so she would not have this offensive thing happening around her; there really wasn't a whole lot more to it than that. For always in her there was a dark place full of despair. And a great driving force to make meaning because there was none.

"Understand, it was not a shallowness we perceived in this woman. It was a youthful belief that she could make the light shine if she tried; that she could shape the world to comfort herself; and it was also a lack of interest in the pain of others. She knew others felt pain, but well, she could not really dwell on it.

"Finally, unable to bear the extent of this obvious duplicity, we turned and studied her, for we must now contend with her. She was not twenty-five years old, this Queen, and her powers were absolute in this land which she had dazzled with her customs from Uruk. And she was almost too pretty to be truly beautiful, for her loveliness overcame any sense of majesty or deep mystery; and her voice contained still a childish ring to it, a ring which evokes tenderness instinctively in others, and gives a faint music to the simplest words. A ring which we found maddening.

"On and on she went with her questions. How did we work our miracles? How did we look into men's hearts? Whence came our magic, and why did we claim that we talked to beings who were invisible? Could we speak in the same manner to her gods? Could we deepen her knowledge or bring her into closer understanding of what was divine? She was willing to pardon us for our savagery if we were to be grateful; if we were to kneel at her altars and lay before her gods and before her what we knew.

"She pursued her various points with a single-mindedness that could make a wise person laugh.

"But it brought up the deepest rage from Mekare. She who had always taken the lead in anything spoke out now.

" 'Stop your questions. You speak in stupidities,' she declared. 'You have no gods in this kingdom, because there are no gods. The only invisible inhabitants of the world are spirits, and they play with you through your priests and your religion as they play with everyone else. Ra, Osiris—these are merely made-up names with which you flatter and court the spirits, and when it suits their purposes they give you some little sign to send you scurrying to flatter them some more.'

"Both the King and Queen stared at Mekare in horror. But Mekare went on:

" 'The spirits are real, but they are childlike and capricious. And they are dangerous as well. They marvel at us and envy us that we are both spiritual and fleshly, which attracts them and makes them eager to do our will. Witches such as we have always known how to use them; but it takes great skill and great power to do it, and this we have and you do not have. You are fools, and what you have done to take us prisoner is evil; it is dishonest; you live in the lie! But we will not lie to you.'

"And then, half weeping, half choking with rage, Mekare accused the Queen before the entire court of duplicity, of massacring our peaceable people simply so that we might be brought here. Our people had not hunted for human flesh in a thousand years, she told this court; and it was a funeral feast that was desecrated at our capture, and all this evil done so that the Queen of Kemet might have witches to talk to, witches of whom to ask questions, witches in her possession whose power she would seek to use for herself.

"The court was in an uproar. Never had anyone heard such disrespect, such blasphemy, and so forth and so on. But the old lords of Egypt, those who still chafed at the ban on sacred cannibalism, they were horrified by this mention of the desecrated funeral feast. And others who also feared the retribution of heaven for not devouring the remains of their parents were struck dumb with fear.

"But in the main, it was confusion. Except for the King and the Queen, who were strangely silent and strangely intrigued.

"Akasha didn't make any answer to us, and it was clear that something in our explanation had rung true for her in the deeper regions of her mind. There flared for the moment a deadly earnest curiosity. *Spirits who pretend to be gods? Spirits who envy the flesh?* As for the charge that she had sacrificed our people needlessly, she didn't even consider it. Again, it did not interest her. It was the spiritual question which fascinated her, and in her fascination the spirit was divorced from the flesh.

"Allow me to draw your attention to what I have just said. It was the spiritual question which fascinated her—you might say the abstract idea; and in her fascination the abstract idea was everything. I do not think she believed that the spirits could be childlike and capricious. But whatever was there, she meant to know of it; and she meant to know of it through us. As for the destruction of our people, she did not care!

"Meantime the high priest of the temple of Ra was demanding our execution. So was the high priest of the temple of Osiris. We were evil; we were witches; and all those with red hair should be burned as had always been done in the land of Kemet. And at once the assemblage echoed these denunciations. There should be a burning. Within moments it seemed a riot would have broken out in the palace.

"But the King ordered all to be quiet. We were taken to our cell again, and put under heavy guard.

"Mekare, enraged, paced the floor, as I begged her not to say any more. I reminded her of what the spirits had told us: that if we went to Egypt, the King and Queen would ask us questions, and if we answered truthfully, which we would, the King and Queen would be angry with us, and we would be destroyed.

"But this was like talking to myself now; Mekare wouldn't listen. Back and forth she walked, now and then striking her breast with her fist. I felt the anguish she felt.

" 'Damnable,' she was saying. 'Evil.' And then she'd fall silent and pace, and then say these words again.

"I knew she was remembering the warning of Amel, the evil one. And I also knew that Amel was near; I could hear him, sense him.

"I knew that Mekare was being tempted to call upon him; and I felt that she must not. What would his silly torments mean to the Egyptians? How many mortals could he afflict with his pinpricks? It was no more than the storms of wind and flying objects which we could already produce. But Amel heard these thoughts; and he began to grow restless.

" 'Be quiet, demon,' Mekare said. 'Wait until I need you!' Those were the first words I ever heard her speak to an evil spirit, and they sent a shiver of horror through me.

"I don't remember when we fell asleep. Only that sometime after midnight I was awakened by Khayman.

"At first I thought it was Amel doing some trick, and I awoke in a frenzy. But Khayman gestured for me to be quiet. He was in a terrible state. He wore only a simple bed gown and no sandals, and his hair was mussed. It seemed he'd been weeping. His eyes were red.

"He sat down beside me. 'Tell me, is this true, what you said of the spirits?' I didn't bother to tell him it was Mekare who said it. People always confused us or thought of us as one being. I merely told him, yes, it was true.

"I explained that there have always been these invisible entities; that they themselves had told us there were no gods or goddesses of which they knew. They had bragged to us often of the tricks they played at Sumer or Jericho or in Nineveh at the great temples. Now and then they would come booming that they *were* this or that god. But we knew their personalities, and when we called them by their old names, they gave up the new game at once.

"What I did not say was that I wished Mekare had never made known such things. What purpose could it serve now?

"He sat there defeated, listening to me, listening as if he had been a man lied to all his life and now he saw truth. For he had been deeply moved when he had seen the spirits strike up the wind on our mountain and he had seen a shower of leaves fall upon the soldiers; it had chilled his soul. And that is always what produces faith, that mixture of truth and a physical manifestation.

"But then I perceived there was an even greater burden upon his conscience, or on his reason, one might say. 'And the massacre of your people, this was a holy war; it was not a selfish thing, as you said.'

"'Oh, no,' I told him. 'It was a selfish and simple thing, I can't say otherwise.' I told him of the tablet sent to us by the messenger, of what the spirits had said, of my mother's fear and her illness, and of my own power to hear the truth in the Queen's words, the truth which she herself might not be able to accept.

"But long before I'd finished, he was defeated again. He knew, from his own observations, that what I was saying was true. He had fought at the King's side through many a campaign against foreign peoples. That an army should fight for gain was nothing to him. He had seen massacres and cities burned; he had seen slaves taken; he had seen men return laden with booty. And though he himself was no soldier, these things he understood.

"But there had been no booty worth taking in our villages; there had been no territory which the King would retain. Yes, it had been fought for our capture, he knew it. And he too felt the distaste for the lie of a holy war against flesh eaters. And he felt a sadness that was even greater than his defeat. He was of an old family; he had eaten the flesh of his ancestors; and he found himself now punishing such traditions among those whom he had known and loved. He thought of the mummification of the dead with repugnance, but more truly he felt repugnance for the ceremony which accompanied it, for the depth of superstition in which the land had been steeped. So much wealth heaped upon the dead; so much attention to those putrefying bodies simply so men and women would not feel guilty for abandoning the older customs.

"Such thoughts exhausted him; they weren't natural to him; what obsessed him finally were the deaths he had seen; executions; massacres. Just as the Queen could not grasp such things, he could not forget them and he was a man losing his stamina; a man drawn into a mire in which he might drown.

"Finally he took his leave of me. But before he went he promised that he would do his best to see that we were released. He did not know how he could do it, but he would try to do it. And he begged me not to be afraid. I felt a great love for him at that moment. He had then the same beautiful face and form which he has now; only then he was dark-skinned and leaner and the curls had been ironed from his hair and it had been plaited and hung long to his shoulders, and he had the air of the court about him, the air of one who commands, and one who stands in the warm love of his prince.

"The following morning the Queen sent for us again. And this time we were brought privately to her chamber, where only the King was with her, and Khayman.

"It was a more lavish place even than the great hall of the palace; it was stuffed to overflowing with fine things, with a couch made of carved leopards, and a bed hung with sheer silk; and with polished mirrors of seemingly magical perfection. And the Queen herself, like a temptress she was, bedecked with finery and perfume, and fashioned by nature into a thing as lovely as any treasure around her.

"Once again she put her questions.

"Standing together, our hands bound, we had to listen to the same nonsense.

"And once again Mekare told the Queen of the spirits; she explained that the spirits have always existed; she told how they bragged of playing with the priests of other lands. She told how the spirits had said the songs and chants of the Egyptians pleased them. It was all a game to the spirits, and no more.

" 'But these spirits! They are the gods, then, that is what you are saying!' Akasha said with great fervor. 'And you speak to them? I want to see you do it! Do it for me now.'

" 'But they are not gods,' I said. 'That is what we are trying to tell you. And they do not abhor the eaters of the flesh as you say your gods do. They don't care about such things. They never have.' Painstakingly I strove to convey the difference; these spirits had no code; they were morally inferior to us. Yet I knew this woman couldn't grasp what I was telling her.

"I perceived the war inside her, between the handmaiden of the goddess Inanna who wanted to believe herself blessed, and the dark brooding soul who believed finally in nothing. A chill place was her soul; her religious fervor was nothing but a blaze which she fed constantly, seeking to warm that chill place.

" 'Everything you say is a lie!' she said finally. 'You are evil women!' She ordered our execution. We should be burnt alive the next day and together, so that we might see each other suffer and die. Why had she ever bothered with us?

"At once the King interrupted her. He told her that he had seen the power of the spirits; so had Khayman. What might not the spirits do if we were so treated? Wouldn't it be better to let us go?

"But there was something ugly and hard in the Queen's gaze. The King's words meant nothing; our lives were being taken from us. What could we do? And it seemed she was angry with us because we had not been able to frame our truths in ways which she could use or take pleasure in. Ah, it was an agony to deal with her. Yet her mind is a common mind; there are countless human beings who think and feel as she did then; and does now, in all likelihood.

"Finally Mekare seized the moment. She did the thing which I did not dare to do. She called the spirits—all of them by name, but so quickly this Queen would never remember the words. She screamed for them to come to her and do her bidding; and she told them to show their displeasure at what was happening to those mortals—Maharet and Mekare—whom they claimed to love.

"It was a gamble. But if nothing happened, if they had deserted us as I feared, well, then she could call on Amel, for he was there, lurking, waiting. And it was the only chance we had finally.

"Within an instant the wind had begun. It howled through the court- yard and whistled through the corridors of the palace. The draperies were torn by it; doors slammed; fragile vessels were smashed. The Queen was in a state of terror as she felt it surround her. Then small objects began to fly through the air. The spirits gathered up the ornaments of her dressing table and hurled them at her; the King stood beside her, striving to protect her, and Khayman was rigid with fear.

"Now, this was the very limit of the spirits' power; and they would not be able to keep it up for very long. But before the demonstration stopped, Khayman begged the King and Queen to revoke the sentence of execution. And on the spot they did.

"At once Mekare, sensing that the spirits were spent anyway, ordered them with great pomp to stop. Silence fell. And the terrified slaves ran here and there to gather up what had been thrown about.

"The Queen was overcome. The King tried to tell her that he had seen this spectacle before and it had not harmed him; but something deep had been violated within the Queen's heart. She'd never witnessed the slightest proof of the supernatural; and she was struck dumb and still now. In that dark faithless place within her, there had been a spark of light; true light. And so old and certain was her secret skepticism, that this small miracle had been for her a revelation of great magnitude; it was as if she had seen the face of her gods.

"She sent the King and Khayman away from her. She said she would speak with us alone. And then she implored us to talk to the spirits so that she could hear it. There were tears in her eyes.

"It was an extraordinary moment, for I sensed now what I'd sensed months ago when I'd touched the clay tablet—a mixture of good and evil that seemed more dangerous than evil itself.

"Of course we couldn't make the spirits speak so that she could understand it, we told her. But perhaps she would give us some questions that they might answer. At once she did.

"These were no more than the questions which people have been putting to wizards and witches and saints ever since. 'Where is the necklace I lost as a child? What did my mother want to tell me the night she died when she could no longer speak? Why does my sister detest my company? Will my son grow to manhood? Will he be brave and strong?'

"Struggling for our lives, we put these questions patiently to the spirits, cajoling them and flattering them to make them pay attention. And we got answers which veritably astonished Akasha. The spirits knew the name of her sister; they knew the name of her son. She seemed on the edge of madness as she considered these simple tricks.

"Then Amel, the evil one, appeared—obviously jealous of all these goings-on—and suddenly flung down before Akasha the lost necklace of which she'd been speaking—a necklace lost in Uruk; and this was the final blow. Akasha was thunderstruck.

"She wept now, holding on to this necklace. And then she begged us to put to the spirits the really important questions whose answers she must know.

"Yes, the gods were made up by her people, the spirits said. No, the names in the prayers didn't matter. The spirits merely liked the music and rhythm of the language—the shape of the words, so to speak. Yes, there were bad spirits who liked to hurt people, and why not? And there were good spirits who loved them, too. And would they speak to Akasha if we were to leave the kingdom? Never. They were speaking now, and she couldn't hear them, what did she expect them to do? But yes, there were witches in the kingdom who could hear them, and they would tell those witches to come to the court at once if that was what she wanted.

"But as this communication progressed, a terrible change came over Akasha.

"She went from jubilance to suspicion and then misery. Because these spirits were only telling her the same dismal things that we had already told her.

" 'What do you know of the life after?' she asked. And when the spirits said only that the souls of the dead either hovered about the earth, confused and suffering, or rose and vanished from it completely, she was brutally disappointed. Her eyes dulled; she was losing all appetite for this. When she asked what of those who had lived bad lives, as opposed to those who had lived good lives, the spirits could give no answer. They didn't know what she meant.

"Yet it continued, this interrogation. And we could sense that the spirits were tiring of it, and playing with her now, and that the answers would become more and more idiotic.

" 'What is the will of the gods?' she asked. 'That you sing all the time,' said the spirits. 'We like it.'

"Then all of a sudden, Amel, the evil one, so proud of the trick with the necklace, flung another great string of jewels before Akasha. But from this she shrank back in horror.

"At once we saw the error. It had been her mother's necklace, and lay on her mother's body in the tomb near Uruk, and of course Amel, being only a spirit, couldn't guess how bizarre and distasteful it could be to bring this thing here. Even now he did not catch on. He had seen this necklace in Akasha's mind when she had spoken of the other one. Why didn't she want it too? Didn't she like necklaces?

"Mekare told Amel this had not pleased. It was the wrong miracle. Would he please wait for her command, as she understood this Queen and he didn't.

"But it was too late. Something had happened to the Queen which was irrevocable. She had seen two pieces of evidence as to the power of the spirits, and she had heard truth and nonsense, neither of which could compare to the beauty of the mythology of her gods which she had always forced herself to believe in. Yet the spirits were destroying her fragile faith. How would she ever escape the dark skepticism in her own soul if these demonstrations continued?

"She bent down and picked up the necklace from her mother's tomb. 'How was this got!' she demanded. But her heart wasn't really in the question. She knew the answer would be more of what she'd been hearing since we had arrived. She was frightened.

"Nevertheless I explained; and she listened to every word.

"The spirits read our minds; and they are enormous and powerful. Their true size is difficult for us to imagine; and they can move with the swiftness of thought; when Akasha thought of this second necklace, the spirit saw it; he went to look for it; after all, one necklace had pleased her, so why not another? And so he had found it in her mother's tomb; and brought it out by means perhaps of some small opening. For surely it could not pass through stone. That was ridiculous.

"But as I said this last part I realized the truth. This necklace had probably been stolen from the body of Akasha's mother, and very possibly by Akasha's father. It had never been buried in any tomb. That is why Amel could find it. Maybe even a priest had stolen it. Or so it very likely seemed to Akasha, who was holding the necklace in her hand. She loathed this spirit that he made known such an awful thing to her.

"In sum, all the illusions of this woman lay now in complete ruin; yet she was left with the sterile truth she had always known. She had asked her questions of the supernatural—a very unwise thing to do—and the supernatural had given her answers which she could not accept; yet she could not refute them either.

" 'Where are the souls of the dead?' she whispered, staring at this necklace.

"As softly as I could I said, 'The spirits simply do not know.'

"Horror. Fear. And then her mind began to work, to do what it had always done—find some grand system to explain away what caused pain; some grand way to accommodate what she saw before her. The dark secret place inside her was becoming larger; it was threatening to consume her from within; she could not let such a thing happen; she had to go on. She was the Queen of Kemet.

"On the other hand, she was angry, and the rage she felt was against her parents and against her teachers, and against the priests and priestesses of her childhood, and against the gods she had worshiped and against anyone who had ever comforted her, or told her that life was good.

"A moment of silence had fallen; something was happening in her expression; fear and wonder had gone; there was something cold and disenchanted and, finally, malicious in her gaze.

"And then with her mother's necklace in hand she rose and declared that all we had said were lies. These were demons to whom we were speaking, demons who sought to subvert her and her gods, who looked with favor upon her people. The more she spoke the more she believed what she was saying; the more the elegance of her beliefs seized her; the more she surrendered to their logic. Until finally she was weeping and denouncing us, and the darkness within had been denied. She evoked the images of her gods; she evoked her holy language.

"But then she looked again at the necklace; and the evil spirit, Amel, in a great rage—furious that she was not pleased with his little gift and was once again angry with us—told us to tell her that if she did us any harm he would hurl at her every object, jewel, wine cup, looking glass, comb, or other such item that she ever so much as asked for, or imagined, or remembered, or wished for, or missed.

"I could have laughed had we not been in such danger; it was such a wonderful solution in the mind of the spirit; and so perfectly ridiculous from a human point of view. Yet it certainly wasn't something that one would want to happen.

"And Mekare told Akasha exactly what Amel had said.

" 'He that can produce this necklace can inundate you in such reminders of suffering,' Mekare said. 'And I do not know that any witch on earth can stop him, should he so begin.'

" 'Where is he?' Akasha screamed. 'Let me see this demon thing you speak to!'

"And at this, Amel, in vanity and rage, concentrated all his power and dove at Akasha, declaring 'I am Amel, the evil one, who pierces!' and he made the great gale around her that he had made around our mother; only it was ten times that. Never had I seen such fury. The room itself appeared to tremble as this immense spirit compressed himself and directed himself into this tiny place. I could hear the cracking of the brick walls. And all over the Queen's beautiful face and arms the tiny bitelike wounds appeared as so many red dots of blood.

"She screamed helplessly. Amel was in ecstasy. Amel could do wondrous things! Mekare and I were in terror.

"Mekare commanded him to stop. And now she heaped flattery upon him, and great thanks, and told him he was very simply the most powerful of all spirits, but he must obey her now, to demonstrate his great wit as well as his power; and that she would allow him to strike again at the right time.

"Meantime, the King rushed to the aid of Akasha; Khayman ran to her; all the guards ran to her. But when the guards raised their swords to strike us down, she ordered them to leave us alone. Mekare and I stood staring at her, silently threatening her with this spirit's power, for it was all that we had left. And Amel, the evil one, hovered above us, filling the air with the most eerie of all sounds, the great hollow laughter of a spirit, that seemed then to fill the entire world.

"Alone in our cell again, we could not think what to do or how to use what little advantage we now had in Amel.

"As for Amel himself, he would not leave us. He ranted and stormed in the little cell; he made the reed mats rustle, and made our garments move; he sent winds through our hair. It was a nuisance. But what frightened me was to hear the things of which he boasted. That he liked to draw blood; that it plumped him up inside and made him slow; but that it tasted good; and when the peoples of the world made blood sacrifice upon their altars he liked to come down and slurp up that blood. After all, it was there for him, was it not? More laughter.

"There was a great recoiling in the other spirits. Mekare and I both sensed this. Except for those who were faintly jealous and demanded to know what this blood tasted like, and why he liked such a thing so much.

"And then it came out—that hatred and jealousy of the flesh which is in so many evil spirits, that feeling that we are abominations, we humans, because we have both body and soul, which should not exist on this earth. Amel ranted of the times when there had been but mountains and oceans and forests and no living things such as us. He told us that to have spirit within mortal bodies was a curse.

"Now, I had heard these complaints among the evil ones before; but I had never thought much about them. For the first time I believed them, just a little, as I lay there and I saw my people put to the sword in my mind's eye. I thought as many a man or woman has thought before and since that maybe it was a curse to have the concept of immortality without the body to go with it.

"Or as you said, on this very night, Marius—life seemed not worth it; it seemed a joke. My world was darkness at that moment, darkness and suffering. All that I was no longer mattered; nothing I looked at could make me want to be alive.

"But Mekare began to speak to Amel again, informing him that she would much rather be what she was than what he was—drifting about forever with nothing important to do. And this sent Amel into a rage again. He would show her what he could do!

" 'When I command you, Amel!' she said. 'Count upon me to choose the moment. Then all men will know what you can do.' And this childish vain spirit was contented, and spread himself out again over the dark sky.

"For three nights and days we were kept prisoner. The guards would not look at us or come near us. Neither would the slaves. In fact, we would have starved had it not been for Khayman, the royal steward, who brought us food with his own hands.

"Then he told us what the spirits had already told us. A great controversy raged; the priests wanted us put to death. But the Queen was afraid to kill us, that we'd loose these spirits on her, and there would be no way she could drive them off. The King was intrigued by what had happened; he believed that more could be learned from us; he was curious about the power of the spirits, and to what uses it could be put. But the Queen feared it; the Queen had seen enough.

"Finally we were brought before the entire court in the great open atrium of the palace.

"It was high noon in the kingdom and the King and Queen made their offerings to the sun god Ra as was the custom, and this we were made to watch. It meant nothing to us to see this solemnity; we were afraid these were the last hours of our lives. I dreamed then of our mountain, our caves; I dreamed of the children we might have borne—fine sons and daughters, and some of them who would have inherited our power—I dreamed of the life that had been taken from us, of the annihilation of our kith and kindred which might soon be complete. I thanked whatever powers that be that I could see blue sky above my head, and that Mekare and I were still together.

"At last the King spoke. There was a terrible sadness and weariness in him. Young as he was, he had something of an old man's soul in these moments. Ours was a great gift, he told us, but we had misused it, clearly, and could be no use to anyone else. For lies, for the worship of demons, for black magic, he denounced us. He would have us burned, he said, to please the people; but he and his Queen felt sorry for us. The Queen in particular wanted him to have mercy on us.

"It was a damnable lie, but one look at her face told us she'd convinced herself that it was true. And of course the King believed it. But what did this matter? What was this mercy, we wondered, trying to look deeper into their souls.

"And now the Queen told us in tender words that our great magic had brought her the two necklaces she most wanted in all the world and for this and this alone she would let us live. In sum, the lie she spun grew larger and more intricate, and more distant from the truth.

"And then the King said he would release us, but first he would demonstrate to all the court that we had no power, and therefore the priests would be appeased.

"And if at any moment an evil demon should manifest himself and seek to abuse the just worshipers of Ra or Osiris, then our pardon should be revoked and we should be put to death at once. For surely the power of our demons would die with us. And we would have forfeited the Queen's mercy which we scarce deserved as it was.

"Of course we realized what was to happen; we saw it now in the hearts of the King and the Queen. A compromise had been struck. And we had been offered a bargain. As the King removed his gold chain and medallion and put it around the neck of Khayman, we knew that we were to be raped before the court, raped as common female prisoners or slaves would have been raped in any war. And if we called the spirits we'd die. That was our position.

" 'But for the love of my Queen,' said Enkil, 'I would take my pleasure of these two women, which is my right; I would do it before you all to show that they have no power and are not great witches, but are merely women, and my chief steward, Khayman, my beloved Khayman, will be given the privilege of doing it in my stead.'

"All the court waited in silence as Khayman looked at us, and prepared to obey the King's command. We stared at him, daring him in our helplessness not to do it—not to lay hands upon us or to violate us, before these uncaring eyes.

"We could feel the pain in him and the tumult. We could feel the danger that surrounded him, for were he to disobey he would surely have died. Yet this was our honor he meant to take; he meant to desecrate us; ruin us as it were; and we who had lived always in the sunshine and peace on our mountain knew nothing really of the act which he meant to perform.

"I think, as he came towards us, I believed he could not do it, that a man could not feel the pain which he felt and still sharpen his passion for this ugly work. But I knew little of men then, of how the pleasures of the flesh can combine in them with hatred and anger; of how they can hurt as they perform the act which women perform, more often than not, for love.

"Our spirits clamored against what was to happen; but for our very lives, we told them to be quiet. Silently I pressed Mekare's hand; I gave her to know that we would live when this was over; we would be free; this was not death after all; and we would leave these miserable desert people to their lies and their illusions; to their idiot customs; we would go home.

"And then Khayman set about to do what he had to do. Khayman untied our bonds; he took Mekare to himself first, forcing her down on her back against the matted floor, and lifting her gown, as I stood transfixed and unable to stop him, and then I was subjected to the same fate.

"But in his mind, we were not the women whom Khayman raped. As his soul trembled, as his body trembled, he stoked the fire of his passion with fantasies of nameless beauties and half remembered moments so that body and soul could be one.

"And we, our eyes averted, closed our souls to him and to these vile Egyptians who had done to us these terrible things; our souls were alone and untouched within our bodies; and all around us, I heard without doubt the weeping of the spirits, the sad, terrible weeping, and in the distance, the low rolling thunder of Amel.

"*You are fools to bear this, witches.*

"It was nightfall when we were left at the edge of the desert. The soldiers gave us what food and drink was allowed. It was nightfall as we started our long journey north. Our rage then was as great as it had ever been.

"And Amel came, taunting us and raging at us; why did we not want him to exact vengeance?

" 'They will come after us and kill us!' Mekare said. 'Now go away from us.' But that did not do the trick. So finally she tried to put Amel to work on something important. 'Amel, we want to reach our home alive. Make cool winds for us; and show us where we can find water.'

"But these are things which evil spirits never do. Amel lost interest. And Amel faded away, and we walked on through the cold desert wind, arm in arm, trying not to think of the miles that lay before us.

"Many things befell us on our long journey which are too numerous here to tell.

"But the good spirits had not deserted us; they made the cooling winds, and they led us to springs where we could find water and a few dates to eat; and they made 'little rain' for us as long as they could; but finally we were too deep in the desert for such a thing, and we were dying, and I knew I had a child from Khayman in my womb, and I wanted my child to live.

"It was then that the spirits led us to the Bedouin peoples, and they took us in, they cared for us.

"I was sick, and for days I lay singing to my child inside my body, and driving away my sickness and my moments of worst remembering with my songs. Mekare lay beside me, holding me in her arms.

"Months passed before I was strong enough to leave the Bedouin camps, and then I wanted my child to be born in our land and I begged Mekare that we should continue our journey.

"At last, with the food and drink the Bedouins had given us, and the spirits to guide us, we came into the green fields of Palestine, and found the foot of the mountain and the shepherd peoples—so like our own tribe—who had come down to claim our old grazing places.

"They knew us as they had known our mother and all our kindred and they called us by name, and immediately took us in.

"And we were so happy again, among the green grasses and the trees and the flowers that we knew, and my child was growing bigger inside my womb. It would live; the desert had not killed it.

"So, in my own land I gave birth to my daughter and named her Miriam as my mother had been named before me. She had Khayman's black hair but the green eyes of her mother. And the love I felt for her and the joy I knew in her were the greatest curative my soul could desire. We were three again. Mekare, who knew the birth pain with me, and who lifted the child out of my body, carried Miriam in her arms by the hour and sang to her just as I did. The child was ours, as much as it was mine. And we tried to forget the horrors we had seen in Egypt.

"Miriam thrived. And finally Mekare and I vowed to climb the mountain and find the caves in which we'd been born. We did not know yet how we would live or what we would do, so many miles from our new people. But with Miriam, we would go back to the place where we had been so happy; and we would call the spirits to us, and we would make the miracle of rain to bless my newborn child.

"But this was never to be. Not any of it.

"For before we could leave the shepherd people, soldiers came again, under the command of the King's high steward, Khayman, soldiers who had passed out gold along the way to any tribe who had seen or heard of the red-haired twins and knew where they might be.

"Once again at midday as the sun poured down on the grassy fields, we saw the Egyptian soldiers with their swords raised. In all directions the people scattered, but Mekare ran out and dropped down on her knees before Khayman and said, 'Don't harm our people again.'

"Then Khayman came with Mekare to the place where I was hiding with my daughter, and I showed him this child, which was his child, and begged him for mercy, for justice, that he leave us in peace.

"But I had only to look at him to understand that he would be put to death if he did not bring us back. His face was thin and drawn and full of misery, not the smooth white immortal face that you see here at this table tonight.

"Enemy time has washed away the natural imprint of his suffering. But it was very plain on that long ago afternoon.

"In a soft, subdued voice he spoke to us. 'A terrible evil has come over the King and the Queen of Kemet,' he said. 'And your spirits have done it, your spirits that tormented me night and day for what I did to you, until the King sought to drive them out of my house.'

"He stretched out his arms to me that I could see the tiny scars that covered him where this spirit had drawn blood. Scars covered his face and his throat.

" 'Oh, you don't know the misery in which I have lived,' he said, 'for nothing could protect me from these spirits; and you don't know the times I cursed you, and cursed the King for what he made me do to you, and cursed my mother that I'd been born.'

" 'Oh, but we have not done this!' Mekare said. 'We have kept faith with you. For our lives we left you in peace. But it is Amel, the evil one, who has done this! Oh, this evil spirit! And to think he has deviled you instead of the King and Queen who made you do what you did! We cannot stop him! I beg you, Khayman, let us go.'

" 'Whatever Amel does,' I said, 'he will tire of, Khayman. If the King and Queen are strong, he will eventually go away. You are looking now upon the mother of your child, Khayman. Leave us in peace. For the child's sake, tell the King and Queen that you could not find us. Let us go if you fear justice at all.'

"But he only stared at the child as if he did not know what it was. He was Egyptian. Was this child Egyptian? He looked at us: 'All right, you did not send this spirit,' he said. 'I believe you. For you do not understand what this spirit has done, obviously. His bedeviling has come to an end. He has gone *into* the King and Queen of Kemet! He is in their bodies! He has changed the very substance of their flesh!'

"For a long time, we looked at him and considered his words, and we understood that he did not mean by this that the King and the Queen were possessed. And we understood also that he himself had seen such things that he could not but come for us himself and try on his life to bring us back.

"But I didn't believe what he was saying. How could a spirit be made flesh!

" 'You do not understand what has happened in our kingdom,' he whispered. 'You must come and see with your own eyes.' He stopped then because there was more, much more, that he wanted to tell us, and he was afraid. Bitterly he said, 'You must undo what has been done, even if it is not your doing!'

"Ah, but we could not undo it. That was the horror. And even then we knew it; we sensed it. We remembered our mother standing before the cave gazing at the tiny wounds on her hand.

"Mekare threw back her head now and called to Amel, the evil one, to come to her, to obey her command. In our own tongue, the twin tongue, she screamed, 'Come out of the King and Queen of Kemet and come to me, Amel. Bow down before my will. You did this not by my command.'

"It seemed all the spirits of the world listened in silence; this was the cry of a powerful witch; but there was no answer; and then we felt it—a great recoiling of many spirits as if something beyond their knowledge and beyond their acceptance had suddenly been revealed. It seemed the spirits were shrinking from us; and then coming back, sad and undecided; seeking our love, yet repelled.

" 'But what is it?' Mekare screamed. 'What is it!' She called to the spirits who hovered near her, her chosen ones. And then in the stillness, as the shepherds waited in fear, and the soldiers stood in anticipation, and Khayman stared at us with tired glazed eyes, we heard the answer. It came in wonder and uncertainty.

" 'Amel has now what he has always wanted; *Amel has the flesh. But Amel is no more.*'

"What could it mean?

"We could not fathom it. Again, Mekare demanded of the spirits that they answer, but it seemed that the uncertainty of the spirits was now turning to fear.

" 'Tell me what has happened!' Mekare said. 'Make known to me what you know!' It was an old command used by countless witches. 'Give me the knowledge which is yours to give.'

"And again the spirits answered in uncertainty:

" 'Amel is in the flesh; and Amel is not Amel; he cannot answer now.'

" 'You must come with me,' Khayman said. 'You must come. The King and Queen would have you come!'

"Mutely, and seemingly without feeling, he watched as I kissed my baby girl and gave her to the shepherd women who would care for her as their own. And then Mekare and I gave ourselves up to him; but this time we did not weep. It was as if all our tears had been shed. Our brief year of happiness with the birth of Miriam was past now—and the horror that had come out of Egypt was reaching out to engulf us once more.

MAHARET closed her eyes for a moment; she touched the lids with her fingers, and then looked up at the others, as they waited, each in his or her own thoughts and considerations, each reluctant for the narrative to be broken, though they all knew that it must.

The young ones were drawn and weary; Daniel's rapt expression had changed little. Louis was gaunt, and the need for blood was hurting him, though he paid it no mind. "I can tell you no more now," Maharet said. "It's almost morning; and the young ones must go down to the earth. I have to prepare the way for them.

"Tomorrow night we will gather here and continue. That is, if our Queen will allow. The Queen is nowhere near us now; I cannot hear the faintest murmur of her presence; I cannot catch the faintest flash of her countenance in another's eyes. If she knows what we do, she allows it. Or she is far away and indifferent, and we must wait to know her will.

"Tomorrow, I'll tell you what we saw when we went into Kemet."

"Until then, rest safe within the mountain. All of you. It has kept my secrets from the prying eyes of mortal men for countless years. Remember not even the Queen can hurt us until nightfall."

Marius rose as Maharet did. He moved to the far window as the others slowly left the room. It was as if Maharet's voice were still speaking to him. And what affected him most deeply was the evocation of Akasha, and the hatred Maharet felt for her; because Marius felt that hatred too; and he felt more strongly than ever that he should have brought this nightmare to a close while he'd had the power to do it.

But the red-haired woman could not have wanted any such thing to happen. None of them wanted to die any more than he did. And Maharet craved life, perhaps, more fiercely than any immortal he'd ever known.

Yet her tale seemed to confirm the hopelessness of it all. What had risen when the Queen stood up from her throne? What was this being that had Lestat in its maw? He could not imagine.

We change, but we do not change, he thought. We grow wise, but we are fallible things! We are only human for however long we endure, that was the miracle and the curse of it.

He saw again the smiling face he had seen as the ice began to fall. Is it possible that he loved as strongly still as he hated? That in his great humiliation, clarity had escaped him utterly? He honestly didn't know.

And he was tired suddenly, craving sleep, craving comfort; craving the soft sensuous pleasure of lying in a clean bed. Of sprawling upon it and burying his face in a pillow; of letting his limbs assemble themselves in the most natural and comfortable position.

Beyond the glass wall, a soft radiant blue light was filling the eastern sky, yet the stars retained their brilliance, tiny and distant though they seemed. The dark trunks of the redwoods had become visible; and a lovely green smell had come into the house from the forest as always happens near dawn.

Far below where the hillside fell away and a clearing full of clover moved out to the woods, Marius saw Khayman walking alone. His hands appeared to glow in the thin, bluish darkness, and as he turned and looked back—up at Marius—his face was an eyeless mask of pure white.

Marius found himself raising his hand in a small gesture of friendship towards Khayman. And Khayman returned the gesture and went on into the trees.

Then Marius turned and saw what he already knew, that only Louis remained with him in the room. Louis stood quite still looking at him as he had earlier, as though he were seeing a myth made real.

Then he put the question that was obsessing him, the question he could not lose sight of, no matter how great was Maharet's spell. "You know whether or not Lestat's still alive, don't you?" he asked. It had a simple human tone to it, a poignant tone, yet the voice was so reserved.

Marius nodded. "He's alive. But I don't really know that the way you think I do. Not from asking or receiving the answer. Not from using all these lovely powers which plague us. I know it simply because I know."

He smiled at Louis. Something in the manner of this one made Marius happy, though he wasn't sure why. He beckoned for Louis to come to him and they met at the foot of the table and walked together out of the room. Marius put his arm around Louis's shoulder and they went down the iron stairs together, through the damp earth, Marius walking slowly and heavily, exactly like a human being might walk.

"And you're sure of it?" Louis asked respectfully.

Marius stopped. "Oh, yes, quite sure." They looked at one another for a moment, and again Marius smiled. This one was so gifted yet not gifted at the same time; he wondered if the human light would go out of Louis's eyes if he ever gained more power, if he ever had, for instance, a little of the blood of Marius in his veins.

And this young one was hungry too; he was suffering; and he seemed to like it, to like the hunger and the pain.

"Let me tell you something," Marius said now, agreeably. "I knew the first moment I ever laid eyes on Lestat that nothing could kill him. That's the way it is with some of us. We can't die." But why was he saying this? Did he believe it again as he had before these trials had begun? He thought back to that night in San Francisco when he had walked down the broad clean-swept pavements of Market Street with his hands in his pockets, unnoticed by mortal men.

"Forgive me," Louis said, "but you remind me of the things they said of him at Dracula's Daughter, the talk among the ones who wanted to join him last night."

"I know," Marius said. "But they are fools and I'm right." He laughed softly. Yes, he did believe it. Then he embraced Louis again warmly. Just a little blood, and Louis might be stronger, true, but then he might lose the human tenderness, the human wisdom that no one could give another; the gift of knowing others' suffering with which Louis had probably been born.

But the night was over now for this one. Louis took Marius's hand, and then turned and walked down the tin-walled corridor to where Eric waited to show him the way.

Then Marius went up into the house.

He had perhaps a full hour more before the sun forced him into sleep, and tired as he was, he would not give it up. The lovely fresh smell of the woods was overpowering. And he could hear the birds now, and the clear singing of a deep creek.

He went into the great room of the adobe dwelling, where the fire had burnt down on the central hearth. He found himself standing before a giant quilt that covered almost half the wall.

Slowly he realized what he was seeing before him—the mountain, the valley, and the tiny figures of the twins as they stood together in the green clearing beneath the burning sun. The slow rhythm of Maharet's speech came back to him with the faint shimmer of all the images her words had conveyed. So immediate was that sun-drenched clearing, and how different it seemed now from the dreams. Never had the dreams made him feel close to these women! And now he knew them; he knew this house.

It was such a mystery, this mixture of feeling, where sorrow touched something that was undeniably positive and good. Maharet's soul attracted him; he loved the particular complexity of it, and he wished he could somehow tell her so.

Then it was as if he caught himself; he realized that he had forgotten for a little while to be bitter, to be in pain. Maybe his soul was healing faster than he had ever supposed it could.

Or maybe it was only that he had been thinking about others—about Maharet, and before that about Louis, and what Louis needed to believe. Well, hell, Lestat probably was immortal. In fact, the sharp and bitter fact occurred to him that Lestat might survive all this even if he, Marius, did not.

But that was a little supposition that he could do without. Where was Armand? Had Armand gone down into the earth already? If only he could see Armand just now. . . .

He went towards the cellar door again but something distracted him. Through an open doorway he saw two figures, very like the figures of the twins on the quilt. But these were Maharet and Jesse, arm in arm before an eastern window, watching motionless as the light grew brighter in the dark woods.

A violent shudder startled him. He had to grip the door frame to steady himself as a series of images flooded his mind. Not the jungle now; there was a highway in the distance, winding north, it seemed, through barren burnt land. And the creature had stopped, shaken, but by what? An image of two red-haired women? He heard the feet begin their relentless tramp again; he saw the feet caked with earth as if they were his feet; the hands caked with earth as if they were his hands. And then he saw the sky catching fire, and he moaned aloud.

When he looked up again, Armand was holding him. And with her bleary human eyes Maharet was imploring him to tell her what he had just seen. Slowly the room came alive around him, the agreeable furnishings, and then the immortal figures near him, who were of it, yet of nothing. He closed his eyes and opened them again.

"She's reached our longitude," he said, "yet she's miles to the east. The sun's just risen there with blazing force." He had felt it, that lethal heat! But she had gone into the earth; that too he had felt.

"But it's very far south of here," Jesse said to him. How frail she looked in the translucent darkness, her long thin fingers hugging the backs of her slender arms.

"Not so far," Armand said. "And she was moving very fast."

"But in what direction does she move!" Maharet asked. "Is she coming towards us?"

She didn't wait for an answer. And it didn't seem that they could give it. She lifted her hand to cover her eyes as if the pain there was now intolerable; and then gathering Jesse to her, and kissing her suddenly, she bid the others good sleep.

Marius closed his eyes; he tried to see again the figure he had seen before. The garment, what was it? A rough thing thrown over the body like a peasant poncho, with a torn opening for the head. Bound at the waist, yes, he'd felt it. He tried to see more but he could not. What he had felt was power, illimitable power and unstoppable momentum, and almost nothing other than that.

When he opened his eyes again the morning shimmered in the room around him. Armand stood close to him, embracing him still, yet Armand seemed alone and perturbed by nothing; his eyes moved only a little as he looked at the forest, which now seemed to press against the house through every window, as if it had crept to the very edge of the porch.

Marius kissed Armand's forehead. And then he did exactly what Armand was doing.

He watched the room grow lighter; he watched the light fill the windowpanes; he watched the beautiful colors brighten in the vast network of the giant quilt.

5

LESTAT:
THIS IS MY BODY;
THIS IS MY BLOOD

HEN I awoke it was quiet, and the air was clean and warm, with the smell of the sea.

I was now thoroughly confused as to time. And I knew from my light-headedness that I had not slept through a day. Also I wasn't in any protective enclosure.

We'd been following the night around the world, perhaps, or rather moving at random in it, as Akasha maybe didn't need at all to sleep.

I needed it, that was obvious. But I was too curious not to want to be awake. And frankly too miserable. Also I'd been dreaming of human blood.

I found myself in a spacious bedroom with terraces to the west and to the north. I could smell the sea and I could hear it, yet the air was fragrant and rather still. Very gradually, I took stock of the room.

Lavish old furnishings, most likely Italian—delicate yet ornamented— were mingled with modern luxuries everywhere I looked. The bed on which I lay was a gilded four-poster, hung with gauzy curtains, and covered with down pillows and draperies of silk. A thick white carpet concealed the old floor.

There was a dressing table littered with glittering jars and silver objects, and a curious old-fashioned white telephone. Velvet chairs; a monster of a television set and shelves of stereo music equipment; and small polished tables everywhere, strewn with newspapers, ashtrays, decanters of wine.

People had lived here up till an hour ago; but now the people were dead. In fact, there were many dead on this island. And as I lay there for a moment, drinking in the beauty around me, I saw the village in my mind where we had been before. I saw the filth, the tin roofs, the mud. And now I lay in this bower, or so it seemed.

And there was death here too. We had brought it.

I got up off the bed and went out onto the terrace and looked down over the stone railing at a white beach. No land on the horizon, only the gently rolling sea. The lacy foam of the receding waves glistening under the moon. And I was in an old weathered palazzo, probably built some four centuries ago, decked with urns and cherubs and covered with stained plaster, a rather beautiful place. Electric lights shone through the green-painted shutters of other rooms. Nestled on a lower terrace just beneath me was a little swimming pool.

And ahead where the beach curved to the left, I saw another old graceful dwelling nestled into the cliffs. People had died in there too. This was a Greek island, I was sure of it; this was the Mediterranean Sea.

When I listened, I heard cries coming from the land behind me, over the crest of the hill. Men being slain. I leaned against the frame of the door. I tried to stop my heart from racing.

Some sudden memory of the slaughter in Azim's temple gripped me—a flash of myself walking through the human herd, using the invisible blade to pierce solid flesh. Thirst. Or was it merely lust? I saw those mangled limbs again; wasted bodies contorted in the final struggle, faces smeared with blood.

Not my doing, I couldn't have . . . But I had.

And now I could smell fires burning, fires like those fires in Azim's courtyard where the bodies were being burnt. The smell nauseated me. I turned towards the sea again and took a deep clean breath. If I let them, the voices would come, voices from all over the island, and from other islands, and from the nearby land, too. I could feel it, the sound, hovering there waiting; I had to push it back.

Then I heard more immediate noise. Women in this old mansion. They were approaching the bedchamber. I turned around just in time to see the double doors opened, and the women, dressed in simple blouses and skirts and kerchiefs, come into the room.

It was a motley crowd of all ages, including young beauties and stout older matrons, and even some rather frail creatures with darkly wrinkled skin and snow white hair. They brought vases of flowers with them; they were placing them everywhere. And then one of the women, a tentative slender thing with a beautiful long neck, moved forward with beguiling natural grace, and began to turn on the many lamps.

Smell of their blood. How could it be so strong and so enticing, when I felt no thirst?

Suddenly they all came together in the center of the room and they stared at me; it was as if they'd fallen into a trance. I was standing on the terrace, merely looking at them; then I realized what they saw. My torn costume—the vampire rags—black coat, white shirt, and the cloak—all spattered with blood.

And my skin, that had changed measurably. I was whiter, more ghastly to look at, of course. And my eyes must have been brighter; or maybe I was being deceived by their naive reactions. When had they seen one of us before?

Whatever . . . it all seemed to be some sort of dream, these still women with their black eyes and their rather somber faces—even the stout ones had rather gaunt faces—gathered there staring at me, and then their dropping one by one to their knees. Ah, to their knees. I sighed. They had the crazed expression of people who had been delivered out of the ordinary; they were seeing a vision and the irony was that they looked like a vision to me.

Reluctantly, I read their thoughts.

They had seen the Blessed Mother. That is what she was here. The Madonna, the Virgin. She'd come to their villages and told them to slaughter their sons and husbands; even the babies had been slaughtered. And they had done it, or witnessed the doing of it; and they were now carried upon a wave of belief and joy. They were witnesses to miracles; they had been spoken to by the Blessed Mother herself. And she was the ancient Mother, the Mother who had always dwelt in the grottoes of this island, even before Christ, the Mother whose tiny naked statues were now and then found in the earth.

In her name they had knocked down the columns of the ruined temples, the ones the tourists came here to see; they had burned the only church on the island; they had knocked out its windows with sticks and stones. Ancient murals had burned in the church. The marble columns, broken into fragments, had fallen into the sea.

As for me, what was I to them? Not merely a god. Not merely the chosen of the Blessed Mother. No, something else. It puzzled me as I stood there, trapped by their eyes, repelled by their convictions, yet fascinated and afraid.

Not of them, of course, but of everything that was happening. Of this delicious feeling of mortals looking at me, the way they had been looking when I'd been on the stage. Mortals looking at me and sensing my power after all the years of hiding, mortals come here to worship. Mortals like all those poor creatures strewn over the path in the mountains. But they'd been worshipers of Azim, hadn't they? They'd gone there to die.

Nightmare. Have to reverse this, have to stop it; have to stop myself from accepting it or any aspect of it!

I mean I could start believing that I was really— But I know what I am, don't I? And these are poor, ignorant women; women for whom television sets and phones are miracles, these are women for whom change itself is a form of miracle. . . . And they will wake up tomorrow and they will see what they have done!

But now the feeling of peace came over us—the women and me. The familiar scent of flowers, the spell. Silently, through their minds, the women were receiving their instructions.

There was a little commotion; two of them rose from their knees and entered an adjoining bath—one of those massive marble affairs that wealthy Italians and Greeks seem to love. Hot water was flowing; steam poured out of the open doors.

Other women had gone to the closets, to take out clean garments. Rich, whoever he was, the poor bastard who had owned this little palace, the poor bastard who had left that cigarette in the ashtray and the faint greasy fingerprints on the white phone.

Another pair of women came towards me. They wanted to lead me into the bath. I did nothing. I felt them touch me—hot human fingers touching me and all the attendant shock and excitement in them as they felt the peculiar texture of my flesh. It sent a powerful and delicious chill through me, these touches. Their dark liquid eyes were beautiful as they looked at me. They tugged at me with their warm hands; they wanted me to come with them.

All right. I allowed myself to be taken along. White marble tile, carved gold fixtures; an ancient Roman splendor, when you got right down to it, with gleaming bottles of soaps and scents lining marble shelves. And the flood of hot water in the pool, with the jets pumping it full of bubbles, it was all very inviting; or might have been at some other time.

They stripped my garments off me. Absolutely fascinating feeling. No one had ever done such a thing to me. Not since I'd been alive and then only when I was a very small child. I stood in the flood of steam from the bath, watching all these small dark hands, and feeling the hairs rise all over my body; feeling the adoration in the women's eyes.

Through the steam I looked into the mirror—a wall of mirror actually, and I saw myself for the first time since this sinister odyssey had begun. The shock was more for a moment than I could handle. *This can't be me.*

I was much paler than I'd imagined. Gently I pushed the women away and went towards the mirror wall. My skin had a pearlescent gleam to it; and my eyes were even brighter, gathering all the colors of the spectrum and mingling them with an icy light. Yet I didn't look like Marius. I didn't look like Akasha. The lines in my face were still there!

In other words I'd been bleached by Akasha's blood, but I hadn't become smooth yet. I'd kept my human expression. And the odd thing was, the contrast now made these lines all the more visible. Even the tiny lines all over my fingers were more clearly etched than before.

But what consolation was this when I was more than ever noticeable, astonishing, unlike a human being? In a way, this was worse than that first moment two hundred years ago, when an hour or so after my death I'd seen myself in a mirror, and tried to find my humanity in what I was seeing. I was just as afraid right now.

I studied my reflection—my chest was like a marble torso in a museum, that white. And the organ, the organ we don't need, poised as if ready for what it would never again know how to do or want to do, marble, a Priapus at a gate.

Dazed, I watched the women draw closer; lovely throats, breasts, dark moist limbs. I watched them touch me all over again. I was beautiful to them, all right.

The scent of their blood was stronger in here, in the rising steam. Yet I wasn't thirsty, not really. Akasha had filled me, but the blood was tormenting me a little. No, quite a lot.

I *wanted* their blood—and it had nothing to do with thirst. I wanted it the way a man can want vintage wine, though he's drunk water. Only magnify that by twenty or thirty or a hundred. In fact, it was so powerful I could imagine taking all of them, tearing at their tender throats one after another and leaving their bodies lying here on the floor.

No, this is not going to take place, I reasoned. And the sharp, dangerous quality of this lust made me want to weep. *What's been done to me!* But then I knew, didn't I? I knew I was so strong now that twenty men couldn't have subdued me. And think what I could do to them. I could rise up through the ceiling if I wanted to and get free of here. I could do things of which I'd never dreamed. Probably I had the fire gift now; I could burn things the way she could burn them, the way Marius said that he could. Just a matter of strength, that's all it was. And dizzying levels of awareness, of acceptance. . . .

The women were kissing me. They were kissing my shoulders. Just a lovely little sensation, the soft pressure of the lips on my skin. I couldn't help smiling, and gently I embraced them and kissed them, nuzzling their heated little necks and feeling their breasts against my chest. I was utterly surrounded by these malleable creatures, I was blanketed in succulent human flesh.

I stepped into the deep tub and allowed them to wash me. The hot water splashed over me deliciously, washing away easily all the dirt that never really clings to us, never penetrates us. I looked up at the ceiling and let them brush the hot water through my hair.

Yes, extraordinarily pleasurable, all of it. Yet never had I been so alone. I was sinking into these mesmerizing sensations; I was drifting. Because really, there was nothing else that I could do.

When they were finished I chose the perfumes that I wanted and told them to get rid of the others. I spoke in French but they seemed to understand. Then they dressed me with the clothes I selected from what they presented to me. The master of this house had liked handmade linen shirts, which were only a little too large for me. And he'd liked handmade shoes as well, and they were a tolerable fit.

I chose a suit of gray silk, very fine weave, and rather jaunty modern cut. And silver jewelry. The man's silver watch, and his cuff links which had tiny diamonds embedded in them. And even a tiny diamond pin for the narrow lapel of the coat. But all these clothes felt so strange on me; it was as if I could feel the surface of my own skin yet not feel it. And there came that déjà vu. Two hundred years ago. The old mortal questions. Why in the hell is this happening? How can I gain control of it?

I wondered for a moment, was it possible not to care what happened? To stand back from it and view them all as alien creatures, things upon which I fed? Cruelly I'd been ripped out of their world! Where was the old bitterness, the old excuse for endless cruelty? Why had it always focused itself upon such small things? Not that a life is small. Oh, no, never, not any life! That was the whole point actually. Why did I who could kill with such abandon shrink from the prospect of seeing their precious traditions laid waste?

Why did my heart come up in my throat now? Why was I crying inside, like something dying myself?

Maybe some other fiend could have loved it; some twisted and conscienceless immortal could have sneered at her visions, yet slipped into the robes of a god as easily as I had slipped into that perfumed bath.

But nothing could give me that freedom, nothing. Her permissions meant nothing; her power finally was but another degree of what we all possessed. And what we all possessed had never made the struggle simple; it had made it agony, no matter how often we won or lost.

It couldn't happen, the subjugation of a century to one will; the design had to be foiled somehow, and if I just maintained my calm, I'd find the key.

Yet mortals had inflicted such horrors upon others; barbarian hordes had scarred whole continents, destroying everything in their path. Was she merely human in her delusions of conquest and domination? Didn't matter. She had inhuman means to see her dreams made real!

I would start weeping again if I didn't stop reaching now for the solution; and these poor tender creatures around me would be even more damaged and confused than before.

When I lifted my hands to my face, they didn't move away from me. They were brushing my hair. Chills ran down my back. And the soft thud of the blood in their veins was deafening suddenly.

I told them I wanted to be alone. I couldn't endure the temptation any longer. And I could have sworn they knew what I wanted. Knew it, and were yielding to it. Dark salty flesh so close to me. Too much temptation. Whatever the case, they obeyed instantly, and a little fearfully. They left the room in silence, backing away as if it weren't proper to simply walk out.

I looked at the face of the watch. I thought it was pretty funny, me wearing this watch that told the time. And it made me angry suddenly. And then the watch broke! The glass shattered; everything flew out of the ruptured silver case. The strap broke and the thing fell off my wrist onto the floor. Tiny glittering wheels disappeared into the carpet.

"Good God!" I whispered. Yet why not?—if I could rupture an artery or a heart. But the point was to control this thing, to direct it, not let it escape like that.

I looked up and chose at random a small mirror, one standing on the dresser in a silver frame. I thought *Break* and it exploded into gleaming fragments. In the hollow stillness I could hear the pieces as they struck the walls and the dresser top.

Well, that was useful, a hell of a lot more useful than being able to kill people. I stared at the telephone on the edge of the dresser. I concentrated, let the power collect, then consciously subdued it and directed it to push the phone slowly across the glass that covered the marble. Yes. All right. The little bottles tumbled and fell as it was pushed into them. Then I stopped them; I couldn't right them however. I couldn't pick them up. Oh, but wait, yes I could. I imagined a hand righting them. And certainly the power wasn't literally obeying this image; but I was using it to organize the power. I righted all the little bottles. I retrieved the one which had fallen and put it back in place.

I was trembling just a little. I sat on the bed to think this over, but I was too curious to think. The important thing to realize was this: it was physical; it was energy. And it was no more than an extension of powers I'd possessed before. For example, even in the beginning, in the first few weeks after Magnus had made me, I'd managed once to move another—my beloved Nicolas with whom I'd been arguing—across a room as if I'd struck him with an invisible fist. I'd been in a rage then; I hadn't been able to duplicate the little trick later. But it was the same power; the same verifiable and measurable trait.

"You are no god," I said. But this increase of power, this new dimension, as they say so aptly in this century. . . . Hmmmm. . . .

Looking up at the ceiling, I decided I wanted to rise slowly and touch it, run my hands over the plaster frieze that ran around the cord of the chandelier. I felt a queasiness; and then I realized I was floating just beneath the ceiling. And my hand, why, it looked like my hand was going through the plaster. I lowered myself a little and looked down at the room.

Dear God, I'd done this without taking my body with me! I was still sitting there, on the side of the bed. I was staring at myself, at the top of my own head. I—my body at any rate—sat there motionless, dreamlike, staring. *Back.* And I was there again, thank God, and my body was all right, and then looking up at the ceiling, I tried to figure what this was all about.

Well, I knew what it was all about, too. Akasha herself had told me how her spirit could travel out of her body. And mortals had always done such things, or so they claimed. Mortals had written of such invisible travel from the most ancient times.

I had almost done it when I tried to see into Azim's temple, *gone there to see,* and she had stopped me because when I left my body, my body had started to fall. And long before that, there had been a couple of other times. . . . But in general, I'd never believed all the mortal stories.

Now I knew I could do this as well. But I certainly didn't want to do it by accident. I made the decision to move to the ceiling again but this time with my body, and it was accomplished at once! We were there together, pushing against the plaster and this time my hand didn't go through. All right.

I went back down and decided to try the other again. Now *only in spirit.* The queasy feeling came, I took a glance down at my body, and then I was rising right through the roof of the palazzo. I was traveling out over the sea. Yet things looked unaccountably different; I wasn't sure this was the literal sky or the literal sea. It was more like a hazy conception of both, and I didn't like this, not one bit. No, thank you. Going home now! Or should I bring my body to me? I tried, but absolutely nothing happened, and that didn't surprise me actually. This was some kind of hallucination. I hadn't really left my body, and ought to just accept that fact.

And Baby Jenks, what about the beautiful things Baby Jenks had seen when she went up? Had they been hallucinations? I would never know, would I?

Back!

Sitting. Side of the bed. Comfortable. The room. I got up and walked around for a few minutes, merely looking at the flowers, and the odd way the white petals caught the lamplight and how dark the reds looked; and how the golden light was caught on the surfaces of the mirrors, all the other lovely things.

It was overwhelming suddenly, the pure detail surrounding me; the extraordinary complexity of a single room.

Then I practically fell into the chair by the bed. I lay back against the velvet, and listened to my heart pounding. Being invisible, leaving my body, I hated it! I wasn't going to do it again!

Then I heard laughter, faint, gentle laughter. I realized Akasha was there, somewhere behind me, near the dresser perhaps.

There was a sudden surge in me of gladness to hear her voice, to feel her presence. In fact I was surprised at how strong these sensations were. I wanted to see her but I didn't move just yet.

"This traveling without your body—it's a power you share with mortals," she said. "They do this little trick of traveling out of their bodies all the time."

"I know," I said dismally. "They can have it. If I can fly with my body, that's what I intend to do."

She laughed again; soft, caressing laughter that I'd heard in my dreams.

"In olden times," she said, "men went to the temple to do this; they drank the potions given them by the priests; it was in traveling the heavens that men faced the great mysteries of life and death."

"I know," I said again. "I always thought they were drunk or stoned out of their minds as one says today."

"You're a lesson in brutality," she whispered. "Your responses to things are so swift."

"That's brutal?" I asked. I caught a whiff again of the fires burning on the island. Sickening. *Dear God.* And we talk here as if this isn't happening, as if we hadn't penetrated their world with these horrors. . . .

"And flying with your body does not frighten you?" she asked.

"It all frightens me, you know that," I said. "When do I discover the limits? Can I sit here and bring death to mortals who are miles away?"

"No," she said. "You'll discover the limits rather sooner than you think. It's like every other mystery. There really is no mystery."

I laughed. For a split second I heard the voices again, the tide rising, and then it faded into a truly audible sound—cries on the wind, cries coming from villages on the island. They had burned the little museum with the ancient Greek statues in it; and with the icons and the Byzantine paintings.

All that art going up in smoke. Life going up in smoke.

I had to see her suddenly. I couldn't find her in the mirrors, the way they were. I got up.

She was standing at the dresser; and she too had changed her garments, and the style of her hair. Even more purely lovely, yet timeless as before. She held a small hand mirror, and she was looking at herself in it; but it seemed she was not really looking at anything; she was listening to the voices; and I could hear them again too.

A shiver went through me; she resembled her old self, the frozen self sitting in the shrine.

Then she appeared to wake; to look into the mirror again, and then at me as she put the mirror aside.

Her hair had been loosened; all those plaits gone. And now the rippling black waves came down free over her shoulders, heavy, glossy, and inviting to kiss. The dress was similar to the old one, as if the women had made it for her out of dark magenta silk that she had found here. It gave a faint rosy blush to her cheeks, and to her breasts which were only half covered by the loose folds that went up over her shoulders, gathered there by tiny gold clasps.

The necklaces she wore were all modern jewelry, but the profusion made them look archaic, pearls and gold chains and opals and even rubies.

Against the luster of her skin, all this ornament appeared somehow unreal! It was caught up in the overall gloss of her person; it was like the light in her eyes, or the luster of her lips.

She was something fit for the most lavish palace of the imagination; something both sensuous and divine. I wanted her blood again, the blood without fragrance and without killing. I wanted to go to her and lift my hand and touch the skin which seemed absolutely impenetrable but which would break suddenly like the most fragile crust.

"All the men on the island are dead, aren't they?" I asked. I shocked myself.

"All but ten. There were seven hundred people on this island. Seven have been chosen to live."

"And the other three?"

"They are for you."

I stared at her. For me? The desire for blood shifted a little, revised itself, included her and human blood—the hot, bubbling, fragrant kind, the kind that— But there was no physical need. I could still call it thirst, technically, but it was actually worse.

"You don't want them?" she said, mockingly, smiling at me. "My reluctant god, who shrinks from his duty? You know all those years, when I listened to you, long before you made songs to me, I loved it that you took only the hard ones, the young men. I loved it that you hunted thieves and killers; that you liked to swallow their evil whole. Where's your courage now? Your impulsiveness? Your willingness to plunge, as it were?"

"Are they evil?" I said. "These victims who are waiting for me?"

She narrowed her eyes for a moment. "Is it cowardice finally?" she asked. "Does the grandeur of the plan frighten? For surely the killing means little."

"Oh, but you're wrong," I said. "The killing always means something. But yes, the grandeur of the plan terrifies me. The chaos, the total loss of all moral equilibrium, it means everything. But that's not cowardice, is it?" How calm I sounded. How sure of myself. It wasn't the truth, but she knew it.

"Let me release you from all obligation to resist," she said. "You cannot stop me. I love you, as I told you. I love to look at you. It fills me with happiness. But you can't influence me. Such an idea is absurd."

We stared at each other in silence. I was trying to find words to tell myself how lovely she was, how like the old Egyptian paintings of princesses with shining tresses whose names are now forever lost. I was trying to understand why my heart hurt even looking at her; and yet I didn't care that she was beautiful; I cared about what we said to each other.

"Why have you chosen this way?" I asked.

"You know why," she said with a patient smile. "It is the best way. It is the only way; it is the clear vision after centuries of searching for a solution."

"But that can't be the truth, I can't believe it."

"Of course it can. Do you think this is impulse with *me?* I don't make my decisions as you do, my prince. Your youthful exuberance is something I treasure, but such small possibilities are long gone for me. You think in terms of lifetimes; in terms of small accomplishments and human pleasures. I have thought out for thousands of years my designs for the world that is now mine. And the evidence is overwhelming that I must proceed as I have done. I cannot turn this earth into a garden, I cannot create the Eden of human imagination—unless I eliminate the males almost completely."

"And by this you mean kill forty percent of the population of the earth? Ninety percent of all males?"

"Do you deny that this will put an end to war, to rape, to violence?"

"But the point . . ."

"No, answer my question. Do you deny that it will put an end to war, to rape, and to violence?"

"Killing everyone would put an end to those things!"

"Don't play games with me. Answer my question."

"Isn't that a game? The price is unacceptable. It's madness; it's mass murder; it's against nature."

"Quiet yourself. None of what you say is true. What is natural is simply what has been done. And don't you think the peoples of this earth have limited in the past their female children? Don't you think they have killed them by the millions, because they wanted only male children so that those children could go to war? Oh, you cannot imagine the extent to which such things have been done.

"And so now they will choose female over male and there will be no war. And what of the other crimes committed by men against women? If there were any nation on earth which had committed such crimes against another nation, would it not be marked for extermination? And yet nightly, daily, throughout this earth these crimes are perpetrated without end."

"All right, that's true. Undoubtedly that's true. But is your solution any better? It's unspeakable, the slaughter of all things male. Surely if you want to rule—" But even this to me was unthinkable. I thought of Marius's old words, spoken long ago to me when we existed still in the age of powdered wigs and satin slippers—that the old religion, Christianity, was dying, and maybe no new religion would rise:

"Maybe something more wonderful will take place," Marius had said, "the world will truly move forward, past all gods and goddesses, past all devils and angels . . ."

Wasn't that the destiny of this world, really? The destiny to which it was moving without our intervention?

"Ah, you are a dreamer, my beautiful one," she said harshly. "How you pick and choose your illusions! Look to the eastern countries, where the desert tribes, now rich on the oil they have pulled up from beneath the sands, kill each other by the thousands in the name of Allah, their god! Religion is not dead on this earth; it never will be. You and Marius, what chess players you are; your ideas are nothing but chess pieces. And you cannot see beyond the board on which you place them in this or that pattern as suits your small ethical souls."

"You're wrong," I said angrily. "Not about us perhaps. We don't matter. You're wrong in all this that you've begun. You're wrong."

"No, I am not wrong," she said. "And there is no one who can stop me, male or female. And we shall see for the first time since man lifted the club to strike down his brother, the world that women would make and what women have to teach men. And only when men can be taught, will they be allowed to run free among women again!"

"There must be some other way! Ye gods, I'm a flawed thing, a weak thing, a thing no better than most of the men who've ever lived. I can't argue for their lives now. I couldn't defend my own. But, Akasha, for the love of all things living, I'm begging you to turn away from this, this wholesale murder—"

"You speak to me of murder? Tell me the value of one human life, Lestat. Is it not infinite? And how many have you sent to the grave? We have blood on our hands, all of us, just as we have it in our veins."

"Yes, exactly. And we are not all wise and all knowing. I'm begging you to stop, to consider . . . Akasha, surely Marius—"

"Marius!" Softly she laughed. "What did Marius teach you? What did he give you? Really give you!"

I didn't answer. I couldn't. And her beauty was confusing me! So confusing to see the roundness of her arms; the tiny dimple in her cheek.

"My darling," she said, her face suddenly tender and soft as her voice was. "Bring to mind your vision of the Savage Garden, in which aesthetic principles are the only enduring principles—the laws that govern the evolution of all things large and small, of colors and patterns in glorious profusion, and beauty! Beauty everywhere one looks. That is nature. And death is everywhere in it.

"And what I shall make is Eden, the Eden all long for, and it shall be better than nature! It shall take things a step further; and the utter abusive and amoral violence of nature shall be redeemed. Don't you understand that men will never do more than dream of peace? But women can realize that dream? My vision is amplified in the heart of every woman. But it cannot survive the heat of male violence! And that heat is so terrible that the earth itself may not survive."

"What if there's something you don't understand," I said. I was struggling, grasping for the words. "Suppose the duality of masculine and feminine is indispensable to the human animal. Suppose the women want the men; suppose they rise against you and seek to protect the men. The world is not this little brutal island! All women are not peasants blinded by visions!"

"Do you think men are what women want?" she asked. She drew closer, her face changing imperceptibly in the play of the light. "Is that what you're saying? If it is so, then we shall spare a few more of the men, and keep them where they may be looked at as the women looked at you, and touched as the women touched you. We'll keep them where the women may have them when they want them, and I assure you they shall not be used as women have been used by men."

I sighed. It was useless to argue. She was absolutely right and absolutely wrong.

"You do yourself an injustice," she said. "I know your arguments. For centuries I have pondered them, as I've pondered so many questions. You think I do what I do with human limitations. I do not. To understand me, you must think in terms of abilities yet unimagined. Sooner will you understand the mystery of splitting atoms or of black holes in space."

"There has to be a way without death. There has to be a way that triumphs over death."

"Now that, my beauty, is truly against nature," she said. "Even I cannot put an end to death." She paused; she seemed suddenly distracted; or rather deeply distressed by the words she'd just spoken. "An end to death," she whispered. It seemed some personal sorrow had intruded on her thoughts. "An end to death," she said again. But she was drifting away from me. I watched her close her eyes, and lift her fingers to her temples.

She was hearing the voices again; letting them come. Or maybe even unable to stop them for a moment. She said some words in an ancient tongue, and I didn't understand them. I was struck by her sudden seeming vulnerability, the way the voices seemed to be cutting her off; the way her eyes appeared to search the room and then to fix on me and brighten.

I was speechless and overwhelmed with sadness. How small had my visions of power always been! To vanquish a mere handful of enemies, to be seen and loved by mortals as an image; to find some place in the great drama of things which was infinitely larger than I was, a drama whose study could occupy the mind of one being for a thousand years. And we stood outside time suddenly; outside of justice; capable of collapsing whole systems of thought. Or was it just an illusion? How many others had reached for such power, in one form or another?

"They were not immortals, my beloved." It was almost an entreaty.

"But it's an accident that we are," I said. "We're things that never should have come into existence."

"Don't speak those words!"

"I can't help it."

"It doesn't matter now. You fail to grasp how little *anything* matters. I give you no sublime reason for what I do because the reasons are simple and practical; how we came into being is irrelevant. What matters is that we have survived. Don't you see? That is the utter beauty of it, the beauty out of which all other beauties will be born, that we have survived."

I shook my head. I was in a panic. I saw again the museum that the villagers on this island had only just burnt. I saw the statues blackened and lying on the floor. An appalling sense of loss engulfed me.

"History does not matter," she said. "Art does not matter; these things imply continuities which in fact do not exist. They cater to our need for pattern, our hunger for meaning. But they cheat us in the end. We must make the meaning."

I turned my back. I didn't want to be drugged by her resolution or her beauty; by the glimmer of light in her jet black eyes. I felt her hands on my shoulders; her lips against my neck.

"When the years have passed," she said, "when my garden has bloomed through many summers and gone to sleep through many winters; when the old ways of rape and war are nothing but memory, and women watch the old films in mystification that such things could ever have been done; when the ways of women are inculcated into every member of the population, naturally, as aggression is now inculcated, then perhaps the males can return. Slowly, their numbers can be increased. Children will be reared in an atmosphere where rape is unthinkable, where war is unimaginable. And then . . . then . . . there can be men. When the world is ready for them."

"It won't work. It can't work."

"Why do you say so? Let us look to nature, as you wanted to do only moments ago. Go out in the lush garden that surrounds this villa; study the bees in their hives and the ants who labor as they have always done. They are female, my prince, by the millions. A male is only an aberration and a matter of function. They learned the wise trick a long time before me of limiting the males.

"And we may now live in an age where males are utterly unnecessary. Tell me, my prince, what is the primary use of men now, if it is not to protect women from other men?"

"What is it that makes you want me here!" I said desperately. I turned around to face her again. "Why have you chosen me as your consort! For the love of heaven, why don't you kill me with the other men! Choose some other immortal, some ancient being who hungers for such power! There must be one. I don't want to rule the world! I don't want to rule anything! I never did."

Her face changed just a little. It seemed there was a faint, evanescent sadness in her that made her eyes even deeper in their darkness for an instant. Her lip quivered as if she wanted to say something but couldn't. Then she did answer.

"Lestat, if all the world were destroyed, I would not destroy you," she said. "Your limitations are as radiant as your virtues for reasons I don't understand myself. But more truly perhaps, I love you because you are so perfectly what is wrong with all things male. Aggressive, full of hate and recklessness, and endlessly eloquent excuses for violence—you are the essence of masculinity; and there is a gorgeous quality to such purity. But only because it can now be controlled."

"By you."

"Yes, my darling. This is what I was born for. This is why I am here. And it does not matter if no one ratifies my purpose. I shall make it so. Right now the world burns with masculine fire; it is a conflagration. But when that is corrected, your fire shall burn ever more brightly—as a torch burns."

"Akasha, you prove my point! Don't you think the souls of women crave that very fire? My God, would you tamper with the stars themselves?"

"Yes, the soul craves it. But to see it in the blaze of a torch as I have indicated, or in the flame of a candle. But not as it rages now through every forest and over every mountain and in every glen. There is no woman alive who has ever wanted to be burnt by it! They want the light, my beauty, the light! And the warmth! But not the destruction. How could they? They are only women. They are not mad."

"All right. Say you accomplish your purpose. That you begin this revolution and it sweeps the world—and mind you I don't think such a thing will happen! But if you do, is there nothing under heaven that will demand atonement for the death of so many millions? If there are no gods or goddesses, is there not some way in which humans themselves—and you and I—shall be made to pay?"

"It is the gateway to innocence and so it shall be remembered. And never again will the male population be allowed to increase to such proportions, for who would want such horrors again?"

"Force the men to obey you. Dazzle them as you've dazzled the women, as you've dazzled me."

"But Lestat, that is just the point; they would never obey. Will you obey? They would die first, as you would die. They would have another reason for rebellion, as if any were ever wanting. They would gather together in magnificent resistance. Imagine a goddess to fight. We shall see enough of that by and by as it is. They cannot help but be men. And I could rule only through tyranny, by endless killing. And there would be chaos. But this way, there shall be a break in the great chain of violence. There shall be an era of utter and perfect peace."

I was quiet again. I could think of a thousand answers but they were all short-circuited. She knew her purpose only too well. And the truth was, she was right in many things she said.

Ah, but it was fantasy! A world without males. What exactly would have been accomplished? Oh, no. No, don't even accept the idea for a moment. Don't even. . . . Yet the vision returned, the vision I'd glimpsed in that miserable jungle village, of a world without fear.

Imagine trying to explain to them what men had been like. Imagine trying to explain that there had been a time when one could be murdered in the streets of the cities; imagine trying to explain what rape meant to the male of the species . . . imagine. And I saw their eyes looking at me, the uncomprehending eyes as they tried to fathom it, tried to make that leap of understanding. I felt their soft hands touching me.

"But this is madness!" I whispered,

"Ah, but you fight me so hard, my prince," she whispered. There was a flash of anger, hurt. She came near to me. If she kissed me again I was going to start weeping. I'd thought I knew what beauty was in women; but she'd surpassed all the language I had for it.

"My prince," she said again in a low whisper. "The logic of it is elegant. A world in which only a handful of males are kept for breeding shall be a female world. And that world will be what we have never known in all our bloody miserable history, in which men now breed germs in vials with which to kill continents in chemical warfare, and design bombs which can knock the earth from its path around the sun."

"What if the women divide along principles of masculine/feminine, the way men so often divide if there are no females there?"

"You know that's a foolish objection. Such distinctions are never more than superficial. Women are women! Can you conceive of war made by women? Truly, answer me. Can you? Can you conceive of bands of roving women intent only on destruction? Or rape? Such a thing is preposterous. For the aberrant few justice will be immediate. But overall, something utterly unforeseen will take place. Don't you see? The possibility of peace on earth has always existed, and there have always been people who could realize it, and preserve it, and those people are women. If one takes away the men."

I sat down on the bed in consternation, like a mortal man. I put my elbows on my knees. Dear God, dear God! Why did those two words keep coming to me? There was no God! I was in the room with God.

She laughed triumphantly.

"Yes, precious one," she said. She touched my hand and turned me around and drew me towards her. "But tell me, doesn't it excite you even a little?"

I looked at her. "What do you mean?"

"You, the impulsive one. You who made that child, Claudia, into a blood drinker, just to see what would happen?" There was mockery in her tone but it was affectionate. "Come now, don't you want to see what will happen if all the males are gone? Aren't you even a little curious? Reach into your soul for the truth. It is a very interesting idea, isn't it?"

I didn't answer. Then I shook my head. "No," I said.

"Coward," she whispered.

No one had ever called me that, no one.

"Coward," she said again. "Little being with little dreams."

"Maybe there would be no war and no rape and no violence," I said, "if all beings were little and had little dreams, as you put it."

She laughed softly. Forgivingly.

"We could argue these points forever," she whispered. "But very soon we will know. The world will be as I would have it be; and we shall see what happens as I said."

She sat beside me. For a moment it seemed I was losing my mind. She slipped her smooth naked arms around my neck. It seemed there had never been a softer female body, never anything as yielding and luscious as her embrace. Yet she was so hard, so strong.

The lights in the room were dimming. And the sky outside seemed ever more vivid and darkly blue.

"Akasha," I whispered. I was looking beyond the open terrace at the stars. I wanted to say something, something crucial that would sweep away all arguments; but the meaning escaped me. I was so drowsy; surely it was her doing. It was a spell she was working, yet knowing it did not release me. I felt her lips again on my lips, and on my throat. I felt the cool satin of her skin.

"Yes, rest now, precious one. And when you wake, the victims will be waiting."

"Victims. . . ." Almost dreaming, as I held her in my arms.

"But you must sleep now. You are young still and fragile. My blood's working on you, changing you, perfecting you."

Yes, destroying me; destroying my heart and my will. I was vaguely conscious of moving, of lying down on the bed. I fell back into the silken pillows, and then there was the silk of her hair near me, the touch of her fingers, and again, her lips on my mouth. Blood in her kiss; blood thundering beneath it.

"Listen to the sea," she whispered. "Listen to the flowers open. You can hear them now, you know. You can hear the tiny creatures of the sea if you listen. You can hear the dolphins sing, for they do."

Drifting. Safe in her arms; she the powerful one; she was the one they all feared.

Forget the acrid smell of the burning bodies; yes, listen to the sea pounding like guns on the beach beneath us; listen to the sound of a rose petal breaking loose and falling onto marble. And the world is going to hell, and I cannot help it, and I am in her arms and I am going to sleep.

"Hasn't that happened a million times, my love?" she whispered. "On a world full of suffering and death, you turned your back as millions of mortals do every night?"

Darkness. Splendid visions taking place; a palace even more lovely than this. Victims. Servants. The mythical existence of pashas, and emperors.

"Yes, my darling, anything that you desire. All the world at your feet. I shall build you palace upon palace; they shall do it; they that worship you. That is nothing. That is the simplest part of it. And think of the hunting, my prince. Until the killing is done, think of the chase. For they would surely run from you and hide from you, yet you would find them."

In the dwindling light—just before dreams come—I could see it. I could see myself traveling through the air, like the heroes of old, over the sprawling country where their campfires flickered.

In packs like wolves they would travel, through the cities as well as the woods, daring to show themselves only by day; for only then would they be safe from us. When night fell, we would come; and we would track them by their thoughts and by their blood, and by the whispered confessions of the women who had seen them and maybe even harbored them. Out in the open they might run, firing their useless weapons. And we would swoop down; we would destroy them one by one, our prey, save for those we wanted alive, those whose blood we would take slowly, mercilessly.

And out of that war shall come peace? Out of that hideous game shall come a garden?

I tried to open my eyes. I felt her kiss my eyelids.

Dreaming.

A barren plain and the soil breaking. Something rising, pushing the dried clods of earth out of its way. I am this thing. This thing walking across the barren plain as the sun sinks. The sky is still full of light. I look down at the stained cloth that covers me, but this is not me. I'm only Lestat. And I'm afraid. I wish Gabrielle were here. And Louis. Maybe Louis could make her understand. Ah, Louis, of all of us, Louis who always knew. . . .

And there is the familiar dream again, the redheaded women kneeling by the altar with the body—their mother's body and they are ready to consume it. Yes, it's their duty, their sacred right—to devour the brain and the heart. Except that they never will because something awful always happens. Soldiers come. . . . I wish I knew the meaning.

BLOOD.

I woke up with a start. Hours had passed. The room had cooled faintly. The sky was wondrously clear through the open windows. From her came all the light that filled the room.

"The women are waiting, and the victims, they are afraid."

The victims. My head was spinning. The victims would be full of luscious blood. Males who would have died anyway. Young males all mine to take.

"Yes. But come, put an end to their suffering."

Groggily I got up. She wrapped a long cloak over my shoulders, something simpler than her own garment, but warm and soft to touch. She stroked my hair with her two hands.

"Masculine—feminine. Is that all there ever was to it?" I whispered. My body wanted to sleep some more. But the blood.

She reached up and touched my cheek with her fingers. Tears again?

We went out of the room together, and onto a long landing with a marble railing, from which a stairs descended, turning once, into an immense room. Candelabra everywhere. Dim electric lamps creating a luxurious gloom.

At the very center, the women were assembled, perhaps two hundred or more of them, standing motionless and looking up at us, their hands clasped as if in prayer.

Even in their silence, they seemed barbaric, amid the European furniture, the Italian hardwoods with their gilt edges, and the old fireplace with its marble scrolls. I thought of her words suddenly: "history doesn't matter; art doesn't matter." Dizzy. On the walls, there ran those airy eighteenth-century paintings, full of gleaming clouds and fat-cheeked angels, and skies of luminescent blue.

The women stood looking past this wealth which had never touched them and indeed meant nothing to them, looking up at the vision on the landing, which now dissolved, and in a rush of whispered noise and colored light, materialized suddenly at the foot of the stairs.

Sighs rose, hands were raised to shield bowed heads as if from a blast of unwelcome light. Then all eyes were fixed upon the Queen of Heaven and her consort, who stood on the red carpet, only a few feet above the assembly, the consort a bit shaken and biting his lip a little and trying to see this thing clearly, this awful thing that was happening, this awful mingling of worship and blood sacrifice, as the victims were brought forth.

Such fine specimens. Dark-haired, dark-skinned, Mediterranean men. Every bit as beautiful as the young women. Men of that stocky build and exquisite musculature that has inspired artists for thousands of years. Ink black eyes and darkly shaved faces; and deep cunning; and deep anger as they looked upon these hostile supernatural creatures who had decreed the death of their brothers far and wide.

With leather straps they'd been bound—probably their own belts, and the belts of dozens of others; but the women had done it well. Their ankles were tethered even, so that they could walk but not kick or run. Naked to the waist they were, and only one was trembling, as much with anger as with fear. Suddenly he began to struggle. The other two turned, stared at him, and started to struggle as well.

But the mass of women closed on them, forcing them to their knees. I felt the desire rise in me at the sight of it, at the sight of leather belts cutting into the dark naked flesh of the men's arms. Why is this so seductive! And the women's hands holding them, those tight menacing hands that could be so soft otherwise. They couldn't fight so many women. Heaving sighs, they stopped the rebellion, though the one who had started the struggle looked up, accusingly, at me.

Demons, devils, things from hell, that is what his mind told him; for who else could have done such things to his world? Oh, this is the beginning of darkness, terrible darkness!

But the desire was so strong. *You are going to die and I am going to do it!* And he seemed to hear it, and to understand it. And a savage hatred of the women rose out of him, replete with images of rape and retribution that made me smile, and yet I understood. Rather completely I understood. So easy to feel that contempt for them, to be outraged that they had dared to become the enemy, the enemy in the age-old battle, they, the women! And it was darkness, this imagined retribution, it was unspeakable darkness, too.

I felt Akasha's fingers on my arm. The feeling of bliss came back; the delirium. I tried to resist it, but I felt it as before. Yet the desire didn't go away. The desire was in my mouth now. I could taste it.

Yes, pass into the moment; pass into pure function; let the bloody sacrifice begin.

The women went down on their knees en masse, and the men who were already kneeling seemed to grow calm, their eyes glazing over as they looked at us, their lips trembling and loose.

I stared at the muscled shoulders of the first one, the one who had rebelled. I imagined as I always do at such moments the feel of his coarse rough-shaven throat when my lips would touch it, and my teeth would break through the skin—not the icy skin of the goddess—but hot, salty human skin.

Yes, beloved. Take him. He is the sacrifice that you deserve. You are a god now. Take him. Do you know how many wait for you?

It seemed the women understood what to do. They lifted him as I stepped forward; there was another struggle, but it was no more than a spasm in the muscles as I took him into my arms. My hand closed too hard on his head; I didn't know my new strength, and I heard the bones cracking even as my teeth went in. But the death came almost instantly, so great was my first draught of blood. I was burning with hunger; and the whole portion, complete and entire in one instant, had not been enough. Not nearly enough!

At once I took the next victim, trying to be slow with it, so that I would tumble into the darkness as I'd so often done, with only the soul speaking to me. Yes, telling me its secrets as the blood spurted into my mouth, as I let my mouth fill before I swallowed. *Yes, brother. I am sorry, brother.* And then staggering forward, I stepped on the corpse before me and crushed it underfoot.

"Give me the last one."

No resistance. He stared up at me in utter quiet, as if some light had dawned in him, as if he'd found in theory or belief some perfect rescue. I pulled him to me—gently, Lestat—and this was the real fount I wanted, this was the slow, powerful death I craved, the heart pumping as if it would never stop, the sigh slipping from his lips, my eyes clouded still, even as I let him go, with the fading images of his brief and unrecorded life, suddenly collapsed into one rare second of meaning.

I let him drop. Now there was no meaning.

There was only the light before me, and the rapture of the women who had at last been redeemed through miracles.

The room was hushed; not a thing stirred; the sound of the sea came in, that distant monotonous booming.

Then Akasha's voice:

The sins of the men have now been atoned for; and those who are kept now, shall be well cared for, and loved. But never give freedom to those who remain, those who have oppressed you.

And then soundlessly, without distinct words, the lesson came.

The ravening lust which they had just witnessed, the deaths they had seen at my hands—that was to be the eternal reminder of the fierceness that lived in all male things and must never be allowed free again. The males had been sacrificed to the embodiment of their own violence.

In sum, these women had witnessed a new and transcendent ritual; a new holy sacrifice of the Mass. And they would see it again; and they must always remember it.

My head swam from the paradox. And my own small designs of not very long ago were there to torment me. I had wanted the world of mortals to know of me. I had wanted to be the image of evil in the theater of the world and thereby somehow do good.

And now I was that image all right, I was its literal embodiment, passing through the minds of these few simple souls into myth as she had promised. And there was a small voice whispering in my ear, hammering me with that old adage: be careful what you wish for; your wish might come true.

Yes, that was the heart of it; all I'd ever wished for was coming true. In the shrine I had kissed her and longed to awaken her, and dreamt of her power; and now we stood together, she and I, and the hymns rose around us. Hosannas. Cries of joy.

The doors of the palazzo were thrown open.

And we were taking our leave; we were rising in splendor and in magic, and passing out of the doors, and up over the roof of the old mansion, and then out over the sparkling waters into the calm sweep of the stars.

I had no fear of falling anymore; I had no fear of anything so insignificant. Because my whole soul—petty as it was and always had been—knew fears I'd never imagined before.

6

THE STORY OF THE TWINS
PART II

S HE was dreaming of killing. It was a great dark city like London or Rome, and she was hurrying through it, on an errand of killing, to bring down the first sweet human victim that would be her own. And just before she opened her eyes, she had made the leap from the things she had believed all her life, to this simple amoral act—killing. She had done what the reptile does when it hoists in its leathery slit of a mouth the tiny crying mouse that it will crush slowly without ever hearing that soft heartbreaking song.

Awake in the dark; and the house alive above her; the old ones saying Come. A television talking somewhere. The Blessed Virgin Mary had appeared on an island in the Mediterranean Sea.

No hunger. Maharet's blood was too strong. The idea was growing, beckoning like a crone in a dark alley. *Killing.*

Rising from the narrow box in which she lay, she tiptoed through the blackness until her hands felt the metal door. She went into the hallway and looked up the endless iron stairs, crisscrossing back over itself as if it were a skeleton, and she saw the sky through the glass like smoke. Mael was halfway up, at the door of the house proper, gazing down at her.

She reeled with it—*I am one of you and we are together*—and the feel of the iron rail under her hand, and some sudden grief, just a fleeting thing, for all she had been before this fierce beauty had grabbed her by the hair.

Mael came down as if to retrieve her, because it was carrying her away.

They understood, didn't they, the way the earth breathed for her now, and the forest sang, and the roots prowled the dark, coming through these earthen walls.

She stared at Mael. Faint smell of buckskin, dust. How had she ever thought such beings were human? Eyes glittering like that. And yet the time would come when she would be walking among human beings again, and she would see their eyes linger and then suddenly move away. She'd be hurrying through some dark city like London or Rome. Looking into the eyes of Mael, she saw the crone again in the alleyway; but it had not been a literal image. No, she saw the alleyway, she saw the killing, purely. And in silence, they both looked away at the same instant, but not quickly, rather respectfully. He took her hand; he looked at the bracelet he'd given her. He kissed her suddenly on the cheek. And then he led her up the stairs towards the mountaintop room.

The electronic voice of the television grew louder and louder, speaking of mass hysteria in Sri Lanka. Women killing men. Even male babies murdered. On the island of Lynkonos there had been mass hallucinations and an epidemic of unexplained deaths.

Only gradually did it dawn on her, what she was hearing. So it wasn't the Blessed Virgin Mary, and she had thought how lovely, when she first heard it, that they can believe something like that. She turned to Mael but he was looking ahead. He knew these things. The television had been playing its words to him for an hour.

Now she saw the eerie blue flicker as she came into the mountaintop room. And the strange spectacle of these her new brethren in the Secret Order of the Undead, scattered about like so many statues, glowing in the blue light, as they stared fixedly at the large screen.

". . . outbreaks in the past caused by contaminants in food or water. Yet no explanation has been found for the similarity of the reports from widely divergent places, which now include several isolated villages in the mountains of Nepal. Those apprehended claim to have seen a beautiful woman, called variously the Blessed Virgin, or the Queen of Heaven, or simply the Goddess, who commanded them to massacre the males of their village, except for a few carefully chosen to be spared. Some reports describe a male apparition also, a fair-haired deity who does not speak and who as yet has no official or unofficial title or name . . ."

Jesse looked at Maharet, who watched without expression, one hand resting on the arm of her chair.

Newspapers covered the table. Papers in French and Hindustani as well as English.

". . . from Lynkonos to several other islands before the militia was called in. Early estimates indicate some two thousand men may have been killed in this little archipelago just off the tip of Greece."

Maharet touched the small black control under her hand and the screen vanished. It seemed the entire apparatus vanished, fading into the dark wood, as the windows became transparent and the treetops appeared in endless, misted layers against the violent sky. Far away, Jesse saw the twinkling lights of Santa Rosa cradled in the dark hills. She could smell the sun that had been in this room; she could feel the heat rising slowly through the glass ceiling.

She looked at the others who were sitting there in stunned silence. Marius glared at the television screen, at the newspapers spread out before him.

"We have no time to lose," Khayman said quickly to Maharet. "You must continue the tale. We don't know when she will come here."

He made a small gesture, and the scattered newspapers were suddenly cleared away, crushed together, and hurtling soundlessly into the fire which devoured them with a gust that sent a shower of sparks up the gaping smokestack.

Jesse was suddenly dizzy. Too fast, all of that. She stared at Khayman. Would she ever get used to it? Their porcelain faces and their sudden violent expressions, their soft human voices, and their near invisible movements?

And what was the Mother doing? Males slaughtered. The fabric of life for these ignorant people utterly destroyed. A cold sense of menace touched her. She searched Maharet's face for some insight, some understanding.

But Maharet's features were utterly rigid. She had not answered Khayman. She turned towards the table slowly and clasped her hands under her chin. Her eyes were dull, remote, as if she saw nothing before her.

"The fact is, she has to be destroyed," Marius said, as if he could hold it in no longer. The color flared in his cheeks, shocking Jesse, because all the normal lines of a man's face had been there for an instant. And now they were gone, and he was visibly shaking with anger. "We've loosed a monster, and it's up to us to reclaim it."

"And how can that be done?" Santino asked. "You speak as if it's a simple matter of decision. You cannot kill her!"

"We forfeit our lives, that's how it's done," Marius said. "We act in concert, and we end this thing once and for all as it should have been ended long ago." He glanced at them all one by one, eyes lingering on Jesse. Then shifting to Maharet. "The body isn't indestructible. It isn't made of marble. It can be pierced, cut. I've pierced it with my teeth. I've drunk its blood!"

Maharet made a small dismissive gesture, as if to say I know these things and you know I know.

"And as we cut it, we cut ourselves?" Eric said. "I say we leave here. I say we hide from her. What do we gain staying in this place?"

"No!" Maharet said.

"She'll kill you one by one if you do that," Khayman said. "You're alive because you wait now for her purpose."

"Would you go on with the story," Gabrielle said, speaking directly to Maharet. She'd been withdrawn all this time, only now and then listening to the others. "I want to know the rest," she said. "I want to hear everything." She sat forward, arms folded on the table.

"You think you'll discover some way to vanquish her in these old tales?" Eric asked. "You're mad if you think that."

"Go on with the story, please," Louis said. "I want to . . ." He hesitated. "I want to *know* what happened also."

Maharet looked at him for a long moment.

"Go on, Maharet," Khayman said. "For in all likelihood, the Mother will be destroyed and we both know how and why, and all this talk means nothing."

"What can prophecy mean now, Khayman?" Maharet asked, her voice low, devitalized. "Do we fall into the same errors that ensnare the Mother? The past may instruct us. But it won't save us."

"Your sister comes, Maharet. She comes as she said she would."

"Khayman," Maharet said with a long, bitter smile.

"Tell us what happened," Gabrielle said.

Maharet sat still, as if trying to find some way to begin. The sky beyond the windows darkened in the interval. Yet a faint tinge of red appeared in the far west, growing brighter and brighter against the gray clouds. Finally, it faded, and they were wrapped in absolute darkness, except for the light of the fire, and the dull sheen of the glass walls which had become mirrors.

"Khayman took you to Egypt," Gabrielle said. "What did you see there?"

"Yes, he took us to Egypt," Maharet said. She sighed as she sat back in the chair, her eyes fixed on the table before her. "There was no escape from it; Khayman would have taken us by force. And in truth, we accepted that we had to go. Through twenty generations, we had gone between man and the spirits. If Amel had done some great evil, we would try to undo it. Or at least . . . as I said to you when we first came to this table . . . we would seek to understand.

"I left my child. I left her in the care of those women I trusted most. I kissed her. I told her secrets. And then I left her, and we set out, carried in the royal litter as if we were guests of the King and Queen of Kemet and not prisoners, just as before.

"Khayman was gentle with us on the long march, but grim and silent, and refusing to meet our gaze. And it was just as well, for we had not forgotten our injuries. Then on the very last night when we camped on the banks of the great river, which we would cross in the morning to reach the royal palace, Khayman called us into his tent and told us all that he knew.

"His manner was courteous, decorous. And we tried to put aside our personal suspicions of him as we listened. He told us of what the demon—as he called it—had done.

"Only hours after we had been sent out of Egypt, he had known that something was watching him, some dark and evil force. Everywhere that he went, he felt this presence, though in the light of day it tended to wane.

"Then things within his house were altered—little things which others did not notice. He thought at first he was going mad. His writing things were misplaced; then the seal which he used as great steward. Then at random moments—and always when he was alone—these objects came flying at him, striking him in the face, or landing at his feet. Some turned up in ridiculous places. He would find the great seal, for instance, in his beer or his broth.

"And he dared not tell the King and Queen. He knew it was our spirits who were doing it; and to tell would be a death sentence for us.

"And so he kept this awful secret, as things grew worse and worse. Ornaments which he had treasured from childhood were now rent to pieces and made to rain down upon him. Sacred amulets were hurled into the privy; excrement was taken from the well and smeared upon the walls.

"He could barely endure his own house, yet he admonished his slaves to tell no one, and when they ran off in fear, he attended to his own toilet and swept the place like a lowly servant himself.

"But he was now in a state of terror. Something was there with him in his house. He could hear its breath upon his face. And now and then he would swear that he felt its needlelike teeth.

"At last in desperation he began to talk to it, beg it to get out. But this seemed only to increase its strength. With the talking, it redoubled its power. It emptied his purse upon the stones and made the gold coins jingle against each other all night long. It upset his bed so that he landed on his face on the floor. It put sand in his food when he wasn't looking.

"Finally six months had passed since we had left the kingdom. He was growing frantic. Perhaps we were beyond danger. But he could not be sure, and he did not know where to turn, for the spirit was really frightening him.

"Then in the dead of night, as he lay wondering what the thing was up to, for it had been so quiet, he heard suddenly a great pounding at his door. He was in terror. He knew he shouldn't answer, that the knocking didn't come from a human hand. But finally he could bear it no longer. He said his prayers; he threw open the door. And what he beheld was the horror of horrors—the rotted mummy of his father, the filthy wrappings in tatters, propped against the garden wall.

"Of course, he knew there was no life in the shrunken face or dead eyes that stared at him. Someone or something had unearthed the corpse from its desert mastaba and brought it there. And this was the body of his father, putrid, stinking; the body of his father, which by all things holy, should have been consumed in a proper funeral feast by Khayman and his brothers and sisters.

"Khayman sank to his knees weeping, half screaming. And then, before his unbelieving eyes, the thing moved! The thing began to dance! Its limbs were jerked hither and thither, the wrappings breaking to bits and pieces, until Khayman ran into the house and shut the door against it. And then the corpse was flung, pounding its fist it seemed, upon the door, demanding entrance.

"Khayman called on all the gods of Egypt to be rid of this monstrosity. He called out to the palace guards; he called to the soldiers of the King. He cursed the demon thing and ordered it to leave him; and Khayman became the one flinging objects now, and kicking the gold coins about in his rage.

"All the palace rushed through the royal gardens to Khayman's house. But the demon now seemed to grow even stronger. The shutters rattled and then were torn from their pivots. The few bits of fine furniture which Khayman possessed began to skitter about.

"Yet this was only the beginning. At dawn when the priests entered the house to exorcise the demon, a great wind came out of the desert, carrying with it torrents of blinding sand. And everywhere Khayman went, the wind pursued him; and finally he looked down to see his arms covered with tiny pinpricks and tiny droplets of blood. Even his eyelids were assaulted. In a cabinet he flung himself to get some peace. And the thing tore up the cabinet. And all fled from it. And Khayman was left crying on the floor.

"For days the tempest continued. The more the priests prayed and sang, the more the demon raged.

"The King and Queen were beside themselves in consternation. The priests cursed the demon. The people blamed it upon the red-haired witches. They cried that we should never have been allowed to leave the land of Kemet. We should be found at all costs and brought back to be burnt alive. And then the demon would be quiet.

"But the old families did not agree with this verdict. To them the judgment was clear. Had not the gods unearthed the putrid body of Khayman's father, to show that the flesh eaters had always done what was pleasing to heaven? No, it was the King and Queen who were evil, the King and Queen who must die. The King and Queen who had filled the land with mummies and superstition.

"The kingdom, finally, was on the verge of civil war.

"At last the King himself came to Khayman, who sat weeping in his house, a garment drawn over him like a shroud. And the King talked to the demon, even as the tiny bites afflicted Khayman and made drops of blood on the cloth that covered Khayman.

" 'Now think what those witches told us,' the King said. 'These are but spirits; not demons. And they can be reasoned with. If only I could make them hear me as the witches could; and make them answer.'

"But this little conversation only seemed to enrage the demon. It broke what little furniture it had not already smashed. It tore the door off its pivots; it uprooted the trees from the garden and flung them about. In fact, it seemed to forget Khayman altogether for the moment, as it went tearing through the palace gardens destroying all that it could.

"And the King went after it, begging it to recognize him and to converse with him, and to impart to him its secrets. He stood in the very midst of the whirlwind created by this demon, fearless and enrapt.

"Finally the Queen appeared. In a loud piercing voice she addressed the demon too. 'You punish us for the affliction of the red-haired sisters!' she screamed. 'But why do you not serve us instead of them!' At once the demon tore at her clothes and greatly afflicted her, as it had done to Khayman before. She tried to cover her arms and her face, but it was impossible. And so the King took hold of her and together they ran back to Khayman's house.

" 'Now, go,' said the King to Khayman. 'Leave us alone with this thing for I will learn from it, I will understand what it wants.' And calling the priests to him, he told them through the whirlwind what we had said, that the spirit hated mankind because we were both spirit and flesh. But he would ensnare it and reform it and control it. For he was Enkil, King of Kemet, and he could do this thing.

"Into Khayman's house, the King and the Queen went together, and the demon went with them, tearing the place to pieces, yet there they remained. Khayman, who was now free of the thing, lay on the floor of the palace exhausted, fearing for his sovereigns but not knowing what to do.

"The entire court was in an uproar; men fought one another; women wept, and some even left the palace for fear of what was to come.

"For two whole nights and days, the King remained with the demon; and so did the Queen. And then the old families, the flesh eaters, gathered outside the house. The King and Queen were in error; it was time to seize the future of Kemet. At nightfall, they went into the house on their deadly errand with daggers raised. They would kill the King and Queen; and if the people raised any outcry, then they would say that the demon had done it; and who could say that the demon had not? And would not the demon stop when the King and Queen were dead, the King and Queen who had persecuted the red-haired witches?

"It was the Queen who saw them coming; and as she rushed forward, crying in alarm, they thrust their daggers into her breast and she sank down dying. The King ran to her aid, and they struck him down too, just as mercilessly; and then they ran out of the house, for the demon had not stopped his persecutions.

"Now Khayman, all this while, had knelt at the very edge of the garden, deserted by the guards who had thrown in with the flesh eaters. He expected to die with other servants of the royal family. Then he heard a horrid wailing from the Queen. Sounds such as he had never heard before. And when the flesh eaters heard these sounds, they deserted the place utterly.

"It was Khayman, loyal steward to the King and Queen, who snatched up a torch and went to the aid of his master and mistress.

"No one tried to stop him. All crept away in fear. Khayman alone went into the house.

"It was pitch-black now, save for the torchlight. And this is what Khayman saw:

"The Queen lay on the floor writhing as if in agony, the blood pouring from her wounds, and a great reddish cloud enveloped her; it was like a whirlpool surrounding her, or rather a wind sweeping up countless tiny drops of blood. And in the midst of this swirling wind or rain or whatever it could be called, the Queen twisted and turned, her eyes rolling up in her head. The King lay sprawled on his back.

"All instinct told Khayman to leave this place. To get as far away from it as he could. At that moment, he wanted to leave his homeland forever. But this was his Queen, who lay there gasping for breath, her back arched, her hands clawing at the floor.

"Then the great blood cloud that veiled her, swelling and contracting around her, grew denser and, all of a sudden, as if drawn into her wounds, disappeared. The Queen's body went still; then slowly she sat upright, her eyes staring forward, and a great guttural cry broke from her before she fell quiet.

"There was no sound whatsoever as the Queen stared at Khayman, except for the crackling of the torch. And then hoarsely the Queen began to gasp again, her eyes widening, and it seemed she should die; but she did not. She shielded her eyes from the bright light of the torch as though it was hurting her, and she turned and saw her husband lying as if dead at her side.

"She cried a negation in her agony; it could not be so. And at the same instant, Khayman beheld that all her wounds were healing; deep gashes were no more than scratches upon the surface of her skin.

" 'Your Highness!' he said. And he came towards her as she crouched weeping and staring at her own arms, which had been torn with the slashes of the daggers, and at her own breasts, which were whole again. She was whimpering piteously as she looked at these healing wounds. And suddenly with her long nails, she tore at her own skin and the blood gushed out and yet the wound healed!

" 'Khayman, my Khayman!' she screamed, covering her eyes so that she did not see the bright torch. 'What has befallen me!' And her screams grew louder and louder; and she fell upon the King in panic, crying, 'Enkil, help me. Enkil, do not die!' and all the other mad things that one cries in the midst of disaster. And then as she stared down at the King, a great ghastly change came over her, and she lunged at the King, as if she were a hungry beast, and with her long tongue, she lapped at the blood that covered his throat and his chest.

"Khayman had never seen such a spectacle. She was a lioness in the desert lapping the blood from a tender kill. Her back was bowed, and her knees were drawn up, and she pulled the helpless body of the King towards her and bit the artery in his throat.

"Khayman dropped the torch. He backed halfway from the open door. Yet even as he meant to run for his life, he heard the King's voice. Softly the King spoke to her. 'Akasha,' he said. 'My Queen.' And she, drawing up, shivering, weeping, stared at her own body, and at his body, at her smooth flesh, and his torn still by so many wounds. 'Khayman,' she cried. 'Your dagger. Give it to me. For they have taken their weapons with them. Your dagger. I must have it now.'

"At once Khayman obeyed, though he thought it was to see his King die once and for all. But with the dagger the Queen cut her own wrists and watched the blood pour down upon the wounds of her husband, and she saw it heal them. And crying out in her excitement, she smeared the blood all over his torn face.

"The King's wounds healed. Khayman saw it. Khayman saw the great gashes closing. He saw the King tossing, heaving his arms this way and that. His tongue lapped at Akasha's spilt blood as it ran down his face. And then rising in that same animal posture that had so consumed the Queen only moments before, the King embraced his wife, and opened his mouth on her throat.

"Khayman had seen enough. In the flickering light of the dying torch these two pale figures had become haunts to him, demons themselves. He backed out of the little house and up against the garden wall. And there it seems he lost consciousness, feeling the grass against his face as he collapsed.

"When he waked, he found himself lying on a gilded couch in the Queen's chambers. All the palace lay quiet. He saw that his clothes had been changed, and his face and hands bathed, and that there was only the dim-mest light here and sweet incense, and the doors were open to the garden as if there was nothing to fear.

"Then in the shadows, he saw the King and the Queen looking down at him; only this was not his King and not his Queen. It seemed then that he would cry out; he would give voice to screams as terrible as those he had heard from others; but the Queen quieted him.

" 'Khayman, my Khayman,' she said. She handed to him his beautiful gold-handled dagger. 'You have served us well.'

"There Khayman paused in his story. 'Tomorrow night,' he said, 'when the sun sets, you will see for yourselves what has happened. For then and only then, when all the light is gone from the western sky, will they appear together in the rooms of the palace, and you will see what I have seen.'

" 'But why only in the night?' I asked him. 'What is the significance of this?'

"And then he told us, that not one hour after he'd waked, even before the sun had risen, they had begun to shrink from the open doors of the palace, to cry that the light hurt their eyes. Already they had fled from torches and lamps; and now it seemed the morning was coming after them; and there was no place in the palace that they could hide.

"In stealth they left the palace, covered in garments. They ran with a speed no human being could match. They ran towards the mastabas or tombs of the old families, those who had been forced with pomp and ceremony to make mummies of their dead. In sum, to the sacred places which no one would desecrate, they ran so fast that Khayman could not follow them. Yet once the King stopped. To the sun god, Ra, he called out for mercy. Then weeping, hiding their eyes from the sun, crying as if the sun burnt them even though its light had barely come into the sky, the King and the Queen disappeared from Khayman's sight.

" 'Not a day since have they appeared before sunset; they come down out of the sacred cemetery, though no one knows from where. In fact the people now wait for them in a great multitude, hailing them as the god and the goddess, the very image of Osiris and Isis, deities of the moon, and tossing flowers before them, and bowing down to them.

" 'For the tale spread far and wide that the King and Queen had vanquished death at the hands of their enemies by some celestial power; that they are gods, immortal and invincible; and that by that same power they can see into men's hearts. No secret can be kept from them; their enemies are immediately punished; they can hear the words one speaks only in one's head. All fear them.

" 'Yet I know as all their faithful servants know that they cannot bear a candle or a lamp too close to them; that they shriek at the bright light of a torch; and that when they execute their enemies in secret, they drink their blood! They drink it, I tell you. Like jungle cats, they feed upon these victims; and the room after is as a lion's den. And it is I, Khayman, their trusted steward, who must gather these bodies and heave them into the pit.' And then Khayman stopped and gave way to weeping.

"But the tale was finished; and it was almost morning. The sun was rising over the eastern mountains; we made ready to cross the mighty Nile. The desert was warming; Khayman walked to the edge of the river as the first barge of soldiers went across. He was weeping still as he saw the sun come down upon the river; saw the water catch fire.

" 'The sun god, Ra, is the oldest and greatest god of all Kemet,' he whispered. 'And this god has turned against them. Why? In secret they weep over their fate; the thirst maddens them; they are frightened it will become more than they can bear. You must save them. You must do it for our people. They have not sent for you to blame you or harm you. They need you. You are powerful witches. Make this spirit undo his work.' And then looking at us, remembering all that had befallen us, he gave way to despair.

"Mekare and I made no answer. The barge was now ready to carry us to the palace. And we stared across the glare of the water at the great collection of painted buildings that was the royal city, and we wondered what the consequences of this horror would finally be.

"As I stepped down upon the barge, I thought of my child, and I knew suddenly I should die in Kemet. I wanted to close my eyes, and ask the spirits in a small secret voice if this was truly meant to happen, yet I did not dare. I could not have my last hope taken from me."

MAHARET tensed.

Jesse saw her shoulders straighten; saw the fingers of her right hand move against the wood, curling and then opening again, the gold nails gleaming in the firelight.

"I do not want you to be afraid," she said, her voice slipping into monotone. "But you should know that the Mother has crossed the great eastern sea. She and Lestat are closer now . . ."

Jesse felt the current of alarm passing through all those at the table. Maharet remained rigid, listening, or perhaps seeing; the pupils of her eyes moving only slightly.

"Lestat calls," Maharet said. "But it is too faint for me to hear words; too faint for pictures. He is not harmed, however; that much I know, and that I have little time now to finish this story. . . ."

7

LESTAT:
THE KINGDOM OF HEAVEN

THE CARIBBEAN. Haiti. The Garden of God.

I stood on the hilltop in the moonlight and I tried not to see this paradise. I tried to picture those I loved. Were they gathered still together in that fairy-tale wood of monster trees, where I had seen my mother walking? If only I could see their faces or hear their voices. Marius, do not be the angry father. Help me! Help us all! I do not give in, but I am losing. I am losing my soul and my mind. My heart is already gone. It belongs to her.

But they were beyond my reach; the great sweep of miles closed us off; I had not the power to overarch that distance.

I looked instead on these verdant green hills, now patched with tiny farms, a picture book world with flowers blooming in profusion, the red poinsettia as tall as trees. And the clouds, ever changing, borne like the tall sailing ships on brisk winds. What had the first Europeans thought when they looked upon this fecund land surrounded by the sparkling sea? That this was the Garden of God?

And to think, they had brought such death to it, the natives gone within a few short years, destroyed by slavery, disease, and endless cruelty. Not a single blood descendant remains of those peaceful beings who had breathed this balmy air, and plucked the fruit from the trees which ripened all year round, and thought their visitors gods perhaps, who could not but return their kindness.

Now, below in the streets of Port-au-Prince, riots and death, and not of our making. Merely the unchanging history of this bloody place, where violence has flourished for four hundred years as flowers flourish; though the vision of the hills rising into the mist could break the heart.

But we had done our work all right, she because she did it, and I because I did nothing to stop it—in the small towns strewn along the winding road that led to this wooded summit. Towns of tiny pastel houses, and banana trees growing wild, and the people so poor, so hungry. Even now the women sang their hymns and, by the light of candles and the burning church, buried the dead.

We were alone. Far beyond the end of the narrow road; where the forest grew again, hiding the ruins of this old house that had once overlooked the valley like a citadel. Centuries since the planters had left here; centuries since they danced and sang and drank their wine within these shattered rooms while the slaves wept.

Over the brick walls, the bougainvillea climbed, fluorescent in the light of the moon. And out of the flagstone floor a great tree had risen, hung with moon blossoms, pushing back with its gnarled limbs the last remnants of the old timbers that had once held the roof.

Ah, to be here forever, and with her. And for the rest to be forgotten. No death, no killing.

She sighed; she said: "This is the Kingdom of Heaven."

In the tiny hamlet below, the women had run barefoot after the men with clubs in hand. And the voodoo priest had screamed his ancient curses as they caught him in the graveyard. I had left the scene of the carnage; I'd climbed the mountain alone. Fleeing, angry, unable any longer to bear witness.

And she had come after, finding me in this ruin, clinging to something that I could understand. The old iron gate, the rusted bell; the brick pillars swathed in vines; things, fashioned by hands, which had endured. Oh, how she had mocked me.

The bell that had called the slaves, she said; this was the dwelling place of those who'd drenched this earth in blood; why was I hurt and driven here by the hymns of simple souls who had been exalted? Would that every such house had fallen to ruin. We had fought. Really fought, as lovers fight.

"Is that what you want?" she had said. "Not ever to taste blood again?"

"I was a simple thing, dangerous yes, but simple. I did what I did to stay alive."

"Oh, you sadden me. Such lies. Such lies. What must I do to make you see? Are you so blind, so selfish!"

I'd glimpsed it again, the pain in her face, the sudden flash of hurt that humanized her utterly. I'd reached out for her.

And for hours we had been in each other's arms, or so it seemed.

And now the peace and the stillness; I walked back from the edge of the cliff, and I held her again. I heard her say as she looked up at the great towering clouds through which the moon poured forth its eerie light: "This is the Kingdom of Heaven."

It did not matter anymore such simple things as lying down together, or sitting on a stone bench. Standing, my arms wound around her, this was pure happiness. And I'd drunk the nectar again, her nectar, even though I'd been weeping, and thinking ah, well, you are being dissolved as a pearl in wine. You're gone, you little devil—you're gone, you know—into her. You stood and watched them die; you stood and watched.

"There is no life without death," she whispered. "I am the way now, the way to the only hope of life without strife that there may ever be." I felt her lips on my mouth. I wondered, would she ever do what she had done in the shrine? Would we lock together like that, taking the heated blood from each other?

"Listen to the singing in the villages, you can hear it."

"Yes."

"And then listen hard for the sounds of the city far below. Do you know how much death is in that city tonight? How many have been massacred? Do you know how many more will die at the hands of men, if we do not change the destiny of this place? If we do not sweep it up into a new vision? Do you know how long this battle has gone on?"

Centuries ago, in my time, this had been the richest colony of the French crown. Rich in tobacco, indigo, coffee. Fortunes had been made here in one season. And now the people picked at the earth; barefoot they walked through the dirt streets of their towns; machine guns barked in the city of Port-au-Prince; the dead in colored cotton shirts lay in heaps on the cobblestones. Children gathered water in cans from the gutters. Slaves had risen; slaves had won; slaves had lost everything.

But it is their destiny; their world; they who are human.

She laughed softly. "And what are we? Are we useless? How do we justify what we are! How do we stand back and watch what we are unwilling to alter?"

"And suppose it is wrong," I said, "and the world is worse for it, and it is all horror finally—unrealizable, unexecutable, what then? And all those men in their graves, the whole earth a graveyard, a funeral pyre. And nothing is better. And it's wrong, wrong."

"Who's to tell you it is wrong?"

I didn't answer.

"Marius?" How scornfully she laughed. "Don't you realize there are no fathers now? Angry or no?"

"There are brothers. And there are sisters," I said. "And in each other we find our fathers and mothers, isn't that so?"

Again she laughed, but it was gentle.

"Brothers and sisters," she said. "Would you like to see your real brothers and sisters?"

I lifted my head from her shoulder. I kissed her cheek. "Yes. I want to see them." My heart was racing again. "Please," I said, even as I kissed her throat, and her cheekbones and her closed eyes. "Please."

"Drink again," she whispered. I felt her bosom swell against me. I pressed my teeth against her throat and the little miracle happened again, the sudden breaking of the crust, and the nectar poured into my mouth.

A great hot wave consumed me. No gravity; no specific time or place. *Akasha.*

Then I saw the redwood trees; the house with the lights burning in it, and in the high mountaintop room, the table and all of them around it, their faces reflected in the walls of dark glass, and the fire dancing. Marius, Gabrielle, Louis, Armand. They're together and they're safe! Am I dreaming this? They're listening to a red-haired woman. And I know this woman! I've seen this woman.

She was in the dream of the red-haired twins.

But I want to see this—these immortals gathered at the table. The young red-haired one, the one at the woman's side, I've seen her too. But she'd been alive then. At the rock concert, in the frenzy, I'd put my arm around her and looked into her crazed eyes. I'd kissed her and said her name; and it was as if a pit had opened under me, and I was falling down into those dreams of the twins that I could never really recall. Painted walls; temples.

It all faded suddenly. *Gabrielle. Mother.* Too late. I was reaching out; I was spinning through the darkness.

You have all of my powers now. You need only time to perfect them. You can bring death, you can move matter, you can make fire. You are ready now to go to them. But we will let them finish their reverie; their stupid schemes and discussion. We will show them a little more of our power—

No, please, Akasha, please, let's go to them.

She drew away from me; she struck me.

I reeled from the shock. Shuddering, cold, I felt the pain spread out through the bones of my face, as if her fingers were still splayed and pressed there. In anger I bit down, letting the pain swell and then recede. In anger I clenched my fists and did nothing.

She walked across the old flags with crisp steps, her hair swaying as it hung down her back. And then she stopped at the fallen gate, her shoulders rising slightly, her back curved as if she were folding into herself.

The voices rose; they reached a pitch before I could stop them. And then they lapsed back, like water receding after a great flood.

I saw the mountains again around me; I saw the ruined house. The pain in my face was gone; but I was shaking.

She turned and looked at me, tensely, her face sharpened, and her eyes slightly narrowed. "They mean so much to you, don't they? What do you think they will do, or say? You think Marius will turn me from my course? I know Marius as you could never know him. I know every pathway of his reason. He is greedy as you are greedy. What do you think I am that I am so easily swayed? I was born a Queen. I have always ruled; even from the shrine I ruled." Her eyes were glazed suddenly. I heard the voices, a dull hum rising. "I ruled if only in legend; if only in the minds of those who came to me and paid me tribute. Princes who played music for me; who brought me offerings and prayers. What do you want of me now? That for you, I renounce my throne, my destiny!"

What answer could I make?

"You can read my heart," I said. "You know what I want, that you go to them, that you give them a chance to speak on these things as you've given me the chance. They have words I don't have. They know things I don't know."

"Oh, but Lestat, I do not love them. I do not love them as I love you. So what does it matter to me what they say? I have no patience for them!"

"But you need them. You said that you did. How can you begin without them? I mean really begin, not with these backward villages, I mean in the cities where the people will fight. Your angels, that's what you called them."

She shook her head sadly. "I need no one," she said, "except . . . Except . . ." She hesitated, and then her face went blank with pure surprise.

I made some little soft sound before I could stop myself; some little expression of helpless grief. I thought I saw her eyes dim; and it seemed the voices were rising again, not in my ears but in hers; and that she stared at me, but that she didn't see me.

"But I will destroy you all if I have to," she said, vaguely, eyes searching for me, but not finding me. "Believe me when I say it. For this time I will not be vanquished; I will not lapse back. I will see my dreams realized."

I looked away from her, through the ruined gateway, over the broken edge of the cliff, and down over the valley. What would I have given to be released from this nightmare? Would I be willing to die by my own hand? My eyes were filled with tears, looking over the dark fields. It was cowardice to think of it; this was my doing! There was no escape now for me.

Stark still she stood, listening; and then she blinked slowly; her shoulders moved as if she carried a great weight inside her. "Why can you not believe in me?" she said.

"Abandon it!" I answered. "Turn away from all such visions." I went to her and took hold of her arms. Almost groggily she looked up. "This is a timeless place we stand in—and those poor villages we've conquered, they are the same as they've been for thousands of years. Let me show you my world, Akasha; let me show you the tiniest part of it! Come with me, like a spy into the cities; not to destroy, but to see!"

Her eyes were brightening again; the lassitude was breaking. She embraced me; and suddenly I wanted the blood again. It was all I could think of, even though I was resisting it; even though I was weeping at the pure weakness of my will. I wanted it. I wanted her and I couldn't fight it; yet my old fantasies came back to me, those long ago visions in which I imagined myself waking her, and taking her with me through the opera houses, and the museums and the symphony halls, through the great capitals and their storehouses of all things beautiful and imperishable that men and women had made over the centuries, artifacts that transcended all evil, all wrongs, all fallibility of the individual soul.

"But what have I to do with such paltry things, my love?" she whispered. "And you would teach me of your world? Ah, such vanity. I am beyond time as I have always been."

But she was gazing at me now with the most heartbroken expression. Sorrow, that's what I saw in her.

"I need you!" she whispered. And for the first time her eyes filled with tears.

I couldn't bear it. I felt the chills rise, as they always do, at moments of surprising pain. But she put her fingers to my lips to silence me.

"Very well, my love," she said. "We'll go to your brothers and sisters, if you wish it. We'll go to Marius. But first, let me hold you one more time, close to my heart. You see, I cannot be other than what I would be. This is what you waked with your singing; this is what I am!"

I wanted to protest, to deny it; I wanted again to begin the argument that would divide us and hurt her. But I couldn't find the words as I looked into her eyes. And suddenly I realized what had happened.

I had found the way to stop her; I had found the key; it had been there before me all the time. It was not her love for me; it was her need of me; the need of one ally in all the great realm; one kindred soul made of the same stuff that she was made of. And she had believed she could make me like herself, and now she knew she could not.

"Ah, but you are wrong," she said, her tears shimmering. "You are only young and afraid." She smiled. "You belong to me. And if it has to be, my prince, I'll destroy you."

I didn't speak. I couldn't. I knew what I had seen; I knew even as she couldn't accept it. Not in all the long centuries of stillness had she ever been alone; had she ever suffered the ultimate isolation. Oh, it was not such a simple thing as Enkil by her side, or Marius come to lay before her his offerings; it was something deeper, infinitely more important than that; she had never all alone waged a war of reason with those around her!

The tears were flowing down her cheeks. Two violent streaks of red. Her mouth was slack; her eyebrows knit in a dark frown, though her face would never be anything but radiant.

"No, Lestat," she said again. "You are wrong. But we must see this through now to the finish; if they must die—all of them—so that you cleave to me, so be it." She opened her arms.

I wanted to move away; I wanted to rail against her again, against her threats; but I didn't move as she came closer.

Here; the warm Caribbean breeze; her hands moving up my back; her fingers slipping through my hair. The nectar flowing into me again, flooding my heart. And her lips on my throat finally; the sudden stab of her teeth through my flesh. Yes! As it had been in the shrine, so long ago, yes! Her blood and my blood. And the deafening thunder of her heart, yes! And it was ecstasy and yet I couldn't yield; I couldn't do it; and she knew it.

8

THE *STORY* OF THE TWINS
CONCLUSION

E FOUND the palace the same as we remembered it, or perhaps a little more lavish, with more booty from conquered lands. More gold drapery, and even more vivid paintings; and twice as many slaves about, as if they were mere ornaments, their lean naked bodies hung with gold and jewels.

"To a royal cell we were now committed, with graceful chairs and tables, and a fine carpet, and dishes of meat and fish to eat.

"Then at sunset, we heard cheers as the King and the Queen appeared in the palace; all the court went to bow to them, singing anthems to the beauty of their pale skin and their shimmering hair; and to the bodies that had miraculously healed after the assault of the conspirators; all the palace echoed with these hymns of praise.

"But when this little spectacle was finished, we were taken into the bedchamber of the royal couple, and for the first time, by the small light of distant lamps, we beheld the transformation with our own eyes.

"We saw two pale yet magnificent beings, resembling in all particulars what they had been when they were alive; but there was an eerie luminescence surrounding them; their skin was no longer skin. And their minds were no longer entirely their minds. Yet gorgeous they were. As you can well imagine, all of you. Oh, yes, gorgeous, as though the moon had come down from heaven and fashioned them with its light. Amid their dazzling gold furniture they stood, draped in finery, and staring at us with eyes that gleamed like obsidian. And then, with a wholly different voice, a voice softly shaded by music, it seemed, the King spoke:

" 'Khayman's told you what has befallen us,' he said. 'We stand before you the beneficiaries of a great miracle; for we have triumphed over certain death. We are now quite beyond the limitations and needs of human beings; and we see and understand things which were withheld from us before.'

"But the Queen's facade gave way immediately. In a hissing whisper she said, 'You must explain this to us! *What has your spirit done?*'

"We were in worse danger than ever from these monsters; and I tried to convey this warning to Mekare, but at once the Queen laughed. 'Do you think I don't know what you are thinking?' she said.

"But the King begged her to be silent. 'Let the witches use their powers,' he said. 'You know that we have always revered you.'

" 'Yes.' The Queen sneered. 'And you sent this curse upon us.'

"At once I averred that we had not done it, that we had kept faith when we left the kingdom, that we had gone back to our home. And as Mekare studied the pair of them in silence, I begged them to understand that if the spirit had done this, he had done it of his own whim.

" 'Whim!' the Queen said. 'What do you mean by such a word as whim? What has happened to us? What are we!' she asked again. Then she drew back her lips for us to see her teeth. We beheld the fangs in her mouth, tiny, yet sharp as knives. And the King demonstrated to us this change as well.

" 'The better to draw the blood,' he whispered. 'Do you know what this thirst is to us! We cannot satisfy it! Three, four men a night die to feed us, yet we go to our bed tortured by thirst.'

"The Queen tore at her hair as if she would give in to screaming. But the King laid his hand on her arm. 'Advise us, Mekare and Maharet,' he said. 'For we would understand this transformation and how it might be used for good.'

" 'Yes,' the Queen said, struggling to recover. 'For surely such a thing cannot happen without reason . . . .' Then losing her conviction, she fell quiet. Indeed it seemed her small pragmatic view of things, ever puny and seeking for justifications, had collapsed utterly, while the King clung to his illusions as men often do, until very late in life.

"Now, as they fell silent, Mekare went forward and laid her hands upon the King. She laid her hands upon his shoulders; and closed her eyes. Then she laid her hands upon the Queen in the same manner, though the Queen glared at her with venom in her eyes.

" 'Explain to us,' Mekare said, looking at the Queen, 'what happened at the very moment. What do you remember? What did you see?'

"The Queen was silent, her face drawn and suspicious. Her beauty had been, in truth, enhanced by this transformation, yet there was something repellent in her, as if she were not the flower now but the replica of the flower made of pure white wax. And as she grew reflective she appeared somber and vicious, and instinctively I drew close to Mekare to protect her from what might take place.

"But then the Queen spoke:

" 'They came to kill us, the traitors! They would blame it on the spirits; that was the plan. And all to eat the flesh again, the flesh of their mothers and fathers, and the flesh for which they loved to hunt. They came into the house and they stabbed me with their daggers, I their sovereign Queen.' She paused as if seeing these things again before her eyes. 'I fell as they slashed at me, as they drove their daggers into my breast. One cannot live with such wounds as I received; and so as I fell to the floor, I knew that I was dead! Do you hear what I am saying? I knew that nothing could save me. My blood was pouring out onto the floor.

" 'But even as I saw it pooling before me, I realized I was not in my wounded body, that I had already left it, that death had taken me and was drawing me upwards sharply as if through a great tunnel to where I would suffer no more!

" 'I wasn't frightened; I felt nothing; I looked down and saw myself lying pale and covered with blood in that little house. Yet I did not care. I was free of it. But suddenly something took hold of me, took hold of my invisible being! The tunnel was gone; I was caught in a great mesh like a fisherman's net. With all my strength I pushed against it, and it gave with my strength but it did not break and it gripped me and held me fast and I could not rise through it.

" 'When I tried to scream I was in my body again! I felt the agony of my wounds as if the knives were cutting me afresh. But this net, this great net, it still had a hold of me, and instead of being the endless thing it had been before, it was now contracted into a tighter weave like the weave of a great silk veil.

" 'And all about me this thing—visible yet invisible—whirled as if it were wind, lifting me, casting me down, turning me about. The blood gushed from my wounds. And it ran into the weave of this veil, just as it might into the mesh of any fabric.

" 'And that which had been transparent was now drenched in blood. And a monstrous thing I saw, shapeless, and enormous, with my blood broadcast throughout it. And yet this thing had another property to it, a center, it seemed, a tiny burning center which was in me, and ran riot in my body like a frightened animal. Through my limbs it ran, thumping and beating. A heart with legs scampering. In my belly it circled as I clawed at myself. I would have cut myself open to get this thing out of me!

" 'And it seemed the great invisible part of this thing—the blood mist that surrounded me and enveloped me—was controlled by this tiny center, twisting this way and that as it scurried within me, racing into my hands one moment and into my feet the next. Up my spine it ran.

" 'I would die, surely I would die, I thought. Then came a moment of blindness! Silence. It had killed me, I was certain. I should rise again, should I not? Yet suddenly I opened my eyes; I sat up off the floor as if no attack had befallen me; and I saw so clearly! Khayman, the glaring torch in his hand!—the trees of the garden—why, it was as if I had never truly seen such simple things for what they were! The pain was gone completely, from inside and from my wounds as well. Only the light hurt my eyes; I could not endure its brilliance. Yet I had been saved from death; my body had been glorified and made perfect. Except that—' And there she stopped.

"She stared before her, indifferent for a moment. Then she said, 'Khayman has told you all the rest.' She looked to the King who stood beside her, watching her; trying to fathom the things she said, just as we tried to fathom them.

" 'Your spirit,' she said. 'It tried to destroy us. But something else had happened; some great power has intervened to triumph over its diabolical evil.' Then again her conviction deserted her. The lies stopped on her tongue. Her face was suddenly cold with menace. And sweetly she said: 'Tell us, witches, wise witches. You who know all the secrets. What is the name for what we are!'

"Mekare sighed. She looked at me. I knew she didn't want to speak now on this thing. And the old warning of the spirits came back. The Egyptian King and Queen would ask us questions and they would not like our answers. We would be destroyed. . . .

"Then the Queen turned her back. She sat down and bowed her head. And it was then, and only then, that her true sadness came to the fore. The King smiled at us, wearily. 'We are in pain, witches,' he said. 'We could bear the burden of this transformation if only we understood it better. You, who have communed with all things invisible; tell us what you know of such magic; help us, if you will, for you know that we never meant to harm you, only to spread the truth and the law.'

"We did not dwell on the stupidity of this statement—the virtue of spreading the truth through wholesale slaughter and so forth and so on. But Mekare demanded that the King now tell what he could recall.

"He spoke of things which you—all of you seated here—surely know. Of how he was dying; and how he tasted the blood from his wife which had covered his face; and of how his body quickened, and wanted this blood, and then how he took it from his wife and she gave it; and then he became as she was. But for him there was no mysterious cloud of blood. There was no thing running rampant within him. 'The thirst, it's unbearable,' he said to us. 'Unbearable.' And he too bowed his head.

"We stood in silence for a moment looking at each other, Mekare and I, and as always, Mekare spoke first:

" 'We know no name for what you are,' she said. 'We know no stories of such a thing ever happening in this world before. But it's plain enough what took place.' She fixed her eyes upon the Queen. 'As you perceived your own death, your soul sought to make its swift escape from suffering as souls so often do. But as it rose, the spirit Amel seized it, this thing being invisible as your soul was invisible; and in the normal course of things you might have easily overcome this earthbound entity and gone on to realms we do not know.

" 'But this spirit had long before wrought a change within himself; a change that was utterly new. This spirit had tasted the blood of humans whom he had pierced or tormented, as you yourself have seen him do. And your body, lying there, and full of blood despite its many wounds, had life still.

" 'And so the spirit, thirsting, plunged down into your body, his invisible form still wedded to your soul.

" 'Still you might have triumphed, fighting off this evil thing as possessed persons often do. But now the tiny core of this spirit—the thing of matter which is the roaring center of all spirits, from which their endless energy comes—was suddenly filled with blood as never in the past.

" 'And so the fusion of blood and timeless tissue was a million times magnified and accelerated; and blood flowed through all his body, both material and nonmaterial, and this was the blood cloud that you saw.

" 'But it is the pain you felt which is most significant, this pain which traveled through your limbs. For surely as inevitable death came to your body, the spirit's tiny core merged with the flesh of your body as its energy had already merged with your soul. It found some special place or organ in which matter merged with matter as spirit had already merged with spirit; and a new thing was formed.'

" 'Its heart and my heart,' the Queen whispered. 'They became one.' And closing her eyes, she lifted her hand and laid it on her breast.

"We said nothing, for this seemed a simplification, and we did not believe the heart was the center of intellect or emotion. For us, it had been the brain which controlled these things. And in that moment, both Mekare and I saw a terrible memory—our mother's heart and brain thrown down and trampled in ashes and dust.

"But we fought this memory. It was abhorrent that this pain should be glimpsed by those who had been its cause.

"The King pressed us with a question. 'Very well,' he said, 'you've explained what has happened to Akasha. This spirit is in her, core wedded perhaps to core. But what is in me? I felt no such pain, no such scurrying demon. I felt . . . I felt only the thirst when her bloodied hands touched my lips.' He looked to his wife.

"The shame, the horror, they felt over the thirst was clear.

" 'But the same spirit is in you, too,' Mekare answered. 'There is but one Amel. Its core resides in the Queen, but it is in you also.'

" 'How is such a thing possible?' asked the King.

" 'This being has a great invisible part,' Mekare said. 'Were you to have seen it in its entirety, before this catastrophe took place, you would have seen something almost without end.'

" 'Yes,' the Queen confessed. 'It was as if the net covered the whole sky.'

"Mekare explained: 'It is only by concentrating such immense size that these spirits achieve any physical strength. Left on their own, they are as clouds over the horizon; greater even; they have now and then boasted to us that they have no true boundaries, though this is not likely the truth.'

"The King stared at his wife.

" 'But how can it be released!' demanded Akasha.

" 'Yes. How can it be made to depart!' the King asked.

"Neither of us wanted to answer. We wondered that the answer was not obvious to them both. 'Destroy your body,' Mekare said to the Queen finally. 'And it will be destroyed as well.'

"The King looked at Mekare with disbelief. 'Destroy her body!' Helplessly he looked at his wife.

"But Akasha merely smiled bitterly. The words came as no surprise to her. For a long moment, she said nothing. She merely looked at us with plain hatred; then she looked at the King. When she looked to us, she put the question. 'We are dead things, aren't we? We cannot live if it departs. We do not eat; we do not drink, save for the blood it wants; our bodies throw off no waste any longer; we have not changed in one single particular since that awful night; we are not alive anymore.'

"Mekare didn't answer. I knew that she was studying them; struggling to see their forms not as a human would see them but as a witch would see them, to let the quiet and the stillness collect around them, so that she might observe the tiny imperceptible aspects of this which eluded regular gaze. Into a trance she fell as she looked at them and listened. And when she spoke her voice was flat, dull:

" 'It is working on your body; it is working and working as fire works on the wood it consumes; as worms work on the carcass of an animal. It is working and working and its work is inevitable; it is the continuance of the fusion which has taken place; that is why the sun hurts it, for it is using all of its energy to do what it must do; and it cannot endure the sun's heat coming down upon it.'

" 'Or the bright light of a torch even,' the King sighed.

" 'At times not even a candle flame,' said the Queen.

" 'Yes,' Mekare said, shaking off the trance finally. 'And you are dead,' she said in a whisper. 'Yet you are alive! If the wounds healed as you say they did; if you brought the King back as you say you did, why, you may have vanquished death. That is, if you do not go into the burning rays of the sun.'

" 'No, this cannot continue!' the King said. 'The thirst, you don't know how terrible is the thirst.'

"But the Queen only smiled bitterly again. 'These are not living bodies now. These are hosts for this demon.' Her lip trembled as she looked at us. 'Either that or we are truly gods!'

" 'Answer us, witches,' said the King. 'Could it be that we are divine beings now, blessed with gifts that only gods share?' He smiled as he said it; he so wanted to believe it. 'Could it not be that when your demon sought to destroy us, our gods intervened?'

"An evil light shone in the Queen's eye. How she loved this idea, but she didn't believe it . . . not really.

"Mekare looked at me. She wanted me to go forward and to touch them as she had done. She wanted me to look at them as she had done. There was something further that she wanted to say, yet she was not sure of it. And in truth, I had slightly stronger powers of the instinctive nature, though less of a gift for words than she.

"I went forward; I touched their white skin, though it repelled me as they repelled me for all that they had done to our people and us. I touched them and then withdrew and gazed at them; and I saw the work of which Mekare spoke, I could even hear it, the tireless churning of the spirit within. I stilled my mind; I cleared it utterly of all preconception or fear and then as the calmness of the trance deepened in me, I allowed myself to speak.

" 'It wants more humans,' I said. I looked at Mekare. This was what she had suspected.

" 'We offer to it all we can!' the Queen gasped. And the blush of shame came again, extraordinary in its brightness to her pale cheeks. And the King's face colored also. And I understood then, as did Mekare, that when they drank the blood they felt ecstasy. Never had they known such pleasure, not in their beds, not at the banquet table, not when drunk with beer or wine. That was the source of the shame. It hadn't been the killing; it had been the monstrous feeding. It had been the pleasure. Ah, these two were such a pair.

"But they had misunderstood me. 'No,' I explained. 'It wants more like you. It wants to go in and make blood drinkers of others as it did with the King; it is too immense to be contained within two small bodies. The thirst will become bearable only when you make others, for they will share the burden of it with you.'

" 'No!' the Queen screamed. 'That is unthinkable.'

" 'Surely it cannot be so simple!' the King declared. 'Why, we were both made at one and the same terrible instant, when our gods warred with this demon. Conceivably, when our gods warred and won.'

" 'I think not,' I said.

" 'You mean to say,' the Queen asked, 'that if we nourish others with this blood that they too will be so infected?' But she was recalling now every detail of the catastrophe. Her husband dying, the heartbeat gone from him, and then the blood trickling into his mouth.

" 'Why, I haven't enough blood in my body to do such a thing!' she declared. 'I am only what I am!' Then she thought of the thirst and all the bodies that had served it.

"And we realized the obvious point; that she had sucked the blood out of her husband before he had taken it back from her, and that is how the thing had been accomplished; that and the fact that the King was on the edge of death, and most receptive, his own spirit shaking loose and ready to be locked down by the invisible tentacles of Amel.

"Of course they read our thoughts, both of them.

" 'I don't believe what you say,' said the King. 'The gods would not allow it. We are the King and Queen of Kemet. Burden or blessing, this magic has been meant for us.'

"A moment of silence passed. Then he spoke again, most sincerely. 'Don't you see, witches? This was destiny. We were meant to invade your lands, to bring you and this demon here, so that this might befall us. We suffer, true, but we are gods now; this is a holy fire; and we must give thanks for what has happened to us.'

"I tried to stop Mekare from speaking. I clasped her hand tightly. But they already knew what she meant to say. Only her conviction jarred them.

" 'It could very likely pass into anyone,' she said, 'were the conditions duplicated, were the man or woman weakened and dying, so that the spirit could get its grip.'

"In silence they stared at us. The King shook his head. The Queen looked away in disgust. But then the King whispered, 'If this is so, then others may try to take this from us!'

" 'Oh, yes,' Mekare whispered. 'If it would make them immortal? Most surely, they would. For who would not want to live forever?'

"At this the King's face was transformed. He paced back and forth in the chamber. He looked at his wife, who stared forward as one about to go mad, and he said to her most carefully, 'Then we know what we must do. We cannot breed a race of such monsters! We know!'

"But the Queen threw her hands over her ears and began to scream. She began to sob, and finally to roar in her agony, her fingers curling into claws as she looked up at the ceiling above her.

"Mekare and I withdrew to the edges of the room, and held tight to each other. And then Mekare began to tremble, and to cry also, and I felt tears rise in my eyes.

" 'You did this to us!' the Queen roared, and never had we heard a human voice attain such volume. And as she went mad now, shattering everything within the chamber, we saw the strength of Amel in her, for she did things no human could do. The mirrors she hurled at the ceiling; the gilded furniture went to splinters under her fists. 'Damn you into the lower world among demons and beasts forever!' she cursed us, 'for what you have done to us. Abominations. Witches. You and your demon! You say you did not send this thing to us. But in your hearts you did. You sent this demon! And he read it from your hearts, just as I read it now, that you wished us evil!'

"But then the King caught her in his arms and hushed her and kissed her and caught her sobs against his chest.

"Finally she broke away from him. She stared at us, her eyes brimming with blood. 'You lie!' she said. 'You lie as your demons lied before. Do you think such a thing could happen if it was not meant to happen!' She turned to the King. 'Oh, don't you see, we've been fools to listen to these mere mortals, who have not such powers as we have! Ah, but we are young deities and must struggle to learn the designs of heaven. And surely our destiny is plain; we see it in the gifts we possess.'

"We didn't respond to what she had said. It seemed to me at least for a few precious moments that it was a mercy if she could believe such nonsense. For all I could believe was that Amel, the evil one, Amel, the stupid, the dull-witted, the imbecile spirit, had stumbled into this disastrous fusion and that perhaps the whole world would pay the price. My mother's warning came back to me. All our suffering came back to me. And then such thoughts—wishes for the destruction of the King and Queen—seized me that I had to cover my head with my hands and shake myself and try to clear my mind, lest I face their wrath.

"But the Queen was paying no mind to us whatsoever, except to scream to her guards that they must at once take us prisoner, and that tomorrow night she would pass judgment upon us before the whole court.

"And quite suddenly we were seized; and as she gave her orders with gritted teeth and dark looks, the soldiers dragged us away roughly and threw us like common prisoners into a lightless cell.

"Mekare took hold of me and whispered that until the sun rose we must think nothing that could bring us harm; we must sing the old songs we knew and pace the floor so that as not even to dream dreams that would offend the King and Queen, for she was mortally afraid.

"Now I had never truly seen Mekare so afraid. Mekare was always the one to rave in anger; it was I who hung back imagining the most terrible things.

"But when dawn came, when she was sure the demon King and Queen had gone to their secret retreat, she burst into tears.

" 'I did it, Maharet,' she said to me. 'I did it. I sent him against them. I tried not to do it; but Amel, he read it in my heart. It was as the Queen said, exactly.'

"There was no end to her recriminations. It was she who had spoken to Amel; she who had strengthened him and puffed him up and kept his interest; and then she had wished his wrath upon the Egyptians and he had known.

"I tried to comfort her. I told her none of us could control what was in our hearts; that Amel had saved our lives once; that no one could fathom these awful choices, these forks in the road; and we must now banish all guilts and look only to the future. How could we get free of this place? How could we make these monsters release us? Our good spirits would not frighten them now; not a chance of it; we must think; we must plan; we must do something.

"Finally, the thing for which I secretly hoped happened: Khayman appeared. But he was even more thin and drawn than before.

" 'I think you are doomed, my red-haired ones,' he said to us. 'The King and Queen were in a quandary over the things which you said to them; before morning they went to the temple of Osiris to pray. Could you not give them any hope of reclamation? Any hope this horror would come to an end?'

" 'Khayman, there is one hope,' Mekare whispered. 'Let the spirits be my witness; I don't say that you should do it. I only answer your question. If you would put an end to this, put an end to the King and Queen. Find their hiding place and let the sun come down upon them, the sun which their new bodies cannot bear.'

"But he turned away, terrified by the prospect of such treason. Only to look back and sigh and say, 'Ah, my dear witches. Such things I've seen. And yet I dare not do such a thing.'

"As the hours passed we went through agony, for surely we would be put to death. But there were no regrets any longer in us for the things we'd said, or the things we'd done. And as we lay in the dark in one another's arms, we sang the old songs again from our childhood; we sang our mother's songs; I thought of my little baby and I tried to go to her, to rise in spirit from this place and be close to her, but without the trance potion, I could not do it. I had never learned such skill.

"Finally dusk fell. And soon we heard the multitude singing hymns as the King and Queen approached. The soldiers came for us. Into the great open court of the palace we were brought as we had been before. Here it was that Khayman had laid his hands upon us and we had been dishonored, and before those very same spectators we were brought, with our hands bound again.

"Only it was night and the lamps burnt low in the arcades of the court; and an evil light played upon the gilded lotus blossoms of the pillars, and upon the painted silhouettes which covered the walls. At last the King and Queen stepped upon the dais. And all those assembled fell to their knees. The soldiers forced us into the same subservience. And then the Queen stepped forward and began to speak.

"In a quavering voice, she told her subjects that we were monstrous witches, and that we had loosed upon this kingdom the demon which had only lately plagued Khayman and tried its evil devilment upon the King and Queen themselves. But lo, the great god Osiris, oldest of all the gods, stronger even than the god Ra, had cast down this diabolical force and raised up into celestial glory the King and the Queen.

"But the great god could not look kindly upon the witches who had so troubled his beloved people. And he demanded now that no mercy be shown.

" 'Mekare, for your evil lies and your discourse with demons,' the Queen said, 'your tongue shall be torn from your mouth. And Maharet, for the evil which you have envisioned and sought to make us believe in, your eyes shall be plucked out! And all night, you shall be bound together, so that you may hear each other's weeping, the one unable to speak, the other unable to see. And then at high noon tomorrow in the public place before the palace you shall be burnt alive for all the people to see.

" 'For behold, no such evil shall ever prevail against the gods of Egypt and their chosen King and Queen. For the gods have looked upon us with benevolence and special favor, and we are as the King and Queen of Heaven, and our destiny is for the common good!'

"I was speechless as I heard the condemnation; my fear, my sorrow lay beyond my reach. But Mekare cried out at once in defiance. She startled the soldiers as she pulled away from them and stepped forward. Her eyes were on the stars as she spoke. And above the shocked whispers of the court she declared:

" 'Let the spirits witness; for theirs is the knowledge of the future—both what it would be, *and what I will!* You are the Queen of the Damned, that's what you are! Your only destiny is evil, as well you know! But I shall stop you, if I must come back from the dead to do it. At the hour of your greatest menace it is I who will defeat you! It is I who will bring you down. Look well upon my face, for you will see me again!'

"And no sooner had she spoken this oath, this prophecy, than the spirits, gathering, began their whirlwind and the doors of the palace were flung open and the sands of the desert salted the air.

"Screams rose from the panic-stricken courtiers.

"But the Queen cried out to her soldiers: 'Cut out her tongue as I have commanded you!' and though the courtiers were clinging to the walls in terror, the soldiers came forward and caught hold of Mekare and cut out her tongue.

"In cold horror I watched it happen; I heard her gasp as it was done. And then with astonishing fury, she thrust them aside with her bound hands and going down on her knees snatched up the bloody tongue and swallowed it before they would tramp upon it or throw it aside.

"Then the soldiers laid hold of me.

"The last things I beheld were Akasha, her finger pointed, her eyes gleaming. And then the stricken face of Khayman with tears streaming down his cheeks. The soldiers clamped their hands on my head and pushed back my eyelids and tore all vision from me, as I wept without a sound.

"Then suddenly, I felt a warm hand lay hold of me; and I felt something against my lips. Khayman had my eyes; Khayman was pressing them to my lips. And at once I swallowed them lest they be desecrated or lost.

"The wind grew fiercer; sand swirled about us, and I heard the courtiers running now in all directions, some coughing, others gasping, and many crying as they fled, while the Queen implored her subjects to be calm. I turned, groping for Mekare, and felt her head come down on my shoulder, her hair against my cheek.

" 'Burn them now!' declared the King.

" 'No, it is too soon,' said the Queen. 'Let them suffer.'

"And we were taken away, and bound together, and left alone finally on the floor of the little cell.

"For hours the spirits raged about the palace; but the King and Queen comforted their people, and told them not to be afraid. At noon tomorrow all evil would be expurgated from the kingdom; and until then let the spirits do what they would.

"Finally, it was still and quiet as we lay together. It seemed nothing walked in the palace save the King and the Queen. Even our guards slept.

"And these are the last hours of my life, I thought. And will her suffering be more than mine in the morning, for she shall see me burn, whereas I cannot see her, and she cannot even cry out. I held Mekare to me. She laid her head against my heartbeat. And so the minutes passed.

"Finally, it must have been three hours before morning, I heard noises outside the cell. Something violent; the guard giving a sharp cry and then falling. The man had been slain. Mekare stirred beside me. I heard the lock pulled, and the pivots creak. Then it seemed I heard a noise from Mekare, something like unto a moan.

"Someone had come into the cell, and I knew by my old instinctive power that it was Khayman. As he cut the ropes which bound us, I reached out and clasped his hand. But instantly I thought, this is not Khayman! And then I understood. 'They have done it to you! They have worked it on you.'

" 'Yes,' he whispered, and his voice was full of wrath and bitterness, and a new sound had crept into it, an inhuman sound. 'They have done it! To put it to the test, they have done it! To see if you spoke the truth! They have put this evil into *me.*' It seemed he was sobbing; a rough dry sound, coming from his chest. And I could feel the immense strength of his fingers, for though he didn't want to hurt my hand, he was.

" 'Oh, Khayman,' I said, weeping. 'Such treachery from those you've served so well.'

" 'Listen to me, witches,' he said, his voice guttural and full of rage. 'Do you want to die tomorrow in fire and smoke before an ignorant populace; or would you fight this evil thing? Would you be its equal and its enemy upon this earth? For what stays the power of mighty men save that of others of the same strength? What stops the swordsman but a warrior of the same mettle? Witches, if they could do this to me, can I not do it to you?'

"I shrank back, away from him, but he wouldn't let me go. I didn't know if it was possible. I knew only that I didn't want it.

" 'Maharet,' he said. 'They shall make a race of fawning acolytes unless they are beaten, and who can beat them save ones as powerful as themselves!'

" 'No, I would die first,' I said, yet even as the words left me I thought of the waiting flames. But no, it was unforgivable. Tomorrow I should go to my mother; I should leave here forever, and nothing could make me remain.

" 'And you, Mekare?' I heard him say. 'Will you reach now for the fulfillment of your own curse? Or die and leave it to the spirits who have failed you from the start?'

"The wind came up again, howling about the palace; I heard the outside doors rattling; I heard the sand flung against the walls. Servants ran through distant passages; sleepers rose from their beds. I could hear the faint, hollow, and unearthly wails of the spirits I most loved.

" 'Be still,' I told them, 'I will not do it. I will not let this evil in.'

"But as I knelt there, leaning my head against the wall, and reasoning that I must die, and must somehow find the courage for it, I realized that within the small confines of this cell, the unspeakable magic was being worked again. As the spirits railed against it, Mekare had made her choice. I reached out and felt these two forms, man and woman, melded like lovers; and as I struggled to part them, Khayman struck me, knocking me unconscious on the floor.

"Surely only a few minutes passed. Somewhere in the blackness, the spirits wept. The spirits knew the final outcome before I did. The winds died away; a hush fell in the blackness; the palace was still.

"My sister's cold hands touched me. I heard a strange sound like laughter; can those who have no tongue laugh? I made no decision really; I knew only that all our lives we had been the same; twins and mirror images of each other; two bodies it seemed and one soul. And I was sitting now in the hot close darkness of this little place, and I was in my sister's arms, and for the first time she was changed and we were not the same being; and yet we were. And then I felt her mouth against my throat; I felt her hurting me; and Khayman took his knife and did the work for her; and the swoon began.

"Oh, those divine seconds; those moments when I saw again within my brain the lovely light of the silver sky; and my sister there before me smiling, her arms uplifted as the rain came down. We were dancing in the rain together, and all our people were there with us, and our bare feet sank into the wet grass; and when the thunder broke and the lightning tore the sky, it was as if our souls had released all their pain. Drenched by the rain we went deep into the cave together; we lighted one small lamp and looked at the old paintings on the walls—the paintings done by all the witches before us; huddling together, with the sound of the distant rain we lost ourselves in these paintings of witches dancing; of the moon coming for the first time into the night sky.

"Khayman fed me the magic; then my sister; then Khayman again. You know what befell me, don't you? But do you know what the Dark Gift is for those who are blind? Tiny sparks flared in the gaseous gloom; then it seemed a glowing light began to define the shapes of things around me in weak pulses; like the afterimages of bright things when one closes one's eyes.

"Yes, I could move through this darkness. I reached out to verify what I beheld. The doorway, the wall; then the corridor before me; a faint map flashed for a second of the path ahead.

"Yet never had the night seemed so silent; nothing inhuman breathed in the darkness. The spirits were utterly gone.

"And never, never again did I ever hear or see the spirits. Never ever again were they to answer my questions or my call. The ghosts of the dead yes, but the spirits, gone forever.

"But I did not realize this abandonment in those first few moments, or hours, or even in the first few nights.

"So many other things astonished me; so many other things filled me with agony or joy.

"Long before the sunrise, we were hidden, as the King and Queen were hidden, deep within a tomb. It was to the grave of Khayman's own father that he took us, the grave to which the poor desecrated corpse had been restored. I had by then drunk my first draught of mortal blood. I had known the ecstasy which made the King and Queen blush for shame. But I had not dared to steal the eyes of my victim; I had not even thought such a thing might work.

"It was five nights later that I made such a discovery; and saw as a blood drinker truly sees for the first time.

"By then we had fled the royal city, moving north all night. And in place after place, Khayman had revealed the magic to various persons declaring that they must rise up against the King and Queen, for the King and Queen would have them believe they alone had the power, which was only the worst of their many lies.

"Oh, the rage Khayman felt in those early nights. To any who wanted the power he gave it, even when he was so weakened that he could scarce walk at our side. That the King and the Queen should have worthy enemies, that was his vow. How many blood drinkers were created in those thoughtless weeks, blood drinkers who would increase and multiply and create the battles of which Khayman dreamed?

"But we were doomed in this first stage of the venture—doomed in the first rebellion, doomed in our escape. We were soon to be separated forever—Khayman, Mekare, and I.

"Because the King and Queen, horrified at Khayman's defection, and suspecting that he had given us the magic, sent their soldiers after us, men who could search by day as well as night. And as we hunted ravenously to feed our newborn craving, our trail was ever easy to follow along the small villages of the riverbank or even to the encampments of the hills.

"And finally not a fortnight after we had fled the royal palace, we were caught by the mobs outside the gates of Saqqâra, less than two nights' walk from the sea.

"If only we had reached the sea. If only we had remained together. The world had been born over again to us in darkness; desperately we loved one another; desperately we had exchanged our secrets by the light of the moon.

"But a trap lay waiting for us at Saqqâra. And though Khayman did manage to fight his way to freedom, he saw that he could not possibly save us, and went deep into the hills to wait his moment, but it never came.

"Mekare and I were surrounded as you remember, as you have seen in your dreams. My eyes were torn from me again; and we feared the fire now, for surely that could destroy us; and we prayed to all things invisible for final release.

"But the King and the Queen feared to destroy our bodies. They had believed Mekare's account of the one great spirit, Amel, who infected all of us, and they feared that whatever pain we might feel would then be felt by them. Of course this was not so; but who could know it then?

"And so into the stone coffins we were put, as I've told you. One to be taken to the east and one to the west. The rafts had already been made to set us adrift in the great oceans. I had seen them even in my blindness; we were being carried away upon them; and I knew from the minds of my captors what they meant to do. I knew also that Khayman could not follow, for the march would go on by day as it had by night, and surely this was true.

"When I awoke, I was drifting on the breast of the sea. For ten nights the raft carried me as I've told you. Starvation and terror I suffered, lest the coffin sink to the bottom of the waters; lest I be buried alive forever, a thing that cannot die. But this did not happen. And when I came ashore at last on the eastern coast of lower Africa, I began my search for Mekare, crossing the continent to the west.

"For centuries I searched from one tip of the continent to the other. I went north in Europe. I traveled up and down along the rocky beaches, and even into the northern islands, until I reached the farthest wastes of ice and snow. Over and over again, however, I journeyed back to my own village, and that part of the story I will tell you in a moment, for it is very important to me that you know it, as you will see.

"But during those early centuries I turned my back upon Egypt; I turned my back upon the King and Queen.

"Only much later, did I learn that the King and Queen made a great religion of their transformation; that they took upon themselves the identity of Osiris and Isis, and darkened those old myths to suit themselves.

" 'God of the underworld' Osiris became—that is, the King who could appear only in darkness. And the Queen became Isis, the Mother, who gathers up her husband's battered and dismembered body and heals it and brings it back to life.

"You've read in Lestat's pages—in the tale Marius told to Lestat as it was told to him—of how the blood gods created by the Mother and Father took the blood sacrifice of evildoers in shrines hidden within the hills of Egypt; and how this religion endured until the time of Christ.

"And you have learned something also of how Khayman's rebellion succeeded, how the equal enemies of the King and Queen whom he had created eventually rose up against the Mother and Father; and how great wars were fought among the blood drinkers of the world. Akasha herself revealed these things to Marius, and Marius revealed them to Lestat.

"In those early centuries, the Legend of the Twins was born; for the Egyptian soldiers who had witnessed the events of our lives from the massacre of our people to our final capture were to tell the tales. The Legend of the Twins was even written by the scribes of Egypt in later times. It was believed that one day Mekare would reappear to strike down the Mother, and all the blood drinkers of the world would die as the Mother died.

"But all this happened without my knowledge, my vigilance, or my collusion, for I was long gone from such things.

"Only three thousand years later did I come to Egypt, an anonymous being, swathed in black robes, to see for myself what had become of the Mother and Father—listless, staring statues, shut up in stone in their underground temple, with only their heads and throats exposed. And to the priestly blood drinkers who guarded them, the young ones came, seeking to drink from the primal fount.

"Did I wish to drink, the young blood drinker priest asked me. Then I must go to the Elders and declare my purity and my devotion to the old worship, declare that I was not a rogue bent upon selfish ends. I could have laughed.

"But oh, the horror to see those staring things! To stand before them and whisper the names Akasha and Enkil, and see not a flicker within the eye or the tiniest twitch of the white skin.

"And so they had been for as long as anyone could remember, and so the priests told me; no one even knew anymore if the myths of the beginning were true. We—the very first children—had come to be called merely the First Brood who had spawned the rebels; but the Legend of the Twins was forgotten; and no one knew the names Khayman or Mekare or Maharet.

"Only one time later was I to see them, the Mother and the Father. Another thousand years had passed. The great burning had just happened when the Elder in Alexandria—as Lestat has told you—sought to destroy the Mother and the Father by placing them in the sun. They'd been merely bronzed by the day's heat as Lestat told it, so strong had they become; for though we all sleep helplessly by day, the light itself becomes less lethal with the passage of time.

"But all over the world blood drinkers had gone up in flames during those daylight hours in Egypt; while the very old ones had suffered and darkened but nothing more. My beloved Eric was then one thousand years; we lived together in India; and he was during those interminable hours severely burned. It took great draughts of my blood to restore him. I myself was bronzed only, and though I lived with great pain for many nights, there was a curious side effect to it: it was then easier for me to pass among human beings with this dark skin.

"Many centuries later, weary of my pale appearance, I was to burn myself in the sun deliberately. I shall probably do it again.

"But it was all a mystery to me the first time it happened. I wanted to know why I had seen fire and heard the cries of so many perishing in my dreams, and why others whom I had made—beloved fledglings—had died this unspeakable death.

"And so I journeyed from India to Egypt, which to me has always been a hateful place. It was then I heard tell of Marius, a young Roman blood drinker, miraculously unburnt, who had come and stolen the Mother and Father and taken them out of Alexandria where no one could ever burn them—or us—again.

"It was not difficult to find Marius. As I've told you, in the early years we could never hear each other. But as time passed we could hear the younger ones just as if they were human beings. In Antioch, I discovered Marius's house, a virtual palace where he lived a life of Roman splendor though he hunted the dark streets for human victims in the last hours before dawn.

"He had already made an immortal of Pandora, whom he loved above all other things on earth. And the Mother and Father he had placed in an exquisite shrine, made by his own hands of Carrara marble and mosaic flooring, in which he burned incense as if it were a temple, as if they were truly gods.

"I waited for my moment. He and Pandora went to hunt. And then I entered the house, making the locks give way from the inside.

"I saw the Mother and Father, darkened as I had been darkened, yet beautiful and lifeless as they'd been a thousand years before. On a throne he'd placed them, and so they would sit for two thousand years, as you all know. I went to them; I touched them. I struck them. They did not move. Then with a long dagger I made my test. I pierced the flesh of the Mother, which had become an elastic coating as my flesh had become. I pierced the immortal body which had become both indestructible and deceptively fragile, and my blade went right through her heart. From right to left I slashed with it, then stopped.

"Her blood poured viscous and thick for a moment; for a moment the heart ceased to beat; then the rupture began to heal; the spilt blood hardened like amber as I watched.

"But most significant, I had felt that moment when the heart failed to pump the blood; I had felt the dizziness, the vague disconnection; the very whisper of death. No doubt, all through the world blood drinkers had felt it, perhaps the young ones strongly, a shock which knocked them off their feet. The core of Amel was still within her; the terrible burning and the dagger, these things proved that the life of the blood drinkers resided within her body as it always would.

"I would have destroyed her then, if it had not been so. I would have cut her limb from limb; for no span of time could ever cool my hatred for her; my hatred for what she had done to my people; for separating Mekare from me. Mekare my other half; Mekare my own self.

"How magnificent it would have been if the centuries had schooled me in forgiveness; if my soul had opened to understand all the wrongs done me and my people.

"But I tell you, it is the soul of humankind which moves towards perfection over the centuries, the human race which learns with each passing year how better to love and forgive. I am anchored to the past by chains I cannot break.

"Before I left, I wiped away all trace of what I had done. For an hour perhaps I stared at the two statues, the two evil beings who had so long ago destroyed my kindred and brought such evil upon me and my sister; and who had known such evil in return.

" 'But you did not win, finally,' I said to Akasha. 'You and your soldiers and their swords. For my child, Miriam, survived to carry the blood of my family and my people forward in time; and this, which may mean nothing to you as you sit there in silence, means all things to me.'

"And the words I spoke were true. But I will come to the story of my family in a moment. Let me deal now with Akasha's one victory: that Mekare and I were never united again.

"For as I have told you, never in all my wanderings did I ever find a man, woman, or blood drinker who had gazed upon Mekare or heard her name. Through all the lands of the world I wandered, at one time or another, searching for Mekare. But she was gone from me as if the great western sea had swallowed her; and I was as half a being reaching out always for the only thing which can render me complete.

"Yet in the early centuries, I knew Mekare lived; there were times when the twin I was felt the suffering of the other twin; in dark dreamlike moments, I knew inexplicable pain. But these are things which human twins feel for each other. As my body grew harder, as the human in me melted away and this more powerful and resilient immortal body grew dominant, I lost the simple human link with my sister. Yet I knew, I knew that she was alive.

"I spoke to my sister as I walked the lonely coast, glancing out over the ice cold sea. And in the grottoes of Mount Carmel I made our story in great drawings—all that we had suffered—the panorama which you beheld in the dreams.

"Over the centuries many mortals were to find that grotto, and to see those paintings; and then they would be forgotten again, to be discovered anew.

"Then finally in this century, a young archaeologist, hearing tell of them, climbed Mount Carmel one afternoon with a lantern in his hand. And when he gazed on the pictures that I had long ago made, his heart leapt because he had seen these very same images on a cave across the sea, above the jungles in Peru.

"It was years before his discovery was known to me. He had traveled far and wide with his bits and pieces of evidence—photographs of the cave drawings from both the Old World and the New; and a vase he found in the storage room of a museum, an ancient artifact from those dim forgotten centuries when the Legend of the Twins was still known.

"I cannot tell you the pain and happiness I experienced when I looked at the photographs of the pictures he had discovered in a shallow cave in the New World.

"For Mekare had drawn there the very same things that I had drawn; the brain, the heart, and the hand so much like my own had given expression to the same images of suffering and pain. Only the smallest differences existed. But the proof was beyond denial.

"Mekare's bark had carried her over the great western ocean to a land unknown in our time. Centuries perhaps before man had penetrated the southern reaches of the jungle continent, Mekare had come ashore there, perhaps to know the greatest loneliness a creature can know. How long had she wandered among birds and beasts before she'd seen a human face?

"Had it been centuries, or millennia, this inconceivable isolation? Or had she found mortals at once to comfort her, or run from her in terror? I was never to know. My sister may have lost her reason long before the coffin which carried her ever touched the South American shore.

"All I knew was that she had been there; and thousands of years ago she had made those drawings, just as I had made my own.

"Of course I lavished wealth upon this archaeologist; I gave him every means to continue his research into the Legend of the Twins. And I myself made the journey to South America. With Eric and Mael beside me, I climbed the mountain in Peru by the light of the moon and saw my sister's handiwork for myself. So ancient these paintings were. Surely they had been done within a hundred years of our separation and very possibly less.

"But we were never to find another shred of evidence that Mekare lived or walked in the South American jungles, or anywhere else in this world. Was she buried deep in the earth, beyond where the call of Mael or Eric could reach her? Did she sleep in the depths of some cave, a white statue, staring mindlessly, as her skin was covered with layer upon layer of dust?

"I cannot conceive of it. I cannot bear to think on it.

"I know only, as you know now, that she has risen. She has waked from her long slumber. Was it the songs of the Vampire Lestat that waked her? Those electronic melodies that reached the far corners of the world? Was it the thoughts of the thousands of blood drinkers who heard them, interpreted them, and responded to them? Was it Marius's warning that the Mother walks?

"Perhaps it was some dim sense collected from all these signals—that the time had come to fulfill the old curse. I cannot tell you. I know only that she moves northward, that her course is erratic, and that all efforts on my part through Eric and Mael to find her have failed.

"It is not me she seeks. I am convinced of it. It is the Mother. And the Mother's wanderings throw her off course.

"But she will find the Mother if that is her purpose! She will find the Mother! Perhaps she will come to realize that she can take to the air as the Mother can, and she will cover the miles in the blink of an eye when that discovery is made.

"But she will find the Mother. I know it. And there can be but one outcome. Either Mekare will perish; or the Mother will perish, and with the Mother so shall all of us.

"Mekare's strength is equal to mine, if not greater. It is equal to the Mother's; and she may draw from her madness a ferocity which no one can now measure or contain.

"I am no believer of curses; no believer of prophecy; the spirits that taught me the validity of such things deserted me thousands of years ago. But Mekare believed the curse when she uttered it. It came from the depths of her being; she set it into motion. And her dreams now speak only of the beginning, of the sources of her rancor, which surely feed the desire for revenge.

"Mekare may bring about the fulfillment; and it may be the better thing for us all. And if she does not destroy Akasha, if we do not destroy Akasha, what will be the outcome? We know now what evils the Mother has already begun to do. Can the world stop this thing if the world understands nothing of it? That it is immensely strong, yet certainly vulnerable; with the power to crush, yet skin and bone that can be pierced or cut? This thing that can fly, and read minds, and make fire with its thoughts; yet can be burnt itself?

"How can we stop her and save ourselves, that is the question. I want to live, as I have always wanted it. I do not want to close my eyes on this world. I do not want those I love to come to harm. Even the young ones, who must take life, I struggle in my mind to find some way to protect them. Is this evil of me? Or are we not a species, and do we not share the desire of any species to live on?

"Hearken to everything that I've told you of the Mother. To what I've said of her soul, and of the nature of the demon that resides in her—its core wedded to her core. Think on the nature of this great invisible thing which animates each one of us, and every blood drinker who has ever walked.

"We are as receptors for the energy of this being; as radios are receptors for the invisible waves that bring sound. Our bodies are no more than shells for this energy. We are—as Marius so long ago described it—blossoms on a single vine.

"Examine this mystery. For if we examine it closely perhaps we can yet find a way to save ourselves.

"And I would have you examine one thing further in regard to it; perhaps the single most valuable thing which I have ever learned.

"In those early times, when the spirits spoke to my sister and me on the side of the mountain, what human being would have believed that the spirits were irrelevant things? Even we were captives of their power, thinking it our duty to use the gifts we possessed for the good of our people, just as Akasha would later believe.

"For thousands of years after that, the firm belief in the supernatural has been part of the human soul. There were times when I would have said it was natural, chemical, an indispensable ingredient in the human makeup; something without which humans could not prosper, let alone survive.

"Again and again we have witnessed the birth of cults and religions—the dreary proclamations of apparitions and miracles and the subsequent promulgation of the creeds inspired by these 'events.'

"Travel the cities of Asia and Europe—behold the ancient temples still standing, and the cathedrals of the Christian god in which his hymns are still sung. Walk through the museums of all countries; it is religious painting and sculpture that dazzles and humbles the soul.

"How great seems that achievement; the very machinery of culture dependent upon the fuel of religious belief.

"Yet what has been the price of that faith which galvanizes countries and sends army against army; which divides up the map of nations into victor and vanquished; which annihilates the worshipers of alien gods.

"But in the last few hundred years, a true miracle has happened which has nothing to do with spirits or apparitions, or voices from the heavens telling this or that zealot what he must now do!

"We have seen in the human animal a resistance finally to the miraculous; a skepticism regarding the works of spirits, or those who claim to see them and understand them and speak their truths.

"We have seen the human mind slowly abandon the traditions of law based upon revelation, to seek ethical truths through reason; and a way of life based upon respect for the physical and the spiritual as perceived by all human beings.

"And with this loss of respect for supernatural intervention; with this credulity of all things divorced from the flesh, has come the most enlightened age of all; for men and women seek for the highest inspiration not in the realm of the invisible, but in the realm of the human—the thing which is both flesh and spirit; invisible and visible; earthly and transcendent.

"The psychic, the clairvoyant, the witch, if you will, is no longer of value, I am convinced of it. The spirits can give us nothing more. In sum, we have outgrown our susceptibility to such madness, and we are moving to a perfection that the world has never known.

"The word has been made flesh at last, to quote the old biblical phrase with all its mystery; but the word is the word of reason; and the flesh is the acknowledgment of the needs and the desires which all men and women share.

"And what would our Queen do for this world with her intervention? What would she give it—she whose very existence is now irrelevant, she whose mind has been locked for centuries in a realm of unenlightened dreams?

"She must be stopped; Marius is right; who could disagree with him?

We must stand ready to help Mekare, not to thwart her, even if it means the end for us all.

"But let me lay before you now the final chapter of my tale in which lies the fullest illumination of the threat that the Mother poses to us all:

"As I've already said, Akasha did not annihilate my people. They lived on in my daughter Miriam and in her daughters, and those daughters born to them.

"Within twenty years I had returned to the village where I'd left Miriam, and found her a young woman who had grown up on the stories that would become the Legend of the Twins.

"By the light of the moon I took her with me up the mountain and revealed to her the caves of her ancestors, and gave her the few necklaces and the gold that was still hidden deep within the painted grottoes where others feared to go. And I told Miriam all the stories of her ancestors which I knew. But I adjured her: stay away from the spirits; stay away from all dealings with things invisible, whatever people call them, and especially if they are called gods.

"Then I went to Jericho, for there in the crowded streets it was easy to hunt for victims, for those who wished for death and would not trouble my conscience; and easy to hide from prying eyes.

"But I was to visit Miriam many times over the years; and Miriam gave birth to four daughters and two sons, and these gave birth in turn to some five children who lived to maturity and of these five, two were women, and of those women eight different children were born. And the legends of the family were told by their mothers to these children; the Legend of the Twins they also learned—the legend of the sisters who had once spoken to spirits, and made the rain fall, and were persecuted by the evil King and Queen.

"Two hundred years later, I wrote down for the first time all the names of my family, for they were an entire village now, and it took four whole clay tablets for me to record what I knew. I then filled tablet after tablet with the stories of the beginning, of the women who had gone back to The Time Before the Moon.

"And though I wandered sometimes for a century away from my homeland, searching for Mekare, hunting the wild coasts of northern Europe, I always came back to my people, and to my secret hiding places in the mountains and to my house in Jericho, and I wrote down again the progress of the family, which daughters had been born and the names of those daughters born to them. Of the sons, too, I wrote in detail—of their accomplishments, and personalities, and sometime heroism—as I did with the women. But of their offspring no. It was not possible to know if the children of the men were truly of my blood, and of my people's blood. And so the thread became matrilineal as it has always been since.

"But never, never, in all this time, did I reveal to my family the evil magic which had been done to me. I was determined that this evil should never touch the family; and so if I used my ever increasing supernatural powers, it was in secret, and in ways that could be naturally explained.

"By the third generation, I was merely a kinswoman who had come home after many years in another land. And when and if I intervened, to bring gold or advice to my daughters, it was as a human being might do it, and nothing more.

"Thousands of years passed as I watched the family in anonymity, only now and then playing the long lost kinswoman to come into this or that village or family gathering and hold the children in my arms.

"But by the early centuries of the Christian era, another concept had seized my imagination. And so I created the fiction of a branch of the family which kept all its records—for there were now tablets and scrolls in abundance, and even bound books. And in each generation of this fictional branch, there was a fictional woman to whom the task of recordkeeping was passed. The name of Maharet came with the honor; and when time demanded it, old Maharet would die, and young Maharet would inherit the task.

"And so I myself was within the family; and the family knew me; and I knew the family's love. I became the writer of letters; the benefactor; the unifier; the mysterious yet trusted visitor who appeared to heal breaches and right wrongs. And though a thousand passions consumed me; though I lived for centuries in different lands, learning new languages and customs, and marveling at the infinite beauty of the world, and the power of the human imagination, I always returned to the family, the family which knew me and expected things from me.

"As the centuries passed, as the millennia passed, I never went down into the earth as many of you have done. I never faced madness and loss of memory as was common among the old ones, who became often like the Mother and Father, statues buried beneath the ground. Not a night has passed since those early times that I have not opened my eyes, known my own name, and looked with recognition upon the world around me, and reached for the thread of my own life.

"But it was not that madness didn't threaten. It was not that weariness did not sometimes overwhelm. It was not that grief did not embitter me, or that mysteries did not confuse me, or that I did not know pain.

"It was that I had the records of my family to safeguard; I had my own progeny to look after, and to guide in the world. And so even in the darkest times, when all human existence seemed monstrous to me and unbearable, and the changes of the world beyond comprehension, I turned to the family as if it were the very spring of life itself.

"And the family taught me the rhythms and passions of each new age; the family took me into alien lands where perhaps I would never have ventured alone; the family took me into realms of art which might have intimidated me; the family was my guide through time and space. My teacher, my book of life. The family was all things."

Maharet paused.

For a moment it seemed she would say something more. Then she rose from the table. She glanced at each of the others, and then she looked at Jesse.

"Now I want you to come with me. I want to show you what this family has become."

Quietly, all rose and waited as Maharet walked round the table and then they followed her out of the room. They followed her across the iron landing in the earthen stairwell, and into another great mountaintop chamber, with a glass roof and solid walls.

Jesse was the last to enter, and she knew even before she had passed through the door what she would see. An exquisite pain coursed through her, a pain full of remembered happiness and unforgettable longing. It was the windowless room in which she'd stood long ago.

How clearly she recalled its stone fireplace, and the dark leather furnishings scattered over the carpet; and the air of great and secret excitement, infinitely surpassing the memory of the physical things, which had forever haunted her afterwards, engulfing her in half-remembered dreams.

Yes, there the great electronic map of the world with its flattened continents, covered with thousands and thousands of tiny glowing lights.

And the other three walls, so dark, seemingly covered by a fine black wire mesh, until you realized what you were seeing: an endless ink-drawn vine, crowding every inch between floor and ceiling, growing from a single root in one corner into a million tiny swarming branches, each branch surrounded by countless carefully inscribed names.

A gasp rose from Marius as he turned about, looking from the great glowing map to the dense and delicately drawn family tree. Armand gave a faint sad smile also, while Mael scowled slightly, though he was actually amazed.

The others stared in silence; Eric had known these secrets; Louis, the most human of them all, had tears standing in his eyes. Daniel gazed in undisguised wonder. While Khayman, his eyes dulled as if with sadness, stared at the map as if he did not see it, as if he were still looking deep into the past.

Slowly Gabrielle nodded; she made some little sound of approval, of pleasure.

"The Great Family," she said in simple acknowledgment as she looked at Maharet.

Maharet nodded.

She pointed to the great sprawling map of the world behind her, which covered the south wall.

Jesse followed the vast swelling procession of tiny lights that moved across it, out of Palestine, spreading all over Europe, and down into Africa, and into Asia, and then finally to both continents of the New World. Countless tiny lights flickering in various colors; and as Jesse deliberately blurred her vision, she saw the great diffusion for what it was. She saw the old names, too, of continents and countries and seas, written in gold script on the sheet of glass that covered the three-dimensional illusion of mountains, plains, valleys.

"These are my descendants," Maharet said, "the descendants of Miriam, who was my daughter and Khayman's daughter, and of my people, whose blood was in me and in Miriam, traced through the maternal line as you see before you, for six thousand years."

"Unimaginable!" Pandora whispered. And she too was sad almost to the point of tears. What a melancholy beauty she had, grand and remote, yet reminiscent of warmth as if it had once been there, naturally, overwhelmingly. It seemed to hurt her, this revelation, to remind her of all that she had long ago lost.

"It is but one human family," Maharet said softly. "Yet there is no nation on earth that does not contain some part of it, and the descendants of males, blood of our blood and uncounted, surely exist in equal numbers to all those now known by name. Many who went into the wastes of Great Russia and into China and Japan and other dim regions were lost to this record. As are many of whom I lost track over the centuries for various reasons. Nevertheless their descendants are there! No people, no race, no country does not contain some of the Great Family. The Great Family is Arab, Jew, Anglo, African; it is Indian; it is Mongolian; it is Japanese and Chinese. In sum, the Great Family is the human family."

"Yes," Marius whispered. Remarkable to see the emotion in his face, the faint blush of human color again and the subtle light in the eyes that always defies description. "One family and all families—" he said. He went towards the enormous map and lifted his hands irresistibly as he looked up at it, studying the course of lights moving over the carefully modeled terrain.

Jesse felt the atmosphere of that long ago night enfold her; and then unaccountably those memories—flaring for an instant—faded, as though they didn't matter anymore. She was here with all the secrets; she was standing again in this room.

She moved closer to the dark, fine engraving on the wall. She looked at the myriad tiny names inscribed in black ink; she stood back and followed the progress of one branch, one thin delicate branch, as it rose slowly to the ceiling through a hundred different forks and twists.

And through the dazzle of all her dreams fulfilled now, she thought lovingly of all those souls who had made up the Great Family that she had known; of the mystery of heritage and intimacy. The moment was timeless; quiet for her; she didn't see the white faces of her new kin, the splendid immortal forms caught in their eerie stillness.

Something of the real world was alive still for her now, something that evoked awe and grief and perhaps the finest love she had ever been capable of; and it seemed for one moment that natural and supernatural possibility were equal in their mystery. They were equal in their power. And all the miracles of the immortals could not outshine this vast and simple chronicle. The Great Family.

Her hand rose as if it had a life of its own. And as the light caught Mael's silver bracelet which she wore around her wrist still, she laid her fingers out silently on the wall. A hundred names covered by the palm of her hand.

"This is what is threatened now," Marius said, his voice softened by sadness, his eyes still on the map.

It startled her, that a voice could be so loud yet so soft. No, she thought, no one will hurt the Great Family. No one will hurt the Great Family!

She turned to Maharet; Maharet was looking at her. And here we are, Jesse thought, at the opposite ends of this vine, Maharet and I.

A terrible pain welled in Jesse. A terrible pain. To be swept away from all things real, that had been irresistible, but to think that all things real could be swept away was unendurable.

During all her long years with the Talamasca, when she had seen spirits and restless ghosts, and poltergeists that could terrify their baffled victims, and clairvoyants speaking in foreign tongues, she had always known that somehow the supernatural could never impress itself upon the natural. Maharet had been so right! Irrelevant, yes, safely irrelevant—unable to intervene!

But now that stood to be changed. The unreal had been made real. It was absurd to stand in this strange room, amid these stark and imposing forms, and say, This cannot happen. This thing, this thing called the Mother, could reach out from behind the veil that had so long separated her from mortal eyes and touch a million human souls.

What did Khayman see when he looked at her now, as if he understood her. Did he see his daughter in Jesse?

"Yes," Khayman said. "My daughter. And don't be afraid. Mekare will come. Mekare will fulfill the curse. And the Great Family will go on."

Maharet sighed. "When I knew the Mother had risen, I did not guess what she might do. To strike down her children, to annihilate the evil that had come out of her, and out of Khayman and me and all of us who out of loneliness have shared this power—that I could not really question! What right have we to live? What right have we to be immortal? We are accidents; we are horrors. And though I want my life, greedily, I want it as fiercely as ever I wanted it—I cannot say that it is wrong that she has slain so many—"

"She'll slay more!" Eric said desperately.

"But it is the Great Family now which falls under her shadow," Maharet said. "It is their world! And she would make it her own. Unless . . ."

"Mekare will come," Khayman said. The simplest smile animated his face. "Mekare will fulfill the curse. I made Mekare what she is, so that she would do it. It is our curse now."

Maharet smiled, but it was vastly different, her expression. It was sad, indulgent, and curiously cold. "Ah, that you believe in such symmetry, Khayman."

"And we'll die, all of us!" Eric said.

"There has to be a way to kill her," Gabrielle said coldly, "without killing us. We have to think on this, to be ready, to have some sort of plan."

"You cannot change the prophecy," Khayman whispered.

"Khayman, if we have learned anything," Marius said, "it is that there is no destiny. And if there is no destiny then there is no prophecy. Mekare comes here to do what she vowed to do; it may be all she knows now or all she can do, but that does not mean that Akasha can't defend herself against Mekare. Don't you think the Mother knows Mekare has risen? Don't you think the Mother has seen and heard her children's dreams?"

"Ah, but prophecies have a way of fulfilling themselves," Khayman said. "That's the magic of it. We all understood it in ancient times. The power of charms is the power of the will; you might say that we were all great geniuses of psychology in those dark days, that we could be slain by the power of another's designs. And the dreams, Marius, the dreams are but part of a great design."

"Don't talk of it as if it were already done," Maharet said. "We have another tool. We can use reason. This creature speaks now, does she not? She understands what is spoken to her. Perhaps she can be diverted—"

"Oh, you are mad, truly mad!" Eric said. "You are going to speak to this monster that roamed the world incinerating her offspring!" He was becoming more frightened by the minute. "What does this thing know of reason, that inflames ignorant women to rise against their men? This thing knows slaughter and death and violence, that is all it has ever known, as your story makes plain. We don't change, Maharet. How many times have you told me. We move ever closer to the perfection of what we were meant to be."

"None of us wants to die, Eric," Maharet said patiently. But something suddenly distracted her.

At the same moment, Khayman too felt it. Jesse studied both of them, attempting to understand what she was seeing. Then she realized that Marius had undergone a subtle change as well. Eric was petrified. Mael, to Jesse's surprise, was staring fixedly at her.

They were hearing some sound. It was the way they moved their eyes that revealed it; people listen with their eyes; their eyes dance as they absorb the sound and try to locate its source.

Suddenly Eric said: "The young ones should go to the cellar immediately."

"That's no use," Gabrielle said. "Besides, I want to be here." She couldn't hear the sound, but she was trying to hear it.

Eric turned on Maharet. "Are you going to let her destroy us, one by one?"

Maharet didn't answer. She turned her head very slowly and looked towards the landing.

Then Jesse finally heard the sound herself. Certainly human ears couldn't hear it; it was like the auditory equivalent of tension without vibration, coursing through her as it did through every particle of substance in the room. It was inundating and disorienting, and though she saw that Maharet was speaking to Khayman and that Khayman was answering, she couldn't hear what they were saying. Foolishly, she'd put her hands to her ears. Dimly, she saw that Daniel had done the same thing, but they both knew it did no good at all.

The sound seemed suddenly to suspend all time; to suspend momentum. Jesse was losing her balance; she backed up against the wall; she stared at the map across from her, as if she wanted it somehow to sustain her. She stared at the soft flow of the lights streaming out of Asia Minor and to the north and to the south.

Some dim, inaudible commotion filled the room. The sound had died away, yet the air rang with a deafening silence.

In a soundless dream, it seemed, she saw the figure of the Vampire Lestat appear in the door; she saw him rush into Gabrielle's arms; she saw Louis move towards him and then embrace him. And then she saw the Vampire Lestat look at her—and she caught the flashing image of the funeral feast, the twins, the body on the altar. He didn't know what it meant! He didn't know.

It shocked her, the realization. The moment on the stage came back to her, when he had obviously struggled to recognize some fleeting image, as they had drawn apart.

Then as the others drew him away now, with embraces and kisses again—and even Armand had come to him with his arms out—he gave her the faintest little smile. "Jesse," he said.

He stared at the others, at Marius, at the cold and wary faces. And how white his skin was, how utterly white, yet the warmth, the exuberance, the almost childlike excitement—it was exactly as it had been before.

PART IV

THE QUEEN
OF THE DAMNED

i

Wings stir the sunlit dust
of the cathedral in which
the Past is buried
to its chin in marble.

STAN RICE
from
"Poem on Crawling into Bed: Bitterness"
Body of Work (1983)

ii

In the glazed greenery of hedge,
and ivy,
and inedible strawberries
the lilies are white; remote; extreme.
Would they were our guardians.
They are barbarians.

STAN RICE
from
"Greek Fragments"
Body of Work (1983)

SHE sat at the end of the table, waiting for them; so still, placid, the magenta gown giving her skin a deep carnal glow in the light of the fire.

The edge of her face was gilded by the glow of the flames, and the dark window glass caught her vividly in a flawless mirror, as if the reflection were the real thing, floating out there in the transparent night.

Frightened. Frightened for them and for me. And strangely, for her. It was like a chill, the presentiment. For her. The one who might destroy all that I had ever loved.

At the door, I turned and kissed Gabrielle again. I felt her body collapse against me for an instant; then her attention locked on Akasha. I felt the faint tremor in her hands as she touched my face. I looked at Louis, my seemingly fragile Louis with his seemingly invincible composure; and at Armand, the urchin with the angel's face. Finally those you love are simply . . . those you love.

Marius was frigid with anger as he entered the room; nothing could disguise this. He glared at me—I, the one who had slain those poor helpless mortals and left them strewn down the mountain. He knew, did he not? And all the snow in the world couldn't cover it up. *I need you, Marius. We need you.*

His mind was veiled; all their minds were veiled. Could they keep their secrets from her?

As they filed into the room, I went to her right hand because she wanted me to. And because that's where I knew I ought to be. I gestured for Gabrielle and Louis to sit opposite, close, where I could see them. And the look on Louis's face, so resigned, yet sorrowful, struck my heart.

The red-haired woman, the ancient one called Maharet, sat at the opposite end of the table, the end nearest the door. Marius and Armand were on her right. And on her left was the young red-haired one, Jesse. Maharet looked absolutely passive, collected, as if nothing could alarm her.

But it was rather easy to see why. Akasha couldn't hurt this creature; or the other very old one, Khayman, who sat down now to my right.

The one called Eric was terrified, it was obvious. Only reluctantly did he sit at the table at all. Mael was afraid too, but it made him furious. He glowered at Akasha, as if he cared nothing about hiding his disposition.

And Pandora, beautiful, brown-eyed Pandora—she looked truly uncaring as she took her place beside Marius. She didn't even look at Akasha. She looked out through the glass walls, her eyes moving slowly, lovingly, as she saw the forest, the layers and layers of dim forest, with their dark streaks of redwood bark and prickling green.

The other one who didn't care was Daniel. This one I'd seen at the concert too. I hadn't guessed that Armand had been with him! Hadn't picked up the faintest indication that Armand had been there. And to think, whatever we might have said to each other, it was lost now forever. But then that couldn't be, could it? We would have our time together, Armand and I; all of us. Daniel knew it, pretty Daniel, the reporter with his little tape recorder who with Louis in a room on Divisadero Street had somehow started all of this! That's why he looked so serenely at Akasha; that's why he explored it moment by moment.

I looked at the black-haired Santino—a rather regal being, who was appraising me in a calculating fashion. He wasn't afraid either. But he cared desperately about what happened here. When he looked at Akasha he was awed by her beauty; it touched some deep wound in him. Old faith flared for a moment, faith that had meant more to him than survival, and faith that had been bitterly burnt away.

No time to understand them all, to evaluate the links which connected them, to ask the meaning of that strange image—the two red-haired women and the body of the mother, which I saw again in a glancing flash when I looked at Jesse.

I was wondering if they could scan my mind and find in it all the things I was struggling to conceal; the things I unwittingly concealed from myself.

Gabrielle's face was unreadable now. Her eyes had grown small and gray, as if shutting out all light and color; she looked from me to Akasha and back again, as if trying to figure something out.

And a sudden terror crept over me. Maybe it had been there all the time. They would never yield either. Something inveterate would prevent it, just as it had with me. And some fatal resolution would come before we left this room.

For a moment I was paralyzed. I reached out suddenly and took Akasha's hand. I felt her fingers close delicately around mine.

"Be quiet, my prince," she said, unobtrusively and kindly. "What you feel in this room is death, but it is the death of beliefs and strictures. Nothing more." She looked at Maharet. "The death of dreams, perhaps," she said, "which should have died a long time ago."

Maharet looked as lifeless and passive as a living thing can look. Her violet eyes were weary, bloodshot. And suddenly I realized why. They were human eyes. They were dying in her head. Her blood was infusing them over and over again with life but it wasn't lasting. Too many of the tiny nerves in her own body were dead.

I saw the dream vision again. The twins, the body before them. What was the connection?

"It is nothing," Akasha whispered. "Something long forgotten; for there are no answers in history now. We have transcended history. History is built on errors; we will begin with truth."

Marius spoke up at once:

"Is there nothing that can persuade you to stop?" His tone was infinitely more subdued than I'd expected. He sat forward, hands folded, in the attitude of one striving to be reasonable. "What can we say? We want you to cease the apparitions. We want you not to intervene."

Akasha's fingers tightened on mine. The red-haired woman was staring at me now with her bloodshot violet eyes.

"Akasha, I beg you," Marius said. "Stop this rebellion. Don't appear again to mortals; don't give any further commands."

Akasha laughed softly. "And why not, Marius? Because it so upsets your precious world, the world you've been watching for two thousand years, the way you Romans once watched life and death in the arena, as if such things were entertainment or theater, as if it did not matter—the literal fact of suffering and death—as long as you were enthralled?"

"I see what you mean to do," Marius said. "Akasha, you do not have the right."

"Marius, your student here has given me those old arguments," she answered. Her tone was now as subdued and eloquent of patience as his. "But more significantly, I have given them a thousand times to myself. How long do you think I have listened to the prayers of the world, pondering a way to terminate the endless cycle of human violence? It is time now for you to listen to what I have to say."

"We are to play a role in this?" Santino asked. "Or to be destroyed as the others have been destroyed?" His manner was impulsive rather than arrogant.

And for the first time the red-haired woman evinced a flicker of emotion, her weary eyes fixing on him immediately, her mouth tense.

"You will be my angels," Akasha answered tenderly as she looked at him. "You will be my gods. If you do not choose to follow me, I'll destroy you. As for the old ones, the old ones whom I cannot so easily dispatch"— she glanced at Khayman and Maharet again—"if they turn against me, they shall be as devils opposing me, and all humanity shall hunt them down, and they shall through their opposition serve the scheme quite well. But what you had before—a world to roam in stealth—you shall never have again."

It seemed Eric was losing his silent battle with fear. He moved as if he meant to rise and leave the room.

"Patience," Maharet said, glancing at him. She looked back at Akasha. Akasha smiled.

"How is it possible," Maharet asked in a low voice, "to break a cycle of violence through more wanton violence? You are destroying the males of the human species. What can possibly be the outcome of such a brutal act?"

"You know the outcome as well as I do," Akasha said. "It's too simple and too elegant to be misunderstood. It has been unimaginable *until now*. All those centuries I sat upon my throne in Marius's shrine; I dreamed of an earth that was a garden, a world where beings lived without the torment that I could hear and feel. I dreamed of people achieving this peace without tyranny. And then the utter simplicity of it struck me; it was like dawn coming. The people who can realize such a dream are women; but only if all the men—or very nearly all the men—are removed.

"In prior ages, such a thing would not have been workable. But now it is easy; there is a vast technology which can reinforce it. After the initial purgation, the sex of babies can be selected; the unwanted unborn can be mercifully aborted as so many of both sexes are now. But there is no need to discuss this aspect of it, really. You are not fools, any of you, no matter how emotional or impetuous you are.

"You know as I know that there will be universal peace if the male population is limited to one per one hundred women. All forms of random violence will very simply come to an end.

"The reign of peace will be something the world has never known. Then the male population can be increased gradually. But for the conceptual framework to be changed, the males must be gone. Who can dispute that? It may not even be necessary to keep the one in a hundred. But it would be generous to do so. And so I will allow this. At least as we begin."

I could see that Gabrielle was about to speak. I tried to give her a silent signal to be quiet, but she ignored me.

"All right, the effects are obvious," she said. "But when you speak in terms of wholesale extermination, then questions of peace become ridiculous. You're abandoning one half of the world's population. If men and women were born without arms and legs, this might be a peaceful world as well."

"The men deserve what will happen to them. As a species, they will reap what they have sown. And remember, I speak of a temporary cleansing—a retreat, as it were. It's the simplicity of it which is beautiful. Collectively the lives of these men do not equal the lives of women who have been killed at the hands of men over the centuries. You know it and I know it. Now, tell me, how many men over the centuries have fallen at the hands of women? If you brought back to life every man slain by a woman, do you think these creatures would fill even this house?

"But you see, these points don't matter. Again, we know what I say is true. What matters—what is relevant and even more exquisite than the proposition itself—is that we now have the means to make it happen. I am indestructible. You are equipped to be my angels. And there is no one who can oppose us with success."

"That's not true," Maharet said.

A little flash of anger colored Akasha's cheeks; a glorious blush of red that faded and left her as inhuman looking as before.

"You are saying that *you* can stop me?" she asked, her mouth stiffening. "You are rash to suggest this. Will you suffer the death of Eric, and Mael, and Jessica, for such a point?"

Maharet didn't answer. Mael was visibly shaken but with anger not fear. He glanced at Jesse and at Maharet and then at me. I could feel his hatred.

Akasha continued to stare at Maharet.

"Oh, I know you, believe me," Akasha went on, her voice softening slightly. "I know how you have survived through all the years unchanged. I have seen you a thousand times in the eyes of others; I know you dream now that your sister lives. And perhaps she does—in some pathetic form. I know your hatred of me has only festered; and you reach back in your mind, all the way back, to the very beginning as if you could find there some rhyme or reason for what is happening now. But as you yourself told me long ago when we talked together in a palace of mud brick on the banks of the Nile River, there is no rhyme or reason. There is nothing! There are things visible and invisible; and horrible things can befall the most innocent of us all. Don't you see—this is as crucial to what I do now as all else."

Again, Maharet didn't answer. She sat rigid, only her darkly beautiful eyes showing a faint glimmer of what might have been pain.

"I shall *make* the rhyme or reason," Akasha said, with a trace of anger. "I shall *make* the future; I shall define goodness; I shall define peace. And

I don't call on mythic gods or goddesses or spirits to justify my actions, on abstract morality. I do not call on history either! I don't look for my mother's heart and brain in the dirt!"

A shiver ran through the others. A little bitter smile played on Santino's lips. And protectively, it seemed, Louis looked towards the mute figure of Maharet.

Marius was anxious lest this go further.

"Akasha," he said in entreaty, "even if it could be done, even if the mortal population did not rise against you, and the men did not find some way to destroy you long before such a plan could be accomplished—"

"You're a fool, Marius, or you think I am. Don't you think I know what this world is capable of? What absurd mixture of the savage and the technologically astute makes up the mind of modern man?"

"My Queen, I don't think you know it!" Marius said. "Truly, I don't. I don't think you can hold in your mind the full conception of what the world is. None of us can; it is too varied, too immense; we seek to embrace it with our reason; but we can't do it. You know a world; but it is not *the* world; it is the world you have selected from a dozen other worlds for reasons within yourself."

She shook her head; another flare of anger. "Don't try my patience, Marius," she said. "I spared you for a very simple reason. Lestat wanted you spared. And because you are strong and you can be of help to me. But that is all there is to it, Marius. Tread with care."

A silence fell between them. Surely he realized that she was lying. I realized it. She loved him and it humiliated her, and so she sought to hurt him. And she had. Silently, he swallowed his rage.

"Even if it could be done," he pressed gently, "can you honestly say that human beings have done so badly that they should receive such a punishment as this?"

I felt the relief course through me. I'd known he would have the courage, I'd known that he would find some way to take it into the deeper waters, no matter how she threatened him; he would say all that I had struggled to say.

"Ah, now you disgust me," she answered.

"Akasha, for two thousand years I have watched," he said. "Call me the Roman in the arena if you will and tell me tales of the ages that went before. When I knelt at your feet I begged you for your knowledge. But what I have witnessed in this short span has filled me with awe and love for all things mortal; I have seen revolutions in thought and philosophy which I believed impossible. Is not the human race moving towards the very age of peace you describe?"

Her face was a picture of disdain.

"Marius," she said, "this will go down as one of the bloodiest centuries in the history of the human race. What revolutions do you speak of, when millions have been exterminated by one small European nation on the whim of a madman, when entire cities were melted into oblivion by bombs? When children in the desert countries of the East war on other children in the name of an ancient and despotic God? Marius, women the world over wash the fruits of their wombs down public drains. The screams of the hungry are deafening, yet unheard by the rich who cavort in technological citadels; disease runs rampant among the starving of whole continents while the sick in palatial hospitals spend the wealth of the world on cosmetic refinements and the promise of eternal life through pills and vials." She laughed softly. "Did ever the cries of the dying ring so thickly in the ears of those of us who can hear them? Has *ever* more blood been shed!"

I could feel Marius's frustration. I could feel the passion that made him clench his fist now and search his soul for the proper words.

"There's something you cannot *see*," he said finally. "There is something that you fail to understand."

"No, my dear one. There is nothing wrong with my vision. There never was. It is you who fail to see. You always have."

"Look out there at the forest!" he said, gesturing to the glass walls around us, "Pick one tree; describe it, if you will, in terms of what it destroys, what it defies, and what it does not accomplish, and you have a monster of greedy roots and irresistible momentum that eats the light of other plants, their nutrients, their air. But that is not the truth of the tree. That is not the whole truth when the thing is seen as part of nature, and by nature I mean nothing sacred, I mean only the full tapestry, Akasha. I mean only the larger thing which embraces all."

"And so you will select now your causes for optimism," she said, "as you always have. Come now. Examine for me the Western cities where even the poor are given platters of meat and vegetables daily and tell me hunger is no more. Well, your pupil here has given me enough of that pap already—the idiot foolishness upon which the complacency of the rich has always been based. The world is sunk into depravity and chaos; it is as it always was or worse."

"Oh, no, not so," he said adamantly. "Men and women are learning animals. If you do not see what they have learned, you're blind. They are creatures ever changing, ever improving, ever expanding their vision and the capacity of their hearts. You are not fair to them when you speak of this as the most bloody century; you are not seeing the light that shines ever more radiantly on account of the darkness; you are not seeing the evolution of the human soul!"

He rose from his place at the table, and came round towards her on the left-hand side. He took the empty chair between her and Gabrielle. And then he reached out and he lifted her hand.

I was frightened watching him. Frightened she wouldn't allow him to touch her; but she seemed to like this gesture; she only smiled.

"True, what you say about war," he said, pleading with her, and struggling with his dignity at the same time. "Yes, and the cries of the dying, I too have heard them; we have all heard them, through all the decades; and even now, the world is shocked by daily reports of armed conflict. But it is the outcry against these horrors which is the light I speak of; it's the attitudes which were never possible in the past. It is the intolerance of thinking men and women in power who for the first time in the history of the human race truly want to put an end to injustice in all forms."

"You speak of the intellectual attitudes of a few."

"No," he said. "I speak of changing philosophy; I speak of idealism from which true realities will be born. Akasha, flawed as they are, they must have the time to perfect their own dreams, don't you see?"

"Yes!" It was Louis who spoke out.

My heart sank. So vulnerable! Were she to turn her anger on him— But in his quiet and refined manner, he was going on:

"It's their world, not ours," he said humbly. "Surely we forfeited it when we lost our mortality. We have no right now to interrupt their struggle. If we do we rob them of victories that have cost them too much! Even in the last hundred years their progress has been miraculous; they have righted wrongs that mankind thought were inevitable; they have for the first time developed a concept of the true family of man."

"You touch me with your sincerity," she answered. "I spared you only because Lestat loved you. Now I know the reason for that love. What courage it must take for you to speak your heart to me. Yet you yourself are the most predatory of all the immortals here. You kill without regard for age or sex or will to live."

"Then kill me!" he answered. "I wish that you would. But don't kill human beings! Don't interfere with them. Even if they kill each other! Give them time to see this new vision realized; give the cities of the West, corrupt as they may be, time to take their ideals to a suffering and blighted world."

"Time," Maharet said. "Maybe that is what we are asking for. Time. And that is what you have to give."

There was a pause.

Akasha didn't want to look again at this woman; she didn't want to listen to her. I could feel her recoiling. She withdrew her hand from Marius; she looked at Louis for a long moment and then she turned to Maharet as if it couldn't be avoided, and her face became set and almost cruel.

But Maharet went on:

"You have meditated in silence for centuries upon your solutions. What is another hundred years? Surely you will not dispute that the last century on this earth was beyond all prediction or imagining—and that the technological advances of that century can conceivably bring food and shelter and health to all the peoples of the earth."

"Is that really so?" Akasha responded. A deep smoldering hate heated her smile as she spoke. "This is what technological advances have given the world. They have given it poison gas, and diseases born in laboratories, and bombs that could destroy the planet itself. They have given the world nuclear accidents that have contaminated the food and drink of entire continents. And the armies do what they have always done with modern efficiency. The aristocracy of a people slaughtered in an hour in a snow-filled wood; the intelligentsia of a nation, including all those who wear eyeglasses, systematically shot. In the Sudan, women are still habitually mutilated to be made pleasing to their husbands; in Iran the children run into the fire of guns!"

"This cannot be all you've seen," Marius said. "I don't believe it. Akasha, look at me. Look kindly on me, and what I'm trying to say."

"It doesn't matter whether or not you believe it!" she said with the first sustained anger. "You haven't accepted what I've been trying to tell you. You have not yielded to the exquisite image I've presented to your mind. Don't you realize the gift I offer you? I would save you! And what are you if I don't do this thing! A blood drinker, a killer!"

I'd never heard her voice so heated. As Marius started to answer, she gestured imperiously for silence. She looked at Santino and at Armand.

"You, Santino," she said. "You who governed the Roman Children of Darkness, when they believed they did God's will as the Devil's henchmen—do you remember what it was like to have a purpose? And you, Armand, the leader of the old Paris coven; remember when you were a saint of darkness? Between heaven and hell, you had your place. I offer you that again; and it is no delusion! Can you not reach for your lost ideals?"

Neither answered her. Santino was horror-struck; the wound inside him was bleeding. Armand's face revealed nothing but despair.

A dark fatalistic expression came over her. This was futile. None of them would join her. She looked at Marius.

"Your precious mankind!" she said. "It has learned nothing in six thousand years! You speak to me of ideals and goals! There were men in my father's court in Uruk who knew the hungry ought to be fed. Do you know what your modern world is? Televisions are tabernacles of the miraculous and helicopters are its angels of death!"

"All right, then, what would your world be?" Marius said. His hands were trembling. "You don't believe that the women aren't going to fight for their men?"

She laughed. She turned to me. "Did they fight in Sri Lanka, Lestat? Did they fight in Haiti? Did they fight in Lynkonos?"

Marius stared at me. He waited for me to answer, to take my stand with him. I wanted to make arguments; to reach for the threads he'd given me and take it further. But my mind went blank.

"Akasha," I said. "Don't continue this bloodbath. Please. Don't lie to human beings or befuddle them anymore."

There it was—brutal and unsophisticated, but the only truth I could give.

"Yes, for that's the essence of it," Marius said, his tone careful again, fearful, and almost pleading. "It's a lie, Akasha; it's another superstitious lie! Have we not had enough of them? And now, of all times, when the world's waking from its old delusions. When it has thrown off the old gods."

"A lie?" she asked. She drew back, as if he'd hurt her. "What is the lie? Did I lie when I told them I would bring a reign of peace on earth? Did I lie when I told them I was the one they had been waiting for? No, I didn't lie. What I can do is give them the first bit of truth they've ever had! I am what they think I am. I am eternal, and all powerful, and shall protect them—"

"Protect them?" Marius asked. "How can you protect them from their most deadly foes?"

"What foes?"

"Disease, my Queen. Death. You are no healer. You cannot give life or save it. And they will expect such miracles. *All you can do is kill.*"

Silence. Stillness. Her face suddenly as lifeless as it had been in the shrine; eyes staring forward; emptiness or deep thought, impossible to distinguish.

No sound but the wood shifting and falling into the fire.

"Akasha," I whispered. "Time, the thing that Maharet asked for. A century. So little to give."

Dazed, she looked at me. I could feel death breathing on my face, death close as it had been years and years ago when the wolves tracked me into the frozen forest, and I couldn't reach up high enough for the limbs of the barren trees.

"You are all my enemies, aren't you?" she whispered. "Even you, my prince. You are my enemy. My lover and my enemy at the same time."

"I love you!" I said. "But I can't lie to you. I cannot believe in it! It is wrong! It is the very simplicity and the elegance which make it so wrong!"

Her eyes moved rapidly over their faces. Eric was on the verge of panic again. And I could feel the anger cresting in Mael.

"Is there not one of you who would stand with me?" she whispered. "Not one who would reach for that dazzling dream? Not even one who is ready to forsake his or her small and selfish world?" Her eyes fixed on Pandora. "Ah, you, poor dreamer, grieving for your lost humanity; would you not be redeemed?"

Pandora stared as if through a dim glass. "I have no taste for bringing death," she answered in an even softer whisper. "It is enough for me to see it in the falling leaves. I cannot believe good things can come from bloodshed. For that's the crux, my Queen. Those horrors happen still, but good men and women everywhere deplore them; you would reclaim such methods; you would exonerate them and bring the dialogue to an end." She smiled sadly. "I am a useless thing to you. I have nothing to give."

Akasha didn't respond. Then her eyes moved over the others again; she took the measure of Mael, of Eric. Of Jesse.

"Akasha," I said. "History is a litany of injustice, no one denies it. But when has a simple solution ever been anything but evil? Only in complexity do we find answers. Through complexity men struggle towards fairness; it is slow and clumsy, but it's the only way. Simplicity demands too great a sacrifice. It always has."

"Yes," Marius said. "Exactly. Simplicity and brutality are synonymous in philosophy and in actions. It is brutal what you propose!"

"Is there no humility in you?" she asked suddenly. She turned from me to him. "Is there no willingness to understand? You are so proud, all of you, so arrogant. You want your world to remain the same on account of your greed!"

"No," Marius said.

"What have I done that you should set yourselves so against me?" she demanded. She looked at me, then at Marius, and finally to Maharet. "From Lestat I expected arrogance," she said. "I expected platitudes and rhetoric, and untested ideas. But from many of you I expected more. Oh, how you disappoint me. How can you turn away from the destiny that awaits you? You who could be saviors! How can you deny what you have seen?"

"But they'd want to know what we really are," Santino said. "And once they did know, they'd rise against us. They'd want the immortal blood as they always do."

"Even women want to live forever," Maharet said coldly. "Even women would kill for that."

"Akasha, it's folly," said Marius. "It cannot be accomplished. For the Western world, not to resist would be unthinkable."

"It is a savage and primitive vision," Maharet said with cold scorn.

Akasha's face darkened again with anger. Yet even in rage, the prettiness of her expression remained. "You have always opposed me!" she said to Maharet. "I would destroy you if I could. I would hurt those you love."

There was a stunned silence. I could smell the fear of the others, though no one dared to move or speak.

Maharet nodded. She smiled knowingly.

"It is you who are arrogant," she answered. "It is you who have learned nothing. It is you who have not changed in six thousand years. It is your soul which remains unperfected, while mortals move to realms you will never grasp. In your isolation you dreamed dreams as thousands of mortals have done, protected from all scrutiny or challenge; and you emerge from your silence, ready to make these dreams real for the world? You bring them here to this table, among a handful of your fellow creatures, and they crumble. You cannot defend them. How could anyone defend them? And you tell us we deny what we see!"

Slowly Maharet rose from the chair. She leant forward slightly, her weight resting on her fingers as they touched the wood.

"Well, I'll tell you what I see," she went on. "Six thousand years ago, when men believed in spirits, an ugly and irreversible accident occurred; it was as awful in its own way as the monsters born now and then to mortals which nature does not suffer to live. But you, clinging to life, and clinging to your will, and clinging to your royal prerogative, refused to take that awful mistake with you to an early grave. To sanctify it, that was your purpose. To spin a great and glorious religion; and that is still your purpose now. But it was an accident finally, a distortion, and nothing more.

"And look now at the ages since that dark and evil moment; look at the other religions founded upon magic; founded upon some apparition or voice from the clouds! Founded upon the intervention of the supernatural in one guise or another—miracles, revelations, a mortal man rising from the dead!

"Look on the effect of your religions, those movements that have swept up millions with their fantastical claims. Look at what they have done to human history. Look at the wars fought on account of them; look at the persecutions, the massacres. Look at the pure enslavement of reason; look at the price of faith and zeal.

"And you tell us of children dying in the Eastern countries, in the name of Allah as the guns crackle and the bombs fall!

"And the war of which you speak in which one tiny European nation sought to exterminate a people. . . . In the name of what grand spiritual design for a new world was that done? And what does the world remember of it? The death camps, the ovens in which bodies were burnt by the thousands. The ideas are gone!

"I tell you, we would be hard put to determine what is more evil— religion or the pure idea. The intervention of the supernatural or the elegant simple abstract solution! Both have bathed this earth in suffering; both have brought the human race literally and figuratively to its knees.

"Don't *you* see? It is not man who is the enemy of the human species. It is the irrational; it is the spiritual when it is divorced from the material; from the lesson in one beating heart or one bleeding vein.

"You accuse us of greed. Ah, but our greed is our salvation. Because we know what we are; we know our limits and we know our sins; you have never known yours.

"You would begin it all again, wouldn't you? You would bring a new religion, a new revelation, a new wave of superstition and sacrifice and death."

"You lie," Akasha answered, her voice barely able to contain her fury. "You betray the very beauty I dream of; you betray it because you have no vision, you have no dreams."

"The beauty is out there!" Maharet said. "It does not deserve your violence! Are you so merciless that the lives you would destroy mean *nothing!* Ah, it was always so!"

The tension was unbearable. The blood sweat was breaking out on my body. I could see the panic all around. Louis had bowed his head and covered his face with his hands. Only the young Daniel seemed hopelessly enraptured. And Armand merely gazed at Akasha as if it were all out of his hands.

Akasha was silently struggling. But then she appeared to regain her conviction.

"You lie as you have always done," she said desperately. "But it does not matter whether you fight on my side. I will do what I mean to do; I will reach back over the millennia and I will redeem that long ago moment, that long ago evil which you and your sister brought into our land; I will reach back and raise it up in the eyes of the world until it becomes the Bethlehem of the new era; and peace on earth will exist at last. There is no great good that was ever done without sacrifice and courage. And if you all turn against me, if you all resist me, then I shall make of better mettle the angels I require."

"No, you will not do it," Maharet said.

"Akasha, please," Marius said. "Grant us time. Agree only to wait, to consider. Agree that nothing must come from this moment."

"Yes," I said. "Give us time. Come with me. Let us go together out there—you and I and Marius—out of dreams and visions and into the world itself."

"Oh, how you insult me and belittle me," she whispered. Her anger was turned on Marius but it was about to turn on me.

"There are so many things, so many places," he said, "that I want to show you! Only give me a chance. Akasha, for two thousand years I cared for you, I protected you . . ."

"You protected yourself! You protected the source of your power, the source of your evil!"

"I'm imploring you," Marius said. "I will get on my knees to you. A month only, to come with me, to let us talk together, to let us examine all the evidence . . ."

"So small, so selfish," Akasha whispered. "And you feel no debt to the world that made you what you are, no debt to give it now the benefit of your power, to alchemize yourselves from devils into gods!"

She turned to me suddenly, the shock spreading over her face.

"And you, my prince, who came into my chamber as if I were the Sleeping Beauty, who brought me to life again with your passionate kiss. Will you not reconsider? For my love!" The tears again were standing in her eyes. "Must you join with them now against me, too?" She reached up and placed her two hands on the sides of my face. "How can you betray me?" she said. "How can you betray such a dream? They are slothful beings; deceitful; full of malice. But your heart was pure. You had a courage that transcended pragmatism. You had your dreams too!"

I didn't have to answer. She knew. She could see it better perhaps than I could see it. And all I saw was the suffering in her black eyes. The pain, the incomprehension; and the grief she was already experiencing for me.

It seemed she couldn't move or speak suddenly. And there was nothing I could do now; nothing to save them; or me. I loved her! But I couldn't stand with her! Silently, I begged her to understand and forgive.

Her face was frozen, almost as if the voices had reclaimed her; it was as if I were standing before her throne in the path of her changeless gaze.

"I will kill you first, my prince," she said, her fingers caressing me all the more gently. "I want you gone from me. I will not look into your face and see this betrayal again."

"Harm him and that shall be our signal," Maharet whispered. "We shall move against you as one."

"And you move against yourselves!" she answered, glancing at Maharet. "When I finish with this one I love, I shall kill those you love; those who should have been dead already; I shall destroy all those whom I can destroy; but who shall destroy me?"

"Akasha," Marius whispered. He rose and came towards her; but she moved in the blink of an eye and knocked him to the floor. I heard him cry out as he fell. Santino went to his aid.

Again, she looked at me; and her hands closed on my shoulders, gentle and loving as before. And through the veil of my tears, I saw her smile sadly. "My prince, my beautiful prince," she said.

Khayman rose from the table. Eric rose. And Mael. And then the young ones rose, and lastly Pandora, who moved to Marius's side.

She released me. And she too rose to her feet. The night was so quiet suddenly that the forest seemed to sigh against the glass.

And this is what I've wrought, I who alone remained seated, looking not at any of them, but at nothing. At the small glittering sweep of my life, my little triumphs, my little tragedies, my dreams of waking the goddess, my dreams of goodness, and of fame.

What was she doing? Assessing their power? Looking from one to the other, and then back to me. A stranger looking down from some lofty height. And so now the fire comes, Lestat. Don't dare to look at Gabrielle or Louis, lest she turn it that way. Die first, like a coward, and then you don't have to see them die.

And the awful part is, you won't know who wins finally—whether or not she triumphs, or we all go down together. Just like not knowing what it was all about, or why, or what the hell the dream of the twins meant, or how this whole world came into being. You just won't ever know.

I was weeping now and she was weeping and she was that tender fragile being again, the being I had held on Saint-Domingue, the one who needed me, but that weakness wasn't destroying her after all, though it would certainly destroy me.

"Lestat," she whispered as if in disbelief.

"I can't follow you," I said, my voice breaking. Slowly I rose to my feet. "We're not angels, Akasha; we are not gods. To be human, that's what most of us long for. It is the human which has become myth to us."

It was killing me to look at her. I thought of her blood flowing into me; of the powers she'd given me. Of what it had been like to travel with her through the clouds. I thought of the euphoria in the Haitian village when the women had come with their candles, singing their hymns.

"But that is what it will be, my beloved," she whispered. "Find your courage! It's there." The blood tears were coursing down her face. Her lip trembled and the smooth flesh of her forehead was creased with those perfectly straight lines of utter distress.

Then she straightened. She looked away from me: and her face went blank and beautifully smooth again. She looked past us, and I felt she was reaching for the strength to do it, and the others had better act fast. I wished for that—like sticking a dagger into her; they had better bring her down now, and I could feel the tears sliding down my face.

But something else was happening. There was a great soft musical sound from somewhere. Glass shattering, a great deal of glass. There was a sudden obvious excitement in Daniel. In Jesse. But the old ones stood frozen, listening. Again, glass breaking; someone entering by one of the many portals of this rambling house.

She took a step back. She quickened as if seeing a vision; and a loud hollow sound filled the stairwell beyond the open door. Someone down below in the passage.

She moved away from the table, towards the fireplace. She seemed for all the world afraid.

Was that possible? Did she know who was coming, and was it another old one? And was that what she feared—that more could accomplish what these few could not?

It was nothing so calculated finally; I knew it; she was being defeated inside. All courage was leaving her. It was the need, the loneliness, after all! It had begun with my resistance, and they had deepened it, and then I had dealt her yet another blow. And now she was transfixed by this loud, echoing, and impersonal noise. Yet she did know who this person was, I could sense it. And the others knew too.

The noise was growing louder. The visitor was coming up the stairs. The skylight and the old iron pylons reverberated with the shock of each heavy step.

"But who is it!" I said suddenly. I could stand it no longer. There was that image again, that image of the mother's body and the twins.

"Akasha!" Marius said. "Give us the time we ask for. Forswear the moment. That is enough!"

"Enough for what!" she cried sharply, almost savagely.

"For our lives, Akasha," he said. "For *all* our lives!"

I heard Khayman laugh softly, the one who hadn't spoken even once.

The steps had reached the landing.

Maharet stood at the edge of the open doorway, and Mael was beside her. I hadn't even seen them move.

Then I saw who and what it was. The woman I'd glimpsed moving through the jungles, clawing her way out of the earth, walking the long

miles on the barren plain. The other twin of the dreams I'd never understood! And now she stood framed in the dim light from the stairwell,
staring straight at the distant figure of Akasha, who stood some thirty feet
away with her back to the glass wall and the blazing fire.

Oh, but the sight of this one. Gasps came from the others, even from
the old ones, from Marius himself.

A thin layer of soil encased her all over, even the rippling shape of her
long hair. Broken, peeling, stained by the rain even, the mud still clung to
her, clung to her naked arms and bare feet as if she were made of it, made
of earth itself. It made a mask of her face. And her eyes peered out of the
mask, naked, rimmed in red. A rag covered her, a blanket filthy and torn,
and tied with a hemp rope around her waist.

What impulse could make such a being cover herself, what tender
human modesty had caused this living corpse to stop and make this simple
garment, what suffering remnant of the human heart?

Beside her, staring at her, Maharet appeared to weaken suddenly all
over as if her slender body were going to drop.

"Mekare!" she whispered.

But the woman didn't see her or hear her; the woman stared at Akasha,
the eyes gleaming with fearless animal cunning as Akasha moved back
towards the table, putting the table between herself and this creature,
Akasha's face hardening, her eyes full of undisguised hate.

"Mekare!" Maharet cried. She threw out her hands and tried to catch
the woman by the shoulders and turn her around.

The woman's right hand went out, shoving Maharet backwards so
that she was thrown yards across the room until she tumbled against the
wall.

The great sheet of plate glass vibrated, but did not shatter. Gingerly
Maharet touched it with her fingers; then with the fluid grace of a cat, she
sprang up and into the arms of Eric, who was rushing to her aid.

Instantly he pulled her back towards the door. For the woman now
struck the enormous table and sent it sliding northward, and then over on
its side.

Gabrielle and Louis moved swiftly into the northwest corner, Santino
and Armand the other way, towards Mael and Eric and Maharet.

Those of us on the other side merely backed away, except for Jesse,
who had moved towards the door.

She stood beside Khayman and as I looked at him now I saw with
amazement that he wore a thin, bitter smile.

"The curse, my Queen," he said, his voice rising sharply to fill the
room.

The woman froze as she heard him behind her. But she did not turn around.

And Akasha, her face shimmering in the firelight, quavered visibly, and the tears flowed again.

"All against me, all of you!" she said. "Not a one who would come to my side!" She stared at me, even as the woman moved towards her.

The woman's muddy feet scraped the carpet, her mouth gaping and her hands only slightly poised, her arms still down at her sides. Yet it was the perfect attitude of menace as she took one slow step after another.

But again Khayman spoke, bringing her suddenly to a halt.

In another language, he cried out, his voice gaining volume until it was a roar. And only the dimmest translation of it came clear to me.

"Queen of the Damned . . . hour of worst menace . . . I shall rise to stop you. . . ." I understood. It had been Mekare's—the woman's—prophecy and curse. And everyone here knew it, understood it. It had to do with that strange, inexplicable dream.

"Oh, no, my children!" Akasha screamed suddenly. "It is not finished!"

I could feel her collecting her powers; I could see it, her body tensing, breasts thrust forward, her hands rising as if reflexively, fingers curled.

The woman was struck by it, shoved backwards, but instantly resisted. And then she too straightened, her eyes widening, and she rushed forward so swiftly I couldn't follow it, her hands out for the Queen.

I saw her fingers, caked with mud, streaking towards Akasha; I saw Akasha's face as she was caught by her long black hair. I heard her scream. Then I saw her profile, as her head struck the western window and shattered it, the glass crashing down in great dagged shards.

A violent shock passed through me; I could neither breathe nor move. I was falling to the floor. I couldn't control my limbs. Akasha's headless body was sliding down the fractured glass wall, the shards still falling around it. Blood streamed down the broken glass behind her. And the woman held Akasha's severed head by the hair!

Akasha's black eyes blinked, widened. Her mouth opened as if to scream again.

And then the light was going out all around me; it was as if the fire had been extinguished, only it hadn't, and as I rolled over on the carpet, crying, my hand clawing at it involuntarily, I saw the distant flames through a dark rosy haze.

I tried to lift my weight. I couldn't. I could hear Marius calling to me, Marius silently calling only my name.

Then I was rising, just a little, and all my weight pressed against my aching arms and hands.

Akasha's eyes were fixed on me. Her head was lying there almost within my reach, and the body lay on its back, blood gushing from the stump of the neck. Suddenly the right arm quivered; it was lifted, then it flopped back down to the floor. Then it rose again, the hand dangling. It was reaching for the head!

I could help it! I could use the powers she'd given me to try to move it, to help it reach the head. And as I struggled to see in the dimming light, the body lurched, shivered, and flopped down closer to the head.

But the twins! They were beside the head and the body. Mekare, staring at the head dully, with those vacant red-rimmed eyes. And Maharet, as if with the last breath in her, kneeling now beside her sister, over the body of the Mother, as the room grew darker and colder, and Akasha's face began to grow pale and ghostly white as if all the light inside were going out.

I should have been afraid; I should have been in terror; the cold was creeping over me, and I could hear my own choking sobs. But the strangest elation overcame me; I realized suddenly what I was seeing:

"It's the dream," I said. Far away I could hear my own voice. "The twins and the body of the Mother, do you see it! The image from the dream!"

Blood spread out from Akasha's head into the weave of the carpet; Maharet was sinking down, her hands out flat, and Mekare too had weakened and bent down over the body, but it was still the same image, and I knew why I'd seen it now, I knew what it meant!

"The funeral feast!" Marius cried. "The heart and the brain, one of you—take them into yourself. It is the only chance."

Yes, that was it. And they knew! No one had to tell them. They knew!

That was the meaning! And they'd all seen it, and they all knew. Even as my eyes were closing, I realized it; and this lovely feeling deepened, this sense of completeness, of something finished at last. Of something known!

Then I was floating, floating in the ice cold darkness again as if I were in Akasha's arms, and we were rising into the stars.

A sharp crackling sound brought me back. Not dead yet, but dying. And where are those I love?

Fighting for life still, I tried to open my eyes; it seemed impossible. But then I saw them in the thickening gloom—the two of them, their red hair catching the hazy glow of the fire; the one holding the bloody brain in her mud-covered fingers, and the other, the dripping heart. All but dead they were, their own eyes glassy, their limbs moving as if through water. And Akasha stared forward still, her mouth open, the blood gushing from her shattered skull. Mekare lifted the brain to her mouth; Maharet put the heart in her other hand; Mekare took them both into herself.

Darkness again; no firelight; no point of reference; no sensation except pain; pain all through the thing that I was which had no limbs, no eyes, no mouth to speak. Pain, throbbing, electrical; and no way to move to lessen it, to push it this way, or that way, or tense against it, or fade into it. Just pain.

Yet I was moving. I was thrashing about on the floor. Through the pain I could feel the carpet suddenly; I could feel my feet digging at it as if I were trying to climb a steep cliff. And then I heard the unmistakable sound of the fire near me; and I felt the wind gusting through the broken window, and I smelled all those soft sweet scents from the forest rushing into the room. A violent shock coursed through me, through every muscle and pore, my arms and legs flailing. Then still.

The pain was gone.

I lay there gasping, staring at the brilliant reflection of the fire in the glass ceiling, and feeling the air fill my lungs, and I realized I was crying again, brokenheartedly, like a child.

The twins knelt with their backs to us; and they had their arms around each other, and their heads were together, their hair mingling, as they caressed each other, gently, tenderly, as if talking through touch alone.

I couldn't muffle my sobs. I turned over and drew my arm up under my face and just wept.

Marius was near me. And so was Gabrielle. I wanted to take Gabrielle into my arms. I wanted to say all the things I knew I should say—that it was over and we had survived it, and it was finished—but I couldn't.

Then slowly I turned my head and looked at Akasha's face again, her face still intact, though all the dense, shining whiteness was gone, and she was as pale, as translucent as glass! Even her eyes, her beautiful ink black eyes were becoming transparent, as if there were no pigment in them; it had all been the blood.

Her hair lay soft and silken beneath her cheek, and the dried blood was lustrous and ruby red.

I couldn't stop crying. I didn't want to. I started to say her name and it caught in my throat. It was as if I shouldn't do it. I never should have. I never should have gone up those marble steps and kissed her face in the shrine.

They were all coming to life again, the others. Armand was holding Daniel and Louis, who were both groggy and unable yet to stand; and Khayman had come forward with Jesse beside him, and the others were all right too. Pandora, trembling, her mouth twisted with her crying, stood far apart, hugging herself as if she were cold.

And the twins turned around and stood up now, Maharet's arm around Mekare. And Mekare stared forward, expressionless, uncomprehending, the living statue; and Maharet said:

"Behold. The Queen of the Damned."

PART V

...WORLD WITHOUT END, AMEN

Some things lighten nightfall
and make a Rembrandt of a grief.
But mostly the swiftness of time
is a joke; on us. The flame-moth
is unable to laugh. What luck.
The myths are dead.
. . . .

STAN RICE
"Poem on Crawling into Bed: Bitterness"
Body of Work (1983)

MIAMI.

A vampire's city—hot, teeming, and embracingly beautiful. Melting pot, marketplace, playground. Where the desperate and the greedy are locked in subversive commerce, and the sky belongs to everyone, and the beach goes on forever; and the lights outshine the heavens, and the sea is as warm as blood.

Miami. The happy hunting ground of the devil.

That's why we are here, in Armand's large, graceful white villa on the Night Island, surrounded by every conceivable luxury, and the wide open southern night.

Out there, across the water, Miami beckons; victims just waiting: the pimps, the thieves, the dope kings, and the killers. The nameless ones; so many who are almost as bad as I am, but not quite.

Armand had gone over at sunset with Marius; and they were back now, Armand playing chess with Santino in the drawing room, Marius reading as he did constantly, in the leather chair by the window over the beach.

Gabrielle had not appeared yet this evening; since Jesse left, she was frequently alone.

Khayman sat in the downstairs study talking with Daniel now, Daniel who liked to let the hunger build, Daniel who wanted to know all about what it had been like in ancient Miletus, and Athens, and Troy. Oh, don't forget Troy. I myself was vaguely intrigued by the idea of Troy.

I liked Daniel. Daniel who might go with me later if I asked him; if I could bring myself to leave this island, which I have done only once since I arrived. Daniel who still laughed at the path the moon made over the water, or the warm spray in his face. For Daniel, all of it—her death even—had been spectacle. But he cannot be blamed for that.

Pandora almost never moved from the television screen. Marius had brought her the stylish modern garments she wore; satin shirt, boots to the knee, cleaving velvet skirt. He'd put the bracelets on her arms, and the rings on her fingers, and each evening he brushed her long brown hair. Sometimes he presented her with little gifts of perfume. If he did not open them for her, they lay on the table untouched. She stared the way Armand did at the endless progression of video movies, only now and then breaking off to go to the piano in the music room and play softly for a little while.

I liked her playing; rather like the Art of the Fugue, her seamless variations. But she worried me; the others didn't. The others had all recovered from what had happened, more quickly than I had ever imagined they could. She'd been damaged in some crucial way before it all began.

Yet she liked it here; I knew she did. How could she not like it? Even though she never listened to a word that Marius said.

We all liked it. Even Gabrielle.

White rooms filled with gorgeous Persian carpets and endlessly intriguing paintings—Matisse, Monet, Picasso, Giotto, Géricault. One could spend a century merely looking at the paintings; Armand was constantly changing them, shifting their positions, bringing up some new treasure from the cellar, slipping in little sketches here and there.

Jesse had loved it here too, though she was gone now, to join Maharet in Rangoon.

She had come here into my study and told me her side of it very directly, asking me to change the names she'd used and to leave out the Talamasca altogether, which of course I wouldn't do. I'd sat silently, scanning her mind as she talked, for all the little things she was leaving out. Then I'd poured it into the computer, while she sat watching, thinking, staring at the dark gray velvet curtains, and the Venetian clock; and the cool colors of the Morandi on the wall.

I think she knew I wouldn't do what she told me to do. She also knew it wouldn't matter. People weren't likely to believe in the Talamasca any more than they would ever believe in us. That is, unless David Talbot or Aaron Lightner came to call on them the way that Aaron had called on Jesse.

As for the Great Family, well, it wasn't likely that any of them would think it more than a fiction, with a touch here and there of truth; that is, if they ever happened to pick up the book.

That's what everybody had thought of *Interview with the Vampire* and my autobiography, and they would think it about *The Queen of the Damned* too.

And that's how it should be. Even I agree with that now. Maharet was right. No room for us; no room for God or the Devil; it should be metaphor—the supernatural—whether it's High Mass at St. Patrick's Cathedral, or Faust selling his soul in an opera, or a rock star pretending to be the Vampire Lestat.

NOBODY knew where Maharet had taken Mekare. Even Eric probably didn't know now either, though he'd left with them, promising to meet Jesse in Rangoon.

Before she left the Sonoma compound, Maharet had startled me with a little whisper: "Get it straight when you tell it—the Legend of the Twins."

That was permission, wasn't it? Or cosmic indifference, I'm not sure which. I'd said nothing about the book to anyone; I'd only brooded on it in those long painful hours when I couldn't really think, except in terms of chapters: an ordering; a road map through the mystery; a chronicle of seduction and pain.

Maharet had looked worldly yet mysterious that last evening, coming to find me in the forest, garmented in black and wearing her fashionable paint, as she called it—the skillful cosmetic mask that made her into an alluring mortal woman who could move with only admiring glances through the real world. What a tiny waist she had, and such long hands, even more graceful, it seemed, for the tight black kid gloves she wore. So carefully she had stepped through the ferns and past the tender saplings, when she might have pushed the trees themselves out of her path.

She'd been to San Francisco with Jessica and Gabrielle; they had walked past houses with cheerful lights; on clean narrow pavements; where people lived, she'd said. How crisp her speech had been, how effortlessly contemporary; not like the timeless woman I had first encountered in the mountaintop room.

And why was I alone again, she'd asked, sitting by myself near the little creek that ran through the thick of the redwoods? Why would I not talk to the others, even a little? Did I know how protective and fearful they were?

They are still asking me those questions now.

Even Gabrielle, who in the main never bothers with questions, never says much of anything. They want to know when I'm going to recover, when I'm going to talk about what happened, when I'm going to stop writing all through the night.

Maharet had said that we would see her again very soon. In the spring perhaps we should come to her house in Burma. Or maybe she'd surprise us one evening. But the point was, we were never to be isolated from one another; we had ways to find each other, no matter where we might roam.

Yes, on that vital point at least everyone had agreed. Even Gabrielle, the loner, the wanderer, had agreed.

Nobody wanted to be lost in time again.

And Mekare? Would we see her again? Would she ever sit with us around a table? Speak to us with a language of gestures and signs?

I had laid eyes upon her only once after that terrible night. And it had been entirely unexpected, as I came through the forest, back to the compound, in the soft purple light just before dawn.

There had been a mist crawling over the earth, thinning above the ferns and the few scattered winter wild flowers, and then paling utterly into phosphorescence as it rose among the giant trees.

And the twins had come through the mist together, walking down into the creek bed to make their way along the stones, arms locked around each other, Mekare in a long wool gown as beautiful as her sister's, her hair brushed and shining as it hung down around her shoulders and over her breasts.

It seemed Maharet had been speaking softly in Mekare's ear. And it was Mekare who stopped to look at me, her green eyes wide and her face for one moment unaccountably frightening in its blankness, as I'd felt my grief like a scorching wind on my heart.

I'd stood entranced looking at her, at both of them, the pain in me suffocating, as if my lungs were being dried up.

I don't know what my thoughts were; only that the pain seemed unbearable. And that Maharet had made some little tender motion to me of greeting, and that I should go my way. Morning coming. The forest was waking all around us. Our precious moments slipping by. My pain had been finally loosened, like a moan coming out of me, and I'd let it go as I'd turned away.

I'd glanced back once to see the two figures moving eastward, down the rippling silver creek bed, swallowed as it were by the roaring music of the water that followed its relentless path through the scattered rocks.

The old image of the dream had faded just a little. And when I think of them now, I think not of the funeral feasts but of that moment, the two sylphs in the forest, only nights before Maharet left the Sonoma compound taking Mekare away.

I was glad when they were gone because it meant that we would be going. And I did not care if I ever saw the Sonoma compound again. My sojourn there had been agony, though the first few nights after the catastrophe had been the worst.

How quickly the bruised silence of the others had given way to endless analysis, as they strained to interpret what they'd seen and felt. How had the thing been transferred exactly? Had it abandoned the tissues of the brain as they disintegrated, racing through Mekare's bloodstream until it found the like organ in her? Had the heart mattered at all?

Molecular; nucleonic; solitons; protoplasm; glittering modern words! Come now, we are vampires! We thrive on the blood of the living; we kill; and we love it. Whether we need to do it or not.

I couldn't bear to listen to them; I couldn't bear their silent yet obsessive curiosity: *What was it like with her? What did you do in those few nights?* I couldn't get away from them either; I certainly hadn't the will to leave altogether; I trembled when I was with them; trembled when I was apart.

The forest wasn't deep enough for me; I'd roamed for miles through the mammoth redwoods, and then through scrub oaks and open fields and into dank impassable woods again. No getting away from their voices: Louis confessing how he had lost consciousness during those awful moments; Daniel saying that he had heard our voices, yet seen nothing; Jesse, in Khayman's arms, had witnessed it all.

How often they had pondered the irony—that Mekare had brought down her enemy with a human gesture; that, knowing nothing of invisible powers, she had struck out as any human might, but with inhuman speed and strength.

Had any of *her* survived in Mekare? That was what I kept wondering. Forget the "poetry of science" as Maharet had called it. That was what I wanted to know. Or had her soul been released at last when the brain was torn loose?

Sometimes in the dark, in the honeycombed cellar with its tin-plated walls and its countless impersonal chambers, I'd wake, certain that she was right there beside me, no more than an inch from my face; I'd feel her hair again; her arm around me; I'd see the black glimmer of her eye. I'd grope in the darkness; nothing but the damp brick walls.

Then I'd lie there and think of poor little Baby Jenks, as *she* had shown her to me, spiraling upwards; I'd see the varicolored lights enveloping Baby Jenks as she looked down on the earth for the last time. How could Baby Jenks, the poor biker child, have invented such a vision? Maybe we do go home, finally.

How can we know?

And so we remain immortal; we remain frightened; we remain anchored to what we can control. It all starts again; the wheel turns; we are *the* vampires; because there are no others; the new coven is formed.

LIKE a gypsy caravan we left the Sonoma compound, a parade of shining black cars streaking through the American night at lethal speed on immaculate roads. It was on that long ride that they told me everything—spontaneously and sometimes unwittingly as they conversed with one another. Like a mosaic it came together, all that had gone before. Even when I dozed against the blue velvet upholstery, I heard them, saw what they had seen.

Down to the swamplands of south Florida; down to the great decadent city of Miami, parody of both heaven and hell.

Immediately I locked myself in this little suite of tastefully appointed rooms; couches, carpet, the pale pastel paintings of Piero della Francesca; computer on the table; the music of Vivaldi pouring from tiny speakers hidden in the papered walls. Private stairway to the cellar, where in the steel-lined crypt the coffin waited: black lacquer; brass handles; a match and the stub of a candle; lining stitched with white lace.

Blood lust; how it hurt; but you don't need it; yet you can't resist it; and it's going to be like this forever; you never get rid of it; you want it even more than before.

When I wasn't writing, I lay on the gray brocade divan, watching the palm fronds move in the breeze from the terrace, listening to their voices below.

Louis begging Jesse politely to describe one more time the apparition of Claudia. And Jesse's voice, solicitous, confidential: "But Louis, it wasn't real."

Gabrielle missed Jesse now that she was gone; Jesse and Gabrielle had walked on the beach for hours. It seemed not a word passed between them; but then, how could I be sure?

Gabrielle was doing more and more little things to make me happy: wearing her hair brushed free because she knew I loved it; coming up to my room before she vanished with the morning. Now and then she'd look at me, probing, anxious.

"You want to leave here, don't you?" I'd ask fearfully; or something like it.

"No," she said. "I like it here. It suits me." When she got restless now she went to the islands, which weren't so very far away. She rather liked the islands. But that wasn't what she wanted to talk about. There was always something else on her mind. Once she had almost voiced it. "But tell me . . ." And then she'd stopped.

"Did I love her?" I asked. "Is that what you want to know? Yes, I loved her."

And I still couldn't say her name.

MAEL came and went.

Gone for a week; here again tonight—downstairs—trying to draw

Khayman into conversation; Khayman, who fascinated everybody. First Brood. All that power. And to think, he had walked the streets of Troy.

The sight of him was continuously startling, if that is not a contradiction in terms.

He went to great lengths to appear human. In a warm place like this, where heavy garments are conspicuous, it isn't an easy thing. Sometimes he covered himself with a darkening pigment—burnt sienna mixed with a little scented oil. It seemed a crime to do so, to mar the beauty; but how else could he slice through the human crowd like a greased knife?

Now and then he knocked on my door. "Are you ever coming out?" he would ask. He'd look at the stack of pages beside the computer; the black letters: *The Queen of the Damned.* He'd stand there, letting me search his mind for all the little fragments, half-remembered moments; he didn't care. I seemed to puzzle him, but why I couldn't imagine. What did he want from me? Then he'd smile that shocking saintly smile.

Sometimes he took the boat out—Armand's black racer—and he let it drift in the Gulf as he lay under the stars. Once Gabrielle went with him, and I was tempted to listen to them, over all that distance, their voices so private and intimate. But I hadn't done it. Just didn't seem fair.

Sometimes he said he feared the memory loss; that it would come suddenly, and he wouldn't be able to find his way home to us. But then it had come in the past on account of pain, and he was so happy. He wanted us to know it; so happy to be with us all.

It seemed they'd reached some kind of agreement down there—that no matter where they went, they would always come back. This would be the coven house, the sanctuary; never would it be as it had been before.

They were settling a lot of things. Nobody was to make any others, and nobody was to write any more books, though of course they knew that was exactly what I was doing, gleaning from them silently everything that I could; and that I didn't intend to obey any rules imposed on me by anybody, and that I never had.

They were relieved that the Vampire Lestat had died in the pages of the newspapers; that the debacle of the concert had been forgotten. No provable fatalities, no true injuries; everybody bought off handsomely; the band, receiving my share of everything, was touring again under its old name.

And the riots—the brief era of miracles—they too had been forgotten, though they might never be satisfactorily explained.

No, no more revelations, disruptions, interventions; that was their collective vow; and please cover up the kill.

They kept impressing that upon the delirious Daniel, that even in a great festering urban wilderness like Miami, one could not be too careful with the remnants of the meal.

Ah, Miami. I could hear it again, the low roar of so many desperate humans; the churning of all those machines both great and small. Earlier I had let its voices sweep over me, as I'd lain stock-still on the divan. It was not impossible for me to direct this power; to sift and focus, and amplify an entire chorus of different sounds. Yet I drew back from it, unable yet to really use it with conviction, just as I couldn't use my new strength.

Ah, but I loved being near to this city. Loved its sleaze and glamour; the old ramshackle hotels and spangled high rises; its sultry winds; its flagrant decay. I listened now to that never ending urban music, a low throbbing hum.

"Why don't you go there, then?"

Marius.

I looked up from the computer. Slowly, just to needle him a little, though he was the most patient of immortal men.

He stood against the frame of the terrace door, with his arms folded, one ankle crossed over the other. The lights out there behind him. In the ancient world had there been anything like it? The spectacle of an electrified city, dense with towers glowing like narrow grids in an old gas fire?

He'd clipped his hair short; he wore plain yet elegant twentieth-century clothes: gray silk blazer and pants, and the red this time, for there was always red, was the dark turtleneck shirt.

"I want you to put the book aside and come join us," he said. "You've been locked in here for over a month."

"I go out now and then," I said. I liked looking at him, at the neon blue of his eyes.

"This book," he said. "What's the purpose of it? Would you tell me that much?"

I didn't answer. He pushed a little harder, tactful though the tone was.

"Wasn't it enough, the songs and the autobiography?"

I tried to decide what made him look so amiable really. Maybe it was the tiny lines that still came to life around his eyes, the little crinkling of flesh that came and went as he spoke.

Big wide eyes like Khayman's had a stunning effect.

I looked back at the computer screen. Electronic image of language. Almost finished. And they all knew about it; they'd known all along. That's why they volunteered so much information: knocking, coming in, talking, then going away.

"So why talk about it?" I asked. "I want to make the record of what happened. You knew that when you told me what it had been like for you."

"Yes, but for whom is this record being made?"

I thought of all the fans again in the auditorium; the visibility; and then those ghastly moments, at her side, in the villages, when I'd been a god without a name. I was cold suddenly in spite of the caressing warmth, the breeze that came in from the water. Had she been right when she called us selfish, greedy? When she'd said it was self-serving of us to want the world to remain the same?

"You know the answer to that question," he said. He drew a little closer. He put his hand on the back of my chair.

"It was a foolish dream, wasn't it?" I asked. It hurt to say it. "It could never have been realized, not even if we had proclaimed her the goddess and obeyed her every command."

"It was madness," he answered. "They would have stopped her; destroyed her; more quickly than she ever dreamed."

Silence.

"The world would not have *wanted* her," he added. "That's what she could never comprehend."

"I think in the end she knew it; no place for her; no way for her to have value and be the thing that she was. She knew it when she looked into our eyes and saw the wall there which she could never breach. She'd been so careful with her visitations, choosing places as primitive and changeless as she was herself."

He nodded. "As I said, you know the answers to your questions. So why do you continue to ask them? Why do you lock yourself here with your grief?"

I didn't say anything. I saw her eyes again. *Why can't you believe in me!*

"Have you forgiven me for all of it?" I asked suddenly.

"You weren't to blame," he said. "She was waiting, listening. Sooner or later something would have stirred the will in her. The danger was always there. It was as much an accident as the beginning, really, that she woke when she did." He sighed. He sounded bitter again, the way he'd been in the first nights after, when he had grieved too. "I always knew the danger," he murmured. "Maybe I wanted to believe she was a goddess; until she woke. Until she spoke to me. Until she smiled."

He was off again, thinking of the moment before the ice had fallen and pinned him helplessly for so long.

He moved away, slowly, indecisively, and then went out onto the terrace and looked down at the beach. Such a casual way of moving. Had the ancient ones rested their elbows like that on stone railings?

I got up and went after him. I looked across the great divide of black water. At the shimmering reflection of the skyline. I looked at him.

"Do you know what it's like, not to carry that burden?" he whispered. "To know now for the first time that I am free?"

I didn't answer. But I could most certainly feel it. Yet I was afraid for him, afraid perhaps that it had been the anchor, as the Great Family was the anchor for Maharet.

"No," he said quickly, shaking his head. "It's as if a curse has been removed. I wake; I think I must go down to the shrine; I must burn the incense; bring the flowers; I must stand before them and speak to them; and try to comfort them if they are suffering inside. Then I realize that they're gone. It's over, finished. I'm free to go wherever I would go and do whatever I would like." He paused, reflecting, looking at the lights again. Then, "What about you? Why aren't you free too? I wish I understood you."

"You do. You always have," I said. I shrugged.

"You're burning with dissatisfaction. And we can't comfort you, can we? It's *their* love you want." He made a little gesture towards the city.

"You comfort me," I answered. "All of you. I couldn't think of leaving you, not for very long, anyway. But you know, when I was on that stage in San Francisco . . ." I didn't finish. What was the use of saying it, if he didn't know. It had been everything I'd ever wanted it to be until the great whirlwind had descended and carried me away.

"Even though they never believed you?" he asked. "They thought you were merely a clever performer? An author with a hook, as they say?"

"They knew my name!" I answered. "It was *my* voice they heard. They saw *me* up there above the footlights."

He nodded. "And so the book, *The Queen of the Damned*," he said.

No answer.

"Come down with us. Let us try to keep you company. Talk to us about what took place."

"You saw what took place."

I felt a little confusion suddenly; a curiosity in him that he was reluctant to reveal. He was still looking at me.

I thought of Gabrielle, the way she would start to ask me questions and stop. Then I realized. Why, I'd been a fool not to see it before. They wanted to know what powers she'd given me; they wanted to know how much her blood had affected me; and all this time I'd kept those secrets locked inside. I kept them locked there now. Along with the image of those dead bodies strewn throughout Azim's temple; along with the memory of the ecstasy I'd felt when I'd slain every man in my path. And along with yet another awful and unforgettable moment: her death, when I had failed to use the gifts to help her!

And now it started again, the obsession with the end. Had she seen me lying there so close to her? Had she known of my refusal to aid her? Or had her soul risen when the first blow was struck?

Marius looked out over the water, at the tiny boats speeding towards the harbor to the south. He was thinking of how many centuries it had taken him to acquire the powers he now possessed. Infusions of her blood alone had not done it. Only after a thousand years had he been able to rise towards the clouds as if he were one of them, unfettered, unafraid. He was thinking of how such things vary from one immortal to another; how no one knows what power is locked inside another; no one knows perhaps what power is locked within oneself.

All very polite; but I could not confide in him or anyone just yet.

"Look," I said. "Let me mourn just a little while more. Let me create my dark images here, and have the written words for friends. Then later I'll come to you; I'll join you all. Maybe I'll obey the rules. Some of them, anyway, who knows? What are you going to do if I don't, by the way, and haven't I asked you this before?"

He was clearly startled.

"You are the damnedest creature!" he whispered. "You make me think of the old story about Alexander the Great. He wept when there were no more worlds to conquer. Will you weep when there are no more rules to break?"

"Ah, but there are always rules to break."

He laughed under his breath. "Burn the book."

"No."

We looked at each other for a moment; then I embraced him, tightly and warmly, and I smiled. I didn't even know why I'd done it, except that he was so patient and so earnest, and there had been some profound change in him as there had been in all of us, but with him it was dark and hurtful as it had been with me.

It had to do with the whole struggle of good and evil which he understood exactly the way I did, because he was the one who had taught me to understand it years ago. He was the one who had told me how we must wrestle forever with those questions, how the simple solution was not what we wanted, but what we must always fear.

I'd embraced him also because I loved him and wanted to be near to him, and I didn't want him to leave just now, angry or disappointed in me.

"You will obey the rules, won't you?" he asked suddenly. Mixture of menace and sarcasm. And maybe a little affection, too.

"Of course!" Again I shrugged. "What are they, by the way? I've forgotten. Oh, we don't make any new vampires; we do not wander off without a trace; we cover up the kill."

"You are an imp, Lestat, you know it? A brat."

"Let me ask you a question," I said. I made my hand into a fist and touched him lightly on the arm. "That painting of yours, *The Temptation of Amadeo,* the one in the Talamasca crypt . . ."

"Yes?"

"Wouldn't you like to have it back?"

"Ye gods, no. It's a dreary thing, really. My black period, you might say. But I do wish they'd take it out of the damned cellar. You know, hang it in the front hall? Some decent place."

I laughed.

Suddenly he became serious. Suspicious.

"Lestat!" he said sharply.

"Yes, Marius."

"You leave the Talamasca alone!"

"Of course!" Another shrug. Another smile. Why not?

"I mean it, Lestat. I'm quite serious. Do not meddle with the Talamasca. Do we understand each other, you and I?"

"Marius, you are remarkably easy to understand. Did you hear that? The clock's striking midnight. I always take my little walk around the Night Island now. Do you want to come?"

I didn't wait for him to answer. I heard him give one of those lovely forbearing sighs of his as I went out the door.

MIDNIGHT. The Night Island sang. I walked through the crowded galleria. Denim jacket, white T-shirt, face half covered by giant dark glasses; hands shoved into the pockets of my jeans. I watched the hungry shoppers dipping into the open doorways, perusing stacks of shining luggage, silk shirts in plastic, a sleek black manikin swathed in mink.

Beside the shimmering fountain, with its dancing plumes of myriad droplets, an old woman sat curled on a bench, paper cup of steaming coffee in her trembling hand. Hard for her to raise it to her lips; when I smiled as I passed she said in a quavering voice: "When you're old you don't need sleep anymore."

A soft whoozy music gushed out of the cocktail lounge. The young toughs prowled the video emporium; blood lust! The raucous zip and flash of the arcade died as I turned my head away. Through the door of the French restaurant I caught the swift beguiling movement of a woman lifting a glass of champagne; muted laughter. The theater was full of black and white giants speaking French.

A young woman passed me; dark skin, voluptuous hips, little pout of a mouth. The blood lust crested. I walked on, forcing it back into its cage. *Do not need the blood. Strong now as the old ones.* But I could taste it; I glanced back at her, saw her seated on the stone bench, naked knees jutting from her tight little skirt; eyes fixed on me.

Oh, Marius was right about it; right about everything. I was burning with dissatisfaction; burning with loneliness. I want to pull her up off that bench: *Do you know what I am!* No, don't settle for the other; don't lure her out of here, don't do it; don't take her down on the white sands, far beyond the lights of the galleria, where the rocks are dangerous and the waves are breaking violently in the little cove.

I thought of what *she* had said to us, about our selfishness, our greed! Taste of blood on my tongue. Someone's going to die if I linger here. . . .

End of the corridor. I put my key into the steel door between the shop that sold Chinese rugs made by little girls and the tobacconist who slept now among the Dutch pipes, his magazine over his face.

Silent hallway into the bowels of the villa.

One of them was playing the piano. I listened for a long moment. Pandora, and the music as always had a dark sweet luster, but it was more than ever like an endless beginning—a theme ever building to a climax which would never come.

I went up the stairs and into the living room. Ah, you can tell this is a vampire house; who else could live by starlight and the glow of a few scattered candles? Luster of marble and velvet. Shock of Miami out there where the lights never go out.

Armand still playing chess with Khayman and losing. Daniel lay under the earphones listening to Bach, now and then glancing to the black and white board to see if a piece had been moved.

On the terrace, looking out over the water, her thumbs hooked in her back pockets, Gabrielle stood. Alone. I went out to her, kissed her cheek, and looked into her eyes; and when I finally won the begrudging little smile I needed, then I turned and wandered back into the house.

Marius in the black leather chair reading the newspaper, folding it as a gentleman might in a private club.

"Louis is gone," he said, without looking up from the paper.

"What do you mean, gone?"

"To New Orleans," Armand said without looking up from the chessboard. "To that flat you had there. The one where Jesse saw Claudia."

"The plane's waiting," Marius said, eyes still on the paper.

"My man can drive you down to the landing strip," Armand said with his eyes still on the game.

"What is this? Why are you two being so helpful? Why should I go get Louis?"

"I think you should bring him back," Marius said. "It's no good his being in that old flat in New Orleans."

"I think you should get out and do something," Armand said. "You've been holed up here too long."

"Ah, I can see what this coven is going to be like, advice from all sides, and everyone watching everyone else out of the corner of an eye. Why did you ever let Louis go off to New Orleans anyway? Couldn't you have stopped him?"

I LANDED in New Orleans at two o'clock. Left the limousine at Jackson Square.

So clean it all was; with the new flagstones, and the chains on the gates, imagine, so the derelicts couldn't sleep on the grass in the square the way they'd done for two hundred years. And the tourists crowding the Café du Monde where the riverfront taverns had been; those lovely nasty places where the hunting was irresistible and the women were as tough as the men.

But I loved it now; always would love it. The colors were somehow the same. And even in this blasted cold of January, it had the old tropical feel to it; something to do with the flatness of the pavements; the low buildings; the sky that was always in motion; and the slanting roofs that were gleaming now with a bit of icy rain.

I walked slowly away from the river, letting the memories rise as if from the pavements; hearing the hard, brassy music of the Rue Bourbon, and then turning into the quiet wet darkness of the Rue Royale.

How many times had I taken this route in the old days, coming back from the riverfront or the opera house, or the theater, and stopping here on this very spot to put my key in the carriage gate?

Ah, the house in which I'd lived the span of a human lifetime, the house in which I'd almost died twice.

Someone up there in the old flat. Someone who walks softly yet makes the boards creak.

The little downstairs shop was neat and dark behind its barred windows; porcelain knickknacks, dolls, lace fans. I looked up at the balcony with its wrought-iron railings; I could picture Claudia there, on tiptoe, looking down at me, little fingers knotted on the rail. Golden hair spilling down over her shoulders, long streak of violet ribbon. My little immortal six-year-old beauty; *Lestat, where have you been?*

And that's what he was doing, wasn't he? Picturing things like that.

It was dead quiet; that is, if you didn't hear the televisions chattering behind the green shutters and the old vine-covered walls; and the raucous noise from Bourbon; a man and a woman fighting deep within a house on the other side of the street.

But no one about; only the shining pavements; and the shut-up shops; and the big clumsy cars parked over the curb, the rain falling soundlessly on their curved roofs.

No one to see me as I walked away and then turned and made the quick feline leap, in the old manner, to the balcony and came down silently on the boards. I peered through the dirty glass of the French doors.

Empty; scarred walls; the way Jesse had left them. A board nailed up here, as though someone had tried once to break in and had been found out; smell of burnt timbers in there after all these years.

I pulled down the board silently; but now there was the lock on the other side. Could I use the new power? Could I make it open? Why did it hurt so much to do it—to think of her, to think that, in that last flickering moment, I could have helped her; I could have helped head and body to come together again; even though she had meant to destroy me; even though she had not called my name.

I looked at the little lock. *Turn, open.* And with tears rising, I heard the metal creak, and saw the latch move. Little spasm in the brain as I kept my eye on it; and then the old door popped from its warped frame, hinges groaning, as if a draft inside had pushed it out.

He was in the hallway, looking through Claudia's door.

The coat was perhaps a little shorter, a little less full than those old frock coats had been; but he looked so very nearly like himself in the old century that it made the ache in me deepen unbearably. For a moment I couldn't move. He might as well have been a ghost there: his black hair full and disheveled as it had always been in the old days, and his green eyes full of melancholy wonder, and his arms rather limp at his sides.

Surely he hadn't contrived to fit so perfectly into the old context. Yet he *was* a ghost in this flat, where Jesse had been so frightened; where she'd caught in chilling glimpses the old atmosphere I'd never forget.

Sixty years here, the unholy family. Sixty years Louis, Claudia, Lestat.

Could I hear the harpsichord if I tried?—Claudia playing her Haydn; and the birds singing because the sound always excited them; and the collected music vibrating in the crystal baubles that hung from the painted glass shades of the oil lamps, and in the wind chimes even that hung in the rear doorway before the curving iron stairs.

Claudia. A face for a locket; or a small oval portrait done on porcelain and kept with a curl of her golden hair in a drawer. But how she would have hated such an image, such an unkind image.

Claudia who sank her knife into my heart and twisted it, and watched as the blood poured down my shirt. *Die, Father. I'll put you in your coffin forever.*

I will kill you first, my prince.

I saw the little mortal child, lying there in the soiled covers; smell of sickness. I saw the black-eyed Queen, motionless on her throne. And I had kissed them both, the Sleeping Beauties! *Claudia, Claudia, come round now, Claudia . . . That's it, dear, you must drink it to get well.*

Akasha!

Someone was shaking me. "Lestat," he said.

Confusion.

"Ah, Louis, forgive me." The dark neglected hallway. I shuddered. "I came here because I was so concerned . . . about you."

"No need," he said considerately. "It was just a little pilgrimage I had to make."

I touched his face with my fingers; so warm from the kill.

"She's not here, Louis," I said. "It was something Jesse imagined."

"Yes, so it seems," he said.

"We live forever; but they don't come back."

He studied me for a long moment; then he nodded. "Come on," he said.

We walked down the long hallway together; no, I did not like it; I did not want to be here. It was haunted; but real hauntings have nothing to do with ghosts finally; they have to do with the menace of memory; that had been my room in there; my room.

He was struggling with the back door, trying to make the old weathered frame behave. I gestured for him to go out on the porch and then I gave it the shove it needed. Locked up tight.

So sad to see the overgrown courtyard; the fountain ruined; the old brick kitchen crumbling, and the bricks becoming earth again.

"I'll fix it all for you if you want," I told him. "You know, make it like it was before."

"Not important now," he said. "Will you come with me, walk with me a little?"

We went down the covered carriageway together, water rushing through the little gutter. I glanced back once. Saw her standing there in her white dress with the blue sash. Only she wasn't looking at me. I was dead, she thought, wrapped in the sheet that Louis thrust into the carriage; she was taking my remains away to bury me; yet there she stood, and our eyes met.

I felt him tugging on me. "No good to stay here any longer," he said.

I watched him close the gate up properly; and then his eyes moved sluggishly over the windows again, the balconies, and the high dormers above. Was he saying farewell, finally? Maybe not.

We went together up to the Rue Ste. Anne, and away from the river, not speaking, just walking, the way we'd done so many times back then. The cold was biting at him a little, biting at his hands. He didn't like to put his hands in his pockets the way men did today. He didn't think it a graceful thing to do.

The rain had softened into a mist.

Finally, he said: "You gave me a little fright; I didn't think you were real when I first saw you in the hallway; you didn't answer when I said your name."

"And where are we going now?" I asked. I buttoned up my denim jacket. Not because I suffered from cold anymore; but because being warm felt good.

"Just one last place, and then wherever you wish. Back to the coven house, I should think. We don't have much time. Or maybe you can leave me to my meanderings, and I'll be back in a couple of nights."

"Can't we meander together?"

"Yes," he said eagerly.

What in God's name did I want? We walked beneath the old porches, past the old solid green shutters; past the walls of peeling plaster and naked brick, and through the garish light of the Rue Bourbon and then I saw the St. Louis Cemetery up ahead, with its thick whitewashed walls.

What did I want? Why was my soul aching still when all the rest of them had struck some balance? Even Louis had struck a balance, and we had each other, as Marius had said.

I was happy to be with him, happy to be walking these old streets; but why wasn't it enough?

Another gate now to be opened; I watched him break the lock with his fingers. And then we went into the little city of white graves with their peaked roofs and urns and doorways of marble, and the high grass crunching under our boots. The rain made every surface luminous; the lights of the city gave a pearl gleam to the clouds traveling silently over our heads.

I tried to find the stars. But I couldn't. When I looked down again, I saw Claudia; I felt her hand touch mine.

Then I looked at Louis again, and saw his eyes catch the dim and distant light and I winced. I touched his face again, the cheekbones, the arch beneath the black eyebrow. What a finely made thing he was.

"Blessed darkness!" I said suddenly. "Blessed darkness has come again."

"Yes," he said sadly, "and we rule in it as we have always done."

Wasn't that enough?

He took my hand—what did it feel like now?—and led me down the narrow corridor between the oldest, the most venerable tombs; tombs that went back to the oldest time of the colony, when he and I had roamed the swamps together, the swamps that threatened to swallow everything, and I had fed on the blood of roustabouts and cutthroat thieves.

His tomb. I realized I was looking at his name engraved on the marble in a great slanting old-fashioned script.

Louis de Pointe du Lac

1766–1794

He rested against the tomb behind him, another one of those little temples, like his own, with a peristyle roof.

"I only wanted to see it again," he said. He reached out and touched the writing with his finger.

It had faded only slightly from the weather wearing at the surface of the stone. The dust and grime had made it all the clearer, darkening each letter and numeral. Was he thinking of what the world had been in those years?

I thought of her dreams, her garden of peace on earth, with flowers springing from the blood-soaked soil.

"Now we can go home," he said.

Home. I smiled. I reached out and touched the graves on either side of me; I looked up again at the soft glow of the city lights against the ruffled clouds.

"You're not going to leave us, are you?" he asked suddenly, voice sharpened with distress.

"No," I said. I wished I could speak of it, all the things that were in the book. "You know, we were lovers, she and I, as surely as a mortal man and woman ever were."

"Of course, I know," he said.

I smiled. I kissed him suddenly, thrilled by the warmth of him, the soft pliant feel of his near human skin. God, how I hated the whiteness of my fingers touching him, fingers that could have crushed him now effortlessly. I wondered if he even guessed.

There was so much I wanted to say to him, to ask him. Yet I couldn't find the words really, or a way to begin. He had always had so many questions; and now he had his answers, more answers perhaps than he could ever have wanted; and what had this done to his soul? Stupidly I stared at him. How perfect he seemed to me as he stood there waiting with such kindness and such patience. And then, like a fool, I came out with it.

"Do you love me now?" I asked.

He smiled; oh, it was excruciating to see his face soften and brighten simultaneously when he smiled. "Yes," he said.

"Want to go on a little adventure?" My heart was thudding suddenly. It would be so grand if— "Want to break the new rules?"

"What in the world do you mean?" he whispered.

I started laughing, in a low feverish fashion; it felt so good. Laughing and watching the subtle little changes in his face. I really had him worried now. And the truth was, I didn't know if I could do it. Without her. What if I plunged like Icarus—?

"Oh, come now, Louis," I said. "Just a little adventure. I promise, I have no designs this time on Western civilization, or even on the attentions of two million rock music fans. I was thinking of something small, really. Something, well, a little mischievous. And rather elegant. I mean, I've been awfully good for the last two months, don't you think?"

"What on earth are you talking about?"

"Are you with me or not?"

He gave another little shake of his head again. But it wasn't a No. He was pondering. He ran his fingers back through his hair. Such fine black hair. The first thing I'd ever noticed about him—well, after his green eyes, that is—was his black hair. No, all that's a lie. It was his expression; the passion and the innocence and the delicacy of conscience. I just loved it!

"When does this little adventure begin?"

"Now," I said. "You have four seconds to make up your mind."

"Lestat, it's almost dawn."

"It's almost dawn *here*," I answered.

"What do you mean?"

"Louis, put yourself in my hands. Look, if I can't pull it off, you won't really be hurt. Well, not that much. Game? Make up your mind. I want to be off now."

He didn't say anything. He was looking at me, and so affectionately that I could hardly stand it.

"Yes or no."

"I'm probably going to regret this, but. . . ."

"Agreed then." I reached out and placed my hands firmly on his arms and I lifted him high off his feet. He was flabbergasted, looking down at me. It was as if he weighed nothing. I set him down.

"*Mon Dieu,*" he whispered.

Well, what was I waiting for? If I didn't try it, I'd never find out. There came a dark, dull moment of pain again; of remembering her; of us rising together. I let it slowly slip away.

I swung my arm around his waist. *Upwards now.* I lifted my right hand, but that wasn't even necessary. We were climbing on the wind that fast.

The cemetery was spinning down there, a tiny sprawling toy of itself with little bits of white scattered all over under the dark trees.

I could hear his astonished gasp in my ear.

"Lestat!"

"Put your arm around my neck," I said. "Hold on tight. We're going west, of course, and then north, and we're going a very long distance, and maybe we'll drift for a while. The sun won't set where we're going for some time."

The wind was ice cold. I should have thought of that, that he'd suffer from it; but he gave no sign. He was merely gazing upwards as we pierced the great snowy mist of the clouds.

When he saw the stars, I felt him tense against me; his face was perfectly smooth and serene; and if he was weeping the wind was carrying it away. Whatever fear he'd felt was gone now, utterly; he was lost as he looked upward; as the dome of heaven came down around us, and the moon shone full on the endless thickening plain of whiteness below.

No need to tell him what to observe, or what to remember. He always knew such things. Years ago, when I'd done the dark magic on him, I hadn't had to tell him anything; he had savored the smallest aspects of it all on his own. And later he'd said I'd failed to guide him. Didn't he know how unnecessary that had always been?

But I was drifting now, mentally and physically; feeling him a snug yet weightless thing against me; just the pure presence of Louis, Louis belonging to me, and with me. And no burden at all.

I was plotting the course firmly with one tiny part of my mind, the way she'd taught me to do it; and I was also remembering so many things; the first time, for example, that I'd ever seen him in a tavern in New Orleans. He'd been drunk, quarreling; and I'd followed him out into the night. And he had said in that last moment before I'd let him slip through my hands, his eyes closing:

"But who are you!"

I'd known I'd come back for him at sunset, that I'd find him if I had to search the whole city for him, though I was leaving him then half dead in the cobblestone street. I had to have him, had to. Just the way I had to have everything I wanted; or had to do everything I'd ever wanted to do.

That was the problem, and nothing she'd given me—not suffering, or power, or terror finally—had changed it one bit.

Four miles from London.

One hour after sunset. We lay in the grass together, in the cold darkness under the oak. There was a little light coming from the huge manor house in the middle of the park, but not much. The small deep-cut leaded windows seemed made to keep it all inside. Cozy in there, inviting, with all the book-lined walls, and the flicker of flames from those many fireplaces; and the smoke belching up from the chimneys into the foggy dark.

Now and then a car moved on the winding road beyond the front gates; and the beams would sweep the regal face of the old building, revealing the gargoyles, and the heavy arches over the windows, and the gleaming knockers on the massive front doors.

I have always loved these old European dwellings, big as landscapes; no wonder they invite the spirits of the dead to come back.

Louis sat up suddenly, looking about himself, and then hastily brushed the grass from his coat. He had slept for hours, inevitably, on the breast of the wind, you might say, and in the places where I'd rested for a little while, waiting for the world to turn. "Where are we?" he whispered, with a vague touch of alarm.

"Talamasca Motherhouse, outside London," I said. I was lying there with my hands cradling my head. Lights on in the attic. Lights on in the main rooms of the first floor. I was thinking, what way would be the most fun?

"What are we doing here?"

"Adventure, I told you."

"But wait a minute. You don't mean to go in there."

"Don't I? They have Claudia's diary in there, in their cellar, along with Marius's painting. You know all that, don't you? Jesse told you those things."

"Well, what do you mean to do? Break in and rummage through the cellar till you find what you want?"

I laughed. "Now, that wouldn't be very much fun, would it? Sounds more like dreary work. Besides, it's not really the diary I want. They can keep the diary. It was Claudia's. I want to talk to one of them, to David

Talbot, the leader. They're the only mortals in the world, you know, who really believe in us."

Twinge of pain inside. Ignore it. The fun's beginning.

For the moment he was too shocked to answer. This was even more delicious than I had dreamed.

"But you can't be serious," he said. He was getting wildly indignant. "Lestat, let these people alone. They think Jesse is dead. They received a letter from someone in her family."

"Yes, naturally. So I won't disabuse them of that morbid notion. Why would I? But the one who came to the concert—David Talbot, the older one—he fascinates me. I suppose I want to know. . . . But why say it? Time to go in and find out."

"Lestat!"

"Louis!" I said, mocking his tone. I got up and helped him up, not because he needed it, but because he was sitting there glowering at me, and resisting me, and trying to figure out how to control me, all of which was an utter waste of his time.

"Lestat, Marius will be furious if you do this!" he said earnestly, his face sharpening, the whole picture of high cheekbones and dark probing green eyes firing beautifully. "The cardinal rule is—"

"Louis, you're making it irresistible!" I said.

He took hold of my arm. "What about Maharet? These were Jesse's friends!"

"And what is she going to do? Send Mekare to crush my head like an egg!"

"You are really past all patience!" he said. "Have you learned anything at all!"

"Are you coming with me or not?"

"You're not going into that house."

"You see that window up there?" I hooked my arm around his waist. Now, he couldn't get away from me. "David Talbot is in that room. He's been writing in his journal for about an hour. He's deeply troubled. He doesn't know what happened with us. He knows something happened; but he'll never really figure it out. Now, we're going to enter the bedroom next to him by means of that little window to the left."

He gave one last feeble protest, but I was concentrating on the window, trying to visualize a lock. How many feet away was it? I felt the spasm, and then I saw, high above, the little rectangle of leaded glass swing out. He saw it too, and while he was standing there, speechless, I tightened my grip on him and went up.

Within a second we were standing inside the room. A small Elizabethan chamber with dark paneling, and handsome period furnishings, and a busy little fire.

Louis was in a rage. He glared at me as he straightened his clothes now with quick, furious gestures. I liked the room. David Talbot's books; his bed.

And David Talbot staring at us through the half-opened door to his study, from where he sat in the light of one green shaded lamp on his desk. He wore a handsome gray silk smoking jacket, tied at the waist. He had his pen in hand. He was as still as a creature of the wood, sensing a predator, before the inevitable attempt at flight.

Ah, now this was lovely!

I studied him for a moment; dark gray hair, clear black eyes, beautifully lined face; very expressive, immediately warm. And the intelligence of the man was obvious. All very much as Jesse and Khayman had described.

I went into the study.

"You'll forgive me," I said. "I should have knocked at the front door. But I wanted our meeting to be private. You know who I am, of course."

Speechless.

I looked at the desk. Our files, neat manila folders with various familiar names: "Théâtre des Vampires" and "Armand" and "Benjamin, the Devil." And "Jesse."

Jesse. There was the letter from Jesse's aunt Maharet lying there beside the folder. The letter which said that Jesse was dead.

I waited, wondering if I should force him to speak first. But then that's never been my favorite game. He was studying me very intensely, infinitely more intensely than I had studied him. He was memorizing me, using little devices he'd learned to record details so that he would remember them later no matter how great the shock of an experience while it was going on.

Tall, not heavy, not slender either. A good build. Large, very well-formed hands. Very well groomed, too. A true British gentleman; a lover of tweed and leather and dark woods, and tea, and dampness and the dark park outside, and the lovely wholesome feeling of this house.

And his age, sixty-five or so. A very good age. He knew things younger men just could not possibly know. This was the modern equivalent of Marius's age in ancient times. Not really old for the twentieth century at all.

Louis was still in the other room, but he knew Louis was there. He looked towards the doorway now. And then back to me.

Then he rose, and surprised me utterly. He extended his hand.

"How do you do?" he said.

I laughed. I took his hand and shook it firmly and politely, observing his reactions, his astonishment when he felt how cold my flesh was; how lifeless in any conventional sense.

He was frightened all right. But he was also powerfully curious; powerfully interested.

Then very agreeably and very courteously he said, "Jesse isn't dead, is she?"

Amazing what the British do with language; the nuances of politeness. The world's great diplomats, surely. I found myself wondering what their gangsters were like. Yet there was such grief there for Jesse, and who was I to dismiss another being's grief?

I looked at him solemnly. "Oh, yes," I said. "Make no mistake about it. Jesse is dead." I held his gaze firmly; there was no misunderstanding. "Forget about Jesse," I said.

He gave a little nod, eyes glancing off for a moment, and then he looked at me again, with as much curiosity as before.

I made a little circle in the center of the room. Saw Louis back there in the shadows, standing against the side of the bedroom fireplace watching me with such scorn and disapproval. But this was no time to laugh. I didn't feel at all like laughing. I was thinking of something Khayman had told me.

"I have a question for you now," I said.

"Yes."

"I'm here. Under your roof. Suppose when the sun rises, I go down into your cellar. I slip into unconsciousness there. You know." I made a little offhand gesture. "What would you do? Would you kill me while I slept?"

He thought about it for less than two seconds.

"No."

"But you know what I am. There isn't the slightest doubt in your mind, is there? Why wouldn't you?"

"Many reasons," he said. "I'd want to know about you. I'd want to talk to you. No, I wouldn't kill you. Nothing could make me do that."

I studied him; he was telling the truth completely. He didn't elaborate on it, but he would have thought it frightfully callous and disrespectful to kill me, to kill a thing as mysterious and old as I was.

"Yes, precisely," he said, with a little smile.

Mind reader. Not very powerful however. Just the surface thoughts.

"Don't be so sure." Again it was said with remarkable politeness.

"Second question for you," I said.

"By all means." He was really intrigued now. The fear had absolutely melted away.

"Do you want the Dark Gift? You know. To become one of us." Out of the corner of my eye I saw Louis shake his head. Then he turned his back. "I'm not saying that I'd ever give it you. Very likely, I would not. But do you want it? If I was willing, would you accept it from me?"

"No."

"Oh, come now."

"Not in a million years would I ever accept it. As God is my witness, no."

"You don't believe in God, you know you don't."

"Merely an expression. But the sentiment is true."

I smiled. Such an affable, alert face. And I was so exhilarated; the blood was moving through my veins with a new vigor; I wondered if he could sense it; did I look any less like a monster? Were there all those little signs of humanity that I saw in others of our kind when they were exuberant or absorbed?

"I don't think it will take a million years for you to change your mind," I said. "You don't have very much time at all, really. When you think about it."

"I will never change my mind," he said. He smiled, very sincerely. He was holding his pen in both hands. And he toyed with it, unconsciously and anxiously for a second, but then he was still.

"I don't believe you," I said. I looked around the room; at the small Dutch painting in its lacquered frame: a house in Amsterdam above a canal. I looked at the frost on the leaded window. Nothing visible of the night outside at all. I felt sad suddenly; only it wasn't anything as bad as before. It was just an acknowledgment of the bitter loneliness that had brought me here, the need with which I'd come, to stand in his little chamber and feel his eyes on me; to hear him say that he knew who I was.

The moment darkened. I couldn't speak.

"Yes," he said in a timid tone behind me. "I *know* who you are."

I turned and looked at him. It seemed I'd weep suddenly. Weep on account of the warmth here, and the scent of human things; the sight of a living man standing before a desk. I swallowed. I wasn't going to lose my composure, that was foolish.

"It's quite fascinating really," I said. "You wouldn't kill me. But you wouldn't become what I am."

"That's correct."

"No. I don't believe you," I said again.

A little shadow came into his face, but it was an interesting shadow. He was afraid I'd seen some weakness in him that he wasn't aware of himself.

I reached for his pen. "May I? And a piece of paper please?"

He gave them to me immediately. I sat down at the desk in his chair. All very immaculate—the blotter, the small leather cylinder in which he kept his pens, and even the manila folders. Immaculate as he was, standing there watching as I wrote.

"It's a phone number," I said. I put the piece of paper in his hand. "It's a Paris number, an attorney, who knows me under my proper name, Lestat de Lioncourt, which I believe is in your files? Of course he doesn't know the things about me you know. But he can reach me. Or, perhaps it would be accurate to say that I am always in touch with him."

He didn't say anything, but he looked at the paper, and he memorized the number.

"Keep it," I said. "And when you change your mind, when you want to be immortal, and you're willing to say so, call the number. And I'll come back."

He was about to protest. I gestured for silence.

"You never know what may happen," I told him. I sat back in his chair, and crossed my hands on my chest. "You may discover you have a fatal illness; you may find yourself crippled by a bad fall. Maybe you'll just start to have nightmares about being dead; about being nobody and nothing. Doesn't matter. When you decide you want what I have to give, call. And remember please, I'm not saying I'll give it to you. I may never do that. I'm only saying that when you decide you want it, then the dialogue will begin."

"But it's already begun."

"No, it hasn't."

"You don't think you'll be back?" he asked. "I think you will, whether I call or not."

Another little surprise. A little stab of humiliation. I smiled at him in spite of myself. He was a very interesting man. "You silver-tongued British bastard," I said. "How dare you say that to me with such condescension? Maybe I should kill you right now."

That did it. He was stunned. Covering it up rather well but I could still see it. And I knew how frightening I could look, especially when I smiled.

He recovered himself with amazing swiftness. He folded the paper with the phone number on it and slipped it into his pocket.

"Please accept my apology," he said. "What I meant to say was that I hope you'll come back."

"Call the number," I said. We looked at each other for a long moment; then I gave him another little smile. I stood up to take my leave. Then I looked down at his desk.

"Why don't I have my own file?" I asked.

His face went blank for a second; then he recovered again, miraculously. "Ah, but you have the book!" He gestured to *The Vampire Lestat* on the shelf.

"Ah, yes, right. Well, thank you for reminding me." I hesitated. "But you know, I think I should have my own file."

"I agree with you," he said. "I'll make one up immediately. It was always . . . just a matter of time."

I laughed softly in spite of myself. He was so courteous. I made a little farewell bow, and he acknowledged it gracefully.

And then I moved past him, as fast as I could manage it, which was quite fast, and I caught hold of Louis, and left immediately through the window, moving out and up over the grounds until I came down on a lonely stretch of the London road.

It was darker and colder here, with the oaks closing out the moon, and I loved it. I loved the pure darkness! I stood there with my hands shoved into my pockets looking at the faint faraway aureole of light hovering over London; and laughing to myself with irrepressible glee.

"Oh, that was wonderful; that was perfect!" I said, rubbing my hands together; and then clasping Louis's hands, which were even colder than mine.

The expression on Louis's face sent me into raptures. This was a real laughing fit coming on.

"You're a bastard, do you know that!" he said. "How could you do such a thing to that poor man! You're a fiend, Lestat. You should be walled up in a dungeon!"

"Oh, come on, Louis," I said. I couldn't stop laughing. "What do you expect of me? Besides, the man's a student of the supernatural. He isn't going to go stark raving mad. What does everybody expect of me?" I threw my arm around his shoulder. "Come on, let's go to London. It's a long walk, but it's early. I've never been to London. Do you know that? I want to see the West End, and Mayfair, and the Tower, yes, let's do go to the Tower. And I want to feed in London! Come on."

"Lestat, this is no joking matter. Marius will be furious. Everyone will be furious!"

My laughing fit was getting worse. We started down the road at a good clip. It was so much fun to walk. Nothing was ever going to take the place of that, the simple act of walking, feeling the earth under your feet, and the sweet smell of the nearby chimneys scattered out there in the blackness; and the damp cold smell of deep winter in these woods. Oh, it was all very lovely. And we'd get Louis a decent overcoat when we reached London, a nice long black overcoat with fur on the collar so that he'd be warm as I was now.

"Do you hear what I'm saying to you?" Louis said. "You *haven't* learned anything, have you? You're more incorrigible than you were before!"

I started to laugh again, helplessly.

Then more soberly, I thought of David Talbot's face, and that moment when he'd challenged me. Well, maybe he was right. I'd be back. Who said I couldn't come back and talk to him if I wanted to? Who said? But then I ought to give him just a little time to think about that phone number; and slowly lose his nerve.

The bitterness came again, and a great drowsy sadness suddenly that threatened to sweep my little triumph away. But I wouldn't let it. The night was too beautiful. And Louis's diatribe was becoming all the more heated and hilarious:

"You're a perfect devil, Lestat!" he was saying. "That's what you are! You are the devil himself!"

"Yes, I know," I said, loving to look at him, to see the anger pumping him so full of life. "And I love to hear you say it, Louis. I need to hear you say it. I don't think anyone will ever say it quite like you do. Come on, say it again. I'm a perfect devil. Tell me how bad I am. It makes me feel so good!"

THE END

The Vampire Chronicles
WILL
CONTINUE.

ABOUT THE AUTHOR

ANNE RICE lives in New Orleans with her husband, the poet and painter Stan Rice, and their son, Christopher.